THE COLLECTED
SHORT STORIES
OF LOUIS L'AMOUR

Bantam Books by Louis L'Amour

THE
COLLECTED SHORT STORIES
OF
LOUIS L'AMOUR

FRONTIER STORIES
Volume 7

Louis L'Amour

BANTAM BOOKS
NEW YORK

The Collected Short Stories of Louis L'Amour, Volume 7, is a work of fiction. Names, characters, places and incidents are the products of the author's imagination or are used fictitiously. Any resemblance to actual events, locales, or persons, living or dead, is entirely coincidental.

2017 Bantam Books Mass Market Edition

Copyright © 2009 by Louis & Katherine L'Amour Trust

Excerpt from *Law of the Desert Born, A Graphic Novel,* by Louis L'Amour text copyright © 2013 by Beau L'Amour, illustrations copyright © 2013 by Louis L'Amour Enterprises, Inc.

Published in the United States by Bantam Books, an imprint of Random House, a division of Penguin Random House LLC, New York.

BANTAM BOOKS and the HOUSE colophon are registered trademarks of Penguin Random House LLC.

Originally published in hardcover in the United States by Bantam Books, an imprint of Random House, a division of Penguin Random House LLC, in 2009.

ISBN 978-0-804-17979-9
ebook ISBN 978-0-553-90705-6

Cover design: Scott Biel
Cover art: Olkyeg Stavrows
Photograph of Louis L'Amour by John Hamilton-Globe Photos, Inc

Printed in the United States of America

randomhousebooks.com

10 9 8

Bantam Books mass market edition: January 2017

CONTENTS

THE COLLECTED
SHORT STORIES
OF LOUIS L'AMOUR

WEST IS WHERE THE HEART IS

J IM LONDON LAY face down in the dry prairie grass, his body pressed tightly against the ground. Heat, starvation, and exhaustion had taken a toll of his lean, powerful body, and although light-headed from their accumulative effects, he still grasped the fact that to survive he must not be seen.

Hot sun blazed upon his back, and in his nostrils was the stale, sour smell of clothes and body long unwashed. Behind him lay days of dodging Comanche war parties and sleeping on the bare ground behind rocks or under bushes. He was without weapons or food, it had been nine hours since he had tasted water, and that was only dew he had licked from leaves.

The screams of the dying rang in his ears, amid the sounds of occasional shots and the shouts and war cries of the Indians. From a hill almost five miles away he had spotted the white canvas tops of the Conestoga wagons and had taken a course that would intercept them. And then, in the last few minutes before he could reach their help, the Comanches had hit the wagon train.

From the way the attack went, a number of the Indians must have been bedded down in the tall grass, keeping out of sight, and then when the train was passing, they sprang for the drivers of the teams. The strategy was perfect, for there was then no chance of the wagon train making its circle. The lead wagons did swing, but two other teamsters were dead and another was fighting for his life, and their wagons could not be turned. The two lead wagons found themselves isolated from the last four and were hit hard by at least twenty Indians. The wagon whose driver was fighting turned over in the tall grass at the edge of a ditch, and the driver was killed.

Within twenty minutes after the beginning of the attack, the fighting was over and the wagons looted, and the Indians were riding away, leaving behind them only dead and butchered oxen, the scalped and mutilated bodies of the drivers, and the women who were killed or who had killed themselves.

Yet Jim London did not move. This was not his first crossing of the plains or his first encounter with Indians. He had fought Comanches before, as well as Kiowas, Apaches, Sioux, and Cheyenne. Born on the Oregon Trail, he had later been a teamster on the Santa Fe. He knew better than to move now. He knew that an Indian or two might come back to look for more loot.

The smoke of the burning wagons bit at his nostrils, yet he waited. An hour had passed before he let himself creep forward, and then it was only to inch to the top of the hill, where from behind a tuft of bunch grass he surveyed the scene before him.

———

NO LIVING THING stirred near the wagons. Slow tendrils of smoke lifted from blackened timbers and wheel spokes. Bodies lay scattered about, grotesque in attitudes of tortured death. For a long time he studied the scene below, and the surrounding hills. And then he crawled over the skyline and slithered downhill through the grass, making no more visible disturbance than a snake or a coyote.

Home was still more than two hundred miles away, and the wife he had not seen in four years would be waiting for him. In his heart, he knew she would be waiting. During the war the others had scoffed at him.

"Why, Jim, you say yourself she don't even know where you're at! She probably figures you're dead! No woman can be expected to wait that long! Not for a man she never hears of and when she's in a good country for men and a bad one for women!"

"No," he said stubbornly. "I'll go home. I'll go back to Jane. I come east after some fixings for her, after some stock for the ranch, and I'll go home with what I set out after."

"You got any young'uns?" The big sergeant was skeptical.

"Nope. I sure ain't, but I wish I did. Only," he added, "maybe I have. Jane, she was expecting, but had a time to go when I left. I only figured to be gone four months."

"And you been gone four years?" The sergeant shook his head. "Forget her, Jim, and come to Mexico with us. Nobody would deny she was a good woman. From what you tell of her, she sure was, but she's been alone and no doubt figures you're dead. She'll be married again, maybe with a family."

Jim London had shaken his head. "I never took up with no other woman, and Jane wouldn't take up with any other man. I'm going home."

He made a good start. He had saved nearly every dime of pay, and he did some shrewd buying and trading when the war was over. He started west with two wagons with six head of mules to the wagon, knowing the mules would sell better in New Mexico than would oxen. He had six cows and a yearling bull, some pigs, chickens, and utensils. He was a proud man when he looked over his outfit, and he hired two boys to help him with the extra wagon and the stock.

Comanches hit them before they were well started. They killed two men, and one woman and stampeded some stock. The wagon train continued, and at forks of Little Creek they were hit again, in force this time, and only Jim London came out of it alive. All his outfit was gone, and he escaped without weapons, food, or water.

He lay flat in the grass at the edge of the burned spot. Again he studied the hills, and then he eased forward and got to his feet. The nearest wagon was upright, and smoke was still rising from it. The wheels were partly burned, the box badly charred, and the interior smoking. It was still too hot to touch.

He crouched near the front wheel and studied the situation, avoiding the bodies. No weapons were in sight, but he had scarcely expected any. There had been nine wagons. The lead wagons were thirty or forty yards off, and the three wagons whose drivers had been attacked were bunched in the middle with one overturned. The last four had burned further than the others.

He saw a dead horse lying at one side with a canteen tied to the saddle. He crossed to it at once, and tearing the canteen loose, he rinsed his mouth with water. Gripping himself tight against further drinking, he rinsed his mouth again and moistened his cracked lips. Only then did he let a mere swallow trickle down his parched throat.

Resolutely he put the canteen down in the shade and went through the saddle pockets. It was a treasure trove. He found a good-sized chunk of almost iron-hard brown sugar, a half dozen biscuits, a chunk of jerky wrapped in paper, and a new plug of chewing tobacco. Putting these things with the canteen, he unfastened the slicker from behind the saddle and added that to the pile.

Wagon by wagon he searched, always alert to the surrounding country and at times leaving the wagons to observe the plain from a hilltop. It was quite dark before he was finished. Then he took his first good drink, for he had allowed himself only nips during the remainder of the day. He took his drink and then ate a biscuit, and chewed a piece of the jerky. With his hunting knife he shaved a little of the plug tobacco and made a cigarette by rolling it in paper, the way the Mexicans did.

Every instinct warned him to be away from the place by daylight, and as much as he disliked leaving the bodies as they were, he knew it would be folly to bury them. If the Indians passed that way again, they would find them buried and would immediately be on his trail.

Crawling along the edge of the taller grass near the depression where the wagon had tipped over, he stopped suddenly. Here in the ground near the edge of the grass was a boot print!

His fingers found it, and then felt carefully. It had been made by a running man, either large or heavily laden. Feeling his way along the tracks, London stopped again, for this time his hand had come in contact with a boot. He shook it, but there was no move or response. Crawling nearer he touched the man's hand. It was cold as marble in the damp night air.

Moving his hand again, he struck canvas. Feeling along it

he found it was a long canvas sack. Evidently the dead man had grabbed this sack from the wagon and dashed for the shelter of the ditch or hollow. Apparently he had been struck by a bullet and killed, but feeling the body again, London's hand came in contact with a belt gun. So the Comanches had not found him! Stripping the belt and gun from the dead man, London swung it around his own hips, and then checked the gun. It was fully loaded, and so were the cartridge loops in the belt.

Something stirred in the grass, and instantly he froze, sliding out his hunting knife. He waited for several minutes, and then he heard it again. Something alive lay here in the grass with him!

A Comanche? No Indian likes to fight at night, and he had seen no Indians anywhere near when darkness fell. No, if anything lived near him now it must be something, man or animal, from the wagon train. For a long time he lay still, thinking it over, and then he took a chance. Yet from his experience the chance was not a long one.

"If there is someone there, speak up."

There was no sound, and he waited, listening. Five minutes passed—ten—twenty. Carefully, then, he slid through the grass, changing his position, and then froze in place. Something was moving, quite near!

His hand shot out, and he was shocked to find himself grasping a small hand with a ruffle of cloth at the wrist! The child struggled violently, and he whispered hoarsely, "Be still! I'm a friend! If you run, the Indians might come!"

Instantly, the struggling stopped. "There!" he breathed. "That's better." He searched his mind for something reassuring to say, and finally said, "Damp here, isn't it? Don't you have a coat?"

There was a momentary silence, and then a small voice said, "It was in the wagon."

"We'll look for it pretty soon," London said. "My name's Jim. What's yours?"

"Betty Jane Jones. I'm five years old and my papa's name is Daniel Jones and he is forty-six. Are you forty-six?"

London grinned. "No, I'm just twenty-nine, Betty Jane."

He hesitated a minute and then said, "Betty Jane, you strike me as a mighty brave little girl. There when I first heard you, you made no more noise than a rabbit. Now do you think you can keep that up?"

"Yes." It was a very small voice but it sounded sure.

"Good. Now listen, Betty Jane." Quietly, he told her where he had come from and where he was going. He did not mention her parents, and she did not ask about them. From that he decided she knew only too well what had happened to them and the others from the wagon train.

"There's a canvas sack here, and I've got to look into it. Maybe there's something we can use. We're going to need food, Betty Jane, and a rifle. Later, we're going to have to find horses and money."

The sound of his voice, low though it was, seemed to give her confidence. She crawled nearer to him, and when she felt the sack, she said, "That is Daddy's bag. He keeps his carbine in it and his best clothes."

"Carbine?" London fumbled open the sack.

"Is a carbine like a rifle?"

He told her it was, and then found the gun. It was carefully wrapped, and by the feel of it London could tell the weapon was new or almost new. There was ammunition, another pistol, and a small canvas sack that chinked softly with gold coins. He stuffed this in his pocket. A careful check of the remaining wagons netted him nothing more, but he was not disturbed. The guns he had were good ones, and he had a little food and the canteen. Gravely, he took Betty Jane's hand and they started.

They walked for an hour before her steps began to drag, and then he picked her up and carried her. By the time the sky had grown gray he figured they had come six or seven miles from the burned wagons. He found some solid ground among some reeds on the edge of a slough, and they settled down there for the day.

After making coffee with a handful found in one of the only partly burned wagons, London gave Betty Jane some of the jerky and a biscuit. Then for the first time he examined his carbine. His eyes brightened as he sized it up. It was a Ball & Lamson Repeating Carbine, a gun just on the market and of which this must have been one of the first sold. It was a seven-shot weapon carrying a .56-50 cartridge. It was only thirty-eight inches in length and weighed a bit over seven pounds.

The pistols were also new, both Prescott Navy six-shooters, caliber .38 with rosewood grips. Betty Jane looked at them and tears welled into her eyes. He took her hand quickly.

"Don't cry, honey. Your dad would want me to use the guns to take care of his girl. You've been mighty brave. Now keep it up."

She looked up at him with woebegone eyes, but the tears stopped, and after a while she fell asleep.

There was little shade, and as the reeds were not tall, he did not dare stand up. They kept close to the edge of the reeds and lay perfectly still. Once he heard a horse walking not far away and heard low, guttural voices and a hacking cough. He caught only a fleeting glimpse of one rider and hoped the Indians would not find their tracks.

———

WHEN NIGHT CAME, they started on once more. He took his direction by the stars and he walked steadily, carrying Betty Jane most of the distance. Sometimes when she walked beside him, she talked. She rambled on endlessly about her home, her dolls, and her parents. Then on the third day she mentioned Hurlburt.

"He was a bad man. My papa told Mama he was a bad man. Papa said he was after Mr. Ballard's money."

"Who was Hurlburt?" London asked, more to keep the child occupied than because he wanted to know.

"He tried to steal Daddy's new carbine, and Mr. Ballard said he was a thief. He told him so."

Hurlburt. The child might be mispronouncing the name, but it sounded like that. There had been a man in Independence by that name. He had not been liked—a big, bearded man, very quarrelsome.

"Did he have a beard, Betty Jane? A big, black beard?"

She nodded eagerly. "At first, he did. But he didn't have it when he came back with the Indians."

"What?" He turned so sharply toward her that her eyes widened. He put his hand on her shoulder. "Did you say this Hurlburt came back with the Indians?"

Seriously, she nodded. "I saw him. He was in back of them, but I saw him. He was the one who shot his gun at Mr. Ballard."

"You say he came back?" London asked. "You mean he went away from the wagons before the attack?"

She looked at him. "Oh, yes! He went away when we stopped by the big pool. Mr. Ballard and Daddy caught him taking things again. They put ropes on him, on his hands and his feet. But when morning came I went to see, and he was gone away. Daddy said he had left the wagons, and he hoped nothing would happen to him."

Hurlburt. He had gone away and then had come back with the Indians. A renegade, then. What had they said of him in Independence? He had been over the trail several times. Maybe he was working with the Indians.

Betty Jane went to sleep on the grass he had pulled for her to lie on, and Jim London made a careful reconnaissance of the area, and then returned and lay down himself. After a long time he dozed, dreaming of Jane. He awakened feeling discouraged, with the last of their food gone. He had not tried the rifle, although twice they had seen antelope. There was too much chance of being heard by Indians.

Betty Jane was noticeably thinner, and her face looked wan as she slept. Suddenly, he heard a sound and looked up, almost too late. Not a dozen feet away a Comanche looked over the reeds and aimed a rifle at him! Hurling himself to one side, he jerked out one of the Navy pistols. The Comanche's rifle bellowed, and then Jim fired. The Indian threw up his rifle and fell over backward and lay still.

Carefully, London looked around. The rim of the hills was unbroken, and there was no other Indian in sight. The Indian's spotted pony cropped grass not far away. Gun in hand, London walked to the Indian. The bullet from the pistol had struck him under the chin and, tearing out the back, had broken the man's neck. A scarcely dry scalp was affixed to his rawhide belt, and the rifle he carried was new.

He walked toward the horse. The animal shied back. "Take it easy, boy," London said softly. "You're all right." Surprisingly, the horse perked up both ears and stared at him.

"Understand English, do you?" he said softly. "Well, maybe you're a white man's horse. We'll see."

He caught the reins and held out a hand to the horse. It hesitated and then snuffed of his fingers. He moved up the reins to it and touched a palm to the animal's back. The bridle was a white man's, too. There was no saddle, however, only a blanket.

Betty Jane was crying softly when he reached her, obviously frightened by the guns. He picked her up and then the rifle and started back toward the horse. "Don't cry, honey. We've got a horse now."

She slept in his arms that night, and he did not stop riding. He rode all through the night until the little horse began to stumble, and then he dismounted and led the horse while Betty Jane rode. Just before daylight they rested.

Two days later, tired, unshaven, and bedraggled, Jim London rode down the dusty street of Cimarron toward the Maxwell House. It was bright in the afternoon sunlight, and the sun glistened on the flanks and shoulders of the saddled horses at the hitch rail. Drawing up before the house, London slid from the saddle. Maxwell was standing on the wide porch staring down at him, and beside him was Tom Boggs, who London remembered from Missouri as the grandson of Daniel Boone.

"You look plumb tuckered, stranger, and that looks like an Injun rig on the horse. Or part of it."

"It is. The Injun's dead." He looked at Maxwell. "Is there a woman around here? This kid's nigh dead for rest and comfort."

"Sure!" Maxwell exclaimed heartily. "Lots of women around! My wife's inside!" He took the sleeping child and called to his wife. As he did so the child's eyes opened and stared, and then the corners of her mouth drew down and she screamed. All three men turned to where she looked.

Hurlburt was standing there gaping at the child as if the earth had opened before him.

"What is it?" Maxwell looked perplexed. "What's the matter?"

"That's the man who killed Mr. Ballard! I *saw* him!"

Hurlburt's face paled. "Aw, the kid's mistook me for somebody else!" he scoffed. "I never seen her before!" He turned to Jim London. "Where'd you find that youngster?" he demanded. "Who are you?"

Jim London did not immediately reply. He was facing Hurlburt and suddenly all his anger and irritation at the trail, the Indians, the awful butchery around the wagons, returned to him and boiled down to this man. A child without parents because of this man.

"I picked that child up on the ground near a burned-out, Injun-raided wagon train," he said. "The same train you left Missouri with!"

Hurlburt's face darkened with angry blood.

"You lie!" he declared viciously. "You lie!"

Jim stared at Hurlburt, his eyes unwavering. "How'd you get here, then? You were in Independence when I left there. No wagons passed us. You had to be with that Ballard train."

"I ain't been in Independence for two years!" Hurlburt blustered. "You're crazy and so's that blasted kid!"

"Seems kind of funny," Maxwell suggested, his eyes cold. "You sold two rifles after you got here, and you had gold money. There's a train due in, the boys tell me; maybe we better hold you until we ask them if you were in Independence."

"Like hell!" Hurlburt said furiously. "I ain't no renegade, and nobody holds me in no jail!"

Jim London took an easy step forward. "These guns I'm wearing, Hurlburt, belonged to Jones. I reckon he'd be glad to see this done. You led those Injuns against those wagons. They found out you was a thief and faced you with it. I got it from Betty Jane, and the kid wouldn't lie about a thing like that. She told me all about it before we got here. So you don't get to go to no jail. You don't get to wait. You get a chance to reach for a gun, and that's all."

Hurlburt's face was ugly. Desperately, he glanced right and left. A crowd had gathered, but nobody spoke for him. He was up against it and he knew it. Suddenly, he grabbed for his guns. Jim London's Prescott Navies leaped from their holsters, and the right one barked, a hard sharp report. Hurlburt backed up two steps, and then fell face down, a blue hole over his eye.

"Good work," Boggs said grimly. "I've had my doubts about that hombre. He never does nothing, but he always has money."

"Staying around?" Maxwell asked, looking at London.

"No," Jim said quietly. "My wife's waiting for me. I ain't seen her since sixty-one."

"Since sixty-one?" Boggs was incredulous. "You heard from her?"

"She didn't know where I was. Anyway, she never learned to write none." He flushed slightly. "I can't, neither. Only my name."

Lucian Maxwell looked away, clearing his throat.

Then he said very carefully, "Better not rush any, son. That's a long time. It'll soon be five years."

"She'll be waiting." He looked at them, one to the other. "It was the war. They took me in the Army, and I fought all through."

"What about the kid?" Boggs asked.

"Come morning she'll be ready, I reckon. I'll take her with me. She'll need a home, and I sort of owe her something for this here rifle and the guns. Also," he looked at them calmly, "I got nine hundred dollars in gold and bills here in my pocket. It's hers. I found it in her daddy's duffle."

He cleared his throat. "I reckon that'll buy her a piece of any place we got and give her a home with us for life. We wanted a little girl, and while my wife, she was expectin', I don't know if anything come of it."

Both men were silent, and finally Maxwell said, "This home of yours, where is it?"

"Up on the North Fork. Good grass, water, and timber. The wife likes trees. I built us a cabin there, and a lean-to. We aimed to put about forty acres to wheat and maybe set us up a mill."

He looked up at them, smiling a little. "Pa was a miller, and he always said to me that folks need bread wherever they are. Make a good loaf," he said, "and you'll always have a good living. He had him a mill up Oregon way."

"North Fork?" Boggs and Maxwell exchanged glances. "Man, that country was run over by Injuns two years ago. Some folks went back up there, but one o' them is Bill Ketchum. He's got a bunch running with him no bettern'n he is. Hoss thieves, folks reckon. Most anything to get the 'coon. You be careful, very careful."

———

WHEN HE ROUNDED the bend below the creek and saw the old bridge ahead of him his mouth got dry and his heart began to pound. He walked his horse, with the child sitting before him and the carbine in its scabbard. At the creek he drew up for just a moment, looking down at the bridge. He built it with his own hands. Then his eyes saw the hand rail on the right. It was cut from a young poplar. He had used cedar. Somebody had worked on that bridge recently.

———

THE CABIN HE had built topped a low rise in a clearing backed by a rocky overhang. He rode through the pines, trying to quiet himself. It might be like they said.

Maybe she had sold out and gone away, or just gone. Maybe she had married somebody else, or maybe the Injuns . . .

The voice he heard was coarse and amused. "Come off it!" the voice said. "From here on you're my woman. I ain't takin' no more of this guff!"

Jim London did not stop his horse when it entered the clearing. He let it walk right along, but he lifted the child from in front of him and said, "Betty Jane, that lady over yonder is your new ma. You run to her now, an' tell her your name is Jane. Hear me?"

He lowered the child to the ground and she scampered at

once toward the slender woman with the wide gray eyes who stood on the step staring at the rider.

The man turned abruptly to see what her expression meant. The lean, rawboned man on the horse had a narrow sun-browned face and a battered hat pulled low. The rider shoved it back now and rested his right hand on his thigh. Ketchum stared at him. Something in that steel-trap jaw and those hard eyes sent a chill through him.

"I take it," London said gravely, "that you are Bill Ketchum. I heard what you said just now. I also heard down the line that you was a horse thief, maybe worse. You get off this place now, and don't ever come back. You do and I'll shoot you on sight. Now get!"

"You talk mighty big." Ketchum stared at him, anger rising within him. Should he try this fellow? Who did he think he was, anyway?

"I'm big as I talk." London said it flatly. "I done killed a man yesterday down to Maxwell's. That's all I figure for this week unless you want to make it two. Start moving now."

Ketchum hesitated, then viciously reined his horse around and started down the trail. As he neared the edge of the woods, rage suddenly possessed him. He grabbed for his rifle and instantly a shot rang out and a heavy slug gouged the butt of his rifle and glanced off.

Behind him the words were plain. "I put that one right where I want it. This here's a seven-shot repeater, so if you want one through your heart, just try it again."

London waited until the man had disappeared in the trees, and a minute more. Only then did he turn to his wife. She was down on the step with her arm around Betty Jane, who was sobbing happily against her breast.

"Jim!" she whispered. "Oh, Jim!"

He got down heavily. He started toward her and then stopped. Around the corner came a boy of four or five, a husky youngster with a stick in his hand and his eyes blazing. When he saw Jim he stopped abruptly. This stranger looked just like the old picture on his mother's table. Only he had on a coat in the picture, a store-bought coat.

"Jim." Jane was on her feet now, color coming back into her face. "This is Little Jim. This is your son."

Jim London swallowed and his throat suddenly filled. He looked at his wife and started toward her. He felt awkward, clumsy. He took her by the elbows. "Been a long time, honey," he said hoarsely, "a mighty long time!"

She drew back a little, nervously. "Let's—I've coffee on. We'll—" She turned and hurried toward the door and he followed.

It would take some time. A little time for both of them to get over feeling strange, and maybe more time for her. She was a woman, and women needed time to get used to things.

He turned his head and almost automatically his eyes went to that south forty. The field was green with a young crop. Wheat! He smiled.

She had filled his cup; he dropped into a seat, and she sat down opposite him. Little Jim looked awkwardly at Betty Jane, and she stared at him with round, curious eyes.

"There's a big frog down by the bridge," Little Jim said suddenly. "I bet I can make him hop!"

They ran outside into the sunlight, and across the table Jim London took his wife's hand. It was good to be home. Mighty good.

THE TURKEYFEATHER RIDERS

JIM SANDIFER SWUNG down from his buckskin and stood for a long minute staring across the saddle toward the dark bulk of Bearwallow Mountain. His was the grave, careful look of a man accustomed to his own company under the sun and in the face of the wind. For three years he had been riding for the B Bar, and for two of those years he had been ranch foreman. What he was about to do would bring an end to that, an end to the job, to the life here, to his chance to win the girl he loved.

Voices sounded inside, the low rumble of Gray Bowen's bass and the quick, light voice of his daughter, Elaine. The sound of her voice sent a quick spasm of pain across Sandifer's face. Tying the buckskin to the hitch rail, he walked up the steps, his boots sounding loud on the planed boards, his spurs tinkling lightly.

The sound of his steps brought instant stillness to the group inside and then the quick tattoo of Elaine's feet as she hurried to meet him. It was a sound he would never tire of hearing, a sound that had brought gladness to him such as he had never known before. Yet when her eyes met his at the door her flashing smile faded.

"Jim! What's wrong?" Then she noticed the blood on his shoulder and the tear where the bullet had ripped his shirt, and her face went white to the lips. "You're hurt!"

"No—only a scratch." He put aside her detaining hand. "Wait. I'll talk to your dad first." His hands dropped to hers, and as she looked up, startled at his touch, he said gravely and sincerely, "No matter what happens now, I want you to know that I've loved you since the day we met. I've thought of little else, believe that." He dropped her hands then and stepped past her into the huge room where Gray Bowen waited, his big body relaxed in a homemade chair of cowhide.

Rose Martin was there, too, and her tall, handsome son, Lee. Jim's eyes avoided them for he knew what their faces were like; he knew the quiet serenity of Rose Martin's face, masking a cunning as cold and calculating as her son's flaming temper. It was these two who were destroying the B Bar, they who had brought the big ranch to the verge of a deadly range war by their conniving. A war that could have begun this morning, but for him.

Even as he began to speak he knew his words would put him right where they wanted him, that when he had finished, he would be through here, and Gray Bowen and his daughter would be left unguarded to the machinations of this woman and her son. Yet he could no longer refrain from speaking. The lives of men depended on it.

Bowen's lips thinned when he saw the blood. "You've seen Katrishen? Had a run-in with him?"

"No!" Sandifer's eyes blazed. "There's no harm in Katrishen if he's left alone. No trouble unless we make it. I ask you to recall, Gray, that for two years we've lived at peace with the Katrishens. We have had no trouble until the last three months." He paused, hoping the idea would soak in that trouble had begun with the coming of the Martins. "He won't give us any trouble if we leave him alone!"

"Leave him alone to steal our range!" Lee Martin flared.

Sandifer's eyes swung. "*Our* range? Are you now a partner in the B Bar?"

Lee smiled, covering his slip. "Naturally, as I am a friend of Mr. Bowen's, I think of his interests as mine."

Bowen waved an impatient hand. "That's no matter! What happened?"

Here it was, then. The end of all his dreaming, his planning, his hoping. "It wasn't Katrishen. It was Klee Mont."

"Who?" Bowen came out of his chair with a lunge, veins swelling. "Mont shot *you*? What for? Why, in heavens' name?"

"Mont was over there with the Mello boys and Art Dunn. He had gone over to run the Katrishens off their Iron Creek holdings. If they had tried that, they would have started a first-class range war with no holds barred. I stopped them."

Rose Martin flopped her knitting in her lap and glanced up at him, smiling smugly. Lee began to roll a smoke, one eyebrow lifted. This was what they had wanted, for he alone had blocked them here. The others the Martins could influence, but not Jim Sandifer.

Bowen's eyes glittered with his anger. He was a choleric man, given to sudden bursts of fury, a man who hated being thwarted and who was impatient of all restraint.

"You stopped them? Did they tell you whose orders took them over there? Did they?"

"They did. I told them to hold off until I could talk with you, but Mont refused to listen. He said his orders had been given him and he would follow them to the letter."

"He did right!" Bowen's voice boomed in the big room. "Exactly right! And you stopped them? *You* countermanded my orders?"

"I did." Sandifer laid it flatly on the line. "I told them there would be no burning or killing while I was foreman. I told them they weren't going to run us into a range war for nothing."

Gray Bowen balled his big hands into fists. "You've got a gall, Jim! You know better than to countermand an order of mine! And you'll leave me to decide what range I need! Katrishen's got no business on Iron Creek, an' I told him so! I told him to get off an' get out! As for this range war talk, that's foolishness! He won't fight!"

"Putting them off would be a very simple matter," Lee Martin interposed quietly. "If you hadn't interfered, Sandifer, they would be off now and the whole matter settled."

"Settled nothin'!" Jim exploded. "Where did you get this idea that Bill Katrishen could be pushed around? The man was an officer in the Army during the war, an' he's fought Indians on the plains."

"You must be a great friend of his," Rose Martin said gently. "You know so much about him."

Gray Bowen stopped in his pacing, and his face was like a

rock. "You been talkin' with Katrishen? You sidin' that outfit?"

"I ride for the brand," Sandifer replied. "I know Katrishen, of course. I've talked to him."

"And to his daughter?" Lee suggested, his eyes bright with malice. "With his pretty daughter?"

Out of the tail of his eye Jim saw Elaine's head come up quickly, but he ignored Lee's comment. "Stop and think," he said to Bowen. "When did this trouble start? When Mrs. Martin and her son came here! You got along fine with Katrishen until then! They've been putting you up to this!"

Bowen's eyes narrowed. "That will be enough of that!" he said sharply. He was really furious now, not the flaring, hot fury that Jim knew so well, but a cold, hard anger that nothing could touch. For the first time Jim realized how futile any argument was going to be. Rose Martin and her son had insinuated themselves too much and too well into the picture of Gray Bowen's life.

"You wanted my report," Sandifer said quietly. "Mont wouldn't listen to my arguments for time. He said he had his orders and would take none from me. I told him then that if he rode forward it was against my gun. He laughed at me, then reached for his gun. I shot him."

Gray Bowen's widened eyes expressed his amazement.

"You shot *Mont*? You beat him to the draw?"

"That's right. I didn't want to kill him, but I shot the gun out of his hand and held my gun on him for a minute to let him know what it meant to be close to death. Then I started them back here."

Bowen's anger was momentarily swallowed by his astonishment. He recalled suddenly that in the three years Sandifer had worked for him there had been no occasion for him to draw a gun in anger. There had been a few brushes with Apaches and one with rustlers, but all rifle work. Klee Mont had seven known killings on his record and had been reputed to be the fastest gunhand west of the Rio Grande.

"It seems peculiar," Mrs. Martin said composedly, "for you to turn your gun on men who ride for Mr. Bowen, taking sides against him. No doubt you meant well, but it does seem strange."

"Not if you know the Katrishens," Jim replied grimly. "Bill was assured he could settle on that Iron Creek holding before he moved in. He was told that we made no claim on anything beyond Willow and Gilita creeks."

"Who," Lee insinuated, "assured him of that?"

"I did," Jim said coolly. "Since I've been foreman, we've never run any cattle beyond that boundary. Iron Mesa is a block that cuts us off from the country south of there, and the range to the east is much better and is open for us clear to Beaver Creek and south to the Middle Fork."

"So you decide what range will be used? I think for a hired hand you take a good deal of authority. Personally, I'm wondering how much your loyalty is divided. Or if it is divided. It seems to me you act more as a friend of the Katrishens—or their daughter."

Sandifer took a step forward. "Martin," he said evenly, "are you aimin' to say that I'd double-cross the boss? If you are, you're a liar!"

Bowen looked up, a chill light in his eyes that Sandifer had never seen there before. "That will be all, Jim. You better go."

Sandifer turned on his heel and strode outside.

———

WHEN SANDIFER WALKED into the bunkhouse, the men were already back. The room was silent, but he was aware of the hatred in the cold, blue eyes of Mont as he lay sprawled in his bunk. His right hand and wrist were bandaged. The Mello boys snored in their bunks, while Art Dunn idly shuffled cards at the table. These were the new hands, hired since the coming of the Martins. Only three of the older hands were in, and none of them spoke.

"Hello—lucky." Mont rolled up on his elbow. "Lose your job?"

"Not yet," Jim said shortly, aware that his remark brought a fleeting anger to Mont's eyes.

"You will!" Mont assured him. "If you are in the country when this hand gets well, I'll kill you!"

Jim Sandifer laughed shortly. He was aware that the older hands were listening, although none would have guessed it without knowing them.

"You called me lucky, Klee. It was you who were lucky in that I didn't figure on killin' you. That was no miss. I aimed for your gunhand. Furthermore, don't try pullin' a gun on me again. You're too slow."

"Slow?" Mont's face flamed. He reared up in his bunk. "Slow? Why, you two-handed bluffer!"

Sandifer shrugged. "Look at your hand," he said calmly. "If you don't know what happened, I do. That bullet didn't cut your thumb off. It doesn't go up your hand or arm; the wound runs *across* your hand."

They all knew what he meant. Sandifer's bullet must have hit his hand as he was in the act of drawing and before the gun came level, indicating that Sandifer had beaten Mont to the draw by a safe margin. That Klee Mont realized the implication was plain, for his face darkened and then paled around the lips. There was pure hatred in his eyes when he looked up at Sandifer.

"I'll kill you!" he said viciously. "I'll kill you!"

As Sandifer started outside, Rep Dean followed him. With Grimes and Sparkman, he was one of the older hands.

"What's come over this place, Jim? Six months ago there wasn't a better spread in the country."

Sandifer did not reply, and Dean built a smoke. "It's that woman," he said. "She twists the boss around her little finger. If it wasn't for you, I'd quit, but I'm thinkin' that there's nothin' she wouldn't like better than for all of the old hands to ask for their time."

Sparkman and Grimes had followed them from the bunkhouse. Sparkman was a lean-bodied Texan with some reputation as an Indian fighter.

"You watch your step," Grimes warned. "Next time Mont will backshoot you!"

They talked among themselves, and as they conversed, he

ran his thoughts over the developments of the past few months. He had heard enough of Mrs. Martin's sly, insinuating remarks to understand how she had worked Bowen up to ordering Katrishen driven off, yet there was no apparent motive. It seemed obvious that the woman had her mind set on marrying Gray Bowen, but for that it was not essential that any move be made against the Katrishens.

Sandifer's limitation of the B Bar range had been planned for the best interests of the ranch. The range they now had in use was bounded by streams and mountain ranges and was rich in grass and water, a range easily controlled with a small number of hands and with little danger of loss from raiding Indians, rustlers, or varmints.

His willingness to have the Katrishens move in on Iron Creek was not without the B Bar in mind. He well knew that range lying so much out of the orbit of the ranch could not be long held tenantless, and the Katrishens were stable, honest people who would make good neighbors and good allies. Thinking back, he could remember almost to the day when the first rumors began to spread, and most of them had stemmed from Lee Martin himself. Later, one of the Mello boys had come in with a bullet hole in the crown of his hat and a tale of being fired on from Iron Mesa.

"What I can't figure out," Grimes was saying, "is what that no-account Lee Martin would be doin' over on the Turkeyfeather."

Sandifer turned his head. "On the Turkeyfeather? That's beyond Iron Mesa! Why, that's clear over the other side of Katrishen's!"

"Sure enough! I was huntin' that brindle steer who's always leadin' stock off into the canyons when I seen Martin fordin' the Willow. He was ridin' plumb careful, an' he sure wasn't playin' no tenderfoot then! I was right wary of him, so I took in behind an' trailed him over to that rough country near Turkeyfeather Pass. Then I lost him."

The door slammed up at the house, and they saw Lee Martin come down the steps and start toward them. It was dusk, but still light enough to distinguish faces. Martin walked up to Sandifer.

"Here's your time." He held out an envelope. "You're through!"

"I'll want that from Bowen himself," Sandifer replied stiffly.

"He doesn't want to see you. He sent this note." Martin handed over a sheet of the coarse brown paper on which Bowen kept his accounts. On it, in Bowen's hand, was his dismissal.

I won't have a man who won't obey orders. Leave tonight.

Sandifer stared at the note, which he could barely read in the dim light. He had worked hard for the B Bar, and this was his answer.

"All right," he said briefly. "Tell him I'm leaving. It won't take any great time to saddle up."

Martin laughed. "That won't take time, either. You'll walk out. No horse leaves this ranch."

Jim turned back, his face white. "You keep out of this, Martin. That buckskin is my own horse. You get back in your hole an' stay there!"

Martin stepped closer. "Why, you cheap bigmouth!"

The blow had been waiting for a long time, but it came fast now. It was a smashing left that caught Martin on the chin and spilled him on his back in the dust. With a muttered curse, Martin came off the ground and rushed, but Sandifer stepped in, blocking a right and whipping his own right into Lee's midsection. Martin doubled over, and Jim straightened him with a left uppercut and then knocked him crashing into the corral fence.

Abruptly, Sandifer turned and threw the saddle on the buckskin. Sparkman swore. "I'm quittin', too!" he said.

"An' me!" Grimes snapped. "I'll be doggoned if I'll work here now!"

Heavily, Martin got to his feet. His white shirt was bloody, and they could vaguely see a blotch of blood over the lower part of his face. He limped away, muttering.

"Sparky," Jim said, low voiced, "don't quit. All of you stay on. I reckon this fight ain't over, an' the boss may need a friend. You stick here. I'll not be far off!"

———

SANDIFER HAD NO plan, yet it was Lee Martin's ride to the Turkeyfeather that puzzled him most, and almost of its own volition, his horse took that route. As he rode he turned the problem over and over in his mind, seeking for a solution, yet none appeared that was satisfactory. Revenge for some old grudge against the Katrishens was considered and put aside; he could not but feel that whatever the reason for the plotting of the Martins, there had to be profit in it somewhere.

Certainly, there seemed little to prevent Rose Martin from marrying Gray Bowen if she wished. The old man was well aware that Elaine was a lovely, desirable girl. The cowhands and other male visitors who came to call for one excuse or another were evidence of that. She would not be with him long, and if she left, he was faced with the dismal prospect of ending his years alone. Rose Martin was a shrewd woman and attractive for her years, and she knew how to make Gray comfortable and how to appeal to him. Yet obviously there was something more in her mind than this, and it was that something more in which Sandifer was interested.

Riding due east Jim crossed the Iron near Clayton and turned west by south through the broken country. It was very late, and vague moonlight filtered through the yellow pine and fir that guarded the way he rode with their tall columns. Twice he halted briefly, feeling a strange uneasiness, yet listen as he might he could detect no alien sound, nothing but the faint stirring of the slight breeze through the needles of the pines and the occasional rustle of a blown leaf. He rode on, but now he avoided the bright moonlight and kept more to the deep shadows under the trees.

After skirting the end of the Jerky Mountains, he headed for the Turkeyfeather Pass. Somewhere off to his left, lost against the blackness of the ridge shadow, a faint sound came to him. He drew up, listening. He did not hear it again, yet his senses could not have lied. It was the sound of a dead branch scraping along leather, such a sound as might be made by a horseman riding through brush.

Sliding his Winchester from its scabbard, he rode forward, every sense alert. His attention was drawn to the buckskin, whose ears were up and who, when he stopped, lifted its head and stared off toward the darkness. Sandifer started the horse forward, moving easily.

To the left towered the ridge of Turkeyfeather Pass, lifting all of five hundred feet above him, black, towering, ominous in the moonlight. The trees fell away, massing their legions to right and left, but leaving before him an open glade, grassy and still. Off to the right Iron Creek hustled over the stones, whispering wordless messages to the rocks on either bank. Somewhere a quail called mournfully into the night, and the hoofs of the buckskin made light whispering sounds as they moved through the grass at the edge of the glade.

Jim drew up under the trees near the creek and swung down, warning the buckskin to be still. Taking his rifle he circled the glade under the trees, moving like a prowling wolf. Whoever was over there was stalking him, watching a chance to kill him or perhaps only following to see where he went. In any case, Jim meant to know who and why.

Suddenly he heard a vague sound before him, a creak of saddle leather. Freezing in place, he listened and heard it again, followed by the crunch of gravel. Then he caught the glint of moonlight on a rifle barrel and moved forward, shifting position to get the unseen man silhouetted against the sky. Sandifer swung his rifle.

"All right," he said calmly, "drop that rifle and lift your hands! I've got you dead to rights!"

As he spoke, the man was moving forward, and instantly the fellow dived headlong. Sandifer's rifle spat fire, and he heard a grunt, followed by a stab of flame. A bullet whipped past his ear. Shifting ground on cat feet, Jim studied the spot carefully.

The man lay in absolute darkness, but listening he could hear the heavy breathing that proved his shot had gone true.

He waited, listening for movement, but there was none. After a while the breathing grew less and he took a chance.

"Better give up!" he said. "No use dyin' there!"

There was silence and then a slight movement of gravel. Then a six-shooter flew through the air to land in the open space between them.

"What about that rifle?" Sandifer demanded cautiously.

"Lost . . . for God's sake, help . . . me!"

There was no mistaking the choking sound. Jim Sandifer got up and, holding his rifle on the spot where the voice had sounded, crossed into the shadows. As it was, he almost stumbled over the wounded man before he saw him. It was Dan Mello, and the heavy slug had torn into his body but seemed not to have emerged.

Working swiftly, Jim got the wounded man into an easier position and carefully pulled his shirt away from the wound. There was no mistaking the fact that Dan Mello was hit hard. Jim gave the wounded man a drink and then hastily built a fire to work by. His guess that the bullet had not emerged proved true, but moving his hand gently down the wounded man's back he could feel something hard near his spine. When he straightened, Mellow's eyes sought his face.

"Don't you move," Sandifer warned. "It's right near your spine. I've got to get a doctor."

He was worried, knowing little of such wounds. The man might be bleeding internally.

"No, don't leave me!" Mello pleaded. "Some varmint might come!" The effort of speaking left him panting.

Jim Sandifer swore softly, uncertain as to his proper course. He had little hope that Mello could be saved, even if he rode for a doctor. The nearest one was miles away, and movement of the wounded man would be very dangerous. Nor was Mello's fear without cause, for there were mountain lions, wolves, and coyotes in the area, and the scent of blood was sure to call them.

"Legs—gone," Mello panted. "Can't feel nothing."

"Take it easy," Jim advised. The nearest place was Bill Katrishen's, and Bill might be some hand with a wounded man. He said as much to Mello. "Can't be more'n three, four miles," he added. "I'll give you back your gun an' build up the fire."

"You—you'll sure come back?" Mello pleaded.

"What kind of coyote do you think I am?" Sandifer asked irritably. "I'll get back as soon as ever I can." He looked down at him. "Why were you gunnin' for me? Mont put you up to it?"

Mello shook his head. "Mont, he—he ain't—bad. It's that Martin—you watch. He's pizen—mean."

———

LEAVING THE FIRE blazing brightly, Jim returned to his buckskin and jumped into the saddle. The moon was higher now, and the avenues through the trees were like roads, eerily lighted. Touching a spur to the horse, Jim raced through the night, the cool wind fanning his face. Once a deer scurried from in front of him and then bounded off through the trees, and once he thought he saw the lumbering shadow of an old grizzly.

The Katrishen log cabin and pole corrals lay bathed in white moonlight as he raced his horse into the yard. The drum of hooves upon the hard-packed earth and his call brought movement and an answer from inside: "Who is it? What's up?"

Briefly, he explained, and after a minute the door opened.

"Come in, Jim. Figured I heard a shot a while back. Dan Mello, you say? He's a bad one."

Hurrying to the corral, Jim harnessed two mustangs and hitched them to the buckboard. A moment later Bill Katrishen, tall and gray haired, came from the cabin, carrying a lantern in one hand and a black bag in the other.

"I'm no medical man," he said, "but I fixed a sight of bullet wounds in my time." He crawled into the buckboard, and one of his sons got up beside him. Led by Sandifer they started back over the way he had come.

Mello was still conscious when they stopped beside him. He looked unbelievingly at Katrishen.

"You come?" he said. "You knowed who—who I was?"

"You're hurt, ain't you?" Katrishen asked testily. Carefully, he examined the man and then sat back on his heels. "Mello," he said, "I ain't one for foolin' a man. You're plumb bad off. That bullet seems to have slid off your hip bone an' tore right through you. If we had you down to the house, we could work on you a durned sight better, but I don't know whether you'd make it or not."

The wounded man breathed heavily, staring from one to the other. He looked scared, and he was sweating, and under it his face was pale.

"What you think," he panted, "all right—with me."

"The three of us can put him on them quilts in the back of the buckboard. Jim, you slide your hands under his back."

"Hold up." Mello's eyes wavered and then focused on Jim. "You watch—Martin. He's plumb—bad."

"What's he want, Mello?" Jim said. "What's he after?"

"G—old," Mellow panted, and then suddenly he relaxed.

"Fainted," Katrishen said. "Load him up."

All through the remainder of the night they worked over him. It was miles over mountain roads to Silver City and the nearest doctor, and little enough that he could do. Shortly before the sun lifted, Dan Mello died.

Bill Katrishen got up from beside the bed, his face drawn with weariness. He looked across the body of Dan Mello at Sandifer.

"Jim, what's this all about? Why was he gunning for you?"

Hesitating only a moment, Jim Sandifer explained the needling of Gray Bowen by Rose Martin, the undercover machinations of her and her tall son, the hiring of the Mellos at their instigation and of Art Dunn and Klee Mont. Then he went on to the events preceding his break with the B Bar. Katrishen nodded thoughtfully, but obviously puzzled.

"I never heard of the woman, Jim. I can't figure why she'd have it in for me. What did Mello mean when he said Martin was after gold?"

"You've got me. I know they are money hungry, but the ranch is—" He stopped, and his face lifted, his eyes narrowing. "Bill, did you ever hear of gold around here?"

"Sure, over toward Cooney Canyon. You know, Cooney was a sergeant in the Army, and after his discharge he returned to hunt for gold he located while a soldier. The Apaches finally got him, but he had gold first."

"Maybe that's it. I want a fresh horse, Bill."

"You get some sleep first. The boys an' I'll take care of Dan. Kara will fix breakfast for you."

The sun was high when Jim Sandifer rolled out of his bunk and stumbled sleepily to the door to splash his face in cold water poured from a bucket into the tin basin. Kara heard him moving and came to the door, walking carefully and lifting her hand to the doorjamb.

"Hello, Jim? Are you rested? Dad an' the boys buried Dan Mello over on the knoll."

Jim smiled at her reassuringly.

"I'm rested, but after I eat I'll be ridin', Kara." He looked up at the slender girl with the rusty hair and pale freckles. "You keep the boys in, will you? I don't want them to be where they could be shot at until I can figure a way out of this. I'm going to maintain peace in this country or die tryin'!"

———

THE BUCKSKIN HORSE was resting, but the iron gray that Katrishen had provided was a good mountain horse. Jim Sandifer pulled his gray hat low over his eyes and squinted against the sun. He liked the smell of pine needles, the pungent smell of sage. He moved carefully, searching the trail for the way Lee Martin's horse had gone the day Grimes followed him.

Twice he lost the trail and then found it only to lose it finally in the sand of a wash. The area covered by the sand was small, a place where water had spilled down a steep mountainside, eating out a raw wound in the cliff, yet there the trail vanished. Dismounting, Sandifer's careful search disclosed a brushed-over spot near the cliff and then a chafed place on a small tree. Here Lee Martin had tied his horse, and from here he must have gone on foot.

It was a small rock, only half as big as his fist, that was the telltale clue. The rock showed where it had lain in the earth but had been recently rolled aside. Moving close, he could see that the stone had rolled from under a clump of brush, the clump moved easily under his hand. Then he saw that although the roots were still in the soil, at some time part of it had been pulled free. The brush covered an opening no more than a couple of feet wide and twice as high. It was a man-made tunnel, but one not recently made.

Concealing the gray in the trees some distance off, Sandifer walked back to the hole, stared around uneasily, and then ducked his head and entered. Once he was inside, the tunnel was higher and wider, and then it opened into a fair-sized room. Here the ore had been stoped out, and he looked around, holding a match high. The light caught and glinted upon the rock, and moving closer he picked up a small chunk of rose quartz seamed with gold!

Pocketing the sample, he walked further in until he saw a black hole yawning before him, and beside it lay a notched pole such as the Indians had used in Spanish times to climb out of mine shafts. Looking over into the hole, he saw a longer pole reaching down into the darkness. He peered over and then straightened. This, then, was what Dan Mello had meant! The Martins wanted gold.

The match flickered out, and standing there in the cool darkness, he thought it over and understood. This place was on land used, and probably claimed, by Bill Katrishen, and it could not be worked unless they were driven off. But could he make Gray Bowen believe him? What would Lee do if his scheme was exposed? Why had Mello been so insistent that Martin was dangerous?

He bent over and started into the tunnel exit and then stopped. Kneeling just outside were Lee Martin, Art Dunn, and Jay Mello. Lee had a shotgun pointed at Jim's body. Jim jerked back around the corner of stone even as the shotgun thundered.

"You dirty, murderin' rat!" he yelled. "Let me out in the open and try that!"

Martin laughed. "I wouldn't think of it! You're right where I want you now, an' you'll stay there!"

Desperately, Jim stared around. Martin was right. He was bottled up now. He drew his gun, wanting to chance a shot at Martin while yet there was time, but when he stole a glance around the corner of the tunnel, there was nothing to be seen. Suddenly, he heard a sound of metal striking stone, a rattle of rock, and then a thunderous crash, and the tunnel was filled with dust, stifling and thick. Lee Martin had closed off the tunnel mouth, and he was entombed alive!

Jim Sandifer leaned back against the rock wall of the stope and closed his eyes. He was frightened. He was frightened with a deep, soul-shaking fear, for this was something against which he could not fight, these walls of living rock around him, and the dead debris of the rock-choked tunnel. He was buried alive.

———

SLOWLY, THE DUST settled from the heavy air. Saving his few matches, he got down on his knees and crawled into the tunnel, but there was barely room enough. Mentally, he tried to calculate the distance out, and he could see that there was no less than fifteen feet of rock between him and escape— not an impossible task if more rock did not slide down from above. Remembering the mountain, he knew that above the tunnel mouth it was almost one vast slide.

He could hear nothing, and the air was hot and close. On his knees he began to feel his way around, crawling until he reached the tunnel and the notched pole. Here he hesitated, wondering what the darkness below would hold.

Water, perhaps? Or even snakes? He had heard of snakes taking over old mines. Nevertheless, he began to descend— down, down into the abysmal blackness below him. He seemed to have climbed down an interminable distance when suddenly his boot touched rock.

Standing upright, one hand on the pole, he reached out. His hand found rock on three sides, on the other, only empty space. He turned in that direction and ran smack into the rock wall, knocking sparks from his skull. He drew back, swearing, and found the tunnel. At the same time, his hand touched something else, a sort of ledge in the corner of the rock, and on the ledge—his heart gave a leap!

Candles!

Quickly, he got out a match and lit the first one. Then he walked into the tunnel. Here was more of the rose quartz, and it was incredibly seamed with gold. Lee Martin had made a strike. Rather, studying the walls, he had found an old mine, perhaps an old Spanish working. Suddenly Jim saw a pick and he grinned. There still might be a way out. Yet a few minutes of exploration sufficed to indicate that there was no other opening. If he was to go out, it must be by the way he came.

Taking the candles with him he climbed the notched pole and stuck a lighted candle on a rock. Then, with a pick at his side, he started to work at the debris choking the tunnel. He lifted a rock and moved it aside, then another.

———

AN HOUR LATER, soaked with sweat, he was still working away, pausing each minute or so to examine the hanging wall. The tunnel was cramped, and the work moved slowly ahead, for every stone removed had to be shoved back into the stope behind him. He reached the broken part overhead, and when he moved a rock, more slid down. He worked on, his breath coming in great gasps, sweat dripping from his face and neck to his hands.

A new sound came to him, a faint tapping. He held still, listening, trying to quiet his breathing and the pound of his heart. Then he heard it again, an unmistakable tapping!

Grasping his pick, he tapped three times, then an interval, then three times again. Then he heard somebody pull at the rocks of the tunnel, and his heart pounded with exultation. He had been found!

———

HOW THE FOLLOWING hours passed Sandifer never quite knew, but working feverishly, he fought his way through the border of time that divided him from the outer world and the clean, pine-scented air. Suddenly, a stone was moved and an arrow of light stabbed the darkness, and with it came the cool air he wanted. He took a deep breath, filling his lungs with air so liquid it might almost be water, and then he went to work, helping the hands outside to enlarge the opening. When there was room enough, he thrust his head and shoulders through and then pulled himself out and stood up, dusting himself off—and found he was facing, not Bill Katrishen or one of his sons, but Jay Mello!

"You?" he was astonished. "What brought you back?"

Jay wiped his thick hands on his jeans and looked uncomfortable.

"Never figured to bury no man alive," he said. "That was Martin's idea. Anyway, Katrishen told me what you done for Dan."

"Did he tell you I'd killed him? I'm sorry, Jay. It was him or me."

"Sure. I knowed that when he come after you. I didn't like it nohow. What I meant, well—you could've left him lie. You didn't need to go git help for him. I went huntin' Dan, when I found you was alive, an' I figured it was like that, that he was dead. Katrishen gave me his clothes, an' I found this—"

It was a note, scrawled painfully, perhaps on a rifle stock or a flat rock, written, no doubt, while Jim was gone for help.

Jay:
   Git shet of Marten. Sandfer's all right. He's gone for hulp to Katrisshn. I'm hard hit. Sandfer shore is wite. So long, Jay, good ridin.

                                        Dan.

"I'm sorry, Jay. He was game."

"Sure." Jay Mello scowled. "It was Martin got us into this, him an' Klee Mont. We never done no killin' before, maybe stole a few hosses or run off a few head of cows."

"What's happened? How long was I in there?" Jim glanced at the sun.

"About five, six hours. She'll be dark soon." Mello hesitated. "I reckon I'm goin' to take out—light a shuck for Texas."

Sandifer thrust out his hand. "Good luck, Jay. Maybe we'll meet again."

The outlaw nodded. He stared at the ground, and then he looked up, his tough, unshaven face strangely lonely in the late-afternoon sun.

"Sure wish Dan was ridin' with me. We always rode together, him an' me, since we was kids." He rubbed a hard hand over his lips. "What d'you know? That girl back to Katrishen's? She put some flowers on his grave! Sure enough!"

He turned and walked to his horse, swung into the saddle, and walked his horse down the trail, a somber figure captured momentarily by the sunlight before he turned away under the pines. Incongruously, Jim noticed that the man's vest was split up the back, and the crown of his hat was torn.

The gray waited patiently by the brush, and then Jim Sandifer untied him and swung into the saddle. It was a fast ride he made back to the ranch on Iron Creek. There he swapped saddles, explaining all to Katrishen. "I'm riding," he said. "There's no room in this country for Lee Martin now."

"Want us to come?" Bill asked.

"No. They might think it was war. You stay out of it, for we want no Pleasant Valley War here. Leave it lay. I'll settle this."

———

HE TURNED FROM the trail before he reached the B Bar, riding through the cottonwoods and sycamores along the creek. Then he rode up between the buildings and stopped beside the corral. The saddle leather creaked when he swung down, and he saw a slight movement at the corner of the corral.

"Klee? Is that you?" It was Art Dunn. "What's goin' on up at the house?"

Jim Sandifer took a long step forward. "No, Art," he said swiftly, "it's me!"

Dunn took a quick step back and grabbed for his gun, but Jim was already moving, expecting him to reach. Sandifer's left hand dropped to Art's wrist, and his right smashed up in a wicked uppercut to the solar plexus.

Dunn grunted and his knees sagged. Jim let go of his wrist then and hooked sharply to the chin, hearing Dunn's teeth click as the blow smashed home. Four times more Jim hit him, rocking his head on his shoulders; then he smashed another punch to the wind and, grabbing Dunn's belt buckle, jerked his gun belt open.

The belt slipped down and Dunn staggered and went to his knees. The outlaw pawed wildly, trying to get at Jim, but he was still gasping for the wind that had been knocked out of him.

The bunkhouse door opened and Sparkman stepped into the light. "What's the matter?" he asked. "What goes on?"

Sandifer called softly, and Sparkman grunted and came down off the steps. "Jim! You here? There's the devil to pay up at the house, man! I don't know what came off up there, but there was a shootin'! When we tried to go up, Mont was on the steps with a shotgun to drive us back."

"Take care of this hombre. I'll find out what's wrong fast enough. Where's Grimes an' Rep?"

"Rep Dean rode over to the line cabin on Cabin Creek to round up some boys in case of trouble. Grimes is inside."

"Then take Dunn an' keep your eyes open! I may need help. If I yell, come loaded for bear an' huntin' hair!"

Jim Sandifer turned swiftly and started for the house. He walked rapidly, circling as he went toward the little-used front door, opened only on company occasions. That door, he knew, opened into a large, old-fashioned parlor that was rarely occupied. It was a showplace, stiff and uncomfortable, and mostly gilt and plush. The front door was usually locked, but he remembered that he had occasion to help move some furniture not long before and the door had been left unlocked. There was every chance that it still was, for the room was so little used as to be almost forgotten.

Easing up on the veranda, he tiptoed to the door and gently turned the knob. The door opened inward, and he stepped swiftly through and closed it behind him. All was dark and silent, but there was light under the intervening door and a sound of movement. With the thick carpet muffling his footfalls, he worked his way across the room to the door.

"How's the old man?" Martin was asking.

His mother replied. "He's all right. He'll live."

Martin swore. "If that girl hadn't bumped me, I'd have killed him and we'd be better off. We could easy enough fix things so that Sandifer would get blamed for it."

"Don't be in such a hurry," Rose Martin intervened. "You're always in such a fret. The girl's here, an' we can use her to help. As long as we have her, the old man will listen, and while he's hurt, she'll do as she's told."

Martin muttered under his breath. "If we'd started by killing Sandifer like I wanted, all would be well," he said irritably. "What he said about the Katrishen trouble startin' with our comin' got the old man to thinkin'. Then I figure Bowen was sorry he fired his foreman."

"No matter!" Rose Martin was brusque. "We've got this place, and we can handle the Katrishens ourselves. There's plenty of time now Sandifer's gone."

Steps sounded. "Lee, the old man's comin' out of it. He wants his daughter."

"Tell him to go climb a tree!" Martin replied stiffly. "You watch him!"

"Where's Art?" Klee protested. "I don't like it, Lee! He's been gone too long. Somethin's up!"

"Aw, forget it! Quit cryin'! You do more yelpin' than a mangy coyote!"

Sandifer stood very still, thinking. There was no sound of Elaine, so she must be a prisoner in her room. Turning, he tiptoed across the room toward the far side. A door there, beyond the old piano, opened into Elaine's room. Carefully, he tried the knob. It held.

At that very instant a door opened in the other room, and he saw light under the door before him. He heard a startled gasp from Elaine and Lee Martin's voice, taunting, familiar.

"What's the matter? Scared?" Martin laughed. "If you'd kept that pretty mouth of yours shut, your dad would still be all right! You tellin' him Sandifer was correct about the Katrishens an' that he shouldn't of fired him!"

"He shouldn't have," the girl said quietly. "If he was here now, he'd kill you. Get out of my room."

"Maybe I ain't ready to go?" he taunted. "An' from now on I'm goin' to come an' go as I like."

His steps advanced into the room, and Jim tightened his grip on the knob. He remembered that lock, and it was not set very securely. Suddenly, an idea came to him. Turning, he picked up an old glass lamp, large and ornate. Balancing it momentarily in his hand, he drew it back and hurled it with a long overhand swing through the window!

Glass crashed on the veranda, and there the lamp hit, went down a step, and stayed there. Inside the girl's room, there was a startled exclamation, and he heard running footsteps from both the girl's room and the old man's. Somebody yelled, "What's that? What happened?" And he hurled his shoulder against the door.

As he had expected, the flimsy lock carried away and he was catapulted through the door into Elaine's bedroom. Catching himself, he wheeled and sprang for the door that opened into the living room beyond. He reached it just as Mont jerked the curtain back, but not wanting to endanger the girl, he swung hard with his fist instead of drawing his gun.

The blow came out of a clear sky to smash Mont on the jaw, and he staggered back into the room. Jim Sandifer sprang through, legs spread, hands wide.

"You, Martin!" he said sharply. "Draw!"

Lee Martin was a killer, but no gunman. White to the lips, his eyes deadly, he sprang behind his mother and grabbed for the shotgun.

"Shoot, Jim!" Elaine cried. "Shoot!"

He could not. Rose Martin stood between him and his target, and Martin had the shotgun now and was swinging it. Jim lunged, shoving the table over, and the lamp shattered in a crash. He fired and then fired again. Flame stabbed the darkness at him, and he fell back against the wall, switching his gun. Fire laced the darkness into a stabbing crimson crossfire, and the room thundered with sound and then died to stillness that was the stillness of death itself.

No sound remained, only the acrid smell of gunpowder mingled with the smell of coal oil and the faint, sickish-sweet smell of blood. His guns ready, Jim crouched in the darkness, alert for movement. Somebody groaned and then sighed deeply, and a spur grated on the floor. From the next room, Gray Bowen called weakly. "Daughter? Daughter, what's happened? What's wrong?"

There was no movement yet, but the darkness grew more familiar. Jim's eyes became more accustomed to it. He could see no one standing. Yet it was Elaine who broke the stillness.

"Jim? Jim, are you all right? Oh, Jim—are you safe?"

Maybe they were waiting for this.

"I'm all right," he said.

"Light your lamp, will you?" Deliberately, he moved, and there was no sound within the room—only outside, a running of feet on the hard-packed earth. Then a door slammed open, and Sparkman stood there, gun in hand.

"It's all right, I think," Sandifer said. "We shot it out."

Elaine entered the room with a light and caught herself with a gasp at the sight before her. Jim reached for the lamp.

"Go to your father," he said swiftly. "We'll take care of this."

Sparkman looked around, followed into the room by Grimes. "Good grief!" he gasped. "They are all dead! All of them!"

"The woman, too?" Sandifer's face paled. "I hope I didn't—"

"You didn't," Grimes said. "She was shot in the back by her own son. Shootin' in the dark, blind an' gun crazy."

"Maybe it's better," Sparkman said. "She was an old hellion."

Klee Mont had caught his right at the end of his eyebrow, and a second shot along the ribs. Sandifer walked away from him and stood over Lee Martin. His face twisted in a sneer, the dead man lay sprawled on the floor, literally shot to doll rags.

"You didn't miss many," Sparkman said grimly.

"I didn't figure to," Jim said. "I'll see the old man and then give you a hand."

"Forget it." Grimes looked up, his eyes faintly humorous.

"You stay in there. An' don't spend all your time with the old man. We need a new setup on this here spread, an' with a new son-in-law who's a first-rate cattleman, Gray could set back an' relax!"

Sandifer stopped with his hand on the curtain. "Maybe you got something there," he said thoughtfully. "Maybe you have!"

"You can take my word for it," Elaine said, stepping into the door beside Jim. "He has! He surely has!"

A MAN NAMED UTAH

THE SMALL GLOW of the lamp over the hotel register, shaded as it was, threw his cheekbones into high relief and left his eyes hollows of darkness. The night clerk saw only a big man, in dusty range clothes, who signed his name in the slow, cramped manner of a man unaccustomed to the pen. Hibbs handed him his key and the man turned and started up the steps.

As he climbed, the light traveled down over his lean hips and picked out the dull luster of walnut-stocked guns, then slid down to worn boots and California-style spurs. When the heels vanished, Hibbs waited no longer but turned the register and peered at the name. Without another instant of delay he came from behind the counter, cast one quick glance up the stairs, and bustled out the door.

The quick, upward glance did not penetrate the darkness. Had it done so, he would have seen the stranger standing in the shadows at the head of the steps, watching him. When Hibbs hurried across the dark street, the rider was at his window, looking down. The clerk disappeared into an alley.

It was a small thing, but the rider knew the wheels had begun to turn. Already they knew of his presence, and already he had gathered his first fragment of a fact. Somebody was almighty interested in his arrival, and that somebody had a working deal with the hotel clerk. Not much to know, but a beginning.

The clerk had hurried on for several hundred feet then turned and stopped by a window with three inches of opening. He tapped lightly with a coin, and at a cautious response, he whispered, "Hibbs, here. Gent just registered as Utah Blaine, El Paso."

"All right."

Disappointed at the lack of reaction, Hibbs waited for something else to be said; then, when it did not come, he added, "He looks salty."

"All right."

Hibbs walked slowly back to the hotel. His round, rather querulous face sagged with vague disappointment.

———

THE MAN BEHIND the darkened window rolled on his side and picked up a carefully prepared cigarette that lay on the table by the bed. When it was lit he lay back, his head on the bunched-up pillow. Against the vague light of the window, the cigarette glowed and he stared up into darkness.

How much longer dared he continue? The pickings were rich, but he was feeling the uneasiness that preceded danger. He had a bag full, no doubt about that. Maybe it was time to pull his stakes.

He knew nothing of Blaine, yet that the man had been asked here was evidence that someone believed he was the man for the job.

Jack Storey had been tough and fast . . . a drunken miner named Peterson had been egged into shooting him in the back. Three other marshals preceded him and they were buried in a neat row on the hill. The man on the bed inhaled deeply and knew he had managed well up to now, but his luck was sure to run out.

He had the gold taken from miners, gamblers, and casual travelers and only Hibbs knew who he was, only he knew the murders and robberies had been engineered by one man. And the clerk could be removed.

So he would quit at last. This was what he had planned when he first came west, to work at a quiet job and amass a fortune by robbery and murder—then he would quit, go east, and live a quiet, ordered life from then on.

From the beginning he had known there was a limit. So far he was unsuspected. He was liked by many. His whole plan had depended on the crimes seeming to be unrelated so they would be considered casual crimes rather than a series planned and carried out by either one man or a gang.

Yet it would be foolish to continue. Three marshals . . . it was too many. Not too many lives, just too many chances. Too many risks of discovery. No matter how shrewd this new man might be, or how dumb, it was time to quit. He would not pull even one more job. He was through. Putting out the stub of his cigarette, he turned over and quietly went to sleep.

————

A SOLID-LOOKING MAN in a black suit and boots was sitting on the creek bank when Utah Blaine rode up. The new marshal's sun-darkened face had a shy grin that livened his features. "Hi, Tom! Mighty good to see you."

"Sure is." The older man gripped his hand. "Long time since the old days on the Neuces."

Blaine started to build a smoke. "So, what're you gettin' me into?"

Tom Church dug at the sand with a stick. "I don't really know. Maybe I'm crazy in the head. We've had fourteen murders this past year, an' it worries me some. This here town was started by my dad, an' he set store by it. We've always had the usual cowpuncher shootin's an' the like of that, but something's different. No other year since we started did we have more'n three or four."

He talked quietly and to the point while Blaine smoked. Nobody in town showed an unusual prosperity. No toughs were hanging around town that couldn't be accounted for. Nobody left town suddenly. Nobody hinted at secrets. The murdered man was always alone, although in two cases he had been left alone only a matter of minutes. All the murdered men had been carrying large sums of money.

A half-dozen men carrying smaller amounts had left town unhindered; only two of the fourteen had made killings at gambling. Others had worked claims, sold herds of cattle or horses. All fourteen had been killed silently, with knife, noose, or club. Which argued a killer who wanted no attention. "This town means a lot to us. My boys are growin' up here, an' two of the men killed were good friends of mine. I think there's a well-organized gang behind it."

"Got a hunch you're wrong, Tom."

"You think there's no connection?"

"I think they tie up, but I don't think it's a gang. I think it is just one man."

"How's that?"

"Look at it. Nobody has flashed any money and nobody has talked while drunk. That's unusual for a gang. You know there's always one wheel that won't mesh. I'll get to work on it."

Tom Church got up and brushed off his pants. "All right, but be careful. We've lost three marshals in the last ten months."

IT WAS TO Utah Blaine's advantage that he did not make a big show of looking for information. He did not throw his weight around. He let people know that he thought the marshal's job was mighty easy if people would just let him be. And while he sat around, he listened.

Hibbs at the hotel might be the key. Hibbs had rushed word of his coming to someone, and Blaine had seen the street he went into. For the first four days Utah Blaine strolled about, rode into the hills, talked little, and listened a lot. He heard a good deal of gossip about conditions of the claims, who was making it and who wasn't. There was talk about cattle and cattle prices. Most of this talk took place on the worn bench outside the barbershop.

It was late on the fourth night that he received his first test as marshal.

Blaine was at a table in a back corner of the saloon when a wide-shouldered young man with red hair smashed through the swinging doors and glared around him. Obviously, he had been drinking, just as obviously, he was not so drunk that his speech was slurred or his reactions slow. "Where's that two-bit marshal?" he demanded.

"Over here. What's on your mind?"

The casual tone upset Red Williams, who was trouble-hunting. Nevertheless, he took three quick steps toward Blaine, and Utah did not move. "You're the marshal? Well, I hear we got to check our guns! You figurin' to take mine away from me? If you do, get started!"

Blaine chuckled. "Red," he said conversationally, "don't you get enough trouble wrestlin' steers? Why don't you fork your bronc and head on for home?"

Red Williams was disturbed. It was not going as expected. Instead of being a hard-eyed marshal who immediately started for him, this man talked like another cowhand. "You tellin' me to get out of town?" he demanded.

"Just advisin'," Utah replied casually. "If you figure to do a day's work tomorrow, you better sleep it off." He pushed his hat back on his head. "I call to mind one time when I rode for Shanghai Pierce. We was—"

"You rode for *Shanghai*?" Red's truculence was forgotten.

"Took a herd over the trail for him in 'sixty-seven," Utah said. "The next year I took one up the trail for Slaughter."

Red Williams swallowed hard, his stomach sick with sudden realization. "You . . . you're *that* Blaine? The one who stopped the herd cuttin' north of Doan's Store?"

"Yeah," Blaine replied quietly. "That was later."

"Wow!" Red backed up, suddenly grinning. "Mister, if that's who you are, this town is off-limits for my kind of trouble!"

———

SQUAW CREEK WAS impressed but not convinced. Twice Blaine quietly talked his way out of trouble that with any other marshal would have meant shooting. Days passed with no gunfights, no brawls, and surprisingly, no robberies and murders.

Once, sitting on the bench in front of the barbershop, he was asked about the killings of Van Hewit and Ned Harris, the two last murders before he took the job of marshal. He shrugged and replied, "I'll handle the crime that comes my way, but I say let the dead past keep its dead."

Before the saloons opened, the benches in front of the barbershop were the usual loafing place. It was there he stopped to gather what facts he could. "Nice idea," he commented. "Gives a man a place to sit and talk."

"Pickard's idea," they told him. "Built 'em for his customers to wait on."

Pickard was a man of medium height, smooth-faced but for a flowing mustache. Square-jawed and square-bodied, he was a friendly man, skillful at his trade, and a good listener. "Mighty fine barber," Tom Church said, "I'll be sorry when he goes."

"He's leavin'?" Blaine asked.

"Brother died, back in Illinois. Got to go back and manage the property."

It was their second meeting since Blaine's arrival, and Church was visibly disturbed. "The rest of the city council, the men who pay your salary, Utah, they're complaining. You've kept it quiet, or it's been quiet, but you've found no killer. I promised that you would."

"You don't catch a killer right away any more than you take a herd to Montana by wishin' it there."

He knew more than he was telling Tom Church. Things were beginning to add up. All the killings had been within five miles of town. All but two had taken place at night or early in the morning. The two had occurred at midday. Five men lived on that street into which Hibbs had gone on the night of his arrival. Childress, Hunt, Newcomb, Jones . . . and Tom Church.

Actually, it was a one-sided street. The houses faced south, which had them looking across the street at the cottonwoods that line Squaw Creek. Behind those cottonwoods were the back doors of the business buildings on Main Street. The saloon, barbershop, marshal's office, harness shop, and general store backed up to the trees.

Hibbs lived in the hotel and did not drink. He was an odd personality, not talkative, and yet he had a habit of always being around when a conversation developed. Unobtrusively, Utah Blaine watched him and waited, knowing his time would come.

Hibbs was never found near the barbershop. For a man so interested in gossip, this was interesting if not odd. Hibbs went to the barbershop only when he needed a haircut.

From the beginning Blaine had known that Hibbs was his key to the situation, yet while watching Hibbs, he had listened and studied the town, and one by one he eliminated the possibilities. The more men he eliminated, the more certain he became of the killer's cunning. He had left no loose ends.

Utah Blaine had learned, long since, how to apply simple logic to a problem. Men were creatures of habit. Therefore he must observe the habits of the possible suspects and watch for any deviation from the usual.

Opportunity was a consideration. Not more than a half-dozen men in town would have been free to move at the hours of the two midday crimes. Childress could not leave his store at the noon hour, and had a wife who insisted upon his being on time for supper. Hunt was a man who habitually drank his supper at the saloon, a convivial soul whose absence would have been noted and commented upon. So it was with most of the others, yet Pickard was a bachelor. He had means of learning, through the talk around the shop, of who had made strikes and who did not, and he could be safely absent at the hours of crimes. Moreover, the cottonwood-cloaked creek bed back of the shop offered an easy means of leaving and returning to town unobserved. All of these were logical reasons for suspicion, but none of it was proof.

On the morning of his tenth day in town, Utah went to the barbershop for a shave. Pickard had gentle hands and he worked carefully and swiftly. He was shaving Utah's throat when Utah said, from under Pickard's left hand, "Goin' to be a break soon. I've got a lead on the man who's been doin' the killing around here."

For only a second the razor stopped moving, and then it continued more slowly. "I thought," Pickard said, "it was the work of casual drifters, or maybe a gang."

"No," Blaine said decidedly, "it's been one man. One mighty shrewd man. He's done it all, and he's been smart enough to protect himself. But every man has to have help, an' I've got a lead on that."

Pickard started to strop his razor, and then the door opened, and closed. "How are you, Mr. Church? Blaine tells me he has a lead on those murders we used to have before he came."

"That right, Utah?"

The razor smoothed a patch on his chin. "Yeah. Fact is, I've had a lead ever since I came to town. From the very hour I got in, you might say."

Pickard finished his job and dusted Blaine's face with powder. Utah sat up in the chair and felt his face. "You sure do give a fine shave, Pickard. . . . Close," he said, looking at the barber, "but not too close."

When they had gone, Blaine and Church walking together, Pickard stared after them. A lead since the very moment . . . he might have seen Hibbs!

Yet, what could he have seen? And suppose he had seen Hibbs come to him? It would prove nothing, and Hibbs could not talk. He would not dare to talk. So there was nothing to worry about. Nevertheless, he did worry.

He had not been fooled by Blaine. The tall gunfighter was too friendly, too casual. His manner did not go with his cold, watchful eyes and the strong-boned face. Alone in the apartment back of his shop, Pickard paced the floor and thought.

It was time to go, but he must be careful. Suppose Blaine was only waiting for him to uncover his loot and so be caught with the goods? Or suppose he frightened Hibbs in some way and forced him to talk? The more he considered, the more he worried. He had been a fool to wait so long. He could have gone long ago. Why, he had over sixty thousand dollars!

Slowly, he went over the problem again. Hibbs might talk, of course, but he had already made plans for Hibbs and it was time he put them into operation. Pickard was a cool-headed man and utterly cold-blooded. He had long known that before he left, Hibbs must die. Aside from the knowledge of Hibbs's past, the one thing he knew was that Hibbs would wait for him to recover the hidden loot, and then Hibbs would try to murder him for it. Pickard knew that idea lay in Hibbs's mind as if he himself had written it there. And to an extent, he had.

If Hibbs betrayed him, he'd never get a chance at the

money. It also allowed him the chance to trap Hibbs. So now to prepare that trap, he had to lead Hibbs out of town into the hills, and then kill him.

———

BLAINE HAD FORMED the habit of riding out of town at least once each day. He varied the times of these rides so as to allow for no easy planning of future crimes or observation of his moves.

First, he rode to the scenes of the crimes and studied the terrain and approaches. There were, of course, no tracks. There had been rain and wind since, but they were not what he was searching for. Nor was he looking for any clue that might have been dropped. He was trying to imagine how the killer would have concealed his loot, for he would not have dared to risk being seen carrying it back into town.

The other rides were short, and they ended in a small clump of juniper atop a ridge outside of Squaw Creek. There, with a pair of field glasses, Utah Blaine watched the town.

The break came suddenly. On one bright and sunny Sunday morning he saw Hibbs come from the hotel and walk across the street. Going down the alley between the buildings, Hibbs turned suddenly into the old, abandoned store building on his right. Not two minutes later he stepped out, only now he had a rifle and a canteen.

Utah Blaine settled himself firmly and watched with care. Hibbs went down into an arroyo and out of town, working his way up the hill right toward Blaine's position! Just when he was sure he must move or be seen, Hibbs stopped and, settling down, began to wait.

Almost an hour passed and then Pickard came from the back door of the barbershop and slid down into the creek bed. Watching, Blaine saw the man working his way downstream, then saw him come out among some boulders. Hibbs got up and began to work his way along the flank of the mountain, keeping Pickard in view. Keeping higher and staying among the junipers, Blaine kept pace with Hibbs. Then the junipers grew more sparse and scattered out. Reluctantly, Blaine swung over the crest and kept the ridge between himself and the two men. From time to time he climbed higher and let his eyes seek out the clerk, then suddenly the man was gone.

Blaine swore bitterly. To cross the ridge within view of either Hibbs or Pickard would ruin the whole plan, and his only chance lay in riding ahead to intercept their trail as it left the ridge, which ended a few miles farther along. So swinging his horse, he rode down into the wash and followed it out until the ridge ended. It was only then that he realized how that ridge had betrayed him.

Some distance back the ridge divided into a rough Y, and he had been following the southernmost of the two arms, while Hibbs had obviously followed along the northern. It was at least two miles across the bottom to the other ridge and it was very hot now, and close to noon.

Before crossing the gap, he studied it with care, but there was no sign of either man. He crossed as quickly as he could, then climbed the far ridge and, taking a chance, mounted the crest. As far as the eye could reach, there was no living thing.

Irritated, he rode down the far side, scouting for tracks. He found none. The two men, and both on foot, had lost him completely. How long since he had lost Hibbs? He checked the sun and his memory. It must have been almost an hour, as best he could figure. Turning back, he rode toward town. He had gone no more than two hundred yards when he drew up sharply.

Before him on the trail lay the sprawled figure of a man, half-covered with the rocky debris of a landslide. Blaine dropped from his horse. It was Hibbs, and he was quite dead. Climbing the hillside, Blaine found scuff marks in the dirt where someone, almost certainly Pickard, had sat, bracing himself while he forced a large boulder from its socket of earth with his heels.

Pickard must have known Hibbs would follow, or had seen him, and had pushed down these boulders, probably coming by later to make sure there was no doubt. Yet allowing for the time it took Hibbs to get to this point on foot, it could have been no more than twenty to thirty minutes ago that he had been killed!

If he rode swiftly now, he might overtake Pickard before he could get back to Squaw Creek!

Yet his ride was in vain. All was quiet when he rode into town and stabled his horse. Pickard was quietly shaving Tom Church and had the job half-done. He glanced up at Blaine and nodded. "Hot day for riding, I guess," he said conversationally. "You can have it. I'd rather stay in my barbershop."

Baffled and irritated, Utah did not trust himself to speak. There was no way the man could have gotten back here that fast. It must be someone else whom he had seen, it must— He stopped. Suppose Pickard had a horse waiting for him out there on the ridge somewhere? And had raced back, changed shirts quickly, and returned to his work as he did each day? But where was the horse? And where had he been concealed?

———

UTAH BLAINE DROPPED in at the saloon for a drink and the first man he saw was Red Williams. The latter grinned, "Howdy, Marshal! No hard feelin's?"

Blaine chuckled. "Why should there be? What are you doin' in town in the middle of the week?"

"Come in after some horses. The boss keeps a half-dozen head of good saddle stock down at his creek barn in case any of the boys need a change of horse."

"Creek barn? Where's that?"

"Just outside of town a ways. We got two outfits, one west of town, an' the other seventeen miles northeast. We switch horses at the creek barn every now and again. It's a line shack right out of town."

"You taking all the horses?"

"Nope. Just four head. We're mighty short of saddle stock right now, the boys haven't rounded up the bunch off the west range yet. Funny thing," he said, "durned kids been ridin' 'em, I guess. One of Tom's best horses is stove up."

Utah Blaine turned his glass in his fingers. "Red, you want to do me a favor?"

"Sure. What is it?"

"Take all those horses with you and keep 'em away from

that line shack for a week. If the boss says anything, I'll explain it."

Red shrugged. "Sure, I'll do it." He looked curiously at Utah. "Wish you'd let me in on it, though."

"Later. But don't even whisper it to anybody, you hear? And don't let anybody see you if you can help it. I've got a feelin' we're goin' to make a murderin' skunk mighty unhappy!"

———

THE DEATH OF Hibbs was amazing to Squaw Creek only because the hotel clerk had been out of town. The curiosity of the loafers at the barbershop was aroused and they speculated at random on what he had been doing in that dusty wash when he was usually at work on the hotel books.

Blaine listened thoughtfully. Then he got up and settled his hat on his head. Inside the barbershop, Pickard was stropping a razor. "I figure he was hunting the loot from those robberies," he said, "and he had some idea where it was . . . only he was too late."

"Too late?" Childress looked up. "You mean somebody found it?" The razor stropping had stopped abruptly.

"Uh-huh," Utah said, weighting his words carefully. "That's just what I mean. . . . Well"—he stepped down off the walk—"be seein' you."

He walked away, feeling their stares on his back. It was rather obvious bait, but would Pickard really have the choice not to bite on it? Could he coolly ignore the possibility that all he had planned so carefully for . . . killed for, might be gone?

Pickard stared out the window after Blaine. What did he mean by that? He was sure that nobody could find the money. It was still there where he'd hidden it, it had to be. . . . He returned to his stropping of the razor, but his mind was not on his work. He scowled. How had Blaine found Hibbs's body so soon? He must have been out in the hills . . . he might even have followed Hibbs.

Yet that could not be, for if he had, he would have been close by when Hibbs was killed . . . or *had* he been close by?

Suppose Blaine was less interested in finding the killer than in finding the loot . . . and keeping it for himself?

Worried now, Pickard grew irritable and restless. If Blaine found that loot, then all his time here was wasted. Pickard would be chained to this barber chair! He would have killed and robbed and risked his life, for nothing!

Yet suppose it was only a trap? That might be Blaine's idea, but it would not work. He knew how . . . he glanced at the building's shadow. Two hours yet to sundown.

———

ALONE IN HIS shop, Pickard worked swiftly. There was no time to lose. Trap or not, he must know whether his loot had been found, and if it was a trap . . . well, they'd find out that their quiet town barber had teeth. He thrust a pistol into his waistband and picked up a shotgun.

When it was dark he slipped from the back of the shop and ducked quickly into the bed of the stream. Hurrying along it, he came out near the TC line shack and crossed quickly to the stable. Quickly, he struck a match and picked up the lantern . . . and then he stopped. The horses were gone!

Pickard froze where he was and the match burned down to his fingers before he dropped it. He had seen Red Williams in town, but he had no idea . . . now there was no other way. He must go on foot.

Suppose somebody came for him while he was gone? He would have to chance that. The shop was closed and he had left everything locked tight. He started down the draw, moving swiftly. At night and without a horse, it seemed much farther than the three miles he had to go, yet despite his hurry, he took his time when reaching the area where the loot was concealed. He waited, listened, then went forward.

Quickly, he moved a rock and reached into the cavity beneath. Instantly, his heart gave a bound. The loot was there! Blaine had been talking through his hat! It was safe! He struck a match, shielding it with his cupped hands. All there . . . should he take it with him now, or should he wait and pick it up, as he had planned, after leaving town?

Much of it was gold, but there was a good bit of paper

money, too. It would be a load, almost a hundred pounds of it, but he could get it back. No, he changed his mind swiftly. He would take one sack of gold, just in case. He could always come back after the rest.

Taking the sack out, he carefully replaced the stone, then lit a match and had a careful look around to make sure the stone was in place and no damp earth was showing. As the match went out his eyes caught a flicker of white on the ground and he guardedly struck another. He stooped . . . merely some whitish-gray mud or damp earth. He dropped the match and, picking up his bag, started back.

Pickard hurried, desperately worried for fear of discovery, and his breath was coming hoarsely when he reached the back door of his shop. He opened the door, stepped in, and turning, he struck a match and lighted the lamp. Just as he replaced the chimney a shock of fear went through him . . . he had left the door *locked*!

Pickard turned sharply, half-crouched like an animal at bay, a sickness turning him faint with shock. Facing him from chairs ranged around the room were Tom Church, Childress, Hunt, and Red Williams!

Clutched in his hand was the sack of stolen gold, and then Utah Blaine spoke. "Drop your guns, Pickard! You are under arrest!"

His years of planning, working, scheming, his murders and robberies, the hot, stifling nights when he waited, when he struck with the knife or club, or tossed the noose over a neck, and strangled . . . all gone! All for nothing! All because . . . !

Like a cat he wheeled and plunged for the door. The move was so swift that Blaine swung, not daring to shoot toward the other men, knelt, and thrust out his foot.

Pickard tripped and sprawled through the door onto the step. Springing to his feet, his hands lacerated from the silvery-gray wood, he grabbed for his gun.

"Hold it!" Blaine yelled.

Pickard's gun swung up . . . and he felt his finger close, and then somebody smashed him a blow in the chest. He staggered, trying to bring his gun to bear, and another blow hit him, half turning him around.

What . . . what th—! His eyes blurred and the gun would not seem to come up and then something struck him on the back of the head and he was on the ground and he was staring up at the stars and then the stars faded and he realized . . . nothing more.

Tom Church stared at the fallen man, white-faced. "Dead center, Utah," he said quietly, "but you had to do it."

"Yeah."

"That's only part of the stolen money," Childress said. "You reckon he spent the rest of it?"

Utah Blaine indicated the dead man's boots, their soles stained with a muddy whitish substance. "I figure it's cached. He left the rest of it, but those white boots will lead us right to it."

"What is that stuff?" Church asked. "Never saw any clay like that around here."

"It's white paint," Blaine replied, "I spilled plenty of it inside the door of the TC barn and corral. I knew he'd come there, and that white paint would leave his marks to trail him by."

Hunt and Williams carefully picked up the body and carried it off down the street. Blaine stood in the alley while Tom Church locked up Pickard's shop. After a moment Childress swore softly. "What's worryin' me now," he said, "is what are we goin' to do for a barber!"

MERRANO OF THE DRY COUNTRY

NOBODY EVEN TURNED a head to look his way as Barry Merrano entered the store. They knew he was there, and their hatred was almost tangible, he felt it pushing against him as he walked to the counter.

Mayer, who kept the store, was talking to Tom Drake, owner of the TD and considered the wealthiest man in the valley; Jim Hill, acknowledged to be its first settler; and Joe Stangle, from the head of the valley. After a moment Mayer left them and walked over to him.

The storekeeper's lips offered no welcoming smile although Barry thought he detected a faint gleam of sympathy in the man's eyes.

In a low voice, Barry gave his order, and several times the others glanced his way, for they could still overhear a part of what he was saying and he was ordering things they could no longer afford.

"I'll have to ask for cash," Mayer said. "With the drouth and all, money's short."

Barry felt a sudden surge of anger. There was a moment when he thought to bring their world crashing about them by asking how long it had been since the others had paid cash. He knew what it would mean. Suddenly they would be faced with the harsh reality of their situation. The Mirror Valley country was broke . . . flat broke.

No sooner had the feeling come than it passed. He had no desire for revenge. They hated him, and he knew why they hated him. They hated him because he was the son of Miguel Merrano, the Mexican vaquero who married the most beautiful and sought-after girl in the valley. They hated him because he had the audacity to return after they had driven his father from the area. They hated him because when they built a fence to keep his cattle from water he had found water elsewhere. Worst of all, he himself had kept up the fence they built, building it even stronger.

They hated him because he had the nerve to tell them they were ruining their land, and that drouth would come and their cattle would die.

"That's all right," he told Mayer, "I have the money and I can pay."

He took his order and paid for it with three gold pieces placed carefully on the counter. Joe Stangle looked at the gold, then stared at him, his eyes mean. "I'd like to know," he said, "where a greaser gets that kind of money. Maybe the sheriff should do some looking around!"

Barry gathered his armful of groceries and put them in a burlap sack. "Maybe he could"—he spoke gently—"and maybe you could, too, Joe. All you'd have to do would be to use your eyes."

He went out, then returned for a second and a third load. "That greaser father of yours knowed what he was doin' when he bought that land," Stangle said.

"The land my father bought was the same sort of land you all have. Once there was good grass everywhere but you overstocked your land and fed it out of existence. Then the brush came in and the underlying roots killed off more grass. When the grass thinned out your stock started eating poison weeds. There's nothing wrong with your land that a few good years won't cure."

"We heard all that preachin' before. No greaser's goin' to come around and tell me how to run my range! Jim Hill an' me were runnin' cattle before you was born!"

Merrano took his last armful of groceries and turned toward the door. White with fury, Joe Stangle stuck out his foot and Barry tripped and sprawled on the floor, spilling his groceries.

Nobody laughed. Tom Drake threw an irritated glance at Stangle, but said nothing.

Barry Merrano got up. His face was very cold and still. "That was a cheap thing to do, Stangle," he said. "There's not much man in you, is there?"

Had he been slapped across the mouth it would have been easier to take. Stangle trembled, and his hand dropped to his gun. Only Jim Hill's grabbing his arm prevented him from shooting Merrano in the back as he walked out the door.

"Yellow!" Stangle sneered. "Yellow, like any greaser!"

"You're wrong, Joe," Hill said quietly, "he's not yellow, nor was his old man."

"He run, didn't he?" Stangle said. "He quit, didn't he?" His voice was hoarse with hatred.

"Yes, he left, but if I recall correctly he backed you down, Joe."

Stangle's face was livid, but Hill turned his back on him and asked Mayer, "I'll have to ask for credit again, Mayer. Can you carry me?"

"I always have." Mayer tried to smile. He had carried them all, but how much longer he could afford to do it he did not know. Only the cash Barry Merrano had spent with him enabled him to meet his own bills, but scarcely that.

———

BARRY MERRANO'S BUCKBOARD rattled out of town, hitting the long, dry road to Willow Springs. It was almost sundown but heat lay over Mirror Valley like a sodden thing, dust hanging heavy in the air. It was always here now, that dust. A few years back, his mother told him, this valley had been a green and lovely place. There had been fat cattle around then, and it was here she had met his father, that pleasant-faced, friendly Mexican—slim, wiry, and elegant— and it was here they had courted and here they were married.

"I'm glad she didn't live to see it," Barry muttered, "it would have broken her heart."

In the rush to get rich from beef cattle the grass had been overgrazed, and the creosote, cat-claw, and tarweed had started to move in. The grass had grown thinner. It had been eaten down, and worn down, wind had whipped the dust from around the roots and rains had washed out the clumps of grass. The water holes, once plentiful, never seemed to fill up or remain full anymore.

"Climate's changing," Drake had suggested to Hill, and the latter nodded his agreement.

"Don't ever recall it being so dry," Hill added.

They watched with sullen impatience when Barry Merrano returned to occupy his father's ranch. And they turned away in contempt when he told them the climate was not changing, but they were simply running more cattle than the range would support.

Willow Springs loomed before him, and Barry kept his eyes averted. It was at Willow Springs where his father and mother first met. It had been green and lovely then, and the pool had been wide and deep. Now most of the willows were dead and where the pool had been, the earth was cracked and gray. There had been no water since early summer.

Turning right at Willow Springs his road became a climb. It was only a trail, two winding ruts across the parched plain. Ahead of him he saw The Fence.

All over the country it was known by no other name. It was simply The Fence, only nowadays it was mentioned rarely.

Seven ranchers had built The Fence, and they had built it when Barry refused to leave.

That was four years ago but to Barry it seemed longer. He had returned, knowing every detail of the hatred Mirror Valley people had felt for his father. He was determined to face it down and win a place for himself; and the land his father left him was all he had. He turned up the draw toward the house Miguel Merrano had built in the basin under the shoulder of Table Mountain.

———

THREE DAYS AFTER his arrival a dozen horsemen had ridden up the draw to tell him he was not wanted. They wanted no Mexicans in Mirror Valley.

He had waited in the door, listening. And then he smiled, looking much more like his Irish mother at that moment. "I'm sorry you've had your ride for nothing," he said. "I'm staying."

"Get out or we'll run you out!" Stangle had shouted.

"Then why waste time talking?" Merrano suggested. "Why don't you start your running?"

With an oath, Stangle had reached for his gun, but his hand got no farther than the butt, then very, very carefully he moved his hand away. Not one of them saw where Merrano had held the shotgun, but suddenly it was there, in Merrano's hands.

"Sorry, gentlemen, but I don't like being shot at. I am not a man of violence, but I've several thousand rounds of ammunition and I hit what I aim at.

"I've noticed that a shotgun has a depressing effect on violent men, as nobody can tell just who is going to get himself ripped open. Now, gentlemen, I've a lot of work to do. Do you go cheerfully or do I have to start a graveyard?"

They went, and Joe Stangle was not the last to leave.

Three days later they built The Fence. They built it across the draw that led from Merrano's adobe in the basin to town. They built it horse-high, hog-tight, and bull-strong. Then six men waited with rifles for somebody to try cutting The Fence.

Barry Merrano came down the draw in his buckboard, and they picked up their rifles for a killing. Before he came to The Fence, Barry pulled up and tumbled a roll of barbed wire from the back of the buckboard. Then, as they watched, suddenly feeling very foolish, Barry Merrano built his own fence, higher, stronger, and tighter. In place of their nine strands of wire he put up fourteen. In the forty feet of width across the draw he put up nine posts to their five. Then he got into his buckboard and drove away.

Cab Casady, forty-five, and accounted one of the toughest men in the valley, laughed. Just as suddenly as he began laughing, he stopped. "We're a pack of fools!" he said with disgust. "And for one, I'm ashamed of myself. I'm going home."

Avoiding each other's eyes the others went to their horses, mounted up and rode away. The Fence was a topic no longer mentioned in conversation.

Yet all wondered what Merrano would do, for there was no way out of the basin unless one walked. For three weeks they waited, and then one day Barry Merrano drove into town for supplies. When they rode out to see, The Fence was still intact.

Jim Hill, although he would not admit it, was relieved. Yet like the others, he was curious. He mounted up and scouted around the country. It was almost a month after that he rode into town. He had a drink in the Faro House and said, "Do you know what that Mex did? He's bored him a hole through the Neck!"

Anybody but Jim Hill they would have called a liar. The Neck was a wall of rock that joined the bulk of Table Mountain to the rest of the range, yet when they rode out to see it, there was a black hole in that red wall of rock.

How could it have been done? It was impossible, yet it had been done.

Nobody mentioned fencing the tunnel mouth.

———

A FEW DAYS later when he passed Willow Springs, Barry Merrano saw a rider emerge from the shabby little grove and start across the trail. When she saw him, she pulled up.

It was Candy Drake.

He stopped the buckskins when he drew close. "How are you, ma'am?" He touched his hat. He started to comment on the heat and the drouth but thought the better of it. Instead he indicated the pinto's leg. "I see that leg is coming along all right."

"Yes, it got well just like you said it would."

He wanted to talk, yet wanted to avoid anything that might give offense. Candy Drake was the prettiest girl in Mirror Valley. He had talked to no one in almost three months, and he admitted to himself that he had been in love with Candy Drake for three years.

"The drouth came the way you said it would, too," she said almost accusingly. "Everything seems to turn out the way you say it will."

He flushed slightly. "Anybody who took the time to look could see this country was in trouble," he said. "This country had been so overgrazed there was no grass to hold what moisture we got. Most of it could have been prevented if work had been started a couple of years ago."

He took off his hat and ran his fingers through his thick, dark hair. "Nobody would listen to me when I offered to help. I was just that damned greaser son of Molly O'Brien's, so what could I know?"

There was a bitterness in his voice that came through no matter how hard he tried to hold it back. He had lived too close to this for too long a time.

Mirror Valley had been outraged when pretty Molly O'Brien had married Miguel Merrano. He had been a top-hand, hired only for the roundup. Pete Drake had his eyes on Molly, and so had others, but she had made promises to no one until she met Merrano.

Miguel bought the Table Mountain place and for four bitter years struggled against the hatred and the prejudice directed against them. Finally, when young Barry was almost two, they had gone away.

Surprisingly, they prospered. Barry heard many tales of Mirror Valley as he was growing up but nothing of the reason for leaving until he was fifteen. He determined then to return and fight it out if it took twenty years.

"My father certainly should know how to run cattle," Candy protested. "He's raised more cattle than you have ever seen."

"I'm twenty-six," Barry said, "and I've a lot to learn, but simply growing old doesn't make one wise. Your father came into a rich, new country and nothing could convince him it would not always stay rich.

"The others were the same. They ran more cattle than the range could support. Once when I was visiting at your place I tried to suggest some changes, but he just thought me a fool."

"But Barry," she protested, "millions of buffalo used to run on these plains, so how could they be spoiled by a few thousand cattle?"

"Your father said the same thing," Barry said, "but you both forget that the buffalo never stopped moving as they grazed. They were constantly moving and as they moved on, the grass had a chance to grow back before they returned again. Now the range is fenced and the cattle are continually feeding over the same ground."

Candy was exasperated. "We always have the same argument," she protested. "Can you talk of anything else?"

"Many things, if you'll listen. Candy, why don't you come over to my place and see for yourself?"

"To your place?" She was shocked, yet as the idea took hold, she was intrigued. Like all in the valley she was curious. What was he doing back there? Nobody had visited the basin since he took over, and they all knew Barry Merrano paid cash for everything. How could he do it?

That he ran cattle, they all knew. He had driven cattle into Aragon to sell and Aragon was out of the way for people from the valley. They knew he did it to avoid meeting them.

"It wouldn't be proper," she said, but as she said it she knew it was a feeble excuse. She had done many things that were often considered improper. "Anyway, that dark tunnel would frighten me. However did you make it?"

"It was not hard. Want to come?"

Her father's disapproval and what might be considered proper was opposed to her curiosity, which resulted in a sweeping victory . . . for her curiosity.

Interested in spite of herself, she followed along. He drove the buckskins into the dark tunnel, and she fell in behind them. The buckskins trotted along undisturbed by the darkness until rounding a small curve they saw light before them. When she emerged from the tunnel she pulled up with a gasp.

The first impression was of size. She had thought of the basin as a small place, yet there must have been thousands of acres within that circle of hills. When she looked again she saw nothing was as it had been.

The basin, in contrast to the country she had left, was green and lovely. A winding road led to a stone cottage that stood on a wide ledge and on either side of the road there were fenced fields, the one on the right of clover, on the left of corn, and the corn was shoulder high as she rode past it on her horse.

The old trees she remembered from a time she had come here as a child, when it was abandoned, but there were younger trees, including a small orchard, carefully set out. The valley of the basin itself was green, with here and there a small pool that caught the sunlight.

"Is that *grass* down there?"

"Most of it. Some is black grama, some is curly mesquite grass. It has always grown in this country but I am careful not to overgraze it. The basin opens at the other end into a canyon and then into Long Valley, the old Navajo sheep range. I made a deal with the Navajo to graze some of it. I run about fifteen head to the section but actually most of this will support twice as many."

Her father should see this, she thought. He would never believe it if she told him.

"But what about water? Where do you get water?"

"This country never has enough, and most of the rain comes in late summer. When I came back I already knew the problem I faced. I did some blasting, built three dams the first summer, damming three draws that open into the basin. Wherever I found a low spot I made some kind of a reservoir. Now I have a couple of small lakes behind the dams and there are pools scattered all over the basin and down into Long Valley. Toward the end of summer most of them do dry up, but by that time the rains are not far off.

"In this country water runs off the hills like off a tin roof so you have to save what you can. Of course, I've drilled a couple of wells, too."

Amazed, she listened with only half her attention. Suddenly, she was frightened. If Joe Stangle saw this place his hatred and envy would be doubled.

She thought of something she had wondered about. "Barry? However did you make that tunnel?"

He chuckled. "Candy, over two-thirds of it was a big, natural cave. I paced it off, then went on top and measured the rock and found I only had a little way to go and much was an upthrust from below that I could take off with a pick.

"As far as the grass goes, I never graze much stock on it at any one time, and I shift them around to give the grass a chance to grow back."

"Don't you have trouble with old Two Moons?"

"Not at all. I explained what I had in mind, and he understood right away. The Navajo have always understood grazing pretty well, and I offered them a fair price."

As they walked back her eyes strayed toward the house. She would have liked to see the inside, but he did not suggest it.

He stripped the harness from the team and turned them into the corral, then saddled a horse. "It's getting late," he said, "I'll ride home with you."

THE RIDE TO the TD was silent, for neither felt like talking. Barry was happy and miserable at the same time. He was in love with Candy; but her father had been one of those who tried to drive him off the place, and her father had lent his tacit consent to building The Fence, if no more than that.

The feeling against him had grown stronger rather than otherwise. The incident in the store would make them turn even further away, and as none of them liked him, most would be only too quick to accept his walking away from Stangle as cowardice.

When they drew up at the gate he said, "I wish you'd come again. And bring your father."

"He wouldn't come, Barry." She was puzzled about her feelings toward him. He had talked more than ever before, and for the first time she had seen something of the kind of man he was, yet she could not quite understand him. He was, she suspected, a much more complex human being than any she had known.

"You're beautiful, Candy." The words came so suddenly that she looked up, surprised by them. "You're so beautiful it hurts. I wish—"

A dark figure loomed near the gate. "Candy? Is that you? Who's that with you?"

"Price? I was just saying good night to Barry Merrano."

"Who?" Astonishment mingled with anger. "Has that dirty Mex been botherin' you? If he has, I'll—!"

"I simply rode home with Miss Drake," Barry said. "There's no reason to get excited."

Price Taylor shoved open the gate and came out. "Listen, greaser! You turn that horse and cut loose for home! Don't you be tellin' me not to get excited! I'll take you off that horse and beat your skull in!"

"Price!" Candy exclaimed. "This is outrageous!"

Taylor was beside Barry's horse. He was a large, somewhat top-heavy young man. As foreman of the TD he had become almost one of the family and he had long looked upon Candy Drake as someone very special and reserved for him, although he had had no encouragement from her and certainly none from Tom Drake, who would have been appalled at the thought. Seeing her in the moonlight with Merrano turned him ugly.

"This is no business for womenfolk! You get along to the house now. I'll take care of this!"

He reached a big hand for Barry and Barry went, much faster than Taylor expected. As Taylor laid hold of him Barry swung his other leg over the saddle and drove his heel into the bigger man's chest, sending him staggering. Then he dropped to the ground.

Coolly, he waited until Taylor recovered his balance. "I'd rather you'd go along to the house," Barry said, "but if you want a licking you can have it."

"A lickin'? *Me?*" Taylor's size had won several brawls for him, and he fancied himself a tough man.

He started for Merrano and a stiff left stopped him, smashing his lips. Taylor dropped into a half-crouch, arms wide to grapple, and moved in. Barry caught the larger man's sleeve and jerked him forward, off-balance, then kicked his foot from under him. Taylor sprawled forward, falling on his hands and knees.

Merrano stood waiting, and Taylor came half erect, then launched himself in a long dive. Merrano sidestepped and waited.

Slowly, carefully, Taylor got up from the ground. Putting

his fists in front of him in an awkward simulation of a boxer, he moved in. Merrano moved to the side and Taylor caught him on the cheekbone with a clumsy swing, but Merrano stood his ground and struck three hard, fast blows to the body, then an uppercut thrown in close that tipped Taylor's chin back.

Taylor bored in, swinging wildly.

Taylor turned, Barry feinted a left and Taylor pawed at the air to knock the punch down, but the feint was followed by a stiff left, then another and another. Taylor was big, but lacked any semblance of fighting skill. He came in, legs spread wide, swinging. Barry hit him with a left, then knocked him down with a right. Taylor got up slowly and Barry knocked him down again.

Taylor got to his knees but was unable to get to his feet. "I'm sorry, Taylor, but you asked for it. You're a game man, but you're no fighter."

Taylor made it to his feet, weaving. Barry thrust out a hand. "As far as I'm concerned, there's no hard feelings. Will you shake?"

Price Taylor ignored the out-thrust hand.

Barry swung to the saddle. "I'm sorry, Candy. I didn't want this to happen."

"You'd better go," she replied coldly.

He swung his horse and rode away, cutting across the plains, gray and empty under a wide white moon.

Taylor wiped his face. "You must think I'm an awful bust, gettin' whipped that way."

Candy shook her head soberly. "No, Price, I don't, but I think we've all made an awful mistake!"

Taylor grunted. "Looks like I made one, anyway."

———

WHEN SHE OPENED the door into the wide living room of the ranch house Candy was surprised to find five or six men talking with her father. Jim Hill was there, and Joe Stangle. Also there were Cab Casady, Rock Dulin, Vinnie Lake, Hardy Benson and a big, powerful man whom she did not know.

"We've got to figure out something or we're finished," Benson was saying. "My cattle are dying like flies!"

"Mine, too," Stangle said, "water holes are dry, and there's no grass."

"If you ask me," Dulin commented, "it ain't only the drouth. There's been some rustlin'."

"There's been no rustling in this country since we got rid of Bert Scovey and his outfit."

"That greaser always has money," Stangle said. "Where's he get it?"

"If you could see that Basin Ranch of his," Candy interrupted, "you wouldn't wonder. You should all have listened to him a long time ago."

Her father looked up sharply. "Candy? What makes you say that? When did you see it?"

"Today," she replied calmly. "He invited me to see it and I did."

"You went into the basin with that low-down Mex?"

"Hold on a minute, Tom!" Stangle lifted a hand. "You mean he's got grass?"

"Yes, he has!" Candy was pleased with the effect of her words. "The whole basin is green and beautiful! He's got water, and lots of it. He's dammed some of the draws, he's dug out some pools, and he has a lot of water. He's even got a grain crop!"

"Grain?" Hill exclaimed. "You mean he's farmin'?"

"Not farming, just raising enough for his own stock. He told me he fed during the winter or just before taking them to market."

"You actually *saw* water and grass?" Hill asked.

"He's done nothing you all couldn't have done, and he's done it all in four years! Certainly, I saw it!"

"You takin' up for him now?" Dulin asked.

"No! I am just telling you he's proved his case. He was right, and you all were wrong."

Stangle leaned forward, intent. "Where'd you say that water was? In Cottonwood Draw?"

"He's dammed both Cottonwood and Spring Valley. He's

planted seedling trees around them to hold the banks and help conserve moisture."

"Well!" Stangle slapped his thigh. "That's it, men! That settles our problem!"

"What do you mean?" Drake looked up hopefully.

"He's got water. Why don't we just take down The Fence and drive our cattle in there? That sneakin' Mexican's got no right to all that water when our cattle are dyin'!"

Casady let his chair legs down hard. "You mean to say you'd have the gall to ask him for water after the way we've treated him?"

"Ask nothin'!" Stangle said. "Just tear down The Fence and let our cattle in. They'd find the water and grass soon enough."

"We couldn't do that," Drake protested, "it wouldn't be right."

"Right?" Stangle's voice was hoarse with bitterness. "Are you so anxious to go broke? You want to watch your cattle die?"

"You'd do a thing like that?" Casady demanded, his eyes going from one to the other.

"I would," Rock Dulin said. "Are you too nice to save your cows?"

Candy stared at Dulin, appalled.

"No, Rock," Casady said quietly, "I'm not too nice. I hope, however, that I know something of fair play. We've bucked that kid and made his life pure hell. We tried to drive him out and he stuck. We fenced him out of our country and still he stayed. He tried to tell us, and we were too damned hard-headed to listen. Now, you would ruin what he has done. How long will that little grass last if we turn our herds in there? We've got seven or eight thousand head between us."

"I don't know, and I don't give a damn!" Stangle said. "He's got no place here in the first place. I've got my cattle to save, and I'll save them."

"He won't stand for it," Hill replied. "He'll fight."

"I hope he does!" Stangle said. "Him and his highfalutin ways! Handin' gold right over the counter! Throwin' it right in our faces!"

"What if he does fight?" Drake asked.

"You fought injuns to get here, didn't you?" Dulin said. "You killed some of Scovey's boys?"

Candy Drake stared in shocked disbelief. "You could do a thing like *that*? Joe Stangle, what kind of a man are you? To wreck all he's done! To destroy everything!"

"It would save our stock, Miss Candy," Benson protested. "We've families to think about. Your pa's in the same fix I am, and I'm head over heels in debt."

"What would you do if he wasn't there? What if I'd not been so foolish as to tell you?"

"But he is there," Dulin replied, "and thanks to you, we know what he's got. There may be water enough to keep our stock alive for a month, and by then the rains might come. I'm for it."

"So am I!" Stangle declared.

"It isn't right," Drake protested. "If he has water it's due to his own hard work, and the water's his."

"Well, Tom, if you want to go broke, the choice is yours," Stangle said. "I'll be damned if I let my cattle die. If you had a water hole you'd let me use it, wouldn't you? Why should he be the only one who's fenced in?"

Casady's dislike was obvious as he stared at Stangle. "And just who built The Fence? Seems to me you had a hand in it, Stangle."

"That cuts no ice." Stangle waved a hand. "We'll tear it down. We'll run our cattle in there, and then we'll see what happens. I'm not going to let my cattle die because he keeps his water fenced up."

"I reckon that speaks for me." Hardy Benson spoke reluctantly. "I'm in debt. I'll lose all I have."

"That says it for me," Vinnie Lake added.

Cab got to his feet. "How about you, Tom?"

Drake hesitated, before his eyes the vision of his dying cattle, the size of the bill he owed Mayer.

"I'll string with the boys," he said.

For a moment Casady looked around at their faces. "I'd rather my cattle died," he said. "Good night, *gentlemen*!"

Dulin started to his feet, his hand reaching for his gun. "I'll kill that—"

"Better not try," Hill said dryly. "You never saw the day you could match Cab with a gun."

He looked around at their faces. "I don't know that I like this, myself."

"It's settled," Stangle declared. "Dulin, Lake, Benson, Drake, and Hill. How about you, McKesson?"

"Sure, I'll ride along, trail my stock with yours. I never liked that Mex, no way."

Tom Drake glanced at him thoughtfully. Curt McKesson was a new man in the valley, a big, somber man with a brooding, sullen face. Drake had seen him angry but once, but that had revealed him to have a vicious, murderous temper. He had beaten a horse to death before anyone could interfere. He disliked the man, and it disturbed him to see how McKesson's eyes followed Candy every move she made. The light in them was not good to see.

Joe Stangle got up, satisfaction showing in his eyes and voice. "We can meet at Willow Springs Monday morning. Once The Fence is down and the cattle started for water there will be no stoppin' them."

Candy watched, feeling sick and empty. She wanted to protest but knew they would not listen. Their own desperation coupled with Stangle's hatred and Dulin's sullen brutality had led them into something most of them would live to regret. Now they were only thinking about delaying their bad times. One by one they filed out and when they had gone she turned on her father.

"Dad, you've got to stop them! You can't let them destroy all that poor boy's work!"

"Poor boy, is it? He's got no right to all that water when our cattle are dying!"

"Who dammed those draws? What have you done to try to save your cattle? All you've done is sit here with the rest of them and sneer at what he thought and what he did!"

"Be quiet!" Drake's voice boomed, his guilt making him even more angry. "I won't have you takin' up for that Mexican. Nor is it your place to question my actions."

"Dad"—Candy's tone was cold—"you'd better understand this. Barry Merrano will fight. If he fights, somebody will get killed. If I were you I'd do a lot of thinking before you start anything. It isn't like it was when you drove out those rustlers. The country has changed."

Despite himself, he knew what she said was the truth. He shook his head irritably. "Nonsense! He's yellow! He won't fight."

He hesitated, thinking. Then he said, "He won't fight. Joe Stangle made a fool of him and he did nothing, nothing at all!"

"Then you'd better go out to the bunkhouse and take a look at Price Taylor. Price thought he wouldn't fight, too."

"What? What do you mean?"

"Barry rode home with me tonight and was leaving me at the gate. He had been a gentleman, no more. Price jumped him, and Barry gave him a beating."

"He whupped Price? Girl, you're crazy!"

"Go look at him. Ask Price if he's yellow. Also, *I* seem to remember you tried to frighten him away before, and he didn't run. He had only an idea to fight for then. Now he's got a place worth having!"

She paused. "Remember this, Dad. He'll fight, and somebody will get killed."

"Bah!" Drake said, but he was disturbed. She knew her father well enough to know that he had not liked the action taken tonight, yet these were the men he knew, men he had worked beside, men with whom he had shared trouble. He had gone along because it offered a way out of bankruptcy and failure, and because there seemed no alternative.

Tom Drake had fought Indians, outlaws, and rustlers, and now he would fight to hold the place, but he knew in his heart that if he were Merrano, he would fight. He did not approve of killing and he believed Merrano would run, yet now, listening to his daughter, he was no longer so sure.

"Dad?" Candy spoke quietly. "I want you to understand. If you go through with this I'll go and fight beside Barry Merrano. I will take a rifle and stand beside him and what happens to him will happen to me."

"What!" He stared at his daughter, consternation in his eyes. In that instant he looked not only into his daughter's eyes but into those of his wife, and something more, he saw a reflection of himself, thirty years before.

Without another word, Candy turned and left the room. The big old man behind her stared after her, hurt, confusion, and doubt struggling in his mind. He sat down suddenly in the big hide chair.

Suddenly he felt old and tired, staring into the fire, trying to think things out and seeing only his dying cattle and the failure of all he had done. The cracked mud in the dried-up water holes, the leafless trees, all his years, all his struggle, all his work and his plans gone.

———

THAT WAS FRIDAY night. Early Saturday morning a buckboard left Mirror Valley and bounced over the stones and through the thick gray dust toward Willow Springs and the turnoff to Merrano's tunnel. Clyde Mayer had made a decision, and he was following through. He knew nothing of the action taken by the ranchers at the TD ranch. He was threatened by foreclosure by the wholesalers, and in this emergency he was turning to the one man in the valley who seemed to have money.

The tunnel was unguarded, and he turned in hesitantly. When he emerged into the bright sunlight Barry Merrano was standing in the door of his house. The sound of hoofs in the tunnel was plainly audible within the house at any time.

Mayer pulled up in the ranch yard and tied the lines to the whipstock. He got down carefully, for he was not as agile as he had once been.

"Howdy, son!" He peered at Barry over his glasses. "Reckon this visit's a surprise."

"Come in," Barry invited. "I'm just back from patching a hole in a dam. A badger dug into it, and the water started to drain out."

"My, my!" Mayer looked around slowly. "Your mother would be right proud, young man! Right proud! She was a fine woman, your mother was!"

"Thanks. That's always good to hear from somebody else. She was a good mother to me."

When they were seated over coffee, Mayer said, "Son, I've come to you for help. The wholesalers have shut off my credit, and they are demanding money. I am low on stock, and the ranchers will be coming in for supplies."

"How much do you need?"

"An awful lot, son. I'd need five thousand dollars. I'd sell you a half interest in my business for it. I know I've been foolish to extend credit, but these are good men, son, and basically they mean well. Every one of them will pay off if it is the last thing they do, but that won't help me now . . . nor them."

"If you don't get the money, you go broke?"

"That's right."

"Then what happens to the ranchers?"

"They'd starve or get out. The drouth's hit this country so bad there isn't a head of cattle fit to sell. It will take two really good years to get them out of the hole they're in. They'd never be able to stick it out. They have no food, no feed, no water."

Merrano stared into his cup, his brown, wind-tanned face thoughtful. After a moment he said, "All right. I'll buy a half interest in your store on one condition. I don't want anybody to know about it."

Mayer hesitated. "What about credit for the ranchers? They are my friends, and I'd hate to turn them down."

"Don't. Give them what they need. Somebody has to have faith in this country. Maybe after this they will learn their lesson and handle their stock sensibly."

Mayer stood up, his relief obvious. "I don't mind telling you, son, I was scared. I hadn't anywhere to turn."

He started for his buckboard and paused before getting into it, "Son, you be careful. That Joe Stangle is a mighty mean man, and so is Dulin."

"Thanks. I'll keep my eyes open."

After Mayer had gone Barry returned to the house and got his Winchester. Then he slipped on his gunbelt. It was time to begin moving the cattle off the Long Valley range and back into the basin. No use to let them feed there too long. In a few weeks he would take thirty head over to Aragon for sale. It would save on feed and water and give him a little more working cash.

He had saddled up and was about to mount when he heard a rattle of horse's hooves. It was Candy Drake.

At her expression he caught her hand. "Candy? What's happened?"

Swiftly, the words tumbling into one another, she told him of the meeting and its result. "Please, Barry! Don't think too hard of Father! All he can see now is his cattle dying!"

"I know," he agreed. "The trouble is that the little water I have wouldn't help much. With that mass of cattle coming in, my smaller pools would be trampled into mud within hours and the bigger pools behind the dams would last no time at all. It would simply add my ruin to the rest of them. Believe me, Candy, I'd like to help.

"There is a way, if they will work. There's water in the White Horse Hills. It would take a lot of work, but they could get at it."

"They wouldn't listen, Barry. Not now."

"There's only one thing I can do now, Candy. They broke my mother's heart on this ground, and they turned Father from a laughter-loving young vaquero into a morose and lonely man.

"There's only one thing I can do, and that's what your father would do or any of the men with him. I am going to fight."

He waved a hand. "There's four years of blood, sweat, and blisters in this. Days and nights when I was so bitterly lonely I thought I'd go insane. I built those dams with my own hands. I gathered the stones for this house, cut and shaped the planks for the floors. I made the chairs. These things are mine, and I'll fight to keep them.

"If a single cow crosses The Fence, that cow will cross over my dead body, but believe me, it won't be lying there alone. Candy, if you can talk to your father, tell him that. Blood won't save his cattle, but if it is blood he wants, that's what he will get."

"They'll kill you, Barry. There are too many of them."

"I won't be alone. This may sound silly, but my mother and father will be with me. This land was theirs before it was mine. The ghosts of a thousand other men who fought for their homes will be there, too!"

"Barry, I told Father that if he came I'd fight with you."

Surprised, he looked up at her. "You said *that*?"

"I did, and I meant it."

Speechless, he hesitated, then shook his head. "No, as much as I'd like it, I can't let you fight against your father. This is my fight. I am obliged for the warning, but you'd better ride on now. But no matter what happens, I'll not forget this."

"All right, I'll go, but Barry, be careful! Joe Stangle hates you! And that other man, Curt McKesson . . . he frightens me!"

For a long time after she was gone, Barry sat staring down the valley, thinking. He would leave the cattle where they were.

Accustomed to working and planning alone he now turned all his thoughts to defense. It was a problem he had considered since his first day, and his position was excellent. Table Mountain and the Neck barred access to Mirror Valley, and only the tunnel and The Fence offered ingress. In the other direction lay the canyon that opened into Long Valley, and he had no worries about that direction. It was a seventy-mile ride, much of it through the reservation lands to get to that approach, and the Indians would resent any armed band crossing their lands.

With cool calculation he began to study his problem.

———

BY NOON ON Saturday he began work, using a double-jack and a drill. These holes he loaded with powder, determined to blast it shut if need be. It was late afternoon before he completed the work.

From the top of Table Mountain he studied the Mirror Valley country with a field glass his father had given him. He could see the dust clouds that told of moving cattle. No cattle had yet reached Willow Springs, which Candy had told him would be the rendezvous point. Yet by Sunday night he knew the cattle would be massed at the opening of the draw.

Returning to the house he lowered a heavy log gate across the tunnel mouth. Mounting his horse and leading a pack-horse, he headed for The Fence.

Once there he studied the terrain with care. The Fence was strong, and his inner fence was stronger. Tearing it out would be no simple job. Climbing the mountain he dug two rifle pits, one forward, the other some distance further back, which he could reach by a hidden route. In each he left am-munition.

No weight of cattle could press down The Fence. It must be torn down or blasted out. Using a crowbar from the pack-horse he pried loose a number of boulders and tumbled them down the steep sides of the draw to a place behind The Fence to widen and deepen the barrier.

Further back, where the draw opened into the basin he dug another rifle pit and tumbled down more stones, but there they were more widely spaced and less of an obstruction. Not until darkness had fallen and he could see the dark mass of advancing cattle did he cease work.

Despite the fact that he feared to leave the barricade, he went back to the house and prepared a meal. He was sitting down to eat when he heard a call from the tunnel.

"Merrano?" The shout reached him clearly. "This is Cab Casady! I want to talk!"

Picking up his rifle, his gun belts still hanging from his hips, he walked to the log gate. "What's the problem?" he asked.

The big man grasped the logs. "Merrano, damn it, I'm no talker! But I do claim some sense of what's right, and I ain't havin' no part of what they're tryin' to do. I got a rifle here and plenty of shells. I came to lend you a hand!"

"You mean that?" He recalled what Candy had said of this man.

"I sure do, boy! You've got sand, and by the Lord Harry I want to show these bullheads that at least one of us won't be stampeded by no hate-filled coyote like Joe Stangle!"

Barry put down his rifle and unlatched the gate. "Come in, Cab! I won't tell you how good it is to see you!"

The two men walked up to the cabin. Over coffee and side meat Barry explained his defenses. Casady chuckled. "I'll like seein' the expression on Joe Stangle's face when he gets to The Fence!" he said.

They took turns guarding the draw, but not until daylight did the cattlemen start to ride up. Barry was at the cabin when he welcomed another visitor . . . two of them, in fact.

Clyde Mayer, driving his old buckboard, a rifle between his knees, drove up the hill when the gate was opened. Beside him on the seat was Candy Drake. She set her lips stubbornly when she saw Barry.

"If you won't let me shoot I can at least make coffee and get food for you. You'll have to eat."

"All right. I'm not sorry you came. Come on, Mayer, we'd better head back for the draw."

He turned to the girl. "Candy, watch the tunnel. If you hear anybody coming, and you can always hear them, tell them to go away. Fire a couple of warning shots and if they don't leave, light the fuses."

Her features were stiff and white, her eyes large. "I'll do it, Barry. They've no business coming here."

Day was breaking into that gray half-light that precedes the dawn. Cab Casady rose from behind a boulder and came to meet them. "Howdy, Mayer! You joined the army?"

"I have."

Casady was a large, broad-shouldered man with twinkling blue eyes. "They're comin' now," he said. "We better look to it."

"Let me do the talking," Barry suggested. "Maybe we can avoid shooting."

"I doubt it," Cab said. "Stangle wants blood."

When the little cavalcade of riders had approached as far as he thought wise he fired a shot that brought them up standing.

"You boys better ride home. Nobody is coming through the wire, today or ever. I don't want to kill anybody, but I'm protecting my property against armed men."

Casady stood up. "I'm here, too, boys. The first man to touch that wire dies!"

Clyde Mayer called out. "Hill? Is that you? I'm no fighting man, but by gravy there's going to be some justice in this country! You take my advice and ride home."

"Mayer?" Hill's tone was incredulous. "You turned traitor, too?"

"I'm upholding justice, and if you've half the sense I gave you credit for you'll turn around and ride home. I like you but you lay a hand on that wire and my bullet will take you right between the eyes!"

There was a hurried conference among the riders. "They can't stop us!" Stangle protested. "They're bluffin'!"

"Count me out," Price Taylor said.

"You yellow?" Dulin sneered.

"You know I'm not yellow," Price Taylor said calmly, "but I've been thinking all the way out here. Merrano whipped me fair and square, and when I was down he didn't put the boots to me but stepped back and let me get up. He made good when we all laughed at him, and he's standing his ground now. As for Mayer, there ain't a fairer, more decent man around than him, and I'll be damned if I'll shoot at him!"

"Then why don't you join him?" Dulin sneered.

Price turned on him. "You called it, Rock! That's just what I'll do! I've made some bad mistakes and I'm no sky pilot, but I never ganged up on a man with guts."

He wheeled his horse and started for the barrier. He lifted a hand. "Don't shoot, Merrano! I'm joinin' you!"

Rock Dulin swore viciously and suddenly he whipped up his rifle and fired.

Price Taylor lurched in the saddle, then slipped over on the ground.

"Damn traitor!" Rock Dulin said. "That'll show 'em!"

Tom Drake stared down at the body of Price Taylor. He had reared the boy. He had helped him mount his first horse. He stared around him in shocked bewilderment. "What are we doing?" he said. "Men, what *are* we doing?"

Dropping from his horse he stumbled to the body of Price Taylor.

Jim Hill was white to the lips. Hardy Benson stared after Tom Drake, his face stupid with shock. He looked as if he had awakened from a nightmare. He turned his eyes to Rock Dulin. "That was murder!" he said. "Nothin' but murder!"

Dulin turned like an animal at bay. His eyes went from man to man. "What's the matter? Are you all turnin' yellow? You started out to do it, now you're quittin'!"

Hill sat his horse, his rifle in his hands. "Price Taylor was a good man. He had a right to his feelin's as much as us. Dulin"—his eyes fastened on the other rancher—"you an' Stangle do what you want, but you lift a gun at me, my boys will string you to the nearest cottonwood, an' that's where you belong! We've been a pack of fools, the lot of us!" He turned in the saddle. "Come on, boys, start 'em for home!"

As the Jim Hill hands began gathering the herd, Tom Drake glanced once at the draw, then turned to his own boys. "A couple of you pick up Price," he said.

Lou Barrow looked over at Drake. "Boss, Price was a good man. Too good to get shot in the back."

"I know, but there's been trouble enough today." He walked his horse to where Jim Hill and Hardy Benson sat. "I seem to be gettin' old these days, Jim. I've been lettin' things get out of hand."

"Yeah. Well, this is it, Tom. We're broke."

Silently, the groups scattered, driving their cattle. Dulin spoke to this one or that one but was ignored, cut off, left out of their thinking.

He turned in cold fury to Stangle. "I got a notion to cut the thing myself!"

"Don't try it," Stangle advised. "If he didn't get you, Cab would. We can get even later."

———

As THE THREE men inside The Fence watched them go, Casady said, "It will be good to get some warm grub." They turned their horses and rode toward the house.

"Dulin has always been a killer. He shot a man in a gun-fight over at Trinidad a few years back," Cab said. "Curt McKesson is another of the same stripe."

Mayer went to his buckboard. "I'll be leaving."

"Watch yourself," Casady advised.

"They daren't bother me," Mayer said. "Without me they can't eat."

Candy was last to go, and Barry rode along with her. At the gate she turned to say good-bye, and he shook his head. "I must talk to your father," he said.

"Do you think that's wise?"

"Maybe not, but he's got a chance to save some of his cattle, if he will listen."

———

DRAKE DID NOT look up when they entered. He was seated in his old hide-bound chair, head hanging.

"Father? Here's someone to see you."

He looked up, raising his head like a cornered bear. "Howdy, Merrano. You're lookin' at an old fool."

"Drake"—Barry squatted against the wall—"if you will work to save your herd you can still do it."

"It would have to be soon, boy. They're dyin' like flies."

"Have you been up in the White Hills lately?"

"The White Hills? Not in five or six years. Nothin' up there but piñon an' juniper."

"I think there's water up there," Barry said. "One time down in Texas I saw them bring in an artesian well in country just like that. If you drilled a well just below that old trapper's cabin I think you'd strike water."

"Never heard of any wells drilled in this country," he said doubtfully.

"I've drilled four," Merrano replied, "all with water."

Drake struck a match and held it to his pipe. "Well, it's high time I owned up to thinkin' I was too smart. We old dogs figured we knew all the tricks."

He puffed on his pipe. "Mind if I ride over and have a look at your place? Candy's told me about it."

"You come at any time. As for well-drilling, I've got an outfit I hauled in two years ago from Aragon."

He rode warily on his homeward way. Despite the peaceful

discussion with Drake he knew that Stangle and Dulin were still his enemies. The two had ridden off together, and Curt McKesson had ridden with them.

———

WHEN TOM DRAKE rode to the basin the next morning, Jim Hill, Vinnie Lake, and Hardy Benson rode with him. They greeted Barry with no more than a nod, and he mounted the steeldust and led them across the basin. Drake pulled in suddenly, pointing to a mound of earth running diagonally across a shallow place on the hill.

"What's the object of that?" he asked.

"Water was starting to make a wash right there," Barry explained, "so I put in that little spreader dam. Causes the water to divide and spread over the hillside and so reaches the roots of more grass.

"Down below where there was a natural hollow, I dug it out a little more with a scraper. Now I've got a pool, although it is drying up now."

"More water in that pool right now than I've got on my whole place!" Hill said.

Barry led them from place to place, showing them the lakes he had dammed in the draws, and the various pools. The first of the wells, where he had a windmill pumping, showed a good flow of water. The second, some distance away, was artesian.

The basin looked green and lovely, and he gestured with a wave of the hand. "That's mostly black grama and curly mesquite grass. I let the cattle run there a few weeks, then move them to another pasture and let this grow back. I only run about a third of the stock you have on the same number of acres, that way my stock is always fat."

"My place is all growed up to cholla cactus now," Drake said.

"Burn that field," Barry advised, "the ashes will help the field and the fire will burn the dry needles off the cholla leaving the green pulp behind. That green pulp is fairly good feed. The Navajos taught me that."

"Then I've got enough cholla on my place to feed all the stock in Christendom," Hill said.

"Son," Drake said, "you've done a job! We should have listened to you a long time back."

————

THE DAYS PASSED swiftly and Barry worked hard, but he was lonely, and even the work failed to help. Each time he returned to the house he kept looking for Candy as he remembered her, making coffee in his kitchen during the fight. At night, alone by the fire, he seemed to see her there. Then one day he rode his horse up the draw and stopped, astonished.

The Fence was gone! Rooted out, wire and posts gone, and the post holes filled in. There might never have been a fence there at all. He pushed his hat back on his head, and shook his head. "Mom," he said aloud, "you'd have liked to see this!"

————

CANDY DRAKE, RIDING her pinto, decided to head for the basin. She knew all about The Fence being down. The burning of the cholla had worked and would be the means of saving at least some of the cattle. Now, if the rains came in time or the drillers struck water, they had a fighting chance.

Yet trouble was mounting. Lou Barrow, filled with fury at Rock Dulin's killing of Price Taylor, had gone to town. Barrow had made a remark about killers, and Dulin had gone for his gun. Barrow was a tough cowhand but no gunman, and Dulin put three bullets into him. Miraculously, Barrow lived.

Rock Dulin swaggered about town, his ranch forgotten, his stock dying. Joe Stangle and Curt McKesson were usually with him.

Candy decided it was time the women took a hand. Alice Benson agreed, and so did the three Lake girls. They organized a big dance and celebration for the purpose of getting everybody together again and wiping out old scores. Candy had taken it upon herself to ride to the basin and invite Barry Merrano.

IN OTHER PARTS of the valley, events were moving in their own way. McKesson had ridden over to Stangle's, and the two sat in the untidy living room over a bottle of whiskey. With nothing on which to feed, Joe Stangle's hatred had turned inward. For days he had been brooding over the thought of Barry Merrano, now the talk of the valley. Joe Stangle's hatred was of long standing, for he had wanted Molly O'Brien and then she had married Miguel Merrano. The fact that Molly had never even noticed his existence made no difference. Deliberately, he provoked trouble with Miguel, confident the Mexican would back down.

The trouble was, he did no such thing. The darkly handsome young Mexican had simply stepped back and told him to go for his gun whenever he was ready.

Suddenly Joe had discovered he was not at all ready. It was one thing to tackle what you thought was a puppy dog, quite another when you found yourself facing a wolf with fangs bared. Stangle looked across eight feet of floor and discovered that courage knows no race or creed.

He had backed down, and although it was not mentioned, he knew he was despised for it. His hatred for Miguel Merrano flowered with the coming of his son.

Now, both men were drunk or nearly so. Hulking Curt McKesson reached for the bottle and so did Stangle. Joe got his hand on it as did Curt. In a sudden burst of fury, Stangle jerked the bottle from McKesson's hand.

McKesson's sullen anger, never far from the surface, exploded into rage and he struck with the back of his hand, the blow knocking Stangle sprawling. McKesson was not wearing a gun, having put it aside in the other room.

Joe Stangle, blind with fury, saw nothing but the great hulking figure. All his bottled-up rage found sudden release in this, and his gun slid into his hand, thumbing the hammer again and again.

The thunderous roar of the six-gun filled the room, and with it the acrid smell of gunsmoke. Then the sound died, the smoke slowly cleared, and Joe Stangle lurched to his feet.

One glance at Curt McKesson was enough. The big man was literally riddled with bullets. Averting his eyes, Joe Stangle picked up the bottle and drained off the last of the whiskey. Without a backward glance, he walked out the door.

Drunk as he was his natural cunning warned him he had no chance of getting away with what had been the killing of an unarmed man. Steps were being taken to elect a sheriff and once that was done neither he nor Rock Dulin would long remain at large. Mounting his horse he started down the valley, filled with a sullen feeling that somehow it was all Barry Merrano's fault.

The trail he was riding, drunk, and filled with sullen rage, intersected that of Candy Drake.

Unknown to either of them, Barry Merrano had ridden out of a draw and glimpsed Candy's pinto at a distance. A deep canyon lay between them although they were less than a mile apart, but with luck he could overtake her at Willow Springs.

As he rode he sang a song he had himself composed, a song made up during his loneliness and when he desperately needed something cheerful of which to think.

> *"Oh, gather 'round closer and fill up your glasses,*
> *And I'll tell you the story of Johnny Go-Day.*
> *He was a young cowhand who rode all the mustangs,*
> *And no bronco they bred could Johnny dismay!"*

In the cancer of envy that festered in the mind of Joe Stangle was a hatred for all better off or more attractive than himself. Most of all, after Barry Merrano, he hated Candy Drake.

She was a girl who spoke to everyone, but Stangle had noticed that she did not particularly enjoy speaking to him. He failed to realize this was due to his own surly manner, and the fact that he had been known to make unpleasant remarks about girls and women. He simply believed she thought herself too good for him.

Riding at a canter Candy approached Willow Springs recalling, as she drew near, that her father had told her they had struck water at this, the first well attempted in the valley.

Riding up to where the drill rig still stood, she swung down, looking at the pool of muddy water and considering what this could mean to the valley.

It was Barry Merrano's drill rig that had brought in this well, and it was on his advice they had fed the cholla to their stock that saved so much of it. The prejudice against him had virtually disappeared. It could mean a new life for him, and might mean—

She did not hear the horse stop at the edge of the brush. Joe Stangle had seen her arrive, knew she was in there alone, in the gathering dusk. He dug into his saddlebag for the pint he carried there and took a pull at the bottle. He was leaving the country, anyway, and he'd show her what was what. Before anybody knew what had happened he'd be long gone.

He pushed his way through the willows, and Candy turned sharply at the unexpected crackling of the dry brush and saw Joe Stangle.

He was not a big man but he was hairy-chested and broad. His face was swollen and the flesh sodden from much drinking, and he was obviously in an ugly mood.

Candy realized her danger, but she was not given to screaming. She backed away warily, wishing her horse were closer. If she turned her back to run he would catch her before she had taken three steps.

He did not speak, just walked toward her.

"What's the matter, Joe? Have you lost something?"

He made no reply, continuing to advance. She stepped back and her boot slipped in the mud and she fell, rolling quickly away and scrambling to her feet.

Drunk he might be, but he could move quickly. "Damn you! You stuck-up—!" She dodged away, but he grabbed at her and caught her wrist. "I'll show you what—!"

In that instant they heard a voice they both knew.

"Oh, there was a young cowhand who used to go riding,
There was a young cowhand named Johnny Go-Day!
He rode a black pony and he never was lonely,
For the girls never said to him 'Johnny, go 'way!'

When they heard his bright laughter their hearts
followed after,
And they called to him 'Johnny! Oh, Johnny, come
stay!' "

Stangle's hand clamped over the girl's mouth before she could cry out a warning. The pinto stood in plain sight, but Joe Stangle's horse was hidden beyond the brush.

Holding her with one powerful arm and hand, a leg pressed before hers and jamming her back against the drill rig, with his free hand he drew his six-shooter.

The song ended and they heard the saddle creak as he dismounted and then as he started through the willows the song continued.

"He rode to town daily and always rode gaily,
And lifted his hat as he cantered along!"

Joe Stangle lifted his six-shooter, took careful aim, and squeezed the trigger.

The firing pin clicked on an empty cartridge. He had emptied his gun into Curt McKesson!

At the click of the cocking hammer Barry stopped dead, and with an oath, Joe Stangle threw the girl from him and grabbed feverishly at his cartridge belt for more shells. In his haste he dropped the first two shells but thrust the others into place.

Wild with fear, Candy dropped to the ground and began to scramble away, crying out, "Look out, Barry! It's Joe Stangle!"

Barry grabbed for his gun, still tied down with the rawhide thong he wore when riding. He slid the thong and drew swiftly.

Dropping to one knee, the other leg thrust out before him, he waited. He could hear the breathing of Candy Drake, but in the darkness of the willow grove he could see nothing. Picking up a stick he threw it to one side. Nothing happened.

He moved slightly, gathering himself to leap aside, and at the sound a stab of flame seemed to leap right at his eyes and a bullet struck a tree behind him with an ugly thud. He fired in reply, and his bullet ricocheted off the drill rig.

He fired again, holding a little lower, and the shot drew a startled movement. He leaped aside, gun poised for another shot. There was an instant of silence, and then a shot. The bullet missed by a fraction of an inch.

Candy lay hugging the ground, and Barry could see her now. Carefully, he shifted position to get further away from her so as not to draw fire in her direction.

Hatred and fear were driving Joe Stangle, but even the courage of a cornered coyote had a breaking point. The liquor fumes had cleared from his mind, and he realized Barry was over there; he had a gun, and he was playing for keeps.

Suddenly what courage he had went out of him like a gust of breath, and like a shadow, he faded back toward the brush and his horse. He wanted desperately to kill, but he did not wish to be killed. He wanted nothing so much as to get a saddle under him and be off. He almost made it.

Merrano, hearing him at last, lunged through the brush after him. Stangle reached his horse and Merrano slid to a stop, and Joe Stangle saw him and tried one last shot. It was there, and he had to try.

Barry fired at the same instant, then he fired again. Joe Stangle's horse leaped away, and Joe Stangle, shot through the belly, all the hatred oozing away with his life's blood, swayed on his feet, the gun slipping from his fingers. Then he fell.

Barry Merrano turned and started back through the willows and then all of a sudden he seemed to step into a hole and he fell.

———

THE CLEAN WHITE bed and the doctor who was putting things away in a black bag were a surprise. Candy was there, and Cab Casady.

"Stangle?" He started to rise.

"He's gone, Barry. He had already killed Curt McKesson in some kind of drunken fight, and was leaving the country."

"Dulin?"

Cab shifted his feet. "I come by and helped Candy get you home. Then I went down to town and run into Rock Dulin. He picked a fight and I had to shoot him."

Cab started for the door. "You two might have something to talk about," he said. "I want to go watch the rain. Seems like it's years since I've seen any."

BLUFF CREEK STATION

T HE STAGE WAS two hours late into Bluff Creek and the station hostler had recovered his pain-wracked consciousness three times. After two futile attempts to move he had given up and lay sprawled on the rough boards of the floor with a broken back and an ugly hole in his side.

He was a man of middle years, his jaw unshaved and his hair rumpled and streaked with gray. His soiled shirt and homespun jeans were dark with blood. There was one unlaced boot on his left foot. The other boot lay near a fireplace gray with ancient ashes.

There were two benches and a few scattered tools, some odd bits of harness, an overturned chair, and a table on which were some unwashed dishes. Near the hostler's right hand lay a Spencer rifle, and beyond it a double-barreled shotgun. On the floor nearby, within easy reach, a double row of neatly spaced shotgun and rifle shells. Scattered about were a number of used shells from both weapons, mute mementos of his four-hour battle with attacking Indians.

Now, for slightly more than two hours there had been no attack, yet he knew they were out there, awaiting the arrival of the stage, and it was for this he lived, to fire a warning shot before the stage could stop at the station. The last shot they fired, from a Sharps .50, had wrecked his spine. The bloody wound in his side had come earlier in the battle, and he had stuffed it with cotton torn from an old mattress.

Outside, gray clouds hung low, threatening rain, and occasional gusts of wind rattled the dried leaves on the trees, or stirred them along the hard ground.

The stage station squatted in dwarfish discomfort at the foot of a bluff, the station was constructed of blocks picked from the slide-rock at the foot of the bluff, and it was roofed with split cedar logs covered with earth. Two small windows stared in mute wonderment at the empty road and at the ragged brush before it where the Indians waited.

Three Indians, he believed, had died in the battle, and probably he had wounded as many more, but he distrusted counting Indian casualties, for all too often they were over-estimated. And the Indians always carried away their dead.

The Indians wanted the stage, the horses that drew it, and the weapons of the people inside. There was no way to warn the driver or passengers unless he could do it. The hostler lay on his back staring up at the ceiling.

He had no family, and he was glad of that now. Ruby had run off with a tinhorn from Alta some years back, and there had been no word from her, nor had he wished for it. Occasionally, he thought of her, but without animosity. He was not, he reminded himself, an easy man with whom to live, nor was he much of a person. He had been a simple, hard-working man, inclined to drink too much, and often quarrel-some when drinking.

He had no illusions. He knew he was finished. The heavy lead slug that had smashed the base of his spine had killed him. Only an iron will had kept life in his body, and he doubted his ability to keep it there much longer. His legs were already dead and there was a coldness in his fingers that frightened him. He would need those fingers to fire the warning shot.

Slowly, carefully, he reached for the shotgun and loaded it with fumbling, clumsy fingers. Then he wedged the shotgun into place in the underpinning of his bunk. It was aimed at nothing, but all he needed was the shot, the dull boom it would make, a warning to those who rode the stage that something was amiss.

He managed to knot a string to the trigger so it could be pulled even if he could not reach it. His extremities would go first and then even if his fingers were useless he could pull the trigger with his teeth.

Exhausted by his efforts he lay back and stared up at the darkening ceiling, without bitterness, waiting for the high, piercing yell of the stage driver and the rumble and rattle of the stage's wheels as it approached the station.

FIVE MILES EAST, the heavily loaded stage rolled along the dusty trail accompanied by its following plume of dust. The humped-up clouds hung low over the serrated ridges. Up on the box, Kickapoo Jackson handled the lines and beside him Hank Wells was riding shotgun. Wells was deadheading it home as there was nothing to guard coming west. He had his revolving shotgun and a rifle with him from force of habit. The third man who rode the top, lying between some sacks of mail, was Marshal Brad Delaney, a former buffalo hunter and Indian fighter.

Inside the stage a stocky, handsome boy with brown hair sat beside a pretty girl in rumpled finery. Both looked tired and were, but the fact that they were recently married was written all over them. Half the way from Kansas City they had talked of their hopes and dreams, and their excitement had been infectious. They had enlisted the advice and sympathy of those atop the coach as well as those who rode inside.

The tall man of forty with hair already gray at the temples was Dr. Dave Moody, heading for the mining camps of Nevada to begin a new practice after several years of successful work in New England. Major Glen Faraday sat beside him at the window. Faraday was a West Point man, now discharged from the army and en route west to build a flume for an irrigation project.

Ma Harrigan, who ran a boardinghouse in Austin and was reputed to make the best pies west of the Rockies, sat beside Johnny Ryan, headed west to the father he had never seen.

Kickapoo Jackson swung the Concord around a bend and headed into a narrow draw. "Never liked this place!" he shouted. "Too handy for injuns!"

"Seen any around?" Delaney asked.

"Nope! But the hostler at Bluff Creek had him a brush with them a while back. He driv 'em off, though! That's a good man, yonder!"

"That's his kid down below," Wells said. "Does he know the kid's comin' west?"

"Know?" Kickapoo spat. "Ryan don't even know he's got a kid! His wife run off with a no-account gambler a few years back! When the gambler found she was carryin' another man's child he just up and left her. She hadn't known about the kid when she left Ryan."

"She never went back?"

"Too proud, I reckon. She waited tables in Kansas City awhile, then got sickly. Reckon she died. The folks the boy lived with asked me to bring him back to his dad. Ol' Ryan will sure be surprised!"

AT BLUFF CREEK all was quiet. Dud Ryan stared up into the gathering darkness and waited. From time to time he could put an eye to a crack and study the road and the area beyond it. They were there . . . waiting.

Delaney and Wells would be riding the stage this trip, and they were canny men. Yet they would not be expecting trouble at the stage station. When they rolled into sight of it there would be a letdown, an easing-off, and the Indians would get off a volley before the men on the stage knew what hit them.

With Brad and Hank out of the picture, and possibly Kickapoo Jackson, the passengers could be slaughtered like so many mice. Caught inside the suddenly stalled stage, with only its flimsy sides to protect them, they would have no chance.

Only one thing remained. He must somehow remain alive to warn them. A warning shot would have them instantly alert, and Hank Wells would whip up his team and they would go through and past the station at a dead run. To warn them he must be alive.

Alive?

Well, he knew he was dying. He had known from the moment he took that large-caliber bullet in the spine. Without rancor he turned the idea over in his mind. Life hadn't given him much, after all. Yet dying wouldn't be so bad if he felt that his dying would do any good.

The trouble was, no man was ever ready to die. There was always something more to do, something undone, even if only to cross the street.

Behind him the years stretched empty and alone. Even the good years with Ruby looked bleak when he thought of them. He had never been able to give her anything, and maybe that was why he drank. Like all kids he had his share of dreams, and he was ready to take the world by the throat and shake it until it gave him the things he desired. Only stronger, more able men seemed always to get what he wanted. Their women had the good things and there had been nothing much he could do for Ruby. Nor much for himself but hard work and privation.

Ruby had stuck by him even after he began to hit the bottle too hard. She used to talk of having a nice house somewhere, and maybe of traveling, seeing the world and meeting people. All he had given her was a series of small mining camps, ramshackle cabins, and nothing much to look forward to but more of the same. His dream, like so many others, was to make the big strike, but he never had.

The tinhorn was a slick talker and Ruby was pretty, prettier than most. He had talked mighty big of the places he would show her, and what they would do. Even when Dud followed him home one night and gave him a beating, Ruby had continued to meet him. Then they ran off.

At the time they had been just breaking even on what he made from odd jobs, and then he got a steady job with the stage line. He rushed home with the news, for it meant he'd have charge of the station at Haver Hill, a cool, pleasant little house where they could raise some chickens and have flower beds as well as a place to raise garden truck. It was always given to a married man, and he had landed it. He rushed home with the news.

The house was empty. He had never seen it so empty because her clothes were gone and there was only the note . . . he still had it . . . telling him she was leaving him.

He gave up Haver Hill then and took a series of remote stations where the work was hard and conditions primitive. His salary wasn't bad and he had saved some money, bought a few horses, and broke teams during his spare time. The stage company itself had bought horses from him, and he was doing well. For the first time he managed to save some money, to get ahead.

There was no word from Ruby although he never stopped hoping she would write. He did not want her back, but he hoped she was doing well and was happy. Also, he wanted her to know how well he was doing.

He did hear about the tinhorn, and it was from Brad Delaney that he got the news. The tinhorn had showed up in El Paso alone. From there he drifted north to Mobeetie, and finally to Fort Griffin. There he had tried to outsmart a man who was smarter, and when caught cheating he tried to outdraw him.

"What happened?" Dud had asked.

"What could happen? He tackled a man who wouldn't take anything from anybody, some fellow who used to be a dentist but was dying of tuberculosis. That dentist put two bullets into that tinhorn's skull, and he's buried in an unmarked grave in Boot Hill."

Dud Ryan wrote to El Paso, but the letter was returned. There was no trace of Ruby. Nobody knew where the tinhorn had come from and the trail ended there. Ryan had about convinced himself that Ruby was dead.

He tried to move, but the agony in his back held him still. If only he could live long enough! Where the hell was the stage? It should have been along hours ago.

He ground his teeth in pain and set his mind on the one thought: *Live! Live! Live!*

Delaney, Wells, and old Kickapoo were too good to die in an ambush. They were strong men, decent men, the kind the country needed. They wouldn't have let him down, and he'd be damned if he would fail them.

I'm tough, he told himself, I'm tough enough to last.

He tried and after a moment succeeded in lifting his hand. His fingers were clumsy and his hand felt cold. There were no Indians in sight but he dared not fire, anyway, for he could never load the gun again. He just had to wait . . . somehow.

He could no longer make out the split logs in the ceiling.

The shadows were darker now, and the room was darker. Was it really that much later? Or was he dying? Was this part of it?

Once he thought he heard a far-off yell, and he gripped the trigger of the shotgun, but the yell was not repeated. His lips fumbled for words fumbled through the thickening fog in his brain. *Live!* he told himself. You've got to *live*!

"Ruby," he muttered, " 's all right, Ruby. I don't blame you."

He worked his mouth but his lips were dry, and his tongue felt heavy in his mouth. "Live!" he whispered. "Please, God! Let me live!"

Something stirred in the brush across the way, and the shadow of movement caught his eye. An Indian was peering toward the station. And then wild and clear he heard Kickapoo's yell. *"Yeeow!"*

Dud Ryan felt a fierce surge of joy. He's made it! By the Lord Harry, he'd—! He tried to squeeze, but his fingers failed him and his hand fell away, fell to the floor.

He could hear the pound of hooves now, and the rattle of the stage.

He rolled over, the stabbing pain from his broken spine wrenching a scream from him, but in a last, terrible burst of energy he managed to grasp the rawhide in his teeth and jerk down. The twin barrels of the shotgun thundered, an enormous bellow of sound in the empty room. Instantly there was a crash of sound from the rolling stage, rifles firing, and all hell breaking loose outside.

———

KICKAPOO JACKSON WAS rolling the stage down the slight hill to Bluff Creek when he heard the roar of the gun. Brad Delaney came up on his knees, rifle in hand, but it was Wells with the revolving shotgun who saw the first Indian. His shotgun bellowed and Delaney's rifle beat out a rapid tattoo of sound, and from below pistols and a rifle were firing.

The attack began and ended in that brief instant of gunfire, for the Indians were no fools and their ambush had failed.

Swiftly, they retired, slipping away in the gathering darkness and carrying three dead warriors with them.

Jackson sawed the team to a halt, and Delaney dropped to the ground and sent three fast shots after the retreating Indians.

Doc Moody pushed open the door and saw the dying man, the rawhide still gripped in his teeth. With a gentle hand he took it away.

"You don't need to tell me, Doc. I've had it." Sweat beaded his forehead. "I've known for . . . hours. Had—had to . . . warn . . ."

Hank Wells dropped to his knees beside Ryan. "Dud, you saved us all, but you saved more than you know. You saved your own son!"

"Son?"

"Ruby had a boy, Dud. Your boy. He's four now, and he's outside there with Ma Harrigan."

"My boy? I saved my boy?"

"Ruby's dead, Ryan," Delaney said. "She was sending the boy to you, but we'll care for him, all of us."

He seemed to hear, tried to speak, and died there on the floor at Bluff Creek Station.

Doc Moody got to his feet. "By rights," he said, "that man should have been dead hours ago."

"Guts," Hank Wells said. "Dud never had much but he always had guts."

Doc Moody nodded. "I don't know how you boys feel about it, but I'm adopting a boy."

"He'll have four uncles, then," Jackson said. "The boy will have to have a family."

"Count us in on that," the newlywed said. "We want to be something to him. Maybe a brother and sister, or something."

THEY'VE BUILT A motel where the stage station stood, and not long ago a grandson and a great-grandson of Dud Ryan walked up the hill where some cedar grew, and stood beside Dud Ryan's grave. They stopped only a few minutes, en route to a family reunion.

There were fifty-nine descendants of Dud Ryan, although the name was different. One died in the Argonne Forest and two on a beach in Normandy and another died in a hospital in Japan after surviving an ambush in what was then known as the Republic of Vietnam. There were eleven physicians and surgeons at the reunion, one ex-governor, two state senators, a locomotive engineer, and a crossing guard. There were two bus drivers and a schoolteacher, several housewives, and a country storekeeper. They had one thing in common: They all carried the blood of Ryan, who died at Bluff Creek Station on a late-October evening.

HERE ENDS THE TRAIL

COLD WAS THE night and bitter the wind and brutal the trail behind. Hunched in the saddle, I growled at the dark and peered through the blinding rain. The agony of my wound was a white-hot flame from the bullet of Korry Gleason.

Dead in the corral at Seaton's he was, and a blessed good thing for the country, too, although had I gone down instead, the gain would have been as great and the loss no greater. Wherever he went, in whatever afterlife there may be for the Korry Gleasons of this world, he'll carry the knowledge that he paid his score for the killing of old Bags Robison that night in Animas.

He'd been so sure, Gleason had, that Race Mallin had bucked it out in gun smoke down Big Band way. He'd heard the rumor all right, so he thought it safe to kill old Bags, and he'd nothing on his mind when he walked, sloshing through the mud toward Seaton's—and then he saw me.

He knew right off, no doubt about that. He knew before he saw my face. He knew even before I spoke. "Good-bye, Korry," I said.

But the lightning flashed as I spoke and he saw me standing there, a big, lean-bodied man wearing no slicker and guns ready to hand. He saw me there with the scar on my jaw, put there by his own spur the night I whipped him in Mobeetie.

He swore and grabbed for his gun and I shot him through the belly, shot him low down, where they die hard, because he'd never given old Bags a chance, old Bags who had been like a father to me . . . who had no father and no mother, nor kith nor kin nor anything. I shot him low and he grabbed iron and his gun swung up and I cursed him like I've never cursed, then I sank three more shots into him, framing the ugly heart of him with lead and taking his bullet in the process.

Oh, he was game, all right! He came of a hard clan, did Korry Gleason, big, bloody, brutal men who killed and fought and drank and built ranches and roads and civilization and then died because the country they built was too big for them to hold down.

So now I'd trail before me and nothing behind me but the other members of the Gleason clan, who, even now, would be after me. The trail dipped down and the wind whipped at my face while the pain of my wound gnawed at my side. My thoughts spun and turned smoky and my brain struggled with the heat haze of delirium.

Gigantic thunder bottled itself up in the mighty canyons of cloud and then exploded in jagged streaks of lightning that stabbed and shimmered among the rock-sided hills. Night and the iron rain and wet rock for a trail, the roaring streams below and the poised boulders, revealed starkly by some momentary flash, then concealed but waiting to go crashing down when the moment came. And through it I rode, more dead than alive, with a good seat in the saddle but a body that lolled and sagged. Under me there was a bronco that was sure-footed on a trail that was a devil's nightmare.

Then there was a light.

Have you ever seen a lighted window flickering through the rain of a lonely land? Have you ever known that sudden rush of heart-glowing warmth at such a sight? There is no other such feeling, and so when I saw it, the weariness and pain seemed warranted and cheap at the price of that distant, promising window.

What lay beyond that light? It did not matter, for since time began, man has been drawn to the sight of human habitation, and I was in an unknown land, and far from anywhere so far as I knew. Then in a lightning flash I saw a house, a barn, and a corral, all black and wet in the whipping rain.

Inside the barn, there was the roar of rain on the roof and the good, friendly smells of horses and hay, of old leather and sacks of grain, and all the smells that make barns what they are. So I slid from my horse and led him into the welcome stillness and closed the door behind us. There I stripped the saddle from him and wiped the rain from his body and shook it from his mane, and then I got fresh hay and stuffed the manger full. "Fill your belly," I told him. "Come dawn we'll be out of here."

Under my slicker, then, I slipped the riding thong from the hammer of my Colt and slid my rifle from the saddle scabbard. The light in the window was welcoming me, but whether friend or enemy waited there, I did not know. A moment after I knocked on the door, it jerked open under my hand and I looked into the eyes of a woman.

Her eyes were magnificent and brown, and she was tall and with poise and her head carried like a princess crowned. She looked at me and she said, "Who are you?" Her voice was low, and when she spoke something within me quivered, and then she said, "What do you want here?"

"Shelter," I said, "a meal if you've got the food to spare. There's trouble following me, but I'll try to be gone before the storm clears. Will you help? Say the word, yes or no."

What she thought I'd no idea, for what could she think of me, big, unshaven, and scarred? And what could she think when my slicker was shed and she saw the two tied-down guns and the mark of blood on the side and the spot where my shirt was torn by the bullet?

"You've been shot," she said.

And then the room seemed to spin slowly in a most sickening fashion and I fell against the wall and grabbed a hook and clung to it, gripping hard, afraid to go down for fear I'd not again get to my feet.

She stepped in close and put her arm about my waist and helped me walk toward the chair, as I refused the bed. I sat while she brought hot water and stripped my shirt from me and looked down at the place where the bullet had come through, and a frightening mess it was, with blood caked to my hide and the wound an ugly sight.

She bathed the wound and she probed for the bullet and somehow she got it out. This was something she had done before, that I could see. She treated my side with something, or maybe it was only her lovely hands and their gentle touch, and as I watched her I knew that here was my woman, if such there was in the world, the woman to walk beside a man, and not behind him. Not one of those who try always to be pushing ahead and who are worth nothing at all as a woman and little as anything else.

She started coffee then and put broth on the fire to warm, and over her shoulder she looked at me. "Who are you, then? And where is it you come from?"

Who was I? Nobody. What was I? Less than nothing. "I'm a drifting man," I said simply enough, "and one too handy with a gun for the good of himself or anyone. I'm riding through. I've always been riding through."

"There's been a killing?"

"Of a man who deserved it. So now I'm running, for though he was a bad lot, there's good men in his line and they'll be after me."

She looked at me coolly, and she said, "You've run out of one fight and into another, unless you move quickly."

"Here?"

"Yes. We have moved in and planted crops and now a cattleman would be driving us out. There are eleven of us— eleven that can fight, and fourteen women, who can help. Some have been killed, my father for one. There are more than thirty tough hands riding with the cattleman, and one of them is Sad Priest."

There was no good in Priest. Him I knew well and nothing about him I liked. "Who is the cattleman?"

"Yanel Webb. It's a big outfit."

"I know them." By now I was eating the broth and drinking coffee and the chill was leaving my bones, but my lids were heavy and there was a weight of sleep on my eyes. She showed me to the bed where her father had slept and helped me off with my boots and guns, and then what happened I never knew, for sleep folded me away into soft darkness.

Though I remembered but fragments, there was a fever that took me and I tossed and turned on the bed for hours. A drink of water from a cup in her gentle hand exhausted me and the medicine in the dressings for my wound stained the sheets. At last I faded off into a dreamless sleep that seemed to go on forever. When next my eyes opened to awareness, there was daylight at the window and a clear sky beyond it and the girl was standing in the door. I had a vague memory of someone knocking on the door, voices, and the pound of hooves receding into the distance.

"You'd best get up. They're coming."

"The Gleasons?"

"Webb and Priest, and his lot. And we're not ready for them. We're all scattered." She dried her palms on her apron. "You'd best slip out. I've saddled your horse."

"And run?"

"It's no fight of yours."

"I'm not a running sort of man. And as to whether it's a fight of mine or not, time will be saying, for you've done me a turn and I pay my debts when I can . . . have you coffee on?"

"My father said there must always be hot coffee in a house."

"Your father was a knowing man."

When I had my boots on and my guns I felt better, favoring my side a bit. When they rode into the yard I was standing in the door with a cup of hot, black coffee in my left hand.

There were at least twenty of them, and armed for business. Tough men, these. Tough men and hard in the belly and eyes. The first of them was Webb, of whom I'd heard talk, and on his left, that lean rail of poison, Sad Priest.

"Morning," I said. "You're riding early."

"We've no talk with you, whoever you are. Where's Maggie Ryan?"

"This morning I'm speaking for her. Is it trouble you're after? If it is"—I smiled at them, feeling good inside and liking the look of them—"you've called at the right door. However, I'll be forgivin'.

"If you turn about now and ride off, I'll be letting you go without risk."

"Let *us* go?" Yanel Webb stared at me as if I was fair daft, and not a bad guess he'd made, for daft I am and always have been. When there's a fight in the offing, something starts rolling around in me, something that's full of gladness and eagerness that will not go down until there's fists or clubs or guns and somebody's won or lost or got themselves a broken skull. "You'll let us go? Get out of here, man! Get out while we see fit to let you!"

That made me laugh. "Leave a scrap when the Priest is in it? That I'd never do, Webb." I stepped out onto the porch, moving toward them, knowing there's something about closeness to a gun that turns men's insides to water and weakness. "How are you, Sad? Forgotten me?"

He opened that scar of a mouth and said, "I've never seen you before—" His voice broke off and he stopped. "Race Mallin . . ."

That made me chuckle. There'd been a change in his eyes then, for he knew me, and I knew myself what was said about me, how I was a gun-crazy fool who had no brains or coolness or reason. A man who wouldn't scare and wouldn't bluff and who would walk down the avenues of hell with dynamite in his pockets and tinder in his hair. Now, no man wants to tackle a man like that, for you know when the chips are down and you've got to fight, he'll die hard and not alone.

Sad Priest was a fast hand with a gun, maybe faster than me, but there'd been other fast men who had died as easily as anyone.

"Right you are. And it looks like some of these boys here will be able to tell it around the bunkhouses next year, the story of how Sad Priest and Yanel Webb died with Race Mallin in an all-out gun battle! What a story that will make for those who yarn around the fires!

"Yanel Webb, all his cattle wasted, his ranch in other hands, his wife a widow, and his baby son an orphan, and Sad Priest, the fastest of them all, facedown in the dirt of a nester's yard with his belly shot full of lead."

Beyond them were the others and I grinned at them. "Oh, don't you lads worry. Some of you favored ones will go along. How many is a guess, but you'd best remember I've ten good bullets here, and while I've gone down three times in gunfights, it was every time with empty guns!

"Tell them, Sad! You were on the Neuces that time when

the four Chambers boys jumped me. They put me down and filled me full of holes and I was six weeks before I could walk, but they buried three of the Chambers and the other one left the country when I left my bed."

"You talk a lot," Webb said sourly.

"It's a weakness of the Irish," I said.

They did not like it. None of them liked it. At such a time no man feels secure and each one is sure you're looking right at him.

"What are you doin' here?" Webb demanded. "This is no fight of yours."

"Why, any one-sided fight is my fight, Yanel," I explained. "I've a weakness for them. I could not stay out of it, and me with the Gleasons behind me."

That I said for the smartness of it. I'm not so crazy as I sound, and wild as I get in a scrap, I knew they'd salt me down if the guns opened here. But my deal was to bluff them, for no man wishes to die, and once the bluff started, to offer them an easy out, a reason for delay.

The Gleasons made a reason. I knew they would figure that if the Gleasons were after me, all they had to do was sit back and let the Gleasons kill me—and any gain in time was a gain for us.

Webb hesitated, soaking it up. He didn't like it, but it was smart, and Priest said something to him under his breath, and probably a warning to let the Gleasons come. Then Webb said, "Why are the Gleasons after you?"

"Korry," I explained, "shot down an old friend of mine when I was down Del Rio way. I met him last night and he was a bit slow."

"That," Webb said, "I'd like to see. We'll camp out and see what happens."

Now, that I'd not expected. I'd believed they would ride out and leave us alone, but with them here ... Maggie Ryan spoke beside me. "What will we do, Race? The others will be here soon, and they are not fighting men, they are quiet, sincere men with families and homes. If there is a fight here, some of them or all of them will die. Webb won't stop killing once he starts."

"It isn't Webb," I said. "It's that cold image of a buzzard beside him, it's Priest that worries me."

Strange is the world that men are born to, and strange the ways of men when trouble comes. Yanel Webb was not a bad man, only a hard man who thought cattle were the only way of life and would stop all others who came into the country. And those with him—they were hard, reckless men, but cowhands, not killers. Fight they would, if they must, but with a decent way out . . . and the Gleasons who were coming. Korry had been the only bad apple in that lot. They knew it as well as I, but they were honor bound to hunt me down, but I'd no stomach for killing honest men.

Across the hard-caked earth of the yard I looked at Sad Priest.

"Maggie," I said, "there's a chance that we can work it out, but only one chance. What stake has Priest in this?"

"Webb's given him land and a job. He's the worst of them, I think."

"How was Webb before he came?"

"Angry, and ordering us off, but he wasn't so strong for killing."

"Maybe," I said, "if Priest were out of it, we could talk."

Then we heard the rattle of hooves on the bridge and the sound of riders and I looked around over my shoulder and saw the Gleasons come into the yard.

There was the weakness from my wound, but no time for weakness now. There they were, the three of them, and they were looking around at what they had ridden into. And then I took my gamble as a man sometimes must. I'm not a talking man when the chips are down and the love of battle is strong within me, but there was more at stake now than me or my desires, for there was a handful of kindly folks and their farms and wishes.

There comes a time to every man when he must drop the old ways and look ahead, so here was I, a man who had ridden and roistered and rustled a few head, who had shot up the wrong side of town on a Saturday night. I'd killed a few hardcases and lived the life of a wild land growing, and now suddenly I could see a chance for my own life: a wife, my own home, my own green and growing land, my own children about the door—maybe all of it lay out there beyond that hot, sunbaked yard where my enemies stood. Twenty-odd men with reasons for killing me, and not one for helping me stay alive.

"Maggie," I said, "I'm a changed man. I'm going out there and talk. Pray if you can, for you're certain to have more of a voice with the Lord than I, for it's got to be blarney rather than bullets if we come out alive from this."

So I walked out there and faced the Gleasons, three hard, tough, honest men. Three men who had ridden here to kill me.

"Pat," I said, "we rode a roundup together. Mickey, you pulled me out from under a steer one time, down Sonora way, an' you, Dave, I've bought you drinks and you've bought them for me. That's why I ran after I'd shot Korry. He had it comin', an' deep in the heart of you, you all know it.

"Korry got what he asked for, and had it not been me, it would have been another, but I ran, for I'd no desire to kill any of you."

"Or to be killed, maybe."

Then I shrugged. "That's a gamble always, but the Chambers boys went down and a fool knows no lack of confidence. Surely, I'm a fool, and a great one."

"Why the palaver?" Pat demanded. "What trick is this?"

"No trick," I said. "Only I've no wish to kill any one of you, nor to kill anyone anymore but one man.

"These"—I gestured at the gathered riders—"are fine up-standing men who've come to rob a girl of her home! To take the roof from a girl who's but recently lost her father!

"They want to run out a lot of fine, homemaking men who are irrigating land and building the country. And they've brought a killer to do their dirty work, a buzzard named Sad Priest!

"I don't want to fight you. I've this fight to think of now. Never yet have I shot an honest man, and I've no wish to begin.

"Only one thing I want now," and when I spoke my eyes

went to Sad Priest across the yard. "I want to kill the man who'd run a girl with no family from her house!"

Oh, I didn't wait for him! Nobody waits for Sad Priest! So when I spoke, I reached, but he drew so fast his gun was up and shooting before I'd more than cleared leather. But I'd known he'd shoot too fast and he did. His bullet tugged at my shirt and I triggered my six-gun, two quick, hammering shots, and then ran!

Right for him, his gun spitting lead and the blood of my bullets showing on his neck and shirtfront, but my running made him miss and only one of the bullets hit me, taking me through the thigh, and I went down and felt another bullet whip past my skull, and then I fired up at him and the bullet split his brisket and his knees let go and he started down just as I rolled on my side and fired into him again at eight feet of distance.

He hit ground then and lay there all sprawled out, and one of the Webb hands started for me and Pat Gleason levered a shell into the barrel of his Winchester. "Hold it, mister!" he said. "That was a fair fight!"

They stood there, all of them, nobody quite knowing what to do, and then Maggie Ryan ran to me and with her hands under my arms I got to my feet. I stepped away from her and pushed her back toward the house. This was not yet over. Blood was running from my side where the other wound had started to bleed.

"Got you twice," Dave Gleason said.

"No," I told him, "the one in my side was Korry's. Only he was a few inches too low."

"Korry got a bullet into you?" Mickey said. "If he did that he had a fair shake. He wasn't fast enough otherwise."

"It's his," I said. "You can see the wound's not fresh."

Yanel Webb stood there with his hands at his sides, not sure of what to say. And his hands waited for him, for he was their boss and they rode for the brand, but knowing their kind I knew their hearts weren't in it.

"Yanel," I said, "Priest was long overdue. Ride home. You've land enough, and when you want eggs and fresh vegetables, come down on the creek and trade with these people.

"You and me," I said, "we've got to grow with the times. The day of the gun and the free range is past. We've got to accept that or go like the buffalo went."

He was reluctant to leave, and he stood there, knowing the truth of what I'd said, and knowing that nothing now stood between him and my first bullet.

"He's calling them fair," Pat Gleason said. "I stand with him on that."

Webb turned to his hands. "Well, boys," he said, "we'd best take Sad along and plant him. I reckon we've played out our hand. These farmers best keep their crops fenced, though." It was his final chance to bluster. "If their fields are eaten or trampled, it's not my lookout!"

They went then, and we watched them ride, and then I faced around and looked at the Gleasons and they looked at me. Maggie Ryan had her arm around me and then she spoke up and said to them, "There's coffee on. Will you come in?"

So we went in and the coffee was hot and black, and there by the table there was warm and pleasant talk of cattle and grass and what a man could do in a green growing valley, with time on his hands.

THE MAN FROM THE DEAD HILLS

THE SAGEBRUSH FLATS shimmered in the white heat of a late-summer sun, and a gray powder of dust lay thick upon the trail. Far away the hills loomed purple against the horizon, but the miles between were dancing with heat waves.

Leosa Barron stood in the door, shaded her eyes against the glare, and searched once more, as she had so often of late, for a figure upon the road. There was nothing. The road was empty of life, vanishing in the far hills where lay a little cow town known as Joe Billy.

She looked away. She must not expect him yet. Even if Tom Andrews received her letter and was able to come, he could not arrive so quickly.

When her housework was finished, during which time she resolutely refused to look at the trail, she walked again to the door. Yet there was nothing but the white dust and the heat. Then her eyes turned back up the even lonelier trail to the badlands, the trail to the dead and empty hills where nothing lived. Her lips parted suddenly, and she stared, refusing at first to believe what she saw between her back fence and the dark cliffs.

Someone was coming. Someone was coming from the direction of the Dead Hills.

Unable to return to the shaded coolness, she waited in the door watching. She was a slender girl, taller than most, and graceful in her movements. She had a friendly mouth, eyes that smiled easily, and lips that could laugh with her eyes. The few freckles scattered over her nose only added a piquant touch to an already charming face.

Much later she was still standing in the doorway when the solitary figure had shaped itself into a man, a man walking.

His hat was gray and battered, his plain wool shirt had a dark spot on the shoulder and was gray with dust. The man was unshaven, and the eyes under the dark brows flashed with a quick, stabbing glance that made her start with something that was almost fear.

The jeans he wore were roughened by wear, and his boots were run-down at the heel. His belt was wide leather, and curiously handworked. Leosa thought she had never seen a man in whom strength was so apparent, strength and ruthlessness.

Yet he wore no gun.

She had been watching him for two miles when he reached the gate. Now he fumbled with the latch and swung it open. He did not speak, but turned back, closing the gate carefully.

As he faced her she knew she was looking at a man exhausted but not beaten, a man whose lips were cracked with thirst, whose flanks were lean with starvation, but a man in whom there burned an indomitable fire, a fire of whose source she knew nothing, and could sense nothing.

Several times she had seen him stagger upon the road, and now as he faced her, his feet wide apart, it suddenly occurred to her that she should be frightened. She was alone here, and this man was from the Dead Hills. Her eyes went to that dark spot on the shoulder, a spot that could be only blood. His face was haggard, a gray mask of dust and weariness from which only the eyes stared, hard and clear.

He walked toward her, and his eyes did not leave hers, fastening to them and clinging as though only their clear beauty kept him alive and on his feet. As in a trance, she saw him stop at the well coping and lift the rope. He staggered, almost losing balance, then she heard the bucket slap on the water.

Quickly she was beside him. "Let me do it— You're nearly dead!"

He smiled then, although the movement of his lips started a tiny trickle of blood from the heat cracks. "Not by a durned sight, ma'am."

But he let her help him. Together they drew up the bucket, then he lifted it and drank, the water slopping over his chin and down his shirtfront. After a minute he put the bucket down and stared at her, then around the place. His eyes returned to her. "You alone here?"

She hesitated. "Yes."

He held the bucket in his hands, and waited. She knew how the body yearns for water and more water when one has been long without it, but this man waited. He impressed her then as a man who could do anything with himself, a man who knew his strength and his weaknesses. His eyes glinted at her, then he lifted the bucket, drank a little more, and put it down.

Turning away from her, he picked up the washbasin and sloshed water into it. Stripping off his shirt, he began to bathe his body. Standing behind him, she could see that there was an ugly wound near the top of his shoulder and a dark stain of dried blood below and around it. Hurrying inside, she secured medicine and clean linen and returned to him.

He accepted her ministrations without comment, only watching her with curious eyes as she cleansed the wound and bandaged his shoulder.

As she worked she was wondering about him. Long ago she had taken a ride into that remote desert country around the Dead Hills. Outlaws had lived there before the gangs were wiped out, but nobody else. There were hideouts near some of the water holes, but those water holes were hard to find unless one knew the country.

To a stranger the region was a waterless horror, a nightmare of grotesque stones and gnarled and blasted cacti, a place where only buzzards and an occasional rattler could be seen.

How far had this man come? What had happened to his horse, and where and how had he been shot?

When she had finished with his wound, she stood back from him and looked up into his eyes. He was smiling, and the expression in his eyes startled her, for it was so different from the lightning of that first glance from the gate. His eyes were warm and friendly, even affectionate. Yet he stepped by her and into the coolness of the room beyond. Without a word he lay down on the divan and was at once asleep.

Returning to the door, she looked down the road again. If Tom Andrews were to arrive in time, there was need that it be soon. If she lost possession of the ranch before he arrived, she had been told there was small chance they would ever recover the property.

Then, almost at sundown, she saw them coming. Not Andrews, but Rorick and Wilson, the men she feared.

They came into the yard riding fast, drawing up without dismounting. "Well"—Van Rorick's voice was cool but triumphant—"are you ready to leave? All packed?"

"I'm not leaving."

Leosa Barron stood straight and still. She knew these men, and for all Rorick's pretended interest in her, she knew there was nothing he would not stoop to do if it obtained results. Lute Wilson was just a tool for Van, and a dangerous man to cross. Yet it was Rorick she feared the most, for she knew the depths of malice in the man, and she had once seen him vent his hatred on a trapped wildcat.

"Then you leave us no choice, Leosa," Rorick replied. "We'll have to move you. If we do that, we might have to handle you rather roughly. You've had plenty of time to leave without trouble."

"I told you I was not going." Leosa stood even straighter. "You will leave this ranch at once!"

Rorick's eyes narrowed a little, but he laughed. It was not a pleasant sound. "If you want to come to my place, I could make you comfortable. If you don't come with me, there will be no place in Joe Billy where they will have you."

Leosa knew the truth of this. Van Rorick was known and feared in the cow town, but more than that, she was herself a stranger, and unkind rumors had been set afloat because of her living alone. She had no doubt that those rumors had been originated by Rorick himself. He knew so well the prejudices of a small town.

"I told you I was staying."

Yet there was no chance of winning. Had Tom Andrews made it, she might have stood them off. She could rely on Tom. Alone against them, she was helpless. And where could she go? She had neither money nor friends. Only Andrews, who had failed her.

"All right, Lute. I guess we move her."

Lute was the first to reach the ground. He turned to face the porch, then stopped, his face stupid with shock.

Surprised, Leosa turned, and found the unshaven stranger at her side. He had belted on her uncle's guns.

"You heard the lady. Get goin'! Get out of here!"

There was a low, ugly sound in the man's voice that frightened her and apparently had something of the same effect upon Lute Wilson, for he froze where he stood, uncertain how to move.

"Leosa," Rorick demanded, "who is this man? What is he doing here?"

The stranger stepped down to the ground, his movements swift and catlike. "Shut up," he said, and his voice was not hard, only somehow more deadly for it.

"Shut up an' get out!"

"My friend"—Rorick's face was a study in controlled fury—"you don't know what you're buttin' into!"

"I can tell a coyote when I see one," the stranger said coolly.

Wilson reached for him. But the stranger sidestepped and smashed him in the stomach with a lifting uppercut that stood Wilson on his toes. Before Rorick could think to move, the stranger smashed a right and left to Wilson's face, and the rider went down in the dust, his face smeared and bloody.

Rorick reached for his gun, reached . . . then stopped, for he was looking into the muzzle of a pistol in the stranger's hand. "Get off your horse," the stranger said quietly, and when Van Rorick, still amazed by the speed of that draw, had dismounted, the stranger said, "Now turn around, take your friend, and start walkin'. When you're out of sight I'll turn your horses loose."

The two men turned, and with Rorick half supporting Wilson, they lurched out of the yard. Together, the newcomer and Leosa stood watching them go, and when they were out of gunshot, the stranger stooped and, lifting the bucket, drank for a long time. It was only when he replaced the bucket that he turned the horses loose, each with a ringing slap on the haunches.

"Those horses will run all the way home, so I figure we've nothin' to bother us for a bit. Meanwhile, you can give me the hang of this so I'll know what's goin' on."

"Your shoulder," she said suddenly. "It's bleeding again!"

"Yeah." He grinned sheepishly. "I reckon I forgot all about it until I began throwing punches. Man, but it hurts!"

"You've had a hard time." She hesitated, wanting to know what had happened to him, but not liking to ask.

Then she hurried about, getting food on the table and making coffee. He sat in a chair near the door and dozed; as she looked at him she marveled at the strength of the man. Nowhere was he bulky, yet his shoulders were compact and hard looking under the faded color of his shirt.

"Do you have a home?" she asked suddenly. "Or are you just drifting?"

His eyes opened sleepily, and he shrugged. "Home?" He shook his head. "I've no home. I always"—his eyes showed a strange wistfulness—"always sort of wanted one."

"I see," she said softly, and she did.

"Who was that man?" he asked suddenly. "What's he want?"

She frowned. "Van was born around here, has lived here most of his life but for some six years. He went away and joined the army, and when he came back, he seems to have become a changed man. Or so they tell me. I've been here but a short time. I guess war does change some men," she added.

He shrugged, watching her. "Maybe. It may, like anything, bring out what's in him. I don't know if it would put anything there that wasn't there before."

"Well, when he came back he moved onto a small spread and began expanding his herd. He prospered, with Lute Wilson to help him. He gets along with some people, rides roughshod over the others. He didn't get along with my uncle, who owned this place. About a year ago my uncle was thrown by a bad horse, just after he had invited me to come here to live with him.

"He died a few days later, and it seems he left some debts. Rorick heard of them, and he bought up the notes and got a lien against this place. He offered to pay me two hundred dollars and give me the notes if I would leave, and I would not.

"You see, there's a valley back of the house that is well watered and every year my uncle got two good cuttings of hay off that piece, and a good deal of grazing after the hay was cut. He also has an orchard and a good-sized garden plot. However, that is only a part of it, for there are some five hundred acres that could be developed into good hay land by putting in a dam on Placer Creek."

"No wonder he wants to get you off," he said dryly. "You could get rich with that amount of hay, and this land." He looked up suddenly. "You haven't even asked who I am."

"Well, I thought you'd tell me if you wanted to. We don't ask many questions around here. Especially," she added, "from men who come out of the Dead Hills."

"I know." He said nothing for a minute, staring out the window. "Better call me Rock," he said. "It's a good name around here."

She laughed. "There's plenty of it, certainly!"

The way he looked at her made her wonder if she'd missed something. "You've no friends to help you?" he said.

"There's one man. His name is Tom Andrews, and he used to ride for my uncle, and he knew my father. I've written to him and he's on his way."

Rock nodded, then he said quietly, "You'd better stop waitin' for him." He drew a wallet from his pocket. "Did you ever see this before?"

She took it in her fingers, and her lips trembled. She had seen it, many times. "Where . . . where did you get this?"

"I found him back in the hills. He'd been wounded, and was in mighty bad shape. I tried to help him, and got shot for my pains. They killed both our horses."

"Who was it?" Leosa asked quickly.

"That"—his eyes were suddenly hard—"is what I'd like to know!" He got to his feet. "About that dam now. How much money would it take?"

"Whiting, he's my lawyer, he said it could be done for a couple of thousand dollars for wages if one used native rock and earth. He said a better dam could be built later, if necessary."

"That makes sense. I'll look the spot over." He touched the guns on his hips. "I'll need these. Is it all right?"

"Of course! Do you . . . does that mean you intend to stay?"

He smiled. "If you'd like me to. I think you need me right now, and I've some resting up to do. I want to get the lay of the land around here."

She nodded. "Please stay on. I don't know what I'd have done today without you. See this through with me and I'll give you a share in the place."

"Now, that there's an interesting idea."

"Good!" Leosa said quickly. "Fifty percent. It won't be worth anything if I lose."

"I'll settle for that." His eyes were thoughtful. "This Rorick got any property around other than his spread?"

"Yes, he owns the Longhorn Hotel and Saloon, and I hear he has an interest in another saloon. There are," she added, "nine saloons in Joe Billy. Nine saloons, four stores, one hotel, one church, and a few other businesses, including a livery stable."

She watched him as he walked toward the empty bunkhouse. Her brow furrowed a little. Was she wrong in accepting the help of a total stranger? In taking as a partner a man she had known but a couple of hours? Who did not even volunteer his full name?

On the other hand, had she a choice? He had at least come to her aid in an hour of need. He had brought Andrews's wallet to her and he seemed ready to accept the task Andrews had been unable to attempt.

Leosa opened the wallet thoughtfully. There was money in it, almost a hundred dollars, and a few pipers. One of them was a scrawled signature on a piece of torn envelope.

Last Will: All my belongings to Leosa Barron, friend and daughter of a friend.

Tom Andrews

The signature was merely a scrawl, and her eyes filled with tears at the thought of Tom, his last thoughts for her, a girl he had known only as a skinny child with freckles and braids. And from him had come this stranger. With a shock of something that was half excitement and half fear, she remembered the sheer brutality of his attack on Wilson, the flashing speed with which the gun had leaped to his hand. Who was he? What was he?

————

IN THE BUNKHOUSE there was an empty bed with folded blankets, and several with no bedding beyond mattresses. Obviously, this was the bunk awaiting Tom Andrews. Rock sat down and studied the room. It was strongly built, as everything seemed to be on this ranch. No effort had been spared to make it strong or comfortable.

He walked to the door and stared toward town. Joe Billy . . . *his town!*

There would be trouble when they knew, and plenty of it. They did not know him now, yet already he had met Rorick and faced him down. His advantage had been surprise, and next time they would be prepared for him. How soon, he wondered, would they realize who he was and why he had come back? All hell would break loose then and Van Rorick would be the one who led it.

In a way, Leosa's fight was his fight. His thoughts went back to the tall, rather shy girl, who had accepted him so readily. He pulled off his shirt and hunted the cabin for shaving gear. He found an old razor, and after a healthy stropping, he shaved. It was dark when he had finished cleaning up, and he walked outside.

Whiting, that was the name of the lawyer that Leosa had mentioned. He would go to him. He walked outside and roped and saddled a horse, then he mounted and rode to the door. "Ridin' to Joe Billy," he said quietly. "You better stay in an' keep a rifle handy."

She watched him ride away, liking the set of his shoulders and the way he rode. Queerly disturbed, she returned inside, pausing to look into the fire. It was strange, having this man here, yet somehow he did not seem strange, and she felt oddly happy. . . . Security, that was it. What else could it be?

———

RANCE WHITING HAD an office over the squat gray bank building. Rock glanced at the tall man who rose to greet him, and instantly liked him. He had a thin face, high cheekbones, and an aquiline nose. His eyes were gray, and friendly. An open volume of Horace sat on the nearby table.

Rock glanced at the title, then at the lawyer. " 'We are dust and shadow,' " he quoted.

Whiting was surprised, and he measured the rider again. The cold green eyes, the shock of dark curly hair, the bronzed features, blunt and strong, the wool shirt under which muscles bulged. "You know Horace?" he asked.

Rock laughed. "Only that. Read it once, an' liked it. I used to read a good deal. Hombre left a flock of books behind an' I was snowed in for the winter. Mostly Shakespeare an' Plato."

"You were looking for an attorney?"

Rock drew several papers from a homemade buckskin wallet, a large wallet he took from the inside of his shirt. It was bloodstained. Without further comment, he handed it to Whiting.

The lawyer opened the papers curiously, then started and glanced up at Rock, then back at the papers. His face was curiously white. He skimmed over the others swiftly, then sat back in his chair, looking up at the man before him. "You know what these will mean, if you produce them? If you even hint they exist?"

Rock nodded.

"It means they'll kill you."

"They can try."

"Who sent you to me?" Whiting was measuring Rock with quick, curious eyes.

"Leosa Barron. I made a deal to help her out for a while."

"Then you're already in trouble! You can't stay there, you know, they'll run you off."

"You mean Rorick and Wilson? They had a pass at runnin' her off today. They didn't get far."

"You stopped them? Alone?"

He shrugged and changed the subject. "I'm going to build that dam for her."

"You are biting off a chunk."

"We'll see."

"What do you want me to call you, young man?"

"My name is Rock."

"Yes . . . yes, I see. Who have you told? Anyone besides Miss Barron?"

"I only told her the last name. Figured it was enough for now."

Whiting lifted the papers, then got to his feet. "When do you want to use these?"

Rock shrugged. "I came to ask your advice, but my idea would be now, down in the Longhorn."

"Now?" Whiting's exclamation faded into a smile. "Yes, it would be amusing. Can you shoot, friend? This is going to blow the top off the town. It might even blow our tops off."

Rock nodded. "It might. Let's do it this way. You put these in a safe place. Then you make out bills to all the folks who owe me money. Make them out particularly to Van Rorick. Then you go down to the Longhorn, and I'll drift in, too. Spring it on him and let's see what happens."

"Not tell them who you are?"

"Not right now. I'm not duckin' a fight, but what I want is to get the picture of things. Also, I'd like to have a showdown with Rorick on Leosa Barron. Because before he gets through, I'm goin' to give him so much trouble he'll forget her."

THE LONGHORN WAS ablaze with light when Rock pushed through the door and walked to the bar. Rorick was there, and he was seated at a table with Lute Wilson, whose face was puffed and swollen out of shape, and another man. Rorick looked up, and Rock felt the shock of his eyes, of the hatred in them.

The bartender served him without comment, and Rock scanned the room. He had never seen it before, but he knew it from the countless tales he had heard. He was barely tasting his drink when the door opened again and Rance Whiting walked in. Without seeming to notice Rock, he went to the bar and ordered a drink, then he glanced around at Rorick. "Van," he said, "I've news for you. News, and a bill."

"A bill?" Rorick was puzzled but wary. "What do I owe you for?"

"Not me. A client. The owner of this property, in fact. You owe him rent for four years on the Longhorn, and on the Placer Saloon, down the street. The total, according to my figures, comes to nine thousand three hundred and seventy dollars."

Rorick's face was ashen, then blood turned it crimson and he started to his feet. "What's this you're givin' me?" he demanded. "I bought this place from Jody Thompson!"

"That was unfortunate," Whiting replied calmly. "You should have investigated his title. He owned neither the buildings nor the land on which they stand. Actually, he was a squatter here, and had no legal rights. This is not, as he supposed, government land. It belongs to my client, and has been in his family for forty years!"

Van Rorick was livid; also, he was frightened. He had built up his influence locally partly on wealth, but mostly on strength. He had little cash, certainly nowhere in the neighborhood of nine thousand dollars. If he were compelled to pay up, he could do so only by selling off all his stock; furthermore, he could be dispossessed here.

His eyes searched Whiting's face. "This is some trick," he protested. "You and that girl have rigged this on me. You won't get away with it!"

Rance shrugged. Glancing toward the far wall of the saloon, he caught the eye of an old man, bearded and gray, who sat there. "Mawson," he asked, "how did this town get its name?"

"Joe Billy?" Mawson got to his feet, enjoying the limelight. "Why, she was named for the son of the man that located the first claims hereabouts. He inherited this chunk of land, something like forty thousand acres, from his father, who got it through marriage to a Valdez gal."

Rorick walked to the bar. He was trapped, but he was thinking swiftly. He should be able to make a deal with Whiting. Certainly, the man had no money. He owed a bar bill, and he owed for supplies down the street. There was sure to be a way to swing it.

Yet even deeper within him, there was a feverish desperation, anger at Whiting for bringing this up, in public, and anger at it coming now when it might frustrate all his plans. His eyes were calm, but inwardly he was seething. There had to be a way . . . and maybe Lute could handle it. Lute, or— his mind returned to the slim and silent man who waited at the table with Wilson—or him.

"Your unsupported statement means nothing," Rorick said, fighting for calmness. "You have some papers? Deeds?"

"I have everything that's necessary," Whiting replied. "When the time comes I'll produce them. Not until then. I intend"—he smiled at Rorick—"to protect my client's interests so they will not disappear until we meet, if must be, in court. That," he added, "would be in Santa Fe."

Van Rorick winced. He dared not show himself in Santa Fe. Did Whiting realize that? But here . . . ? Anything might happen.

"We can make a deal, Rance," he said quietly. "I can't pay that money now, and I'm sure you don't want to hurry me. I can pay a part of it, and make a deal for the rest."

Whiting shook his head. "No, the saloon is doing business," he said. "Some of that profit can go to my client as well as to you. All he wants from you is the arrears in rent."

He paused, his eyes studying Rorick. "That, or you leave the country."

"What!" Rorick's lips thinned down. "So that's it? I'll see you in hell first! And whoever your client is!"

"You have five days. No more." Whiting finished his drink and placed the glass on the bar.

After Whiting had gone, Van Rorick stood at the bar for a few minutes, and for the first time recalled that the stranger from Leosa Barron's ranch was in the room, and that he had entered just before Whiting! Was there a tie-up there? No sooner had the thought entered his mind than he was sure such was the case. That this had come up when the stranger arrived was too much for a coincidence.

Whiting, and this man. Who was he, then? Rorick was thinking swiftly. Somehow, he must get rid of both. After all, hadn't he managed to rid himself of Tom Andrews? With Whiting out of it and whatever papers he had in his possession, he would be even more secure.

Thanks to his carefully planted rumors, Leosa Barron was disliked by all the women of the town, and suspected by most of the men. The presence of Rock on her ranch would make those suspicions seem fact. Moreover, his mysterious arrival would help . . . but whatever was done must be done carefully to avert all suspicion from himself. And there was a way . . . with them gone, he could always claim Whiting had tried to defraud him.

———

ROCK LEFT THE saloon and, without returning to see Whiting, headed for the ranch. He had anticipated trouble, and knew that Rorick would not take this lying down. The man's sudden quiet disturbed him more than he cared to admit.

At daybreak Rock was riding, and by noon he had made a careful survey of the site chosen for the dam. It was a good spot, no doubt about it, and looking at the massive stone walls above, he had an idea how it could be done.

He said nothing to Leosa, but after a quick lunch, took some giant powder from a cache near the house and returned to the mountain. By nightfall he had his first set of holes in, and had them charged.

Leosa, a new warmth in her eyes, reported no sign of Wilson or Rorick. A passing neighbor, one of the few who condescended to speak, had told her there was a rumor that Art Beal and Milt Blue, the outlaws, were in the vicinity, that Blue had been seen riding near Joe Billy.

Leosa said this last with averted eyes. She was remembering that flashing draw, and the fact that Rock had come out of the Dead Hills. Milt Blue was a known killer, and a deadly man with a gun. She had never seen him nor heard a description, but she was afraid now. Afraid for Rock. Was he . . . could he be Milt Blue?

Yet if the rumors meant anything to him, he said nothing. "Art Beal hasn't been around much," he commented. "Disappeared a while back. Blue killed another man down to El Paso, only a month ago."

The following day, Rock returned and put in his second round of holes. When he had them charged, he studied the situation below. If the rock broke right, he would have a fairly good dam across the canyon. Then another charge, to help things along, and in no time the creek itself would finish the dam by piling up silt, brush, and weeds to fill up the holes and gaps in the rocks.

Rock carefully lighted his fuses, then descended the rock face to the bottom of the draw. The fuses were long, for he had wanted to get both shots off approximately together. The climb to the opposite side took him little time, and in a matter of a minute he had spit those fuses and then slid rapidly down the steep declivity to the bottom. He turned and started up the draw, then glanced back.

Light glinted high on the rock, and instinctively, he hurled himself to the right. A rifle spoke, its distant bark swallowed by the huge, all-engulfing roar as the first set of powder-charged holes let go. It was an enormous sound, magnified and echoed again and again by the walls of the canyon, but Rock did not hear it. He was going over headfirst into the rocks. He landed facedown, slid a short distance, then his body ceased to slide and he lay sprawled out and unconscious among the greasewood and boulders at one side of the draw.

Beyond him rocks fell, then ceased to fall, and dust rose slowly, in a great cloud. When it stopped rising, there was a wall across the canyon, low in the middle, but high enough. The mountain stream, trickling down its normal bed, found the way blocked, it turned right, searching for a way under or through, but discovered no way to accommodate the swelling strength of water behind it. Spreading left, it found no way out, and so began to back up in a slowly widening and deepening pool.

———

IT WAS DARK when the lapping water reached the nest of rocks where the fallen man lay. Cold fingers encircled his outflung hand, crept up his arm with exploring tentacles, and flattened out, creeping along his side and toward his face.

A coyote, prowling nearby and sniffing blood, paused to stare at the man's dark body. Curious, he came near, stepping daintily to keep his feet from the water. When the man moved, drawing back a hand, the coyote drew back and trotted swiftly off.

It was the cold touch of the water that roused Joe Billy Rock. Water against his face and water along his ribs. For an instant he lay still, and then the meaning of the creeping coldness came to him with a rush, and he jerked back and lunged to his feet. The startled reaction that brought him up also brought a rush of pain to his head. His fingers lifted and explored. The bullet had caused chips of rock to pepper his face and arm, but there was at least one other cut caused by his fall, and his whole body was stiff and numb.

He staggered, splashing, toward higher ground. There he looked back, and saw that almost an acre of water had already gathered behind his crude dam. A little work would make it more effective.

Memory returned, and he realized he had been shot at. Shot at the instant before the explosion by someone perched on the very rocks he was blasting! Whoever that unknown marksman had been, he was dead now. Survival, where he had been perched, was out of the question.

A half hour of staggering and falling brought him to his horse, which looked up quickly at the sight of him, tossing his head at the smell of blood. It was no more than fifteen minutes of riding to the house. All was dark and still.

Carefully, Rock considered this. Had Leosa been at home, she would certainly have a light. Moreover, she would be awaiting supper. The time he roughly estimated to be nine or past, but she knew he was working and would have heard the explosion. Had she gone out looking for him? Stealthily, he rode nearer, then dismounted. Ten minutes of careful searching proved the house, barn, and the whole ranch was empty. The stove was cold, no dishes on the table. No evidence that a meal had been prepared.

Squinting against the stinging pain in his cheek and forehead, he tried to assemble his thoughts. Somehow they must have gotten her out of here, believing him dead. Van Rorick had acted to seize the ranch.

The gray he was riding had a liking for the trail and he let him take it. He ran like a scared rabbit until the town lights were plain, then Rock slowed him to a canter and then a walk. He swung down from the horse near the livery barn, loosened his guns in his holsters, and started up the street. Voices made him draw back into the shadows. Between two buildings he waited while two men drew near.

"Hear about that gal out to the old Barron place? One said she was Barron's niece? She skipped out with that tough-lookin' hand who's been hanging around there. Somebody said they was seen on the road to Cimarron, ridin' out of the country."

"Good riddance, I'd say. I hear she carried on plenty!"

Rock stared after them. Rorick was shrewd. His story was already going the rounds, and it was a plausible yarn. But what had happened to Leosa?

He started up the street, moving more cautiously now. First, he must see Whiting. The lawyer would know what to do, and would start a search here. Then he would head for Rorick's own ranch.

It was possible that Rorick had killed the girl at once, or that Lute Wilson had. But the man on the rock before the explosion was probably Lute. Rorick was too smart to take such chances himself. It had been only bad luck that got Lute, however, for the man could not have known of the loaded holes and spitted fuses.

Rock climbed the stairs, then pushed open the lawyer's door. Rance Whiting's office was dark and still. Fumbling in his pocket, he got a match and lighted it. Whiting was sprawled on the floor, his shirt bloody, his face white as death.

Dropping to his knees, Rock found the lawyer had been stabbed twice, once in the back, once in the chest. The room was in wild disorder.

Working swiftly, Rock got water and bathed the wounds, then bandaged them. The lawyer was still alive, and the first thing was to get the bleeding stopped. When he had him resting easily on the bed, Rock turned to the door. He was opening it when he heard the lawyer's hoarse cry.

Instantly, he turned back. "The papers," Whiting whispered, "they . . ." His voice trailed feebly away. He had fainted.

Leaving the light burning, Rock ran down the outside stairs to the street, glanced once at the saloon, and then ran up the street to old Doc Spencer's home. In a few minutes he had the old man started toward Whiting's office.

Joe Rock stared at the Longhorn. This was his town. He owned the whole townsite by inheritance, and he intended to keep it, especially that part usurped by Van Rorick. He walked swiftly to the saloon and, from a position near the window, studied the interior. Rorick was there but he didn't appear happy. The same slight-figured man who had been with him before was with him now. Lute was not, which was all the assurance Rock needed that the man was dead. It was undoubtedly his failure to return that worried Rorick.

Circling swiftly, he came to the rear door, but reached it only to hear the front door open and close. When he looked in, Rorick and his friend had gone.

From the street came a sound of horses' hooves and then two men rode down the street and out of town. Hurrying to his own horse, Rock swung into the saddle and, kicking his feet into the stirrups, started in pursuit.

Rorick set a fast pace. Rock let his mind leap ahead, trying to get the drift of the other man's thinking. Wilson had not returned, and that could mean he had failed. It could also mean Wilson and Rock had killed each other. Rorick swung toward the Barron homestead, and drew up, staring toward it.

Rock was no more than a hundred yards away and could see the men outlined against the sky.

Seeing the house dark, they evidently decided that Rock had not returned there. They pushed on. When they reached the now dry creek, Rock heard a startled exclamation, and then the riders turned toward the dam. He saw them ride up to it and look around, heard a low-voiced conversation of which he could guess the sense but understand no word. Then they mounted and rode on.

The course they followed now led deeper and deeper into the rocky canyons to the north. This was lonely country, and was not, Rock was aware, toward Rorick's ranch. Suddenly the two men rode down into a hollow and disappeared.

Rock drew up, straining his eyes into the night, holding his breath for any sound. There was none. He walked his horse a short way, and was about to go farther when his eyes caught a vague suggestion of light. Turning, he worked his way through some willows and saw among some boulders the darker blotch of a cabin from which gleamed two lighted windows!

Swinging down, Rock stole toward the house, ghostlike in the night. She had to be here! His heart pounding, his mouth dry, all the fear he had been feeling all evening was now tight and cold within him. What if something had happened to her? What if she had been killed?

A door opened and a man stepped out. He was a stranger. "I'll put the horses up," he said over his shoulder, "an' grub's ready."

The fellow carried a lantern and he walked toward a rock barn that stood close under a cliff. Joe Rock followed, and moved in behind him. The man placed the lantern on the ground and reached for a bridle.

In that instant Rock's forearm went across his throat and jammed a knee into the startled man's back, jerking him off balance. Then Rock turned him loose, but before he could get breath to yell a warning, Rock slugged him in the wind. He doubled up, and Rock struck him again. Then he grabbed him by the throat and shoved him against the wall. He was trembling with fury. "Is that girl in there? Is she safe?"

The fellow gasped and choked. "She . . . she's all right! Don't kill me! For Lord's sake, man!"

"Who's in there?" Rock demanded in a hoarse whisper.

"Just them two. Beal 'n' Milt Blue."

Joe Rock froze. Then he said carefully, "Who did you say? Art Beal and Milt Blue? The outlaws?"

"They ain't sky pilots," the man said, growling.

"You mean Beal is the hombre known in town as Rorick?"

"Yeah, maybe." The man was talking freely now. "He said there'd be no trouble. I ain't no outlaw! I just needed a few dollars."

Roughly, Rock bound and gagged the man. He was aware now of his real danger, and of Leosa's danger. If Rorick was Art Beal, that accounted for some of the six years he had been away from Joe Billy, and also let Rock know just what sort of a man Rorick was. Yet for all of that, the real risk lay in facing Milt Blue, the gunslinger.

He left the man bound on the dirt floor of the barn, and started for the house. He carried the lantern with him, wanting them to believe he was their helper. As he neared the door he shifted the lantern to his left hand and drew his gun. Then he opened the door and stepped in.

Only Leosa was looking toward the door, and her eyes widened. Her expression must have warned them, for as one man they turned. Instantly, as though it had been rehearsed, Leosa threw her body against Rorick, knocking him off balance.

Rock had his feet spread and his gun ready. "Drop it, Blue!" he yelled.

The gunman grabbed iron. His gun leaped free with amazing speed, and as the muzzle cleared the holster Rock shot him in the stomach. He was slammed back by the force of the bullet, but fought doggedly and bitterly to get his gun up. Despite the fierce struggle against the wall, where Leosa fought desperately with Rorick, Rock took his time. He fired again. Blue's eyes glazed and the gun slid from his hand.

Rock turned and instantly Leosa let go and stepped back. Van Rorick stared across the room. "You think you've won!" he cried. "Well, you haven't! I got the papers! I burned them!

Burned every last one of them! You've lost everything! And I sold my claim on her place, so you'll lose that, too! And now I'm going to kill you."

His right hand had dangled behind him, and now it swung up, clutching a gun. Rock's pistol leaped in his hand, and the room thundered with a shot. Rorick's face twisted and he stepped back, shocked with realization. Awareness of death hit him, and his eyes widened, then his mouth dropped open and he crumpled to the floor.

Rock caught Leosa in his arms and hurried her to the door.

———

DOC SPENCER MET them when they reached the top of the office stairs. "He's in bad shape, but he'll pull through," he told them. "Few minutes ago he was conscious, an' he said to tell you the papers are stuck behind his volume of Horace. Those he left for Rorick to find were fakes he fixed up. He figured on somethin' like this."

They walked back down the steps to the silent street. Almost unconsciously, they were holding hands.

"Rock," Leosa asked gently, "what will you do now? You own the town? I heard you did."

"I'm goin' to give all these folks who shape up right deeds to their property. It ain't worth so much, anyway. The Longhorn I'll sell."

"What about you?" she asked, looking up at him.

"Me? . . . Why, I was thinkin' of ranchin' an' watchin' hay crops grow out on the Barron place . . . with my wife."

HIS BROTHER'S DEBT

"**Y**OU'RE YELLOW, CASADY!" Ben Kerr shouted. "Yellow as saffron! You ain't got the guts of a coyote! Draw, curse you. Fill your hand so I can kill you!" Kerr stepped forward, his big hands spread over his gun butts. "Go ahead, *reach*!"

Rock Casady, numb with fear, stepped slowly back, his face gray. To right and left were the amazed and incredulous faces of his friends, the men he had ridden with on the O Bar, staring unbelieving.

Sweat broke out on his face. He felt his stomach retch and twist within him. Turning suddenly, he plunged blindly through the door and fled.

Behind him, one by one, his shamefaced, unbelieving friends from the O Bar slowly sifted from the crowd. Heads hanging, they headed homeward. Rock Casady was yellow. The man they had worked with, sweated with, laughed with. The last man they would have suspected. Yellow.

Westward, with the wind in his face and tears burning his eyes, his horse's hoofs beating out a mad tattoo upon the hard trail, fled Rock Casady, alone in the darkness.

Nor did he stop. Avoiding towns and holding to the hills, he rode steadily westward. There were days when he starved and days when he found game, a quail or two, killed with unerring shots from a six-gun that never seemed to miss. Once he shot a deer. He rode wide of towns and deliberately erased his trail, although he knew no one was following him or cared where he went.

Four months later, leaner, unshaven, and saddle weary, he rode into the yard of the Four Spoke Wheel. Foreman Tom Bell saw him coming and glanced around at his boss, big Frank Stockman.

"Look what's comin'. Looks like he's lived in the hills. On the dodge, maybe."

"Huntin' grub, most likely. He's a strappin' big man, though, an' looks like a hand. Better ask him if he wants a job. With Pete Vorys around, we'll have to be huntin' strangers or we'll be out of help!"

The mirror on the wall of the bunkhouse was neither cracked nor marred, but Rock Casady could almost wish that it was. Bathed and shaved, he looked into his own tortured eyes and then looked away.

People had told him many times that he was a handsome man, but when he looked into his eyes he knew he looked into the eyes of a coward.

He had a yellow streak.

The first time—well, the first time but one—that he had faced a man with a gun he had backed down cold. He had run like a baby. He had shown the white feather.

Tall, strongly built, skillful with rope or horse, knowing with stock, he was a top hand in any outfit. An outright genius with guns, men had often said they would hate to face him in a shoot-out. He had worked hard and played rough, getting the most out of life until that day in the saloon in El Paso when Ben Kerr, gunman and cattle rustler, gambler and bully, had called him, and he had backed down.

———

TOM BELL WAS a knowing and kindly man. Aware that something was riding Casady, he told him his job and left him alone. Stockman watched him top off a bad bronc on the first morning and glanced at Bell.

"If he does everything like he rides, we've got us a hand!"

And Casady did everything that well. A week after he had hired out he was doing so much work as any two men. And the jobs they avoided, the lonely jobs, he accepted eagerly.

"Notice something else?" Stockman asked his foreman one morning. "That new hand sure likes the jobs that keep him away from the ranch."

Stockman nodded. "Away from people. It ain't natural, Tom. He ain't been to Three Lakes once since he's been here."

Sue Landon looked up at her uncle. "Maybe he's broke!" she exclaimed. "No cowhand could have fun in town when he's broke!"

Bell shook his head. "It ain't that, Sue. He had money when he first come in here. I saw it. He had anyway two hundred dollars, and for a forty-a-month cowpoke, that's a lot of money!"

"Notice something else?" Stockman asked. "He never packs a gun. Only man on the ranch who doesn't. You'd better warn him about Pete Vorys."

"I did." Bell frowned. "I can't figure this hombre, Boss. I did warn him, and that was the very day he began askin' for all the bad jobs. Why, he's the only man on the place who'll fetch grub to Cat McLeod without bein' bullied into it!"

"Over in that Rock Canyon country?" Stockman smiled. "That's a rough ride for any man. I don't blame the boys, but you've got to hand it to old Cat. He's killed nine lions and forty-two coyotes in the past ninety days! If he keeps that up we won't have so much stock lost!"

"Too bad he ain't just as good on rustlers. Maybe," Bell grinned, "we ought to turn him loose on Pete Vorys!"

———

ROCK CASADY KEPT his palouse gelding moving steadily. The two packhorses ambled placidly behind, seemingly content to be away from the ranch. The old restlessness was coming back to Casady, and he had been on the Four Spoke only a few weeks. He knew they liked him, knew that despite his taciturn manner and desire to be alone, the hands liked him as well as did Stockman or Bell.

He did his work and more, and he was a hand. He avoided poker games that might lead to trouble and stayed away from town. He was anxiously figuring some way to be absent from the ranch on the following Saturday, for he knew the whole crowd was going to a dance and shindig in Three Lakes.

While he talked little, he heard much. He was aware of impending trouble between the Four Spoke Wheel outfit and the gang of Pete Vorys. The latter, who seemed to ride the country as he pleased, owned a small ranch north of Three Lakes, near town. He had a dozen tough hands and usually spent money freely. All his hands had money, and while no one dared say it, all knew he was rustling.

Yet he was not the ringleader. Behind him there was someone else, someone who had only recently become involved, for recently there had been a change. Larger bunches of cattle were being stolen, and more care was taken to leave no trail. The carelessness of Vorys had given way to more shrewd operation, and Casady overheard enough talk to know that Stockman believed a new man was directing operations.

He heard much of Pete Vorys. He was a big man, bigger than Rock. He was a killer with at least seven notches on his gun. He was pugnacious and quarrelsome, itching for a fight with gun or fists. He had, only a few weeks before, whipped Sandy Kane, a Four Spoke hand, within an inch of his life. He was bold, domineering, and tough.

The hands on the Four Spoke were good men. They were hard workers, willing to fight, but not one of them was good enough to tackle Vorys with either fists or gun.

Cat McLeod was scraping a hide when Rock rode into his camp in Blue Spring Valley. He got up, wiping his hands on his jeans and grinning.

"Howdy, son! You sure are a sight for sore eyes! It ain't no use quibblin', I sure get my grub on time when you're on that ranch! Hope you stay!"

Rock swung down. He liked the valley and liked Cat.

"Maybe I'll pull out, Cat." He looked around. "I might even come up here to stay. I like it."

McLeod glanced at him out of the corners of his eyes. "Glad to have you, son. This sure ain't no country for a young feller, though. It's a huntin' an' fishin' country, but no women here, an' no likker. Nothin' much to do, all said an' done."

CASADY UNSADDLED IN silence. It was better, though, than a run-in with Vorys, he thought. At least, nobody here knew he was yellow. They liked him and he was one of them, but he was careful.

"Ain't more trouble down below, is there? That Vorys cuttin' up much?" The old man noted the gun Rock was wearing for the trip.

"Some. I hear the boys talkin' about him."

"Never seen him yourself?" Cat asked quizzically. "I been thinkin' ever since you come up here, son. Might be a good thing for this country if you did have trouble with Vorys. You're nigh as big as him, an' you move like a catamount. An' me, I know 'em! Never seen a man lighter on his feet than you."

"Not me," Rock spoke stiffly. "I'm a peace-lovin' man, Cat. I want no trouble with anybody."

McLeod studied the matter as he worked over his hide. For a long time now he had known something was bothering Rock Casady. Perhaps this last remark, that he wanted no trouble with anybody, was the answer?

Cat McLeod was a student of mankind as well as the animals upon whom he practiced his trade. In a lifetime of living along the frontier and in the world's far places, he had learned a lot about men who liked to live alone and about men who sought the wilderness. If it was true that Rock wanted no trouble, it certainly was not from lack of ability to handle it.

There had been that time when Cat had fallen, stumbling to hands and knees. Right before him, not three feet from his face and much nearer his outstretched hands, lay one of the biggest rattlers Cat had ever seen. The snake's head jerked back above its coil, and then, with a gun's roar blasting in his ears, that head was gone and the snake was a writhing mass of coils, showing only a bloody stump where the head had been!

Cat had gotten to his feet gray faced and turned. Rock Casady was thumbing a shell into his gun. The young man grinned.

"That was a close one!" he had said cheerfully.

McLeod had dusted off his hands, staring at Casady. "I've heard of men drawin' faster'n a snake could strike, but that's the first time I ever seen it!"

Since then he had seen that .44 shoot the heads off quail and he had seen a quick shot with the rifle break a deer's neck at two hundred yards.

Now his mind reverted to their former topic. "If that Vorys is tied in with some smart hombre, there'll be hell to pay! Pete was never no great shakes for brains, but he's tough, tough as all get out! With somebody to think for him, he'll make this country unfit to live in!"

Later that night, McLeod looked over his shoulder from the fire. "You know," he said, "if I was wantin' a spread of my own an' didn't care much for folks, like you, I'd go down into the Pleasant Valley Outlet, south of here. Lonely, but she's sure grand country!"

———

TWO DAYS LATER Rock was mending a bridle when Sue Landon walked over to him. She wore jeans and a boy's shirt, and her eyes were bright and lovely.

"Hi!" she said brightly. "You're the new hand? You certainly keep out of the way. All this time on the ranch and I never met you before!"

He grinned shyly. "Just a quiet hombre, I reckon," he said. "If I had it my way I'd be over there with Cat all the time."

"Then you won't like the job I have for you!" she said. "To ride into Three Lakes with me, riding herd on a couple of packhorses."

"Three Lakes?" He looked up so sharply it startled her. "Into town? I never go into town, ma'am. I don't like the place. Not any town."

"Why, that's silly! Anyway, there's no one else, and Uncle Frank won't let me go alone with Pete Vorys around."

"He wouldn't bother a girl, would he?"

"You sure don't know Pete Vorys!" Sue returned grimly. "He does pretty much what he feels like, and everybody's afraid to say anything about it. But come on—you'll go?"

Reluctantly, he got to his feet. She looked at him curiously, not a little piqued. Any other hand on the ranch would have jumped at the chance, and here she had deliberately made sure there were no others available before going to him. Her few distant glimpses of Rock Casady had excited her interest, and she wanted to know him better.

Yet as the trail fell behind them, she had to admit she was getting no place. For shyness there was some excuse, although usually even the most bashful hand lost it when alone with her. Rock Casady was almost sullen, and all she could get out of him were monosyllables.

THE TRUTH WAS that the nearer they drew to Three Lakes the more worried Rock grew. It had been six months since he had been in a town, and while it was improbable he would see anyone he knew, there was always a chance. Cowhands were notoriously footloose and fancy-free. Once the story of his backing out of a gunfight got around, he would be through in this country, and he was tired of running.

Yet Three Lakes looked quiet enough as they ambled placidly down the street and tied up in front of the general store. He glanced at Sue tentatively.

"Ma'am," he said, "I'd sure appreciate it if you didn't stay too long. Towns make me nervous."

She looked at him, more than slightly irritated. Her trip with him, so carefully planned, had thus far come to nothing, although she had to admit he was the finest-looking man she had ever seen, and his smile was quick and attractive.

"I won't be long. Why don't you go have a drink? It might do you good!" She said the last sentence a little sharply, and he looked quickly at her, but she was already flouncing into the store, as well as any girl could flounce in jeans.

Slowly he built a cigarette, studying the Hackamore Saloon over the way. He had to admit he was tempted, and probably he was foolish to think that he would get into trouble or that anyone would know him. Nevertheless, he sat down suddenly on the edge of the boardwalk and lighted his smoke.

He was still sitting there when he heard the sound of booted heels on the boardwalk and then heard a raucous voice.

"Hey! Lookit here! One of them no-'count Four Spokers in town! I didn't think any of them had the sand!"

In spite of himself, he looked up, knowing instantly that this man was Pete Vorys.

He was broad in the shoulders, with narrow hips. He had a swarthy face with dark, brilliant eyes. That he had been drinking was obvious, but he was far from drunk. With him were two tough-looking hands, both grinning cynically at him.

Vorys was spoiling for a fight. He had never been whipped and doubted there lived a man who could whip him in a tooth-and-nail knockdown and drag-out battle. This Four Spoker looked big enough to be fun.

"That's a rawhide outfit, anyway," Vorys sneered. "I've a mind to ride out there sometime, just for laughs. Wonder where they hooked this ranny?"

Despite himself, Rock was growing angry. He was not wearing a gun, and Vorys was. He took the cigarette out of his mouth and looked at it. Expecting trouble, a crowd was gathering. He felt his neck growing red.

"Hey, you!" Vorys booted him solidly in the spine, and the kick hurt. At the same time, he slapped Casady with his sombrero. Few things are more calculated to enrage a man.

Rock came to his feet with a lunge. As he turned, with his right palm he grabbed the ankle of Vorys' boot, and with his left fist he smashed him in the stomach, jerking up on the leg. The move was so sudden, so totally unexpected, that there was no chance to spring back. Pete Vorys hit the board-walk flat on his shoulder blades!

A whoop of delight went up from the crowd, and for an instant, Pete Vorys lay stunned. Then with an oath he came off the walk, lunging to his feet.

Rock sprang back, his hands wide. "I'm not packin' a gun!" he yelled.

"I don't need a gun!" Vorys yelled. It was the first time he had ever hit the ground in a fight and he was furious.

He stepped in, driving a left to the head. Rock was no boxer. Indeed, he had rarely fought except in fun. He took that blow now, a stunning wallop on the cheekbone. At the same moment, he let go with a wicked right swing. The punch caught Vorys on the chin and rocked him to his heels.

More astonished than hurt, he sprang in and threw two swings for Rock's chin, and Casady took them both coming in. A tremendous light seemed to burst in his brain, but the next instant he had Pete Vorys in his hands. Grabbing him by the collar and the belt, he heaved him to arm's length overhead and hurled him into the street. Still dazed from the punches he had taken, he sprang after the bigger man, and seizing him before he could strike more than an ineffectual punch, swung him to arm's length overhead again, and slammed him into the dust!

Four times he grabbed the hapless bully and hurled him to the ground while the crowd whooped and cheered. The last time, his head clearing, he grabbed Vorys' shirtfront with his left hand and swung three times into his face, smashing his nose and lips. Then he lifted the man and heaved him into the water tank with such force that water showered around him.

Beside himself, Rock wheeled on the two startled men who had walked with Vorys. Before either could make a move, he grabbed them by their belts. One swung on Rock's face, but he merely ducked his head and heaved. The man's feet flew up and he hit the ground on his back. Promptly, Rock stacked the other atop him.

The man started to get up, and Rock swung on his face, knocking him into a sitting position. Then grabbing him, he heaved him into the water tank with Vorys, who was scrambling to get out. Then he dropped the third man into the pool and, putting a hand in Vorys' face, shoved him back.

For an instant then while the street rocked with cheers and yells of delight, he stood, panting and staring. Suddenly, he was horrified. In his rage he had not thought of what this would mean, but suddenly he knew that they would be hunting him now with guns. He must face a shoot-out or skip the country!

Wheeling, he shoved through the crowd, aware that someone was clinging to his arm. Looking down, he saw Sue beside him. Her eyes were bright with laughter and pride.

"Oh, Rock! That was wonderful. Just *wonderful*!"

"Let's get out of town!" he said quickly. "Now!"

So pleased was she by the discomfiture of Pete Vorys and his hands by a Four Spoker that she thought nothing of his haste. His eye swelling and his nose still dripping occasional drops of blood, they hit the trail for the home ranch. All the way, Sue babbled happily over his standing up for the Four Spoke and what it meant, and all the while all he could think of was the fact that on the morrow Vorys would be looking for him with a gun.

He could not face him. It was far better to avoid a fight than to prove himself yellow, and if he fled the country now, they would never forget what he had done and always make excuses for him. If he stayed behind and showed his yellow streak, he would be ruined.

Frank Stockman was standing on the steps when they rode in. He took one look at Rock's battered face and torn shirt and came off the steps.

"What happened?" he demanded. "Was it that Pete Vorys again?"

Tom Bell and two other hands were walking up from the bunkhouse, staring at Rock. But already, while he stripped the saddles from the horses, Sue Landon was telling the story, and it lost nothing in the telling. Rock Casady of the Four Spoke had not only whipped Pete Vorys soundly, but he had ducked Pete and two of his tough hands in the Three Lakes water tank!

The hands crowded around him, crowing and happy, slapping him on the back and grinning. Sandy Kane gripped his hand.

"Thanks, pardner," he said grimly, "I don't feel so bad now!"

Rock smiled weakly, but inside he was sick. It was going to look bad, but he was pulling out. He said nothing, but after supper he got his own horse, threw the saddle aboard, and then rustled his gear. When he was all packed, he drew a deep breath and walked toward the ranch house.

Stockman was sitting on the wide veranda with Bell and Sue. She got up when he drew near, her eyes bright. He avoided her glance, suddenly aware of how much her praise and happiness meant to him. In his weeks on the Four Spoke, while he had never talked to her before today, his eyes had followed her every move.

"How are you, son?" Stockman said jovially. "You've made this a red-letter day on the Four Spoke! Come up an' sit down! Bell was just talking here; he says he needs a segundo, an' I reckon he's right. How'd you like the job? Eighty a month?"

He swallowed. "Sorry, Boss. I got to be movin'. I want my time."

"You *what*?" Bell took his pipe from his mouth and stared.

"I got to roll my hoop," he said stiffly. "I don't want trouble."

Frank Stockman came quickly to his feet. "But listen, man!" he protested. "You've just whipped the best man around this country! You've made a place for yourself here! The boys think you're great! So do I! So does Tom! As for Sue here, all she's done is talk about how wonderful you are! Why, son, you came in here a drifter, an' now you've made a place for yourself! Stick around! We need men like you!"

Despite himself, Casady was wavering. This was what he had always wanted and wanted now, since the bleak months of his lonely riding, more than ever. A place where he was at home, men who liked him, and a girl. . . .

"Stay on," Stockman said more quietly. "You can handle any trouble that comes, and I promise you, the Four Spoke will back any play you make! Why, with you to head 'em we can run Pete Vorys and that slick partner of his, that Ben Kerr, clean out of the country!"

Casady's face blanched. "*Who?* Did you say, *Ben Kerr*?"

"Why, sure!" Stockman stared at him curiously, aware of the shocked expression on Rock's face. "Ben Kerr's the hombre who come in here to side Vorys! He's the smart one who's puttin' all those fancy ideas in Pete's head! He's a brother-in-law of Vorys or something!"

Ben Kerr—here!

THAT SETTLED IT. He could not stay now. There was no time to stay. His mind leaped ahead. Vorys would tell his story, of course. His name would be mentioned, or if not his name, his description. Kerr would know, and he wouldn't waste time. Why, even now . . .

"Give me my money!" Casady said sharply. "I'm movin' out right now! Thanks for all you've offered, but I'm ridin'! I want no trouble!"

Stockman's face stiffened. "Why, sure," he said, "if you feel that way about it!" He took a roll of bills from his pocket and coolly paid over the money; then abruptly he turned his back and walked inside.

Casady wheeled, his heart sick within him, and started for the corral. He heard running steps behind him and then a light touch on his arm. He looked down, his eyes miserable, into Sue's face.

"Don't go, Rock!" she pleaded gently. "Please don't go! We all want you to stay!"

He shook his head. "I can't, Sue! I can't stay. I want no gun trouble!"

There—it was out.

She stepped back, and slowly her face changed. Girl that she was, she still had grown up in the tradition of the West. A man fought his battles with gun or fist; he did not run away.

"Oh?" Her amazed contempt cut him like a whip. "So that's it? You're afraid to face a gun? Afraid for your life?" She stared at him. "Why, Rock Casady," her voice lifted as realization broke over her, "you're *yellow*!"

Hours later, far back in the darkness of night in the mountains, her words rang in his ears. She had called him yellow! She had called him a coward!

Rock Casady, sick at heart, rode slowly into the darkness. At first he rode with no thought but to escape, and then as his awareness began to return, he studied the situation. Lee's Ferry was northeast, and to the south he was bottled by the Colorado Canyon. North it was mostly Vorys' range, and west lay Three Lakes and the trails leading to it. East, the

Canyons fenced him off also, but east lay a lonely, little-known country, ridden only by Cat McLeod in his wanderings after varmints that preyed upon Four Spoke cattle. In that wilderness he might find someplace to hole up. Cat still had plenty of supplies, and he could borrow some from him. . . . Suddenly he remembered the canyon Cat had mentioned, the Pleasant Valley Outlet.

He would not go near Cat. There was game enough, and he had packed away a few things in the grub line when he had rolled his soogan. He found an intermittent stream that trailed down a ravine toward Kane Canyon, and followed it. Pleasant Valley Outlet was not far south of Kane. It would be a good hideout. After a few weeks, when the excitement was over, he could slip out of the country.

In a lonely canyon that opened from the south wall into Pleasant Valley Canyon, he found a green and lovely spot. There was plenty of driftwood and a cave hollowed from the Kaibab sandstone by wind and water. There he settled down. Days passed into weeks, and he lived on wild game, berries, and fish. Yet his mind kept turning northwestward toward the Four Spoke, and his thoughts gave him no rest.

On an evening almost three weeks after his escape from the Four Spoke, he was putting his coffee on when he heard a slight sound. Looking up, he saw old Cat McLeod grinning at him.

"Howdy, son!" he chuckled. "When you head for the tall timber you sure do a job of it! My land! I thought I'd never find you! No more trail 'n' trout swimmin' upstream!"

Rock arose stiffly. "Howdy, Cat. Just put the coffee on." He averted his eyes and went about the business of preparing a meal.

Cat seated himself, seemingly unhurried and undisturbed by his scant welcome. He got out his pipe and stuffed it full of tobacco. He talked calmly and quietly about game and fish and the mountain trails.

"Old Mormon crossin' not far from here," he said. "I could show you where it is."

After they had eaten, McLeod leaned back against a rock.

"Lots of trouble back at the Four Spoke. I reckon you was the smart one, pullin' out when you did."

Casady made no response, so McLeod continued. "Pete Vorys was some beat up. Two busted ribs, busted nose, some teeth gone. Feller name of Ben Kerr came out to the Four Spoke huntin' you. Said you was a yella dog an' he knowed you of old. He laughed when he said that, an' said the whole Four Spoke outfit was yella. Stockman, he wouldn't take that, so he went for his gun. Kerr shot him."

Rock's head came up with a jerk. "Shot Stockman? He killed him?" There was horror in his voice. This was his fault—*his*!

"No, he ain't dead. He's sure bad off, though. Kerr added injury to insult by runnin' off a couple of hundred head of Four Spoke stock. Shot one hand doin' it."

———

A LONG SILENCE FOLLOWED in which the two men smoked moodily. Finally, Cat looked across the fire at Rock.

"Son, there's more'n one kind of courage, I say. I seen many a dog stand' up to a grizzly that would hightail it from a skunk. Back yonder they say you're yella. Me, I don't figure it so."

"Thanks, Cat," Rock replied simply, miserably. "Thanks a lot, but you're wrong. I am yellow."

"Reckon it takes pretty much of a man to say that, son. But from what I hear you sure didn't act it against Pete an' his riders. You walloped the tar out of them!"

"With my hands it's different. It's—it's—guns."

McLeod was silent. He poked a twig into the fire and re-lighted his pipe.

"Ever kill a man, son?" His eyes probed Rock's, and he saw the young rider's head nod slowly. "Who was it? How'd it happen?"

"It was—" He looked up, his face drawn and pale. "I killed my brother, Cat."

McLeod was shocked. His old eyes went wide. "You killed your brother? Your *own* brother?"

Rock Casady nodded. "Yeah," he said bitterly, "my own brother. The one person in this world that really mattered to me!"

Cat stared, and then slowly his brow puckered. "Son," he said, "why don't you tell me about it? Get it out of your system, like."

For a long while Rock was silent. Then he started to speak.

"It was down in Texas. We had a little spread down there, Jack and me. He was only a shade older, but always protectin' me, although I sure didn't need it. The finest man who ever walked, he was.

"Well, we had us a mite of trouble, an' this here Ben Kerr was the ringleader. I had trouble with Ben, and he swore to shoot me on sight. I was a hand with a gun, like you know, an' I was ready enough to fight, them days. One of the hands told me, an' without a word to Jack, I lit into the saddle an' headed for town.

"Kerr was a gunslick, but I wasn't worried. I knew that I didn't have scarcely a friend in town an' that his whole outfit would be there. It was me against them, an' I went into town with two guns an' sure enough on the prod.

"It was gettin' late when I hit town. A man I knowed told me Ben was around with his outfit and that nobody was goin' to back me one bit, them all bein' scared of Ben's boys. He told me, too, that Ben Kerr would shoot me in the back as soon as not, he bein' that kind.

"I went huntin' him. Kidlike, an' never in no fight before, I was jumpy, mighty jumpy. The light was bad. All of a sudden, I saw one of Ben's boys step out of a door ahead of me. He called out, 'Here he is, Ben! Take him!' Then I heard runnin' feet behind me, heard 'em slide to a halt, an' I wheeled, drawin' as I turned, an' fired." His voice sank to a whisper.

Cat, leaning forward, said, "You shot? An' then . . . ?"

"It was Jack. It was my own brother. He'd heard I was in town alone, an' he come runnin' to back me up."

Cat McLeod stared up at the young man, utterly appalled. In his kindly old heart he could only guess at the horror that must have filled Casady, then scarcely more than a boy, when he had looked down into that still, dead face and seen his brother.

"Gosh, son." He shook his head in amazed sympathy. "It ain't no wonder you hate gunfights! It sure ain't! But . . . ?" He scowled. "I still don't see. . . ." His voice trailed away.

Rock drew a deep breath. "I sold out then and left the country. Went to ridin' for an outfit near El Paso. One night I come into town with the other hands, an' who do I run into but Ben Kerr? He thought I'd run because I was afraid of him, an' he got tough. He called me—right in front of the outfit. I was goin' to draw, but all I could see there in front of me was Jack, with that blue hole between his eyes! I turned and ran."

Cat McLeod stared at Rock and then into the fire. It was no wonder, he reflected. He probably would have run, too. If he had drawn he would have been firing on the image of the brother. It would have been like killing him over again.

"Son," he said slowly, "I know how you feel, but stop a minute an' think about Jack, this brother of yours. He always protected you, you say. He always stood up for you. Now don't you suppose he'd understand? You thought you was all alone in that town. You'd every right in the world to think that was Ben Kerr behind you. I would have thought so, an' I wouldn't have wasted no time shootin', neither.

"You can't run away from yourself. You can't run no further. Someday you got to stand an' face it, an' it might as well be now. Look at it like this: Would your brother want you livin' like this? Hunted an' scared? He sure wouldn't! Son, ever' man has to pay his own debt an' live his own life. Nobody can do it for you, but if I was you, I'd sort of figure my brother was dead because of *Ben Kerr,* an' I'd stop runnin'!"

Rock looked up slowly. "Yeah," he agreed, "I see that plain. But what if when I stepped out to meet him, *I look up an' see Jack's face again?*"

His eyes dark with horror, Rock Casady turned and plunged downstream, stumbling, swearing in his fear and loneliness and sorrow.

AT DAYLIGHT, OLD Cat McLeod opened his eyes. For an instant, he lay still. Then he realized where he was and what he had come for, and he turned his head. Rock Casady, his gear and horse, were gone. Stumbling to his feet, McLeod slipped on his boots and walked out in his red flannels to look at the trail.

It headed south, away from Three Lakes, and away from Ben Kerr. Rock Casady was running again.

THE TRAIL SOUTH to the canyon was rough and rugged. The palouse was sure-footed and had a liking for the mountains, yet seemed undecided, as though the feeling persisted that he was going the wrong way.

Casady stared bleakly ahead, but he saw little of the orange and red of the sandstone cliffs. He was seeing again Frank Stockman's strong, kindly face and remembering his welcome at the Four Spoke. He was remembering Sue's hand on his sleeve and her quick smile, and old Tom Bell, gnarled and worn with handling cattle and men. He drew up suddenly and turned the horse on the narrow trail. He was going back.

"Jack," he said suddenly aloud, "stick with me, boy. I'm sure goin' to need you now!"

SANDY KANE, GRIM lipped and white of face, dismounted behind the store. Beside him was Sue Landon.

"Miss Sue," he said, "you get that buyin' done fast. Don't let none of that Vorys crowd see you. They've sure taken this town over since they shot the boss."

"All right, Sandy." She looked at him bravely and then squeezed the older man's hand. "We'll make it, all right." Her blue eyes darkened. "I wish I'd been a man, Sandy."

The girl started to enter the store, but then caught the cowhand's hand.

"Sandy," she said faintly, "look!"

A tall man with broad shoulders had swung down before the store. He tied his horse with a slipknot and hitched his guns into place. Rock Casady, his hard young face bleak and desperate, stared carefully along the street.

It was only three blocks long, this street. It was dusty and warm with the noonday sun. The gray-fronted buildings looked upon the dusty canal that separated them, and a few saddled horses stamped lazily, flicking their tails at casual flies. It was like that other street, so long ago.

Casady pulled the flat brim of his black hat a little lower over his eyes. Inside he felt sick and faint. His mouth was dry. His tongue trembled when it touched his lips. Up the street a man saw him and got slowly to his feet, staring as if hypnotized. The man backed away and then dove into the Hackamore Saloon.

Rock Casady took a deep breath, drew his shoulders back, and started slowly down the walk. He seemed in a trance where only the sun was warm and the air was still. Voices murmured. He heard a gasp of astonishment, for these people remembered that he had whipped Pete Vorys, and they knew what he had come for.

He wore two guns now, having dug the other gun and belt from his saddlebags to join the one he had only worn in the mountains. A door slammed somewhere.

BEN KERR STARED at the face of the man in the door of the saloon.

"Ben, here comes that yellow-backed Casady! And he's wearin' a gun!"

"He is, is he?" Kerr tossed off his drink. "Fill that up, Jim! I'll be right back. This will only take a minute!"

He stepped out into the street. "Come to get it this time?" he shouted tauntingly. "Or are you runnin' again?"

Rock Casady made no reply. His footsteps echoed hollowly on the boardwalk, and he strode slowly, finishing the walk at the intersecting alley, stepping into the dust and then up on the walk again.

Ben Kerr's eyes narrowed slightly. Some sixth sense warned him that the man who faced him had subtly changed. He lifted his head a little and stared. Then he shrugged off the feeling and stepped out from the building.

"All right, yellabelly! If you want it!" His hand swept down in a flashing arc and his gun came up.

Rock Casady stared down the street at the face of Ben Kerr, and it was only the face of Kerr. In his ear was Jack's voice: "Go ahead, kid! Have at it!"

Kerr's gun roared and he felt the hot breath of it bite at his face. And then suddenly, Rock Casady laughed! Within him all was light and easy, and it was almost carelessly that he stepped forward. Suddenly the .44 began to roar and buck in his hand, leaping like a live thing within his grasp. Kerr's gun flew high in the air, his knees buckled, and he fell forward on his face in the dust.

Rock Casady turned quickly toward the Hackamore. Pete Vorys stood in the door, shocked to stillness.

"All right, Pete! Do you want it or are you leavin' town?"

Vorys stared from Kerr's riddled body to the man holding the gun.

"Why, I'm leavin' town!" Vorys said. "That's my roan, right there. I'll just . . ." As though stunned, he started to mount, and Rock's voice arrested him.

"No, Pete. You walk. You hoof it. And start now!"

The bully of Three Lakes wet his lips and stared. Then his eyes shifted to the body in the street.

"Sure, Rock," he said, taking a step back. "I'll hoof it." Turning, stumbling a little, he started to walk. As he moved, his walk grew swifter and swifter as though something followed in his tracks.

Rock turned and looked up, and Sue Landon was standing on the boardwalk.

"Oh, Rock! You came back!"

"Don't reckon I ever really left, Sue," he said slowly. "My heart's been right here all the time!"

She caught his arm, and the smile in her eyes and on her lips was bright. He looked down at her.

Then he said aloud. "Thanks, Jack!"

She looked up quickly. "What did you say?"

He grinned at her. "Sue," he said, "did I ever tell you about my brother? He was one grand hombre! Someday, I'll tell you." They walked back toward the horses, her hand on his arm.

THE BLACK ROCK
COFFIN MAKERS

JIM GATLIN HAD been up the creek and over the mountains, and more than once had been on both ends of a six-shooter. Lean and tall, with shoulders wide for his height and a face like saddle leather, he was, at the moment, doing a workmanlike job of demolishing the last of a thick steak and picking off isolated beans that had escaped his initial attack. He was a thousand miles from home and knew nobody in the town of Tucker.

He glanced up as the door opened and saw a short, thick-bodied man. The man gave one startled look at Jim and ducked back out of sight. Gatlin blinked in surprise, then shrugged and filled his coffee cup from the pot standing on the restaurant table.

Puzzled, he listened to the rapidly receding pound of a horse's hoofs, then rolled a smoke, sitting back with a contented sigh. Two hundred and fifty-odd miles to the north was the herd he had drifted up from Texas. The money the cattle had brought was in the belt around his waist and his pants pockets. Nothing remained now but to return to Texas, bank the profit, and pick up a new herd.

The outer door opened again, and a tall girl entered the restaurant. Turning right, she started for the door leading to the hotel. She stopped abruptly as though his presence had only then registered. She turned, and her eyes widened in alarm. Swiftly, she crossed the room to him. "Are you insane?" she whispered. "Sitting here like that when the town is full of Wing Cary's hands? They know you're coming and have been watching for you for days!"

Gatlin looked up, smiling. "Ma'am, you've sure got the wrong man, although if a girl as pretty as you is worried about him, he sure is a lucky fellow. I'm a stranger here. I never saw the place until an hour ago!"

She stepped back, puzzled, and then the door slammed open once more, and a man stepped into the room. He was as tall as Jim, but thinner, and his dark eyes were angry. "Get away from him, Lisa! I'm killin' him—right now!"

The man's hand flashed for a gun, and Gatlin dove sidewise to the floor, drawing as he fell. A gun roared in the room; then Gatlin fired twice.

The tall man caught himself, jerking his left arm against his ribs, his face twisted as he gasped for breath. Then he wilted slowly to the floor, his gun sliding from his fingers.

Gatlin got to his feet, staring at the stranger. He swung his eyes to the girl staring at him. "Who is that hombre?" he snapped. "What's this all about? Who did he think I was?"

"You—you're not—you aren't Jim Walker?" Her voice was high, amazed.

"Walker?" He shook his head. "I'm sure as hell not. The name is Gatlin. I'm just driftin' through."

There was a rush of feet in the street outside. She caught his hand. "Come! Come quickly! They won't listen to you! They'll kill you! All the Cary outfit are in town!"

She ran beside him, dodging into the hotel, and then swiftly down a hall. As the front door burst open, they plunged out the back and into the alley behind the building. Unerringly, she led him to the left and then opened the back door of another building and drew him inside. Silently, she closed the door and stood close beside him, panting in the darkness.

Shouts and curses rang from the building next door. A door banged, and men charged up and down outside. Jim was still holding his gun, but now he withdrew the empty shells and fed two into the cylinder to replace those fired. He slipped a sixth into the usually empty chamber. "What is this place?" he whispered. "Will they come here?"

"It's a law office," she whispered. "I work here part-time, and I left the door open myself. They'll not think of this place." Stealthily, she lifted the bar and dropped it into place.

"Better sit down. They'll be searching the streets for some time."

He found the desk and seated himself on the corner, well out of line with the windows. He could see only the vaguest outline of her face. His first impression of moments before was strong enough for him to remember she was pretty. The gray eyes were wide and clear, her figure rounded yet slim. "What is this?" he repeated. "What was he gunnin' for me for?"

"It wasn't you. He thought you were Jim Walker, of the XY. If you aren't actually him, you look enough like him to be a brother, a twin brother."

"Where is he? What goes on here? Who was that hombre who tried to gun me down?"

She paused, and seemed to be thinking, and he had the idea she was still uncertain whether to believe him or not. "The man you killed was Bill Trout. He was the badman of Paradise country and *segundo* on Wing Cary's Flying C spread. Jim Walker called him a thief and a murderer in talking to Cary, and Trout threatened to shoot him on sight. Walker hasn't been seen since, and that was four days ago, so everybody believed Walker had skipped the country. Nobody blamed him much."

"What's it all about?" Gatlin inquired.

"North of here, up beyond Black Rock, is Alder Creek country, with some rich bottom hay land lying in several corners of the mountains. This is dry country, but that Alder Creek area has springs and some small streams flowing down out of the hills. The streams flow into the desert and die there, so the water is good only for the man who controls the range."

"And that was Walker?"

"No, up until three weeks ago, it was old Dave Butler. Then Dave was thrown from his horse and killed, and when they read his will, he had left the property to be sold at auction and the money to be paid to his nephew and niece back in New York. However, the joker was, he stipulated that Jim Walker was to get the ranch if he would bid ten thousand cash and forty thousand on his note, payable in six years."

"In other words, he wanted Walker to have the property?" Jim asked. "He got first chance at it?"

"That's right. And I was to get second chance. If Jim didn't want to make the bid, I could have it for the same price. If neither of us wanted it, the ranch was to go on public auction, and that means that Cary and Horwick would get it. They have the money, and nobody around here could outbid them."

The street outside was growing quieter as the excitement of the chase died down. "I think," Lisa continued, "that Uncle Dave wanted Jim to have the property because Jim did so much to develop it. Jim was foreman of the XY acting for Dave. Then, Uncle Dave knew my father and liked me, and he knew I loved the ranch, so he wanted me to have second chance, but I don't have the money, and they all know it. Jim had some of it, and he could get the rest. I think that was behind his trouble with Trout. I believe Wing deliberately set Trout to kill him, and Jim's statements about Bill were a result of the pushing around Bill Trout had given him."

The pattern was not unfamiliar, and Gatlin could easily appreciate the situation. Water was gold in this country of sparse grass. To a cattleman, such a ranch as Lisa described could be second to none, with plenty of water and grass and good hay meadows. Suddenly, she caught his arm. Men were talking outside the door.

"Looks like he got plumb away, Wing. Old Ben swears there was nobody in the room with him but that Lisa Cochrane, an' she never threw that gun, but how Jim Walker ever beat Trout is more'n I can see. Why, Bill was the fastest man around here unless it's you or me."

"That wasn't Walker, Pete. It couldn't have been!"

"Ben swears it was, an' Woody Hammer busted right through the door in front of him. Said it was Jim, all right."

Wing Cary's voice was irritable. "I tell you, it couldn't have been!" he flared. "Jim Walker never saw the day he dared face Trout with a gun," he added. "I've seen Walker draw an' he never was fast."

"Maybe he wasn't," Pete Chasin agreed dryly, "but Trout's dead, ain't he?"

"Three days left," Cary said. "Lisa Cochrane hasn't the

money, and it doesn't look like Walker will even be bidding. Let it ride, Pete. I don't think we need to worry about anything. Even if that was Walker, an' I'd take an oath it wasn't, he's gone for good now. All we have to do is sit tight."

The two moved off, and Jim Gatlin, staring at the girl in the semidarkness, saw her lips were pressed tight. His eyes had grown accustomed to the dim light, and he could see around the small office. It was a simple room with a desk, chair, and filing cabinets. Well-filled bookcases lined the walls.

He got to his feet. "I've got to get my gear out of that hotel," he said, "and my horse."

"You're leaving?" she asked.

Jim glanced at her in surprise. "I've already killed one man, and if I stay, I'll have to kill more or be killed myself. There's nothing here for me."

"Did you notice something?" she asked suddenly. "Wing Cary seemed very sure that Jim Walker wasn't coming back, that you weren't he."

Gatlin frowned. He had noticed it, and it had him wondering. "He did sound mighty sure. Like he might *know* Walker wasn't coming back."

They were silent in the dark office, yet each knew what the other was thinking. Jim Walker was dead. Pete Chasin had not known it. Neither, obviously, had Bill Trout.

"What happens to you then?" Gatlin asked suddenly. "You lose the ranch?"

She shrugged. "I never had it, and never really thought I would have it, only . . . well, if Jim had lived . . . I mean, if Jim got the ranch we'd have made out. We were very close, like brother and sister. Now I don't know what I can do."

"You haven't any people?"

"None that I know of." Her head came up suddenly. "Oh, it isn't myself I'm thinking of; it's all the old hands, the ranch itself. Uncle Dave hated Cary, and so do his men. Now he'll get the ranch, and they'll all be fired, and he'll ruin the place! That's what he's wanted all along."

Gatlin shifted his feet. "Tough," he said, "mighty tough." He opened the door slightly. "Thanks," he said, "for getting me out of there." She didn't reply, so after a moment, he stepped out of the door and drew it gently to behind him.

There was no time to lose. He must be out of town by daylight and with miles behind him. There was no sense getting mixed up in somebody else's fight, for all he'd get out of it would be a bellyful of lead. There was nothing he could do to help. He moved swiftly, and within a matter of minutes was in his hotel room. Apparently, searching for Jim Walker, they hadn't considered his room in the hotel, so Gatlin got his duffel together, stuffed it into his saddlebags, and picked up his rifle. With utmost care, he eased down the back stairs and into the alley.

The streets were once more dark and still. What had become of the Flying C hands, he didn't know, but none were visible. Staying on back streets, he made his way carefully to the livery barn, but there his chance of cover grew less, for he must enter the wide door with a light glowing over it.

After listening, he stepped out and, head down, walked through the door. Turning, he hurried to the stall where his powerful black waited. It was the work of only a few minutes to saddle up. He led the horse out of the stall and caught up the bridle. As his hand grasped the pommel, a voice stopped him.

"Lightin' out?"

It was Pete Chasin's voice. Slowly, he released his grip on the pommel and turned slightly. The man was hidden in a stall. "Why not?" Gatlin asked. "I'm not goin' to be a shootin' gallery for nobody. This ain't my range, an' I'm slopin' out of here for Texas. I'm no trouble hunter."

He heard Chasin's chuckle. "Don't reckon you are. But it seems a shame not to make the most of your chance. What if I offered you five thousand to stay? Five thousand, in cash?"

"Five thousand?" Gatlin blinked. That was half as much as he had in his belt, and the ten thousand he carried had taken much hard work and bargaining to get. Buying a herd, chancing the long drive.

"What would I have to do?" he demanded.

Chasin came out of the stall. "Be yourself," he said, "just

be yourself—but let folks think you're Jim Walker. Then you buy a ranch here . . . I'll give you the money, an' then you hit the trail."

Chasin was trying to double-cross Cary! To get the ranch for himself!

Gatlin hesitated. "That's a lot of money, but these boys toss a lot of lead. I might not live to spend the dough."

"I'll hide you out," Chasin argued. "I've got a cabin in the hills. I'd hide you out with four or five of my boys to stand guard. You'd be safe enough. Then you could come down, put your money on the line, an' sign the papers."

"Suppose they want Walker's signature checked?"

"Jim Walker never signed more'n three, four papers in his life. He left no signatures hereabouts. I've took pains to be sure."

Five thousand because he looked like a man. It was easy money, and he'd be throwing a monkey wrench into Wing Cary's plans. Cary, a man he'd decided he disliked. "Sounds like a deal," he said. "Let's go!"

———

THE CABIN ON the north slope of Bartlett Peak was well hidden, and there was plenty of grub. Pete Chasin left him there with two men to guard him and two more standing by on the trail toward town. All through the following day, Jim Gatlin loafed, smoking cigarettes and talking idly with the two men. Hab Johnson was a big, unshaven hombre with a sullen face and a surly manner. He talked little, and then only to growl. Pink Stabineau was a wide-chested, flat-faced jasper with an agreeable grin.

Gatlin had a clear idea of his own situation. He could use five thousand, but he knew Chasin never intended him to leave the country with it and doubted if he would last an hour after the ranch was transferred to Chasin himself. Yet Gatlin had been around the rough country, and he knew a trick or two of his own. Several times he thought of Lisa Cochrane, but avoided that angle as much as he could.

After all, she had no chance to get the ranch, and Walker was probably dead. That left it between Cary and Chasin.

The unknown Horwick of whom he had heard mention was around, too, but he seemed to stand with Cary in everything.

Yet Gatlin was restless and irritable, and he kept remembering the girl beside him in the darkness and her regrets at breaking up the old outfit. Jim Gatlin had been a hand who rode for the brand; he knew what it meant to have a ranch sold out from under a bunch of old hands. The home that had been theirs gone, the friends drifting apart never to meet again, everything changed.

He finished breakfast on the morning of the second day, then walked out of the cabin with his saddle. Hab Johnson looked up sharply. "Where you goin'?" he demanded.

"Ridin'," Gatlin said briefly, "an' don't worry. I'll be back."

Johnson chewed a stem of grass, his hard eyes on Jim's. "You ain't goin' nowheres. The boss said to watch you an' keep you here. Here you stay."

Gatlin dropped his saddle. "You aren't keepin' me nowheres, Hab," he said flatly. "I've had enough sittin' around. I aim to see a little of this country."

"I reckon not." Hab got to his feet. "You may be a fast hand with a gun, but you ain't gittin' both of us, and you ain't so foolish as to try." He waved a big hand. "Now you go back an' set down."

"I started for a ride," Jim said quietly, "an' a ride I'm takin'." He stooped to pick up the saddle and saw Hab's boots as the big man started for him. Jim had lifted the saddle clear of the ground, and now he hurled it, suddenly, in Hab's path. The big man stumbled and hit the ground on his hands and knees, then started up.

As he came up halfway, Jim slugged him. Hab tottered, fighting for balance, and Gatlin moved in, striking swiftly with a volley of lefts and rights to the head. Hab went down and hit hard, then came up with a lunge, but Gatlin dropped him again. Blood dripped from smashed lips and a cut on his cheekbone.

Gatlin stepped back, working his fingers. His hard eyes flicked to Pink Stabineau, who was smoking quietly, resting on one elbow, looking faintly amused. "You stoppin' me?" Gatlin demanded.

Pink grinned. "Me? Now where did you get an idea like that? Take your ride. Hab's just too persnickety about things. Anyway, he's always wantin' to slug somebody. Now maybe he'll be quiet for a spell."

There was a dim trail running northwest from the cabin and Gatlin took it, letting his horse choose his own gait. The black was a powerful animal, not only good on a trail but an excellent roping horse, and he moved out eagerly, liking the new country. When he had gone scarcely more than two miles, he skirted the edge of a high meadow with plenty of grass, then left the trail and turned off along a bench of the mountain, riding due north.

Suddenly, the mountain fell away before him, and below, in a long finger of grass, he saw the silver line of a creek, and nestled against a shoulder of the mountain, he discerned roofs among the trees. Pausing, Jim rolled a smoke and studied the lie of the land. Northward, for all of ten miles, there was good range. Dry, but not so bad as over the mountain, and in the spring and early summer it would be good grazing land. He had looked at too much range not to detect, from the colors of the valley before him, some of the varieties of grass and brush. Northwest, the range stretched away through a wide gap in the mountains, and he seemed to distinguish a deeper green in the distance.

Old Dave Butler had chosen well, and his XY had been well handled, Gatlin could see as he rode nearer. Tanks had been built to catch some of the overflow from the mountains and to prevent the washing of valuable range. The old man, and evidently Jim Walker, had worked hard to build this ranch into something. Even while wanting money for his relatives in the East, Butler had tried to ensure that the work would be continued after his death. Walker would continue it, and so would Lisa Cochrane.

ALL MORNING HE rode, and well into the afternoon, studying the range but avoiding the buildings. Once, glancing back, he saw a group of horsemen riding swiftly out of the mountains from which he had come and heading for the XY. Reining in, he watched from a vantage point among some huge boulders. Men wouldn't ride that fast without adequate reason.

Morosely, he turned and started back along the way he had come, thinking more and more of Lisa. Five thousand was a lot of money, but so far he had played the game straight. Still, why think of that? In a few days, he'd have the money in his pocket and be headed for Texas. He turned on the brow of the hill and glanced back, carried away despite himself by the beauty of the wide sweep of range.

Pushing on, he skirted around and came toward the cabin from the town trail. He was riding with his mind far away when the black snorted violently and shied. Jim drew up, staring at the man who lay sprawled in the trail. It was the cowhand Pete Chasin had left on guard there. He'd been shot through the stomach, and a horse had been ridden over him.

Swinging down, a quick check showed the man was dead. Jim grabbed up the reins and sprang into the saddle. Sliding a six-gun from its holster, he pushed forward, riding cautiously. The tracks told him that a party of twelve horsemen had come this way.

He heard the wind in the trees, the distant cry of an eagle, but nothing more. He rode out into the clearing before the cabin and drew up. Another man had died here. It wasn't Stabineau or Hab Johnson, but the other guard, who must have retreated to this point for aid.

Gun in hand, Gatlin pushed the door open and looked into the cabin. Everything was smashed, yet when he swung down and went in, he found his own gear intact, under the overturned bed. He threw his bedroll on his horse and loaded up his saddlebags. He jacked a shell into the chamber of the Winchester and was about to mount up when he heard a muffled cry.

Turning, he stared around, then detected a faint stir among the leaves of a mountain mahogany. Warily, he walked over and stepped around the bush.

Pink Stabineau, his face pale and his shirt dark with blood, lay sprawled on the ground. Curiously, there was still a faint touch of humor in his eyes when he looked up at Gatlin. "Got me," he said finally. "It was that damned Hab. He sold us out . . . to Wing Cary. The damn dirty—!"

Jim dropped to his knees and gently unbuttoned the man's shirt. The wound was low down on the left side, and although he seemed to have lost much blood, there was a chance. Working swiftly, he built a fire, heated water, and bathed and then dressed the wound. From time to time, Pink talked, telling him much of what he suspected, that Cary would hunt Chasin down now and kill him.

"If they fight," Jim asked, "who'll win?"

Stabineau grinned wryly. "Cary . . . he's tough, an' cold as ice. Pete's too jumpy. He's fast, but mark my words, if they face each other, he'll shoot too fast and miss his first shot. Wing won't miss!

"But it won't come to that. Wing's a cinch player. He'll chase him down an' the bunch will gun him to death. Wing's bloodthirsty."

Leaving food and a canteen of water beside the wounded man and giving him two blankets, Jim Gatlin mounted. His deal was off then. The thought left him with a distinct feeling of relief. He had never liked any part of it, and he found himself without sympathy for Pete Chasin. The man had attempted a double cross and failed.

Well, the road was open again now, and there was nothing between him and Texas but the miles. Yet he hesitated, and then turned his horse toward the XY. He rode swiftly, and at sundown was at the ranch. He watched it for a time, and saw several hands working around, yet there seemed little activity. No doubt they were waiting to see what was to happen.

Suddenly, a sorrel horse started out from the ranch and swung into the trail toward town. Jim Gatlin squinted his eyes against the fading glare of the sun and saw the rider was a woman. That would be Lisa Cochrane. Suddenly, he swung the black and, touching spurs to the horse, raced down the mountains to intercept her.

Until that moment, he had been uncertain as to the proper course, but now he knew. Yet for all his speed, his eyes were alert and watchful, for he realized the risk he ran. Wing Cary would be quick to discover that as long as he was around and alive, there was danger, and even now the rancher might have his men out, scouring the country for him. Certainly, there were plausible reasons enough, for it could be claimed that he had joined with Chasin in a plot to get the ranch by appearing as Jim Walker.

———

LISA'S EYES WIDENED when she saw him. "I thought you'd be gone by now. There's a posse after you!"

"You mean some of Cary's men?" he corrected.

"I mean a posse. Wing has men on your trail, too, but they lost you somehow. He claims that you were tied up in a plan with Pete Chasin to get the ranch, and that you killed Jim Walker!"

"That *I* did?" His eyes searched her face.

She nodded, watching him. "He says that story about your being here was all nonsense, that you actually came on purpose, that you an' Chasin rigged it that way! You'll have to admit it looks funny, you arriving right at this time and looking just like Jim."

"What if it does?" he demanded impatiently. "I never heard of Jim Walker until you mentioned him to me, and I never heard of the town of Tucker until a few hours before I met you."

"You'd best go, then," she warned. "They're all over the country. Sheriff Eaton would take you in, but Wing wouldn't, nor any of his boys. They'll kill you on sight."

"Yeah," he agreed. "I can see that." Nevertheless, he didn't stir, but continued to roll a cigarette. She sat still, watching him curiously. Finally, he looked up. "I'm in a fight," he admitted, "and not one I asked for. Cary is making this a mighty personal thing, ma'am, an' I reckon I ain't figurin' on leavin'." He struck a match. "You got any chance of gettin' the ranch?"

"How could I? I have no money!"

"Supposin'," he suggested, squinting an eye against the smoke, "you had a pardner—with ten thousand dollars?"

Lisa shook her head. "Things like that don't happen," she said. "They just don't."

"I've got ten thousand dollars on me," Gatlin volunteered, "an' I've been pushed into this whether I like it or not. I say we ride into Tucker now an' we see this boss of yours, the lawyer. I figure he could get the deal all set up for us tomorrow. Are you game?"

"You—you really have that much?" She looked doubtfully at his shabby range clothes. "It's honest money?"

"I drove cattle to Montana," he said. "That was my piece of it. Let's go."

"Not so fast!" The words rapped out sharply. "I'll take that money, an' take it now! Woody, get that girl!"

For reply Jim slapped the spurs to the black and, at the same instant, slapped the sorrel a ringing blow. The horses sprang off together in a dead run. Behind them, a rifle shot rang out, and Jim felt the bullet clip past his skull. "Keep goin'!" he yelled. "Ride!"

At a dead run, they swung down the trail, and then Jim saw a side trail he had noticed on his left. He jerked his head at the girl and grabbed at her bridle. It was too dark to see the gesture, but she felt the tug and turned the sorrel after him, mounting swiftly up the steep side hill under the trees. There the soft needles made it impossible for their horses' hoofs to be heard, and Jim led the way, pushing on under the pines.

That it would be only a minute or so before Cary discovered his error was certain, but each minute counted. A wall lifted on their right, and they rode on, keeping in the intense darkness close under it, but then another wall appeared on their left, and they were boxed in. Behind them they heard a yell, distant now, but indication enough their trail had been found. Boulders and slabs of rock loomed before them, but the black horse turned down a slight incline and worked his way around the rocks. From time to time, they spoke to each other to keep together, but he kept moving, knowing that Wing Cary would be close behind.

The canyon walls seemed to be drawing closer, and the boulders grew larger and larger. Somewhere Jim heard water running, and the night air was cool and slightly damp on his face. He could smell pine, so he knew that there were trees about and they had not ridden completely out of them. Yet Jim was becoming worried, for the canyon walls towered above them, and obviously there was no break.

The black began to climb and in a few minutes walked out on a flat of grassy land. The moon was rising, but as yet there was no light in this deep canyon.

Lisa rode up beside him. "Jim"—it was the first time she had ever called him by name—"I'm afraid we're in for it now. Unless I'm mistaken, this is a box canyon. I've never been up here, but I've heard of it, and there's no way out."

"I was afraid of that." The black horse stopped as he spoke, and he heard water falling ahead. He urged the horse forward, but he refused to obey. Jim swung down into the darkness. "Pool," he said. "We'll find some place to hole up and wait for daylight."

They found a group of boulders and seated themselves among them, stripping the saddles from their horses and picketing them on a small patch of grass behind the boulders. Then, for a long time, they talked, the casual talk of two people finding out about each other. Jim talked of his early life on the Neuces, of his first trip into Mexico after horses when he was fourteen, and how they were attacked by Apaches. There had been three Indian fights that trip, two south of the border and one north of it.

He had no idea when sleep took him, but he awakened with a start to find the sky growing gray and to see Lisa Cochrane sleeping on the grass six feet away. She looked strangely young, with her face relaxed and her lips slightly parted. A dark tendril of hair had blown across her cheek. He turned away and walked out to the horses. The grass was thick and rich there.

He studied their position with care and found they were on a terrace separated from the end wall of the canyon only by the pool, at least an acre of clear, cold water into which a small fall poured from the cliff above. There were a few trees, and some of the scattered boulders they had encountered the previous night. The canyon on which they had come was a wild jumble of boulders and brush surmounted on either side by cliffs that lifted nearly three hundred feet. While escape might be impossible if Wing Cary attempted, as he surely would, to guard the opening, their own position was secure, too, for one man with a rifle might stand off an army from the terrace.

After he had watered the horses, he built a fire and put water on for coffee. Seeing some trout in the pool, he tried his luck, and from the enthusiasm with which they went for his bait, the pool could never have been fished before, or not in a long time. Lisa came from behind the boulders just as the coffee came to a boil. "What is this? A picnic?" she asked brightly.

He grinned, touching his unshaven jaw. "With this beard?" He studied her a minute. "But I'd never guess you spent the night on horseback or sleeping at the end of a canyon," he said. Then his eyes sobered. "Can you handle a rifle? I mean, well enough to stand off Cary's boys if they tried to come up here?"

She turned quickly and glanced down the canyon. The nearest boulders to the terrace edge were sixty yards away, and the approach even that close would not be easy. "I think so," she said. "What are you thinking of?"

He gestured at the cliff. "I've been studyin' that. With a mite of luck, a man might make it up there."

Her face paled. "It isn't worth it. We're whipped, and we might as well admit it. All we can do now is sit still and wait until the ranch is sold."

"No," he said positively. "I'm goin' out of here if I have to blast my way out. They've made a personal matter out of this, now, and"—he glanced at her—"I sort of have a feeling you should have that ranch. Lookin' at it yesterday, I just couldn't imagine it without you. You lived there, didn't you?"

"Most of my life. My folks were friends of Uncle Dave's, and after they were killed, I stayed on with him."

"Did he leave you anything?" he asked.

She shook her head. "I . . . I think he expected me to marry Jim. . . . He always wanted it that way, but we never felt like that about each other, and yet Jim told me after Uncle Dave died that I was to consider the place my home, if he got it."

As they ate, he listened to her talk while he studied the cliff. It wasn't going to be easy, and yet it could be done.

A shout rang out from the rocks behind them, and they both moved to the boulders, but there was nobody in sight. A voice yelled again that Jim spotted as that of Wing Cary. He shouted a reply, and Wing yelled back, "We'll let Lisa come out if she wants, an' you, too, if you come with your hands up!"

Lisa shook her head, so Gatlin shouted back, "We like it here! Plenty of water, plenty of grub! If you want us, you'll have to come an' get us!"

In the silence that followed, Lisa said, "*He* can't stay, not if he attends the auction."

Jim turned swiftly. "Take the rifle. If they start to come, shoot an' shoot to kill! I'm going to take that chance!"

Keeping out of sight behind the worn gray boulders, Gatlin worked his way swiftly along the edge of the pool toward the cliff face. As he felt his way along the rocky edge, he stared down into the water. That pool was deep, from the looks of it. And that was something to remember.

At the cliff face, he stared up. It looked even easier than he thought, and at one time and another, he had climbed worse faces. However, once he was well up the face, he would be within sight of the watchers below . . . or would he?

———

HE PUT A hand up and started working his way to a four-inch ledge that projected from the face of the rock and slanted sharply upward. There were occasional clumps of brush growing from the rock, and they would offer some security. A rifle shot rang out behind him, then a half dozen more, farther off. Lisa had fired at something and had been answered from down the canyon.

The ledge was steep, but there were good handholds, and he worked his way along it more swiftly than he would have believed possible. His clothing blended well with the rock, and by refraining from any sudden movements, there was a chance that he could make it.

When almost two hundred feet up the face, he paused, resting on a narrow ledge, partly concealed by an outcropping. He looked up, but the wall was sheer. Beyond, there was a chimney, but almost too wide for climbing, and the walls looked slick as a blue clay sidehill. Yet study the cliff as he would, he could see no other point where he might climb farther. Worse, part of that chimney was exposed to fire from below.

If they saw him, he was through. He'd be stuck, with no chance of evading their fire. Yet he knew he'd take the chance. Squatting on the ledge, he pulled off his boots, and running a loop of piggin' string through their loops, he slung them from his neck. Slipping thongs over his guns, he got into the chimney and braced his back against one side, then lifted his feet, first his left, then his right, against the opposite wall.

Whether Lisa was watching or not, he didn't know, but almost at that instant she began firing. The chimney was, at this point, all of six feet deep and wide enough to allow for climbing, but very risky climbing. His palms flat against the slippery wall, he began to inch himself upward, working his feet up the opposite wall. Slowly, every movement a danger, his breath coming slow, his eyes riveted on his feet, he began to work his way higher.

Sweat poured down his face and smarted in his eyes, and he could feel it trickling down his stomach under his wool shirt. Before he was halfway up, his breath was coming in great gasps, and his muscles were weary with the strain of opposing their strength against the walls to keep from falling. Then, miraculously, the chimney narrowed a little, and climbing was easier.

He glanced up. Not over twenty feet to go. His heart bounded, and he renewed his effort. A foot slipped, and he felt an agonizing moment when fear throttled him and he seemed about to fall. To fall meant to bound from that ledge and go down, down into that deep green pool at the foot of the cliff, a fall of nearly three hundred feet.

Something smacked against the wall near him and from below there was a shout. Then Lisa opened up, desperately, he knew, to give him covering fire. Another shot splashed splinters in his face and he struggled wildly, sweat pouring from him, to get up those last few feet. Suddenly, the rattle of fire ceased and then opened up again. He risked a quick glance and saw Lisa Cochrane running out in the open, and as she ran, she halted and fired.

She was risking her life, making her death or capture inevitable, to save him.

Suddenly, a breath of air was against his cheek, and he hunched himself higher, his head reaching the top of the cliff. Another shot rang out and howled off the edge of the rock beside him. Then his hands were on the edge, and he rolled over on solid ground, trembling in every limb.

There was no time to waste. He got to his feet, staggering, and stared around. He was on the very top of the mountain, and Tucker lay far away to the south. He seated himself and got his boots on, then slipped the thongs from his guns. Walking as swiftly as his still-trembling muscles would allow, he started south.

There was a creek, he remembered, that flowed down into the flatlands from somewhere near there, an intermittent stream, but with a canyon that offered an easy outlet to the plain below. Studying the terrain, he saw a break in the rocky plateau that might be it and started down the steep mountainside through the cedar, toward that break.

A horse was what he needed most. With a good horse under him, he might make it. He had a good lead, for they must come around the mountain, a good ten miles by the quickest trail. That ten miles might get him to town before they could catch him, to town and to the lawyer who would make the bid for them, even if Eaton had him in jail by that time. Suddenly, remembering how Lisa had run out into the open, risking her life to protect him, he realized he would willingly give his own to save her.

He stopped, mopping his face with a handkerchief. The canyon broke away before him, and he dropped into it, sliding and climbing to the bottom. When he reached the bottom, he started off toward the flat country at a swinging stride. A half hour later, his shirt dark with sweat, the canyon suddenly spread wide into the flat country. Dust hung in the air, and he slowed down, hearing voices.

"Give 'em a blow." It was a man's voice speaking. "Hear any more shootin'?"

"Not me." The second voice was thin and nasal. "Reckon it was my ears mistakin' themselves."

"Let's go, Eaton," another voice said. "It's too hot here. I'm pinin' for some o' that good XY well water!"

Gatlin pushed his way forward. "Hold it, sheriff! You huntin' me?"

Sheriff Eaton was a tall, gray-haired man with a handlebar mustache and keen blue eyes. "If you're Gatlin, an' from the looks of you, you must be, I sure am! How come you're so all-fired anxious to get caught?"

Gatlin explained swiftly. "Lisa Cochrane's back there, an' they got her," he finished. "Sheriff, I'd be mighty pleased if you'd send a few men after her, or go yourself an' let the rest of them go to Tucker with me."

Eaton studied him. "What you want in Tucker?"

"To bid that ranch in for Lisa Cochrane," he said flatly. "Sheriff, that girl saved my bacon back there, an' I'm a grateful man! You get me to town to get that money in Lawyer Ashton's hands, an' I'll go to jail!"

Eaton rolled his chaw in his lean jaws. "Dave Butler come over the Cut-Off with me, seen this ranch, then, an' would have it no other way but that he come back here to settle. I reckon I know what he wanted." He turned. "Doc, you'll git none of that XY water today! Take this man to Ashton, then put him in jail! An' make her fast!"

Doc was a lean, saturnine man with a lantern jaw and cold eyes. He glanced at Gatlin, then nodded. "If you say so, sheriff. Come on, pardner."

They wheeled their horses and started for Tucker, Doc turning from the trail to cross the desert through a thick tangle of cedar and sagebrush. "Mite quicker thisaway. Ain't nobody ever rides it, an' she's some rough."

It was high noon, and the sun was blazing. Doc led off, casting only an occasional glance back at Gatlin. Jim was puzzled, for the man made no show of guarding him. Was he deliberately offering him the chance to make a break? It looked it, but Jim wasn't having any. His one idea was to get to Tucker, see Ashton, and get his money down. They rode on, pushing through the dancing heat waves, no breeze stirring the air, and the sun turning the bowl into a baking oven.

Doc slowed the pace a little. "Hosses won't stand it," he commented, then glanced at Gatlin. "I reckon you're honest. You had a chance for a break an' didn't take it." He grinned wryly. "Not that you'd have got far. This here ol' rifle o' mine sure shoots where I aim it at."

"I've nothin' to run from," Gatlin replied. "What I've said was true. My bein' in Tucker was strictly accidental."

The next half mile they rode side by side, entering now into a devil's playground of boulders and arroyos. Doc's hand went out, and Jim drew up. Buzzards roosted in a tree not far off the trail, a half dozen of the birds. "Somethin' dead," Doc said. "Let's have a look."

Two hundred yards farther and they drew up. What had been a dappled gray horse lay in a saucerlike depression among the cedars. Buzzards lifted from it, flapping their great wings. Doc's eyes glinted, and he spat. "Jim Walker's mare," he said, "an' his saddle."

They pushed on, circling the dead horse. Gatlin pointed. "Look," he said, "he wasn't killed. He was crawlin' away."

"Yeah"—Doc was grim—"but not far. Look at the blood he was losin'."

They got down from their horses, their faces grim. Both men knew what they'd find, and neither man was looking forward to the moment. Doc slid his rifle from the scabbard. "Jim Walker was by way o' bein' a friend o' mine," he said. "I take his goin' right hard."

The trail was easy. Twice the wounded man had obviously lain still for a long time. They found torn cloth where he had ripped up his shirt to bandage a wound. They walked on until they saw the gray rocks and the foot of the low bluff. It was a cul-de-sac.

"Wait a minute," Gatlin said. "Look at this." He indicated the tracks of a man who had walked up the trail. He had stopped there, and there was blood on the sage, spattered blood. The faces of the men hardened, for the deeper impression of one foot, the way the step was taken, and the spattered blood told but one thing. The killer had walked up and kicked the wounded man.

They had little farther to go. The wounded man had nerve, and nothing had stopped him, He was backed up under a clump of brush that grew from the side of the bluff, and he lay on his face. That was an indication to these men that Walker had been conscious for some time, that he had sought a place where the buzzards couldn't get at him.

Doc turned, and his gray white eyes were icy. "Step your boot beside that track," he said, his rifle partly lifted.

Jim Gatlin stared back at the man and felt cold and empty inside. At that moment, familiar with danger as he was, he was glad he wasn't the killer. He stepped over to the tracks and made a print beside them. His boot was almost an inch shorter and of a different type.

"Didn't figger so," Doc said. "But I aimed to make sure."

"On the wall there," Gatlin said. "He scratched somethin'."

Both men bent over. It was plain, scratched with an edge of whitish rock on the slate of a small slab, *Cary done* . . . and no more.

Doc straightened. "He can wait a few hours more. Let's get to town."

———

Tucker's street was more crowded than usual when they rode up to Ashton's office and swung down. Jim Gatlin pulled open the door and stepped in. The tall, gray-haired man behind the desk looked up. "You're Ashton?" Gatlin demanded.

At the answering nod, he opened his shirt and unbuckled his money belt. "There's ten thousand there. Bid in the XY for Cochrane an' Gatlin."

Ashton's eyes sparkled with sudden satisfaction. "You're her partner?" he asked. "You're putting up the money? It's a fine thing you're doing, man."

Gatlin turned to Doc, but the man was gone. Briefly, he

explained what they had found and added, "Wing Cary's headed for town now."

"Headed for town?" Ashton's head jerked around. "He's here. Came in about twenty minutes ago!"

Jim Gatlin spun on his heel and strode from the office. On the street, pulling his hat brim low against the glare, he stared left, then right. There were men on the street, but they were drifting inside now. There was no sign of the man called Doc or of Cary.

Gatlin's heels were sharp and hard on the boardwalk. He moved swiftly, his hands swinging alongside his guns. His hard brown face was cool, and his lips were tight. At the Barrelhouse, he paused, put up his left hand, and stepped in. All faces turned toward him, but none was that of Cary. "Seen Wing Cary?" he demanded. "He murdered Jim Walker."

Nobody replied, and then an oldish man turned his head and jerked it down the street. "He's gettin' his hair cut, right next to the livery barn. Waitin' for the auction to start up."

Gatlin stepped back through the door. A dark figure, hunched near the blacksmith shop, jerked back from sight. Jim hesitated, alert to danger, then quickly pushed on.

The red and white barber pole marked the frame building. Jim opened the door and stepped in. A sleeping man snored with his mouth open, his back to the street wall. The bald barber looked up, swallowed, and stepped back.

Wing Cary sat in the chair, his hair half-trimmed, the white cloth draped around him. The opening door and sudden silence made him look up. "You, is it?" he said.

"It's me. We found Jim Walker. He marked your name, Cary, as his killer."

Cary's lips tightened, and suddenly a gun bellowed, and something slammed Jim Gatlin in the shoulder and spun him like a top, smashing him sidewise into the door. That first shot saved him from the second. Wing Cary had held a gun in his lap and fired through the white cloth. There was sneering triumph in his eyes, and as though time stood still, Jim Gatlin saw the smoldering of the black-rimmed circles of the holes in the cloth.

He never remembered firing, but suddenly Cary's body

jerked sharply, and Jim felt the gun buck in his hand. He fired again then, and Wing's face twisted and his gun exploded into the floor, narrowly missing his own foot.

Wing started to get up, and Gatlin fired the third time, the shot nicking Wing's ear and smashing a shaving cup, spattering lather. The barber was on his knees in one corner, holding a chair in front of him. The sleeping man had dived through the window, glass and all.

Men came running, and Jim leaned back against the door. One of the men was Doc, and he saw Sheriff Eaton, and then Lisa tore them aside and ran to him. "Oh, you're hurt! You've been shot! You've . . . !"

His feet gave away slowly, and he slid down the door to the floor. Wing Cary still sat in the barbershop, his hair halfclipped.

Doc stepped in and glanced at him, then at the barber. "You can't charge him for it, Tony. You never finished!"

THE LION HUNTER
AND THE LADY

THE MOUNTAIN LION stared down at him with wild, implacable eyes and snarled deep in its chest. He was big, one of the biggest Morgan had seen in his four years of hunting them. The lion crouched on a thick limb not over eight feet above his head.

"Watch him, Cat!" Lone John Williams warned. "He's the biggest I ever seen! The biggest in these mountains, I'll bet!"

"You ever seen Lop-Ear?" Morgan queried, watching the lion. "He's half again bigger than this one!" He jumped as he spoke, caught a limb in his left hand and then swung himself up as easily as a trapeze performer.

The lion came to its feet then and crouched, growling wickedly, threatening the climbing man. But Morgan continued to mount toward the lion.

"Give me that pole," Morgan called to the older man. "I'll have this baby in another minute."

"You watch it," Williams warned. "That lion ain't foolin'!"

Never in the year he had been working with Cat Morgan had Lone John become accustomed to seeing a man go up a tree after a mountain lion. Yet in that period Morgan had captured more than fifty lions alive and had killed as many more. Morgan was not a big man as big men are counted, but he was tall, lithe, and extraordinarily strong. He had no hesitation climbing trees, cliffs, or rocky slopes after the big cats, for which he was named, and had made a good thing out of supplying zoo and circus animal buyers.

With a noose at the end of the pole, and only seven feet below the snarling beast, Morgan lifted the pole with great care. The lion struck viciously and then struck again, and in that instant after the second strike, Morgan put the loop around his neck and drew the noose tight. Instantly the cat became a snarling, clawing, spitting fury, but Morgan swung down from the tree, dragging the beast after him.

Before the yapping dogs could close with him, Lone John tossed his own loop, snaring the lion's hind legs. Morgan closed with the animal, got a loop around the powerful fore-legs, and drew it tight. In a matter of seconds the mountain lion was neatly trussed and muzzled, with a stick thrust into its jaws between its teeth, and its jaws tied shut with rawhide. Then Morgan drew a heavy sack around the animal and then tied it at the neck, leaving the lion's head outside.

Straightening, Cat Morgan took out the makin's and began to roll a smoke. "Well," he said, as he put the cigarette between his lips, "that's one more and one less."

Hard-ridden horses sounded and then a half dozen riders burst from the woods and a yell rent the air. "Got 'em, Dave! Don't move, you!" The guns the men held backed up their argument, and Cat Morgan relaxed slowly, his eyes straying from one face to another, finally settling on the big man who rode last from out of the trees.

This man was not tall, but blocky and powerful. His neck was thick and his jaw wide. He was clean-shaven, unusual in this land of beards and mustaches. His face wore a smile of unconcealed satisfaction now, and swinging down he strode toward them. "So, you finally got caught, didn't you? Now how smart do you feel?"

"Who do you think we are?" Morgan asked coolly. "I never saw you before!"

"I reckon not, but we trailed you right here. You've stole your last horse! Shake out a loop, boys! We'll string 'em up right here."

"Be careful with that talk," Lone John said. "We ain't horse thieves an' ain't been out of the hills in more'n a year. You've got the wrong men."

"That's tough," the big man said harshly, "because you hang, here and now."

"Maybe they ain't the men, Dorfman. After all, we lost the trail back yonder a couple of miles." The speaker was a slender man with black eyes and swarthy face.

Without turning Dorfman said sharply, "Shut up! When I want advice from a breed, I'll ask it!"

His hard eyes spotted the burlap sack. The back of it lay toward him, and the lion's head was faced away from him. All he saw was the lump of the filled sack. "What's this? Grub?" He kicked hard at the sack, and from it came a snarl of fury.

Dorfman jumped and staggered back, his face white with shock. Somebody laughed, and Dorfman wheeled, glaring around for the offender. An old man with gray hair and a keen, hard face looked at Morgan. "What's in that sack?" he demanded.

"Mountain lion," Cat replied calmly. "Make a good pet for your loudmouthed friend." He paused and then smiled tolerantly at Dorfman. "If he wouldn't be scared of him!"

Dorfman's face was livid. Furious that he had been frightened before these men, and enraged at Morgan as the cause of it, he sprang at Morgan and swung back a huge fist. Instantly, Cat Morgan stepped inside the punch, catching it on an upraised forearm. At the same instant he whipped a wicked right uppercut to Dorfman's wind. The big man gasped and paled. He looked up, and Morgan stepped in and hooked hard to the body and then the chin. Dorfman hit the ground in a lump.

Showing no sign of exertion, Morgan stepped back. He looked at the older man. "He asked for it," he said calmly. "I didn't mind, though." He glanced at Dorfman, who was regaining his breath and his senses, and then his eyes swung back to the older man. "I'm Cat Morgan, a lion hunter. This is Lone John Williams, my partner. What Lone John said was true. We haven't been out of the hills in a year."

"He's tellin' the truth." It was the half-breed. The man was standing beside the tree. "His hounds are tied right back here, an' from the look of this tree they just caught that cat. The wood is still wet where the bark was skinned by his boots."

"All right, Loop." The older man's eyes came back to Morgan. "Sorry. Reckon we went off half-cocked. I've heard of you."

A wiry, yellow-haired cowhand leaned on his pommel. "You go up a tree for the cats?" he asked incredulously. "I wouldn't do it for a thousand dollars!"

Dorfman was on his feet. His lips were split and there was a cut on his cheekbone. One eye was rapidly swelling. He glared at Morgan. "I'll kill you for this!" he snarled.

Morgan looked at him. "I reckon you'll try," he said. "There ain't much man in you, just brute and beef."

The older man spoke up quickly. "Let's go, Dorf! This ain't catchin' our thief!"

As the cavalcade straggled from the clearing, the man called Loop loitered behind. "Watch yourself, Morgan," he said quietly. "He's bad, that Dorfman. He'll never rest until he kills you, now. He won't take it lyin' down."

"Thanks." Cat's gray-green eyes studied the half-breed. "What was stolen?"

Loop jerked his head. "Some of Dorfman's horses. Blooded stock, stallion, three mares, and four colts."

Morgan watched them go and then walked back down the trail for the pack animals. When they had the cat loaded, Lone John left him to take it back to camp.

Mounting his own zebra dun, Morgan now headed down-country to prospect a new canyon for cat sign. He had promised a dealer six lions and he had four of them. With luck he could get the other two this week. Only one of the hounds was with him, a big, ugly brute that was one of the two best lion dogs he had. A mongrel, Big Jeb was shrewd beyond average. He weighed one hundred and twenty pounds and was tawny as the lions he chased.

The plateau was pine clad, a thick growth that spilled over into the deep canyon beyond, and that canyon was a wicked jumble of wrecked ledges and broken rock. At the bottom he could hear the roar and tumble of a plunging mountain stream, although he had never seen it.

There was no trail. The three of them, man, dog, and horse, sought a path down, working their way along the rim over a thick cover of pine needles. At last Cat Morgan saw the slope fall away steeply, but at such a grade that he could walk the horse to the bottom. Slipping occasionally on the needles, they headed down.

Twice Jeb started to whine as he picked up old lion smell, but each time he was dissuaded by Cat's sharp-spoken command.

There was plenty of sign. In such a canyon as this it should take him no time at all to get his cats. He was walking his horse and rolling a smoke when he heard the sound of an ax.

It brought him up standing.

It was impossible! There could be nobody in this wild area, nobody! Not in all the days they had worked the region had they seen more than one or two men until they encountered the horse-thief hunters.

Carefully, he went on, calling Jeb close to the horse and moving on with infinite care. Whoever was in this wilderness would be somebody he would want to see before he was seen. He remembered the horse thieves whose trail had been lost. Who else could it be?

Instantly, he saw evidence of the correctness of his guess. In the dust at the mouth of the canyon were tracks of a small herd of horses!

Certainly, the thief had chosen well. Nobody would ever find him back in here. The horses had turned off to the right. Following, Cat went down, through more tumbled rock and boulders, and then drew up on the edge of a clearing.

It was after sundown here. The shadows were long, but near the far wall was the black oblong of a cabin, and light streamed through a window and the wide-open door.

Dishes rattled, the sound of a spoon scraping something from a dish, and he heard a voice singing. A woman's voice!

Amazed, he started walking his horse nearer, yet the horse had taken no more than a step when he heard a shrill scream, a cry odd and inhuman, a cry that brought him up short. At the same instant, the light in the house went out and all was silent. Softly, he spoke to his horse and walked on toward the house.

He heard the click of a back drawn hammer, and a cool, girl's voice said, "Stand right where you are, mister! And if you want to get a bullet through your belt buckle, just start something!"

"I'm not moving," Morgan said cautiously. Something strange was going on here.

"What do you want, anyway? Who are you?" she demanded.

"Cat Morgan. I'm a lion hunter. As for bein' invited, I've been a lot of places without bein' invited. Let me talk to your dad or your husband."

"You'll talk to me. Lead your horse and start walkin' straight ahead. My eyes are mighty good, so if you want to get shot, just try me."

With extreme care, Morgan walked on toward the house. When he was within a dozen paces a shrill but harsh voice cried, "Stand where you are! Drop your guns!"

Impatiently, Morgan replied, "I'll stand where I am, but I won't drop my guns. Who the hell is out there?"

Someone moved, and later there was a light. Then the girl spoke. "Come in, you!"

She held a double-barreled shotgun and she was well back inside the door. A tall, slender but well-shaped girl, she had rusty-red hair and a few scattered freckles. She wore a buckskin shirt that failed to conceal the lines of her lovely figure.

Her inspection of him was cool, careful. Then she looked at the big dog that had come in and stood alongside him. "Lion hunter? You the one who has that pack of hounds I hear nearby every day?"

He nodded. "I've been runnin' lions up on the plateau. Catchin' 'em, too." Cat looked carefully around.

She stared. "*Catching* them? *Alive?* Sounds to me like you have more nerve than sense. What do you want live lions for?"

"Sell 'em to some circus or zoo. They bring anywhere from three to seven hundred dollars, dependin' on size and sex. That beats punchin' cows."

She nodded. "It sure does, but I reckon punchin' cows is a lot safer."

"How about you?" he said. "What's a girl doin' up in a

place like this? I didn't have any idea there was anybody back in here."

"Nor has anybody else up to now. You ain't going to tell, are you? If you go out of here an' tell, I'll be in trouble. Dorfman would be down here after me in a minute."

"For stealin' horses?" Morgan asked shrewdly.

Her eyes flashed. "They are not his horses! They are mine! Every last one of them!" She lowered the gun a trifle. "Dorfman is both a bully and a thief! He stole my dad's ranch, then his horses. That stallion is mine, and so are the mares and their get!"

"Tell me about it," he suggested. Carefully, he removed his hat.

She studied him doubtfully and then lowered the gun. "I was just putting supper on. Draw up a chair."

"Let's eat!" a sharp voice yelled. Startled, Cat turned and for the first time saw the parrot in the cage.

"That's Pancho," she explained. "He's a lot of company."

Her father had been a trader among the Nez Perce Indians, and from them he obtained the splendid Appaloosa stallion and the mares from which his herd was started. When Karl Dorfman appeared, there had been trouble. Later, while she was east on a trip, her father had been killed by a fall from a horse. Returning, she found the ranch sold and the horses gone.

"They told me the stallion had thrown him. I knew better. It had been Dorfman and his partner, Ad Vetter, who found Dad. And then they brought bills against the estate and forced a quick sale of all property to satisfy them. The judge worked with them. Shortly after, the judge left and bought a ranch of his own. Dad never owed money to anyone. I believe they murdered him."

"That would be hard to prove. Did you have any evidence?"

"Only what the doctor said. He told me the blows could not have been made by the fall. He believed Dad had been struck while lying on the ground."

Cat Morgan believed her. Whether his own dislike of Dorfman influenced it, he did not know. Somehow the story rang true. He studied the problem thoughtfully.

"Did you get anything from the ranch?"

"Five hundred dollars and a ticket back east." Anger flashed in her eyes as she leaned toward him to refill his cup. "Mr. Morgan, that ranch was worth at least forty thousand dollars. Dad had been offered that much and refused it."

"So you followed them?"

"Yes. I pretended to accept the situation, but discovered where Dorfman had gone and followed him, determined to get the horses back, at least."

————

IT WAS EASIER, he discovered two hours later, to ride to the secret valley than to escape from it. After several false starts, he succeeded in finding the spot where the lion had been captured that day, and then hit the trail for camp. As he rode, the memory of Dorfman kept returning—a brutal, hard man, accustomed to doing as he chose. They had not seen the last of him. That he knew.

Coming into the trees near the camp, Cat Morgan grew increasingly worried, for he smelled no smoke and saw no fire. Speaking to the horse, he rode into the basin and drew up sharply. Before him, suspended from a tree, was a long black burden!

Clapping the spurs to the horse he crossed the clearing and grabbed the hanging figure. Grabbing his hunting knife, he slashed the rope that hung him from the tree and then lowered the old man to the ground. Loosening his clothes, he held his hand over the old man's heart. Lone John was *alive*!

Swiftly, Morgan built a fire and got water. The old man had not only been hanged, but had been shot twice through the body and once through the hand. But he was still alive.

The old man's lids fluttered, and he whispered, "Dorfman. Five of 'em! Hung me—heard somethin'—they done—took off." He breathed hoarsely for a bit. "Figured it—it was you—reckon."

"*Shhh!* Take it easy now, John. You'll be all right."

"No. I'm done for. That rope—I grabbed it—held my weight till I plumb give out."

The wiry old hand gripping his own suddenly eased its grip, and the old man was dead.

Grimly, Cat got to his feet. Carefully, he packed what gear had not been destroyed. The cats had been tied off a few yards from the camp and had not been found. He scattered meat to them, put water within their reach, and returned to his horse. A moment only, he hesitated. His eyes wide open to what lay ahead, he lifted the old man across the saddle of a horse and then mounted his own. The trail he took led to Seven Pines.

It was the gray hour before the dawn when he rode into the town. Up the street was the sheriff's office. He knocked a long time before there was a reply. Then a hard-faced man with blue, cold eyes opened the door. "What's the matter? What's up?"

"My partner's been murdered. Shot down, then hung."

"Hung?" The sheriff stared at him, no friendly light in his eyes. "Who hung him?"

"Dorfman. There were five in the outfit."

The sheriff's face altered perceptibly at the name. He walked out and untied the old man's body, lowering it to the stoop before the office. He scowled. "I reckon," he said dryly, "if Dorfman done it he had good reason. You better light out if you want to stay in one piece."

Unbelieving, Morgan stared at him. "You're the sheriff?" he demanded. "I'm chargin' Dorfman with murder. I want him arrested."

"You want?" The sheriff glared. "Who the devil are you? If Dorfman hung this man he had good reason. He's lost horses. I reckon he figured this hombre was one of the thieves. Now you slope it afore I lock you up."

Cat Morgan drew back three steps, his eyes on the sheriff. "I see. Lock me up, eh? Sheriff, you'd have a mighty hard job lockin' me up. What did you say your name was?"

"Vetter, if it makes any difference."

"Vetter, eh? Ad Vetter?" Morgan was watching the sheriff like a cat.

Sheriff Vetter looked at him sharply. "Yes, Ad Vetter. What about it?"

Cat Morgan took another step back toward his horses, his eyes cold now. "Ad Vetter—a familiar name in the Nez Perce country."

Vetter started as if struck. "What do you mean by that?"

Morgan smiled. "Don't you know," he said, chancing a long shot, "that you and Dorfman are wanted up there for murderin' old man Madison?"

"You're a liar!" Sheriff Vetter's face was white as death and Morgan could almost see the thought in the man's mind and knew that his accusation had marked him for death. "If Dorfman finds you here, he'll hang you, too."

Cat Morgan backed away slowly, watching Vetter. The town was coming awake now, and he wracked his brain for a solution to the problem. Obviously, Dorfman was a man with influence here, and Ad Vetter was sheriff. Whatever Morgan did or claimed was sure to put him in the wrong. And then he remembered the half-breed, Loop, and the older man who had cautioned Dorfman the previous afternoon.

A man was sweeping the steps before the saloon, and Morgan stopped beside him. "Know a man named Loop? A breed?"

"Sure do." The sweeper straightened and measured Morgan. "Huntin' him?"

"Yeah, and another hombre. Older feller, gray hair, pleasant face but frosty eyes. The kind that could be mighty bad if pushed too hard. I think I heard him called Dave."

"That'll be Allen. Dave Allen. He owns the D over A, west of town. Loop lives right on the edge of town in a shack. He can show you where Dave lives."

Turning abruptly, Morgan swung into the saddle and started out of town. As he rounded the curve toward the bridge, he glanced back. Sheriff Vetter was talking to the sweeper. Cat reflected grimly that it would do him but little good, for unless he had talked with Dorfman the previous night, and he did not seem to have, he would not understand Morgan's reason for visiting the old rancher. And Cat knew that he might be wasting his time.

He recognized Loop's shack by the horse in the corral and drew up before it. The breed appeared in the door, wiping an ear with a towel. He was surprised when he saw Cat Morgan, but he listened as Morgan told him quickly about the hanging of Lone John Williams and Vetter's remarks.

"No need to ride after Allen," Loop said. "He's comin' down the road now. Him and Tex Norris."

At Loop's hail, the two riders turned abruptly toward the cabin. Dave Allen listened in silence while Cat repeated his story, only now he told all, not that he had seen the girl or knew where she was, but that he had learned why the horses were stolen, and then about the strange death of old man Madison. Dave Allen sat his horse in silence and listened. Tex spat once, but made no other comment until the end. "That's Dorfman, Boss! I never did cotton to him!"

"Wait." Allen's eyes rested thoughtfully on Cat. "Why tell me? What do you want me to do?"

Cat Morgan smiled suddenly, and when Tex saw that smile he found himself pleased that it was Dorfman this man wanted and not him. "Why, Allen, I don't want you to do anythin'! Only, I'm not an outlaw. I don't aim to become one for a no-account like Dorfman, nor another like this here Vetter. You're a big man hereabouts, so I figured to tell you my story and let you see my side of this before the trouble starts."

"You aim to go after him?"

Morgan shook his head. "I'm a stranger here, Allen. He's named me for a horse thief, and the law's against me, too. I aim to let them come to me, right in the middle of town!"

Loop walked back into his cabin, and when he came out he had a Spencer .56, and mounting, he fell in beside Morgan. "You'll get a fair break," he said quietly, his eyes cold and steady. "I aim to see it. No man who wasn't all right would come out like that and state his case. Besides, you know, that old man Williams struck me like a mighty fine old gent."

DORFMAN WAS STANDING on the steps as they rode up. One eye was barely open, the other swollen. That he had been talking to Vetter was obvious by his manner, although the sheriff was nowhere in sight. Several hard-case cowhands loitered about, the presence creating no puzzle to Cat Morgan.

Karl Dorfman glared at Allen. "You're keepin' strange company, Dave."

The old man's eyes chilled. "You aimin' to tell me who I should travel with, Dorfman? If you are, save your breath. We're goin' to settle more than one thing here today."

"You sidin' with this here horse thief?" Dorfman demanded.

"I'm sidin' nobody. Last night you hanged a man. You're going to produce evidence here today as to why you believed him guilty. If that evidence isn't good, you'll be tried for murder."

Dorfman's face turned ugly. "Why, you old fool! You can't get away with that! Vetter's sheriff, not you! Besides," he sneered, "you've only got one man with you."

"Two," Loop said quietly, "I'm sidin' with Allen—and Cat Morgan, too."

Hatred blazed in Dorfman's eyes. "I never seen no good come out of a breed yet!" he flared. "You'll answer for this!"

Dave Allen dismounted, keeping his horse between himself and Dorfman. By that time a good-sized crowd had gathered about. Tex Norris wore his gun well to the front, and he kept his eyes roving from one to the other of Dorfman's riders. Cat Morgan watched but said nothing.

Four men had accompanied Dorfman, but there were others here who appeared to belong to his group. With Allen and himself there were only Tex and Loop, and yet, looking at them he felt suddenly happy. There were no better men than these, Tex with his boyish smile and careful eyes, Loop with his long, serious face. These men would stick. He stepped then into the van, seeing Vetter approach.

Outside their own circle were the townspeople. These, in the last analysis, would be the judges, and now they were saying nothing. Beside him he felt a gentle pressure against his leg, and looking down saw Jeb standing there. The big dog had never left him. Morgan's heart was suddenly warm and his mind was cool and ready.

"Dorfman!" His voice rang in the street. "Last night you hung my ridin' partner! Hung him for a horse thief, without evidence or reason! I charge you with murder!

"The trail you had followed you lost, as Dave Allen and Loop will testify! Then you took it upon yourself to hang an old man simply because you wanted revenge for that beating I gave you!"

His voice was loud in the street, and not a person in the crowd but could hear every syllable. Dorfman shifted his feet, his face ugly with anger, yet worried, too. Why didn't Vetter stop him? Arrest him?

"Moreover, the horses you were searching for were stolen by you from Laurie Madison, in Montana! They were taken from the ranch after that ranch had been illegally sold, and after you and Vetter had murdered her father."

"That's a lie!" Dorfman shouted. He was frightened now. There was no telling how far such talk might carry. Once branded, a man would have a lot of explaining to do. Suppose what Morgan had told Vetter was true? That they were wanted in Montana? Suppose something had been uncovered?

He looked beyond Morgan at Allen, Loop, and Tex. They worried him, for he knew their breed. Dave Allen was an Indian fighter, known and respected. Tex had killed a rustler only a few months ago in a gun battle. Loop was cool, careful, and a dead shot.

"That's a lie," he repeated. "Madison owed me money. I had papers agin' him!"

"Forged papers! We're reopenin' the case, Dorfman, and this time there won't be any fixed judge to side you!"

Dorfman felt trapped. Twice Cat Morgan had refused to draw when he had named him a liar, but Dorfman knew it was simply because he had not yet had his say. Of many things he was uncertain, but of one he was positive. Cat Morgan was not yellow.

Before he spoke again, Sheriff Ad Vetter suddenly walked into sight. "I been investigatin' your claim," he said to Morgan, "and she won't hold water. The evidence shows you strung up the old man yourself."

Cat Morgan shrugged. "Figured somethin' like that from you, Vetter. What evidence?"

"Nobody else been near the place. That story about a gal is all cock and bull. You had some idea of an alibi when you dragged that in here."

"Why would he murder his partner?" Allen asked quietly. "That ain't sense, Ad."

"They got four lions up there. Them lions are worth money. He wanted it all for himself."

Cat Morgan smiled, and slowly lifting his left hand, he tilted his hat slightly. "Vetter," he said, "you got a lot to learn. Lone John was my partner only in the campin' and ridin'. He was workin' for me. I catch my own cats. I got a contract with Lone John. Got my copy here in my pocket. He's goin' to be a hard man to replace because he'd learned how to handle cats. I liked that old man, Sheriff, and I'm chargin' Dorfman with murder like I said. I want him put in jail—now."

Vetter's face darkened. "You givin' orders now?"

"If you've got any more evidence against Morgan," Allen interrupted, "trot it out. Remember, I rode with Dorfman on that first posse. I know how he felt about this. He was frettin' to hang somebody, and the beatin' he took didn't set well."

Vetter hesitated, glancing almost apologetically at Dorfman. "Come on, Dorf," he said. "We'll clear you. Come along."

An instant only the rancher hesitated, his eyes ugly. His glance went from Allen back to Cat Morgan, and then he turned abruptly. The two men walked away together. Dave Allen looked worried and he turned to Morgan. "You'd better get some evidence, Cat," he said. "No jury would hang him on this, or even hold him for trial."

IT WAS LATE evening in the cabin and Laurie filled Cat's cup once more. Outside, the chained big cats prowled restlessly, for Morgan had brought them down to the girl's valley to take better care of them, much to the disgust of Pancho, who stared at them from his perch and scolded them wickedly.

"What do you think will happen?" Laurie asked. "Will they come to trial?"

"Not they—just Dorfman. Yes, I've got enough now so that I can prove a fair case against him. I've found a man who will testify that he saw him leave town with four riders and head for the hills, and that was after Allen and that crowd had returned. I've checked that rope they used, and it is Dorfman's. He used a hair rope, and most everybody around here uses rawhide riatas. Several folks will swear to that rope."

"Horse thief," Pancho said huskily. "Durned horse thief!"

"Be still," Laurie said, turning on the parrot. "You be still!"

Jeb lifted his heavy head and stared curiously, his head cocked, at the parrot, who looked upon Jeb with almost as much disfavor as the cats.

"These witnesses are all afraid of Dorfman, but if he is brought to trial, they will testify."

Suddenly, Pancho screamed, and Laurie came to her feet, her face pale. From the door there was a dry chuckle. "Don't scream, lady. It's too late for that!" It was Ad Vetter's voice!

Cat Morgan sat very still. His back was toward the door, his eyes on Laurie's face. He was thinking desperately.

"Looks like this is the showdown." That was Dorfman's voice. He stepped through the door and shoved the girl. She stumbled back and sat down hard on her chair. "You little fool! You wouldn't take that ticket and money and let well enough alone! You had to butt into trouble! Now you'll die for it, and so will this lion-huntin' friend of yours."

The night was very still. Jeb lay on the floor, his head flattened on his paws, his eyes watching Dorfman. Neither man had seemed to notice the parrot. "Allen will be askin' why you let Dorfman out," Morgan suggested, keeping his voice calm.

"He don't know it," Vetter said smugly. "Dorf'll be back in jail afore mornin', and in a few days when you don't show up as a witness against him, he'll be freed. Your witnesses won't talk unless you get Dorf on trial. They are scared. As for Dave Allen, we'll handle him later, and that breed, too."

"Too bad it won't work," Morgan said, yet even as he spoke he thought desperately that this was the end. He didn't have a chance. Nobody knew of this place, and the two of them could be murdered here, buried, and probably it would be years before the valley was found. Yet it was Laurie of whom he was thinking now. It would be nothing so easy as murder for her, not to begin with. And knowing the kind of men Dorfman and Vetter were, he could imagine few things worse for any girl than to be left to their mercy.

He made up his mind then. There was no use waiting. No use at all. They would be killed; the time to act was now. He might get one or both of them before they got him. As it was he was doing nothing, helping none at all.

"You two," he said, "will find yourselves looking through cottonwood leaves at the end of a rope!"

"*Horse thief!*" Pancho screamed. "Durned horse thief!"

Both men wheeled, startled by the unexpected voice, and Cat left his chair with a lunge. His big shoulder caught Dorfman in the small of the back and knocked him sprawling against the pile of wood beside the stove. Vetter whirled and fired as he turned, but the shot missed, and Morgan caught him with a glancing swing that knocked him sprawling against the far wall. Cat Morgan went after him with a lunge, just as Dorfman scrambled from the wood pile and grabbed for a gun. He heard a fierce growl and whirled just as Jeb hurtled through the air, big jaws agape.

The gun blasted, but the shot was high and Jeb seized the arm in his huge jaws and then man and dog went rolling over and over on the floor. Vetter threw Morgan off and came to his feet, but Morgan lashed out with a left that knocked him back through the door. Dorfman managed to get away from the dog and sprang through the door just as Ad Vetter came to his feet, grabbing for his gun.

Cat Morgan skidded to a stop, realizing even as his gun flashed up that he was outlined against the lighted door. He felt the gun buck in his hand, heard the thud of Vetter's bullet in the wall beside him, and saw Ad Vetter turn half around and fall on his face. At the same moment a hoarse scream rang out behind the house, and darting around, Morgan saw a dark figure rolling over and over on the ground among the chained lions!

Grabbing a whip, he sprang among them, and in the space of a couple of breaths had driven the lions back. Then he caught Dorfman and dragged him free of the beasts. Apparently blinded by the sudden rush from light into darkness, and mad to escape from Jeb, the rancher had rushed right into the middle of the lions. Laurie bent over Morgan. "Is— is he *dead*?"

"No. Get some water on, fast. He's living, but he's badly bitten and clawed." Picking up the wounded man he carried him into the house and placed him on the bed. Quickly, he cut away the torn coat and shirt. Dorfman was unconscious but moaning.

"I'd better go for the doctor," he said.

"There's somebody coming now, Cat. Riders."

Catching up his rifle, Morgan turned to the door. Then he saw Dave Allen, Tex, and Loop with a half dozen other riders. One of the men in a dark coat was bending over the body of Ad Vetter.

"The man who needs you is in here," Morgan said. "Dorfman ran into my lions in the dark."

Dave Allen came to the door. "This clears you, Morgan," he said, "and I reckon a full investigation will get this lady back her ranch, or what money's left, anyway. And full title to her horses.

"Loop," he added, "was suspicious. He watched Vetter and saw him slip out with Dorfman and then got us and we followed them. They stumbled onto your trail here, and we came right after, but we laid back to see what they had in mind."

"Thanks." Cat Morgan glanced over at Laurie, and their eyes met. She moved quickly to him. "I reckon, Allen, we'll file a claim on this valley, both of us are sort of attached to it."

"Don't blame you. Nice place to build a home."

"That," Morgan agreed, "is what I've been thinkin'."

BILL CAREY RIDES WEST

THE MAN ON the flea-bitten mustang was a gone gosling. That was plain in the way he sat his horse, in the bloodstained bandage on his head and the dark stain on his left shoulder.

The horse was gone, too. The mustang was running raggedly, running the heart out of him to get the man away. The mount swept down through the pines and juniper, hit the bare slope, and stumbled, throwing the rider free.

He hit the ground hard, rolled over twice, and lay still.

JANE CONWAY HAD come to the door of her ranch house when she heard the rattle of flying hoofs. She stood there, shading her eyes up the hill against the sun. No rider was in sight.

"Anybody coming, Janie?" Her father's voice was weak, worn-out with pain and helplessness. "Thought I heard a horse runnin'?"

"I thought so, too," she agreed, puzzled, "but there's nobody in sight."

She went back to preparing supper. It would soon be dark, and they must save the little coal oil they had. There was no telling when they could get more.

UP ON THE hillside, consciousness returned slowly to the wounded man. Somehow, he had rolled over on his back, and he was looking up into a star-sprinkled sky. Cool wind stirred his hair, and he rolled over, getting his right hand under him. Then he pushed himself to his knees.

He felt for his guns. They were still there. Slowly and painfully, for his left arm was stiff and sore, he pushed shells into the two empty guns. Then he got to his feet.

The mustang was dead. He looked down at the little gray horse and found tears in his eyes, though he wasn't a crying man.

"You had nerve, boy," he said softly. "You wasn't much, and I hadn't had you long, but you had the heart of a champion!"

His rifle was in the boot, and he got it out. Then gently he worked the saddle loose. Shouldering it, he staggered painfully to a clump of juniper and dropped the saddle out of sight. For a minute he hesitated, staring down at the heavy saddlebags. He touched one with his toe and it jingled faintly. Gold. Well, it wouldn't do him much good.

———

DOWNHILL HE HEARD metal strike against metal, then the sound of a bucket being dipped into the water—the splat as the side of it struck the surface, then the heavy gulp as the bucket filled. It was a still, cool night. Chambering a shell in his rifle, he started downhill.

No dog barked, and he was puzzled. A ranch in this lonely place would certainly have a dog. When he got closer he could see the house, small and neat, could see the rail corral, the log barn. But there was no bunkhouse. That simplified matters. Bill Carey wasn't wanting any shooting now.

He crossed the hard-packed earth, puzzled by the lack of light. It was early, judging by the stars, and he had been unconscious only a short time.

Something moved in the doorway, and he froze, his rifle covering the bit of white he could see.

"Stand still," he said, his voice low and hard. "I don't want to shoot, but I will if I have to."

"You don't have to shoot," a girl's voice replied. "Who are you? What do you want?"

A woman! Carey frowned, then he moved a step nearer. "Are you alone?" he said, low voiced. "Tell the truth!"

"I always tell the truth," she replied coolly. "Did Ryerson send you?"

"Ryerson?" He was puzzled, yet he lifted his head a little, some response coming to him as he heard the name. "Who's Ryerson?"

"If you don't know that," Jane Conway replied drily, "you're a stranger. Come in."

He walked forward, watching her keenly. The girl made no effort to move until he could almost touch her, then she saw the bandage on his head.

"Oh, you're hurt!" she exclaimed. "What happened? Did your horse throw you?"

"No." He looked at her, watching the effect of his words. "I was shot. By a posse," he added grimly. "I robbed a bank."

"Well"—Jane's voice was even—"every man to his own taste. You better let me have a look at your head."

He stepped into the darkness and waited, hearing her moving about. She went to a window, and he saw the grayness blanked out. Then another window. Then she closed the door. A moment later and a match flared.

They looked at each other then. Jane Conway was a tall girl with gray eyes and ash-blond hair. She was pretty, but too thin, a result of the heat and too much work.

She saw a big man with broad and powerful shoulders, and the biceps revealed through the torn sleeve were a bulge of muscle. His face was haggard and hard, unshaven, with a jaw on which there was a stain of blood. This had evidently run down from under the bandage and dried in the stubble on his cheek.

"Sit down," she said sternly, "and don't worry. There is no law here."

"No law?" He seated himself, stared up at her. "What do you mean, no law?"

She smiled without bitterness. "These are the Shafter Hills," she said. "Haven't you heard?"

He had heard. The Shafter Hills. A patch of wooded and lonely hills, and among them the Hawk's Nest, the place where Hawk Shafter and his outlaws holed up. A nest of the most vicious criminals unhung.

Ryerson! The name struck him now like a blow. Tabat Ryerson! He was here! Bill Carey smiled grimly. He would be. Troubles never came singly.

"You mentioned Ryerson?" he asked. "What about him?"

Jane looked down at him. She could hear her father's even breathing. He was resting. That was something.

"If you were one of his crowd," she said, as though to herself, "you'd not come here."

As she took the bandage from his head and began to bathe it with warm water, she told him, "Tabat Ryerson is Hawk Shafter's right-hand man. He's a killer. Some say he's taking over from the old man. I thought he might have sent someone for me when I heard you coming. Then I knew if he had, you'd come on a horse. He said he was coming for me tonight or tomorrow—to take me to the Nest."

The warm water felt good, and her fingers were gentle.

"You want to go?" Bill Carey asked.

"No." Gently she began combing his tangled hair. "No woman would willingly go to Tabat Ryerson. He's a brute. I'll kill him if I can. I'll kill myself if I can't get him."

He looked at her, shocked. Yet what he saw in her face told him she would do what she said. And she was right. Ryerson was a beast.

"He's been running this country," she went on, softly, "ever since the Hawk had his fall from a bronc. Shafter gave more and more power to Tabat. Every herd that's rustled means beef for him; every robbery means a percentage for him."

She began taking his shirt from his shoulders. There was no nonsense about her. She did what was to be done.

"He'll kill you if he finds you here," she said. "You'd better mount and ride when you've eaten."

"My horse is dead," he said simply. "Run to death."

"We've got several. There's a big black that will carry you. Take him and welcome."

"I can pay," he assured her grimly.

"I don't want stolen money," she replied. "Not any part of it. I'm giving him to you. A man as big as you," she added, "should do more than steal!"

Stung, he looked up quickly. "The bank foreclosed on my

ranch. It was legal, but it wasn't right. He'd told me he'd give me more time. In the spring, maybe I could've made it."

"Listen!" Her voice quickened. "They are coming!"

She looked at him anxiously.

"Go!" she said quickly. "Out the back! You can wait until we're gone, then take the black and go!"

He stood up, huge and formidable in the darkness as she doused the light.

"No," he said sullenly. "I don't run well on no empty stomach."

"Open up, Janie!" The voice outside was sharp and ugly. "Tabat sent us down to get you."

Bill Carey opened the door and stepped outside. He stood there in the vague light of the rising moon.

"Get out!" he snarled. "Get out—*fast*!"

"Who the devil are you?" a man's voice demanded.

Bill Carey's hand made a casual gesture, but the gun that suddenly filled it was not casual.

"You know the lingo this iron speaks," he said. "Get out! And tell Tabat Ryerson to leave this girl alone or I'll kill him!"

"You?" Anger crowded amusement in the man's voice. "Kill Ryerson?"

"Tell him to stay away," Carey continued, his voice ugly, "and tell Hawk Shafter an hombre from Laredo sent that word. If Tabat don't understand that, Shafter will! Now get!"

The two men backed their horses, turned them. A little way off they stopped, talking low voiced.

Carey watched them, his eyes narrow. "I got a rifle," he called drily. "If you two want to get planted, you can do it mighty easy!"

Their horses started moving, and he listened a long time. When he walked inside the girl had lighted the lamp again and was dishing up some food. He watched the steam rise from the coffee she poured into the thick white cup.

When she had put frijoles, potatoes, and cornbread on the tin plate he sat down and started to eat. He did not talk, but ate with the steady eating of a big man who was very, very hungry.

"Ryerson won't take that," Jane said warningly. "He'll come himself next time!"

"Uh-huh. I reckon he will." Bill leaned back in the chair and looked up at her quiet, rather pretty face. "But he won't come until morning. I know Ryerson." He chuckled cynically. "Some men ain't so big as the shadow they throw."

Bill Carey got up from the chair and looked down at the rag rug on the floor.

"Better get some sleep," he advised. "I'll sleep here."

She started to protest, then turned away without speaking. In a few minutes she was back with a blanket. Using his holsters and rolled belt for a pillow, he pulled the blanket over him and stretched out on the floor. . . .

———

DAWN WAS GRAY in the eastern sky when he got up from the floor. After folding the blanket and buckling on his gun belts, he walked outside. Gray serpents of mist lay along the low places and wound back up into the trees along the mountain. The air was fresh, cool.

Bill Carey walked down to the barn and watered the stock. It was merely a matter of lifting a small board and letting water run into the trough in the corral. He forked hay over to the horses, and then studied the country with a knowing eye.

It was a good place for a ranch. There was plenty of water, and the gentle slope toward the creek was subirrigated by water from the mountain. There would be green grass here most of the year. A man could really make a place like this pay. It was even better than his own ranch, so recently lost.

His eyes were somber as he studied the dim trail that led toward the Hawk's Nest. So this was to be it. The old enmity between Tabat Ryerson and himself was to come to a head here, after all this time.

It was a feeling of long standing, this between him and Tabat. Five times they had fought with their fists, and four times Tabat, who was older and stronger, had whipped him. The fifth time, in Tombstone, he had given Ryerson a beating. Tabat had sworn to kill him if they met again.

Yet Tabat Ryerson knew, even as old Hawk Shafter knew,

that Bill Carey was a dangerous man with a six-gun. Had Carey been a vain man there could have been eleven notches on his guns.

Four were for members of a gang which had tried to rustle his cattle. He had cornered them, and in the subsequent fight all four had died in the mountain cabin where they had holed up. Carey, shot three times, had ridden back to town for help.

Three others he killed had been badmen who tried to run a town where he had been marshal. The other four had been gunmen, two of them Hawk Shafter's men, who had tried him out—one in Silver City, two in Sonora, and the last in Santa Fe.

When Bill walked back to the cabin the old man was awake. Jane was working over the fireplace, preparing breakfast.

"How's it, old-timer?" Carey asked, looking down at the grim, white-mustached old man. "Feelin' better?"

"A mite. My heart's bad. Ain't so pert as I used to be." He looked at Carey shrewdly. "You on the dodge? Janie told me some of it."

Carey nodded. "Don't worry. After a bit I'll be on my way."

Conway shook his head. "Ain't that, son. We'd mighty like to have you stay. Place needs a man around, and like I say, I ain't so pert no more." His face became grave. "Them outlaws is bad, son. Ride across my place every once in a while. Regular trail through here. Wasn't so bad when old Hawk was up and around. This Ryerson's poison mean."

———

BILL CAREY WAS drinking coffee when he heard them coming. He was sitting there without a shirt, as Jane had taken his to wash. He got up, a big, brown, powerful man, and walked to the door. He was catlike on his feet, but when he got there, he put his rifle down alongside the door and leaned against the doorjamb, watching the horsemen.

Ryerson could be spotted at a distance. He sat a horse the same as he always had. Carey watched him and the other outlaws with hard, cynical eyes. There was no fear in him, no excitement. This was not a new story, but one he could face without a tremor. He knew he could kill Tabat Ryerson without remorse. The man lived for cruelty and crime. He was nothing but a rattlesnake.

Three men. Carey smiled drily. Tabat must think well of himself. They reined in, and all three dropped to the ground. Bill did not move.

Then Ryerson took two steps, but froze and his face changed. Bill could not be sure whether it was a fear or fury that filled the man he faced as recognition came.

"You, is it?" Ryerson demanded. "What are you butting in here for?"

Carey straightened, and a slow smile came to his hard mouth.

"Maybe because I like these folks," he drawled. "Maybe because I don't like you."

"Don't ask for it, Carey," Ryerson snapped. "Get on your horse and take out, and we'll let you go."

Bill chuckled and ran his fingers through his thick hair.

"Don't wait for me to leave, Tabby," he said drily. "I like this place. Looks like the place a man could build to something."

"You and me can't live in the same country!" Ryerson snarled. "It ain't big enough for the two of us!"

"Uh-huh," Carey agreed. "You sure hit the nail on the head that time. And I'm staying. So if I was you, Tabat Ryerson, I'd fork that mangy bronc you're riding and take out— pronto!"

"You're telling me?" Ryerson's fury was a thing to behold. "Why, you—"

―――――

ALL THREE OUTLAWS went for their guns. Carey's six-shooter bellowed from the doorway, but the thin, tigerlike man on the right had flashed a fast gun, and his shot burned past Carey's stomach. Tabat Ryerson's quick, responsive jerk saved his life. Carey's second shot knocked the tiger man reeling, and a third pinned him to the ground.

Ryerson had leaped to one side, triggering his pistol. He shot wildly, and splinters splattered in Bill's face.

He whipped back inside the door, snapped a quick shot at Tabat, then went through the house with a lunge and slid through the back window just as the other man came around the corner. Bill's feet hit the ground at the instant they saw each other, and both fired.

Bill shot low, and his bullet hit the big man above the belt buckle and knocked him to the ground. The outlaw was game and rolled over, trying to get his feet under him. The second shot was through his lungs and the fellow went down, bloody froth mounting to his lips.

Carey slid to the corner and, crouching, looked around it. A shot split the edge of the log over his head; then he heard a sudden rattle of horse's hoofs and rounded the corner to see Tabat Ryerson racing into the junipers.

He swore softly, knowing it had been only a beginning. Tabat knew who he was now. He would come back loaded for bear. Bill Carey walked toward the man on the ground, his gun ready.

The thin, wiry fellow who had spoiled his first shot was dead.

Carey walked back to the man behind the house. He also was dead. Bill scowled. Two gone, but they were two men who had been killed uselessly. Had it been Ryerson, these two might have lived.

Janie was beside him suddenly, her eyes wide and frightened.

"Are you all right?" she said anxiously.

Her wide gray eyes, frightened for him, stirred him strangely.

"Uh-huh," he said. "They didn't shoot too straight. Neither did I," he added bitterly. "I missed Tabat!"

"You think he'll come back?"

"Sure he'll come back—with help!"

She poured him fresh coffee and he studied the red crease across his stomach. Scarcely a drop of blood showed. The merest graze of the skin. But when she saw it, her face paled.

"You and the old man better get up in the pines," he said. "I'll hold it here."

"No." She shook her head with finality. "This is our home. Besides, Dad can't be moved."

"You're stubborn," he said. "A man could like a girl like you."

She smiled faintly. "Are you making love to me, Bill Carey?"

He flushed, then grinned. "Maybe. If I knew how, I reckon I would. I ain't so much, though. Just a would-be rancher who got gypped out of his ranch and robbed a bank."

"I think you're a good man at heart, Bill."

"Maybe." He shrugged. "I was raised right. Reckon I've come a long way since then."

He glanced at the hills. He was worried. Sheriff Buck Walters wasn't the man to give up. He had been close behind Bill yesterday. What had happened?

His eyes drifted down across the swell of the grassland toward the cottonwood-lined stream far below. The mist still lay in thin, emaciated streamers along the edge of the trees. A man could love this country. He narrowed his eyes, seeing white-faced cattle feeding over that broad, beautiful range. Yes, a man could do a lot here.

Regret stirred within him. That bank. Why did a man have to be such a hotheaded fool? He had been gypped, he knew. He had been tricked into asking for that loan, and he suspected there had been some rustling of his cattle. Well, that didn't matter now. No matter who had been in the right before, robbing the bank had put him in the wrong. He was over the line now, the thin line that divided so many men of the early west into the law-abiding and the lawless.

Reason told him he was one with Tabat Ryerson and the Shafter Hills gang now, but everything within him rebelled against it.

Thinking of old Hawk Shafter, he wondered. The old man was an outlaw, but he had also been a square shooter. Maybe, if—

Carey pushed away the thought. Getting into the Hawk's Nest would be almost impossible.

Sheriff Walters kept returning to his mind. The grim, hard-bitten old lawman would never leave a hot trail. Remembering the sheriff made Bill remember the gold and his saddle. Glancing down the empty trail, he turned and started up the mountain. His left arm was stiff, although he could use it. The bullet had gone through the muscle atop his shoulder. His head wound had been only a graze.

When he reached the junipers, he went into the thick tangle where he had hidden his saddle. The saddle was there, but the saddlebags were flat and empty!

Tabat Ryerson!

He had seen the outlaw come this way. Somehow, in hunting a hiding place from gunfire, the outlaw had found these bags, and had removed the gold.

Carey picked up the bags, and a white piece of paper dropped out. On it was written:

Thanks. You won't need this here where you're going.
                                                    Tabat.

Grimly Bill Carey swung his saddle to his right shoulder and clumped down the mountain, staggering over the rocks. Might as well saddle that big black and be ready. When Walters came, he wouldn't have much time.

Walters! Ryerson! Carey grinned. If the two came at once, that would be something. He chuckled, and the thought kept stirring in his mind.

Walters could have lost his trail the other side of the mountain. Probably even now he was striking around for it. Carey recalled that he had ridden over a long rock ledge back there, and his trail might have been even better hidden than he believed.

If Buck Walters had seen him, he would have come right over here. And Tabat—

Carey dropped the saddle on the hard ground and, picking up his hair rope, shook out a loop. When he had roped the black and led the mount out of the corral, he turned to see Janie standing in the doorway watching him gravely.

Their eyes met briefly; then she turned and walked back into the house, her face grave and serious.

He flushed suddenly. She thought he was leaving. She thought he was running away. Stubbornly he saddled the black, then swung into the saddle. The outlaw bunch might get here before he could find the sheriff. It was a chance he would have to take. His eyes strayed to the door again, and he turned the horse that way.

Janie stepped into the doorway.

"You got a rifle?" he demanded. His voice was harsh without his wanting it so.

She nodded, without speaking.

"Then hand me mine," he said. "If they come, be durned sure it's Ryerson's gang, then use that rifle. Be sure, because it might be a posse."

He held his rifle in his hand and, turning the black, rode off up the mountain down which he had come the night before. Three times he looked back. Each time the trail was empty of dust, and each time he could see the slim, erect figure of the girl in the doorway.

When he had been riding for no more than a half hour, he saw the posse—a tight little knot of some fifteen men, led by a tall, white-haired old man on a sorrel horse. Buck Walters. Beside the white-haired man was a thin, dried-out wisp of a half-breed. Antonio Deer! With that tracker on his trail, it was a wonder they hadn't closed in already.

He looked downhill, then grinned and lifted his rifle. He aimed and fired almost in the same instant, shooting at a tree a dozen feet away from the sheriff. The sorrel reared suddenly; then he saw the posse scatter out, hesitate only an instant, and then, with a whoop, start for him.

He was several hundred yards away and knew the country now. He wheeled his horse and took off through the brush at right angles to the trail, then cut back as though to swing toward the direction from which they had come. Whipping the black around a clump of juniper, he straightened out on the trail for home.

They would be cautious in the trees, he knew. That would delay them a little, at least.

When he came out on the mountainside above the Conway cabin, his heart gave a leap. Down the trail was a cloud of dust, and the horsemen were already within a quarter of a mile of the cabin!

———

TOUCHING SPURS TO the black he started downhill at breakneck speed, hoping against hope they wouldn't see him. Yet he had gone no more than a hundred yards when he heard a distant yell and saw several men cut away from the main body and start for him.

A rifle spoke.

The lead horse stumbled and went down, and Bill Carey saw a tiny puff of smoke lift from a cabin window.

The horsemen broke, scattering wide, but advancing on the house. The black was in a dead run now, and Bill lifted his rifle and took a snapshot at the approaching horsemen who were coming on undaunted by the girl's shot.

At that distance and from a running horse, he didn't expect a hit, nor did he make one, but the shot slowed the horsemen up, as he had hoped. Then he was nearing the cabin, and he saw two more horsemen break from the woods and start for him. They were close up, and he blasted a shot with the rifle held across his chest, and saw one man throw up his hands and plunge to the ground.

The other wheeled his horse, and Bill Carey fired three times as swiftly as he could chamber the shells. He saw the horse go down, throwing the man headlong into the mesquite.

Then the black was charging into the yard, and Bill Carey hit the ground running and made the cabin. The door slammed open as if it had been timed for his arrival, and he lunged inside.

Janie looked up at him, her eyes flashing; then as he crossed to the window, she dropped the bar in place.

A shot splattered glass and punched a hole in the bottom of the washbasin. Another thudded into the log sill below the window. Kneeling beside it, Carey put two quick shots into the brush beyond the corral, and drew back to reload.

Suddenly, from outside, there was a startled yell. Peering out through the window he could see a long stream of horsemen pouring out of the woods and coming down the hill.

Startled, Janie glanced at him.

"The posse!" he said grimly.

Her father was up on one elbow, cursing feebly at his helplessness. A man started from the brush, and Janie's rifle spoke. The fellow stumbled, then scrambled back into the mesquite.

Outside everything was a bedlam of roaring guns now. Somewhere a horse screamed in pain, and shots thudded into the cabin wall.

Jerking out his six-guns, Bill Carey sprang for the door. He threw it open and snapped a quick shot at a man peering around the corral. The fellow let go and dropped flat on his face, arms outspread.

The fight was moving away. Both outlaws and posse were mounted, and it was turning into a running fight.

Bill Carey crouched near the house, his face twisted in a scowl. Tabat Ryerson had come back to kill him. It wasn't like Tabat to run, not at this stage of the game. He would never leave now without killing Carey, or being killed.

Where was he?

Carey slid along the cabin wall, pressed close to the logs. The space between the house and corral was empty, except for a dead horse, lying with its back toward him. There was no movement in the corral. The dead man lay by the corner; another lay across the water trough.

The barn! Carey lunged from shelter and made the corral in a quick sprint. He went around the corral, still running, and dived for the side wall of the barn. When he reached it, he lifted himself slowly, trying to get a look into the window.

Carey could see nothing. Sunlight fell through the open door and across the shafts of an old buckboard. Wisps of hay hung down from the small loft overhead. There was nothing. No movement. No sign of anything human.

The firing had faded into the distance now, and was growing desultory. Somebody was winning and, knowing Buck

Walters and the hard-bitten posse behind him, Bill Carey thought he knew who it was.

Bill Carey eased around the corner and glanced at the door of the barn. When he went through that door he was going to be outlined, stark and clear in the sunlight. But he was going through. Suddenly, he was mad clear through. He had never liked sneaking around. He liked to meet trouble face to face and blast it out, and the devil take the unfortunate or the slow of hand!

He lunged around the doorpost and went through that path of sunlight with a lunge that carried him into the shadow even as a gun bellowed. Dust fell from overhead, but he had seen the flash of the gun. Tabat Ryerson was behind the buckboard!

CAREY STEPPED BACK into the open, firing as he moved. He could see only a vague outline, but he salted that outline down with lead and snapped a few shots around it just for luck. He felt a slug hit him and went to his knees. Then he was up, and standing there swaying, he thumbed shells into a gun and heard Ryerson's gun bellow. Something knocked him back into the corner of the stall; then Tabat came out into the open and Bill drilled him four times over the shirt pocket with four fast-triggered shots, all of them within the outline of the pocket itself.

Tabat folded and went down, and with his heart shot to pieces, he still had life in him. He stared up at Carey, his eyes blazing. "You always had my number, curse you!" he gasped. "I hate the life of you, but you're a mule-tough hombre!"

He sagged, and the light went out of his eyes. Bill Carey automatically thumbed shells into his guns, staring down at the bullet-riddled body. The man was fairly ballasted with lead.

"You're a right tough man, yourself!" he said softly. "A right tough man!"

Carey walked out into the sunlight and saw Sheriff Buck Walters and several of his men riding into the yard. He holstered his guns, and stood there waiting, his mouth tight.

Janie was standing in the doorway, standing as he had seen her so many times, as he knew he could never forget her.

Suddenly Bill Carey felt strange and lonely. Walters looked down.

"Looks like you had a bad time, Bill," he said drily, "tackling all these bandits. I want to apologize, too."

"For what?" Carey stared up at the hard-riding sheriff.

"Why," Buck said innocently, "for thinking you was a thief! Old Hankins swore it was you robbed him, but he's so mean he can't see straight. When we found all that gold in Ryerson's saddlebags, we knew it was him was the thief. He being an outlaw, anyway, stands to reason we was wrong. Anyway, when we seen you this morning you was riding a big black, and that bandit didn't have no black horse."

"Funny, ain't it," Carey agreed, looking cynically at the old sheriff, "how a man can make mistakes?"

"Sure is," Walters agreed. "Even a salty hombre like you might make one." The sheriff patted his horse on the shoulder. "But there'd be no reason for him to make two!"

Bill Carey glanced at Janie Conway, her eyes shining with gladness.

"Why, Buck, I reckon you're right as rain!" Bill said. "I think if I was to leave this here ranch, I'd be making another one! Maybe you all better ride over here sometime and pay us a visit!"

"Us?" Walters looked at him, then at the girl. "Oh! Yeah, I see what you mean." Buck swung his horse around, then glanced down again. "Can she bake a cherry pie?"

"Can she?" Carey grinned. "Why, man, when we get married, she—"

He looked toward the door, and the girl had disappeared.

"Don't bother me, Sheriff," he said, grinning. "Can't you see I'm a family man?"

THE MARSHAL OF SENTINEL

A T EIGHT O'CLOCK Marshal Fitz Moore left his house and walked one block west to Gard's Saloon. It was already open and Fitz glimpsed Gard's swamper sweeping up debris from the previous night. Crossing the street the marshal paused at the edge of the boardwalk to rub out his cigar on the top of the hitching rail. As he did so he turned his eyes but not his head, glancing swiftly up the narrow street alongside the saloon. The gray horse was gone.

Fitz Moore hesitated, considering this, estimating time and probabilities. Only then did he turn and enter the restaurant just ahead of him.

The Fred Henry gang of outlaws had been operating in this corner of the territory for more than two years, but the town of Sentinel had thus far escaped their attention. Fitz Moore, who had been marshal of Sentinel for more than half that time, had taken care to study the methods of Henry and his men. In recent raids the marshal had been slain within minutes before the raid began, or just at the moment the gang arrived.

A persistent pattern of operation had been established and invariably the raids had been timed to coincide with the availability of large sums of money. Such a time had come to Sentinel, as Fitz Moore had reason to know.

So, unless all his reasoning had failed, the town was marked for a raid within the next two hours. And he was marked for death.

Fitz Moore was a tall, spare man with a dark, narrow face and carefully trimmed mustache. Normally his face was still and cold, only his eyes seeming alive and aware.

As he entered the restaurant he removed his black, flat-crowned hat. His frock coat was unbuttoned, offering easy access to the Smith & Wesson Russian .44. The gun was belted high and firmly on his left side just in front of his hipbone, butt to the right, holster at a slight angle.

Three men and two women sat at a long community table but only one murmured a greeting. Jack Thomas glanced up and said, "Good morning, Marshal," his tone low and friendly.

Acknowledging the greeting, the marshal seated himself at the far end of the table and accepted the cup of coffee poured by the Chinese cook.

With his mind closed to the drift of conversation from the far end of the table, he considered the situation that faced him. His days began in the same identical manner, with a survey of the town from each of the six windows of his house. This morning he had seen the gray horse tied behind Peterson's unused corral, where it would not be seen by a casual glance.

With field glasses the marshal examined the horse. It was streaked with the salt of dried sweat, evidence of hard riding. There were still some dark, damp spots indicating the horse had been ridden not long before, and the fact that it was still bridled and saddled indicated it would be ridden soon again. The brand was a Rocking R, not a local brand.

When Fitz Moore had returned to his living room he had seated himself and for an hour he read, occasionally glancing out of the window. The gray horse had not been moved in that time.

At eight when he left for breakfast the horse was still there, but by the time he had walked a block it was gone. And there lingered in the air a faint smell of dust.

Where was the horse?

Down the arroyo, of course, as it gave easy access to the forest and the mountain canyons where there was concealment and water. Taking into consideration the cool night, the sweat-streaked horse . . . not less than six miles to the point of rendezvous.

The rider of the gray had obviously been making a final check with a local source of information. To return to the rendezvous, discuss the situation and return, gave him roughly two hours, perhaps a bit more. He would deal in minimums.

The marshal lighted a cigar, accepted a fresh cup of coffee and leaned back in his chair. He was a man of simple tastes and many appreciations. He knew little of cattle and less of mining, but two things he did know. He knew guns and he knew men.

He was aware of the cool gray eyes of the young woman, the only person present whom he did not know by sight. There was about her a haunting familiarity that disturbed him. He tasted his coffee and glanced out the window. Reason warned him he should be suspicious of any stranger in town at such a time, yet every instinct told him he need not be suspicious of her.

The Emporium Bank would be open in about an hour. A few minutes later Barney Gard would leave his saloon and cross the street with the receipts from Saturday and Sunday. It could be a considerable sum.

The Emporium safe would be unlocked by that time and, as they had been accepting money from ranchers and dust from miners, there would be plenty of cash on hand. In approximately one hour there would be no less than twenty thousand dollars in spendable cash within easy reach of grasping fingers and ready guns.

The Henry gang would, of course, know this. By now they were in the saddle, leaving their camp.

He did not know the name of the stranger who played poker with the Catfish Kid, but he had known the face. It had been the face of a man he had seen in Tascosa with Fred Henry, the bandit leader, some two years ago. Tied to this was the fact that the Rocking R was a brand registered to one Harvey Danuser, alias Dick Mawson, the fastest gunhand in the Henry outfit.

He was suddenly aware that a question had been directed to him. "What would you do, Marshal," Jack Thomas was asking, "if the Henry gang raided Sentinel?"

Fitz Moore glanced at the end of his cigar, then lifted his eyes to those of Jack Thomas. "I think," he said mildly, "I should have to take steps."

The marshal was not a precipitate man. Reputed to be both fast and accurate with a gun, he had yet to be proved locally. Once, not so long ago, he had killed the wrong man. He hoped never to make such a mistake again.

So far he had enforced the peace in Sentinel by shrewd judgment of character, appreciation of developing situations, and tactical moves that invariably left him in command. Authorized to employ an assistant, he had not done so. He preferred to work as he lived . . . alone.

He was, he acknowledged, but only to himself, a lonely man. If he possessed any capacity for affection or friendship it had not been obvious to the people of Sentinel. Yet this was an added strength. No one presumed to take him lightly or expect favoritism.

Long ago he had been considered a brilliant conversationalist and, in a time when a cowboy's saddlebags might carry a volume of the classics as often as Ned Buntline, he was known as a widely read man. He had been a captain in the cavalry of the United States, a colonel in a Mexican revolution, a shotgun messenger for Wells Fargo, and a division superintendent for the Butterfield Stage Line.

Naturally, he knew of the Henry gang. They had been operating for several years but only of late had they shown a tendency to shoot first and talk later. This seemed to indicate that at least one of the gang had become a ruthless killer.

Three marshals had been killed recently, each one shot in the back, an indication that a modus operandi had been established. First kill the marshal, then rob the town. With the marshal out of action it was unlikely resistance could be organized before the outlaws had escaped.

Fitz Moore dusted the ash from his cigar. He thought the gray horse had been standing long enough to let the sweat dry, which meant the horse had been ridden into town before daybreak. At that hour everything was closed and he had seen nobody on the street, and that seemed to indicate the rider had gone in somewhere. And that meant he not only knew where to go at that hour but that he would be welcomed.

So the Henry gang had an accomplice in Sentinel. When the rider of the gray horse left town that accomplice had undoubtedly been awake. With a raid imminent it was unlikely he would risk going back to sleep. What more likely place for him to be than right in this cafe? Here he could not only see who was around but would have a chance to judge the temper of the marshal.

Had anyone entered before he arrived? Fitz Moore knew everyone in the room except the girl with the gray eyes. She was watching him now.

Each of the others had a reason to be here at this hour. Barney Gard had opened his saloon and left it to the ministrations of his swamper. Jack Thomas directed the destinies of the livery stable. Johnny Haven, when he wasn't getting drunk and trying to tree the town, was a hard-working young cowhand and thoroughly trustworthy.

The older of the two women present was Mary Jameson, a plump and gossipy widow, the town's milliner, dressmaker, and Niagara of conversation. When she finished her breakfast she would walk three doors down the street and open her shop.

But what of the girl with the gray eyes? Her face was both delicate and strong, her hair dark and lovely, and she had an air of being to the manor born. Perhaps it was because she did possess that air, like someone from the marshal's own past, that she seemed familiar. And also, he thought reluctantly, she was just the sort of girl—

It was too late now, and there was no use thinking of it. He was not fool enough to believe there could be any such girl for him now. Not after all these years. And there was an antagonism in her eyes that he could not account for.

The marshal glanced thoughtfully at Johnny Haven. The young cowboy was staring sourly at his plate or devoting his attention to his coffee. Over his right temple was a swelling and a cut. This, coupled with a hangover, had left Johnny in a disgruntled mood. Last night had been the end of his monthly spree, and the swelling and the cut were evidences of the marshal's attention.

Johnny caught the marshal's glance and scowled. "You

sure leave a man with a headache, Marshal. Did you have to slug me with a gun barrel?"

Fitz Moore dusted the ash from his cigar. "I didn't have an ax handle and nothing else would have been suitable for the job." He added casually, "Of course, I could have shot you."

Johnny was perfectly aware of the fact and some marshals would have done exactly that. Coming from Fitz Moore it was almost an apology.

"Is it so easy to kill men?" It was the girl with the gray eyes who spoke, her tone low and modulated but shaded with contempt.

"That depends," Fitz Moore replied with dignity, "on who is doing the shooting and the circumstances."

"I think"—and there was a flash of anger in her eyes— "that you would find it easy to kill. You might even enjoy killing. If you were capable of feeling anything at all."

The depth of feeling in her words was so obvious that, surprised, Johnny turned to look at her. Her face had gone pale, her eyes large.

The marshal's expression did not change. He knew Johnny understood, as any westerner would. Johnny Haven had himself given cause for shooting on more than one occasion. He also knew that what Marshal Fitz Moore had just said to him was more of an explanation than he had given any man. Fitz Moore had arrested Johnny Haven six times in as many months, for after every payday Johnny came to town hunting trouble. Yet Fitz Moore knew that Johnny Haven was simply a wild youngster with a lot of good stuff in him, one who simply needed taming and a sense of responsibility.

The girl's tone carried an animosity for which none of them could account, and it left them uneasy.

Barney Gard got to his feet and dropped a dollar on the table. Johnny Haven and then the milliner followed him out. Jack Thomas loitered over his coffee.

"That Henry outfit has me worried, Marshal," he said. "You want me to get down the old scatter-gun, just in case?"

Fitz Moore watched Barney Gard through the window. The saloon keeper had paused on the walk to talk to Johnny Haven. Under the stubble of beard Johnny's face looked clean and strong, reminding the marshal, as it had before, of the face of another young man, scarcely older.

"It won't be necessary," Fitz Moore replied. "I'll handle them in my own way, in my own time. It's my job, you know."

"Isn't that a bit foolish? To refuse help?"

The contempt in her voice stirred him, but he revealed nothing. He nodded gravely. "I suppose it might be, ma'am, but I was hired to do the job and take the risks."

"Figured I'd offer," Thomas said, unwilling to let the matter drop. "You tell me what you figure to do, and I'll be glad to help."

"Another time." The marshal tasted his coffee again and looked directly at the girl. "You are new in Sentinel. Will you be staying long?"

"No."

"Do you have relatives here?"

"No."

He waited, but no explanation was offered. Fitz Moore was puzzled and he studied her from the corners of his eyes. There was no sound in the room but the ticking of the big, old-fashioned clock.

The girl sat very still, the delicate line of her profile bringing to him a faint, lost feeling, a nostalgia from his boyhood when such women as she rode to hounds, when there was perfume on the air, blue grass, picket fences . . .

And then he remembered.

Thomas got to his feet. He was a big, swarthy man, always untidy, a bulge of fat pushing his wide belt. "You need any help, Marshal, you just call on me."

Fitz Moore permitted himself one of his rare smiles. "If there is any trouble, Jack," he said gently, "you will be the first to know."

The clock ticked off the seconds after the door closed, and then the marshal broke the silence.

"Why have you come here? What can you do in this place?"

"All I have is here. Just a little west of here. I left the stage to hire a rig, and then I heard your name and I wanted to see what manner of man it would be who would kill his best friend."

He got to his feet. At that moment he knew better than ever what loneliness could mean.

"You judge too quickly. Each man must be judged against the canvas of his own time, his own world."

"There is only one way to judge a killer."

"Wait. Wait just a little while and you will see what I mean. And please . . . stay off the street today. If you need a rig I will see you get a responsible man." He walked to the door and paused with his hand on the knob. "He used to tell me about you. We talked often of you, and I came to feel I knew you. I had hoped, before it happened, that someday we would meet. But in a different world than this.

"What will happen today I want you to see. I do not believe you lack the courage to watch what happens nor to revise your opinion if you feel you have been mistaken. Your brother, as you were advised in my letter, was killed by accident."

"But you shot him! You were in a great hurry to kill."

"I was in the midst of a gun battle. He ran up behind me."

"To help you."

"I believed him to be a hundred miles away, and in the town where we were I had no friends. It was quick. At such a time, one acts."

"Kill first," she said bitterly, "look afterward."

His features were stiff. "I am afraid that is what often happens. I am sorry."

He lifted the latch. "When you see what happens today, try to imagine how else it might be handled. If you cannot see this as I do, then before night comes you will think me even more cruel than you do now. But you may understand, and where there is understanding there is no hate."

Outside the door he paused and surveyed the street with care. Not much longer now.

Across from him was Gard's Saloon. One block down was his office and across the street from it his small home. Just a little beyond was an abandoned barn. He studied it thoughtfully, glancing again at Gard's with the bank diagonally across the street from the saloon, right past the milliner's shop.

It would happen here, upon this dusty street, between these buildings. Here men would die, and it was his mission to see that good men lived and had their peace, and the bad were kept from crime. As for himself, he was expendable . . . but which was he, the good or the bad?

Fitz Moore knew every alley, every door, every corner in this heat-baked, alkali-stamped cluster of life that would soon become the arena. His eyes turned again to the barn. It projected several feet beyond the otherwise carefully lined buildings. The big door through which hay had once been hoisted gaped wide.

So little time!

He knew what they said about him. "Ain't got a friend in town," he had overheard Mrs. Jameson say. "Lives to hisself in that old house. Got it full of books, folks say. But kill you quick as a wink, he would. He's cold . . . mighty cold."

Was he?

When first he came to the town he found it a shambles, wrecked by a passing trail-herd crew. It had been terrorized by two dozen gamblers and gunmen, citizens robbed by cardsharps and thieves. Robbery had been the order of the day and murder all too frequent. Now it had been six months since the last murder. Did that count for nothing?

He took out a fresh cigar and bit off the end. What was the matter with him today? He had not felt like this in years. Was it what they say happens to a drowning man and his whole life was passing before his eyes, just before the end? Or was it simply that he had seen Julia Heath, the sum and total of all he had ever wanted in a girl? And realizing who she was, realized also how impossible it had become?

They had talked of it, he and Tom Heath, and Tom had written to Julia, suggesting she come west because he had found the man for her. And two weeks later Tom was dead with his, with Fitz Moore's, bullet in his heart.

The marshal walked along the street of false-fronted, weather-beaten buildings. Squalid and dismal as they might seem to a stranger they were the center of the world for those who lived in the country around. Here where mountains and desert met, the town was changing. It was growing with the hopes of its citizens and with the changing of times and needs. This spring, for example, flowers had been planted in the yard of a house near the church, and trees had been trimmed in another.

From a haphazard collection of buildings catering to the needs of a transient people, the town of Sentinel was acquiring a sense of belonging, a consciousness of the future. The days of cattle drives were soon to be gone and where they had walked men would build and plant and harvest.

Fitz Moore turned into the empty alley between the Emporium and the general store. Thoughts of his problem returned. With the marshal dead the town would be helpless until men could gather, choose a leader, and act. For the moment the town would be helpless.

But how did they plan to kill him? That it had been planned he was sure, but it must be done soon and quickly, for the marshal would be the focal point of resistance.

The loft of the abandoned barn commanded a view of the street. The outlaws would come into town riding toward the barn and somewhere along that street the marshal of Sentinel would be walking, covered by a hidden rifleman.

He climbed up the stairs to the barn loft. The dust on the steps had been disturbed. At the top a board creaked under his boot. A rat scurried away. The loft was wide and empty, only dust and wisps of hay, a few cobwebs.

From that wide door the raid might be stopped, but this was not the place for him. His place was down there in that hot, dusty street where his presence would count. Much remained to be done and there was but little time.

Returning to his quarters, Fitz Moore thrust an extra gun into his pocket and belted on a third. Then he put two shotguns into a wool sack. Nobody would be surprised to see him carrying the sack, for he used it to bring firewood from the pile back of Gard's.

Jack Thomas was seated in a chair in front of the livery stable. Barney Gard came from the saloon, glanced at the marshal as if to assure himself of his presence, then went back inside. Fitz Moore paused, relighting his dead cigar, surveying the street over the match and under the brim of his hat.

The topic of what might happen here if the Henry gang attempted to raid was not a new one. There had been much speculation. Several men aside from Thomas had brought up the subject, trying to feel him out, to discover what he thought, what he might plan to do.

Jack Thomas turned his head to watch the marshal. He was a big, easygoing man with a ready smile. He had been one of the first to offer his services.

Johnny Haven, seated on the steps of the saloon's porch, looked up at the marshal, grinning. "How's the town clown?" he asked.

Moore paused beside him, drawing deep on the cigar and permitting himself a glance toward the loft door, almost sixty yards away and across the street. Deliberately, he had placed himself in line with the best shooting position.

"Johnny," he said, "if anything happens to me, I want you to have this job. If nothing happens to me I want you for my deputy."

Young Haven could not have been more astonished, but he was also deeply moved. He looked up at the marshal as if he thought his mind had been affected by the heat. Aside from the words the very fact that the marshal had ventured a personal remark was astonishing.

"You're twenty-six, Johnny, and it's time you grew up. You've played at being the town roughneck long enough. I've looked the town over, and I've decided you're the man for the job."

Johnny ... Tom. He tried to avoid thinking of them together but there was a connection. Tom had been a good man, too. Now he was a good man gone. Johnny was a good one, no question about it. He had heard many stories of how dependable he was out on the range, but Johnny was walking the hairline of the law. A step too far and he could become an outlaw.

Johnny Haven was profoundly impressed. To say that he both respected and admired this tall, composed man was no more than the truth. After Moore arrested him the first time Johnny had been furious enough to kill him, but each time he came into town he found himself neatly boxed and helpless.

Nor had Moore ever taken unfair advantage, never striking one blow more than essential, never keeping the cowhand in jail an hour longer than necessary. And Johnny Haven was honest enough to realize he could never have handled the situation as well.

Anger had dissolved into reluctant admiration. Only stubbornness and the pride of youth had prevented him from giving up the struggle.

"Why pick on me?" He spoke roughly to cover his emotion. "You won't be quitting."

There was a faint suggestion of movement from the loft. The marshal glanced at his watch. Two minutes to ten.

"Johnny—?" The sudden change of tone brought Johnny's head up sharply. "When the shooting starts there are two shotguns in this sack. Get behind the water trough and use one of them. Shoot from under the trough, it's safer."

Two riders walked their horses into the upper end of the street, almost a block away. Two men on powerful horses, much better horses than were usually found on any cow ranch.

Three more riders emerged from the space between the buildings, coming from the direction of Peterson's corral. One of them was riding a gray horse. They were within twenty yards when Barney Gard came from his saloon carrying two canvas bags. He was starting for the bank, and one of the riders reined his horse around to come between Gard and his goal.

"Shotgun in the sack, Gard." The marshal's tone was conversational.

Then, sunlight glinted on a rifle barrel in the loft door. Fitz Moore took one step forward and drew. The thunder of the rifle merged a little late with the bark of his own gun. The rifle clattered, falling, and an arm fell loosely from the loft door.

The marshal's turn was abrupt, yet smooth. "All right, Henry!" His voice was like the blare of a trumpet in the narrow street. "You've asked for it! Now *take* it!"

There was no request for surrender. The rope awaited these men, death rode their hands and their guns.

As one man they went for their guns. The marshal leaped into the street, landing flat-footed and firing. The instant of surprise was his, and they were mounted on nervous horses. His first shot had killed the man in the loft, the second killed Fred Henry.

Behind and to his right a shotgun's deep roar blasted the sun-filled morning. The man on the gray horse died falling, his gun throwing a useless shot into the hot, still air.

A rider leaped his horse at the marshal but Fitz Moore stood his ground and fired. The rider's face seemed to disintegrate under the impact of the bullet.

And then there was silence. The roaring of guns was gone and only the faint smells lingered, the acrid tang of gunpowder, of blood in the dust, the brighter crimson of blood on a saddle.

Johnny Haven got up slowly from behind the horse trough. Barney Gard stared around as if just awakened, the canvas bags at his feet, his hands gripping the shotgun Johnny had thrown him.

There was a babble of sound then and people running into the street, and a girl with gray eyes watching. Those eyes seemed to reach across the street and into the heart of the marshal.

"Only one shot!" Barney Gard exclaimed. "I got off only one shot and missed that one!"

"The Henry gang wiped out!" yelled an excited citizen. "Wait until Thomas hears that!"

"He won't be listenin'," somebody said. "They got him."

Fitz Moore turned like a duelist. "I got him," he said flatly. "He was their man. He tried all morning to find out what I'd do if they showed up. Besides, he was hostler at the livery stable at the time of the holdup at the Springs."

AN HOUR LATER Johnny Haven followed the marshal into the street. Four men were dead, two were in jail.

"How did you know, Marshal?"

"You learn, Johnny. You learn or you die. That's your lesson for today. Learn to be in the right place at the right time and keep your own counsel. You'll be getting my job." His cigar was gone. He bit the end from another and continued.

"Jack Thomas was the only man the rider of the gray horse could have visited without crossing the street. No outlaw would have left the horse he would need for a quick getaway on the wrong side of the street."

When he returned to the eating house Julia Heath was at her table again. She was white and shaken.

"I am sorry, Julia, but now you know how little time there is when guns are drawn. These men came to steal the money honest men worked to earn, and they would have killed again as they have killed before. Such men know only the law of the gun." He placed his hands on the table. "I should have recognized you at once, but I never imagined, after what happened, that you would come. I had forgotten about Tom's ranch. He was proud of you, and he was my best friend."

"But you killed him."

Marshal Moore gestured toward the street. "It was like that. Guns exploding, a man dying almost at my feet, then someone rushing up behind me in a town where I had no friends. I fired at a man who was shooting at me, turned and fired at one running up behind me. I killed my best friend, your brother."

She knew now how it must have been for this man, and she was silent.

"And now?" she asked finally.

"My job goes to Johnny Haven, but I shall stay here and try to help the town grow. This fight should end it for a while. In the meantime the town can mature, settle down, and become a place to live in instead of just a place to camp for the night."

"I—I guess it's worth doing."

"It is." He put down his unlighted cigar. "You will be driving over to settle Tom's estate. When you come back you might feel like stopping off again. If you do, I'll be waiting to see you."

She looked at him, looking beyond the coldness, the stillness, seeing the man her brother must have known. "I think I shall. I think I will stop . . . when I come back."

Out in the street a man was raking dust over the blood. Back of the barn an old hen cackled, and somewhere a pump began to complain rustily, drawing clear water from a deep, cold well.

NO REST FOR THE WICKED

THE BAT-WING DOORS slammed open as if struck by a charging steer and he stood there, framed for an instant in the doorway, a huge man with a golden beard.

Towering five inches over six feet and weighing no less than two hundred and fifty pounds, he appeared from out of the desert like some suddenly reincarnated primeval giant.

He was dirty, not with the dirt of indigence, but with the dust and grime of travel. He smelled of the trail, and his cheekbones had a desert bronze upon them. As he strode to the bar there was something reckless and arrogant about him that raised the hackles on the back of my neck.

Stopping near me he called for a bottle, and when he had it in his hand he poured three fingers into a water glass and took it neat. He followed with its twin before he paused to look around.

He glanced at the tables where men played cards, and then at the roulette wheel. His eyes rested on the faces of the gamblers, and then at last, they swung around to me. Oh, I knew he was coming to me! He had seen me when he came in, but he saved me for last.

His look measured me and assayed me with a long, deliberately contemptuous glance. For I am a big man, too, and the difference between us was slight.

Yet where he was golden, I was black, and where the heat had reddened his cheekbones, I was deep-browned by sun and wind. We measured each other like two strange mastiffs, and neither of us liked the other.

He looked from my eyes to the star on my chest, and to the gun low-slung on my leg. He grinned then, a slow, insulting grin. "The town clown," he said.

"Exactly," I replied, and smiled at him. For I could see it

then, knew it was coming, and I could afford to wait. He measured me again when he saw that I did not anger.

He changed suddenly, shrugging, and smiled. "No offense," he said, and his smile seemed genuine. "I've got a loose tongue." He reached in his pocket and drew out three pieces of ore and rolled them on the bar. "Besides, I feel too good to make trouble for anybody today. I've found the Lost Village Diggings."

His voice had not lifted a note, and yet had he shouted the words he could have received no more attention. Every head turned; men came to their feet; all eyes were on him, all ears listening.

"The Lost Village Diggings!" Old Tom Curtis grabbed the stranger by the arm. "You've found 'em? You actually have? Where?"

The big man chuckled. "Didn't aim to get you folks upset," he said. "Look for yourself." He nudged the ore with his fist. "How's that look?"

Curtis grabbed up the ore. His eyes were hot with excitement. He was almost moaning in his reverence. "Why! Why, it must run three or four thousand dollars to the ton! *Look* at it!"

The chunks of ore were ribbed with gold, bright and lovely to see, but I spared the gold only a glance. My eyes were on the stranger, and I was waiting.

They crowded around him, shouting their questions, eager to see and to handle the ore. He poured another drink, looked at me, then grinned. He lifted the glass in a silent toast.

Yet I think it bothered him. The rest of them were crazy with gold fever, but I was not. And he didn't understand it.

The Lost Village Diggings! Stories of lost mines crop up wherever one goes in the Southwest, but this one was even more fantastic than most. In 1609 three Franciscan friars, accompanied by an officer and sixteen soldiers, started north out of Mexico.

Attacked by Apaches, they turned back, and finally were surrounded among rough mountains by the Indians. During the night they attempted to escape and became lost. By daylight they found themselves moving through utterly strange country, and their directions seemed all wrong. All of them felt curiously confused.

Yet they had escaped the Indians. Thankfully, they kept on, getting deeper and deeper into unfamiliar country. On the third day they found themselves in a long canyon through which wound a stream of fresh, clear water. There were wide green meadows, rich soil, and a scattering of trees. Weary of their flight, they gratefully settled down for a rest. And then they found gold.

The result was, instead of going on, they built houses and a church, and remained to mine the rich ore and reduce it to raw gold. Accompanied by one of the Indians who had come with them, for there had been a dozen of these, four soldiers attempted to find a way out to Mexico. All were killed but one, who returned. Attracted by the healing of one of the Franciscans, several Tarahumares came to live among them, and then more. Several of the soldiers took wives from the Indian girls and settled down. Lost to the outside world, the village grew, cultivated fields, and was fairly prosperous. And they continued to mine gold.

Yet a second attempt to get out of the valley also failed, with three men killed. It was only after thirty years had passed that an Indian succeeded. He got through to Mexico and reported the village. Guiding the party on the return trip, he was bitten by a snake and died.

In 1750 two wandering Spanish travelers stumbled upon a faint trail and followed it to the village. It had grown to a tight, neatly arranged settlement of more than one hundred inhabitants. The travelers left, taking several villagers with them, but they likewise were killed by Apaches. Only one man got through, adding his story to the legend of the Lost Village. From that day on it was never heard of again.

"All my life," Old Tom Curtis said, "I've hoped I'd find that Village! Millions! Millions in gold there, all stored and waiting to be took! A rich mine! Maybe several of 'em!"

The big man with the golden beard straightened up. "My name's Larik Feist," he said. "I found the Lost Village by accident. I was back in the Sierra Madres, and I wounded a boar. I chased after him, got lost, and just stumbled on her."

"Folks still there?" Curtis asked eagerly.

"Nobody," Feist said. "Not a soul. Dead for years, looks like." He leaned against the bar and added three fingers to his glass. "But I found the mine—two of 'em! I found their *arrastra,* too!"

"But the gold?" That was Bob Wright, owner of the livery stable. "Did you find the gold?"

"Not yet," Feist admitted, "but she's got to be there."

There was an excited buzz of talk, but I turned away and leaned against the bar. There was nothing I could say, and nobody who would believe me. I knew men with the gold fever; I'd seen others have it. So I waited, knowing what was coming, and thinking about Larik Feist.

"Sure," Feist said, "I'm goin' back. Think I'm crazy? Apaches? Never seen a one, but what if I did? No Apache will keep me away from there. But I got to get an outfit."

"I'll stake you," Wright said quickly. "I'll furnish the horses and mules."

Men crowded around, tendering supplies, equipment, guns, experience. Feist didn't accept; he just shook his head. "First thing I need," he said, "is some rest. I won't even think about it until morning."

He straightened up and gathered his samples. Reluctantly, the others drew back. Feist looked over at me. "What's the matter, Marshal?" he taunted. "No gold fever?"

"Once," I said, "I had it."

"He sure did!" Old Tom Curtis chuckled. "Why, he was only a boy, but he sure spent some time down there. Say! He'd be a good man to take along! The marshal sure knows the Sierra Madres!"

Feist had started to move away. Now he stopped. His face had a queer look. "You've been there?" he demanded.

"Yes." I spoke quietly. "I've been there."

———

THAT WAS THE beginning of it. Larik Feist avoided me, but his plans went forward rapidly. A company was formed with Feist as president, Wright as treasurer, and Dave Neil as vice-president. When I heard that, I walked down to Neil's house. Marla was out in the yard, picking flowers.

"Your dad home?"

She straightened and nodded to me. It seemed she was absent-minded—not like she usually was when I came around. I stood there, and I looked myself over in her eyes. A big man with wide, thick shoulders and a chest that stretched his shirt tight. With a brown, wind-darkened face and green eyes, a shock of black, curly, and usually untrimmed hair, a battered black sombrero, flat crowned, a faded checked shirt, jeans, and boots with run-down heels.

Feist was different. He had the trail dust off him now and a new outfit of clothes, bought on credit. He looked slick and handsome; his hair was trimmed. He was the talk of the town, with all the girls making big eyes at him. They all knew me. They all knew Lou Morgan, who was half-Irish and half-Spanish.

"Yes, Dad's inside talking to Larik," she said. "Isn't he wonderful?"

That hurt. I'd always figured on Marla being my girl. We'd gone dancing together, we'd been riding together, and we'd talked some about the future—when I'd made my stake and owned a ranch.

"Wonderful?" I shook my head. "That doesn't seem like the right word."

"Oh, Lou!" She was impatient. "Don't be like that! Here Larik comes to town and offers us all a chance to be rich, and you stand around—they all told me how you acted—just like . . . like . . . like you were jealous of him!"

"Why should I be jealous?" I asked.

Her eyes chilled a little. "Oh? You don't think I'm worth being jealous over?"

That made me look at her again. "Oh! So you're in this, too? It's not only all the town's money he wants, but you, too."

"You've no right to talk that way! I like Larik! He's wonderful! And he's doing something for us all!"

Right then I couldn't trust myself to talk. I just walked by her and went into the house. Neil was there, seated at the table with Feist, Wright, Curtis, and John Powers. They all had money on the table, and some sort of legal-looking papers.

"What's the money for?" I asked, quiet-like.

"We're buyin' into Mr. Feist's mine," Powers said. "You'd better dig down in that sock of yours and get a piece of this, Lou. We'll need a good man to protect that gold." Powers turned to Feist and jerked a head at me. "Lou, here, is about the fastest thing with a gun this side of Dodge."

Feist looked up at me, his eyes suddenly cold and careful.

Me, I didn't look at him. "Neil," I said, "do you mean to tell me you men are all paying good cash for something you've never seen? That you're buyin' a pig in a poke?"

"Never seen?" Neil said. "What does that matter? We've seen the gold, haven't we? We all know the Lost Village story, and—"

"All you know," I said, "is an old legend that's been told around for years. You're all like a pack of kids taken in by a slick-talking stranger. Feist"—I looked across the table at him—"you're under arrest. Obtaining money under false pretenses."

Neil lunged to his feet. His face was flushed with anger. "Lou, what's the matter? Have you gone crazy?"

All of them were on their feet protesting. Only Larik Feist had not moved, but for the first time he looked worried.

It was Marla who made it worse. "Dad," she said, "pay no attention to him. Lou's jealous. He's made big tracks around here so long he can't stand for anybody to take the limelight."

That made me red around the gills because it was so untrue. "You think what you like, but I'm taking Feist now."

Feist looked at me, a long measuring look from those cold, careful eyes. He had it in his mind.

"Don't go for that gun," I said quietly. "I want you tried in a court of law, not dead on this floor."

Powers put a hand on Feist's arm. "Go along with him," he said. "And don't worry. We'll take care of you. Far as that goes, we can call a meeting and throw him out of office."

"I'm arresting Feist," I said patiently. "You do whatever you want."

"On what evidence?" Neil demanded.

"I'll present the evidence when it's needed," I said. "Take my word for it, I've evidence for a conviction. This man has never been to Lost Village. He didn't get his gold there. And there's no gold there, anyway, but a little placer stuff."

Whether they heard me or not, I don't know. They were all around me, yelling at me, shaking their fingers in my face. And they were all mad. Neil was probably the maddest of all. Marla, when I looked at her, just turned her head away.

Feist got up when I told him to, and walked out ahead of me. "I might have expected this," he said. "But you won't get away with it."

"Yes, I will. And when they discover what you tried to put over, I'll have trouble keeping you from getting lynched."

When he was locked in a cell, I walked back to my desk and sat down.

Ever feel like the whole world was against you? Well, that's the way I felt then. My girl had turned her back on me. The town's leading citizens—the men I'd worked for, been friends with and protected—they all hated me. And they could throw me out of office, that was true. All they needed was to get the council together.

It was ten miles to the nearest telegraph, but when the stage went out that night, I had a letter on it.

Up and down the street men were gathered in knots, and when they looked at me they glared and muttered. So I walked back to my office and sat down. Feist was stretched on his cot, and he never moved.

Every night now, for months, Marla Neil had brought me a pot of coffee at eight o'clock. When eight drew near, I began to feel both hungry and miserable. There'd be no Marla tonight, that was something I could bet. And then, there she was, a little cool, but with her coffeepot.

"Marla!" I sat up straight. "Then you—?" I got to my feet. "You're not mad at me? Believe me, Marla, when you all know the truth, you won't be. Listen, I can ex—"

She drew back. "Drink your coffee," she said, "or it will get cold. I'll talk to you tomorrow." She turned and hurried away.

So I sat down, ate a cookie, and then poured out the coffee.

It was black and strong, the way I like it . . . very black, and very strong. . . .

———

My MOUTH TASTED funny when I awoke, and I had trouble getting my eyes open. When I got them open I rolled and caught myself just in time. It wasn't my bed I was in. I was on a jail cot.

My head felt like it weighed a ton, but I lifted it and looked around. I was in a cell. Larik Feist's cell.

That brought me to my feet with a lurch. I charged the door.

Locked.

Taking that door in my two hands I shook it until the whole door rattled and banged. I shouted, but there was no sound from outside. I swore. Then I looked around. There was a note on the floor.

I picked it up and read:

You wouldn't listen to us. I hated to do this, but you'd no right to keep the whole town from getting rich just because of your pigheaded jealousy.

It didn't need any signature, for by that time I was remembering that the last thing I had done was drink some coffee Marla had brought me.

The door rattled and I yelled, but nobody answered. I went to the window and looked out. Nobody was stirring, but I knew all those who lived in town weren't gone. They probably had orders to ignore me.

Then I remembered something else. This jail was old and of adobe. I'd been trying for months to get the council to vote the money to make repairs. These bars— As I've said, I weigh two hundred and thirty pounds and none of it anything but bone and muscle. I grabbed those bars and bowed my back, but they wouldn't stir. Yet I knew they weren't well seated. Then I picked up the cot and smashed it, and taking one of the short iron pieces, I used it as a lever between the bars. That did the trick.

In five minutes I was on the street, then back inside after my guns. This time I belted on two of them, grabbed my Winchester, and ran for the livery stable.

Abel was there, but no Wright. I grabbed Abel. "Which way did they go?" I yelled at him.

"Lou!" he protested, pulling back. "You let go of me. I ain't done nothing! And you leave those folks alone. We all going to be rich."

I dropped him, because I remembered something very suddenly. Larik Feist had changed his clothes after he came to town. Had he taken the old ones with him after he got a complete outfit? I made a run for Powers' store, but it was closed. I put one foot against the doorjamb and took the knob in my hands— It came loose, splintering the jamb.

The clothes were there. A worn, dirty shirt, jeans, boots, and a coat. Right there I sat down and looked them over.

Not that I didn't know where they were going now. The Sierra Madres were far south of the border, and nobody except a few Indians and Mexicans who live there knew them better than I. What I wanted to know was where Feist had come from, because one thing I knew. He had not come up from Mexico.

From our town the country slopes gradually away to the Border. It's a long valley running deep into Mexico, and from my usual seat at the jail door I could look down that valley. Yesterday, before Feist appeared, I had been sitting there, and Larik Feist had not come up that valley. Nothing bigger than a mouse or rattlesnake had been moving out there.

Also, just before noon, Luke Fair drove his buckboard in from Tombstone, and he had seen nobody for fifty miles, he said. The fact remained, all things considered, the only way Feist could have come was by train. The railroad was just ten miles away. And I'd spotted soot on his ears, which he'd not washed off.

The dust on his clothes was not desert dust—no more than he could have picked up coming from the railroad. And there were some cinders in the cuffs of his jeans. All his clothes were old except for the coat. It had a label from an El Paso store.

Tracking that party into Mexico offered no problem, but I had another idea. Feist, if I was right, and I was betting my shirt on it, would get his hands on the money that had been put up. Then he would light out and leave them stranded. And I had just a hunch where he would go.

Luke Fair was in front of his shack when I walked up. "You played hob," he said.

I spoke fast: "Luke, get a horse and a couple of pack mules. Take grub and plenty of water. Then light out after that bunch. By the time you get to them, they'll be mighty glad to see you."

Luke looked at me. The fact that he was here and not with them showed he had brains. "What do you mean?"

"I mean," I said, "that about fifty miles south of the Border you'll find that bunch. They'll probably be out of water and afoot."

He took his pipe out of his mouth. "I don't get you."

"That Feist," I said, "was a swindler. He never saw the Sierra Madres. He rigged that story, and that gold never came from Lost Village because there's no gold there, and never was."

"How do you know that?"

"Luke, what was my ma's name?"

"Why"—he looked sort of odd—"it was Ibañez."

"Sure, and Luke, do you know what the name of that officer was who went with the Franciscan friars?"

"No."

"It was Ibañez. Luke, I've had a map to Lost Village ever since I was six. My father went there when he was a boy. I went there, too. There was a village, but folks left it when the springs went dry. There never was any mining close by. The mine they took the gold from was ten miles from the village itself, and it's being worked right now by the Sonora Mining Company."

"Well, I'll be blasted!" Luke just sat there looking at me. "Why didn't you tell them?"

"I started to, but they wouldn't listen. Most of it I didn't want to tell until the trial. I didn't want this gent to know what he was facing. I had no idea they'd go off the way they did."

"If I was you," he said, "I'd let 'em get back the best they can."

"They might not get back," I told him, but he knew that as well as I did. He got up and began gathering his duffel.

"What about you?" he asked.

That made me grin. "Luke, that gent will head for El Paso unless I'm clean off my rocker. He'll ditch them about the second day out and he'll head through the hills toward El Paso. He'll take a straight route, and about noon of the second day after he leaves them, he'll stop for water at a little *pozo,* a place called Coyote Spring. And, Luke, when he gets there, I'll be sitting close by."

IF YOU LOOK on a good big map, and if you pick a place about midway between the Animas and The Alamo Huaco Mountains, and then measure off about twenty-eight miles or so south of the border, you'll find Pozo de Coyote.

The spring is in a plain, but the country is rough and broken, and the ground slopes off a little into a sort of hollow. The *pozo* is in the bottom. At noon, on the second day after I figured Larik Feist would have left them, I was sitting back in the brush with my field glasses and a rifle.

He was more than an hour late getting to the *pozo,* but I was taking it easy back in a tall clump of cholla and mesquite when I heard his horse. It was hot—a still, blazing noon in the desert—when he drew up at the water hole. Lifting my Winchester, I put a bullet into the sand at his feet. He jerked around and jumped for his rifle, but as he lifted it, I smashed two shots at the stock and he dropped it as if it was hot. The stock was splintered. He stood still, his hands lifted.

Getting to my feet, I walked down the hill. Once he made a motion as if to go for his gun, but I fired the rifle from the hip and grooved the leather of his holster. When I stepped into the open we were thirty yards apart.

His face was flushed with heat and fury, and he glared at

me, the hatred a living thing in his eyes. "You, is it? I might have guessed."

"What kept you so long, Feist?" I said. "I've been waiting for you."

"How'd you get here? How'd you know I'd be coming this way?"

"Simple." I smiled at him, taking my time. Then I let him have it, about the map I had, how the Lost Village was not lost, and how there was no mine at all there, and no gold, and never had been.

"So you knew all the time?" It made him furious to think that. "Now what are you going to do?"

"Take you in. I wired Tucson about you. They are checking with other places. You'll be wanted someplace." My rifle tilted a little. "Drop your gun belts," I told him. "Or, if you feel lucky, try to draw."

Gingerly, he moved his hands to his belt buckle, and unfastening it, he let the belt drop. Then, stepping carefully, he moved away. I closed in and picked up the belt, then shucked shells from the gun, and stuck the belt and gun in my saddlebag. Then I spoke again to Larik Feist: "Now get ready to travel, fellow."

THREE DAYS LATER I rode into town with Larik Feist tied to his saddle. He had made one break to escape, and had taken a bad beating. His eyes were swollen shut and his beard matted with blood and sand. He looked like he had been dragged through a lava bed on his face.

There was nobody in sight. Soon a few people, mostly women, came to the doors to watch.

Luke Fair strolled out finally. I handed him the pouch containing the money I'd recovered.

"Where's everybody? Did you find 'em?"

Fair grinned at me. "Found 'em just like you said, afoot and out of water. He'd stolen their horses and canteens, but I rounded up the horses that he'd turned loose, and we started back."

"But where are they?"

He chuckled. "Mining," he said. "Working one of the richest ledges I ever saw. We started back, but about ten miles below the border, Powers sits down for a rest and crumbles a piece of rotten quartz, and it was fairly alive with gold. So they all staked claims an' they all figure that they're going to get rich."

He started to walk toward the bank, then stopped. "Marla's in town," he said.

When I'd jailed Feist, I thought about it. Suddenly, I knew what I was doing. The law could have Feist and they could have their marshal's job.

———

MARLA OPENED THE door for me, and she'd never looked prettier. Some of it was last-minute fixin'—I could easily see that.

My badge was in my hand. "Give that to your dad," I said. "He and Powers wanted a new marshal—now they can get him."

"But they were angry, Lou!" she protested. "They weren't thinking!"

"Be the same way next time. Feist is in jail. You can turn him over to the law, or hang him, or let him rot there, or turn him loose, for all of me."

Marla looked at me. She didn't know what to say. She was pretty and she knew it, but suddenly that meant nothing at all to me and she saw it. And believe me, it was the only thing she had, the only weapon and the only asset. I could see that then, which I couldn't see before.

"Where are you going?" she asked, hesitantly.

My horse was standing there and I stepped into the saddle. "Why," I said, "I've been setting here since I was a kid talking to folks who'd been places. Once I made a trip to Tombstone, but this time, I'm really traveling. I'm going clear to Tucson!"

So I rode out of town, and I never looked back.

Not once.

LONG RIDE HOME

BEFORE HIM ROLLED the red and salmon unknown, the vast, heat-waved unreality of the raw desert, broken only by the jagged crests of the broken bones of upthrust ledges. He saw the weird cacti and the tiny puffs of dust from the hooves of his grulla, but Tensleep Mooney saw no more.

Three days behind him was the Mexican border, what lay ahead he had no idea. Three days behind him lay the Rangers of Texas and Arizona, and a row of graves, some new buried, of men he had killed. But Tensleep Mooney of the fast gun and the cold eye was southbound for peace, away from the fighting, the bitterness, the struggle. He was fleeing not the law alone, but the guns of his enemies and the replies his own must make if he stayed back there.

Here no peon came, and rarely even the Indians. This was a wild and lonely land, born of fire and tempered with endless sunlight, drifting dust-devils and the bald and brassy sky. Sweat streaked his dust-caked shirt, and there were spots flushed red beneath his squinted eyes, and pinkish desert dust in the dark stubble of his unshaven jaws.

Grimly, he pointed south, riding toward something he knew not what. In his pocket, ten silver pesos; in his canteen, a pint of brackish water remaining; in the pack on the stolen burro, a little sowbelly, some beans, rice, and enough ammunition to fight.

Behind him the Carrizal Mountains, behind him the green valleys of the Magdalena, and back along the line, a black horse dead of a rifle bullet, his own horse lying within a half minute's buzzard flight of the owner of the horse he now rode, a bandit who had been too optimistic for his health. And back at Los Chinos, a puzzled peon who had sold a mule and beans to a hard-faced Yanqui headed south.

Mooney had no destination before him. He was riding out of time, riding out of his world into any other world. What lay behind him was death wherever he rode, a land where the law sought him, and the feuding family of his enemies wanted vengeance for their horse-thieving relatives he had killed.

The law, it seemed, would overlook the killing of a horse thief. It would even overlook the killing of a pair of his relatives if they came hunting you, but when it came to the point of either eliminating the males of a big family or being eliminated oneself, they were less happy. Tensleep Mooney had planted seven of them and had been five months ducking bullets before the Rangers closed in; and now, with discretion, Mooney took his valor south of the border.

TWO DAYS HAD passed in which he saw but one lonely rancho; a day since he came across any living thing except buzzards and lizards and an occasional rattler. He swung eastward, toward the higher mountains, hunting a creek or a water hole where he could camp for the night, and with luck, for a couple of days' rest.

The country grew rougher, the cacti thicker, the jagged ridges sloped up toward the heights of the mountains. The brush was scattered but head high, and then he saw a patch of greener brush ahead and went riding toward it, sensing water in the quickened pace of his grulla.

Something darted through the brush, and he shucked his gun with an instinctive draw that would have done credit to Wes Hardin—but he pushed on. He wanted water and he was going to have it if he had to fight for it.

The something was an Indian girl, ragged, thin and wide-eyed. She crouched beside a man who lay on the sand, a chunk of rock in her hand, waiting at bay with teeth bared like some wild thing.

Mooney drew his horse to a stop and holstered his gun. She was thin, emaciated. Her cheekbones were startling against the empty cheeks and sunken eyes. She was barefoot, and the rags she wore covered a body that no man would have looked at twice. On the sand at her feet lay an old Indian, breathing hoarsely. One leg was wrapped in gruesomely dirty rags, and showed blood.

"What's the matter, kid?" he said in hoarse English. "I won't hurt you."

She did not relent, waiting, hopeless in her courage, ready to go down fighting. It was a feeling that touched a responsive chord in Tensleep, of the Wyoming Mooneys. He grinned and swung to the ground, holding a hand up, palm outward. "Amigo," he said, hesitantly. His stay in Texas had not been long and he knew little Spanish and had no confidence in that. "Me amigo," he said, and he walked up to the fallen man.

The man's face was gray with pain, but he was conscious. He was Indian, too. Tarahumara, Mooney believed, having heard of them. He dropped beside the old man and gently began to remove the bandage. The girl stared at him, then began to gasp words in some heathen, unbelievable language.

Mooney winced when he saw the wound. A bullet through the thigh. And it looked as ugly as any wound he had seen in a long time. Turning to the trees, Mooney began to gather dry sticks. When he started to put them together for a fire the girl sprang at him wildly and began to babble shrill protest, pointing off to the west as she did so. "Somebody huntin' you, is there?" Tensleep considered that, looked at the man, the girl, and considered himself, then he chuckled. "Don't let it bother you, kid," he said. "If we don't fix this old man up fast, he'll die. Maybe it's too late now. An'," here he chuckled again, "if they killed all of us, they wouldn't accomplish much."

The fire was made of dry wood and there was little smoke. He put water on to get hot. Then when the water was boiling he went to a creosote bush and got leaves from it and threw them into the water. The girl squatted on her heels and watched him tensely. When he had allowed the leaves to boil for a while, he bathed the wound in the concoction. He knew that some Indians used it for an antiseptic for burns and wounds. The girl watched him, then darted into the brush and after several minutes came back with some leaves which she dampened and then began to crush into a paste. The old man lay very still, his face more calm, his eyes on Mooney's face.

Tensleep looked at the wide face, the large soft eyes that could no doubt be hard on occasion, and the firm mouth. This was a man—he had heard many stories of the endurance of these Tarahumara Indians. They would travel for fabulous miles without food, they possessed an unbelievable resistance to pain in any form. When the wound was thoroughly bathed, the girl moved forward with the paste and signified that it should be bound on the wound. He nodded, and with a tinge of regret he ripped up his last white shirt—the only one he had owned in three years—and bound the wound carefully. He was just finishing it when the girl caught his arm. Her eyes were wide with alarm, but he saw nothing. And then, as he listened, he heard horses drawing nearer and he got to his feet and slid his Winchester from its scabbard. His horse had stopped among the uptilted rocks that surrounded the water hole.

There were three of them, a well-dressed man with a thin, cruel face and two hard-faced vaqueros. "Ah!" The leader drew up. He looked down at the old Indian and said, *"Perro!"* Then his hand dropped to his gun and Tensleep Mooney drew.

The Mexican stopped, his hand on his own gun, looking with amazement into the black and steady muzzle of Tensleep's Colt. A hard man himself, he had seen many men draw a pistol, but never a draw like this. His eyes studied the man behind the gun and he did not like what he saw. Tensleep Mooney was honed down and hard, a man with wide shoulders, a once broken nose, and eyes like bits of gray slate.

"You do not understand," the Mexican said coolly. "This man is an Indio. He is nothing. He is a dog. He is a thief."

"Where I come from," Mooney replied, "we don't shoot helpless men. An' we don't run Injuns to rags when they're afoot an' helpless. We," his mouth twisted wryly, "been hard on our own Injuns, but mostly they had a fightin' chance. I figure this hombre deserves as much."

"You are far from other gringos," the Mexican suggested,

"and I am Don Pedro," he waved a hand, "of the biggest hacienda in one hundred miles. The police, the soldiers, all of them come when I speak. You stop me now and there will not be room enough in this country for you to hide, and then we shall see how brave you are."

"That's as may be," Mooney shrugged, his eyes hard and casual. "You can see how big my feet are right now if you three want to have at it. I'll holster my gun, an' then you can try, all three of you. Of course," Mooney smiled a pleasant, Irish smile, "you get my first shot, right through the belly."

Don Pedro was no fool. It was obvious to him that even if they did kill the gringo it would do nothing for Don Pedro, for the scion of an ancient house would be cold clay upon the Sonora desert: It was a most uncomfortable thought, for Don Pedro had a most high opinion of the necessity for Don Pedro's continued existence.

"You are a fool," he said coldly. He spoke to his men and swung his horse.

"An' you are not," Mooney said, "if you keep ridin'."

Then they were gone and he turned to look at the Indians. They stared at him as if he were a god, but he merely grinned and shrugged. Then his face darkened and he kicked the fire apart. "We got to move," he said, waving a hand at the desert, "away."

He shifted the pack on the burro and loaded the old man on the burro's back. "This may kill you, Old One," he said, "but unless I miss my guess, that hombre will be back with friends."

The girl understood at once, but refused to mount with him, striking off at once into the brush. "I hope you know where you're goin'," he said, and followed on, trusting to her to take them to a place of safety.

She headed south until suddenly they struck a long shelf of bare rock, then she looked up at him quickly, and gestured at the rock, then turned east into the deeper canyons. Darkness fell suddenly but the girl kept on weaving her way into a trackless country—and she herself seemed tireless.

His canteen was full, and when the girl stopped it was at a good place for hiding, but the *tinaja* was dry. He made coffee and the old man managed to drink some, then drank more, greedily.

He took out some of the meat and by signs indicated to the girl what he wanted. She was gone into the brush only a few minutes and then returned with green and yellow inflated stems. "Squaw cabbage!" he said. "I'll be durned! I never knowed that was good to eat!" He gestured to indicate adding it to the stew and she nodded vigorously. He peeled his one lone potato and added it to the stew.

All three ate, then rolled up and slept. The girl sleeping close to her father, but refusing to accept one of his blankets.

They started early, heading farther east. "Water?" he questioned. "Agua?"

She pointed ahead, and they kept moving. All day long they moved. His lips cracked, and the face of the old man was flushed. The girl still walked, plodding on ahead, although she looked in bad shape. It was late afternoon when she gestured excitedly and ran on ahead. When he caught up with her, she was staring at a water hole. It was brim full of water, but in the water floated a dead coyote.

"How far?" he asked, gesturing.

She shook her head, and gestured toward the sky. She meant either the next afternoon or the one following. In either case, there was no help for it. They could never last it out.

"Well, here goes," he said, and swinging down he stripped the saddle from the horse. Then while the girl made her father comfortable, he took the dead coyote from the water hole, and proceeded to build a fire, adding lots of dry wood. When he had a good pile of charcoal, he dipped up some of the water in a can, covered the surface to a depth of almost three inches with charcoal, and then put it on the fire. When it had boiled for a half hour, he skimmed impurities and the charcoal, and the water below looked pure and sweet. He dipped out enough to make coffee, then added charcoal to the remainder. When they rolled out in the morning the water looked pure and good. He poured it off into his canteen and they started on.

Now the girl at last consented to climb up behind him, and

they rode on into the heat of a long day. Later, he swung down and walked, and toward night the girl slipped to the ground. And then suddenly the vegetation grew thicker and greener. The country was impossibly wild and lonely. They had seen nothing, for even the buzzards seemed to have given up.

Then the girl ran on ahead and paused. Tensleep walked on, then stopped dead still, staring in shocked amazement.

Before him, blue with the haze of late evening, lay a vast gorge, miles wide, and apparently, also miles deep! It stretched off to the southwest in a winding splendor, a gorge as deep as the Canyon of the Colorado, and fully as magnificent.

The girl led him to a steep path and unhesitatingly she walked down it. He followed. Darkness came and still she led on, and then suddenly he saw the winking eye of a fire! They walked on, and the girl suddenly called out, and after a minute there was an answering hail. And then they stopped on a ledge shaded by towering trees. Off to the left was the vast gorge; somewhere in its depths a river roared and thundered. Indians came out of the shadows, the firelight on their faces. Behind them was the black mouth of a cave, and something that looked like a wall with windows.

The old man was helped down from the burro and made comfortable. An old woman brought him a gourd dish full of stew and he ate hungrily. The Tarahumaras gathered around, unspeaking but watching. They seemed to be waiting for something, and then it came.

A man in a sombrero pushed his way through the Indians and stopped on the edge of the fire. Obviously an Indian also, he was dressed like a peon. "I speak," he said. "This man an' the girl say much thank you. You are good hombre."

"Thanks," Mooney said, "I was glad to do it. How do I get out of here?"

"No go." The man shook his head. "This man, Don Pedro, he will seek you. Here you must wait . . . here." He smiled. "He will not come. Here nobody will come."

Tensleep squatted beside the fire. That was all right, for a while, but he had no desire to remain in this canyon for long.

He could guess that the gorge would be highly unsafe for anyone who tried to enter without permission of the Tarahumaras. But to get out?

"How about downstream?" He pointed to the southwest. "Is there a way?"

"Sí, but it is long an' ver' difficult. But you wait. Later will be time enough."

They brought him meat and beans, and he ate his fill for the first time in days. Squatting beside the fire he watched the Indians come and go, their dark, friendly eyes on his face, half-respectful, half-curious. The girl was telling them of all that happened, and from her excited gestures he could gather that the story of his facing down Don Pedro and his vaqueros was losing nothing in the telling.

For two days Mooney loitered in the gorge. Here and there along the walls were ledges where crops had been planted. Otherwise the Indios hunted, fished in the river, and went into the desert to find plants. Deeper in the canyon the growth was tropical. There were strange birds, jaguars, and tropical fruit. Once he descended with them, clear to the water's edge. It was a red and muddy stream, thinning down now as the rainy season ended, yet from marks on the walls he could see evidence that roaring torrents had raged through here, and he could understand why the Indios suggested waiting.

"Indio," he said suddenly on the third day, "I must go. Ain't no use my stayin' here longer. I got to ride on."

The Indian squatted on his heels and nodded. "Where you go now?"

"South." He shrugged. "It ain't healthy for me back to the north."

"I see." Indio scratched under his arm. "You are bueno hombre, Señor." From his shirt pocket he took a piece of paper on which an address had been crudely lettered. "Thees rancho," he said, "you go to there. Thees woman, she is Indio, like me. She ver' . . . ver' . . . how you say? Rico?"

"Yeah, I get you." Mooney shrugged. "All I want is a chance to lay around out of sight an' work a little for my grub. Enough to keep me goin' until I go back north." He rubbed his jaw. "Later, if I can get some cash I might go to

Vera Cruz and take a boat for New Orleans, then back to Wyomin'. Yeah, that would be best."

Indio questioned him, and he explained, drawing a map in the dirt. The Indian nodded, grasping the idea quickly. He seemed one of the few who had been outside of the canyon for any length of time. He had, he said, worked for this woman to whom Mooney was to go. She was no longer young, but she was very wise, and her husband dead. Most of those who worked for her were Tarahumaras.

They left at daybreak, and the girl came to the door of the house-cave to motion to him. When he entered, the old Indian lay on the floor on a heap of skins and blankets. He smiled and held up a hand whose grip was surprisingly strong, and he spoke rapidly, then said something to the girl. When she came up to Mooney she held in her hands a skin-wrapped object that was unusually heavy. It was, Mooney gathered, a present. Awkwardly, he thanked them, then came out and mounted.

Once more his pack was rounded and full. Plenty of beans, some jerky, and some other things the Indians brought for him. All gathered together on the ledge to wave good-bye. Indio led him down a steep path, then into a branch canyon, and finally they started up.

It was daylight again before they reached the rancho for which they had started, and they had traveled nearly all day and night. Lost in the chaparral, Tensleep was astonished to suddenly emerge into green fields of cotton. Beyond them were other fields, and some extensive orchards. And then to the wall-enclosed rancho itself.

The old woman had evidently been apprised of his coming, for she stood on the edge of the patio to receive him. She was short, like the other women of her people, but there was something regal in her bearing that impressed Mooney.

"How do you do?" she said, then smiled at his surprise. "Yes, I speak the English, although not well." Later, when he was bathed and shaved, he walked into the wide old room where she sat and she told him that when fourteen, she had been adopted by the Spanish woman who had lived here before her. She had been educated at home, then at school, and finally had married a young Mexican. He died when he was fifty, but she had stayed on at the ranch, godmother to her tribe.

Uneasily, Mooney glanced through the wide door at the long table that had been set in an adjoining room. "I ain't much on society, ma'am," he said. "I reckon I've lived in cow camps too long, among men-folks."

"It's nothing," she said. "There will come someone tonight whom I wish you to meet. Soon he goes north, over the old Smuggler's Crossing into the Chisos Mountains beyond the Rio Grande, and then to San Antonio. You can go with him, and so to your own country."

Suddenly, she started to talk to him of cattle and of Wyoming and Montana. Startled, he answered her questions and described the country. She must have been sixty at least, although Tarahumara women, he had noticed, rarely looked anywhere near their true ages, preserving their youth until very old. She seemed sharp and well informed, and he gathered that she owned a ranch in Texas, and was thinking of sending a herd over the trail to Wyoming.

Suddenly, she turned on him. "Señor, you are a kind man. You are also a courageous one. You seem to know much of cattle and of your homeland. We of the Tarahumara do not forget quickly, but that does not matter now. You will take my herd north. You will settle it on land in Wyoming, buying what you need, you will be foreman of my ranch there."

Mooney was stunned. He started to protest, then relaxed. Why should he protest? He was a cattleman, she was a shrewd and intelligent woman. Behind her questioning there had been a lot of good sense, and certainly, it was a windfall for him. At twenty-seven he had nothing but his saddle, a horse and a burro—and experience.

"I am not a fool, señor," she said abruptly. "You know cattle, you know men. You have courage and consideration. Also, you know your own country best. There is much riches in cattle, but the grass of the northland fattens them best. This is good for you, I know that. It is also good for me. Who else do I know who knows your land of grass and snow?"

When he gathered his things together, she saw the skin-wrapped package. Taking it in her graceful brown fingers she cut the threads and lifted from the skin an image, not quite six inches high, of solid gold.

Mooney stared at it. Now where did those Indians get anything like that?

"From the caves," she told him when he spoke his thought. "For years we find them. Sometimes one here, sometimes one there. Perhaps at one time they were all together, somewhere. It is Aztec, I think, or Toltec. One does not know. It is ver' rich, this thing."

When dinner was over he stood on the edge of the patio with Juan Cabrizo. He was a slim, wiry young man with a hard, handsome face. "She is shrewd, the Old One," he said. "She makes money! She makes it like that!" He snapped his fingers. "I work for her as my father worked for old Aguila, who adopted her. She was ver' beautiful as a young girl." His eyes slanted toward Mooney. "This Don Pedro? You must be careful, sí? Ver' careful. He is a proud and angry man. I think he knows where you are."

At daybreak they rode northeast, and Cabrizo led the way, winding through canyons, coming suddenly upon saddles, crossing ranges into long empty valleys. For two days they rode, and on the second night as they sat by a carefully shielded fire, Mooney nodded at it. "Is that necessary? You think this Don Pedro might come this far?"

Cabrizo shrugged. "I think only the Rio Grande will stop him. He is a man who knows how to hate, amigo; and you have faced him down before his vaqueros. For this he must have your heart."

There were miles of sun and riding, miles when the sweat soaked his shirt and the dust caked his face and rimmed his eyes. And then there was a cantina at Santa Teresa.

Juan lifted a glass to him at the bar of the cantina. "Soon, señor, tomorrow perhaps, you will cross into your own country! To a happy homecoming!"

Tensleep Mooney looked at his glass, then tossed it off. It was taking a chance, going back into Texas, but still, he had crossed the border from Arizona, and they no doubt would not guess he was anywhere around. Moreover, he had crossed as an outlaw, now he returned as a master of three thousand head of cattle.

"Señor!" Cabrizo hissed. "Have a care! It is *he!*"

Tensleep Mooney turned slowly. Don Pedro had come in the door and with him were four men.

Mooney put down his glass and stepped swiftly around the table. Don Pedro turned to face him, squinting his eyes in the bright light. And then the barrel of Mooney's gun touched his belt and he froze, instantly aware. "You're a long ways from home, Don Pedro," he said. "You chasin' another Indian?"

"No, señor." Don Pedro's eyes flashed. "I chase you! And now I have caught you."

"Or I've caught you. Which does it look like?"

"I have fifty men!"

"An' if they make one move, you also have, like I warned you before, a bellyful of lead."

Don Pedro stood still, raging at his helplessness. His men stood around, not daring to move. "Perhaps you are right," he admitted coldly. "Because I am not so skillful with the gun as you."

"You have another weapon?"

"I?" Don Pedro laughed. "I like the knife, señor. I wish I could have you here with the knife, alone!"

Tensleep chuckled suddenly, the old lust for battle rising in his throat like a strong wine, stirring in his veins. "Why, sure! Tell your men we will fight here, with the knife. If I win, I am to go free."

Don Pedro stared at him, incredulous. "You would dare, señor?"

"Will they obey you? Is your word good?"

"My word?" Don Pedro's nostrils flared. "Will they obey me?" He wheeled on them, and in a torrent of Spanish told them what they would do.

Cabrizo said, "He tells them, amigo. He tells them true, but this you must not. It is a way you would die."

Coolly, Mooney shucked his gun belts and placed them on the bar beside Cabrizo. Then from a scabbard inside his belt he drew his bowie knife. "The gent that first used this knife," he said, "killed eight men with it without gettin' out of bed where he was sick. I reckon I can slit the gullet of one man!"

Don Pedro was tall, he was lean and wiry as a whip, and he moved across the floor like a dancer. Mooney grinned and his slate-gray eyes danced with a hard light.

Don Pedro stepped in quickly, light glancing off his knife blade, stepped in, then thrust! And Mooney caught the blade with his own bowie and turned it aside. Pedro tried again, and Mooney again caught the blade and they stood chest to chest, their knives crossed at the guard. Mooney laughed suddenly and, exerting all the power in his big, work-hardened shoulders, thrust the Mexican away from him. Pedro staggered back, then fell to a sitting position.

Furious, he leaped to his feet and lunged, blind with rage. Mooney sidestepped, slipped, and hit the floor on his shoulder. Pedro sprang at him but Mooney came up on one hand and stabbed up. He felt the knife strike, felt it slide open in the stomach of Don Pedro, and then for one long minute their eyes held. Not a foot apart, Don Pedro's whole weight on the haft of Mooney's knife. "Bueno!" Don Pedro said hoarsely. "As God wills!" Slowly, horribly, he turned his eyes toward his men. "Go home!" he said in Spanish. "Go home to my brother. It was my word!"

Carefully, Tensleep Mooney lowered the body to the floor and withdrew the knife. Already the man was dead. "What kind of cussedness is it," he said, "that gets into a man? He had nerve enough." But remembering the Indian, he could find no honest regret for Pedro, only that this had happened.

"Come, amigo," Cabrizo said softly, "it is better we go. It is a long ride to Wyoming, no?"

"A long ride," Tensleep Mooney agreed, "an' I'll be glad to get home."

MISTAKES CAN KILL YOU

MA REDLIN LOOKED up from the stove. "Where's Sam? He still out yonder?"

Johnny rubbed his palms on his chaps. "He ain't comin' to supper, Ma. He done rode off."

Pa and Else were watching him, and Johnny saw the hard lines of temper around Pa's mouth and eyes. Ma glanced at him apprehensively, but when Pa did not speak, she looked to her cooking. Johnny walked around the table and sat down across from Else.

When Pa reached for the coffeepot he looked over at Johnny. "Was he alone, boy? Or did he ride off with that no-account Albie Bower?"

It was in Johnny neither to lie nor to carry tales. Reluctantly, he replied. "He was with somebody. I reckon I couldn't be sure who it was."

Redlin snorted and put down his cup. It was a sore point with Joe Redlin that his son and only child should take up with the likes of Albie Bower. Back in Pennsylvania and Ohio the Redlins had been good God-fearing folk, while Bower was no good, and came from a no-good outfit. Lately, he had been flashing money around, but he claimed to have won it gambling at Degner's Four Star Saloon.

"Once more I'll tell him," Redlin said harshly. "I'll have no son of mine traipsin' with that Four Star outfit. Pack of thieves, that's what they are."

Ma looked up worriedly. She was a buxom woman with a round apple-cheeked face. Good humor was her normal manner. "Don't you be sayin' that away from home, Joe Redlin. That Loss Degner is a gunslinger, and he'd like nothin' so much as to shoot you after you takin' Else from him."

"I ain't afeerd of him." Redlin's voice was flat. Johnny

knew that what he said was true. Joe Redlin was not afraid of Degner, but he avoided him, for Redlin was a small rancher, a onetime farmer, and not a fighting man. Loss Degner was bad all through and made no secret of it. His Four Star was the hangout for all the tough element, and Degner had killed two men since Johnny had been in the country, as well as pistol whipping a half dozen more.

It was not Johnny's place to comment, but secretly he knew the older Redlin was right. Once he had even gone so far as to warn Sam, but it only made the older boy angry.

Sam was almost twenty-one and Johnny but seventeen, but Sam's family had protected him and he had lived always close to the competence of Pa Redlin. Johnny had been doing a man's work since he was thirteen, fighting a man's battles, and making his own way in a hard world.

Johnny also knew what only Else seemed to guess, that it was Hazel, Degner's red-haired singer, who drew Sam Redlin to the Four Star. It was rumored that she was Degner's woman, and Johnny had said as much to Sam. The younger Redlin had flown into a rage and whirling on Johnny had drawn back his fist. Something in Johnny's eyes stopped him, and although Sam would never have admitted it, he was suddenly afraid.

Like Else, Johnny had been adrift when he came to the R Bar. Half dead with pneumonia, he had come up to the door on his black gelding, and the Redlin's hospitality had given him a bed and the best care the frontier could provide, and when Johnny was well, he went to work to repay them. Then he stayed on for the spring roundup as a forty-a-month hand.

He volunteered no information, and they asked him no questions. He was slightly built and below medium height, but broad shouldered and wiry. His shock of chestnut hair always needed cutting, and his green eyes held a lurking humor. He moved with deceptive slowness, for he was quick at work, and skillful with his hands. Nor did he wait to be told about things, for even before he began riding he had mended the buckboard, cleaned out and shored up the spring, repaired the door hinges, and cleaned all the guns.

"We collect from Walters tomorrow," Redlin said suddenly. "Then I'm goin' to make a payment on that Sprague place and put Sam on it. With his own place he'll straighten up and go to work."

Johnny stared at his plate, his appetite gone. He knew what that meant, for it had been in Joe Redlin's mind that Sam should marry Else and settle on that place. Johnny looked up suddenly, and his throat tightened as he looked at her. The gray eyes caught his, searched them for an instant, and then moved away, and Johnny watched the lamplight in her ash blonde hair, turning it to old gold.

He pushed back from the table and excused himself, going out into the moonlit yard. He lived in a room he had built into a corner of the barn. They had objected at first, wanting him to stay at the house, but he could not bear being close to Else, and then he had the lonely man's feeling for seclusion. Actually, it had other advantages, for it kept him near his horse, and he never knew when he might want to ride on.

That black gelding and his new .44 Winchester had been the only incongruous notes in his getup when he arrived at the R Bar, for he had hidden his guns and his best clothes in a cave up the mountain, riding down to the ranch in shabby range clothes with only the .44 Winchester for safety.

He had watched the ranch for several hours despite his illness before venturing down to the door. It paid to be careful, and there were men about who might know him.

Later, when securely in his own room, he had returned to his cache and dug out the guns and brought his outfit down to the ranch. Yet nobody had ever seen him with guns on, nor would they, if he was lucky.

The gelding turned its head and nickered at him, rolling its eyes at him. Johnny walked into the stall and stood there, one hand on the horse's neck. "Little bit longer, boy, then we'll go. You sit tight now."

There was another reason why he should leave now, for he had learned from Sam that Flitch was in town. Flitch had been on the Gila during the fight, and he had been a friend of Card Wells, whom Johnny had killed at Picacho. Moreover, Flitch had been in Cimarron a year before that when Johnny, only fifteen then, had evened the score with the men who had killed his father and stolen their outfit. Johnny had gunned two of them down and put the third into the hospital.

Johnny was already on the range when Sam Redlin rode away the next morning to make his collection. Pa Redlin rode out with Else and found Johnny branding a yearling. Pa waved and rode on, but Else sat on her horse and watched him. "You're a good hand, Johnny," she said when he released the calf. "You should have your own outfit."

"That's what I want most," he admitted. "But I reckon I'll never have it."

"You can if you want it enough. Is it because of what's behind you?"

He looked up quickly then. "What do you know of me?"

"Nothing, Johnny, but what you've told us. But once, when I started into the barn for eggs, you had your shirt off and I saw those bullet scars. I know bullet scars because my own father had them. And you've never told us anything, which usually means there's something you aren't anxious to tell."

"I guess you're right." He tightened the girth on his saddle. "There ain't much to tell, though. I come west with my pa, and he was a lunger. I drove the wagon myself after we left Independence. Clean to Caldwell, then on to Santa Fe. We got us a little outfit with what Pa had left, and some mean fellers stole it off us, and they killed Pa."

Joe Redlin rode back to join them as Johnny was swinging into the saddle. He turned and glanced down at the valley. "Reckon that range won't get much use, Johnny," he said anxiously, "and the stock sure need it. Fair to middlin' grass, but too far to water."

"That draw, now," Johnny suggested. "I been thinkin' about that. It would take a sight of work, but a couple of good men with teams and some elbow grease could build them a dam. There's a sight of water comes down when it rains, enough to last most of the summer if it was dammed. Maybe even the whole year."

The three horses started walking toward the draw, and Johnny pointed out what he meant. "A feller over to Mobeetie did that one time," he said, "and it washed his dam out twice, but the third time she held, and he had him a little lake, all the year around."

"That's a good idea, Johnny." Redlin studied the setup and then nodded. "A right good idea."

"Sam and me could do it," Johnny suggested, avoiding Pa Redlin's eyes.

Pa Redlin said nothing, but both Johnny and Else knew that Sam was not exactly ambitious about extra work. A good hand, Sam was, strong and capable, but he was big-headed about things and was little inclined to sticking with a job.

"Reminds me," Pa said, glancing at the sun. "Sam should be back soon."

"He might stop in town," Else suggested, and was immediately sorry she had said it for she could see the instant worry on Redlin's face. The idea of Sam Redlin stopping at the Four Star with seven thousand dollars on him was scarcely a pleasant one. Murder had been done there for much, much less. And then Sam was overconfident. He was even cocky.

"I reckon I'd better ride in and meet him," Redlin said, genuinely worried now. "Sam's a good boy, but he sets too much store by himself. He figures he can take care of himself anywhere, but that pack of wolves . . ." His voice trailed off to silence.

Johnny turned in his saddle. "Why, I could just as well ride in, Pa," he said casually. "I ain't been to town for a spell, and if anything happened, I could lend a hand."

Pa Redlin was about to refuse, but Else spoke up quickly. "Let him go, Pa. He could do some things for me, too, and Johnny's got a way with folks. Chances are he could get Sam back without trouble."

That's right! Johnny's thoughts were grim. Send me along to save your boy. You don't care if I get shot, just so's he's been saved. Well, all right, I'll go. When I come back I'll climb my gelding and light out. Up to Oregon. I never been to Oregon.

Flitch was in town. His mouth tightened a little, but at that, it would be better than Pa going. Pa always said the wrong thing, being outspoken like. He was a man who spoke his mind, and to speak one's mind to Flitch or Loss Degner would mean a shooting. It might be he could get Sam out of town all right. If he was drinking it would be hard. Especially if that redhead had her hands on him.

"You reckon you could handle it?" Pa asked doubtfully.

"Sure," Johnny said, his voice a shade hard, "I can handle it. I doubt if Sam's in any trouble. Later, maybe. All he'd need is somebody to side him."

"Well," Pa was reluctant, "better take your Winchester. My six-gun, too."

"You hang on to it. I'll make out."

Johnny turned the gelding and started back toward the ranch, his eyes cold. Seventeen he might be, but four years on the frontier on your own make pretty much of a man out of you. He didn't want any more shooting, but he had six men dead on his back trail now, not counting Comanches and Kiowas. Six, and he was seventeen. Next thing, they would be comparing him to the Kid or to Wes Hardin.

He wanted no gunfighter's name, only a little spread of his own where he could run a few cows and raise horses, good stock, like some he had seen in East Texas. No range ponies for him, but good blood. That Sprague place now . . . but that was Sam's place, or as good as his. Well, why not? Sam was getting Else, and it was little enough he could do for Pa and Ma, to bring Sam home safe.

He left the gelding at the water trough and walked into the barn. In his room he dug some saddle gear away from a corner and, out of a hiding place in the corner, he took his guns. After a moment's thought, he took but one of them, leaving the newer pistol, a .44 Russian, behind. He didn't want to go parading into town with two guns on him, looking like a sure-enough shooter. Besides, with only one gun and the change in him, Flitch might not spot him at all.

Johnny was at the gate riding out when Else and Pa rode up. Else looked at him, her eyes falling to the gun on his hip. Her face was pale and her eyes large. "Be careful, Johnny. I had to say that because you know how hotheaded Pa is. He'd get killed, and he might get Sam killed."

That was true enough, but Johnny was aggrieved. He

looked her in the eyes. "Sure, that's true, but you didn't think of Sam, now, did you? You were just thinking of Pa."

Her lips parted to protest, but then her face seemed to stiffen. "No, Johnny, it wasn't only Pa I thought of. I did think of Sam. Why shouldn't I?"

That was plain enough. Why shouldn't she? Wasn't she going to marry him? Wasn't Sam getting the Sprague place when they got that money back safe?

He touched his horse lightly with a spur and moved on past her. All right, he would send Sam back to her, if he could. It was time he was moving on, anyway.

The gelding liked the feel of the trail and moved out fast. Ten miles was all, and he could do that easy enough, and so he did it, and Johnny turned the black horse into the street and stopped before the livery stable, swinging down. Sam's horse was tied at the Four Star's hitchrail. The saddlebags were gone.

Johnny studied the street and then crossed it and walked down along the buildings on the same side as the Four Star. He turned quickly into the door.

Sam Redlin was sitting at a table with the redhead, the saddlebags on the table before him, and he was drunk. He was very drunk. Johnny's eyes swept the room. The bartender and Loss Degner were standing together, talking. Neither of them paid any attention to Johnny, for neither knew him. But Flitch did.

Flitch was standing down the bar with Albie Bower, but none of the old Gila River outfit. Both of them looked up, and Flitch kept looking, never taking his eyes from Johnny. Something bothered him, and maybe it was the one gun.

Johnny moved over to Sam's table. They had to get out of here fast, before Flitch remembered. "Hi, Sam," he said. "Just happened to be in town, and Pa said if I saw you, to side you on the way home."

Sam stared at him sullenly. "Side me? You?" He snorted his contempt. "I need no man to side me. You can tell Pa I'll be home later tonight." He glanced at the redhead. "Much later."

"Want I should carry this stuff home for you?" Johnny put his hand on the saddlebags.

"Leave him be!" Hazel protested angrily. "Can't you see he don't want to be bothered? He's capable of takin' care of himself, an' he don't need no kid for gardeen!"

"Beat it," Sam said. "You go on home. I'll come along later."

"Better come now, Sam." Johnny was getting worried, for Loss Degner had started for the table.

"Here, you!" Degner was sharp. "Leave that man alone! He's a friend of mine, and I'll have no saddle tramp annoying my customers!"

Johnny turned on him. "I'm no saddle tramp. I ride for his pa. He asked me to ride home with him—now. That's what I aim to do."

As he spoke he was not thinking of Degner, but of Flitch. The gunman was behind him now, and neither Flitch, fast as he was, nor Albie Bower was above shooting a man in the back.

"I said to beat it." Sam stared at him drunkenly. "Saddle tramp's what you are. Folks never should have let you in."

"That's it," Degner said. "Now get out! He don't want you nor your company."

There was a movement behind him, and he heard Flitch say, "Loss, let me have him. I know this hombre. This is that kid gunfighter, Johnny O'Day, from the Gila."

Johnny turned slowly, his green eyes flat and cold. "Hello, Flitch. I heard you were around." Carefully, he moved away from the table, aware of the startled look on Hazel's face, the suddenly tight awareness on the face of Loss Degner. "You lookin' for me, Flitch?" It was a chance he had to take. His best chance now. If shooting started, he might grab the saddlebags and break for the door and then the ranch. They would be through with Sam Redlin once the money was gone.

"Yeah." Flitch stared at him, his unshaven face hard with the lines of evil and shadowed by the intent that rode him hard. "I'm lookin' for you. Always figured you got off easy, made you a fast rep gunnin' down your betters."

Bower had moved up beside him, but Loss Degner had drawn back to one side. Johnny's eyes never left Flitch. "You in this, Loss?"

Degner shrugged. "Why should I be? I was no Gila River gunman. This is your quarrel. Finish it between you."

"All right, Flitch," Johnny said. "You want it. I'm givin' you your chance to start the play."

The stillness of a hot midafternoon lay on the Four Star. A fly buzzed against the dusty, cobwebbed back window. Somewhere in the street a horse stamped restlessly, and a distant pump creaked. Flitch stared at him, his little eyes hard and bright. His sweat-stained shirt was torn at the shoulder, and there was dust ingrained in the pores of his face.

His hands dropped in a flashing draw, but he had only cleared leather when Johnny's first bullet hit him, puncturing the Bull Durham tag that hung from his shirt pocket. The second shot cut the edge of it, and the third, fourth, and fifth slammed Albie Bower back, knocking him back step by step, but Albie's gun was hammering, and it took the sixth shot to put him down.

Johnny stood over them, staring down at their bodies, and then he turned to face Loss Degner.

Degner was smiling, and he held a gun in his hand from which a thin tendril of smoke lifted. Startled, Johnny's eyes flickered to Sam Redlin.

Sam lay across the saddlebags, blood trickling from his temples. He had been shot through the head by Degner under cover of the gun battle, murdered without a chance.

Johnny O'Day's eyes lifted to Loss Degner's. The saloon-keeper was still smiling. "Yes, he's dead, and I've killed him. He had it coming, the fool! Thinking we cared to listen to his bragging! All we wanted was that money, and now we've got it. Me—Hazel and I! We've got it."

"Not yet." Johnny's lips were stiff and his heart was cold. He was thinking of Pa, Ma, and Else. "I'm still there."

"You?" Degner laughed. "With an empty gun? I counted your shots, boy. Even Johnny O'Day is cold turkey with an empty gun. Six shots—two for Flitch, and beautiful shooting, too, but four shots for Albie, who was moving and shooting, not so easy a target. But now I've got you. With you dead, I'll just say Sam came here without any money, that he got shot during the fight. Sound good to you?"

Johnny still faced him, his gun in his hand. "Not bad," he said, "but you still have me here, Loss. And this gun ain't empty!"

Degner's face tightened and then relaxed. "Not empty? I counted the shots, kid, so don't try bluffing me. Now I'm killing you." He tilted his gun toward Johnny O'Day, and Johnny fired once, twice . . . a third time. As each bullet hit him, Loss Degner jerked and twisted, but the shock of the wounds, and death wounds they were, was nothing to the shock of the bullets from that empty gun.

He sagged against the bar and then slipped floorward. Johnny moved in on him. "You can hear me, Loss?" The killer's eyes lifted to his. "This ain't a six-shooter. It's a Walch twelve-shot Navy gun, thirty-six caliber. She's right handy, Loss, and it only goes to show you shouldn't jump to conclusions."

Hazel sat at the table, staring at the dying Degner. "You better go to him, Red," Johnny said quietly. "He's only got a minute."

She stared at him as he picked up the saddlebags and backed to the door.

Russell, the storekeeper, was on the steps with a half dozen others, none of whom he knew. "Degner killed Sam Redlin," he said. "Take care of Sam, will you?"

At Russell's nod, Johnny swung to the saddle and turned the gelding toward home.

He wouldn't leave now. He couldn't leave now. They would be all alone there, without Sam. Besides, Pa was going to need help on that dam. "Boy," he touched the gelding's neck, "I reckon we got to stick around for a while."

THE MAN FROM BATTLE FLAT

A T HALF-PAST FOUR Krag Moran rode in from the canyon trail, and within ten minutes half the town knew that Ryerson's top gunhand was sitting in front of the Palace.

Nobody needed to ask why he was there. It was to be a showdown between Ryerson and the Squaw Creek nesters, and the showdown was to begin with Bush Leason.

The Squaw Creek matter had divided the town, yet there was no division where Bush Leason was concerned. The big nester had brought his trouble on himself and if he got what was coming to him nobody would be sorry. That he had killed five or six men was a known fact.

Krag Moran was a lean, wide-shouldered young man with smoky eyes and a still, Indian-dark face. Some said he had been a Texas Ranger, but all the town knew about him for sure was that he had got back some of Ryerson's horses that had been run off. How he would stack up against a sure-thing killer like Bush Leason was anybody's guess.

Bush Leason was sitting on a cot in his shack when they brought him the news that Moran was in town. Leason was a huge man, thick through the waist and with a wide, flat, cruel face. When they told him, he said nothing at all, just continued to clean his double-barreled shotgun. It was the gun that had killed Shorty Grimes.

Shorty Grimes had ridden for Tim Ryerson, and between them Ryerson and Chet Lee had sewed up all the range on Battle Flat. Neither of them drifted cattle on Squaw Creek, but for four years they had been cutting hay from its grass-rich meadows, until the nesters had moved in.

Ryerson and Lee ordered them to leave. They replied the land was government land open to filing. Hedrow talked for the nesters, but it was Bush Leason who wanted to talk, and Bush was a troublemaker. Ryerson gave them a week and, when they didn't move, tore down fences and burned a barn or two.

In all of this Shorty Grimes and Krag Moran had no part. They had been repping on Carol Duchin's place at the time. Grimes had ridden into town alone and stopped at the Palace for a drink. Leason started trouble, but the other nesters stopped him. Then Leason turned at the door. "Ryerson gave us a week to leave the country. I'm giving you just thirty minutes to get out of town! Then I come a-shooting!"

Shorty Grimes had been ready to leave, but after that he had decided to stay. A half hour later there was a challenging yell from the dark street out front. Grimes put down his glass and started for the door, gun in hand. He had just reached the street door when Bush Leason stepped through the back door and ran forward, three light, quick steps.

Bush Leason stopped there, still unseen. "Shorty!" he called softly.

Pistol lowered, unsuspecting, Shorty Grimes had turned, and Bush Leason had emptied both barrels of the shotgun into his chest.

One of the first men into the saloon after the shooting was Dan Riggs, editor of *The Bradshaw Journal*. He knew what this meant, knew it and did not like it, for he was a man who hated violence and felt that no good could come of it. Nor had he any liking for Bush Leason. He had warned the nester leader, Hedrow, about him only a few days before.

Nobody liked the killing but everybody was afraid of Bush. They had all heard Bush make his brags and the way to win was to stay alive. . . .

Now Dan Riggs heard that Krag Moran was in town, and he got up from his desk and took off his eye-shade. It was no more than ninety feet from the front of the print shop to the Palace and Dan walked over. He stopped there in front of Krag. Dan was a slender, middle-aged man with thin hands and a quiet face. He said:

"Don't do it, son. You mount up and ride home. If you kill Leason that will just be the beginning."

"There's been a beginning. Leason started it."

"Now, look here—" Riggs protested, but Krag interrupted him.

"You better move," he said, in that slow Texas drawl of his. "Leason might show up any time."

"We've got a town here," Riggs replied determinedly. "We've got women and homes and decent folks. We don't want the town shot up and we don't want a lot of drunken killings. If you riders can't behave yourselves, stay away from town! Those farmers have a right to live, and they are good, God-fearing people!"

Krag Moran just sat there. "I haven't killed anybody," he said reasonably, his face a little solemn. "I'm just a-sittin' here."

Riggs started to speak, then with a wave of exasperated hands he turned and hurried off. And then he saw Carol Duchin.

Carol Duchin was several things. By inheritance, from her father, she owned a ranch that would make two of Ryerson's. She was twenty-two years old, single, and she knew cattle as well as any man. Chet Lee had proposed to her three times and had been flatly refused three times. She both knew and liked Dan Riggs and his wife, and she often stopped overnight at the Riggs home when in town. Despite that, she was cattle, all the way.

Dan Riggs went at once to Carol Duchin and spoke his piece. Right away she shook her head. "I won't interfere," she replied. "I knew Shorty Grimes and he was a good man."

"That he was," Riggs agreed sincerely, "I only wish they were all as good. That was a dastardly murder and I mean to say so in the next issue of my paper. But another killing won't help things any, no matter who gets killed."

Carol asked him: "Have you talked to Bush Leason?"

Riggs nodded. "He won't listen either. I tried to get him to ride over to Flagg until things cooled off a little. He laughed at me."

She eyed him curiously.

"What do you want me to do?"

"Talk to Krag. For you, he'll leave."

"I scarcely know him." Carol Duchin was not planning to tell anyone how much she did know about Krag Moran, nor how interested in the tall rider she had become. During his period of repping with her roundup he had not spoken three words to her, but she had noticed him, watched him, and listened to her riders talk about him among themselves.

"Talk to him. He respects you. All of them do."

Yes, Carol reflected bitterly, he probably does. And he probably never thinks of me as a woman.

She should have known better. She was the sort of girl no man could ever think of in any other way. Her figure was superb, and she very narrowly escaped genuine beauty. Only her very coolness and her position as owner had kept more than one cowhand from speaking to her. So far only Chet Lee had found the courage. But Chet never lacked for that.

She walked across the street toward the Palace, her heart pounding, her mouth suddenly dry. Now that she was going to speak to Krag, face to face, she was suddenly frightened as a child. He got to his feet as she came up to him. She was tall for a girl, but he was still taller. His mouth was firm, his jaw strong and clean boned. She met his eyes and found them smoky green and her heart fluttered.

"Krag," her voice was natural, at least, "don't stay here. You'll either be killed or you'll kill Bush. In either case it will be just one more step and will just lead to more killing."

His voice sounded amused, yet respectful, too. "You've been talking to Dan Riggs. He's an old woman."

"No," suddenly she was sure of herself, "no, he's telling the truth, Krag. Those people have a right to that grass, and this isn't just a feud between you and Leason. It means good men are going to be killed, homes destroyed, crops ruined, and the work of months wiped out. You can't do this thing."

"You want me to quit?" He was incredulous. "You know this country. I couldn't live in it, nor anywhere the story traveled."

She looked straight into his eyes. "It often takes a braver man not to fight."

He thought about that, his smoky eyes growing somber. Then he nodded. "I never gave it any thought," he said seriously, "but I reckon you're right. Only I'm not that brave."

"Listen to Dan!" she pleaded. "He's an intelligent man! He's an editor! His newspaper means something in this country and will mean more. What he says is important."

"Him?" Krag chuckled. "Why, ma'am, that little varmint's just a-fussin'. He don't mean nothing, and nobody pays much attention to him. He's just a little man with ink on his fingers!"

"You don't understand!" Carol protested.

———

BUSH LEASON WAS across the street. During the time Krag Moran had been seated in front of the Palace, Bush had been doing considerable serious thinking. How good Krag was, Bush had no idea, nor did he intend to find out, yet a showdown was coming and from Krag's lack of action he evidently intended for Bush to force the issue.

Bush was not hesitant to begin it, but the more he considered the situation the less he liked it. The wall of the Palace was stone, so he could not shoot through it. There was no chance to approach Krag from right or left without being seen for some time before his shotgun would be within range. Krag had chosen his position well, and the only approach was from behind the building across the street.

This building was empty, and Bush had gotten inside and was lying there watching the street when the girl came up. Instantly, he perceived his advantage. As the girl left, Krag's eyes would involuntarily follow her. In that instant he would step from the door and shoot Krag down. It was simple and it was foolproof.

"You'd better go, ma'am," Krag said. "It ain't safe here. I'm staying right where I am until Leason shows."

She dropped her hands helplessly and turned away from him. In that instant, Bush Leason stepped from the door across the street and jerked his shotgun to his shoulder. As he did so, he yelled.

Carol Duchin was too close. Krag shoved her hard with his left hand and stepped quickly right, drawing as he stepped and firing as his right foot touched the walk.

Afterward, men who saw it said there had never been anything like it before. Leason whipped up his shotgun and yelled, and in the incredibly brief instant, as the butt settled against Leason's shoulder, Krag pushed the girl, stepped away from her, and drew. And he fired as his gun came level.

It was split-second timing and the fastest draw that anybody had ever seen in Bradshaw; the .45 slug slammed into Bush Leason's chest just as he squeezed off his shot, and the buckshot *whapped* through the air, only beginning to scatter and at least a foot and a half over Krag Moran's head. And Krag stood there flatfooted and shot Bush again as he stood leaning back against the building. The big man turned sideways and fell into the dust off the edge of the walk.

As suddenly as that it was done. And then Carol Duchin got to her feet, her face and clothes dusty. She brushed her clothes with quick, impatient hands, and then turned sharply and looked at Krag Moran. "I never want to see you again!" she flared. "Don't put a foot on my place! Not for any reason whatever!"

Krag Moran looked after her helplessly, took an involuntary step after her, and then stopped. He glanced once at the body of Bush Leason and the men gathered around it. Then he walked to his horse. Dan Riggs was standing there, his face shadowed with worry. "You've played hell!" he said.

"What about Grimes?"

"I know, I know! Bush was vicious. He deserved killing, and if ever I saw murder it was his killing of Grimes, but that doesn't change this. He had friends, and all of the nesters will be sore. They'll never let it alone."

"Then they'll be mighty foolish." Krag swung into the saddle, staring gloomily at Carol Duchin. "Why did she get mad?"

He headed out of town. He had no regrets about the killing. Leason was a type of man that Krag had met before, and they kept on killing and making trouble until somebody shot too fast for them. Yet he found himself upset by the worries of Riggs as well as the attitude of Carol Duchin. Why was she so angry? What was the matter with everybody?

Moran had the usual dislike for nesters possessed by all cattlemen, yet Riggs had interposed an element of doubt, and he studied it as he rode back to the ranch. Maybe the nesters had an argument, at that. This idea was surprising to him, and he shied away from it.

As the days passed and the tension grew, he found himself more and more turning to thoughts of Carol. The memory of her face when she came across the street toward him and when she pleaded with him, and then her flashing and angry eyes when she got up out of the dust.

No use thinking about her, Moran decided. Even had she not been angry at him, what could a girl who owned the cattle she owned want with a drifting cowhand like himself? Yet he did think about her. He thought about her too much. And then the whole Bradshaw country exploded with a bang. Chet Lee's riders, with several hotheads from the Ryerson outfit, hit the nesters and hit them hard. They ran off several head of cattle, burned haystacks and two barns, killed one man, and shot up several houses. One child was cut by flying glass. And the following morning a special edition of *The Bradshaw Journal* appeared.

ARMED MURDERERS RAID
SLEEPING VALLEY

Blazing barns, ruined crops and death remained behind last night after another vicious, criminal raid by the murderers, masquerading as cattlemen, who raided the peaceful, sleeping settlement on Squaw Creek.

Ephraim Hershman, 52 years old, was shot down in defense of his home by gunmen from the Chet Lee and Ryerson ranches when they raided Squaw Valley last night. Two other men were wounded, while young Billy Hedrow, 3 years old, was severely cut by flying glass when the night-riders shot out the windows. . . .

Dan Riggs was angry and it showed all the way through the news and in the editorial adjoining. In a scathing attack he named names and bitterly assailed the ranchers for their tactics, demanding intervention by the territorial governor.

Ryerson came stamping out to the bunkhouse, his eyes hard and angry. "Come on!" he yelled. "We're going in and show that durned printer where he gets off! Come on! Mount up!"

———

CHET LEE WAS just arriving in town when the cavalcade from the Ryerson place hit the outskirts of Bradshaw. It was broad daylight, but the streets of the town were empty and deserted.

Chet Lee was thirty-five, tough as a boot, and with skin like a sunbaked hide. His eyes were cruel, his lips thin and ugly. He shoved Riggs aside and his men went into the print shop, wrecked the hand press, threw the type out into the street, and smashed all the windows out of the shop.

Though he had ridden along, Krag Moran now stood aside awaiting the end of the destruction. Nobody made a move to harm Dan Riggs, who stood pale and quiet at one side. He said nothing to any of them until the end, and then it was to Ryerson.

"What good do you think this will do?" he asked quietly. "You can't stop people from thinking. You can't throttle the truth. In the end it always comes out. Grimes and Leason were shot in fights, but that last night was wanton murder and destruction of property."

"Oh, shut up!" Ryerson flared. "You're getting off lucky!"

Lee's little eyes brightened suddenly. "Maybe," he said, "a rope is what this feller needs!"

Dan Riggs looked at Lee without shifting an inch. "It would be like you to think of that," he said, and Lee struck him across the mouth.

Riggs got slowly to his feet, blood running down his lips. "You're fools," he said quietly. "You don't seem to realize that if you can destroy the property of others, they can destroy it for you. Or do you realize that when any freedom is destroyed for others, it is destroyed for you, too.

"You've wrecked my shop, ruined my press. Tyrants and bullies have always tried that sort of thing, especially when they are in the wrong."

Nobody said anything, Ryerson's face was white and stiff, and Krag felt suddenly uneasy. Riggs might be a fool but he had courage. It had been a rotten thing for Chet Lee to hit him when he couldn't fight back.

"We fought for the right of a free press and free speech back in seventy-six," Dan Riggs persisted. "Now you would try to destroy the free press because it prints the truth about you. I tell you now, you'll not succeed."

They left him standing there among the ruins of his printing shop and all he owned in the world, and then they walked to the Palace for a drink. Ryerson waved them to the bar.

"Drinks are on me!" he said. "Drink up!"

Krag Moran edged around the crowd and stopped at Ryerson's elbow. "Got my money, boss?" he asked quietly. "I've had enough."

Ryerson's eyes hardened. "What kind of talk is that?"

Chet Lee had turned his head and was staring hard at Moran. "Don't be a fool!"

"I'm not a fool. I'm quitting. I want my money. I'll have no part in that sort of thing this morning. It was a mean, low trick."

"You pointing any part of that remark at me?" Lee turned carefully, his flat, wicked eyes on Krag. "I want to know."

"I'm not hunting trouble." Krag spoke flatly. "I spoke my piece. You owe me forty bucks, Ryerson."

Ryerson dug his hand into his pocket and slapped two gold eagles on the bar. "That pays you off! Now get out of the country! I want no part of turncoats! If you're around here after twenty-four hours, I'll hunt you down like a dog!"

Krag had started to turn away. Now he smiled faintly. "Why, sure! I reckon you would! Well, for your information, Ryerson, I'll be here!"

Before they could reply, he strode from the room. Chet Lee stared after him. "I never had no use for that saddle tramp, anyway!"

Ryerson bit the end off his cigar. His anger was cooling

and he was disturbed. Krag was a solid man. Despite Lee, he knew that. Suddenly he was disturbed—or had it been ever since he saw Dan Riggs's white, strained face? Gloomily, he stared down at his whiskey. What was wrong with him? Was he getting old? He glanced at the harsh face of Chet Lee— why wasn't he as sure of himself as Lee? Weren't they here first? Hadn't they cut hay in the valley for four years? What right had the nesters to move in on them?

KRAG MORAN WALKED outside and shoved his hat back on his head. Slowly, he built a smoke. Why, he was a damned fool! He had put himself right in the middle by quitting. Now he would be fair game for Leason's friends, with nobody to stand beside him. Well, that would not be new. He had stood alone before he came here, and he could again.

He looked down the street. Dan Riggs was squatted in the street, picking up his type. Slowly, Krag drew on his cigarette; then he took it from his lips and snapped it into the gutter. Riggs looked up as his shadow fell across him. His face was still dark with bitterness.

Krag nodded at it. "Can you make that thing work again? The press, I mean."

Riggs stared at the wrecked machine. "I doubt it," he said quietly. "It was all I had, too. They think nothing of wrecking a man's life."

Krag squatted beside him and picked up a piece of the type and carefully wiped off the sand. "You made a mistake," he said quietly. "You should have had a gun on your desk."

"Would that have stopped them?"

"No."

"Then I'm glad I didn't have it. Although," there was a flicker of ironic humor in his eyes, "sometimes I don't feel peaceful. There was a time this afternoon when if I'd had a gun—"

Krag chuckled. "Yeah," he said, "I see what you mean. Now let's get this stuff picked up. If we can get that press started, we'll do a better job—and this time I'll be standing beside you."

Two days later the paper hit the street, and copies of it swiftly covered the country.

BIG RANCHERS WRECK JOURNAL PRESS

Efforts of the big ranchers of the Squaw Creek Valley range to stifle the free press have proved futile. . . .

There followed the complete story of the wrecking of the press and the threats to Dan Riggs. Following that was a re-hash of the two raids on the nesters, the accounts of the killings of Grimes and Leason, and the warning to the state at large that a full-scale cattle war was in the making unless steps were taken to prevent it.

Krag Moran walked across the street to the saloon, and the bartender shook his head at him. "You've played hob," he said. "They'll lynch both of you now."

"No, they won't. Make mine rye."

The bartender shook his head. "No deal. The boss says no selling to you or Riggs."

Krag Moran's smile was not pleasant. "Don't make any mistakes, Pat," he said quietly. "Riggs might take that—I won't. You set that bottle out here on the bar or I'm going back after it. And don't reach for that shotgun! If you do, I'll part your hair with a bullet."

The bartender hesitated and then reached carefully for the bottle. "It ain't me, Krag," he objected. "It's the boss."

"Then you tell the boss to tell me." Krag poured drink, tossed it off, and walked from the saloon.

When Moran crossed the street, there was a sorrel mare tied in front of the shop. He glanced at the brand and felt his mouth go dry. He pushed open the door and saw her standing there in the half shadow—and Dan Riggs was gone.

"He needed coffee," Carol said quietly. "I told him I'd stay until you came back."

He looked at her and felt something moving deep within him, an old feeling that he had known only in the lonesome hours when he had found himself wanting someone, something . . . and this was it.

"I'm back." She still stood there. "But I don't want you to go."

She started to speak, and then they heard the rattle of hoofs in the street and suddenly he turned and watched the sweeping band of riders come up the street and stop before the shop. Chet Lee was there, and he had a rope.

Krag Moran glanced at Carol. "Better get out of here," he said. "This will be rough." And then he stepped outside.

They were surprised and looked it. Krag stood there with his thumbs hooked in his belt, his eyes running over them. "Hi!" he said easily. "You boys figure on using that rope?"

"We figure on hanging an editor," Ryerson said harshly.

Krag's eyes rested on the old man for an instant. "Ryerson," he said evenly, "you keep out of this. I have an idea if Chet wasn't egging you on, you'd not be in this. I've also an idea that all this trouble centers around one man, and that man is Chet Lee."

Lee sat his horse with his eyes studying Krag carefully. "And what of it?" he asked.

Riggs came back across the street. In his hand he held a borrowed rifle, and his very manner of holding it proved he knew nothing about handling it. As he stepped out in front of the cattlemen, Carol Duchin stepped from the print shop. "As long as you're picking on unarmed men and helpless children," she said clearly, "you might as well fight a woman, too!"

Lee was shocked. "Carol! What are you doin' here? You're *cattle*!"

"That's right, Chet. I run some cows. I'm also a woman. I know what a home means to a woman. I know what it meant to Mrs. Hershman to lose her husband. I'm standing beside Riggs and Moran in this—all the way."

"Carol!" Lee protested angrily. "Get out of there! This is man's work! I won't have it!"

"She does what she wants to, Chet," Krag said, "but you're going to fight me."

Chet Lee's eyes came back to Krag Moran. Suddenly he saw it there, plain as day. This man had done what he had failed to do; he had won. It all boiled down to Moran. If he was out of the way . . . "Boss," it was one of Ryerson's men, "look out."

Ryerson turned his head. Three men from the nester outfit stood ranged at even spaces across the street. Two of them held shotguns, one a Spencer rifle. "There's six more of us on the roofs," Hedrow called down. "Anytime you want to start your play, Krag, just open the ball."

Ryerson shifted in his saddle. He was suddenly sweating, and Krag Moran could see it. Nevertheless, Moran's attention centered itself on Chet Lee. The younger man's face showed his irritation and his rage at the futility of his position. Stopped by the presence of Carol, he was now trapped by the presence of the nesters.

"There'll be another day!" He was coldly furious. "This isn't the end!"

Krag Moran looked at him carefully. He knew all he needed to know about the man he faced. Chet Lee was a man driven by a passion for power. Now it was the nesters, later it would be Ryerson, and then, unless she married him, Carol Duchin. He could not be one among many; he could not be one of two. He had to stand alone.

"You're mistaken, Chet," Moran said. "It ends here."

———

CHET LEE'S EYES swung back to Krag. For the first time he seemed to see him clearly. A slow minute passed before he spoke. "So that's the way it is?" he said softly.

"That's the way it is. Right now you can offer your holdings to Ryerson. I know he has the money to buy them. Or you can sell out to Carol, if she's interested. But you sell out, Chet. You're the troublemaker here. With you gone I think Ryerson and Hedrow could talk out a sensible deal."

"I'll talk," Hedrow said quietly, "and I'll listen."

Ryerson nodded. "That's good for me. And I'll buy, Chet. Name a price."

Chet Lee sat perfectly still. "So that's the way it is?" he repeated. "And if I don't figure to sell?"

"Then we take your gun and start you out of town," Krag said quietly.

Lee nodded. "Yeah, I see. You and Ryerson must have had this all figured out. A nice way to do me out of my ranch. And your quitting was all a fake."

"There was no plan," Moran said calmly. "You've heard what we have to say. Make your price. You've got ten minutes to close a deal or ride out without a dime."

Chet Lee's face did not alter its expression. "I see," he said. "But suppose something happens to you, Krag? Then what? Who here could make me toe the line? Or gamble I'd not come back?"

"Nothing's going to happen to me." Krag spoke quietly. "You see, Chet, I know your kind."

"Well," Chet shrugged, glancing around, "I guess you've got me." He looked at Ryerson. "Fifty thousand?"

"There's not that much in town. I'll give you twelve, and that's just ten thousand more than you hit town with."

"Guess I've no choice," Chet said. "I'll take it." He looked at Krag. "All right if we go to the bank?"

"All right."

Chet swung his horse to the right, but as he swung the horse he suddenly slammed his right spur into the gelding's ribs. The bay sprang sharply left, smashing into Riggs and knocking him down. Only Krag's quick leap backward against the print shop saved him from going down, too. As he slammed home his spur, Chet grabbed for his gun. It came up fast and he threw a quick shot that splashed Krag Moran's face with splinters; then he swung his horse and shot, almost point blank, into Krag's face!

But Moran was moving as the horse swung, and as the horse swung left, Moran moved away. The second shot blasted past his face and then his own guns came up and he fired, two quick shots. So close was Chet Lee that Krag heard the slap of the bullets as they thudded into his ribs below the heart.

Lee lost hold of his gun and slid from the saddle, and the horse, springing away, narrowly missed stepping on his face.

Krag Moran stood over him, looking down. Riggs was climbing shakily to his feet, and Chet was alive yet, staring at Krag.

"I told you I knew your kind, Chet," Krag said quietly. "You shouldn't have tried it."

Carol Duchin was in the cafe when Krag Moran crossed the street. He had two drinks under his belt and he was feeling them, which was rare for him. Yet he hadn't eaten and he could not remember when he had.

She looked up when he came through the door and smiled at him. "Come over and sit down," she said. "Where's Dan?"

Krag smiled with hard amusement. "Getting money from Ryerson to buy him a new printing outfit."

"Hedrow?"

"Him and the nesters signed a contract to supply Ryerson with hay. They'd have made a deal in the beginning if it hadn't been for Chet. Hedrow tried to talk business once before. I heard him."

"And you?"

He placed his hat carefully on the hook and sat down. He was suddenly tired. He ran his fingers through his crisp, dark hair. "Me?" He blinked his eyes and reached for the coffee-pot. "I am going to shave and take a bath. Then I'm going to sleep for twenty hours about, and then I'm going to throw the leather on my horse and hit the trail."

"I told you over there," Carol said quietly, "that I didn't want you to go."

"Uh-uh. If I don't go now," he looked at her somberly, "I'd never want to go again."

"Then don't go," she said.

And he didn't.

DEATH SONG OF THE SOMBRERO

STRETCH MAGOON, SIX-FOOT-FIVE in his sock feet and lean as a buggy whip, put his grulla mustang down the bank of the wash, and cut diagonally across it toward the trail up the bank. His long, melancholy face seemed unusually sad.

When the grulla scrambled up the bank, Stretch kept him to a slow-paced walk. The sadness remained in his eyes, but they were more watchful, almost expectant.

The ramshackle house he was approaching was unpainted and dismal. Sadly in need of repair, the grounds around were dirty and unkempt, the corral a patchwork of odds and ends of rails, the shed that did duty for a barn little more than a roof over some rails where three saddles rode.

Magoon's eyes caught the saddles first, and the hard bronze of his face tightened. He reined up in the space between the shack and the shed. A big man loomed in the door, a bearded man with small, ugly eyes. "Howdy," he said. "Wantin' somethin'?"

"Uh-huh." Stretch dug out the makin's and began to build a smoke. "Wantin' t' tell you all somethin'." He finished his job, put the cigarette in his mouth, and struck a match on the side of his jeans. Then he looked up. Two men were there now; the bigger man had stepped outside, and a runty fellow with sandy hair and a freckled, ugly face stood in the door. One hand was out of sight.

"As of this mornin', come daylight," he said, "I'm ramroddin' the Lazy S."

"You're what?" The big man walked two steps closer. "You mean, you're the foreman? What's become of Ketchell?"

Stretch Magoon looked sadly down at the big man. "Why, Weidman, Ketchell did what I knowed he would do sooner or later. He was a victim of bad judgment. Ever' time that man played a hand of poker, I could see it comin'."

"Get t' the point!" Weidman demanded harshly. "What happened?"

"We had us a mite of an argument," Stretch said calmly, "an' Ketchell thought I was bluffin'. He called. We both drawed a new hand an' I led with two aces—right through the heart."

"Y' killed Burn Ketchell?" Weidman demanded incredulously. "I don't believe it!"

"Well"—Stretch dropped his left hand to the reins—"dead or not, they are havin' a buryin'. I reckon if he ain't dead he'll be some sore when he wakes up an' finds all that dirt in his face." He turned the mouse-colored mustang. "Oh yeah! That reminds me. We had the argument over suggestin' t' you that your Sombrero brand could be run mighty easy out of a Lazy S."

"Y' accusin' us o' rustlin'?" Weidman demanded. His eyes flickered for an instant, and Stretch felt a little shiver of relief go through him. He knew where that third man was now. It had had him bothered some. The third man was beside the corner of the corral.

His eyes dropped, and his heart gave a leap. The sun was beyond the corral, and he could see the shadow of that corner on the hard ground. He almost grinned as his eyes caught the flicker of movement.

"I ain't accusin' you o' nothin'. I ain't sure. If I was sure, I wouldn't be settin' here talkin'. I'd be stringin' your thick neck t' a cottonwood. What I'm doin' is givin' you a tip that the fun's over now. You can change your brand or leave the country. I ain't p'tic'lar which."

"Why, you—" Weidman's face was mottled and ugly, but he made the mistake of trusting too much to his dry-gulch attempt, and when Stretch Magoon drew, it was so fast he didn't have a chance to match him. He was depending too much on that shot from the corral corner.

Magoon's eyes had been on the shadow, unnoticed by Weidman. Stretch had seen the rifle come up from past the corner of the corral, had waited it out, waited until it froze. Then he drew and fired in the same instant.

He fired across his body, and too quickly. It had to be a snap shot because he needed to get his gun around and on the other two men. As it was, his bullet struck the man's hand just where his left thumb lay along the rifle barrel.

Very neatly it clipped the tip of the thumb and continued past to cut a furrow in the man's cheek, cut the lobe from his ear, and bury itself in the ground beyond. It had the added effect of a blow behind the ear, and the marksman rolled over on the ground, knocked momentarily unconscious by the blow.

Weidman's gun was only half out, and Red Posner had not even started to draw when Magoon's gun swung back in line. Weidman froze, then, very delicately, spread his fingers and let his gun slip back into its holster. His face was gray under the stubble of beard.

"No hard feelin's," Stretch said quietly, "but I'm repeatin'. Change your brand or git!"

He swung his horse and, watching warily, rode to the wash. Then, instead of following the trail up the other side, he whipped the mustang around and rode rapidly down the wash for a quarter of a mile. There it branched away to the left, and he took the branch. Well back in the cedars, he rode out of the wash and cut across country toward town.

Despite himself, he was disturbed. Something about the recent action had not gone as he had expected. Barker had sent for him two weeks before, when the missing cattle from the Lazy S had begun to mount rapidly in numbers. In those two weeks, Stretch had ascertained two things: first, that Lazy S cattle were being branded, and then, while the brands were still fresh, drifted into the breaks across the range near the Sombrero spread of Lucky Weidman.

Second, he had trailed Burn Ketchell and had actually caught him in the act of venting a brand. The change from a Lazy S to a Sombrero was all too simple for a handy man with a running iron.

It was merely a matter of making an inverted U over the top bend of the Lazy S to make the crown of the Sombrero, and then running a burned line from the top of the S around and down to the lower tip. It was simple, perfectly simple.

Burn Ketchell had been the brains behind the rustling. With Burn out of the way, Stretch had believed the rustling would be ended. Now, because of that attempted killing, he was not so sure.

Lucky Weidman was crooked and he was dirty, but he was no fool. He would never have taken a chance of having Magoon killed on his place after rustling had been discovered, unless he had friends—and friends in places to do him some good.

———

TINKERVILLE WAS AN unsightly cowtown sprawled on a flat at the mouth of Tinker Canyon. Recently silver had been discovered up the canyon and the town had experienced a slight boom. With the boom the town had received an overflow of boomers, a number of whom were from the East and new to Western ways. One of these was the tall, precise, gray-mustached man who became sheriff, Ben Rowsey.

Another was the tall, handsome Paul Hartman.

New to the country himself, Stretch Magoon, itinerant range detective, had looked the town over when he arrived. Paul Hartman, only six months a resident of Tinkerville, was the acknowledged big man of the town.

He had loaned money to Sam Tinker, who owned the Tinker House and had founded the town in Indian days. He bought stock in the mining ventures. He grubstaked three prospectors, he started a weekly newspaper, and he bought a controlling interest in the Longhorn Bar.

Another newcomer was Kelly Jarvis, who owned the Lazy S, of which Dean Barker was manager.

Kelly was twenty-one years old, lovely, and fresh from the East. Her father had been a salty old range rider, tough and saddle-worn. He had made a mint of money, and had lavished it on Kelly. She was named for a companion of her father's. A story she told, and no one questioned.

Within two hours after she reached town, Kelly was being

shown around by Paul Hartman. He was handsome and agreeable.

Stretch Magoon knew all of this. Tall, sad, and quiet, he got around, listened, and rarely asked a question. When he did, the questions were casual and calculated to start a flow of talk that usually ended in Magoon's learning a lot more than anyone planned to tell him.

He was having a drink in the Longhorn when Ben Rowsey walked up to him. "Magoon," Rowsey demanded sharply, "what's the straight of that shootin' out at the Lazy S?"

Magoon was surprised. In the West, rustling usually ended promptly with either a rope or a bullet. Not a man given to violence himself, he acted according to the code of the country. He had presented evidence of vented brands to Barker, had proved that Ketchell's orders had sent the cattle into the breaks near the Sombrero, and had been riding with Barker and County Galway when he found Ketchell. Ketchell had not seen Barker and Galway, and had tried to shoot it out.

"Nothin' much t' tell. I found him ventin' a brand, an' he went for a gun. He was too slow."

"You'll have to understand, Magoon," Rowsey said sharply, "that gunplay is a thing of the past out here. There's goin' t' be an investigation. You have witnesses?"

"Uh-huh." Magoon was mildly surprised but not alarmed. "Barker an' Galway were comin' up behind me an' saw the whole play."

Rowsey's eyes narrowed. "Galway, is it? His evidence won't be good in this county. He's been mixed up in too many shootin' scrapes himself."

The door opened then, and Paul Hartman came in. "Oh, hello, Magoon. Just the man I was looking for. Miss Jarvis wishes to see you."

Stretch walked outside into the sunlight. Kelly Jarvis, a vision in red hair and dark green riding habit, was sitting a sorrel horse at the door. Hartman and Sheriff Rowsey followed him out.

"You wanted t' see me, ma'am?" He looked sadly up into her violet eyes. They were cold now.

"Yes, I did. I understand you were hired by Dean Barker to

find who was rustling on my ranch. Also, that you killed my foreman. I don't want hired killers on my property. You're fired."

"Fired?" Magoon's long, melancholy face did not change. "I was hired by Barker, ma'am. I reckon I'll let him fire me."

"Barker," Kelly Jarvis said crisply, "has already been fired!"

Magoon looked up at her; then he pushed his battered hat back on his head. "I reckon," he said sadly, "that's all the reward a feller can expect after givin' the best years o' his life t' that ranch like Barker done. I reckon that's all anybody can expect from a girl who was named for a mule!"

Kelly's face turned crimson with embarrassment. "Who told you that?" she flared angrily.

Paul Hartman stepped up abruptly. "That's enough out of you!" he said sharply. "Get going!" He put a hand on Stretch Magoon's shoulder and shoved.

It was an unfortunate thing. Even an unhappy thing. Paul Hartman was a widely experienced young man, yet not unacquainted with the rough and seamy side of life. When his shoulder blades hit the dust of the street a good six feet off the boardwalk, he was jarred from head to heel, jarred as he had never been before.

"Here!" Rowsey interrupted sharply. "Y' can't—"

Chicken Livers, the town loafer, was smiling. "The dude put his hand on him," he said dryly. "He shouldn't a done it."

Hartman got up, brushing off his clothes. Then, quietly, he removed his coat. "I'm going to teach you something!" he snapped, his eyes blazing. "It's about time some of you hicks learned how to talk to a gentleman!"

Hartman had boxed a good deal, but they had been polite boxing matches, between friends. Stretch Magoon had learned his fighting by extensive application, and while a good deal of boxing skill was included, none of it had been politely learned. The left jab that made a bloody puffball of Paul Hartman's lips wasn't in the least polite, and the right uppercut that lifted into Hartman's solar plexus and picked his feet clear of the boardwalk was crude, to say the least. Even a little vulgar.

Sheriff Ben Rowsey too was unaccustomed to Western ways. He had been appointed by a board of which Hartman was the chairman and the directing voice. He was, however, something of a fighting man himself. He helped pick Hartman up from the street and dust him off. Aloud, he voiced his sadness at the unfortunate affair. Mentally, he acknowledged it had been months, years even, since he had seen two nicer punches. For the first time, and not without adequate reason, he began to wonder about Paul Hartman.

Kelly Jarvis was an angry young lady. Her red hair and Irish ancestry, and perhaps something of the nature that had caused her father to name her for his favorite mule, helped to make her angry.

It took her something over an hour to find that she was much less angry at Stretch Magoon for knocking Hartman into the middle of the street than she was at Hartman for allowing himself to be disposed of so thoroughly. Heroes live by doing, and Paul Hartman had not done.

———

"THE WAY I figger it," Stretch was saying to Galway, "is this Paul Hartman has been talking to her. She ain't been here long, an' he is the hombre that knows it all. So she listens."

"But what's the idea?" Galway asked. "What's his ante?"

"That," Magoon admitted, "is the point. Maybe he is just a smart lad tryin' t' take over a pretty filly, an' maybe there's something more behind it. I aim t' see."

He was not the only one who was doing some thinking. Kelly was sitting at lunch, and for the first time since coming West, she was using her own pretty red head.

New to the West, she had let Paul Hartman advise her. Now she was wondering. After all, Dean Barker had worked for her since her father had died when she was but fourteen. His reports, poorly written, but always legible, had been coming with regularity, and somehow, she recalled, the ranch had always shown a profit. Now, on the strength of a new friend's advice, she had discharged him, and had discharged the man Barker hired to investigate the rustling of her cattle.

It was true Stretch Magoon had killed her foreman. Hartman had told her Magoon was a professional killer. But was he? She recalled then that her father had once killed two men trying to rustle his cattle. Another thing came up to irritate her: How had Magoon known that her father had named her for a mule?

It was irritating that he knew. But it was also puzzling.

After lunch, Kelly Jarvis mounted her horse and took to the hills. The green riding habit and hat were left behind in the room at Tinker House. She wore a pair of jeans, boots, a boy's shirt, and a hat. And for the first time since she was fourteen, when her father had let her ride alone, she was carrying a pistol.

It had been seven years since she had been West, but she found as she rode that her knowledge had not been lost. She had grown up on the back of a cow pony, and she could use a rope and could ride as well as many a cowhand.

She rode into the brakes that divided her range from that of the new Sombrero outfit. Once, dismounting at a spring to get a drink, she drew a Lazy S in the mud with a stick, then performed the two simple movements essential to change it to a Sombrero. She had to admit that Stretch Magoon had a point. If Lucky Weidman was honest, as Hartman maintained, it was mighty funny he had chosen the Sombrero for a brand.

RED POSNER, WEIDMAN'S right-hand man, had a face like a horned toad and a disposition like a burro with the colic. He left thinking to his betters, collected his money, drank it up, then rustled more cattle to get more money to buy more whiskey. He was very busy venting a brand on a Lazy S steer when Kelly Jarvis rode down into the clearing.

They saw each other at the same instant, but Red, having a guilty conscience, had the quicker reaction. He hauled iron and threw down on the girl. In a matter of minutes she was on her back in the dust, roped and hogtied with Red's piggin' strings.

When he had her, he paused. There she was, roped and

tied. But what now? What to do with her? That he had a lot of ideas on the subject went without saying, but Red Posner had learned that doing things without Lucky Weidman's say-so was very apt to lead to trouble. He tied the girl in her saddle and rode back to the shack on the dry wash.

From Lucky Weidman's viewpoint, it could not have been worse. Had Red Posner come to him and told him he had the girl, he would have instantly framed a rescue and rushed her back to town, to become the hero of the hour—even if he had to shoot Red. Which, as he considered it, was not a bad idea anyway.

Red, however, being simple even if crooked, had ridden right up to Lucky and started telling what had happened. There was no question but what the girl knew they were working together. There was no chance to saddle this on Magoon. Moreover, this was something Hartman could never fix. Rustling cows was one thing; capturing and holding a girl was another.

While Lucky puzzled over this situation, Stretch Magoon was thinking.

Long and lean and unhappy looking, Stretch had a memory as long as his stretch of limb. As an itinerant range detective and law officer, he had a mind filled with odds and ends of lore, and with a veritable mass of data on wanted men and stolen goods. He was thinking as he whittled, and he sat beside Chicken, asking frequent questions and fitting it into the jigsaw of information in his mind.

Chicken Livers had a little mining claim. From time to time he washed out a bit of color. It kept him in food and liquor and free of the awful entangling bonds of labor. Chicken was a philosopher, a dreamer, a man who observed his fellow men with painstaking care. He was no moralist. He was no gossip. He observed and he remembered.

If Livers had observed a murder, he might have been interested in the method and the motive. He would never have dreamed of reporting it. It was a world in which people did strange things. If murder was one of them, it was no business of his.

On this day, however, drawn by the companion whittling

of the long-legged range detective and the fact that someone was actually interested in him, Chicken Livers was giving forth.

He remembered, for instance, the very day Paul Hartman had come to town. "Alone, was he?" No. Not alone, but the other man had left him on the outskirts. "Plenty of money?" Uh-huh, plenty. All in twenty-dollar bills. Spankin' new ones, too. "Any friends?" Not right away. Talked with Sam Tinker. Then one day got in a confab with Lucky Weidman, sort of by accident. Only maybe it was not an accident. Weidman had stood around a good deal, like he was waiting.

"Could Weidman have been the man he left on the edge o' town?" Could be. Big feller. 'Bout the size o' Weidman.

After a while Magoon got up and sauntered down to the Longhorn, where Sheriff Ben Rowsey was having a drink. Magoon bought one, then looked at Ben. "I take it," Magoon said, "that you're an honest man?"

"I aim t' be!" Rowsey said.

"I take it that if'n you knew a man was a crook, you'd lay hand on him, no matter who he was?"

"That's right!" Rowsey was sincere. "If it was my own brother!"

"Then," Magoon said, "suppose y' wire El Paso for a description o' the teller an' two gunmen who robbed the bank at Forsyth last May; then check up a little."

With that, Stretch Magoon walked out to his horse and swung aboard. Sheriff Ben stood there with his drink, puckering his brows over it, then tossed it off, straightened up, and walked down to the stage station where they'd just put in one of those telegraph outfits.

THE GRULLA WAS a trail-liking mustang, and he took to the hills. Magoon had no love for towns and he liked to get out and go. He skirted the plain near the Lazy S headquarters and then turned into the hills, keeping to the high slopes among the cedar and studying terrain with eyes like a hawk's. So it was that after an hour of riding in the hills he noted the thin wisp of smoke from the dying fire where Red Posner had done his work.

In twenty minutes he was on the scene, puzzling over the second set of tracks. Finally, he found, in the welter of dust and tracks, a partly trampled-out boot print made by a small boot.

There were some marks of ropes on the ground. A tight coil had been turned three times around something. That mark, too, had been partly erased, not by intention, but just by the hoofprints of horses. Then one horse had gone off, and from the way the other followed, always the same distance and never farther behind, it was a led horse.

When two horsemen came into a clearing from opposite directions and go out like that, one of the riders is dead, hurt, or a prisoner.

Stretch Magoon started down the trail made by those tracks. He had a fair idea where they had gone, and about how long before. He followed them because he was afraid they might stop before they reached the Sombrero ranch house. He was pretty certain who the first rider was, and that small boot print could only mean that the prisoner was Kelly Jarvis.

———

LUCKY WEIDMAN WAS mad. He was mad clear through, but he was also worried. Until now his tracks had been well covered, or fairly well covered, with Hartman's help. The disappearance of the girl would set the country on its ears.

He cursed Posner for branding cattle when he should have remained quiet, forgetting that he had told him to go ahead. He cursed Hartman for not keeping the girl in town, cursed Posner for not killing her on the spot, and cursed Stretch Magoon most of all.

Tinny Curtis was going around with a bandage around his neck under his ear, and a bandage on his hand. The wound had been slight, but the missing earlobe was painful and Curtis was trembling for revenge.

Posner sat on the steps, his face heavy with sullen rage. Lucky had given him a cursing, and he didn't like it.

Kelly Jarvis was inside, a bundle of girl dropped on a dirty bed that smelled of Weidman's huge bulk. Bitterly, she regretted ever knowing Paul Hartman or discharging Magoon.

Out in front, on the hard-packed dirt, the three men stared at each other, hating themselves and everybody else.

There was, of course, just one thing to do. Take the girl up into the mountains, drop her into a deserted mine shaft, and then act innocent. And that wasn't going to be simple.

Into that circle of hell and hatred walked Stretch Magoon.

He had left the grulla in the wash and crept up on foot, knowing the advantage of surprise. He glimpsed the girl on the bed, and she glimpsed him. He had no heroic ideas about slipping in, untying her, and making a break for it. He knew he couldn't get through the window and across the room without making some noise. He had one chance, and he was a man who believed in direct methods.

Stretch Magoon stepped around the corner. "Hello, boys," he said, and went for his gun.

There was no heroism in him. He was a man with a job to do. It was characteristic of the West to give a man a break, but even men of the West found it convenient to ignore that principle on occasion. And when one man faces three is not a time to start giving breaks.

The three of them, seething with hatred as they were, didn't lag far behind. Magoon's first shot was for Posner. He didn't want the coyotes yapping at his heels trying to hamstring him when he went after the old grizzly.

Red Posner hopped around like the horned toad he resembled, but his gun never got into action, he took a bullet through the teeth, and it was immediately apparent that he found the lead indigestible.

Tinny Curtis was sitting down, nursing his jaw. He never got to his feet. The bullet that got him took him right in the brisket and went right out through his spine.

Lucky Weidman *was* lucky; he was also careful. He got his gun out, but Magoon was thin, and his first shot missed; the second knocked Magoon back into the wall of the shack, and then Magoon swung his gun onto Weidman and let one bullet chase another one through his big stomach. His fifth and last shot, Magoon missed completely. Then he threw the gun and, with Weidman firing, went into him swinging wildly. He saw the red blaze of the gun, felt the heat on his face, and he felt his fists smashing into that big face. Weidman went down, and Magoon lit just past him, on his knees, then he slid forward into the dust.

A half-hour later he was still lying there, more dead than alive, when Sheriff Ben Rowsey rode in with a warrant for the arrest of Weidman and Posner. With him rode Sam Tinker, Chicken Livers, and a scattering of townspeople.

When Magoon was able to talk, Rowsey told him, "Hartman's in jail. You were right about figuring he was that missin' teller. Weidman an' Posner were the other two."

Kelly was bending over him. He looked at her sadly and she said, "Hurry up and get well. I've put Dean Barker back on the job. I've got some plans for you too, when you get up."

"I reckon," Magoon said woefully, "that I know better than t' argue with a girl who was named for a mule!"

Her face flushed. "Who told you that?" she demanded.

"Your pa," he said. "I rode for him three years steady, after you left!"

THE OUTLAWS OF MESQUITE

ILT COGAR WAS at the corral catching the paint when Thacker walked down from the store. "You'd better get out of this town, boy. They are fixin' to make trouble for you."

Milt turned around and looked at the big, clumsy man, his shirt stuffed into his trousers and held there by a rope belt. Thacker never seemed to have a full beard and always seemed to need a shave. His watery blue eyes looked vague. He rolled his quid in his jaws and spat.

"It's what I'm tellin' you, son. You done me a favor or two."

"Why should they be after me?" Cogar demanded. He was a lean young man with a dark, leatherlike face. His eyes were almost black, and keen.

"Spencer wants your horses. You know that. He sets a sight of store by good horseflesh, and he's had a thorn in his side ever since you rode into the valley. Anyway, you're a stranger, and this country don't cotton to strangers."

Milt Cogar hitched his gun belts and stared at Thacker. "Thanks. I'll not forget it. But betwixt the two of us, this country has good reason to be afraid of strangers."

Thacker's eyes shifted uneasily. "Don't you be sayin' that aloud. Not around here. And don't you tell nobody what I said."

Thacker drifted off down toward his shack, and Milt Cogar stood there, uncertainly. He was not ready to drift, nor did he like being pushed, but he had sensed the undercurrent of feeling against him.

Mesquite was a rustler town. It was a holdup man's town, and he was a wild horse wrangler and a drifter. He threw the saddle on the paint and cinched it down. All the while he was thinking of Jennie Lewis, for she was the reason he had stayed on at Mesquite.

Milt Cogar was no trouble-hunting man. He knew that of himself and he told that to himself once more. In nearly thirty years of drifting, he had kept clear of most of the trouble that came his way. Not that he hadn't had his share, for times came when a man couldn't dodge fights. This could be that kind of time.

Dan Spencer was ramrodding the town. He was the big wheel. Milt had seen the big man's eyes trailing him down the dusty corner of road that did duty as Mesquite's main street. There were only four buildings on that street, and a dozen houses. Jennie lived in the house back under the cottonwoods with Joe and Mom Peters.

Spencer wasn't only big and rough. He was slick. He was slicker than blue mud on a sidehill, only he didn't look it. Milt was a top hand at reading sign, and he could read the tracks years left across a man's face. He knew what manner of a man Dan Spencer was, and what to expect from the others, from Record and Martinez.

It was a mean little place, this valley. The scattering of ugly, unpainted frame buildings, the hillsides covered with scrub pine and juniper, the trail a dusty pathway through the pine and huge, flat-faced boulders. There was a waterhole, and it was that which had started the town. And somewhere back in the cliff and brush country there was a canyon where Spencer and his boys backed up their stolen cattle.

Thacker was right. He should throw a leg over his horse right now and light a shuck out of here. If he stayed, there would be trouble, and he was no gunfighter like Spencer or Record, nor a knife-in-the-belly killer like Martinez. He should light out of here right now, but there was Jennie Lewis.

Jennie was eighteen now, a slim, lovely girl with soft gray eyes and ash-blond hair. She looked like the wind could blow her away but there was quick, bubbling laughter in her, and a look in her eyes that touched something away down inside of a man.

She was a casualty of the trail. Cholera had wiped out her family, and Joe Peters had found her, ten years old and frightened, and carried her home. Only now she was big enough and old enough for Spencer to see, and what Dan Spencer wanted, he took.

Nobody in town would stop Spencer. There were twenty-seven people in Mesquite, but those who weren't outlaws were shy, frightened people who made themselves obscure and came and went as silently as possible, fearful of speaking lest Dan Spencer lay eyes upon them.

———

THAT WAS HOW it had been until Milt Cogar rode into town with his catch of wild horses, sixteen head of them, and all fine stock, and most of them broke to ride. Milt was going on through, but he stopped by the waterhole with his horses, and while they drank he talked with Jennie.

"You've beautiful horses," she said wistfully. "I never saw anything so beautiful, not even the horses that Spencer has."

"They are nice." Cogar was a man unused to the sound of his voice, for he lived much alone. "That's one of the reasons why I catch them. I like working with horses."

She was standing near one of them, and the black put out a friendly nose, and she touched it. The horse did not shy.

"You would never guess they had ever been wild," she said wonderingly. "They are so gentle."

"Most horses are nice folks, ma'am," he said. "They like people. You teach one he doesn't have to be afraid, and right away he gets mighty curious and friendly. For the first few days you just keep them around, no sudden movements, no violence. Just keep a firm hand on them, and feed them well.

"Horses when frightened can't think, not even so much as people, but once they know a man, they'll trust him to take them anywhere at all."

She looked at him thoughtfully. "You must be a kind man," she said gently. "Most men around here break their horses rough."

He flushed and looked away, feeling the slow red on his face and neck and hating himself for being self-conscious. "I don't know about that, ma'am."

Hurriedly, he tried to change the subject. "Your folks live here?"

A shadow touched her face. "No, they are dead, long ago. I live with Joe Peters. He and Mom took me in when I was a child." Her eyes went to his. "You aren't staying here?"

"I was figuring on drifting through," he said, "down toward the canyon country. I got me a little place down there, and I figured to rest up for a while."

"It must be nice to go wherever you want," she said slowly, shifting the heavy wooden bucket in her hands. "This is an awful place!"

The sudden feeling in her voice shocked him. "Why don't you leave?"

"I can't. Dan Spencer wouldn't let me, not even if I found a way to get out."

"Spencer? What's he to you?" Milt Cogar pushed his black hat back on his head and looked at her, seeing the softness in her eyes, and the worry, too. Yet it was more than worry: it was fear.

"He runs Mesquite and everybody in it. He . . . wants me."

"Do you want him? You aim to marry him?"

She flushed anew. "I've not much to say about it here. If he wants me, there's nobody to stop him. As for the rest of it, he hasn't said anything about marrying."

Milt Cogar felt chill anger rising within him. "Who does this Spencer think he is?" he demanded. "Nobody can take a girl unless she wants to go! This country's free!"

"Not in Mesquite, it isn't! This is Dan Spencer's town, and nothing happens in it he don't like. You'd better keep him from seeing your horses, too. He'll want them."

"He'll trip himself up gettin' them!" Cogar said decisively. His eyes went to Jennie's face. "Ma'am, why don't you mount up and ride out of here? If you want to go, I'll see you get safe to the Ferry. Once across the river, you can head down toward Prescott or somewhere you'd be safe."

"Oh, if I only could—" Her voice died, and Milt looked up. A burly, heavy-shouldered man with two guns was standing across the waterhole.

"If you could what?" the burly man asked. Then his eyes

shifted to Milt, and from him to his horses, which he studied with a slow, appraising look, then back to Cogar. "Who are you?"

Milt looked at him with careful eyes. There was danger in this man, but he had faced danger before.

"I'm a man ridin' through," Milt said. "Who are you?"

Spencer stiffened. "Dan Spencer's the name, and I run this town."

Milt lifted his eyes insultingly toward the collection of miserable shacks. "Must keep you busy," he said.

"Not too busy but what I could teach you some manners!" Spencer's voice rang harshly. He walked around the water-hole, hands swinging at his sides. "Jennie, you go on home!"

Only an instant did the girl hesitate, apprehension for Cogar in her eyes. Then she began backing away.

Spencer stopped, a dozen feet from Milt, and dropped his hand to his gun butt—then the hand froze where it was, and Dan Spencer's eyes bulged. He was looking into the muzzle of a .44 Winchester carbine. "Unbuckle your belt, and be careful!" Milt warned.

Dan Spencer's face was gray. Very slowly he moved his fingers to the belt and unbuckled it, letting the Colts fall. "Now take a step toward me," Cogar commanded.

The big man complied. Color was coming back into his face and with it the realization that Milt Cogar had shown him up in front of the girl. Yet there was little he could do. His guns were on the ground behind him now.

"Now, let me tell you something, Spencer." Cogar spoke quietly, but coldly. "You let me alone. I'm passin' through Mesquite. I may decide to stay over a couple of days, but don't let that give you any ideas, because if you get tough with me, I'll kill you! Now pull your freight."

When Spencer was gone, Milt stooped and shucked the shells from Spencer's guns, then from the belt, shoving the shells into his pocket—all but a few. He stood there by his horses and, taking out his knife, worked for a few minutes over those shells. Then he fed them back into the guns. When he was about to mount and ride on, he heard a low call from the brush. It was Jennie.

He mounted and rode over to where she waited, leaving his horses tied in groups of four.

"You'd better go quickly!" she warned. "He'll kill you! It isn't only him alone. He has other men. Two of them are John Record and Pablo Martinez. Both are killers and with him nearly all the time."

Cogar looked down at the girl. He was a tall, spare man with a quiet, desert man's face.

"This is no place for a girl. You want to leave?" he said.

Hope flashed into her eyes. "Oh, I'd love to! But I've nowhere to go, and even if I wanted to, Spencer wouldn't allow it. Mom has wanted Joe to smuggle me away, but he's afraid."

"Well, you get back to your house and get together whatever you want to take along, but not much of it. You fix us a mite of grub, too. Then you slip out of the house, come daybreak, and meet me by that white boulder I can see just below town. I'll take you out of here, and see you get safe to help. You ain't afraid of me?"

Jennie looked at him quickly. "No, I guess not. You look like an honest man. Also I'm remembering you treat your horses kind. I trust you. Anyway," she added, "there's nobody else."

He grinned. "That makes it simple. You be there, now. We may have to ride fast."

———

WHEN MILT COGAR had his horses bedded down on the edge of Mesquite, he studied the place warily. There was a saloon, a general store, a blacksmith shop, and an eating house. Leaving his carbine concealed near a clump of mesquite, he hitched his guns to an easier position and headed up the street. A heavy-bodied man with a stubble of beard showed on the saloon stoop. Milt avoided the place, rightly guessing it would be Spencer's hangout, and walked to the restaurant and went in.

A fat man with freckles and a fringe of sandy hair around a bald spot was cooking over an iron range. He glanced up.

"Fix me some grub," Milt suggested. "I'm sure hungry."

Red nodded briefly and, grabbing a big plate, ladled out a

thick chunk of beef, a couple of scoops of beans, and some potatoes. Then he poured a cup of coffee from a battered coffeepot and picked up some sourdough bread.

Cogar ate in silence for a while, then glanced up. "You one of Dan Spencer's outfit?"

Red stiffened. "I run my own shebang. If Spencer wants to eat, I feed him. That's all I have to do with him."

"I heard this was his town."

"It is. All but me." The door pushed open as he spoke, and Thacker came in. He sat down heavily on a chair across the table from Milt Cogar.

"Nice horses you got," he said tentatively.

Milt glanced up, taking in Thacker with a glance. "They'll do," he agreed.

"Don't need a hand, do you? Sixteen horses are a bunch for one man."

"My horses are gentle. I can handle them."

Thacker's face flushed a slow red, and he glanced toward the sandy-haired cook. He said softly:

"I could use a mite of work now. I'm sort of short."

Milt Cogar could sense the big man's embarrassment and it stirred his quick generosity. "Might lend you a bit," he suggested, keeping his own voice low. "Would ten dollars help?"

Thacker's face glowed red, but there was surprise and gratitude in his eyes. "I ain't no hand to borry," he said, "and you ridin' through like you are." He spoke hesitantly. "I reckon I hadn't better."

Cogar pushed a gold piece across the table. "Take it, man, and welcome. I've been staked a couple of times with no chance to pay back, so forget about paying me. When you have it, stake some other hombre."

When Thacker had gone, Red turned around. "Heard that," he said, then jerked his head toward the way Thacker had gone. "He ain't much good, either, but he's got him a boy he fair worships. He'll buy grub for that kid with the money, you can bank on it."

It was later, by the corral, that Thacker had come to Cogar with his warning. It was unnecessary, for Milt knew what he was facing. He also knew he was going to ride out of that town with Jennie Lewis or there would be blood on the streets. Yet he was no fighting man unless pushed. He wanted to get her away without trouble, yet when he faced the facts, he knew that Spencer grated on his nerves, that the thought of the man ruling the helpless people of the town angered him.

Carefully, he looked over his horses, checking to see if any had injured feet, and stopping to talk and pet each one of them. They were fine stock, and would sell well, yet he never gentled a bunch like this without hating to part with them.

Up the street he could see lights going on in the saloon. He felt better with the meal under his belt, and he inspected his gun again. Spencer, Record, and Martinez, and half the town at least in cahoots with them. Nor could he expect any help. It was his game.

Milt backed up against a corral post and faced the town. He could watch from here. The horses liked to see him close. He dozed a little, knowing trouble would come later, if at all. For a while they would wait for him at the saloon, and that was a place he had no intention of going.

Darkness crawled over the hills and pushed patrols of shadow between the buildings and along the edge of the woods. More lights came on. Behind him a horse stamped and blew, and somewhere out on the desert, a blue quail called softly, inquiringly.

It was very quiet. A tin bucket rattled somewhere, and he could smell the oil on his guns. Once he got up and walked among his horses, talking softly to them. His eyes shifted toward the light in the cabin where Jennie lived.

It seemed strange, having a woman to think about. He was a lonely man, and like so many lonely men he knew how to value love, attention, and the nearness of someone. He remembered the dusty spun gold of her hair, and the slim figure under the faded dress. There was something fine about her, something that spoke of another world than the world of Mesquite, Dan Spencer, and his followers.

He grinned ruefully. After all, she was not his to think about. He had only offered to help her, and once she was safely away—well, who was he to expect interest from such a girl as that?

A door opened and closed, and he glanced toward the saloon, making out a dark figure on the porch. The pale blotch above it was the man's face, looking toward him. Yet the watcher could not see Milt, for the blackness of his body would merge with the blackness of the corral corner.

They were beginning to wonder if he was coming, and when. He sat perfectly still, keeping his ears ready for the slightest sound. He did not look directly at the figure, but near it, and he did not allow his gaze to become fixed. He must be wary and ready always.

Had it not been for the weariness of his horses he might have started with Jennie at night, but the horses needed rest, and tomorrow would be a hard, long day. Doubly hard if Spencer elected to pursue.

The man on the porch returned inside, and Milt Cogar arose and moved around to get the stiffness from his muscles. Suddenly, an idea came to him, and he turned toward the corral, staring within. His own horses were outside, but inside were a half-dozen cow ponies used by Spencer and others. For an instant, Cogar considered, and then he got busy.

A sorrel with a white face had stayed close to the corral bars and several times he had patted it a little. Now he went inside and, catching the halter, led it out and tied it near his own horses. By soft talk and easy movements, he succeeded in getting two more outside where he tied them in plain view of the saloon. Then he took the first four of his own horses and, walking them carefully, led them away down the trail.

When he was out of sight of the town, he tied them and returned. In four trips he had led all of his own horses to the same place. Then he untied the first four, knowing they would stay together. After that he walked back and saddled his gray gelding. The paint he had caught earlier was already saddled and waiting. He had bought the extra saddle from a busted cowhand down Las Vegas way, but now it was to come in handy.

He retrieved his rifle and slid it into the scabbard. Then he sat down and lit a cigarette. Twice in the next hour or so a man came to the saloon door and looked out. Each time he let the cigarette glow brightly.

From where he sat he could see the corner of the water trough in the corral, and a glow caught his eye. For a few minutes he studied it curiously, and then recognized it. The glow was that greenish, phosphorescent light from damp, rotten wood, such as he had often seen in swampy country, or after a period of heavy rains. Many times he had seen branches like that, greenish, ghostly fingers reaching into the darkness.

It gave him another idea and he got to his feet again and walked off a short distance. It was still visible. This would be just the added touch he would need to make his escape effective. He broke off a small bit of the wood and fastened it into the corral post where he had been sitting, and then moved out into the street. The glow was still visible, not so bright as a cigarette, but enough to fool anyone taking a casual glance toward the corral. They were, he was sure, waiting for him to fall asleep.

Once the phosphorescent wood was in place, he moved swiftly. Getting into the saddle, he led the gray horse behind him and moved across the valley toward the Peters cabin, where Jennie Lewis lived. Dismounting then, he concealed his horses in the timber, and moved up to the house. A quick glance through the windows, and he saw no one but Jennie, carrying dishes away from the table, and the two older people.

Stepping up to the back door, he tapped gently. There was a moment of silence within, then a question. "Who is it?" At his reply, the door opened and he stepped inside.

"We've got to go now," he said quickly. "My horses aren't ready for it, but Spencer's bunch are watching me, and we've got a chance to get away that may give us an hour or so of start."

Joe Peters was staring at him, his face pale. "Hope you make it!" he said. "I hate to think what Spencer will do when we don't tell him you're gone! He's apt to kill us both, or whup us!"

"We'll fix that," Cogar replied. "We'll tie you both. You can say I threw a gun on you."

"Sure!" Peters said. "Sure thing!" He turned to his wife. "Mom, you let me tie you, and then this hombre can tie me."

Jennie had not hesitated. When he spoke she had turned and gone into her room, and now she came out. Startled, he saw she had a pistol belt around her hips.

"Pa's gun," she said, at his question. "It might come in handy!"

They rode swiftly until they reached the edge of the settlement, and then swung around toward where Milt Cogar had left his horses. As they drew alongside, Milt got down to unfasten the ropes that tied them in groups of four. They might have to run, and he wanted nothing to tangle them up.

Suddenly, a dark figure moved from the shadow of the mesquite, and a low voice spoke softly. "I've got you covered. If you move I'll shoot!"

It was not Dan Spencer. But Record, perhaps?

"Who's moving?" he said calmly. "You're doin' a fool thing, buttin' in on this deal."

"Am I?" The man stepped out from the darkness of the mesquite, and Cogar could see his face. The man was slim, wiry and hard-jawed. The gun he held brooked no argument. "Anyway, I'm in. Dan Spencer will be pleased to find I've stopped you from gettin' away with his girl."

Milt Cogar held himself very still. There was only one way he could come out of this alive, and it required a gamble with his life at stake. The moment would come. In the meanwhile, he tried the other way, for which he had no hope.

"Folks won't let you steal this girl," he said. "They'll stand for everything but that."

"They'll stand for that, too," the man said. "Now turn around!"

"Stay where you are!" Jennie's voice was low, penetrating. "Johnny Record, I've got you covered. Drop that gun or I'll kill you!"

Record stiffened, but before he could realize that as long as Cogar was covered there was a stalemate, the girl's voice snapped again.

"You drop that gun before I count three or I'll shoot! One! Two! Thr—"

Her count ended as Record let go of his gun. Milt stepped up and retrieved it. Swiftly then, he spun Record around and tied him tightly, hand and foot.

In the saddle and moving away, he glanced through the darkness toward Jennie. "I reckon as a hero I don't count for much, you gettin' us out of that fix!"

"What else could I do? Anyway, I'd never have had the courage unless you were taking me away like this. With a man to help, I'm brave enough, I guess."

THEY RODE ON, holding a steady if not fast pace. There was small chance of them losing any pursuit. That would have to be met when it came. He couldn't leave his horses behind, for they were all he had. He might need the money from their sale to help Jennie. She would be friendless and alone.

The desert was wide and white in the moonlight, with only the dark, beckoning fingers of the giant cactuses or the darker blotches of the mesquite or distant mountains. He turned off the trail he had been following, heading into the canyon country. This would be rough going, but there were places ahead where one might stand off an army.

Foothills crept out into the desert toward them, and they started the horses into a deep draw between two parted arms of hills. The rock walls grew higher and higher, and they lost the light, having only a small rectangle of starlit sky overhead. Milt took no time to rest, but pushed the horses relentlessly, taking no time for anything but getting on.

He knew where he was going, and he knew he must make it by daylight. Jennie said nothing, but he could sense her weariness, judging it to an extent by his own, for her strength would not be equal to his.

Finally, the canyon opened out into a wide flat valley in the mountains, and he moved the horses into the tall grass, giving them no rest, but pushing them diagonally across it. They were mounting toward the far wall of the valley before he drew up.

"We'll stop here, Jennie," he said, "but we daren't have a fire."

He divided the blankets and rolled up in his. In a moment, he was sound asleep. He was unworried about the horses, for they would be too tired to go far.

The sun on his face awakened him, and he came to a sitting position with a start. Jennie was sitting about a dozen feet away with his rifle across her knees.

Milt stared at her, red-faced. "I slept like a tenderfoot!" he said, abashed.

"I'm not used to sleeping out, so I awakened early, that's all. There was no need you being awake. Anyway, they just came into the valley."

"Spencer?"

"Three of them. They came out of the ravine over there and are scouting for our trail. They haven't found it yet."

"Probably not. There's wild horses in this valley and their herd tracks are everywhere." Jennie looked tired but her eyes were bright. "We'll saddle up and get going."

When they were moving again, he hugged the wall of the canyon, knowing they would scarcely be visible against its darkness. They pushed on steadily, and from time to time his eyes strayed to the girl. She rode easily in the saddle, her willowy body yielding to every movement of the horse.

He found he liked having her there. He had never realized how nice it was to know there was someone beside you, someone who mattered. That was the trouble. It was going to be lonesome when she was gone. To avoid that thought, he turned in his saddle and glanced back. They were coming, all three of them, and he had no more than a mile or two of leeway before they would catch up.

Milt's mind was quick, and he knew this valley. The hollow up ahead was the only possible chance. He rode up and turned the horses into it, backing them into the trees along the hillside out of range. Jennie had followed his glance when he looked back, and her face was pale.

When the horses were safely under the trees, he walked

back to the crest of the rise. It was a poor place for defense, yet nothing else offered. In the bottom of the hollow one was safely out of range unless they circled around and got on the mountain behind it. If that happened, there would be small chance for either of them. Still, Milt thought as he nestled down into the grass, there were only three outlaws.

They came on, riding swiftly, and he knew they had seen the two of them ride into the hollow. Jennie moved up beside him.

"I can load your rifle," she whispered, "while you stand them off with the six-guns."

He nodded to indicate he understood, and lifted the .44 Winchester. When they were within rifle range, he sighted at them, then took the gun from his shoulder and let them come closer. At last he lifted the rifle again and put a shot into the ground ahead of them. They drew up.

"That won't get you no place!" Spencer roared. "You turn that girl loose and we'll let you go!"

Cogar made no reply, merely waiting. There was some talk down below, and then he called out. "You've come far enough. Don't advance any further!"

One of them, probably Martinez, although Milt could not be sure, wheeled his horse and started for the hollow at a dead run. Milt lifted the rifle and fired.

The rifle leaped in his hand, and Martinez yelled and threw up his hands. He went off the horse as it veered sharply and cut away across the grass. Martinez staggered to his feet and, one arm hanging limp, started back toward the other two outlaws.

Cogar let him go. He was not a killer, and wanted only to be let alone.

Four more horsemen were coming up, and were scarcely more than a half mile away. They came on, and drew up with Spencer, where they began to talk.

"That makes six of them out there, not counting Martinez," Cogar said. "Looks like we're in for it."

"You could let them have me," Jennie suggested. Her cheek was pillowed on her forearm, and her wide eyes on his face.

He did not take his eyes from them. "Don't talk foolishness! I said I'd take you away, and I will. My promises are good."

"Is your promise the only reason?"

"Maybe it is and maybe it ain't. Womenfolks always have to see things personal-like. If you can be got out of this alive, I'll get you out."

"You know, you're really quite good-looking."

"Huh?" He looked around, startled at the incongruous remark. Then as it hit him, he flushed.

"Oh, forget it! Looks ain't gettin' us out of this hole! What I'm afraid of is they'll get somebody on the mountain behind us, or else they'll fire the grass."

"Fire the grass?" Her head jerked up and her face went white. "Oh, no! They wouldn't burn us!"

"That outfit? They'd do anything if they got good and riled."

Some sort of a plan seemed to have been arrived at. Dan Spencer shouted again:

"One more chance! Come out with your hands up and we'll turn you loose! Otherwise we're comin' after you!"

They were barely within rifle range, and Milt Cogar knew the chips were down. His reply was a rifle shot that clipped a white hat from the head of a newcomer. They all hit dirt then.

"I wanted to get him then," Milt muttered. "That wasn't to scare him."

Milt was scared, he admitted to himself. He was as scared as he'd ever been, yet in another way, he wasn't. There was no way out that he could see, and if they fired the grass the only chance was a run for the horses and a wild break in an attempt to outrun the attackers. But there was small chance of that working, for there were too many of them. An idea came suddenly.

"You slip back there," he said. "Get the horses down into the hollow. We may have to make a break for it."

She glanced at him quickly, and then without a word, slid back down the slope and got to her feet. He heard a rifle spang, but what happened to the bullet, he didn't know, and then there was a volley and he knew what happened to all the rest. Two whipped by right over his head, and one of them burned him across the shoulders. He rolled over and crept to another position. He could see nothing to shoot at, yet a moment later there was a movement down below, and he fired twice, fast as he could lever the rifle.

The movement stopped, and he rolled over again, getting himself to a new position. If they got to the edge of the hollow, he was done for, but he couldn't watch all the terrain. A bullet nipped the grass over his head and he fired at the sound.

Stealing a quick glance backward, he saw Jennie coming out of the trees into the hollow with the horses. They seemed disturbed by the firing, and halted not far away.

Spencer yelled then, and instantly, without replying, Milt snapped a shot at the spot, then one left and one right of it. He heard a startled yelp, but doubted from the sound that his shot had more than burned the renegade.

"Get to your horse but keep your head down!" he warned Jennie. "Now listen: we're going out of here, you and I, and fast when we go. We're going to start our horses right down there into the middle of them, and try to crash through. It's a wild chance, but from the way they act, they are scattering out to get all around us. If they do, we won't have much chance. If we run for it now, right at them, they may get us, but we'll have a chance of stampeding their horses."

He swung into the saddle and they turned the herd of fifteen horses toward the enemy, then with whoops and yells, started them on a dead run for Spencer. The rim of the hollow and the tall grass gave them a few precious moments of invisibility, so when the horses went over the rise they were at a dead run.

Milt Cogar, a six-gun in each hand, blazed away over the heads of the horses at the positions of the attackers. He saw instantly that he had been right, for men were already moving on foot off to left and right to surround the hollow.

With a thunder of racing hoofs, the horses charged down on Spencer's position, nostrils flaring, manes flowing in the wind of their furious charge.

Milt saw Dan Spencer leap to his feet and throw up a gun,

but his shot went wild, and the next instant he turned and fled. Johnny Record had started to move off to the right, but he turned when he saw the charging horses, and threw his rifle to his shoulder. Cogar snapped a shot at him, and the yells of the men ahead swerved the horses.

There was a moment of startled horror as Record saw death charging upon him, and then he dropped his rifle and started to run. He never made it, and Milt heard his death scream as he went down under the lashing hoofs. And then the herd was racing away down the valley.

"Milt!" Jennie's cry was agonized.

He swung his horse and looked back. The gray had fallen with her, spilling her over on the ground even as she screamed. And running toward her was Dan Spencer.

Milt Cogar's horse was beside her in three bounds and he dropped from the saddle, drawing as he hit ground. His first shot was too quick, and he missed. Spencer skidded to a halt, his face triumphant.

"Now we'll see!" he shouted.

The veins swelled in his forehead, and his eyes were pinpoints of steel. His gun bucked in his hand, and Milt's leg went out from under him, but even as his knee hit ground, he fired. His bullet caught Spencer in the diaphragm, and knocked him back on his heels. Both men fired again, but Dan Spencer's shot bit into the earth just in front of Cogar, and he thumbed his gun, aiming low down at the outlaw's body. Spencer backed up, his jaw working, his eyes fiercely alive. Then a bloody froth came to his lips, and Milt, cold and still inside, fired once more. The outlaw's knees gave way and he pitched over on his face.

Milt stared at the fallen man, fumbling at his belt for more cartridges. His fingers seemed very clumsy, but he finally filled the empty chambers. Jennie was hobbling toward him.

"I've sprained my ankle," she said, "but it's nothing!"

She dropped beside him, and gasped when she saw the blood on his trouser leg. "You're hurt!" she exclaimed.

"Not much," he told her. "Who's that coming?"

Her head came up sharply. Then her face whitened with relief. "It's Joe Peters! And Thacker!"

The two men walked up, the slender Peters looking even smaller beside the rope-girthed bulk of Thacker. Both men had rifles.

"You two all right?" Thacker demanded. The hesitation and fear seemed to have left him. "We hurried after you to help, but we got here late."

"What happened to the other men with Spencer?" Cogar asked.

"The horses got both Martinez and Record. We found one other man dead, one wounded. We kilt one our ownselves, and caught up the rest."

Red came up. "Reckon you started somethin', mister," he said to Milt. "When you took Jennie away so's Spencer couldn't have her, we decided it was right mean of us to let a stranger protect our women. So Thacker here, he seen Joe Peters, and a few others. Then we got together at my eatin' place and started cleanin' the town. We done a good job!"

Thacker grinned, well pleased with himself. "You two can come back if you want," he suggested. "This here deserves a celebration."

"Why, I'd like to come back, sometime," Milt said, "but right now I've got to get my horses down to my own ranch and into the pasture there. I'd take Jennie to see the place, if she'll go."

"A ranch might be nice," Jennie said. Her eyes smiled at him, but there was something grave and serious in their depths. "I might like it."

"Only if you come, I might want to keep you," Milt said. "It isn't going to be the same after this."

"Why should it?" Jennie said.

The gray had gotten to his feet and was shaking himself. Milt walked over to him, and his hand trembled as he examined the gelding's legs. When he straightened up, Jennie was facing him, and her lips looked soft and inviting.

"I reckon," Thacker said, pleased, "that we'll have to celebrate without them!"

MURPHY PLAYS HIS HAND

B RAD MURPHY HAD been a prisoner in the box canyon for three months when he heard the yell.

He jerked erect so suddenly that he dropped his gold pan, spilling its contents. Whirling about, he saw the three horsemen on the rim and he ran toward the cliff, shouting and waving his arms.

One of the men dismounted and came to the edge of the ninety-foot precipice.

"What's the trouble?" he yelled.

"Can't get out!" Murphy yelled. "Slide wiped out the trail to the rim. I been a prisoner here for months!"

"Made a strike?" The man on the rim gestured toward the stream and the gold pan.

Instinct made Brad hesitate.

"No," he said cautiously. "Only a little color."

The man walked back and then he returned to the cliff edge, knotting together the ends of two riatas. While he was doing that, Brad Murphy walked back to the camp and picked up his rifle. On a sudden hunch he thrust his pistol inside his shirt and under his belt. Then he picked up the sack of dust and nuggets. It wasn't a large sack, but it weighed forty pounds.

When they got him to the rim, the man who had done the talking stared at the heavy sack, his eyes curious. He lifted his eyes to Brad's face, and the eyes were small, cruel, and sparkling with sardonic humor.

"My name's Butch Schaum," he said quietly. "What's yourn?"

"Murphy," Brad replied. "Brad Murphy."

The thin-faced man on the buckskin jerked his head up and turned toward Brad.

"You the Brad Murphy used to be in Cripple Creek?"

Brad nodded. "Yeah, I was there for a spell. You're Asa Moffitt." His eyes shifted to the third man on the paint. "And you'll be Dave Cornish."

"Know us all, do you?" Schaum said; his eyes flickered over Brad's height, taking in his great breadth of shoulder, the powerful hands. Then straying to the rifle.

Murphy shrugged. "Who doesn't know the Schaum gang? You've been ridin' these hills for several years." He rubbed his hands on his pants. "Any of you got a smoke?"

Schaum offered the makings. "Go on an' Dave can ride behind Asa," he said. "His horse'll carry double. I'll take the sack."

"No." Brad looked up and his green eyes were steady, hard. "I'll do that myself."

"Be too heavy on the hoss," Schaum declared.

"I'll carry the sack," Murphy replied, "and walk."

"Ain't necessary," Moffitt interrupted. "My hoss'll take the weight. It's only six miles to the shack."

———

GRIMLY BRAD MURPHY kept his rifle in his hands. They didn't know it was empty. They didn't know he had run out of the heavy .40-65 ammunition over two months ago.

Too much was known about Butcher Schaum. The man and his henchmen were cruel as Yaquis. They were killers, outlaws of the worst sort. Three years ago they had held up the bank in Silver City, killing the cashier and escaping with several thousand dollars. They killed one of the posse that followed them. In Tascosa, Dave Cornish had shot a man over a horse.

In Cripple Creek, where Brad Murphy had known Asa Moffitt, Asa was suspected of a series of robberies and killings. Escape from the canyon was now a case of out of the frying pan, into the fire. These men were not wondering what was in the sack; the only thing that could be that heavy was gold.

That gold would more than pay Brad for the three lonely months in the box canyon. It was gold enough to buy the ranch he wanted, and to stock it. His stake, the one he had sought for so long, was here. Now he and Ruth would have their own home. And a home for their son as well.

He suffered from no illusions. These men would kill him in an instant for his gold. They had delayed this long only because they had him, helpless, or practically so. Of course, there had been Asa's manner when he mentioned his name. Asa Moffitt knew about Brad Murphy. And Moffitt's queer reaction at the mention of his name had been a warning to Schaum.

"Ever have any more trouble with the Howells crowd?" Moffitt asked.

It was, Brad knew, a means of telling Schaum who he was. They would remember. His gunfight with the three Howells boys had made history.

"A little," he replied shortly. "Two cousins of theirs follered me to Tonopah."

"What happened?" Butcher Schaum demanded. Moffitt's question had told him at once who Murphy was.

"They trailed me to a water hole near the Dead Mountains. I planted 'em there."

Butcher Schaum felt a little chill go through him at the calm, easy way in which Brad Murphy spoke. Schaum was ruthless, cold-blooded, and a killer. Moreover, he was fast enough. But he had never killed three men in one gun battle, nor even two.

For this reason, nobody was going to move carelessly around Murphy. After all, Murphy knew who Schaum was. He knew what to expect. Getting that gold wasn't going to be that simple. Getting it would mean killing Brad Murphy.

THE SHACK WAS tucked in a cozy niche in the cliff face. The level of the plateau broke off sharply, and under the lip of rock, the shack was built of stone and crude mortar. It was not easy to approach, hard to get away from, and was built for defense. Any posse attacking the Schaum gang here could figure on losing some men. You couldn't come within fifty yards of it without being under cover of a rifle. And that approach was from only one direction.

They swung down, and Butcher noted how carefully Brad kept them in front of him. He did it smoothly, bringing a grudging admiration to Butcher's eyes. This hombre was no fool. The sack never left his hand.

He followed them into the cabin.

"I'd like a horse," he said. "My wife and kid must think I'm dead. This is the longest I've been away."

"Too late to travel now," Cornish said. "That trail's plumb dangerous in the dark. We'll get a horse for you in the mornin'."

———

HIS RIFLE BESIDE him, Brad sat at the table as Moffitt went about getting supper. The sack of gold lay on the floor at Brad's side.

"How do we know you won't tell the law where we're holed up?" Cornish demanded.

"You know better'n that," Murphy replied shortly. "You boys gave me a hand. I never—" he added coolly, "bother nobody that don't bother me."

It was a warning, flat, cold, plain as the rocky ridge that lined the distant sky. They took it, sitting very still. Moffitt put some beans and baton on the table and several slabs of steak.

Brad Murphy had chosen a seat that kept his back to the wall. It had been a casual move, but one that brought a hard gleam to Asa Moffitt's eyes. His thin, cruel face betrayed no hint of what he was thinking, but he knew, even better than the others, what they were facing.

Idly, they gossiped about the range, but when the meal was over, Butcher looked up from under his thick black brows.

"How about some poker?" he asked. "Just to pass the time."

Cornish brought over a pack of cards and shuffled. Murphy cut, and they dealt. They played casually, almost carelessly. They had been playing for almost an hour, with luck seesawing back and forth, when Asa suddenly got up. "How about some coffee?" he said.

Brad had just drawn two cards, and he looked up only as Asa was putting Brad's rifle in the rack.

"I'll just set this rifle out of the way," he said, with a malicious gleam in his eye. "I reckon you won't be needin' it."

Schaum chuckled, deep in his throat. He won a small pot, and his eyes were bright and hungry as he looked at Brad Murphy.

"You fellows have played a lot of poker," Brad drawled. Coolly, he began rolling a smoke. "Ain't never wise to call unless you're pretty sure what the other feller's holdin'."

Cornish stared at him. "What do you mean by that?" he asked sharply.

"Me?" Brad looked surprised. "Nothin' but what I say. Only," he added, "it'd sure make a man feel mighty silly if he figured an hombre had a couple of deuces, then called and found him holdin' a full house."

Butcher Schaum's eyes were cautious. Somehow, Murphy was too confident, too sure of himself. Maybe it would be easier to get the gold by winning it over the table. He fumbled the cards in his big hands, then dealt.

Brad Murphy, his eyes half closed, heard the flick of the card as it slipped off the bottom of the deck. He smiled at Schaum, just smiled, and Butcher Schaum felt something turn over inside of him. He was a hard man, but in Murphy's place he would have been scared. He knew it. Only once he had been cornered like that, and he had been scared. Luckily, some friends arrived to save him. This hombre wasn't scared. He was cool, amused.

Schaum picked up his cards, glanced at them, and straightened in his chair, his face slowly going red under the deep tan. The three kings he had slipped from the bottom of the deck, all marked by his thumbnail, had suddenly become deuces!

Trying to be casual, he turned a card in his hand. The mark was there!

He looked up, and Brad Murphy was smiling at him, smiling with a hard humor. Brad Murphy had dealt last. Obviously, he had detected the marks and added his own, to the deuces.

Suddenly, Butcher Schaum knew there was going to be a showdown. He wasn't going to wait. To the devil with it!

He tossed his cards onto the table. Brad Murphy looked up, surprised.

"Murphy." Schaum leaned over the table. "You figger to be a purty smart hombre. You know us boys ain't no lily-fingered cowpokes. We been owl-hootin' for a long time now. You got a lot of gold in that poke. We want a split."

Brad smiled. "I'm right grateful," he said, "for you pullin' me out of that canyon, and I wouldn't mind payin' you for a horse. But the future of this gold has already been accounted for, and I ain't makin' any sort of split."

He shifted a little in the seat, turning his body. One hand placed two double eagles on the table, taken from the pocket of his jeans. He then shifted his winnings from the game to the same pile. "Now, if you boys want to let me have the horse," he said, "I'll split the breeze out of here. Like I say, it's been a long time since I seen my wife and kid."

"You play a pretty good hand of poker," Schaum said, "but it's you that's bucking a full house. Asa's over there by the door. Yore rifle's gone. Cornish and me here, we figure we're in a good spot ourselves. It's three to one, and them ain't good odds for you."

"No," Brad admitted, "they ain't. Specially with Asa off on my side like that. The odds are right bad, I reckon. Almost," he added, "as bad as when the Howells boys tried me."

He smiled at Schaum. "There was three of them, too."

"Split your poke," Schaum said. "Ten pounds o' that for each of us. That's plenty of a stake."

"I'm not splittin' anything, Butcher," Murphy said quietly. "If you shorthorns want to be paid for draggin' me out of that hole, there it is." He gestured to what was on the table. "But I worked down in the heat and misery for this gold. I aim to keep it."

"We're holdin' the best hand, Brad," Schaum said. "So set back and make it easy on yourself. You divvy up, or we take it all."

"No," Murphy replied, "I'm holdin' the only hand, Butcher. You three got me cornered. You might get me, but that wouldn't help you—you'd be dead!"

"Huh? What do you mean?" Butcher sat up, his lips tight.

"Why, the six-shooter I'm holdin', Butch. She's restin' on my knee, pointin' about an inch under yore belt buckle." He tapped the underside of the table with the barrel.

He shoved back in his chair a little, then stood up, the Army Colt .45 balanced easily in his hand. "I'm takin' a horse, boys, an' I wouldn't figure on nothin' funny; this gun's mighty easy on the trigger."

Waving Asa around with the other two, he gathered his sack with his left hand and edged around the table toward the door. Slowly, he backed to the door, his gun covering them.

He stepped back. Butcher Schaum, his face swollen with fury, stared at him, his right hand on the table, fingers stretched like a claw, and stiff with rage.

He stepped back again, quickly this time. His foot hung. Too late he remembered the raised doorsill, he fell backward, grabbing at the air. Then a gun blasted and something struck him alongside the head. With his last flicker of consciousness, he hurled the sack of gold at the slope that reared itself alongside the cabin. It struck, gravel rattled, and he felt blackness close over him, soft, folding, deadening.

———

THE FIRST THING he realized was warmth. His back was warm. Then his eyes flickered open, blinding sunlight struck them, and they closed.

He was lying, his head turned sideways, sprawled face-down on the hard-packed earth outside the cabin door. It was daylight.

Butcher Schaum's voice broke into his growing realization. "Where'd he put that durned sack?" he snarled angrily. "My shot got him right outside the door, he didn't have no more'n two steps, an' now that gold is plumb gone."

"You sure he's dead?" Asa protested.

"Look at his head!" Cornish snapped. "If he ain't dead he will be. I couldn't get no pulse last night. He's dead all right."

"Should we bury him?" Asa suggested. "I don't like to see him lying like that."

"Go ahead, if you want to," Schaum snarled. "I'm huntin' that gold. When I get it, I'm leavin'. You can stay if you want to. The buzzards'll take care of him. Leave him lay."

His head throbbing with pain, Brad lay still. How bad was he hurt? What was wrong with his head? It felt stiff and sore, and the pain was like a red-hot iron pressed against his skull.

Something crawled over his hand. His eyes flickered. An ant. Horror went through him. Ants! In a matter of minutes they'd be all over him. If there was an open wound—yet he dare not move. His gun? He had lost it in falling. No telling where it was now. If he tried to move they would kill him.

He could hear the three men moving as they searched. Schaum began to curse viciously.

"Where could it get to?" he bellowed angrily. "He didn't go no more'n a few feet."

Other ants were coming now, crawling over his arm toward his head. He knew now that he was cut there. The bullet must have grazed his skull, ripping the scalp open and drenching him with blood, making it appear that he was shot through the head.

Piercing pain suddenly went through him. The ants had gone to work. He forced himself to lie still. His teeth gritted, and he lay, trying not to tense himself.

"I'll bet he throwed that sack down the gully," Cornish said suddenly. "It couldn't be no place else."

He could hear them then, cursing and sliding to get to the bottom of the gully that curved close to the cabin from the left. The bank against which he had thrown the sack was to the right.

Two of them gone. The ants were all over him now, and he could not stand the agony much longer. It was turning his head into a searing sheet of white-hot pain.

Where was Moffitt? He could hear no sound. Then, as he was about to move, he heard a step, so soft he could scarcely detect it. Then another step, and Asa Moffitt was bending over him.

"In his shirt," Moffitt muttered. "Where the gun was!"

Moffitt caught him by the coat and jerked him over on his back. "Ants gittin' him," he muttered. "Too bad he ain't alive." Asa knelt over him, and pulled his shirt open, cursing when he saw no sack. Then he thrust a hand into Brad's pants pocket.

It was the instant Brad had waited for. He exploded into action. A fist caught Asa on the head and knocked him sprawling. Lunging to his feet, Brad jumped for the man, slugging him twice before he could get to a standing position, and then as Asa grabbed at him, Brad jerked his knee into the outlaw's face.

Asa cried out sharply, falling over on his back, and Brad stooped over him, slugging him again as the man continued to yell, then he jerked Asa's gun from his holster and, wheeling, ran for the rim of the gully.

His own gun lay nearby, and then he saw the standing horse. Grabbing up his own gun, he raced for the horse.

A shot rang out, and he saw Cornish come lunging over the rim of the gully. He tried a shot, saw that he'd missed. Realizing all chance of escape was gone, he ran for the house. Another gun roared, and then he plunged through the door and slammed it shut. Panting, he dropped the bar into place.

Outside he could hear shouts of anger, and Butcher Schaum fired at the door. From beside a window he snapped a hasty shot at Schaum, and smiled grimly as the man sprang for cover.

There was a tin pan filled with water near the door and he ducked his head into it, rinsing out his hair and washing the wound. From time to time he took a glimpse from the window. Obviously, there was a council of war going on down on the edge of the gully.

Freeing himself of some of the ants, he reloaded his pistol. A rifle stood by the door, and he picked it up. Digging around he found some .44-.40s and shoved cartridges into the magazine.

Hastily, he took stock. He had enough grub here for days. He had ammunition enough. They would know that as well as he. From the front the place was almost invulnerable. He glanced up, and his face tightened. The roof was made of rough planking and piled over with straw thatch. Fire dropped from the shelving cliff behind could burn him out.

How long would it take them to think of that? They wouldn't leave without the gold, he knew. And regardless of where it had gotten to, he wasn't leaving without it either.

The bank was in view of the window. He could cover it. The fact remained that they would never let him get away alive, and it would not take them long to resign themselves to burning him out. Much of their own gear was inside, which would cause some hesitation. It would be a last resort for them—but the end of him.

His only way out would be straight ahead, across that fifty yards of open space. Not more than one would go to the shelf above, and the other two would be waiting to cut him down.

Not more than one? His eyes narrowed. Was there a way to the top of the cliff? Hastily, he took a glance outside, caught a bit of movement in the brush, and put two quick shots into it with his rifle. Then he tried two more shots, spaced at random along the edge of the gully, merely as a warning.

Reloading the rifle, he went to the back of the cabin. The back wall was the cliff itself. Trying to recall the looks of the place, he remembered there had been some vines or brush suspended from the shelf. Perhaps he could get up under the edge of those vines! Taking a hasty glance through the window, he went to the back of the house.

There was a place where a plank was too short. Standing atop a chair, he began pulling at the thatch. It was well placed, and his fingers were soon raw from tugging at it, yet he was making progress.

From time to time he returned to the window. Several times, shots came into the cabin.

"Give yourself up, Murphy, and we'll split that gold any way you want it," Schaum yelled.

"You go to blazes!" he roared back. He was seething with anger. "It's you or me now, so don't try none of your tricks! I ain't leavin' here now until all three of you are dead or my prisoners. Unless you want to hightail it out of here, I'm gittin' you, Schaum!"

A volley of rifle shots was the reply. He crouched below the stone sill, and when the volley ended, he tried a quick shot. A reply burned his shoulder, and he shot again, then put down the rifle and returned to his digging at the thatch.

Soon he had a hole he could peer up through. A wild grapevine hung down from the brush overhead, trailing down from the bending branches of the brush. Up in back of it was a hollow in the rock. It might offer a foothold. The hollow was right under the very shelf of rock he had seen on nearing the cabin. It would be invisible from in front of the cabin if he could get up behind that brush. There would be an instant when he would be half revealed. The instant when he reached up to get his hands on the brush or rock.

The day wore on, and he dug up some biscuits and munched them cheerfully. He found a couple of cartridge belts and slung them to his hips, holstering the guns. Then he stuffed his pockets with rifle shells.

"Gettin' hungry out there?" he yelled. "I got lots of chow!"

A string of vile curses replied to him, and he studied the terrain ahead of him through the crack of the door. A dozen bullet holes let little swords of light into the shadows inside.

He went to the bucket and drank, then he stripped and brushed more ants from him. Dressing again, he glanced from the window. The saddled horse was gone. As he listened, he heard the sounds of a rapidly ridden horse leaving. Then a shout from Schaum.

"Yore last chance, Murphy!" Schaum shouted. "Come out or we burn you out."

He did not want them to think that he had planned for that. He fired two quick shots from the window, and drew one shot in reply. Then he heard something hit the roof. Hastily, he got up on the chair. Smoke came to his nostrils. He thrust his head up and got a whiff of smoke, then a blast of flame and heat! Thrusting his rifle through the hole, he struggled to pull himself up.

He got his shoulders through, then his six-guns hung. The thatch in front was roaring now and the fire was spreading toward him. Wildly, he ripped at it to make the hole larger. Then, getting a hand in a rock crevice, he tugged himself up.

The rock crumbled in his fingers, and with a wild gasp of despair he felt himself sliding back. Desperately, his hand shot out, caught a handful of brush. His arms jerked in their sockets, and then, slowly, he dragged himself up.

With his feet clinging precariously to a tiny ledge, he glanced back. His rifle lay where he had left it and as the fire spread across the roof the shells in the magazine began to explode . . . he heard yelling, what they thought was going on he couldn't imagine, maybe they thought he was still shooting at them. Hand over hand, he pulled himself up into the hollow under the shelf.

The roof below was a roaring furnace now. The slightest slip would send him plunging into the flames. Smoke rose in a stifling cloud. He pulled himself higher until the shelf was directly over his back. As he clung there, fighting for breath, he heard footsteps grate on the rock only a few inches over his head.

There would be no chance to get over the edge of the shelf as long as that man remained there. Clinging to the brush, his feet resting on a small ledge, only a couple of inches wide, he turned his head. A black hole gaped in the stone face. A hole scarcely large enough for a man's body, a hole under the shelf of rock.

Carefully, taking his whole weight on his arms, he lifted his feet and thrust them into the hole. Catching his toes behind a minor projection of rock, he drew himself back inside.

Dropping his feet, he felt around. Inside the opening, the hole was several feet deep. He drew back until he was on his knees, only his head in the opening. Less smoke was coming toward him now. He could hear shouts from below, and one from above him.

"See him?" The voice was that of Cornish.

"Blamed fool burned to death," Schaum said in astonishment. "He never even showed."

"I'm coming down!" Cornish shouted.

"You stay there," Schaum bellowed. "I don't like the look of this!"

Brad felt of the walls and top of the hole he was in. At the back it slanted down and around. But feeling at the top in back, he felt earth and roots. It was probably not more than two feet to the surface there, or very little more.

Where was Cornish? The question was answered when he heard the man shout another question at Schaum. He was probably at least thirty feet away.

Removing a spur, Brad Murphy dug at the earth. He worked carefully, avoiding sound. He dug at the soft earth, letting it fall to the bottom of the hole. Much of it fell on his own legs, cushioning the little sound. He had worked but a few minutes when taking a small root, he pulled down, a tiny hole appeared, and earth cascaded around him. Pistol ready, he waited for an instant to see if Cornish had heard him. There was no sound or movement, and he tugged at another root. More dirt cascaded around him. That time there was a muffled gasp and he heard pounding feet.

His gun was ready and it was all that saved him. Dave Cornish, his eyes wide and frightened, was staring down into the hole at him, gun in hand.

The man was petrified by astonishment. The man he thought had burned in the cabin below was coming up through the earth. Before Cornish could realize what was truly happening, Brad acted. The gun was ready. He shoved it up, and even as Cornish started from his shock, the six-gun bellowed.

The close confines of the hole made a terrific blast, and acrid fumes cut at Murphy's nostrils. Cornish fell forward, and bracing his shoulders against the earth atop the hole, Brad shoved himself through. He scrambled out, rolling over flat.

ONE LOOK AT Dave Cornish was enough. The man was dead. He had been shot right through the heart. Excited shouts came from below. The shot, muffled by the earth, had reached them but dimly. Yet they were alarmed.

"Butcher!" Murphy yelled.

Schaum was walking toward the smoldering cabin, Moffitt a few feet behind him.

Butcher Schaum froze; terror had turned his face to an ugly mask as he raised his eyes.

He dropped a hand for a gun, and Brad Murphy whipped up his own. Shots stabbed into the hot still air, something struck his shoulder, and he staggered one step, then fired. Schaum swayed drunkenly, tried to get a gun up, and then Brad fired again.

Behind him, Asa Moffitt swept up a pistol and emptied it in a terror-stricken blast of fire. Then he turned and ran for the gully.

Remorselessly, Brad Murphy waited an instant, then fired. Once, twice! The outlaw and murderer fell, rolled over, and lay sprawled out on the lip of the gully.

Calmly, Brad Murphy reloaded. He found the paint horse standing not far away, and mounting, rode down to the smoldering ruins.

A few minutes of search and he found his gold. The bag had hit and slid down the bank. It was lying there covered partially by dirt, visible but not likely to attract attention.

Shaking his head, he swung into the saddle and turned the horse toward town.

"Horse," he said, "you're takin' me home. I got to buy me a ranch for Ruth and my boy. . . . I reckon," he added, "they'll be right glad to see me."

He turned the horse down the trail. The nearest town was thirty miles away. Behind him the smoke lifted slowly toward the sky where a buzzard circled lazily in the wavering heat. Gravel rattled, and the horse felt good between Brad's legs, and he liked the heavy feeling of the gold.

SECRET OF SILVER SPRINGS

I T WAS AN hour after sunup when Dud Shafter rode the roan gelding up to the water hole at Pistol Rock. The roan had come up the basin at a shuffling trot, but the man who waited there knew that both horse and man had come far and fast over rough trails.

The waiting man, Navarro, could understand that. The trail this rider had left behind him lay through some of the roughest country in the Southwest, a journey made no easier by the fact that several Apache bands were raiding and their exact location was anyone's guess. He glanced appraisingly at the sweat-stained, sun-faded blue shirt the red-haired man wore, noted the haggard lines of the big-boned, freckled face, and the two walnut-butted guns in their worn holsters.

As the man drew up, Navarro indicated the fire. "Coffee, señor? There is plenty."

Shafter stared down at the Mexican with hard blue eyes, and when he swung down he kept the horse between them. He stripped the saddle from the horse and rubbed it down briskly with a handful of desert grass, then walked toward the fire. He had not even for an instant turned his back on the Mexican.

"Don't mind if I do," he said at last.

Squatting, he placed his cup on a flat rock, then lifting the pot with his left hand, he poured the cup full of scalding black coffee. Replacing the pot alongside the coals, he glanced across the fire at Navarro and lifted the cup.

"Luck!" he said.

After a moment, he put the cup down and dug in his pocket for the makings.

"You make a good cup of coffee," he said.

Navarro lifted a deprecating shoulder and one eyebrow.

His eyes had never left the big man's carefully moving hands. It was simply something to say; Navarro was a good cook, coffee was the least of his achievements . . . and he had other abilities as well.

The Mexican wore buckskin breeches, hand-tooled boots, and one ivory-butted gun. His felt sombrero was fastened under his chin with a rawhide thong.

The sound of another horse approaching brought the heads of both men up sharply. Navarro touched his lips with his tongue, and Dud Shafter shifted his weight to face the opening into the basin.

A buckskin horse came through the opening at a walk, and a man sat that horse with a double-barreled express shotgun across his saddle bows. The man was a Negro.

"Howdy!" Shafter said.

"Join us," Navarro added.

The Negro grinned and swung to the ground. He was shorter than either of the others, but of such powerful build that his weight would have equaled that of Shafter, who was a big man in any company.

He wore a six-shooter in an open-toed holster, but as he dismounted and moved up to the fire, he kept his shotgun in his hand. He carried his own cup, as did the others, and when he squatted to pour the coffee, the shotgun was ready to his hand.

Navarro smiled, revealing even white teeth under the black of his mustache. These were men of his own kind. After a moment or two, he took a burlap sack off his saddle and began to cook. Slowly he assembled a meal, such a meal as the two strangers had certainly not seen in many weeks. Tortillas were heated on a flat rock, lean shredded beef was cooked with peppers and onions, frijoles that he had soaked since he had camped the previous night were split into three portions. As Navarro worked his magic he carefully watched his new companions.

"It takes money," he suggested, "to travel far. I know where there is money!"

Dud Shafter's chill blue eyes lifted in a curious, speculative glance. "It takes money. That's the truth."

"If you're travelin' "—the other man wiped off his seamed black hands—"and you know where there is money for the takin', you're a lucky man!"

"One man cannot get this money," Navarro hinted. "Three men might."

Dud Shafter let the idea soak in, staring into the fire. He picked up a mesquite stick and thrust it into the coals, watching a tongue of flame lick greedily at the dry wood.

He looked around casually. "Would this money be nearby?" he asked.

"Sixty miles by this road, but by a way I and only a few others know, it is but twenty. There is an Apache path through the mountains. We could ride over this trail, make our collection, and return. We could get water and some rest here, then head for the Blues."

"You don't think others know this trail . . . others we might have to worry about?" Dud asked.

Navarro shrugged. "Who knows. But we will be careful. At the right moment we will hide our tracks. Also, in going there we will learn the path well. It is a chance that I believe in."

Dud Shafter rolled the idea over in his mind. He was not above driving off a few steers, especially if he didn't know whose they were. But this sounded like crime, straight from the shoulder, out-and-out theft. Not his style, but he *was* going to need money. There was trouble down his back trail and a winter with no work in his future.

"There is an express box," Navarro informed him, "on a stage. In that box are two small payrolls . . . small for payrolls, but good money for us. More than seven thousand dollars. Before the stage arrives at Lobo station, it passes through Cienaga Pass. That is the place."

After a moment Shafter nodded and then the Negro did too. He didn't really like the idea but he was willing to go along. What he did like, however, was the Mexican's food.

NAVARRO LED OFF because he knew the route. Dud Shafter and the Negro, who had said his name was Benzie, followed. Navarro led them into the cedars along the mountainside back of Pistol Rock, then crossed the hill and cut down its side into a sandy wash. Seven miles farther, he led them into a tangle of mesquite, cat-claw, and yeso. Steadily, their trail tended toward the blank face of the cliff, yet when they reached it, Navarro turned south for two miles, then entered a canyon. The canyon ended in a jumble of rocks, and beyond the tumbled pile of boulders was the cliff.

"Looks like you miscalculated," Dud said. "There ain't no way through there."

"Wait, *compadre*." Navarro chuckled. "Just wait!"

They rode on into the gathering dark, weaving a way among the boulders toward the face of the cliff.

The walls to right and left closed in, and the darkness shouldered its shadows toward their horses. Then a boulder-strewn, cedar-cloaked hillside lifted toward the sheer wall of rock, and the Mexican started up. Within only a few feet of the cliff, he turned his horse at right angles and started down a steep slope that led right up to the face. Concealed by the boulder-strewn hill was a path that slanted steeply down, then turned to a crevasse between two walls of rock. It was a trail that no man would ever suspect was there.

Between the walls, so close together their stirrups grazed the rock on either side, it was dark and cool. There was dampness in the air.

"It is like this for miles," Navarro said. "No danger of going astray."

They rode on and Dud nodded in the saddle, his horse plodding steadily forward. Finally, after nearly an hour's ride, the crevasse widened into a canyon, and they still rode on. Then the canyon narrowed to a crevasse again, and they passed by a trickle of water. When they had gone only a little way farther, Navarro halted.

Dud Shafter, startled from a half sleep, slid a gun into his hand. He glared around in the darkness.

"There is no trouble," Navarro said. "The trail is there." He pointed toward the black mouth of a cave. "We will enter the cave and each of you will go exactly seventy-seven steps from the time your horse starts onto the rock floor, it will be very dark. Then you must turn left. You will see an opening covered with vines, push them aside and ride through."

Navarro led the way and they rode into darkness. The echoes from the other horses' hooves made it hard for Dud to count and he discovered it was better to plug his ears with his fingertips and feel the footsteps of his horse than to try to follow the confusing sounds in the cave. At seventy-seven he reined over and momentarily dragged his left knee against the rock.

"Guess that Mex has got a bigger horse than mine," he grumbled.

Now the footfalls of their horses splashed in shallow water, then there was a dim light ahead and they pushed the vines aside and emerged into the evening air. A small trickle of water ran out from under the cover of vines and soaked the ground around their horses' hooves.

Navarro turned to face them. "We will stop here," Navarro said. "And I will tell you the way back in case I should be killed. You must follow the streambed in the cave and let your horse take thirty steps—no more.

"Turn your horse sharply right and ride straight ahead, and after you have been riding into darkness for a few minutes, you will see the trail down which we have come."

"Suppose I take more than thirty steps?" Shafter asked.

Navarro shrugged. "You will find yourself in a great cavern, the floor is crumbling and filled with many holes. One man I knew made that mistake, and his horse and he went through the floor. We heard him scream as he fell. He fell a long way, señor."

"I'll count the thirty steps," Shafter said dryly.

They bedded down and slept until dawn, then rolled out. Dud was the first one up, collecting greasewood and a few pieces of dead cedar for a fire. When he had the fire going he looked around and took stock of their position.

They had camped in what appeared to be a box canyon, and they were in the upper end of the canyon with a lovely green meadow of some thirty acres spread out before them. Not far away was a ruined adobe house and a pole corral.

When they had rested and eaten another of Navarro's

meals, they mounted and the Mexican rode into the meadow. The ruined adobe stood among ancient trees and beside a pool, crystal clear. Dud glanced around with appreciation.

"It's a nice place," he said thoughtfully. "A right nice place!"

In a wooden beam over the adobe's door was carved a brand. "PV9" it read.

Benzie nodded, and shifted his shotgun. He carried it like part of himself, like an extension of his arm. He spoke little but never seemed to miss a trick.

————

LATER, THEY SWUNG down behind a clump of juniper on the crest of a low hill just off the stage road. Here the team would be slowed to a walk. It would be the best place.

They rode back into the juniper and dismounted. There was plenty of time. Benzie sat on the dead trunk of a tree and lit a smoke, staring bleakly off across the blue-misted bottomland of desert that stretched away toward purple hills. He had never stolen anything before.

Navarro stretched at full length on the sparse grass, his hat over his face. Dud Shafter idly flipped his knife into the end of the log. Shafter wondered about his Mexican and Negro companions, but asked no questions—and they volunteered no information.

Shafter swore softly and stared down the road. There was a warrant out for his arrest back along the trail. He hadn't stolen that bunch of cattle but he'd been with the men who did. He might as well stick up the stage; might as well have the pay as well as the blame. Still, this was a point, a branching road where a man turned toward the owl hoot or along a trail with honest men. Warrant or not, he was sitting in a fork of that road right now.

Keen as Dud's ears were, Benzie heard them first. He started up. "Some men are comin'," he said.

Navarro was off the ground like a cat. Dud ground his cigarette into the sand and moved to his horse's head, a hand over the nostrils. The three stood there like statues, waiting, listening.

At least four horses, Dud thought, listening to the hoof-beats. There was no noise of rigging or rattle of wheels . . . it was not the stage. The horses slowed and stopped.

"This is the best place," a voice said. "We'll draw back into the trees." Over some brush Dud glimpsed a flash of white as one of them moved; the man who had spoken was wearing a light-colored hat.

Holding his breath, every sense alert, Dud Shafter waited. Navarro looked at him, a droll, humorous glint in his eyes. The new men took the brush on the opposite side of some rocks. The air was clear, and a man's words could have been distinguished at a much greater distance but the voice echoed slightly.

"They'll be slowin' up right here." The same voice was speaking. "We make it a clean sweep. Joe, you take the driver. Pete, the messenger. Nobody must be left alive to tell who did it. Above all, get that old man. We'll make him talk!"

There was silence, and the three men on the other side of the trail stared at each other. Here was a complication. To speak aloud would be to give themselves away. Even the movement of their horses might have that result, for if a hoof struck stone, that would mean discovery, and each of them knew from what had been said that the men across the way were utterly ruthless.

Taking careful steps, Dud moved over to Navarro. Benzie leaned his head near.

"We don't want no killing on our hands," Dud whispered. "Stealing is one thing, killing another . . . especially if we ain't gonna get the money."

Navarro and Benzie both nodded.

"Looks like they be wantin' an old man for some reason."

Dud Shafter stared unhappily at his boots. The struggle within him was short and one-sided.

"You fellers can do as you're a-might to," he said at last. "I'm a-going to butt in."

"We are partners, no?" Navarro shrugged. "We are with you!"

Benzie nodded. It had an odd kind of logic and none of

them was about to let someone else get away with a robbery they had planned, even if it meant losing the prize themselves.

At that moment, they heard the rattle of wheels and a shout from the stage driver. The three leaped for their saddles even as the first shot sounded. Racing their horses through the brush, they heard a burst of firing. Then their own guns opened up.

Dud Shafter came out of the scrub with both guns ready. A big, bearded man loomed before him and turned sharply in his saddle to stare with rolling eyes; Shafter fired twice. The big man went out of the saddle and his horse leaped away.

Behind Dud, Benzie's shotgun coughed hoarsely, and he could hear the sharp reports from Navarro's smoothly handled pistol. There was a flash of light from the trees and a crashing of brush. In a matter of seconds, it was all over, and four men lay on the ground. Dud stared at the brush, for there had been a fifth. The man with the white hat was gone!

He swung down, and the passengers poured from the coach. The shotgun messenger walked up and thrust out his hand.

"Thanks, partners! You-all saved our bacon! That outfit came in shootin'!"

"You hurt?" Dud asked, staring at the man's pale face.

"Winged me," the messenger said.

Shafter turned, feeding shells into his guns, and saw the passengers gathering around. A tall man in a beaver hat, a flamboyantly dressed woman, a solid-looking man with a heavy gold chain, a hard hat, and muttonchop whiskers. Then an old man with a beard, and a young girl evidently his daughter.

This must be the man the robbers had mentioned. He was short with pleasant blue eyes and a glint of humor in his face.

"Some shootin', boys! Thank you."

Dud walked slowly from one dead man to the other. None of them was familiar to Dud.

The man with the muttonchop whiskers thrust out his hand.

"My name is Wendover," he said. "James T. Wendover of

Wells Fargo. You men saved our shipment and I can assure you you'll be rewarded. Can you tell us where you live?"

Shafter hesitated, then with a jerk of his thumb, he indicated the box canyon where they had camped beside the ruined adobe.

"We got us a sort of a ranch back up in there," he said. "The three of us."

"Good! Now what do you call it, and what is your name?"

"My name's Shafter," Dud replied. "The ranch is the—"

"The Silver Springs Ranch," Navarro added smoothly.

At the name, the old man started and his eyes hardened as he stared from one to the other. Puzzled, Shafter noticed the girl had put her hand on her father's arm, and the grateful light was gone from her eyes.

Wendover turned away to where the other woman passenger was dressing the messenger's wound. That left Shafter and his companions standing with the old man and the girl.

She stared at him with accusing eyes. "So you're the ones!"

Shafter shook his head. "I don't know what you mean, ma'am," he said simply, "but we probably ain't. Actually, we're just sort of riding through, like."

"You told that man you owned Silver Springs!" she protested indignantly.

"No, señorita," Navarro protested. "We have to tell him something. We could very much use the reward. It is a good place to wait."

"We'd been warned to expect trouble," the old man said. "My name is Fanning, and this is my granddaughter, Beth. Silver Springs belonged to my brother, a long time ago. We were goin' to get off when we got there, but the driver wasn't exactly sure where it was. Are we there now?"

"Yeah," Dud agreed, "this is it. But you folks better know this. Them fellers we shot it out with, they were aiming to kill everybody on that stage, when we overheard 'em. What they was after was you, Mr. Fanning. They said they were going to make you talk."

"So that was it?" Fanning's jaw hardened. "Well, I'd like to find who was behind this! He's the man I want!"

"One of 'em got away," Benzie suggested. "Could be 'twas him."

Navarro and Benzie appointed themselves a burial committee for the dead men, and Dud walked back to the stage to unload the baggage belonging to Fanning and Beth. Wendover was obviously nervous, wanting to get on to the stage station at Lobo Wells.

Leading the Fannings' horses that had been tied to the back of the stage, and with the girl's bag in his hand and a couple more hung to the saddle horn, Shafter led the way back toward the ruined adobe. As he walked, he explained about the little valley, and the condition of things, but Beth was not disturbed. She walked into the ruined building, took a quick look around, and then came out.

"We can fix it up!" she said. "You'll help, won't you?"

Dud, caught flat-footed, assured her that he would.

"Good!" Beth said. "Now if you'll get on your horse and ride down to that stage station and just get us some supplies—" She opened her purse, searching for money.

He turned and started for the Wells. Yet as he rode his thoughts were only occasionally with the girl. He was thinking more of the man in the white hat, and the fact that Fanning knew something, something that would cause men to contemplate murder.

The stage station was one of four buildings at Lobo Wells. There was a rest house and eating place in the station, and the station's office and a storeroom. The other buildings were the Lobo Saloon, the freight office of Bert Callan, and the Mickley General Store. Dud swung down at the hitching rail in front of Mickley's and walked in.

Ben Mickley was in low conversation with a tall man in a fringed buckskin coat. Both men turned to look him over, seeing his big-boned freckled face and the shock of rust-red hair under his battered sombrero. As he collected his order, he was conscious of their scrutiny.

"New around here, ain't you?" Mickley suggested conversationally.

Dud grinned at the proprietor. "Not that new. I spent a moment or two out there tying my horse up," he said, and added tentatively, "going to start ranching on the Silver Springs place."

"I'm afraid not."

Shafter's eyes shifted to the man in the buckskin jacket. He was smooth-featured with a drooping mustache and dark eyes. His jaw was hard, and there was a tightness in his expression that Shafter read as well as he read the low-hung, tied-down guns. The man was bareheaded.

"I reckon yes." Shafter's voice was calm. "We moved in there, my pards and me, and we figure to stay. We're riding for Jim Fanning, who owns the place."

"Corb Fanning filed on that place, a long time ago," said the hard-jawed man. "He was killed, and it lapsed. That spring now belongs to me."

"Lapsed?"

"I filed on it, mister. It's private property now . . . my property."

Dud did not smile. He did not even feel like smiling. He turned around to face the other man, and in his dusty, trail-worn clothes, with his uncut red hair and big freckled hands, he looked like what he was—a hard-bitten man who had cut his eyeteeth on a gun butt.

"Where's your hat, stranger?" he asked quietly.

"Don't you go to proddin' him! That's Bert Callan and he's no stranger to me. He runs the freight company hereabouts." Mickley warned Dud, "And I don't want any shooting in my store. You understand?"

The icy blue eyes held Callan's and Shafter spoke slowly. His hand rested lightly on his gun butt.

"All right, Mickley, throw that sack of stuff over your back, and walk out the door ahead of me—alongside of this hombre. Unless this hombre wants to try some six-foot distance shootin'!"

Bert Callan stared into the cold blue eyes and decided uncomfortably that he didn't want to try it. At a distance, yes, but six feet? Neither of them would live. It was out of the question. He shrugged and followed Ben Mickley to the door.

Dud Shafter threw the sack of groceries over his saddle bows.

"Now you two can go back inside," he said coolly.

"You-all better move off that spring and fast!" Callan's face flushed dark with anger and his hand moved toward his gun.

"You just put on that white hat, if it's yours, and come on up. You come up and tell us to move!"

He swung a leg over his horse and turned the horse into the trail. Then, at a canter, he moved out of town.

Ben Mickley stared after him, hard-eyed. "That's a mean one, Bert. You better soft-pedal it with him!"

"Mean, huh!" Callan flared. "The man's a fool! Go to shootin' in there, we'd both die!"

"That's right," Mickley said thoughtfully, "you would."

————

SHAFTER RODE UP to Silver Springs shortly after sundown; as he drew up to the adobe, he saw a man move in the shadows. It was Benzie, with his shotgun.

"All right?" Benzie asked. "No trouble?"

Navarro walked up as Dud explained briefly.

"There will be trouble," he ended. "They want this place. In fact, they may own it."

Beth Fanning called to them.

"Come and get it before I throw it away!"

When they were eating, she looked over at Dud.

"What did you three plan on doing? Riding on when you get your money?"

He detected the worry in her voice and leaned back on his elbow, placing his plate and coffee cup on the ground.

"Maybe we'd better stick around," he said. He looked over at Jim Fanning. "You want to tell us what this is all about?"

Fanning hesitated, chewing slowly. "Reckon you fellers have helped us a mite," he finally said. "What do you think, Beth? This is your say-so as much as mine."

The girl lifted her eyes and looked at Dud for a long moment, then at Navarro and Benzie.

"Why, tell them," she said, "I like them all, and we have to trust our friends."

Dud swallowed and looked away, and he saw Benzie's face lighten a little. The Negro looked up, waiting. It was something, Shafter thought, being trusted that way. Especially when you didn't deserve it. A little one way or the other, and they might have robbed that stage themselves.

"We've got a map," Fanning said. "My brother, Corbin, he filed on this place. He come west with six wagons, and he aimed to stay right here. He brought a sight of money along, gold coin it was. Had it hid in his own wagon, nigh to forty thousand dollars of it. It was cached here on the place, and he sent me the location in a letter."

"What happened to him?" Navarro asked softly.

"Injuns. At least they say it was Injuns. Now that these fellers are lookin' for me, I don't know. Beth and I came here to restart the place and that money was goin' to help us do it."

"Can you find it?" Dud asked. He was thinking of forty thousand dollars, and that all three of them were broke. It was a lot of money. How far could Navarro be trusted? Or Benzie? Or himself?

"Maybe. Now that I'm settin' here the directions aren't as clear as I'd like."

"You could let us help you," he said. "But maybe it would be a good idea to have us ride out of here an' you find it on your own . . . you shouldn't trust anyone you don't know."

"No," Beth interrupted. "You saved our lives. I say we should get it now and deposit it with the Wells Fargo. Then it's their worry."

Shafter nodded. "Well, that's best, I'm sure."

He scowled, remembering the man in the white hat and the man at the stage station. Too bad their glimpse of the rider who escaped had been so fleeting. He had taken no part in the fighting, and when Shafter and the others broke from the brush, he had fled at once, as if fearing to be seen.

When morning had come, Jim Fanning left the breakfast table and returned with a fold of papers. They all walked outside. Carefully he laid out the letter in a patch of sunlight.

"This here drawing," he said slowly, "don't nowhere make sense as I'd like. There's the 'dobe all right. Over yonder is the flat-faced cliff, an' here's the stream from Silver Springs. But lookee here, this says, 'GOLD BURIED UNDER THE . . . NE.' The ink is smudged, it don't make sense."

Navarro looked up sharply, his eyes meeting Shafter's across the fire. Slowly he got up and walked around the fire and knelt over the map. Dud knew what he was thinking, and what Benzie must have in mind. The cave was under a vine, or behind a vine, if you wanted it that way.

Shafter stared down at the map. In the cave, then. But he didn't speak up and neither did the others.

"Look out!" he said softly. "Watch it!"

Dud got to his feet and Jim Fanning smothered the letter in his fist. Navarro and Benzie got up, too. A tight-knit bunch of riders were walking their horses up the canyon toward them. One of the two men in the lead was Bert Callan.

Eight of them. No, there was another rider following.

Nine to four, and a girl in the way of the shooting. Dud Shafter's jaw set hard.

"Callan—he's one of them men—will want me," he said quietly. "The rest of you stay out."

"We're partners, amigo," Navarro said softly. "Your fight is my fight."

Benzie moved out toward the adobe, then halted. Jim Fanning was by the fire, and the girl close to him.

"So? Caught up with you, did we?" Callan stared hard at Shafter. "You're on my place and we're gonna clear you out. First, though, we're gonna have a talk with the old man here."

There could be no backing down. One sign of weakness and none of them had a chance. Then he recognized the ninth rider.

"You in this, too, Mickley?" Dud demanded sharply. "If you're not, ride out of here!"

"You've got gold hidden on this place," Mickley said. "Let us have it and you can all go on your way. If there's shootin', you'll all die—and so will the girl."

"And so will some of you," Dud replied stiffly. "I think we can handle it."

"No," Navarro said suddenly. "I do not wish to die!"

Shafter could scarcely believe his ears. He would have backed the Mexican to a standstill in any kind of a fight, but here he was giving up!

Before he could speak, Navarro said quickly:

"I will tell you, señors, so do not shoot! I think of the lady, of course!"

Callan snorted, but Mickley nodded eagerly.

"Of course! So where is the gold?"

Navarro reached over and took the letter from Fanning's surprised fingers before the older man could close his fist.

"Here! You see? It says the gold is under the vine."

Mickley stared at the letter over Navarro's shoulder. The other men held their guns steady. If that had been Navarro's plan—to take them by surprise and shoot—it was wasted. This bunch had their rifles over their saddle horns, ready for action. No, there was no question, much as Dud hated to admit it, Navarro had gone yellow.

"Under the vine?" Callan stared. "What vine?"

"But surely, señor," Navarro protested, "you know of the vine that covers the cave mouth? It is there, where the spring flows from the rock. Behind that hanging vine there is a cave. And I think I know where the gold is!"

"You know?" Mickley stared at him suspiciously. "Where?"

"There is a ledge, señor, with something upon it. You walk in, say forty paces on your horse, and there you are!"

Forty paces! Shafter's face stiffened, then relaxed, and he tried to keep the gleam from his eyes.

"Damn you!" Shafter burst out furiously. "You sold us out!"

"Let's go!" Mickley said eagerly. "Let's get it!"

"The box will be ver' heavy, señor," Navarro warned. He rolled a smoke with nerveless fingers. "It will take several men."

"That's right," Mickley agreed. The storekeeper bound up a piece of a canvas ground sheet around a three-foot stick to make a torch. "You"—he motioned to three of the men—"you come and help move the money. Bert, you stay and keep an eye on these folks. I don't trust 'em. Nor you," he added, turning on the Mexican. "Come with us!" He handed Navarro the stick and set a match to the bundle on the end.

Navarro's face paled, and his eyes lifted to meet Dud's. He started to speak, to voice a protest, but Navarro gave a slight, almost imperceptible shake of his head.

"Of course, señor," he said gently. "Why not?"

Mickley turned abruptly toward the cave entrance. As he turned, the bright silver on the butt of his pistol caught Dud's eye. He remembered the flash he had seen during the robbery. It was Mickley! The store owner had planned all this!

Dud Shafter stared after him, and Benzie swallowed, his eyes wide and white. Neither Fanning nor Beth understood, and they could only believe Dud looked so because of the betrayal.

"They'd better find it," Bert Callan warned. He sat his horse beside the remaining three men.

Well, Navarro's attempt to cut the odds had helped some. It was three to four now, if the shooting started. If only Beth were out of the way!

He looked at her, trying to warn her with his eyes, but she failed to grasp his meaning, and moved closer.

He glanced around, and saw with panic that the group had disappeared behind the vine. Mentally, he counted their steps. Suddenly his hard, freckled face turned grim.

"Run, Beth!" he yelled.

Callan's face blanched, then suddenly his hands swept down for his guns and they came up spouting fire. But too slow, for Dud Shafter's gun was blasting almost before Callan's cleared the holster!

But at the same instant, there was a great crash of falling rock from within the cave, and screams of agony! Then more falling rock, and in the midst of it the roar of guns as Shafter, Benzie, and Fanning opened up on the remaining riders!

Shafter's first shot struck Callan high in the chest and rocked him in the saddle, unsettling his aim so that Callan's bullet went wild. Then Dud, firing low and fast, triggered two more slugs into the gunman. Suddenly, loose in the saddle, as though all his bones and muscles had turned to jelly, Callan rolled and fell, like a sack of wheat into the grass.

The first blast of Benzie's shotgun had blown a rider clear out of his saddle even as his hands lifted his rifle, and for the rest, that was enough. The two remaining men held their hands high.

Dud turned, thumbing shells into his gun, and started at a stumbling run toward the cave. One of his legs felt numb and he remembered a stunning shock when something had struck his knee as the shooting began. Yet as he reached the cave mouth, the vines were shoved aside and three men rushed out. Two of the would-be robbers, and behind them— Navarro!

Shafter let out a whoop of joy and held his gun on the two riders, but they had no fight left in them. They looked pale and sick.

Dud stared at the Mexican. "You're safe? I thought you'd betrayed us, then I thought you'd committed suicide!"

Navarro looked white and shaky himself, and his black eyes were large in his handsome face.

"You forget, amigo, that I knew what was to happen! At the moment we reached the thirtieth step, I stopped and, holding my torch high, pointed ahead! There was a ledge, and on it a fallen rock that in the shadows did not look unlike a chest. They rushed forward, and *poof!* They were gone! It was awful, señor! A horrifying thing which I hope never to see again!"

"Mickley? Mickley was the man who wore the white hat. When he started for the cave, I recalled the flash of silver from his gun, the same I saw on the trail!"

"*Sí,* Mickley and one other, who was close behind them. These? They were frightened and ran. It was most terrible, amigo."

They walked back to the adobe. Beth, her face stark-white, her teeth biting her lower lip, was standing beside Benzie, who held the two riders under his shotgun.

"You two"—Shafter motioned with his six-gun to the men from the cave—"line up over there with them others!"

They obeyed, avoiding the bodies of Callan and the man Benzie had killed. Dud's hard face was remorseless.

"Your boss died back in the cave," he said, "and there's the other one." He motioned to Callan. "Now who do you hombres work for?"

A lanky man in a worn vest swallowed and said, "Shafter, I reckon we all done run out of a job! We shore have!"

"Then I'll give you one." Dud Shafter's voice was quiet. "Plant these two hombres over against the cliff and plant 'em deep. Then if I was you, I'd climb into leather and light a shuck. They tell me," he added grimly, "they are hiring hands up in the Wind River country."

Gingerly, Shafter examined his knee. It was already turning black, but evidently a chunk of rock from the foundation of the house had ricocheted against his leg, for there was no sign of a bullet.

Fanning shrugged hopelessly. "An ugly fracas," he said, "and we ain't no closer to the gold!"

Dud glanced up, pulling down his pant leg. "I don't know where it is but I'll lay a bet Navarro knows! He wouldn't have taken them into the cave unless he knew that wasn't the right place."

"*Si.*" The Mexican nodded. Turning, he pointed to the brand chiseled into the cliff behind the adobe. "See? Corb Fanning's brand—the PV Nine—which the vaqueros, of which I was one, shortened to call the Pea Vine! Where else would a man bury his gold but under his own brand?"

MEN TO MATCH THE HILLS

CAP MOFFIT WAS a careful man. That he was forty-two years old and still alive proved that beyond a doubt, for Cap Moffit was a professional killer.

He had learned the lesson of care from his first professional killing. In that case—and he had been fifteen years younger—Cap had picked a fight with his victim and shot him down and been nearly lynched as a result.

From that day on, Cap Moffit planned every killing as painstakingly as a great general might plan a battle. And he no longer made mistakes, knowing he need make but one. Over the years he had developed a technique, a carefully worked out pattern of operation.

He rode into the country over back trails, located the man he was to kill, and then spied upon him from cover until all his habits were known. Then, and only then, did Cap Moffit move in for the kill.

He always waited until his man was alone. He always caught him without cover in case the first shot was not a kill. He waited until his man was on the ground, so that a startled horse could not carry off a wounded man, or deliver the body too soon among friends. And also because it made that first shot more certain.

He never approached the body after a man fell, always went immediately away. And so far he had never failed.

Slightly below medium height, he was of slender build, and his face was narrow and quiet, with pale blue eyes and a tight, thin-lipped mouth. He invariably wore a narrow-brimmed gray hat, scuffed and solid, a gray vest over a blue cotton shirt, and faded jeans outside of boots with run-down heels. His gray coat was usually tied over his bedroll behind his saddle.

Cap Moffit lay comfortably on his stomach in a slight depression in the partial shade of the pines that crested Elk Ridge. Below him, in the long, green valley, was the T U Ranch, and living alone on that ranch was the man he was to kill. He was a man unknown to Moffit, although Cap knew his name was Jim Bostwick.

"Don't figure him for an easy one," his employer had warned. "The man's no gunfighter, but he gives me the impression that he's been around. He's tough, and he won't scare at all. We tried that."

The advice bored Cap. It mattered not at all who or what Jim Bostwick was. He would have no chance to show himself as wise or tough. Once the situation was known, Cap Moffit would kill him, and that would be that. Of this, Cap Moffit had been sure.

Now, after five days of watching the ranch, he was no longer so positive. Men, he had discovered, were creatures of habit. All the little practices of living sooner or later fell into a pattern, and once that pattern was known, it was comparatively easy to find a point at which a man was usually motionless and within range.

For the first three days Jim Bostwick had come from the house at five-thirty in the morning and fed his horse a bait of oats and corn. He curried the horse while it finished the grain. Not many men took the time to care for a horse so thoroughly. That completed, he brought a wooden bucket from the house and, walking to the spring which was forty steps from the door, he filled the bucket and returned. Only then did he prepare breakfast.

By the second day Cap Moffit had decided that if the practice continued, the place for the killing was at the corral while Bostwick was currying the horse. The pole corral offered no cover, the man was practically motionless, and there was good cover for Moffit within forty yards. If the first shot failed there was time to empty the gun before Bostwick could reach shelter. And Cap Moffit had never missed once since he had entered his present profession. He did not dare miss.

Moreover, the spot he had selected for himself offered easy access and retreat over low ground, so he could not be seen reaching his objective. On the third day the pattern was repeated, and Cap Moffit decided if it held true one more day he would act.

He had taken every care to conceal his own presence. His camp was six miles away and carefully hidden. He never used the same vantage point on two successive days. He kept his fieldglasses shaded so their glass would not reflect light.

Yet, despite all his care, he had given himself away, and now the hunter was also the hunted.

On THE MORNING of the fourth day, Jim Bostwick came from the house before Cap Moffit was settled into shooting position. Instead of going to the corral, he went around the house and disappeared from sight behind it. Puzzled by the sudden change Cap waited, sure the frame of habit would prove too strong and that the man would return to his usual ways. Suddenly, his eyes caught a movement at the corral and he was startled to see the horse eating from a bucket. Now, what the hell!

Jim Bostwick was nowhere in sight.

Then suddenly he appeared, coming from the spring with a bucket of fresh water. At the corner of the cabin he stopped and shaded his eyes, looking up the trail. Was he expecting visitors?

Bostwick disappeared within the house, and smoke began to climb from the chimney. Cap Moffit lit a cigarette and tried to puzzle it out. If Bostwick followed his usual pattern now he would devote more than an hour to eating and cleaning up afterward. But why had he gone around the house? How had he reached the corral without being seen? And the spring? Could he possibly be aware that he was being watched?

Moffit dismissed that possibility. No chance of it, none at all. He had given no indication of his presence.

Nevertheless, men do not change a habit pattern lightly, and something had changed that of Bostwick, at least for a few minutes. And why had he looked so carefully up the trail? Was he expecting someone?

No matter. Moffit would kill Bostwick, and he would not wait much longer. Just enough to see if anyone did come.

Moffit was rubbing out his first cigarette of the day when his eye caught a flicker of movement. A big man, even bigger than Bostwick, was standing on the edge of the brush. He carried a rifle, and he moved toward the house. The fellow wore a buckskin shirt, had massive chest and shoulders, and walked with a curious, sidelong limp. At the door he suddenly ducked inside. Faintly, Moffit heard a rumble of voices, but he was too far away to hear anything that was said.

He scowled irritably. Who was the man in the buckskin shirt? What did *he* want?

——————

HAD HE BUT known it, there was only one man in the cabin. That man was Bostwick himself. Stripping off the buckskin shirt, he removed the other shirts and padding he had worn under it and threw the worn-out hat to a hook. He was a big, tough man, to whom life had given much in trouble and hard work. He had come here to hold down this ranch for a friend until that friend could get back to make his own fight for it, a friend whose wife was fighting for her life now, and for the life of their child.

Jim Bostwick knew Charley Gore wanted this ranch and that he would stop at nothing to get it. They had tried to scare him first, but that hadn't worked. Gore had tried to ride him into a fight in town, when Gore was surrounded by his boys, and Bostwick had refused it. Knowing the game as he did, and knowing Gore, Bostwick had known this would not be the end of it.

Naturally wary, he had returned to the ranch, and days had gone by quietly. Yet he remained alert. And then one morning as he had started for the corral, he had caught a flash of something out of the corner of his eyes. He had not stopped nor turned his head, but when he was currying the horse he got a chance to study the rim of Elk Ridge without seeming to.

What he had seen was simple enough. A bird had started to light in a tree, then had flown up and away. Something was in that tree or was moving on the ground under it.

It could have been any one of many things.

Cap MOFFIT WAS a student of men and their habits. In the case of Jim Bostwick he had studied well, but not well enough. In the first place he had not guessed that Bostwick had a habit of suspicion, and that he also had a habit of liking to walk in the dark.

It was simply that he liked the cool of night, the stars, the stillness of it. He had walked at night after supper ever since he was a boy. And so it was that the night after the bird had flown up Jim Bostwick, wearing moccasins for comfort, took a walk. Only that night he went further afield.

He had been walking west of the ranch when he smelled dust. There was no mistaking it. He paused, listening, and heard the faint sound of hoofbeats dwindling away into distance.

At the point where he now stood was the junction between two little-used trails, and the hoofbeats had sounded heading south down the Snow Creek trail. But where could the rider have come from? The only place, other than the ranch, would be high on Elk Ridge itself.

Puzzled, Jim Bostwick made his way back to the ranch. If this rider had been on Elk Ridge that morning, and had caused that bird to fly up, he must have spent the day there. What was he doing there? Obviously he had been watching the ranch. Yet, Bostwick thought, he could have been mistaken about the bird. A snake or a mountain lion might have caused it to fly up. But he doubted it.

The following morning, an hour before day, he was not in the cabin. He was lying among the rocks above Snow Creek trail, several miles from the ranch, his horse hidden well back in the brush. He did not see the rider, for the man kept off the trail in the daylight, but he heard him. Heard him cough, heard his horse's hoofs strike stone, and knew from the sound that the rider had gone up through the trees to Elk Ridge.

When the rider was safely out of the way, Jim Bostwick went out and studied the tracks. He then returned to the horse he had been riding and started back for the ranch, but he circled wide until he could ride down into the arroyo that skirted the north side of the ranch. This arroyo was narrow and invisible from the top of the ridge. In a grassy spot near the ranch house, he turned the horse into a small corral. It was where Tom Utterback kept his extra riding stock.

Then he crept back to the ranch house and went about his chores in the usual way, careful to indicate no interest in the ridge. He was also careful not to stand still where he would long be visible.

Inside the house, he prepared breakfast and considered the situation carefully. Obviously he was being watched. There was no point in watching him unless somebody meant to kill him. If the killer was that careful, he was obviously a dangerous man, and not to be taken lightly.

Why had he not made an attempt? Because he was stalking. Because he had not yet found the right opportunity.

Bostwick sat long over his coffee and mentally explored every approach to the situation. Putting himself in the unseen killer's place, he decided what he would do, and the following morning he began his puzzling tactics. Going around the house, he had gone down to the arroyo, then slipped back and, by using available cover, got the feed to his own horse. The ruse of the buckskin shirt had been used to make the watcher believe another man had entered the house. If he was correct in his guess that the killer was a careful man, the fellow would wait until he knew Bostwick was alone.

Bostwick was playing for time, working out a solution. Somehow he had to find out when the killer expected to kill, and from where. It was not long before he arrived at the same solution that had come to Cap Moffit.

The one time he could be depended upon to be at a given spot, not too far from cover, was when he curried his horse. That black was the love of his life, and he cared for the horse as he would for a child. The logical place was from the bed of the T U Creek. Flowing as it did from Elk Ridge, it presented a natural approach. Searching it, Bostwick found a few faint tracks. The killer had been down this way, had made sure of his ground.

Jim Bostwick prepared supper that night with a scowl on his face. Something, some idea, nagged at his consciousness but was not quite realized. There was something he had missed, but one thing he was sure of. Whoever the killer was, he had been hired by Charley Gore.

Now it has been said that Jim Bostwick was no gunfighter. Those who knew him best knew that Jim Bostwick was a tough man, easygoing usually, but get him mad and he would walk into a den of grizzlies and drag the old man grizzly out by the scruff of his neck. He was that kind of man. Angered, he had an unreasoning courage that was absolutely without fear of consequences or death.

Jim Bostwick was growing angry now. He didn't like being hunted, and he liked even less the thought behind it, and the man behind it. He was going to get this killer, and then he was going to get Charley Gore.

Yet he was not without the usual rough, ironic cowboy sense of humor so common in the west. The killer was up there on the hill hiding in the brush, and all the time the intended victim knew it. Suddenly, he began to chuckle. An idea had come to him, one he would enjoy.

Getting his pick and shovel he went out beside the house at a place just far enough away, but one which allowed no nearby cover, and commenced to dig. High on Elk Ridge, Cap Moffit stared down at Bostwick, puzzled by the digging. He became more puzzled as the hole became outlined. It was about six feet long and probably no more than half that wide. Jim Bostwick was digging a grave!

While digging, the idea that had been nagging at Bostwick's memory flowered suddenly. There had been other cases such as this. Lone men murdered without a clue, killed by some hidden marksman who then had vanished. There had been a family of three, slain one after another, over in the Panhandle.

Cap Moffit!

JIM BOSTWICK WALKED into the cabin and put the coffeepot on the stove. Nothing much was known about Cap Moffit. He was a rumor, perhaps a legend. A rancher had hinted once, at the beginning of a range war, that the proper way to end one was to send for Moffit. It had been a casual remark, yet it seemed to have information behind it. After that, there had been other stories, guarded, indefinite. It seemed that some of the more powerful cattlemen knew where they could get a killer when one was wanted.

Cap Moffit had been suspected of the Panhandle killings. His method had been talked about—the careful planning, the unerring marksmanship, the cold efficiency.

Now Jim Bostwick was sure the same man was lying up there on Elk Ridge. Of course, there were other killers for hire, but none with Moffit's careful, almost precise manner of killing. Realizing who he had to deal with sharpened his attention. If that was Cap Moffit, this was going to be anything but easy.

Cap had the reputation of shooting but once—and he did not miss.

Yet that in itself might be an advantage if Bostwick could continue to prevent him from getting the chance he wanted—or lead him into a trap, believing he had it.

He got a slab of wood and carved on it. Then he took it out and placed it at the head of the open grave. From the top of the ridge, Moffit saw it. A cold, unimaginative man except when it came to killing, Cap Moffit was puzzled. Anything he did not understand disturbed him, and he did not understand this. For the first time he made a change in his plans. He decided to crawl close enough to read what was carved on the slab through his fieldglasses.

Bostwick came out, saddled up, always keeping the horse between himself and the available shelter. Then he mounted and rode away. Using the cut of the T U Creek, Cap Moffit came down the mountain and got into position under a huge old cottonwood and lifted his glass.

Cut deep and blackened with soot the words were plain, all too plain!

HERE LIES
CAP MOFFIT, KILLER
SHOT DOWN
UPON
THIS SPOT
APRIL 1877

Cap Moffit lowered his glasses and wiped his eyes. He was crazy! It couldn't be! His second long look told the same story, and he lowered the glasses. He was known! Jim Bostwick knew him!

He looked again at the carved slab. An eerie feeling stole over him. It was unnatural. It was crazy. A man looking at his own grave marker. Only the date was blank, but the month was this month, the year this year. It was a warning—and it might be a prophecy.

Cap Moffit drew back and shook his head irritably. He was a fool to be disturbed by such a thing. Bostwick thought he was smart! Why, the fool! He'd show him!

Yet how had Bostwick known him? How could he be so sure?

Cap Moffit rolled a smoke and lit it, irritation strong within him, yet there was underlying worry, too. Had he known that at that very minute Jim Bostwick was scouting the ridge top, he would have been even more worried.

———

JIM BOSTWICK HAD gambled on Moffit's curiosity, and to some extent he did not care. There was a hard heedlessness about Jim Bostwick when aroused. He did not like being hunted. He did not like the necessity of being careful to avoid that assassin's bullet. Leaving the ranch, he had taken the trail toward town, but he had not followed it far; instead he had turned left and ridden round the end of Elk Ridge and mounted through the trees on the southern side.

Shortly, he had found Moffit's trail, knowing the tracks from those he had seen before. Now he rode with caution, his Winchester in his hand. Soon he found Moffit's horse, and on the inspiration of a moment, he stripped off saddle and bridle and turned the animal loose. Then he followed the trail of the walking man and found his various hideouts on the ridgetop.

Rightly, he deduced that the killer was down below, but he guessed wrong. Even as he found the last place where Moffit had rested under the big pine, Moffit was coming back up the gully of the T U Creek. He was coming slowly and carefully as was his wont, but his mind was preoccupied. He did not like the thought that his prospective victim knew who he was. What if he talked? What if, even now, he had gone to town to report to the sheriff?

Even as this thought struck him, Moffit noticed something else. He had reached the back slope of the ridge, and he noticed a black saddled horse standing some two hundred yards away. Yet even as he saw the horse, the black's head jerked up, its ears pricked, and it looked at him.

Something moved in the brush near the horse's head, and Cap Moffit's rifle came up, leaping to his shoulder. He saw the leaping body of Jim Bostwick, and he fired. The black sprang away, running, and Bostwick dropped, but as he hit ground, he fired!

The bullet clipped leaves not inches from his head, and Cap Moffit dropped to the ground. He slid downhill a few feet, then got up and, running lightly, circled toward his horse. He had no wish to fight a gun battle on that brush-covered, boulder-strewn mountainside. Such a battle would be too indefinite, for there not only marksmanship would be important, but woodcraft as well.

Moffit ran lightly toward his horse, then stopped. The horse was gone. An empty bridle and saddle awaited him!

Furious, he dropped back a few feet and took shelter among the rocks. He was fairly trapped! Unless—unless he could get Bostwick's horse.

It had run off, but would not go far. Probably his bullet had burned it. Yet he must be careful, for even now Bostwick might be coming down the mountain. The man would rightly deduce that the ambusher would head for his horse, so even now he might be drawing near.

Cap Moffit began to sweat. Something had gone wrong this time, and it would take all his ingenuity to get himself out of it alive. The man hunting him was no fool.

———

JIM BOSTWICK, WARNED by the quick swing of the black's head, had dropped. It was that dropping movement which drew the shot. Instantly, he rolled over and began to crawl, worming his way a full thirty yards before he stopped.

His own bullet had been an instinctive reply, and he had no idea how close it had come. Yet there was nothing in him that warned him to retreat. His only idea was to get the killer for hire who had come here to kill him.

The woods were still, and the sun was hot. Here under the trees, now that the breeze had died, it was sticky and still. The air was sultry, and sweat trickled down his face. His neck itched from dust and from pine needles picked up when he rolled over. There was the acrid smell of gunpowder from his rifle, and the silence of the woods. His horse had stopped running somewhere off among the trees.

Jim Bostwick waited. Patience and alertness would win now. Here in the woods, anything might happen. His throat felt dry and he wished for a drink. Somewhere he thought he heard a faint sound, but he did not move. He was lying on brown, parched pine needles in the blazing hot sun. Around him were the sharp edges and corners of rock thrust from the earth of the ridge, and not far away were larger boulders and a huge fallen log. It offered better cover, but more suspicious cover than he now had.

He waited. Somewhere an eagle cried. Something tiny scurried among the leaves. Then all was still.

His horse would come back to him. The black was trained to do just that. Yet even as he realized the black would soon be coming, another thought occurred. Cap Moffit would try to catch the horse and get away! Or kill him!

Moffit was cunning. Suppose he realized the horse was going back to Bostwick? And that he had only to wait and be guided by the horse? The black would find him, for a horse can smell out a trail as well as some dogs, if the trail is not an old one. More than once Jim Bostwick had seen horses do just that.

The sun was blazing hot. There was no breeze. The rocks glistened with desert varnish, smooth as mirrors. Far away he heard the horse walking. Bostwick did not like waiting. It had not been his way to wait, but to barge right in, swinging or shooting, and letting things happen as they would. This was Cap Moffit's game. The cool, careful killer's game.

Moffit would be coming. Moffit *had* to kill him now. He forced himself to lie still. The black was nearer now. Somewhere he heard a faint whisper of sound, the brushing of jeans on a rock or branch. He slid his hand back to the trigger guard of the rifle, gripped the gun with two hands, ready to leap and shoot.

There was no further sound. The horse had stopped. Probably the black had seen Moffit.

Bostwick waited, sweating, his back cooking under the direct rays of the spring sun. Every muscle was tensed and ready for action. Suddenly there was a flashing movement and a gun blasted, a rifle bullet cut through his hat brim and burned along his back. Instantly he fired, not holding his shots, one in the center, then quickly left and right of the spot from which the shot had come.

Another bullet notched his ear and he rolled over, down the south side of the ridge, trying to avoid the next shot until he could get to his feet. A bullet smashed dirt into his eyes and he fired blindly.

Rolling over, he lunged to his feet and dived for the shelter of some rocks. A bullet smashed into the rocks and ricocheted almost in his face, whining past his ear with a scream like a banshee. He hit ground and behind him he heard Moffit running to get another shot. The rifle roared behind him and he felt his rifle smashed from his hands and saw its stock was splintered.

He lunged to his feet again and threw himself in a long dive for some brush as the rifle bellowed again. He felt the shock of that bullet and knew that he was hit. Moffit wasn't stopping, but was coming on. Bostwick whirled and grabbed for his six-shooter.

As it came into his hand, he threw himself to his feet just as Moffit ran into the open. Jim Bostwick braced himself with the world rolling under him and the sweat in his eyes and the smell of blood in his nostrils, and he threw lead from his .44 and saw dust jump from Moffit's shirt. The smaller man fell back and hit the ground, but shot from the ground. Jim Bostwick felt the shock of that bullet, but he fired as he was falling, and missed.

He rolled over into the brush and, filled with sudden panic that he might get caught there in the open, he fought and scrambled his way through the brush. Fighting to get to shelter, he left a trail of scratched earth and blood behind him.

When he could stop, he rolled over to a sitting position and reloaded his six-shooter. There was no sound. He knew that Cap Moffit was not dead, but that one of them would die here, perhaps both. His gun loaded, he looked to his wounds. He had a hole through the fleshy upper part of his thigh, and it was bleeding badly. He plugged that with a handkerchief, torn to use on both sides, then examined his chest.

He was afraid the bullet had struck him in a vital spot, for the shock of it had turned him sick. However, he was fortunate. The bullet had struck his hip bone and ricocheted off, making a nasty open wound, but nothing deep. He drew the lips of the wound together and bound it with his torn shirt.

There was neither sound nor movement. His canteen was on his horse, and the horse would come if he called. The black was probably waiting for just that.

Jim Bostwick checked his belt. His six-shooter now held six shells, for he was going to be using it, not carrying it, and there were still twenty-odd shells in his belt. If he could not win with that number, he would never win.

Rage welled up in him and suddenly, heedless of consequences, he shouted, "I'm going to kill you, Cap! You've drygulched your last man!"

"Come and get me, then!" Moffit taunted. "You're so full of holes now you won't last the night!"

Jim Bostwick rubbed his unshaven jaw. He rolled over, thrusting his six-shooter in his belt. His arms were strong and unhurt, he could drag himself, or hobble if he could get up on his good leg.

Slowly and painfully, he worked his way along the side of the ridge into the deeper brush and trees. Dust and sweat caked his face, but his jaw was set and frozen against the biting pain. In a dense clump of brush, he waited. The horse was his ace-in-the-hole. The black would not leave, and he could call to him. Had Moffit been active, he might have reached the horse, but smelling of blood, there was small chance of any stranger getting near.

Under the bushes, Bostwick lowered himself and lay on

the pine needles, panting hoarsely. He must not pass out—he must stay alert. Cap Moffit had not only money for a reason now, but he must kill Bostwick or die himself.

Pain welled up and went through the rancher. He gritted his teeth against it, and against the weakness that was in him. Soon he would start out. He would get going.

A faint coolness touched his face, a stirring breath of air. He lifted his head and looked around. There was a bank of clouds over the mountains, piled-up thunderheads. The coolness touched his face again, breeze with the smell of rain in it. The country could use rain. The grass needed it. His head sank forward.

―――

ONLY A MINUTE it seemed, yet when he opened his eyes it was black—black and wet. It was raining. He had passed out.

His eyes had opened to darkness and a vast roaring that filled the world, a roaring of gigantic masses of wind and almost continuous thunder. Like a solid wall the wind swept the ridge, bending the huge trees like willows and sweeping the rocks with icy scythes of driving rain, pounding the earth and lashing at his cowering, rain-drenched body.

Suddenly, below the awful roar of the wind along the towering ridge, he heard another sound—faint, but definite. A vast bursting flare of lightning illuminated the ridge with blinding incandescent light. Through the flare there was a vicious whiplash of vivid blue flame, and his brain seemed split apart by a rending crash!

The huge pine near which he had been lying seemed to burst under his eyes and the towering mass of the tree toppled, falling away from him, leaving the dead-white fractured center exposed to the rain and the wind. Lightning whipped at the ridge, and the earth and rocks smelled of brimstone and charred pine needles.

And below the roar he heard again that whisper of sound. Lightning flared, and in the white glare he saw Cap Moffit, eyes wide and staring, Cap Moffit, poised and waiting for the flare, gun in hand. Even as he glimpsed him, Moffit fired!

The bullet missed, and Jim Bostwick rolled over, grabbing wildly, desperately, for his own gun. Wildly he fired, hurling three fast shots at the place from which the shot had come. With a lunge he made it to his feet, shot out a hand, and grabbed the lightning-blasted stump even as lightning flared again. They shot as one man, then Bostwick let go his hold and lunged through the driving wall of rain at the spot where he had seen Moffit. They came together, and Bostwick struck wickedly with his gunbarrel and missed, falling forward. He rolled over quickly and saw the dark figure swaying above him. Moffit fired, the blast of flame only feet from Bostwick's face. He felt the wicked sting of burning powder and felt the blow of the bullet as it struck him.

Huge billowing clouds rolled low over the ridge, and the whiplike flashes of lightning danced like dervishes of flame along the ridge. The forest would have been aflame had it not been for the great masses of water that were driven along it.

Moffit fired again, but he was weaving like one of the bushes around them and the shot missed. Bostwick rolled over. Grimly he struggled, moaning with eagerness to get up, to get his hands on Moffit. He swung out a wild, clutching hand and grabbed one of the killer's ankles. He jerked and the man fell and, bloody and wounded as Bostwick was, he clawed to grab a hold on the man's throat. There was another vivid streak of lightning, then Moffit's gun roared. . . .

CONSCIOUSNESS RETURNED, BUT slowly. Jim Bostwick lay flat on his face on the rocks of the ridge, swept bare by the violence of wind and rain. Around him, where all had been rushing wind and roaring rain, there was dead stillness. His head thudded with hammer-blows of agony. His shoulder and arm were stiff, one leg seemed useless, and every movement seared him with pain.

The rain had ceased. The wind had gone. The might of the thunder in the lonely ravines to the south and west had turned to the far-off mumbling of a puppy. Storm-tossed clouds scattered the skies and vied with the stars for attention. And

Jim Bostwick lay sprawled and alone on the ridge, his body spent, weakened from loss of blood and the whipping rain. And then he put out a hand and found his gun. Somehow he got his knees under him and lifted himself. He spun the cylinder of the gun and it turned.

Fumbling with clumsy fingers, he worked the ejector rod and pushed out the empty shells. Then he loaded the gun with care from his belt. There was nobody near him. He could see that. Wherever Moffit was, he was not here.

Jim Bostwick fumbled around, feeling, then he found a broken limb. Using it for a crutch, he got to his feet.

Blackie would have gone. The storm would have driven him off. Bostwick knew that straight ahead of him and more than a thousand feet down was the ranch, and if he was to live, he must get back to that ranch.

It was no use to try going around by the trail. He would never make it. Somehow he must fumble and fall and feel his way to the bottom. How long it took him, he did not know, but he knew when he reached it, and his fingers found something else. A horse's track!

If a track was here, it had to be made since the storm. He called out, risking a shot from Moffit, if he was still alive and nearby. He called again, and again. Then he heard a low whinny and the *clop, clop* of hoofs.

"Blackie!" he whispered. "Blackie!"

The horse snorted and shied, then came nearer, snuffling in the darkness. He reached up, and the horse shied again. He spoke his name and Blackie stood still. One hand got the stirrup, and then he pulled himself into the wet saddle.

"Home, Blackie!" he whispered and, as if waiting for just that, the black turned and started out across the little valley toward the house.

Sagging over the pommel, he still managed to cling to it, and when the black stopped at the steps of the house, he almost fell from the saddle. And when he hit the steps *his* hand struck the face. He grabbed for a gun, then stopped. The face was still, the body unmoving, but warm.

In the still, cold light from a vague gray predawn, he stared down at the crumpled figure. It was Cap Moffit.

JIM BOSTWICK CHUCKLED, a hoarse, choking sound. "You—you couldn't take it!" he sneered.

Turning over, he reached with his good hand for the girth and managed to get it loose and let the saddle fall. Then he pulled the black's head down and got the bridle off.

"Take a roll, boy," he whispered, "and rustle some grub."

He got the door open, then got a hand on Moffit's collar and dragged him inside, leaving one boot caught on the step with a spur. He got Moffit's gun and put them both near his hand.

It took him an hour to get his wounds uncovered, and another hour to get them bathed and dressed, after a fashion. As he worked, he looked grimly at the unconscious man. "I'm still moving," he said, "I'm going to come through."

When he had his wounds dressed, he went to work on Moffit. He was working on nerve, he knew that, and nothing but nerve. He kept himself going, forced himself to keep moving. He got the wounded man fixed up and got water heating on the stove, then slumped in a chair, his face haggard and bearded, his eyes hollow, his hair tangled with mud and blood—the last bullet had cut his scalp open and given him what was probably a mild concussion. He stared across at the unconscious killer, his eyes bleak.

When the water was hot, he made coffee and laced it with whisky and burned his mouth gulping a cup of it, then another. Then he pulled himself, sliding the chair by gripping the wall, until he was close to Cap Moffit. He tied the wounded killer's wrists and ankles. Some time later, sprawled on the bed, he passed out again.

HOURS LATER, WITH daylight streaming in the door from a sinking sun, he awakened. His eyes went at once to Moffit. The wounded man lay on the floor, glaring at him.

Bostwick swung his feet to the floor and stared blearily at Moffit. "Trussed up like a dressed chicken!" he sneered. "A hell of a gunman you are!"

Moffit stared at him. "You don't look so good yourself!" he retorted.

Bostwick caught the ledge along the wall with his good hand and pulled himself erect. He slapped the gun in his waistband. "I still got a gun," he said, and crept along the wall to the kitchen where he got the fire going, then fell into a chair. "You ain't so hot with a short gun," he said.

"I got *you*."

Bostwick chuckled. "Yeah, you're holding me, ain't you? I'm dead, ain't I? You two-bit imitation of a killer, you never saw the day you could kill me."

Moffit shook his head. "Maybe you're right," he said. "You must have three bullets in you now."

"Four hits you made." Bostwick chuckled. "I'm carrying no lead."

His stomach felt sick, but he managed to get water on the stove and make coffee. When he fell back in the chair again he felt weak and sicker.

"You better set still," Moffit said. "You're all in." He paused. "Whyn't you shoot me when you had the chance?"

"Aw"—Bostwick stared at him, grim humor in his eyes—"I like a tough man. I like a fighter. You did pretty good up on that mountain last night, pretty good for a drygulching killer."

Cap Moffit said nothing. For the first time the words of another man hurt. He stared down at his sock feet, and he had no reply to make.

"You going to turn me in for a hanging?" he finally asked.

"Naw." Bostwick poured coffee into a cup and slid it across the table. "Somebody'll shoot you sure as the Lord made little apples. You ever come back around here and I will. This here Tom Utterback who owns this spread, he's a good man."

"He's got a good man for a friend."

———

Two SICK, WOUNDED men struggled through four days, but it was Bostwick who struggled the hardest. Moffit watched him, unbelieving. It was impossible that any man could be so tenacious of life, so unbelievably tough. Yet this big, hard man was not giving up. No man, Moffit felt suddenly, could kill such a man. There was something in him, something black, bitter and strong, something that would not die.

On the sixth morning, Cap Moffit was gone. He had taken a gray from the other corral and he had gone off, riding his recovered saddle—wounded, but alive.

Tom Utterback rode up to the ranch on the ninth day. He stared at the pale shadow of a man who greeted him, gun in hand. He stared at the bloody bandage on the leg.

"You wasn't in that gunfight in town, was you?" he demanded.

"What gunfight?"

"Stranger name of Cap Moffit. He had some words with Charley Gore and two of his boys. They shot it out."

"They get him?"

"Don't know. He was shot up bad, but he rode out on his own horse."

"What happened to Gore?"

Utterback shook his head. "That stranger was hell on wheels. He killed Gore and one of his men and wounded the other."

"Yeah, he was a good man, all right." Jim Bostwick backed up and sat down in a chair. "Make some coffee, will you? And a decent meal. I'm all in."

A few minutes later he opened his eyes. He looked up at the ceiling, then out the door where another sun was setting.

"I'm glad he got away," he muttered.

TRAIL TO SQUAW SPRINGS

JIM BOSTWICK WAS packing a grouch, and he didn't care who knew it. The rain that began with a cloudburst had degenerated into a gully-washing downpour that for forty-eight hours showed no indication of letup. Bostwick, riding a flea-bitten cantankerous roan, was headed for the mountains to file a claim.

Rain slanted dismally across the country before him, pounding on his back and shoulders, beating on his waxed canvas slicker until his back was actually sore. Under a lowering gray sky the rain drew a metallic veil over the country, turning the road into a muddy path across what had been desert two days ago and would be desert again within two hours after the rain ended.

Bostwick swore at the roan, who merely twitched his ears, being familiar with cowhands and their ways. He knew the cussing didn't mean anything, and he knew the man who rode him took better care of him than any rider he'd had.

Bostwick swore because he wanted breakfast, wanted a drink, because he hadn't slept the night before, because he needed a shave and his face itched, and he swore on general principles.

His boss on the Slash Five had given him five days off in which to file on his claim, get drunk or whatever he pleased, and it looked like it would rain the whole five days, which Bostwick took as a personal affront.

Bostwick was a cowhand. Not a top hand, just a good, six-days-a-week, fourteen-hours-a-day cowhand who could handle a rope or a branding iron, dig post-holes, mend fences, clean water holes, shoe a horse, and play a fair hand of bunk-house poker.

He was twenty-nine years old, had never married, and he

made forty dollars a month. Several times a month he managed to get good and drunk. And every drunk began or ended with a fistfight. To date he was breaking even on the fights.

He wore a gun but had never drawn it in anger in his life. He had killed only one man he knew of, an Indian who was trying to steal his horse. That was when he was sixteen and coming West in a covered wagon.

At five eleven and weighing one hundred and seventy pounds his method of fighting was simple, to wade in swinging until something hit the dirt, either him or the other fellow. He fought because he enjoyed it and never carried a grudge that lasted longer than the headache.

The rain-blackened lava flow on his left ended and the trail curved around it into a huddle of nondescript buildings, for the most part unpainted and weather-beaten. This was the town of Yellowjacket.

The main street was empty, empty except for a covered wagon whose off wheels were on higher ground, giving a precarious tilt to the wagonbed. A man in a tattered slicker stood before the wagon talking to a girl whose face was barely revealed through the parted canvas.

"He doesn't plan to give them back, Ruthie," the old man was saying. "He doesn't aim to ever give them back. He says we owe him because he fed them."

The thin, querulous voice carried through the rain to Bostwick, who turned his eyes to them. There was something about the large dark eyes and the thin child's face that disturbed him. As he drew abreast of them the old man looked up at him out of faded blue eyes, then back to the girl.

"You'd better get into the wagon, Grandad. We can't do anything until the storm breaks."

Bostwick rode to the livery stable, stripped the gear from the roan and rubbed the horse reasonably dry with handfuls of hay, but the ungrateful beast nipped at his elbow and, as he departed the stall, took a playful kick at him that he evaded more from habit than attention. Without looking back he slogged through the mud to the saloon. There was no sound from the wagon as he went by.

The Yellowjacket Saloon was a bar fifteen feet long with a row of bottles behind, mud mixed with sawdust on the plank floor and a potbellied stove glowing red like an expectant boil. Behind the bar there was a big man with a polished face and a handlebar mustache. His hair started midway on the top of his head and was jet-black. He had big, square fists and his hands and arms were white as a woman's.

A man dozed in a chair against the wall, his hat over his eyes, another slept with his head on a card table. At the other table four men played a lackluster game in a desultory fashion with a dog-eared deck of cards. From time to time one or the other of them would turn his head to spit at a box of sawdust, and from time to time one of them hit it.

Bostwick removed his hat, slapped the raindrops from it with a blow against his leg and said, "Gimme a shot of rye." The bartender glanced at Jim's broken nose as he poured the drink.

A man in a mackinaw who sat near the glowing stove took his pipe from his mouth. "Just the same, I think it's mighty mean of him to take their horses. How are they going to get out of here?"

A man with a streaked blond mustache glanced cynically at the first speaker. "You know Pennock. He doesn't plan for them to leave, not a-tall!"

"He seen that girl," the man in the mackinaw said. "Ain't many women come to Yellowjacket. Besides, that old man was all set to file on Squaw Springs, and Pennock figures that's his'n."

Jim Bostwick downed his drink. Squaw Springs? That was the claim he'd planned to file on.

He let the bartender refill his glass. "He filed on Squaw Springs?"

"Pennock? Why should he? Who's going to butt in when he says it's his'n? They say that gun of his packs seven notches, or could if he wished it."

"It could," the bartender said. "We all know two notches that could go on it. Sandy Chase tried Pennock's game and came up a loser."

"Ought to be a law against killin' when the ground's all

froze up. Grave diggin' no pleasure any time, but in frozen ground?"

"Makes for shallow graves," somebody said, "better when Judgment Day comes."

"That girl ain't no more'n sixteen or seventeen. It's a damn shame."

"You go tell that to Pennock."

Nobody replied to that. Well, it was none of his fuss. Besides, they planned to file on his claim, as did Pennock.

"Where's the grub-pile?" he asked.

"Two doors down." He glanced again at the broken nose. "You a fighter?"

Bostwick buttoned his slicker. "Only when I'm pushed."

He started for the door and heard the man in the mackinaw say, "He killed Chase over a woman. What was the other one about?"

"Feller aimed to file on Squaw Springs. Pennock brought some sort of a charge against him, and the feller got riled. Figured he was a tough case and maybe in his home country he was."

"He was too far from home, then. I'm not hunting any beef with Jack Pennock!"

Jim pulled his hat low over his eyes. Shoulders hunched against the rain, he slopped through the mud to the light already showing from the boardinghouse window. The covered wagon was directly across the street and, as he glanced over, he saw the girl getting down from the wagon. Averting his eyes he ducked into the door.

A big-bosomed woman with a red, Irish face pointed at the mat. "Wipe your feet, an' wipe 'em good!"

Meekly, Bostwick did as he was told. Taking off his hat and slicker he hung them from pegs near the door and seated himself at the long table.

"You're early, stranger," the Irish woman said, "but you look hungry, so set up. I'll feed you."

Bostwick looked up as the door closed. It was the girl from the wagon. She had dark hair and large dark eyes. Her face was oval and quite pretty. She had a coffeepot in her hand.

She looked at him, then turned hastily away as if she had seen too many of his kind. Bostwick flushed.

"Ma'am? Can I buy some coffee? Grandad's having a chill."

"I shouldn't wonder, sloppin' around in the rain like he's been doin'. You two goin' to pay Jack Pennock what he asks?"

Her lips, delicate as rose petals, trembled. "We can't. We just don't have it."

The woman filled the coffeepot and waved payment aside. "You take it along, honey. I wouldn't know what to charge for that little dab of coffee."

"But I—! I do want to pay."

"You go along now. It's all right."

When the girl had gone, she brought food to Bostwick. "It's a shame!" she said. "A downright shame!"

Jim Bostwick helped himself to a slab of beef and some mashed potatoes. "Who is this Pennock?" he asked, without looking up.

The woman turned to look at him. "He's the town marshal. More, he's the boss around here, and folks know it."

"Nobody stands against him?"

"Some tried. Things happened to them. Jack Pennock is a hard man."

He was getting bored by that repeated comment. "When did those folks get here?"

"Yesterday. Pennock took their horses, impounded them for being in the street all night. Back when the mining boom was on, the town council passed that rule because the streets were so crowded at night a body couldn't get through. After the boom died people forgot about it until Pennock was elected marshal, then he dug into the town laws and dug up a lot of regulations, all of which show profit for him."

The door opened and the man in the mackinaw came in followed by his blond-mustached friend. Jim was aware of their attention.

"Howdy, Kate!"

"Howdy, Harbridge! How are you, Grove? How's Emma doin'?"

"Ailin'," Grove replied cheerfully.

The bartender came in and behind him, another man. Talk around the table died and Bostwick looked up. The newcomer was a big man, heavy-shouldered with bold black eyes. Instinctively, Bostwick knew this was Pennock. The man sat down near him and instantly Bostwick felt the stirring of an inner rebellion. There was something deep within him that deeply resented such men.

Bostwick was, as many an American has been before and since, a man who resented authority. He knew its necessity and tried to conform but when that authority became domineering, as this man obviously was, Bostwick's resentment grew.

More than that, very big men who used their size to overawe others irritated him. That accounted for the fact that he had lost as many fights as he had, for he was always choosing the biggest, toughest ones. Large men put him on edge, and he was on edge now.

"Stranger in town?" Pennock asked abruptly.

"No." Bostwick could not have told why he chose to deliberately antagonize the man. "I been in town more'n an hour."

Pennock did not reply, but Bostwick was aware of a subdued stir down the table. He reached over and took the coffeepot almost out of Pennock's hand and filled his cup. The big man's eyes hardened, and he studied Bostwick carefully.

"Don't look at me," Jim said, "I put my horse in the barn."

Somebody snickered and Pennock said, "I didn't ask about your horse. Seems to me, stranger, you're somewhat on the prod."

"Me?" Bostwick looked surprised. "I'm not huntin' trouble. I'm not expectin' trouble, either. Of course, if I was an old man with a pretty young granddaughter I might feel different."

Pennock put his cup down hard. "I don't like that remark. If you're huntin' trouble you're sure headed right at it."

"I ain't huntin' trouble, but there's no law against a man thinkin' out loud. I'm just of the opinion that a town that will make trouble for a sick old man and his granddaughter is pretty small stuff."

"Nobody asked you," Pennock said.

Pennock had an ugly expression in his eyes, but Bostwick was suddenly aware that Pennock was in no hurry to push trouble. That was an interesting point. Because he was a stranger? Because the attack had surprised him? Because Pennock was a sure-thing man who had no desire to tackle tough strangers? It was a point worthy of some thought.

Talk started up again, and Kate came around and laid an enormous slab of apple pie on Bostwick's plate. When he looked up, she was smiling.

No man such as Pennock just happens. Each has a past and perhaps somewhere back down the line Pennock was wanted. Or maybe he had taken water for somebody—

"Pennock?" he muttered. "That name does sound familiar." Bostwick looked him over coolly. "Been around here long?"

Pennock's lips thinned out, yet he fought back his anger. "I'll ask the questions here. What do you want in Yellowjacket?"

"Just passin' through."

"A drifter?"

"No, I'm with a big outfit south of here, below the Bradshaws. The Slash Five."

Grove looked up at the mention of the name. "Ain't that the outfit that treed Weaver?"

It had been a fight with some tinhorn gamblers, but Bostwick lied, "We didn't like the town marshal. He gave one of our boys a rough time, so we just naturally moved in."

Kate asked, "What happened to the marshal?"

"Him? Oh, we hung him!" Bostwick said carelessly. "That is, we hung the body. I figure he was already dead because we dropped a loop on him and drug him maybe three hundred yards with some of the boys shootin' into him as we drug him. He was a big feller, too."

"What's that got to do with it?" Pennock's face had lost color but none of the meanness in his eyes.

"Huh? Oh, not much! Only them big fellers don't hang so good. Bodies are too heavy. This feller's head pulled off. Would you believe it? Right off!"

Pete and Shorty would get a hoot out of that story. Just

wait until he told them! They'd never hung anybody or dragged anybody. A couple of the tinhorns tried to shoot it out but Shorty was, for a cowhand, mighty good with a gun. He nailed one, and Pete wounded the other one. Then they had pitched all the rest of the tinhorns' gear into the street and ran them out of town in their sock feet.

He was aware the others were enjoying his baiting of the town marshal. He was enjoying it himself, and with a good meal inside him he had lost his grouch. But none of this was getting him anywhere closer to Squaw Springs—nor was it getting that girl and her grandad out of trouble.

It was then he remembered they were planning to file on Squaw Springs themselves, so if somehow he got them out of trouble—

He stopped abruptly. Now who said he was getting them out of trouble? What business was it of his? A man could get himself killed, butting into such things.

But saying he did get them out of trouble, then they would be going after the same claim he wanted!

It was a good claim. The spring had a fine flow of excellent water, and the land lay well for farming or grazing. A man could do something with it, fruit trees, maybe. A place like his folks had back East.

Pennock wanted that claim, too, and any way a man looked at it Pennock was in the way.

Jack Pennock finished eating and went outside, ignoring Bostwick. Pennock stopped outside the boardinghouse window picking his teeth with the ivory toothpick that had been hanging from his watchchain. He was looking across the street at the covered wagon. That decided Bostwick. He would get them out of trouble first and then decide about the claim.

"You better lay off Pennock," Harbridge warned him. "He's a killer. He'll be out to get you now, one way or the other.

"He'll get out that book of city laws and find something he can hang onto you."

Bostwick had a sudden thought. "Is there just one of them law books? I mean, does anybody else have a copy?"

"I have, I think," Kate replied dubiously. "My old man was mayor during the boom days. I believe he had one."

"You have a look. I'll talk to that girl."

There was worry in Kate's eyes. "Now you be careful, young man! Don't take Pennock lightly!"

"I surely won't. I ain't anxious to get hurt. You see," he said ruefully, "I had my heart set on Squaw Springs myself!"

He splashed across the street to the wagon and rapped on the wagonbox. Dusk was falling but he could see her expression change from fear to relief as she saw him.

"Ma'am, how much does that marshal want for your horses?"

"He said fifty dollars."

"How's your grandad?"

"Not very good." She spoke softly. "I'm worried."

"Maybe we better get him inside Kate's house. It's cold and damp out here."

"Oh, but we can't! If we leave the wagon the marshal will take it, too."

"You get him fixed to move," Bostwick said. "You leave that marshal to me."

When he explained to Kate she agreed readily but then wondered, "What about the wagon?"

"I'll find a way," he said doubtfully.

"I found that book," Kate said, "for whatever good it will do you."

It was not really a book, just a few handwritten sheets stapled together. It was headed boldly: *City Ordnances*.

Bostwick was a slow reader at best, but he seated himself and began to work his way through the half-dozen pages of what a long-ago town council had decreed for Yellowjacket.

Later, when he had grandad safely installed in the room where Kate's husband had once lived, he had a long talk with Kate.

"I'll do it! I'll do it or me name's not Katie Mulrennan!"

———

WATCHING HIS CHANCE to move unseen, Bostwick ran through the mud and crawled into the wagon, burrowing down amidst the bedding and odds and ends of household furniture. He had been there but a few minutes when he heard a splashing of hoofs and a rattle of trace-chains. Pennock was, as he had expected, hitching grandad's team to the wagon.

Crouching back of the seat, he waited. Pennock had learned of his moving grandad into Kate's but had no idea Bostwick was inside the wagon.

It was dark and wet, and the big man was watching his footing as he started to clamber into the wagon. He missed seeing the hand that shot out of the darkness and grabbed the lines from his hand, nor the foot until it smashed into his chest.

Pennock let out a choking yell and grabbed at the leg as he toppled backward into the mud.

Scrambling to the seat, Bostwick slapped the horses with the lines, and the heavy wagon started with a jerk.

Behind him there was an angry shout. Glancing back Bostwick saw the big man lunge after the wagon, then slip and fall facedown in the mud. Then the team was running, and the wagon was out of town on the trail to Squaw Springs.

Jim Bostwick drove for thirty minutes until he came to what he was looking for, an abandoned barn that had stood there since the boom days. He drove over the gravel approach and into the door in the end of the barn. Fortunately, somebody had used the barn during the summer and there was hay in the manger. He unhitched the horses and tied them to the manger, and then going outside, he eliminated what tracks he could find. The rain would do the rest.

When he had finished he went back to town riding one horse and leading the other. He took them to the livery stable, then scouted the boardinghouse, but as Kate had foretold, most of the townspeople were present.

When he entered, Jack Pennock half-started to his feet but Bostwick had a thumb hooked in his belt near his gun, and slowly Pennock sat down again.

"You the one who drove that wagon off?"

"I was. And I was completely within my rights."

Astonishment replaced anger on Pennock's face. "What do you mean . . . *rights*?"

"You quiet down, Pennock. We've got business." Bostwick glanced at Kate. "Are you ready, judge?"

"Judge?" Pennock's hands rested flat on the table. He looked like an old bull at bay. "What's going on here?"

Kate Mulrennan banged the table with a hammer. "Court's now in session!"

Pennock looked from one to the other. "What kind of tom-foolery is this?" he demanded.

"It means," Bostwick replied, "that the town council met this afternoon and appointed me the town marshal according to the regulation set forth in the city ordnances of Yellow-jacket, which decrees—read it, Katie."

The aforesaid town council shall meet on the fifth day of January, or as soon thereafter as possible, and shall appoint a judge, a town marshal and town clerk. These officials shall hold office only until the fifth of January following, at which time the council shall again meet and reappoint or replace these officials as they shall see fit.

Bostwick's eyes never left Pennock. It was the first time the man's bluff had been called, and he was expecting trouble. Appointed to the office almost three years before, he had run the town as he saw fit and had pocketed the fines.

"That means," Jim went on, "that you are no longer the town marshal and I am. It also means that for two years you have been acting without authority. As there was no meeting of the town council in that time we will waive that part of it, but we must insist on an accounting of all the fines and monies collected by you."

"What? You're a pack of crazy fools!"

"According to regulations you get ten percent of all collected. Now we want an accounting."

Jack Pennock clutched the edge of the table. Month after month he had bullied these people, fining them as well as strangers, and no man dared deny him. Now this stranger had come to Yellowjacket and in one day his power had crumbled to nothing.

But had it? Need he let it be so? Watching Pennock, Bostwick judged that he had been wary of tackling a tough man who might be a gunfighter, but driven into a corner, Pennock had no choice. It was run or fight.

"I haven't the money." Pennock was very cool now. "So you'll pay hell collecting it."

"We thought of that, so you have a choice. Pay up or leave town tomorrow by noon."

"Suppose I decide to pay no attention to this kangaroo court?"

"Then it becomes my job," Bostwick replied quietly, "as the newly elected town marshal . . ."

Jack Pennock got to his feet. Bostwick had to hand it to him. When the chips were down Pennock was going to fight for what he had. "You won't have to come looking for me, Bostwick. I'll be out there waiting for you."

Pennock started for the door and Kate called out, "Hold up a minute, Jack! You owe me a dollar for grub. Now pay up, you cheapskate!"

Pennock's face was livid. He hesitated, then shaking with anger he tossed a dollar on the table and walked out.

"Well, Jim," Harbridge said, "you said if it came to this that you'd handle it. Now you've got it to do."

"He's a dangerous man with a gun. Sandy Chase was good, but he wasn't good enough. I never would've had the nerve to go through with this if Kate hadn't told us you'd face him, if need be."

"Are you fast?" Grove asked.

"No, I'm not. Probably I'm no faster than any of you, but I'll be out there and he'd better get me quick or I'll take him."

Bostwick disliked to brag, but these men needed to believe. If he failed them they would take the brunt of Pennock's anger.

When they had trooped out of the room and gone to their homes, Bostwick sat down again, suddenly scared. He looked up to see Ruth watching him.

"I heard what was said. You've done this for me . . . for us, haven't you?"

Bostwick's hard features flushed. "Ma'am, I ain't much, and I'm no braver than most, it's just that when I see a man like him something gets into me."

"I wish we had a few more like you!" Kate said.

She gestured to the table. "You set, I've some more of that pie." She looked around at Ruthie. "You, too, you look like you could do with some nourishment."

When the sun hung over the street, Bostwick stood in a doorway thinking what a damned fool he was. Why, Shorty, who laid no claims to being good with a gun, was better than he was. Yet he had walked into this with his eyes open.

He must make no effort at a fast draw. He was not fast, and he would be a fool to try.

He might have time for one shot only, and he must be sure that shot would kill. Jim Bostwick was a man without illusions. He knew he was going to take some lead, and he had to be prepared for it.

He was a good shot with a pistol, better than most when shooting at targets, only this time the target would be shooting back. He had faced that before and wasn't looking forward to it. Not at all.

The sun was baking the wetness from the street and from the false-fronted buildings. Somewhere a piano was playing. He stepped into the street.

"Bostwick!"

The call was from *behind* him! Jack Pennock had been lurking somewhere near the livery stable and had outsmarted him, played him for a sucker.

Jack was standing there, big and rough, a pistol in his hand. And he was smiling at the success of his trick. Jack fired.

Take your time! The words rang in his mind like a bell. He lifted his bone-handled gun and fired just as Jack let go with his second shot. Something slugged Bostwick in the leg as he realized Jack had missed his first shot!

His eyes were on that toothpick on Jack's watchchain. He

squeezed off a shot even as he fell, then he was getting up, bracing himself for another careful shot.

Jack seemed to be weaving, turning his side to him like a man on a dueling field. Bostwick fired from where his gun was, shooting as a man points a finger. This time there was no mistake. Where the toothpick had hung there was a widening stain now, and he fired again, then went to his knees, losing his grip on his gun.

Somewhere a door slammed, and he heard running feet. He reached out for his gun, but his hand closed on nothing. He smelled the warm, wet earth on which his face rested, and he felt somebody touch his shoulder.

———

"I THINK HE'S waking up," somebody said, some woman.

He moved then and a bed creaked and when his eyes opened he was looking up at a ceiling and he heard Ruthie saying, "Oh, Katie! He's awake! He's awake!"

"Awake and hungry," he grumbled.

He looked at Ruthie. "How's your grandad?"

"He died . . . only a little while after your fight. He said you were a good man."

"Jack Pennock? Did I—?"

"You hit him four times. He's been buried these two weeks."

"*Two weeks?* You mean I've been here two weeks?"

"You have. Two weeks and a day, to be exact." She took his hand. "Jim? Kate told me that you planned to file on Squaw Springs yourself."

"Forget it. That will be a good place for you, and as for me, I'm just a forty-dollar-a-month cowhand."

"We could do it together."

"Well, you know how folks talk. You being a young girl, and all."

"What if we were married?" she suggested doubtfully.

"Well," he admitted cautiously, "that might do it." He stole a look at her from the corners of his eyes. "Did you ever take a good look at me? Even when I'm shaved—"

"You are shaved, silly!" She laughed at him. "Kate shaved you. She said she always wondered what you looked like under all that brush."

He lifted a hand. It was true. He had been shaved. "You think you could marry a man like me?"

"Well," she said, "just to stop the talk—"

WEST OF THE PILOT RANGE

WARD MCQUEEN LET the strawberry roan amble placidly down the hillside toward the spring in the cottonwoods. He pulled his battered gray sombrero lower over his eyes and squinted at the meadow.

There were close to three hundred head of white-faced cattle grazing there and a rider on a gray horse was staring up toward him. The man carried a rifle across his saddle, and as McQueen continued to head down the hillside, the rider turned his horse and started quickly forward.

He was a powerfully built man with a thick neck and a shock of untrimmed red hair. His hard, little, blue eyes stared at McQueen.

"Who are yuh?" the redhead demanded. "Where yuh goin'?"

McQueen brought the roan to a stop. The redhead's voice angered him and he was about to make a sharp reply when he noticed a movement in the willows along the stream and caught the gleam of a rifle. "I'm just ridin' through," he replied quietly. "Why?"

"Which way yuh come from?" The redhead was suspicious. "Lots of rustlers around here."

McQueen chuckled. "Well, I ain't one," he said cheerfully. "I been ridin' down Arizona way. Thought I'd change my luck by comin' north."

"Saddle tramp, eh?" Red grinned a little himself, revealing broken yellow teeth. "Huntin' a job?"

"Might be." McQueen looked at the cattle. "Your spread around here?"

"No. We're drivin' 'em west. The boss bought 'em down Wyomin' way. We could use a hand. Forty a month and grub, bonus when we git there."

"Sounds good," McQueen admitted. "How far you drivin'?"

" 'Bout a hundred miles further." Red hesitated a little. "Come talk to the boss. We got a couple of riders, but we'll need another, all right."

They started down the hill toward the cottonwoods and willows. Ward McQueen glanced thoughtfully at the cattle. They were in good shape. It was unusual to see cattle in such good shape after so long a drive. And the last seventy-five miles of it across one of the worst deserts in the West. Of course, they might have been here several days, and green grass, rest, and water helped a lot.

———

A TALL MAN in black stepped from the willows as they approached. There was no sign of a rifle, yet Ward was certain it was the same man. Rustlers or Indians would have a hard time closing in on this bunch, he thought.

"Boss," Red said, "this here's a saddle tramp from down Arizony way. Huntin' him a job. I figgered he might be a good hand to have along. This next forty miles or so is Injun country."

The man stared at McQueen through close-set, black eyes, and one hand lifted to the carefully trimmed mustache.

"My name is Hoyt," he said sharply. "Iver Hoyt. I do need another hand. Where yuh from?"

"Texas. Been ridin' south of Santa Fe and over Arizona way." He took out the makin's and started to build a cigarette.

Hoyt was a sharp-looking man with a hard, ratlike face. He wore a gun under his Prince Albert coat.

"All right, Red, put him to work." Hoyt looked up at Red. "Work him on the same basis as the others, understand?"

"Sure," Red said, grinning. "Oh, sure. The same way."

Hoyt turned and strode away through the trees toward a faint column of smoke that arose from beyond the willows.

Red turned. "My name's Red Naify," he said. "What do I call you?"

"I'm Ward McQueen. They call me Ward. How's it for grub?"

"Sure thing." Red turned his horse through the willows. McQueen followed, frowning thoughtfully.

There was no danger about the cattle drifting. They had just crossed a desert, if Red's story was true, and there was no grass within miles as green and lush as this in the meadow. And water was scarce. So why had Naify been out there with the cattle close to grub call? And why had Iver Hoyt been down in the trees with a rifle?

It was on the edge of Indian country, he knew. There had been rumors of raids by a band of Piute warriors from the Thousand Spring Valley, north of here. He shrugged. What the devil? He was probably being unduly suspicious about the outfit.

Two riders were sitting over the fire when he approached. One was a squat man with a bald head. The other a slim, pleasant-looking youngster who looked up, grinning.

"That there is 'Baldy' Jackson," Naify said. "He's cook and nightrider usually. The kid is Bud Fox. Baldy an' Bud, this is Ward McQueen."

Baldy's head came up with a jerk and he almost dropped the frying pan. Naify looked at him in surprise and so did Bud. Baldy looked around slowly, his eyes slanting at Ward, without expression.

"Howdy," he said, and turned back to his cooking.

Bud Fox brought up an armful of wood and began poking sticks into the fire. He glanced at Baldy curiously, but the cook did not look up again.

When they had finished eating, Hoyt saddled a fresh horse and mounted up. Red Naify got up and sauntered slowly over to the edge of camp, out of hearing distance. The two talked seriously while Bud Fox lay with his head on his saddle, dozing. Baldy picked idly at his teeth, staring into the fire. Once or twice the older man looked up, glancing toward the two standing at the edge of the willows.

He picked up a heavier stick and placed it on the fire.

"You from Lincoln?" he asked, low-voiced. "I knowed of a McQueen, right salty. He rid for John Chisum."

"Could be," McQueen admitted softly. "Where you from?"

Baldy looked up out of wise eyes. "Animas. Rid with

'Curly Bill' some, but I ain't no rustler no more. I left the owlhoot."

Red Naify was walking back. He looked at Ward thoughtfully.

"Yuh tired?" he asked suddenly. "I been workin' these boys pretty regular. How's about you night-herdin'?"

"Uh-huh." McQueen got up and stretched. "I didn't come far today. No use a man ridin' the legs off his hoss when he ain't got to get noplace particular."

Naify chuckled. "That's right."

———

WARD MCQUEEN SADDLED up and rode out toward the herd. He was very thoughtful. He couldn't help feeling that something was wrong. He shook his head. Baldy Jackson might or might not be off the owlhoot, but there was someone around whom Baldy didn't trust.

Idly, he let the roan circle the herd, bringing a few straying steers closer to the main herd. There was plenty of grass. It was a nice, comfortable spot to hole up for a few days.

An hour later, as the sun was just out of sight, he had an idea. Picking out one of the steers McQueen rode in and roped it. In a matter of seconds the young steer was tied. With a bit of stick he dug into the dirt on one hoof. A few minutes of examination, and he got up and turned the steer loose. It struggled erect and hiked back to the herd.

Ward McQueen mounted again, his face thoughtful. That critter had never crossed the alkali desert! There was no caked alkali dust on the hoof, none of it in the hair on the animal's leg. Wherever the cattle had come from, it hadn't been across the vast, salt plain where animals sank to their knees in the ashy waste. They had traveled in fairly good country, which meant they had come down from the north.

There was three hundred head of prime beef here, and it had been moved through pretty good country.

It was almost two o'clock in the morning and he had started back toward the camp when he saw the lean height of young Bud Fox walking toward him. He spotted him in the moonlight and reined in, waiting.

"How's it go?" Bud asked cheerfully. "I woke up and thought maybe yuh'd like some coffee?" He held up a cup and held another for himself.

McQueen swung down and ground-hitched the roan.

"Tastes mighty good!" he said, after a pull at the coffee. He glanced up at Bud. "How long you and Baldy been with this herd?"

"Not long," Bud said. "We joined 'em here, too. We was ridin' down from the Blue Mountains, up Oregon way. Hoyt and Naify was already here. Said they'd been here a couple of days. Had two punchers when they come, they told us, but the punchers quit and headed for Montana."

"Yuh ever punch cows in Montana?" McQueen asked.

"Nope. Not me."

McQueen watched Bud walk back to camp and then forked the roan and started off, walking the horse. The stories of Baldy and Bud sounded straight enough. Baldy was admittedly from New Mexico and Arizona. Bud Fox said he had never ridden in Montana, and he looked like a southern rider. On the other hand, Red Naify, the foreman, who said he had driven in from Wyoming, rode a big horse and carried a thick, hemp lariat. Both were more typical of Montana cowhands.

It was almost daylight when McQueen heard the shot.

He had rounded the herd and was nearing the willows when the sudden *spang* of a rifle stabbed the stillness.

The one shot, then silence.

Touching spurs to the roan, he whipped it through the willows to the camp. Red Naify was standing, pistol in hand, at the edge of the firelight, staring into the darkness.

Both Baldy and Bud were sitting up in their blankets, and Baldy had his rifle in his hand.

"Where'd that shot come from?" McQueen demanded.

"Up on the mountain. It was some distance off," Naify said.

"Sounded close by to me," Bud retorted. "I'da sworn it was right close up in them trees."

"It was up on the mountain," Naify growled. He looked around at McQueen. "Them cows all right?"

"Sure thing. I'll go back."

"Wait." Fox rolled out of his blankets. "I'll go out. You been out all night."

"We're movin' in a couple of hours," Red Naify said. "Let him go back."

Ward McQueen turned the roan and rode back to the herd. It was not yet daylight. He could see the campfire flickering through the trees.

———

THE HERD WAS quiet. Some of the cattle had started up at the shot, but the stillness had quieted them again. Most of them were bedded down. With a quick glance toward the fire, McQueen turned the roan toward the mountain.

Skirting some clumps of piñon and juniper, he rode into the trees. It was gray, and the ground could be seen, but not well. He knew what he was looking for. If there had been a man, there must have been a horse. Perhaps the shot had been a miss. In any event, there had been no sound of movement in the stillness that followed. The roan's ears were keen, and he had given no indication of hearing anything.

He was riding through a clump of manzanita when he heard a horse stamp. He caught his own horse's nose, then ground-hitched it, and walked through the trees.

It was a fine-looking black horse, all of sixteen hands high, with a silver-mounted saddle. A Winchester '73 was in the scabbard, and the saddlebags were hand-tooled leather.

Working away from the horse, McQueen started toward the edge of the woods. He was still well under cover when he saw the dark outline of the body. He glanced around, listened, then moved closer. He knelt in the gray dimness of dawn. The man was dead.

He was a young man, dressed in neat, expensive black. He wore one gun and it was in its holster. Gently, McQueen rolled the man on his back. He had been handsome as well as young, with a refined, sensitive face. Not, somehow, a Western face.

Slipping his hand inside the man's coat, McQueen withdrew a flat wallet. On it, in neat gold lettering, was the name

Dan Kermitt. Inside, there was a sheaf of bills and other papers.

Suddenly McQueen heard a light footstep. Quickly, he slid the wallet into his shirt and stood up. Red Naify was standing on the edge of the woods.

"Looks like somebody got who he was shootin' at," McQueen said quietly. "Know him?"

Naify walked forward on cat feet. He looked down, then he shrugged.

"Never saw him afore!" He looked up, his piglike eyes gleaming. It was light enough now for McQueen to see their change of expression. "Did you kill him?"

"Me?" For an instant McQueen was startled. "No. I never saw this hombre before."

"Yuh could've," Red said, insinuatingly. "There wasn't nobody to see."

"So could you," McQueen replied. "So could you!"

"I got an alibi." Red grinned suddenly. "What the devil? I don't care who killed him. Injuns, probably. Find anythin' on him?"

"Just startin' to look," McQueen replied carefully. How much had Red seen?

Naify stooped over the body and fanned it with swift, skillful fingers. In the right-hand pocket he found a small wallet containing a few bills and some gold coin. Ward McQueen stared at it thoughtfully, and when Naify straightened, he asked a question.

"Anythin' to tell who he was?"

"Not a thing. I'll jest keep this until somebody calls for it." He pocketed the money. "Yuh want to bury him?"

"Yeah. I'll bury him." McQueen stared down at the body. This was no place to bury a nice young man like this. But then, the West did strange things to people, bringing a strange grave to many a man.

"Hey." Red paused. "He should have a hoss. I better have a look around."

"Leave it to me," McQueen said quietly. "You got the money. I already found the hoss."

Red Naify hesitated, and for an instant his face was harsh

and cruel. McQueen watched him, waiting. It was coming, sooner or later, and it could be now as well as later.

Naify shrugged, and started to turn away, then looked back. "Was it—the hoss, I mean—a big black?"

"Yeah," McQueen told him, unsmiling. "So yuh did know him?"

Naify's face darkened. "No. Only I seen somebody follerin' us that was ridin' a big black. Could've been him." He strode off toward camp.

Carrying the young man to a wash in the steep bank, he placed the body on the bottom, then caved dirt over it.

"Not much of a grave, friend," he said softly, "but I'll come back an' do her proper." He turned and as he walked away he added quietly, "And when I do, amigo, yuh can rest easy."

———

STANDING IN THE brush near the black horse, he took out the flat leather wallet and opened it. He thrust his hand inside, then gulped in amazement. He was staring down at a sheaf of thousand-dollar bills!

Swiftly, he counted. Twenty-five of them, all new and crisp. There were two letters and a few odds and ends of no importance. He opened one letter, in feminine handwriting. It was short and to the point.

> We have gone ahead to Fort Mallock. Come there with the money, as Kim has located a good ranch. I don't know what we'd have done without Iver, however, as ever since Father was killed, he has advised and helped me. The cattle are coming west with two of the most trustworthy hands, Chuck and Stan Jones.
>
> Ruth

Replacing the wallet in his shirt, Ward McQueen swung into the saddle. He rode the black horse back to where his own horse waited, then leading his horse, he rode back to the camp.

Red Naify looked up at him, and then glanced at the horse, envy and greed shining in his eyes. Baldy looked up, too, and his eyes narrowed a little, but he said nothing. Bud Fox was already bunching the herd to start them moving.

Naify mounted up and joined him while McQueen ate. Twice he glanced up from his food to Baldy.

"Say," he said finally, "where was Red when yuh first looked up after that shot?"

"Red?" Baldy looked up, and put his big red hands on his hips. "Red wasn't in sight. Then I looked around, and he was standin' there. He could've been there all the time, but I don't think he was."

McQueen nodded up the hillside. "There was a dead man up there. He'd been lookin' us over from the cover of the trees. Right nice-lookin' gent. No rustler."

"Yuh think somebody's pullin' a steal?" Baldy asked shrewdly, stowing away the camp gear in the chuck wagon.

"Don't you?" Ward said quietly.

"Uh-huh. So what happens?" Baldy asked.

"My guess would be they don't intend to let us have no part of the profits. To us, the deal is supposed to be on the level. We don't know that it ain't," he added. "Actually, we don't know a thing."

"Uh-huh." Baldy crawled up on the wagon. "So we keep our eyes peeled, huh?"

"And a six-shooter handy," McQueen agreed grimly.

He tied the black horse to the wagon, then swung aboard the roan as the chuck wagon rumbled out after the cattle. McQueen started the roan after the herd at a canter, scowling thoughtfully.

The letter had referred to two trusted hands, Chuck and Stan Jones. Trusted men didn't ride away and leave a herd. Not to go back to Montana or anywhere. What had happened to them, then? Where were they?

The trail wound slowly up toward the pass in the Toana range. The cattle moved slowly, reluctant to leave the green meadows bordering Pilot Creek. There was little time for thinking as two old steers had no intention of leaving the creek and made break after break trying to get away.

Late in the afternoon, Bud Fox rode up beside McQueen. He lighted a smoke, then glanced across the herd at Naify.

"Nice hoss yuh got back there," he commented casually. "Hombre what owned him's dead, I s'pose?"

"Uh-huh. I buried him. A darned good rifle shot killed him."

Bud rode quietly. "Yuh know," he said softly, "I been wonderin' a mite. When Baldy and me come up the trail, we got us a glimpse of somethin'. Way north of where we was, but on the Montana trail. We seen us some buzzards circlin'— like maybe a dead critter was lyin' there."

"Or dead men." Ward McQueen's voice was grim. "Men who might object to what was goin' to be done with these cows."

"Uh-huh," Fox agreed, "like that. Or maybe riders the boss didn't have no intention of payin'. On a long drive, yuh know, ain't nobody goin' to be surprised if a cowpoke never comes back. He could've gone on to Californy, or maybe south of the Colorado country. Or he could've just started driftin'."

———

THE HERD MOVED steadily westward, camping one night at Flower Lake, a grass-covered and spring-fed swamp, then moving on up the steep slopes of the Pequops through a scattered forest of mountain mahogany, juniper, and piñon. Ward McQueen, his battered gray hat pulled low over his eyes, his lean-jawed face ever more quiet, ever more watchful.

Red Naify held to the point, rarely leaving it even for a few minutes. The blocky, hard-faced foreman rode cautiously, and once, when they sighted several horsemen, he let the herd veer southward, away from them.

On the west side of the Pequops the herd ambled slowly across a sage-covered valley toward the distant violet and purple of mountains, and finally, almost in the shadow of the Humboldt Range, the herd was circled for a night stop on the edge of Snow Water Lake.

Naify rode back. "Bed 'em down here," he said. "We'll spend the night and let 'em feed some more. No use losin' too much beef on this move."

"Where's Mallock?" McQueen asked suddenly.

Naify turned his head and looked squarely at him. "Don't worry about it. We ain't goin' near Mallock!"

Thoughtfully, Ward watched Red ride away. Red Naify knew nothing of the letter in McQueen's pocket. In that simple statement he had given himself away. The girl was waiting at Fort Mallock for the cattle. Iver Hoyt was probably with her. He was the trusted adviser, and he was stealing her herd!

In McQueen's pocket, given to him by a friend before he ever started for this country, was a map. It showed Mallock, the fort built only a short time before, to be not far beyond the Humboldt Mountains. He made a sudden decision.

Wheeling his horse, he rode to the chuck wagon, where Baldy had unhitched the team. The cattle were drinking, and Bud Fox was sitting his horse nearby, rolling a smoke.

"Listen," he said, reining in the roan beside the wagon. "I'm ridin' out of here. I got me an idea. You two better keep plenty close watch. I figger this is where she happens!"

Fox nodded. "Red said he'd be back sometime tomorrow or the day after. That we was to sit tight. Where yuh goin'?"

"Fort Mallock. I'm ridin' the black."

It was dark when the black horse cantered down the dusty street of the little community that had grown up around the fort. Ward McQueen rode up to the hitching rail and swung down. He hitched his belt and loosened his guns. He had just stepped up on the walk when a wiry, broad-shouldered man stepped out from the batwing doors.

For an instant the man stood stock-still, his eyes on the black horse, then his eyes shifted to McQueen.

"Your hoss, podner?" he queried gently.

McQueen felt something inside him tighten. There was something in the faint suggestion of that voice that warned him. This man was dangerous.

"I'm ridin' him," he replied quietly.

"Where'd you get him?" the stranger asked, stepping away from in front of the door.

"Before I answer that," McQueen said quietly, "s'pose you tell me why you're askin'."

The young man stared back at him, and McQueen decided there was something in the black eyes and brown, young face that he liked.

"My name," the young man said evenly, "is Kim Sartain. And the man who owned that hoss, and that saddle, was a friend of mine!"

"So you're Kim," McQueen said softly. "You know an hombre name of Iver Hoyt?"

Sartain's face darkened and his eyes grew cautious. "Yeah, I know him. A friend of yours?"

"No." McQueen looked at him thoughtfully. "You know where Ruth Kermitt is?"

"Yeah."

"Then take me to her. I'll talk there."

Leading the black horse, Ward McQueen followed Kim. The young man walked alongside him, his left side toward McQueen, who grinned to himself at this precaution.

"You don't take no chances, Sartain," he said. "But I think we're on the same side."

Kim's hard face did not relent. "I'll know that when you tell me where you got that hoss."

McQueen tied the horse to a hitching rail, followed Sartain into a small hotel, and into a back parlor, a small, comfortably furnished room. There was a girl sitting on the divan, and she rose quickly when they came in.

McQueen halted, his face suddenly blank. He had expected anything but the tall, lovely girl who faced him. Probably twenty years old, she was erect, poised, and lovely, her black hair gathered in a loose knot at the nape of her neck, her blue eyes wide.

Kim spoke, his voice flat. "This hombre wants to talk with you, ma'am. He rode into town on Dan's hoss."

"Ma'am," McQueen said quietly, "I'm afraid I'm bringin' bad news."

"It's Dan! Something's happened to Dan!" Ruth Kermitt came toward him quickly.

McQueen's face flushed, then paled a little. "He's—he's been killed, ma'am. Shot!"

Her face turned deathly white, and she fell back a step, her eyes still wide. Swiftly, Kim crossed to her side.

"Ma'am," he said. "Better hold yourself together. We got to get this hombre's yarn. He may need killin' hisself." He spoke this last in a low, dangerous tone.

Briefly, with no details, McQueen explained, saying nothing about the herd except to mention the names of the men riding with it.

Kim stared at him. "A herd of three hundred white-faces? And *with Red Naify*? Who're those others you mentioned?"

"Baldy Jackson and Bud Fox. Good men. Naify told us the other riders rode off and left 'em."

"Like the devil they did!" Kim snapped. "Somebody's lyin', ma'am!"

"We'd better get Iver," Ruth said hesitantly. "He always knows what to do."

Ward McQueen shook his head. "If you mean Iver Hoyt, ma'am, I wouldn't get him. He's a crook, tryin' to rustle them cattle hisself."

Ruth stiffened and her eyes flashed.

"You don't know what you're saying!" she said sharply. "He's been a very good friend! My only friend, aside from Kim here. And *he* wasn't found riding Dan's horse!"

"I reckon not," McQueen replied grimly, "but he—"

The door opened suddenly to interrupt him, and Iver Hoyt stepped in, two men crowding in behind him.

"Ruth!" he said. "Dan's horse is outside!" His eyes found Ward McQueen and his lips tightened. "Ruth, who is this man?"

"Don't you remember me?" McQueen said gently. "That Texas rider you hired back at Pilot Creek. The one you told Red Naify to work on the same basis as the others."

"You're crazy!" Hoyt snapped. "I never saw you before in my life. As for Red Naify, the man's an outlaw! A rustler!"

"If I never saw you before," McQueen said quietly, "how do I know your gun butt's got the head of a longhorn steer on it? How do I know you ride a bay hoss with three white stockin's?"

Kim stood with his thumbs hooked in his belt. "I've noticed that steer's head, Hoyt. And he sure enough has your hoss spotted."

"He's a liar!" Hoyt snarled, his hands poised. "I never saw him before!"

"I'll take care of that liar business in due time," McQueen said softly. "In the meantime, tell us what happened to Chuck and Stan Jones!"

Ruth looked up quickly, staring at Hoyt. Iver Hoyt's face tightened.

"They went back to Montana!" he snapped.

"They were coming on here, Iver," Ruth Kermitt said quietly. "You know they'd promised to work for me. They wouldn't break a promise. Neither of them would."

Hoyt stiffened and his eyes turned hard. "So? You don't believe me either? We'll discuss this in the mornin'!" He turned abruptly and walked from the room, followed by the two men with him.

"Ma'am, I think I better get back to them cattle," Ward McQueen suggested suddenly. "Hoyt'll try to steal 'em, and soon. In fact, I think he'll try it sooner now than he'd planned."

"I'll go back with you," Kim said. "I think you're smokin' some skunks out of this tree, podner!"

———

It WAS ALMOST daylight when they rode down the slope of the mountain near Secret Pass and cut across the plain toward Snow Water. They were still almost a half mile away when a volley of shots rang out.

McQueen touched spurs to the black and whipped it around some tall sage and started on a dead run for the camp. Then, ahead, there was another shot. Then another and another.

He sighted the wagon and slowed down. Kim Sartain was behind him, and suddenly McQueen glimpsed the moonlight on Baldy's head. At the same instant he saw the gleam of a lifted rifle.

"Hold it!" he yelled. "It's me!"

He swung down. "What happened?"

Baldy grinned. "After yuh left, we got to thinkin', so when it come dark we rolled up some sacks and left them on the ground near the fire. Then we moved back in the sagebrush. A few minutes ago some rannies come up and let go with a volley into those dummies. A half minute later I see one of 'em move closer for a look, and I let him have it."

Suddenly a voice called out of the darkness. "Hey, Baldy!" It was Red Naify calling. "Put down yore guns. It's all right. They run off when they saw me and the boss comin'."

McQueen fell back into the deep shadows under the wagon.

"Get out of sight, Kim," he whispered. "They didn't see us come in. Call 'em in, Baldy, but be careful."

At that moment there was a soft voice from the shadows in the direction Ward and Sartain had come.

"I'm going to wait here. I want to see this, too."

It was Ruth Kermitt! She had followed them out from town. Well, maybe it was the best way, McQueen thought.

"Come on in," Baldy said, "but come slow."

Red Naify, his blocky, powerful body looking even bigger in the dancing firelight, came first. After him, only a step behind but to the right, was Iver Hoyt.

"Glad yuh boys ain't turned in yet," Red said. "We're goin' to move these cows."

"Tonight?" Baldy objected. "Where to?"

"Up in the Humboldts," Hoyt said. "I know the place." He looked around. "Who was shootin'?"

"That's what we wondered." Bud Fox had his thumbs in his gun belt. His eyes shifted from Naify to Hoyt. "Lucky they didn't get us."

Ward, crouching under the wagon, could see what was coming. Naify had casually moved two steps farther to the left. Baldy and Bud were going to be caught in a cross fire. He stepped from under the wagon and straightened, hearing Kim move out also.

One step took him into the firelight. "Fall back, you two," he said quietly. "I'm takin' over!"

"And me," Kim said. "Don't forget me."

"You're an awful fool, Hoyt," Ward McQueen said suddenly. "Why don't you ask Naify what he did with the money he took off Dan Kermitt."

Hoyt's eyes suddenly blazed up. "Naify, did you get that fifty thousand?"

"Fifty thousand?" Stark incredulity rang in Red Naify's voice. "Why, I only got sixty dollars!" Suddenly his eyes gleamed. "Boss, *he's* got it! He's got it right there in his pocket!"

Iver Hoyt smiled suddenly. "So, we won't lose after all! Boys, come in!"

There was a sound of movement, and four more men stepped into the circle of light. One of them tossed a bundle of brush on the fire, and it blazed up.

"Think you're pretty smart, don't you, Hoyt?" McQueen said quietly. "Yuh engineered this whole steal, didn't you?"

"Of course," Hoyt admitted proudly. "We stole old Kermitt blind up in Montana. He was too fresh from the East to know what was happenin' to him. Then he found us that night and I had to kill him."

Suddenly a new voice sounded. "You four back up against the wagon and stay out of this. I've got a double-barrel shotgun here, and if there is one move out of you, I'll let you have both barrels!"

RUTH KERMITT STOOD there. Tall, splendid in the firelight, she looked like a portrait of all the pioneer women of any age. The shotgun she held was steady and she waved the four back.

"I'll second that motion, ma'am," Bud Fox said quietly, "with a six-gun!"

Baldy spoke suddenly and his voice drawled.

"This is goin' to be pretty. Real pretty," he said. "Hoyt, you know who this ranny is you're talkin' to? This here's Ward McQueen. Think back a ways. Where'd you hear that name afore?"

Baldy paused, and he saw a frown appear on Iver Hoyt's face.

"Ward, you had a bosom friend in Larry White, didn't

you?" he said to McQueen then. "Well, Iver Hoyt's full name is Iver Hoyt Harris!"

"Ike Harris!" Ward McQueen's face suddenly went stone cold. "Kim," he said suddenly, and his voice rang loud, "as a favor, let me have them both! *Now!*"

It was Hoyt who moved first. At the mention of Larry White's name, his face went dead pale, and his hand, twitching nervously, shot down for his gun.

McQueen's six-guns seemed to leap from their holsters, spewing jagged darts of fire. Hoyt, caught full in the chest by a leaden slug, was smashed back to his heels, and then another slug caught him in the face, and another in the throat.

Coolly, ignoring Red Naify, he poured fire into the killer of his friend. Then he took one swinging step, bringing himself around to face Naify.

Red, a leer on his face, was waiting.

"Yuh dirty coyote!" he snarled.

Both men's guns belched flame. Red swayed on his feet, and then Ward McQueen stepped forward, firing as coolly as though on a target range. He stepped again, and each time his foot planted, his guns roared. Smashed back by the heavy slugs Red Naify staggered, then toppled to his knees.

His face a bloody mess from a bullet that had burned a hole through the right side of his face below the eye, he lifted his gun and fired again. The bullet hit McQueen and he staggered, but bracing himself, he brought one gun down and triggered it again. The dart of fire seemed almost to touch Red's face, and he toppled over on his face in the dust, his gun belching one last grass-cutting shot as his fist closed in agony.

Ward McQueen staggered a little and then, stooping with great care, picked up his hat.

"The devil," he said, "only three bullet holes! Wyatt Earp had five after his battle with Curly Bill's gang at the water hole."

Ruth Kermitt ran to his side. "You're hurt! Oh, you're hurt!" she exclaimed.

He turned to look at her, and then suddenly everything faded out.

When he opened his eyes again it was morning. Ruth sat beside him, her eyes heavy with weariness. She put a cool cloth on his forehead and wiped his face off with another.

"You must lie still," she told him. "You've lost a lot of blood."

"Of course, if you say so, ma'am," he assured her. "I'll lay right quiet."

Baldy Jackson looked at him and snorted.

"Look at that, would you!" he exploded. "And that's the ranny crawled three miles with seven holes in him after his Galeyville fight! Just goes to show you what a woman'll do to a man!"

MCQUEEN OF THE TUMBLING K

WARD MCQUEEN REINED in the strawberry roan and squinted his eyes against the sun. Salty sweat made his eyes smart, and he dabbed at them with the end of a bandanna. Kim Sartain was hazing a couple of rambunctious steers back into line. Bud Fox was walking his horse up the slope to where Ward waited, watching the drive.

Fox drew up alongside him and said, "Ward, d'you remember that old brindle ladino with the scarred hide? This here is his range but we haven't seen hide nor hair of him."

"That's one old mossyhorn I won't forget in a hurry. He's probably hiding back in one of the canyons. Have you cleaned them out yet?"

"Uh-huh, we surely have. Baldy an' me both worked 'em, and no sign. Makes a body mighty curious."

"Yeah, I suppose you've got a point. It ain't like him to be away from the action. He'd surely be down there makin' trouble." He paused, suddenly thoughtful. "Missed any other stock since I've been gone?"

Fox shrugged. "If there's any missin' it can't be but a few head, but you can bet if that old crowbait is gone some others went along. He ramrods a good-sized herd all by himself."

Baldy Jackson joined them on the slope. He jerked his head to indicate a nearby canyon mouth, "Seen some mighty queer tracks over yonder," he said, "like a man afoot."

"We'll go have a look," McQueen said. "A man afoot in this country? It isn't likely."

He started the roan across the narrow valley, with Baldy and Bud following.

The canyon was narrow and high walled. Parts of it were choked with brush and fallen rock, with only the winding watercourse to offer a trail. In the spreading fan of sand where the wash emptied into the valley, Baldy drew up.

Ward looked down at the tracks Baldy indicated. "Yes, they do look odd," said Ward. "Fixed him some homemade footgear. Wonder if that's his blood or some critter?" Leading the roan he followed the tracks up the dry streambed.

After a few minutes, he halted. "He's been hurt. Look at the tracks headed this way. Fairly long, steady stride. I'd guess he's a tall man. But see here? Goin' back the steps are shorter an' he's staggerin'. He stopped twice in twenty yards, each time to lean against something."

"Reckon we'd better follow him?" Baldy looked at the jumble of boulders and crowded brush. "If he doesn't aim to be ketched he could make us a powerful lot of trouble."

"We'll follow him anyway. Baldy, you go back an' help the boys. Tell Kim an' Tennessee where we're at. Bud will stay with me. Maybe we can track him down, an' he should be grateful. It looks like he's hurt bad."

They moved along cautiously for another hundred yards. Bud Fox stopped, mopping his face. "He doesn't figure on bein' followed. He's makin' a try at losin' his trail. Even tried to wipe out a spot of blood."

Ward McQueen paused and looked up the watercourse with keen, probing eyes. There was something wrong about all this. Obviously the man was injured. Just as obviously he was trying, even in his weakened condition, to obliterate his trail. That meant that he expected to be followed and that those who followed were enemies.

Pausing to study the terrain he ran over in his mind the possibilities from among those whom he knew. Who might the injured man be? And whom did he fear?

They moved on, working out the trail in the close, hot air of the canyon. The tracks split suddenly and disappeared on a wide ledge of stone where the canyon divided into two.

"We're stuck," Fox said, "he won't leave tracks with those makeshift shoes of his, and there's nowhere he can go up the canyons."

The right-hand branch ended in a steep, rocky slide, impossible to climb without hours of struggle, and the left branch ended against the sheer face of a cliff against whose base lay a heaped-up pile of boulders and rocky debris.

"He may have doubled back or hidden in the brush," Fox added.

Ward shrugged. "Let's go back. He doesn't want to be found, but hurt like he is he's apt to die out here without care."

Deliberately, he had spoken loudly. Turning their mounts they rode back down the canyon to rejoin the herd.

RUTH KERMITT WAS waiting on the steps when they left the grassy bottom and rode up to the bunkhouse. With her was a slender, narrow-faced man in a black frock coat. As Ward drew up, the man's all-encompassing glance took him in, then slid away.

"Ward, this is Jim Yount. He's buying cattle and wants to look at the herd you just brought in."

"Howdy," Ward said, agreeably. He glanced at Yount's horse and then at the tied-down gun.

Two more men sat on the steps of the bunkhouse, a big man in a checkered shirt and a slim redhead with a rifle across his knees.

"We're looking to buy five hundred to a thousand head," Yount commented. "We heard you had good stock."

"Beef?"

"No, breeding, mostly. We're stockin' a ranch. I'm locatin' the other side of Newton's place."

Ward commented, "We have some cattle. Or rather, Miss Kermitt has. I'm just the foreman."

"Oh?" Yount looked around at Ruth with a quick, flashing smile. "Miss, is it? Or are you a widow?"

"Miss. My brother and I came here together, but he was killed."

"Hard for a young woman to run a ranch alone, isn't it?" His smile was sympathetic.

"Miss Kermitt does very well," Ward replied coolly, "and she isn't exactly alone."

"Oh?" Yount glanced at McQueen, one eyebrow lifted.

"No," he said after a minute, "I don't expect you could say she was alone as long as she had cattle on the place, and cowhands."

Ruth got up quickly, not liking the look on Ward's face. "Mr. Yount? Wouldn't you like some coffee? Then we can talk business."

When they had gone inside Ward McQueen turned on his heel and walked to the bunkhouse, leading his horse. He was mad and he didn't care who knew it. The thin-faced redhead looked at him as he drew near.

"What's the matter, friend? Somebody steal your girl?"

Ward McQueen halted and turned slowly. Baldy Jackson got up quickly and moved out of line. The move put him at the corner of the bunkhouse, leaving Yount's riders at the apex of a triangle of which McQueen and himself formed the two corners.

"Miss Kermitt," McQueen's tone was cold, "is my boss. She is also a lady. Don't get any funny notions."

The redhead chuckled. "Yeah, and our boss is a ladies' man! He knows how to handle 'em." Deliberately, he turned his back on Baldy. "Ever been foreman on a place like this, Dodson? Maybe you or me will have a new job."

Ward walked into the bunkhouse. Bud Fox was loitering beside the window. He, too, had been watching the pair.

"Don't seem the friendly type," Bud commented, pouring warm water into the tin washbasin. "Almost like they wanted trouble!"

"What would be the idea of that?" Ward inquired.

Bud was splashing in the basin and made no reply, but Ward wondered. Certainly their attitude was not typical. He glanced toward the house, and his lips tightened. Jim Yount was a slick-talking sort and probably a woman would think him good-looking.

Out beyond the ranch house was a distant light, which would be Gelvin's store in Mannerhouse. Gelvin had ranched the country beyond Newton's. Suddenly, McQueen made up his mind. After chow he would ride into Mannerhouse and have a little talk with Gelvin.

Supper was served in the ranch house as always and was a

quiet meal but for Ruth and Jim Yount, who laughed and talked at the head of the table.

Ward, seated opposite Yount, had little to say. Baldy, Bud, and Tennessee sat in strict silence. Only Red Lund, seated beside Pete Dodson, occasionally ventured a remark. At the foot of the table, lean, wiry Kim Sartain let his eyes rove from face to face.

When supper was over, Ward moved outside into the moonlight and Kim followed. "What goes on?" Kim whispered. "I never did see anybody so quiet."

Ward explained, adding, "Yount may be a cattle buyer, but the two riders with him are no average cow-punchers. Red Lund is a gunhand if I ever saw one, and Dodson's right off the Outlaw Trail or I miss my guess." He hitched his belt. "I'm ridin' into town. Keep an eye on things, will you?"

"I'll do that." He lowered his tone. "That Lund now? I don't cotton to him. Nor Yount," he added.

Gelvin's store was closed but McQueen knew where to find him. Swinging down from the saddle, he tied his horse and pushed through the batwing doors. Abel was polishing glasses behind the bar, and Gelvin was at a table with Dave Cormack, Logan Keane, and a tall, lean-bodied stranger. They were playing poker.

Two other strangers lounged at the bar. They turned to look at him as he came in.

"Howdy, Ward! How's things at the Tumblin' K?"

The two men at the bar turned abruptly and looked at Ward again, quick, searching glances. He had started to speak to Gelvin, but something warned him and instead he walked to the bar.

"Pretty good," he replied. "Diggin' some stuff out of the breaks today. Tough work. All right for a brushpopper, but I like open country."

He tossed off his drink, watching the two men in the bar mirror. "They tell me there's good range beyond the Newtons. I think I'll ride over and see if there's any lyin' around loose."

Gelvin glanced up. He was a short, rather handsome man with a keen, intelligent face.

"There's plenty that you can have for the taking. That country is going back to desert as fast as it can. Sand moving in, streams drying up. You can ride a hundred miles and never find a drink. Why," he picked up the cards and began to shuffle them, ". . . old Coyote Benny Chait came in two or three weeks ago. He was heading out of the country. He got euchred out of his ranch by some slick card handler. He was laughin' at the man who won it, said he'd get enough of the country in a hurry."

The two men at the bar had turned and were listening to Gelvin. One of them started to speak and the other put a cautioning hand on his arm.

"Who was it won the ranch? Did he say?"

"Sure!" Gelvin began to deal. "Some driftin' cardsharp by the name of—"

"You talk too much!" The larger of the two men at the bar stepped toward the card table. "What d'you know about the Newton country?"

Startled by the unprovoked attack, Gelvin turned in his chair. His eyes went from one to the other of the two men. Ward McQueen had picked up the bottle.

"What is this?" Gelvin asked, keeping his tone even. These men did not seem to be drunk, yet he was experienced enough to know he was in trouble, serious trouble. "What did I say? I was just commenting on the Newton country."

"You lied!" The big man's hand was near his gun. "You lied! That country ain't goin' back! It's as good as it ever was!"

Gelvin was a stubborn man. This man was trying to provoke a fight, but Gelvin had no intention of being killed over a trifle. "I did not lie," he replied coolly. "I lived in that country for ten years. I came in with the first white men, and I've talked with the Indians who were there earlier. I know of what I speak."

"Then you're sayin' I'm a liar?" The big man's hand spread over his gun.

Ward McQueen turned in one swift movement. His right hand knocked the bottle spinning toward the second man and as he kept swinging around, his right hand grabbed the big man by the belt. With a heave he swung the big man off balance and whirled him, staggering, into the smaller man, who had sprung back to avoid the bottle.

The big man staggered again, fell, and then came up with a grunt of fury. Reaching his feet his hand went to his gun, then froze. He was looking into a gun in Ward McQueen's hand.

"That was a private conversation," Ward said mildly. "In this town we don't interfere. Understand?"

"If you didn't have the drop on me you wouldn't be talkin' so big!"

Ward dropped his six-gun into its holster. "All right, now you've got an even break."

The two men faced him, and suddenly neither liked what they saw. This was no time for bravery, they decided. "We ain't lookin' for trouble," the smaller man said. "We just rode into town for a drink."

"Then ride out," Ward replied. "And don't butt into conversations that don't concern you."

"Hollier 'n' me," the big man started to speak but then suddenly stopped and started for the door.

Ward stepped back into the bar. "Thanks, Gelvin. You told me something I needed to know."

"I don't get it," Gelvin protested. "What made them mad?"

"That card shark you mentioned? His name wouldn't be Jim Yount, would it?"

"Of course! How did you know?"

The tall stranger playing cards with Gelvin glanced up and their eyes met. "You wouldn't be the Ward McQueen from down Texas way, would you?"

"That's where I'm from. Why?"

The man smiled pleasantly. "You cut a wide swath down thataway. I heard about your run-in with the Maravillas Canyon outfit."

McQueen was cautious when he took the trail to the Tumbling K, but he saw nothing of the two men in the saloon. Hollier . . . he was the smaller one. There had been a Hollier who escaped from a lynch mob down Uvalde way a few years back. He had trailed around with a man called Packer, and the larger of these two men had a P burned on his holster with a branding iron.

What was Jim Yount's game? Obviously, the two men from the saloon were connected with him somehow. They had seemed anxious Yount's name not be spoken, and they seemed eager to quiet any talk about the range beyond the Newtons.

The available facts were few. Yount had won a ranch in a poker game. Gelvin implied the game was crooked. The ranch he won was going back to desert. In other words, he had won nothing but trouble. What came next?

The logical thing for a man of Yount's stamp was to shrug off the whole affair and go on about his business. He was not doing that, which implied some sort of a plan. Lund and Dodson would make likely companions to Packer and Hollier. Yount was talking of buying cattle, but he was not the sort to throw good money after bad. Did they plan to rustle the cattle?

One thing was sure. It was time he got back to the ranch to alert the boys for trouble. It would be coming sooner, perhaps, because of what happened tonight. But what about Ruth? Was she taken with Yount? Or simply talking business and being polite? Did he dare express his doubts to her?

The Tumbling K foreman was riding into the ranch yard when the shot rang out. Something had struck a wicked blow on his head, and he was already falling when he heard the shot.

HIS HEAD FELT tight, constricted, as if a tight band had been drawn around his temples. Slowly, fighting every inch of the way, he battled his way to consciousness. His lids fluttered, then closed, too weak to force themselves open. He struggled against the heaviness and finally got his eyes open. He was lying on his back in a vague half-light. The air felt damp, cool.

Awareness came. He was in a cave or mine tunnel. Turning his head carefully, he looked around. He was lying on a crude pallet on a sandy floor. Some twenty feet away was a narrow shaft of light. Nearby, his gun belt hung on a peg driven into the wall and his rifle leaned against the wall.

The rift of light was blotted out and someone crawled into the cave. A man came up and threw down an armful of wood. Then he lighted a lantern and glanced at McQueen.

"Come out of it, did you? Man, I thought you never would!"

He was lean and old, with twinkling blue eyes and almost white hair. He was long and tall. Ward noted the footgear suddenly. This was the man they had trailed up the canyon!

"Who are you?" he demanded.

The man smiled and squatted on his heels. "Charlie Quayle's the name. Used to ride for Chait, over in the Newtons."

"You're the one we trailed up the canyon the other day. Yesterday, I believe it was."

"I'm the man, all right, but it wasn't yesterday. You've been lyin' here all of two weeks, delirious most of the time. I was beginning to believe you'd never come out of it."

"Two weeks?" McQueen struggled to sit up, but the effort was too much. He sank back. "Two weeks? They'll figure I'm dead back at the ranch. Why did you bring me here? Who shot me?"

"Hold your horses! I've got to wash up and fix some grub." He poured water in a basin and began to wash his face and hands. As he dried his hands he explained. "You was shot, and I ain't sure who done it. Two of them rustlin' hands of Yount's packed you to the canyon and dropped you into the wash. Then they caved sand over you and some brush. But they weren't about to do more than need be, so figurin' you were sure enough dead, they rode off.

"I was almighty curious to know who'd been killed, so I pulled the brush away and dug into the pile and found you was still alive. I packed you up here, and mister, it took some packin'! You're a mighty heavy man."

"Were you trailin' them when they shot me?"

"No. To tell you the truth I was scoutin' the layout at the ranch, figurin' to steal some coffee when I heard the shot. Then I saw them carry you off, so I follered."

Quayle lighted his pipe. "There's been some changes," he

added. "Your friend Sartain has been fired. So have Fox and that bald-headed gent. Tennessee had a run-in with Lund, and Lund killed him. Picked a fight and then beat him to the draw. Yount is real friendly with Ruth Kermitt and he's runnin' the ranch. One or more of those tough gunmen of his is there all the time."

Ward lay back on his pallet. Kim Sartain fired! It didn't seem reasonable. Kim had been with Ruth Kermitt longer than any of them! He had been with them when Ruth and her brother came over the trail from Montana.

Kim had been with her through all that trouble at Pilot Range when Ward himself had first joined them. Kim had always rode for the brand. Now he had been fired, run off the place!

And Tennessee killed!

What sort of girl was Ruth Kermitt? She had fired her oldest and most loyal hands and taken on a bunch of rustlers with a tinhorn gambler for boss. And to think he had been getting soft on her! He'd actually been thinking she was the girl for him, and the only reason he'd held on was because he had no money, nothing to offer a woman. Well, this showed what a fool he would have been.

"You've got a hard head," Quayle was saying, "or you'd be dead by now. That bullet hit right over your eye and skidded around your skull under the skin. Laid your scalp open. You had a concussion, too. I know the signs. And you lost blood."

"I've got to get out of here!" Ward said. "I've got to see Ruth Kermitt."

"You'd be better off to sit tight and get well. Right now she's right busy with that there Yount. Rides all over the range with him, holdin' hands more'n half the time. Everybody's seen 'em. And if she fired all the rest of her hands you can be sure she doesn't want her foreman back."

He was right, of course. What good would it do to even talk to a woman who would fire such loyal hands as she had?

"Where d' you fit into all this?"

Quayle sliced bacon into a frying pan. "Like I told you, I rode for Chait. Yount rooked him out of his ranch, but as a matter of fact, Chait was glad to get shut of it. When Yount found what he'd won he was sore. Me, I'd saved me nigh on a year's wages an' was fixin' to set up for myself. One of those hands of Yount's, he seen the money and trailed me down, said it was ranch money. We had us a fight and they got some lead into me. I got away an' holed up in this here canyon."

All day McQueen rested in the cave, his mind busy with the problem. But what could he do? If Ruth Kermitt had made her choice it was no longer any business of his. The best thing he could do was to get his horse and ride out of there, just drop the whole thing.

It was well after dark before Quayle returned, but he had news and was eager to talk.

"That Yount is takin' over the country! He went into Mannerhouse last night huntin' Gelvin, but Gelvin had gone off with that stranger friend of his that he plays poker with all the time.

"Yount had words with Dave Cormack and killed him. They say this Yount is greased lightning with a gun. Then Lund an' Pete Dodson pistol-whipped Logan Keane. Yount told them he was runnin' the Tumblin' K and was going to marry Ruth Kermitt, and he was fed up with the talk about him and his men. He thinks he's got that town treed, an' maybe he has. Takes some folks a long time to get riled."

Ruth to marry Jim Yount! Ward felt a sharp pang. He realized suddenly that he was in love with Ruth. Now that he realized it he knew he had been in love with her for a long time. And she was to marry Yount!

"Did you see anything of Kim Sartain?"

"No," Quayle replied, "but I heard the three of them rode over into the Newtons."

Ward McQueen was up at daybreak. He rolled out of his blankets, and although his head ached he felt better. No matter. It was time to be up and doing. His long period of illness had at least given him rest, and his strength was such that he recovered rapidly. He oiled his guns and reloaded them. Quayle watched him preparing to travel but said nothing until he pulled on his boots.

"Better wait until sundown if you're huntin' trouble," he said. "I got a hoss for you. Stashed him down in the brush."

"A horse? Good for you! I'm going to have a look at the ranch. This deal doesn't figure right to me."

"Nor me." Quayle knocked the ash from his pipe. "I seen that girl's face today. They rid past as I lay in the brush. She surely didn't look like a happy woman. Not like she was ridin' with a man she loved. Maybe she ain't willin'."

"I don't like to think she'd take up with a man like Yount. Well, tonight I ride."

"*We* ride!" Quayle insisted. "I didn't like gettin' shot up any more than you-all. I'm in this fight, too."

"I can use the help, but what I'd really like you to do is hunt down Kim Sartain and the others. I can use their help. Get them back here for a showdown. Warn them it won't be pretty."

Where Quayle had found the quick-stepping buckskin Ward neither knew nor cared. He needed a horse desperately, and the buckskin was not only a horse but a very good one.

Whatever Yount's game was he had been fast and thorough. He had moved in on the Tumbling K, had Ward McQueen dry-gulched, had Ruth Kermitt fire her old hands, replaced them with his own men, and then rode into Mannerhouse and quieted all outward opposition by killing Dave Cormack and beating another man.

If there was to have been opposition it would have been Cormack and Keane who would have led it. Tennessee, too, had been killed, but Tennessee was not known in town, and that might be passed off as a simple dispute between cow-hands. Yount had proved to be fast, ruthless and quick of decision. As he acted with the real or apparent consent of Ruth Kermitt there was nothing to be done by the townspeople in the village of Mannerhouse.

Probably, with Cormack and Keane out of the picture and Gelvin off God knew where, they were not inclined to do anything. None of them were suffering any personal loss, and nothing was to be gained by bucking a man already proved to be dangerous. Obviously, the gambler was in control. He had erred in only two things. He had failed to kill Charlie Quayle and to make sure that McQueen was dead.

The buckskin had a liking for the trail and moved out fast. Ward rode toward the Tumbling K, keeping out of sight. Quayle had ridden off earlier in the day to find Kim, Baldy, and Bud Fox. The latter two were good cowhands and trustworthy, but the slim, dark-faced youngster, Kim Sartain, was one of the fastest men with a gun Ward had ever seen.

"With him," Ward told the buckskin, "I'd tackle an army!"

He left the buckskin in a clump of willows near the stream and then crossed on stepping-stones, working his way through the brush toward the Tumbling K ranch house.

He had no plan of action, nor anything on which to base a plan. If he could find Ruth and talk to her or if he could figure out what it was that Yount was trying to accomplish, it would be a beginning.

The windows were brightly lit. For a time he lay in the brush studying the situation. An error now would be fatal, if not to him, at least to their plans.

There would be someone around, he was sure. Quayle had said one of the gunmen was always on the ranch, for the gambler was a careful man.

A cigarette glowed suddenly from the steps of the bunkhouse. Evidently the man had just turned toward him. Had he inadvertently made a sound? At least he knew that somebody was there, on guard.

Ward eased off to the left until the house was between himself and the guard. Then he crossed swiftly to the side of the house. He eased a window open slightly.

Jim Yount was playing solitaire at the dining room table. Red Lund was oiling a pistol. Packer was leaning his elbows on the table and smoking, watching Yount's cards.

"I always wanted a ranch," Yount was saying, "and this is it. No use gallivanting around the country when a man can live in style. I'd have had it over in the Newtons if that damned sand bed I got from Chait had been any good. Then I saw this place. It was too good to be true."

"You worked fast," Packer said, "but you had a streak of

luck when Hollier an' me got McQueen. From what I hear, he was nobody to fool around with."

Yount shrugged. "Maybe so, but all sorts of stories get started and half of them aren't true. He might be fast with a gun, but he had no brains, and it takes brains to win in this kind of game."

He glanced at Lund. "Look, that Logan Keane outfit lies south of Hosstail Creek, and it joins onto this one. Nice piece of country, thousands of acres with good water, running right up to the edge of town.

"Keane's scared now. Once me and Ruth Kermitt are married so our title to this ranch is cinched we'll go to work on Keane. We'll rustle his stock, run off his hands, and force him to sell. I figure the whole job shouldn't take more than a month, at the outside."

Red glanced up from his pistol. "You get the ranches, what do we get?"

Yount smiled. "You don't want a ranch, and I do, but I happen to know that Ruth has ten thousand dollars cached. You boys," for a moment his eyes held those of Red Lund, "can split that among you. You can work out some way of dividing it even up all around."

Lund's eyes showed his understanding, and McQueen glanced at Packer, but the big horse thief showed no sign of having seen the exchange of glances. Ward could see how the split would be made, it would be done with Red Lund's six-shooter. They would get the lead, he'd take the cash.

It had the added advantage to Jim Yount of leaving only one witness to his treachery.

Crouched below the window, Ward McQueen calculated his chances. Jim Yount was reputed to be a fast man with a gun. Red Lund had already proved his skill. Packer would also be good, even if not an artist like the others. Three to one made the odds much too long, and at the bunkhouse would be Hollier and Pete Dodson, neither a man to be trifled with.

A clatter of horse's hoofs on the hard-packed trail, and a horseman showed briefly in the door and was ushered into the room. It was the lean stranger who had played poker with Gelvin and Keane.

"You Jim Yount? Just riding by and wanted to tell you there's an express package at the station for Miss Kermitt. She can drop in tomorrow to pick it up if she likes."

"Express package? Why didn't you bring it out?"

"Wouldn't let me. Seems like it's money or something like that. A package of dinero that's payment for some property in Wyoming. She's got to sign for it herself. They won't let anybody else have it."

Yount nodded. "All right. She's asleep, I think, but come morning I'll tell her."

The rider went out and a few minutes later Ward heard his horse's hoofs on the trail.

"More money?" Packer grinned. "Not bad, Boss! She can pick it up for us and we'll split it."

Red Lund was wiping off his pistol. "I don't like it," he spoke suddenly. "Looks like a move to get us off the ranch and the girl into town."

Yount shrugged. "I doubt it, but suppose that's it? Who in town has the guts or the skill to tackle us? Personally, I believe it's the truth, but if it ain't, why worry? We'll send Packer in ahead to scout. If there's any strangers around he can warn us. I think it's all right. We'll ride in tomorrow."

An hour later, and far back on a brush-covered hillside, Ward McQueen bedded down for the night. From where he lay he could see anybody who arrived at or left the ranch. One thing he knew, tomorrow was to be the payoff.

At daylight he was awake and watching, his buckskin saddled and ready. It had been a damp, uncomfortable night, and he stretched, trying to get the chill from his muscles. The sunshine caught reflected light from the window. Hollier emerged and began roping horses in the corral. He saddled his own, Ruth's brown mare, and Yount's big gray.

Ward McQueen tried to foresee what would happen. He was convinced, as was Red Lund, that the package was a trick. There were only nine buildings on the town's main street, scarcely more than two dozen houses scattered about.

The express and stage office was next to the saloon. Gelvin's store was across the street.

Whatever happened, Ruth would be in danger. She would

be with Yount, closely surrounded by the others. To fire on them was to endanger her.

And where did that young rider stand? He had been called Rip, and he had known of McQueen's gun battle in Maravillas Canyon. Ward was sure he was not the aimless drifter he was supposed to be. His face was too keen, his eyes too sharp. If he had baited a trap with money, he had used the only bait to which these men would rise. But what was he hoping to accomplish?

There were no men in Mannerhouse who could draw a gun in the same league with Yount or Lund.

Gelvin would try, if he was there, but Gelvin had only courage, and no particular skill with a handgun, and courage alone was not enough.

It was an hour after daylight when Packer mounted his paint gelding and started for town. Ward watched him go, speculating on what must follow. He had resolved upon his own course of action. His was no elaborate plan. He intended to slip into town and at the right moment kill Jim Yount and, if possible, Red Lund.

The only law in Mannerhouse was old John Binns, a thoroughly good man of some seventy years who had been given the job largely in lieu of a pension. He had been a hardworking man who owned his home and a few acres of ground, and he had a wife only a few years younger.

Mannerhouse had never been on the route of train drives, land booms, or mining discoveries, and in consequence the town had few disturbances or characters likely to cause them. The jail had been used but once, when the town first came into being, and few citizens could remember the occasion. John Binns's enforcement of the law usually was a quiet suggestion to be a little less noisy or to "go home and sleep it off."

Ward McQueen, a law-abiding man, found himself faced with a situation where right, justice, and the simple rules of civilized society were being pushed aside by men who did not hesitate to kill. One prominent citizen had been murdered, another pistol-whipped. Their stated intention was to do more of the same, to say nothing of Jim Yount's plan to marry Ruth, and his implication had been that it was simply a means to seize her land. Once they had won what they wished, there was no reason to believe the violence would cease. Gangrene had infected the area, and the only solution open to Ward McQueen was to amputate.

Yet he was no fool. He knew something of the gun skills of the men he would face. Even if he was killed himself he must eliminate them. The townspeople could take care of such as Hollier and Packer.

If he succeeded, Kim Sartain could handle the rest of it, and would. That was Kim's way.

Mounting the buckskin he started down the trail toward Mannerhouse, only a few miles away. When he had ridden but a few hundred yards he saw from his vantage point above the ranch that three riders were also headed for town. Jim Yount, Ruth, and a few yards behind, Red Lund.

Pete Dodson, riding a sorrel horse, was also headed for town but by another route. Jim Yount was taking no chances.

The dusty main street of Mannerhouse lay warm under the morning sun. On the steps of the Express Office, Rip was sunning himself. Abel, behind his bar, watched nervously both his window and his door. He was on edge and aware, aware as a wild animal is when a strange creature nears its lair. Trouble was in the wind.

Gelvin's store was closed, unusual for this time of day. Abel glanced at Rip, and his brow furrowed. Rip was wearing two tied-down guns this morning, unusual for him.

Abel finished polishing the glass and put it down, glancing nervously at Packer. Suddenly Packer downed the drink and got to his feet. Walking to the door he glanced up and down the street. All was quiet, yet the big man was worried. A man left the post office and walked along the boardwalk to the barbershop and entered. The sound of the closing door was the only sound. A hen pecked at something in the mouth of the alley near Gelvin's store. As he watched he saw Pete Dodson stop his horse behind Gelvin's. Pete was carrying a rifle. Packer glanced over at Rip, noting the guns.

Packer turned suddenly, glaring at Abel. "Give me that scatter-gun you got under the bar!"

"Huh?" Abel was frightened. "I ain't got—"

"Don't give me that! I want that gun!"

There was an instant when Abel considered covering Packer or even shooting him, but the big man frightened him and he put the shotgun on the bar. Packer picked it up and tiptoed to the window and put the gun down beside it. Careful to make no sound, he eased the window up a few inches. His position now covered Rip's side and back.

Abel cringed at what he had done. He liked Rip. The lean, easygoing, friendly young man might now be killed because of him. He'd been a coward. He should have refused, covered Packer, and called Rip inside. Now, because of him a good man might be murdered, shot in the back. What was going on, anyway? This had been such a quiet little town.

Jim Yount rode up the street with Ruth beside him. Her face was pale and strained, and her eyes seemed unnaturally large. Red Lund trailed a few yards behind. He drew up and tied his horse across the street.

From the saloon Abel could see it all. Jim Yount and Ruth Kermitt were approaching Rip from the west. North and west was Red Lund. Due north and in the shadow of Gelvin's was Pete Dodson. In the saloon was Packer. Rip was very neatly boxed, signed, and sealed. All but delivered.

Jim Keane, Logan's much older brother, was the express agent. He saw Jim Yount come, saw Red Lund across the street.

Rip got up lazily, smiling at Ruth as she came up the steps with Jim Yount.

"Come for your package, Miss Kermitt?" he asked politely. "While you're here would you mind answering some questions?"

"By whose authority?" Yount demanded sharply.

Ward McQueen, crouched behind the saloon, heard the reply clearly. "The State of Texas, Yount," Rip replied. "I'm a Texas Ranger."

Jim Yount's short laugh held no humor. "This ain't Texas, and she answers no questions."

Ward McQueen opened the back door of the saloon and stepped inside.

Packer, intent on the scene before him, heard the door open. Startled and angry, he whirled around. Ward McQueen, whom he had buried, was standing just inside the door. The shotgun was resting on the windowsill behind Rip. Packer went for his six-gun, but even as he reached he knew it was hopeless. He saw the stab of flame, felt the solid blow of the bullet, and felt his knees turn to butter under him. He pitched forward on his face.

Outside all hell broke loose. Ruth Kermitt, seeing Rip's situation, spurred her horse to bump Yount's, throwing him out of position. Instantly, she slid from the saddle and threw herself to the ground near the edge of the walk.

All seemed to have begun firing at once. Yount, cursing bitterly, fired at Rip. He in turn was firing at Red Lund. Ward stepped suddenly from the saloon and saw himself facing Yount, who had brought his mount under control. He fired at Yount, and a bullet from Dodson's rifle knocked splinters from the post in front of his face.

Yount's gun was coming into line and McQueen fired an instant sooner. Yount fired and they both missed. Ward's second shot hit Yount, who grabbed for the pommel. Ward walked a step forward, but something hit him and he went to his knee. Red Lund loomed from somewhere and Ward got off another shot. Lund's face was covered with blood.

There was firing from the stage station and from Gelvin's store. There was a thunder of hoofs, and a blood-red horse came charging down the street, its rider hung low like an Indian, shooting under the horse's neck.

Yount was down, crawling on his belly in the dust. He had lost hold of his six-shooter, but his right hand held a knife and he was crawling toward Ruth. McQueen's six-shooter clicked on an empty chamber. How many shots were left in his other gun? He lifted it with his left hand. Something was suddenly wrong with his right. He rarely shot with his left hand, but now—

Yount was closer now. Ruth was staring across the street, unaware. McQueen shot past Ruth, squeezing off the shot with his left hand. He saw Yount contract sharply as the bullet struck. McQueen fired again and the gambler rolled over on his side and the knife slipped from his fingers.

Abel ran from the saloon with the shotgun, and Gelvin from his store, with a rifle. Then Ruth was running toward him and he saw Kim Sartain coming back up the street, walking the red horse. He tried to rise to meet Ruth, but his knees gave way and he went over on his face, thinking how weak she must think him. He started to rise again, and blacked out.

When he could see again Ruth was beside him. Kim was squatting on his heels. "Come on, Ward!" he said. "You've only been hit twice and neither of 'em bad. Can't you handle lead anymore?"

"What happened?"

"Clean sweep, looks like. Charlie Quayle got to us and we hightailed it to the ranch. Hollier wanted to give us trouble but we smoked him out. I believe there were others around, but if there were they skipped the country.

"Whilst they were cleanin' up around I took it on the run for town. Halfway there I thought I heard a shot and when I hit the street everybody in town was shootin', or that's what it looked like. Reg'lar Fourth of July celebration!

"Pete Dodson is dead, and Red Lund's dying with four bullets in him. Yount's alive, but he won't make it either. Packer's dead."

Ward's head was aching and he felt weak and sick, but he did not want to move, even to get out of the street. He just wanted to sit, to forget all that had taken place. With fumbling fingers, from long habit, he started to reload his pistols. Oddly, he found one of them contained three live shells. Somehow he must have reloaded, but he had no memory of it.

Rip came over. "My name's Coker, Ward. I couldn't figure any other way to bust up Yount's operation so I faked that package to get them into town, hoping I could get her away from them. I didn't figure they'd gang up on me like they did."

They helped him up and into the saloon. Gelvin brought

the doctor in. "Yount just died," Gelvin said, "cussing you and everybody concerned."

He sat back in a chair while the doctor patched him up. Again he had lost blood. "I've got to find a bed," he said to Kim. "There must be a hotel in town."

"You're coming back to the ranch," Ruth said. "We need you there. They told me you left me, Ward. Jim Yount said you pulled out and Kim with you. I hadn't seen him, and Yount said he'd manage the ranch until I found someone. Then he brought his own men in and fired Kim, whom I hadn't seen, and I was surrounded and scared. If you had been there, or if I'd even known you were around, I—"

"Don't worry about it." Ward leaned his head back. All he wanted was rest.

Baldy Jackson helped him into a buckboard, Bud Fox driving. "You know that old brindle longhorn who turned up missin'? Well, I found him. He's got about thirty head with him, holed up in the prettiest little valley you ever did see. Looks like he's there to stay."

"He's like me," Ward commented, "so used to his range he wouldn't be happy anywhere else."

ROUNDUP IN TEXAS

THE INSTANT WARD McQueen saw the horsemen in the basin below, his heart leaped with quick apprehension. That would be Kim Sartain astride the sorrel, and the other riders, three of them, had him neatly boxed.

Touching spurs to the strawberry roan, McQueen went down the hill at a dead run, then slowed up as he neared the group. He saw Yost's face flash with anger and disappointment as the man recognized him. Ward drew up.

"All right, boys," he said. "Break it up!"

In a moment the situation had changed appreciably. The three riders had Sartain in such a position that he would be covered from three sides if he started to fire.

There would be no chance for escape.

Ernie Yost's expression showed his uncertainty. The odds still favored them three to two, but now one of the three, Ike Taylor, had his back to McQueen. Ward had stopped his horse to the left rear of Sartain, and could fire at all three men without endangering Sartain. Taylor was now in the middle, between Ward and the guns of his two friends.

"If any shootin' starts, boss," Kim suggested quietly, "I'll take Yost!"

Ernie's face flamed with dark blood, but he hesitated. He was no fool. Kim Sartain had once flashed a gun in his presence at Sotol, against a half-crazed Mexican killer who had Kim covered, but the Mexican never got off a shot.

As for Ward McQueen, the foreman of the Tumbling K had held a reputation in Texas long before he went off to Wyoming and Nevada. He was known to be a deadly gunfighter. Taylor was as good as dead if shooting started, and without Taylor, Ernie Yost wanted no part of it.

Yost spoke calmly. "This rider of yours is on the prod, McQueen. He ordered us off the range."

"What business have you here?" McQueen demanded. Ike Taylor was sweating blood in his present position. He started to shift around.

McQueen's voice was sharp. "Ike, you sit still or I'll drill you!"

Taylor swallowed and sat still, his eyes haunted. He was filled with regrets, wishing he were in Sotol, or any other place but here.

Yost's face had darkened again. "A man has a right to ride anywhere he wants!"

"No, he doesn't!" McQueen wasn't hedging. Had he arrived thirty seconds later, Sartain might have been dead. "You don't run any cattle, Yost. You have no business on this range at any time. We're working cattle here, and we don't like rustlers. Now you get off and stay off!"

Yost was bursting with hatred. His hands trembled as he strove to compose himself. "Some day you'll go too far, Ward!"

"Call it when you're ready!" Ward answered sharply. He stepped his horse nearer at a walk. He was angry and ready. "Why not now?"

No one had ever accused Ernie Yost of cowardice, yet in this situation, he could see no hope. He had never faced deadlier gunmen than Ward McQueen and his dark-faced *segundo,* Kim Sartain.

"All right," he flared suddenly. "I'll stay off!" He turned his horse with a jerk and started to walk away. Villani and Taylor wasted no time in following.

The two riders sat on their horses and watched until they were over the rise. "Reckon we ought to follow?" Sartain wondered.

"No. Let's get back. There's work to do."

Sartain glanced up at him. "You showed up at the right time, boss," he said dryly. "Another minute and they would have had me."

"They were set for a killing, all right," Ward agreed. "I don't savvy it. Ever had any trouble with them?"

"Not until I ordered them off." Sartain was puzzled. "But there's more to this than meets the eye."

They rode away. But as they topped the rise, Ward removed his hat and anxiously mopped his brow as he stared down at the dusty herd below them. When Ward had bought that stock from Old Dick Gerber, it had looked like a godsend. Long ago, he had worked for Gerber, and knew the tight-fisted old rancher well. That was before Ward had gone to Nevada and become foreman of the Tumbling K, Ruth Kermitt's ranch.

In all his dealings, the old man had seemed to be strictly honest and reliable, so when he showed McQueen a tally book, and the records amounted to over four thousand head, Ward decided to buy. The price seemed reasonable enough. Ward had, however, insisted upon a guarantee. At first Gerber had balked, but finally agreed to guarantee three thousand head.

The guarantee was something on which Ward would never have insisted had he been buying the herd for himself. He just wanted to be sure that Ruth got her money's worth. The price he paid had been for four thousand head, the whole procedure handled in the somewhat loose and careless manner typical of the West of that era.

Now, however, the number of cattle was running far below four thousand, and McQueen could not understand it. He still firmly believed that Dick Gerber's count was honest, and knowing the old man, he knew that Gerber's methods were not slipshod.

"The tally's fallin' short, ain't it?" Sartain asked. He knew McQueen was worried. "Do you suppose Yost would know anything about that?"

"How could he? Our own boys are handlin' this roundup. Yost hasn't been around—just my riders and the few of Gerber's I kept on to handle the branding."

Buying as he had, without waiting for the completed tally, he had saved money, for Gerber had insisted that the deal be made before the roundup. The difference was considerable. Now it could take all their profit away.

The ranch in Nevada had been making money steadily, and

410 / Louis L'Amour

it had been Ruth Kermitt's idea to stock it with more cattle. They could, she suggested, pick up a herd in Texas and drift it north, letting it feed as it moved.

McQueen liked the plan. With luck they could sell enough cattle at the railheads in Kansas or Nebraska to pay expenses, and possibly, with luck, even pay for the herd.

Buying cattle on the range could often prove very profitable, for in many cases the completed tally would run higher than the estimate. McQueen, knowing Gerber, had little hope of exceeding the tally.

Bud Fox and "Baldy" Jackson, the two hands that had come south with them, were drifting their way. "Brought in about thirty head," Bud volunteered as they drew near.

"Any unbranded stock?"

"Nope. Gerber must have figured wrong on that, because most of the stuff we're findin' has to be vented."

"Where is that KT rep?" Ward asked. He started to build a smoke, studying the cattle thoughtfully.

"Buff Colker?" Jackson rubbed a hand over his bald pate. "He's off to Sotol, as always. Said he had to mail a letter."

Sartain chuckled. "Shucks, Baldy! You're just jealous because you can't go in, too."

"Jealous?" Baldy snorted. "Of that Kansas City cowhand?"

"Buff sure ain't around much," Bud Fox agreed. "He takes his reppin' job easy."

"If those outfits he's workin' for can stand it, we can," McQueen said. "How's it look back in the breaks, Bud?"

"Cleaned out, almost. There's a few steers around that we might pick up, but most of them are wild as deer."

"Forget them," Ward advised, "they aren't worth it. We could waste a month combing that chaparral an' never get them out."

Kim Sartain spoke thoughtfully. "You know that Colker hombre sure puzzles me. He says he goes to Sotol, but remember that time you sent me in after some smokin' for the boys? Well, Buff was supposed to be there, too, but I didn't see him."

"Maybe you just didn't run into him," Bud said.

"In Sotol?" Sartain stared at Fox with utmost disgust. "You couldn't hide a pack rat in that place! You could cover the whole durned town under a Mexican's saddle blanket!"

Ward McQueen reined in and lounged loosely in the saddle, staring unhappily at the herd. Tonight he would ride in and have a talk with Ruth. He would have to tell her that his deal had been a poor one. Scowling, he tried to think if there was any spot they had somehow missed. Still, with Perkins, Gallatin, Jensen, and Lopez working for them, all men who knew this range, there was small chance of overlooking anything.

When the hands finished bunching the herd, Kim drifted his way again. "Riding into Sotol, boss?"

McQueen slanted his eyes at the casual young rider. "Yeah, what about it?"

"Nothin'." Kim shrugged carelessly. "Figured you might let me ride along. Sort of wash some of the dust out of my throat!"

Ward grinned. Few men cared so little for drinking as Kim Sartain. The rider was a top hand, but he liked a good fight, and Ward knew he was thinking of Yost.

"I don't want any trouble, Kim. You know how Miss Kermitt is."

Sartain turned his horse, riding toward the ranch house beside McQueen. "Boss, when are you and Miss Kermitt tyin' the knot?"

Ward looked around. "We don't plan on gettin' married until we get back to Nevada." He shrugged. "Maybe after she hears what a bad deal I made for her, she won't want to."

"Boss," Kim said hesitantly, "did you ever figure that maybe this Gerber lied? He wouldn't swear there was over three thousand."

Ward spat and swung the horse up to the corral. "Did you ever see the time you could swear to how many head you had on a ranch? I never could."

Sartain got down and began stripping the saddle from his sorrel. "I could guess within a thousand head," he replied.

Ward McQueen stopped a moment and frowned uneasily. Maybe he had been wrong in trusting Gerber. After all, the old man was notoriously tight-fisted, and he might not be above dishonesty with a man who came from so far away, and was on his way back. The thought rankled McQueen.

———

RUTH KERMITT WAS waiting for him on the steps of the hotel when he cantered up the street and swung down. She was smiling as he joined her.

"After you talk to me," he said, "you may not look so happy. Have you eaten?"

"Yes, but I want some more coffee with you."

She was a tall girl, her dark hair gathered in a loose knot at the nape of her neck. Her wide, blue eyes examined his face as he lifted his cup. She could see the lines of weariness etched there, the worry in his eyes.

"What's wrong, Ward?" she asked.

He sighed. "We bought four thousand head accordin' to Gerber's tally book. We won't get more than three thousand."

Her lips tightened. "Oh! I was afraid of something like that."

"Me, I'd have sworn by Gerber."

The door to the room smashed back suddenly, and Ward looked around. Five men had come into the cafe. In the lead, his blue eyes flashing from his brown, wind-burned face, his untrimmed white hair falling to his shoulders, was Old Dick Gerber. Behind him were four hard-faced riders.

Gerber sighted Ward and crossed the room swiftly.

"McQueen!" Gerber's voice rang in the narrow room. "It's come to my ears that you say I lied about my tally on that herd! Did you call me a liar?"

As Ward McQueen carefully got to his feet, the door opened quietly behind him.

"I'm with you, boss." It was Kim Sartain's voice.

"No, Dick, I didn't say you lied."

"The great McQueen, takin' water!" sneered one of the riders. A big man known as Black.

Ward's eyes shifted to Black. "I'm not takin' water. It's just I've known Dick Gerber a lot longer than I expect to know you."

His eyes turned to Gerber's. "Dick, you sold me four thousand head of cattle according to your tally. I took your word and the word of your book. I worked for you, an' that tally book of yours was somethin' to swear by. I had no doubts."

Gerber stared at him, still resentful. "What's the fuss about, then?" he demanded.

"Because we've had our roundup, an' we've only netted three thousand head."

"Three thousand?" Gerber stared. "Ward, you're crookin' me! If you only found three thousand head, you've snuck some off somewheres." His mouth tightened. "Ah? Maybe that's it? Maybe you figure to get me on that guarantee! Well, I won't stand for it, Ward!"

Ward's face flushed. "All I want is a square deal."

"He's askin' for trouble, Gerber," Black said. "Let me have him."

"Listen, big ears," Sartain took a step into the room, "if you're so anxious to throw iron, suppose you come out in the street an' throw it with me?"

"*Kim!*" Ward barked. "Stop it!" Ward wheeled on Black. "And you shut up! Gerber, get that man out of here, and get him out fast! If we start shootin' in this room, nobody will get out alive. And we've a woman here, remember that!"

Dick Gerber's anger left him. Realization broke over him that what Ward said was true. Ruth Kermitt was there. To throw a gun when a woman was present was out of reason.

"Quiet down!" Gerber snapped. "You, Black, mind what I say." He turned back to McQueen. "I'm sorry, Ward. Maybe I went off half-cocked, but I sure ain't the man to bunco anybody. I figure you of all people knew that."

"Mr. Gerber," Ruth said quietly, "just before you came in Ward was saying that even though there was a problem he would swear by you."

The old man looked around. "I guess I'm a fool," he said, and dropped into a chair. "I never figured on makin' a shootin' match of it, Ward. I was just too mad to think."

"Forget it and let's have a talk." Ward glanced at Sartain. "Kim, we don't want any trouble."

"That goes for you boys, too," Gerber told his men. "Ward an' me'll find some peaceful way to handle this."

As the hands trooped out, the door pushed open and into the room swaggered a big man, broad shouldered and blond. He was nattily dressed in black and he smiled when he saw Ruth.

"Oh, Miss Kermitt! I was looking for you. They told me in the office that you had come in here with one of the hands. Are you ready now?"

Ward McQueen looked around, astonished. The man was Buff Colker, the rep for the KT outfit, but he had never looked like this on the range. Then, as Colker's meaning swept over him, his face flushed and he glanced around at Ruth.

"Why, yes, Mr. Colker, just one minute." She turned quickly to Ward and put her hand on his. "I wasn't sure that you'd be in tonight," she said, "and Mr. Colker asked if he might call. Do you mind?"

For a moment Ward McQueen sat still, resentment burning within him. He had a half notion to say that he certainly did mind. Then he shrugged it off.

"No," he said, "I've got to talk with Gerber, anyway."

Yet as she arose and walked with Buff Colker into the other room, he glared after them. "Make a nice-lookin' couple," Gerber suggested thoughtfully. "She ain't married, is she?"

"We came here to talk about cattle." McQueen's voice had a faint rasp.

"Sure," Gerber agreed. He pulled his tally book from his pocket. "Got money, that young Colker has. I often wonder why he works for the KT, but maybe he figures to go into the cattle business."

He put on his glasses and peered at the book. "Now let's see: there were a couple of hundred head in Seminole Canyon. Did you get those out?"

TWO HOURS LATER Ward McQueen stalked into the saloon, irritated and unhappy. Despite their discussion and the careful checking of the record Gerber had kept, there was no accounting for the missing cattle. Yet a thousand head of cattle cannot just vanish, nor can they be hidden with ease.

Sartain was sitting alone at a card table idly riffling a deck of cards. He had his flat-brimmed gray hat shoved back on his head and was watching Black like a cat. The big gunman looked around when Ward came in, and watched as he walked over and dropped into a chair with Kim.

Sartain riffled the cards through his fingers and, without looking up, commented, "That Black has money. He buys drinks pretty free for a forty-dollar cowhand."

He has money. The words flitted through McQueen's mind, and then were lost as the door shoved open and Ernie Yost came in, accompanied by Villani and Taylor.

Taylor averted his eyes hastily. One of the three, McQueen reflected, was content to let well enough alone. Watching them, Ward was struck by the fact that Yost, staring straight across the bar, was speaking out of the corner of his mouth. The man beside him was Black.

Black's eagerness for trouble and a few words exchanged with Yost lingered in Ward's brain. What was between those two? Was Black tied in with Yost? What was going on around here?

"Let's leave, Kim. We've got a hard day tomorrow."

Mounting, they turned down the trail toward the ranch, but as he glanced back, Ward saw Ruth saying good night to Colker on the steps of the hotel. "He's got money." That was what Gerber had said of Colker. It was also what Sartain had said of Black. Could there be a tie-up there? Did their money come from the same source? Or was jealousy leading him down a blind alley?

What was the source of Black's money? The man had the earmarks of an owlhoot.

"Glad you got me out of there," Kim said, "I reckon I'm sleepier'n I thought."

Sleepier was right. *Sleep—er.*

Ward's dark mood was gone in a flash. He jerked around in the saddle. "Kim, have you been over to that herd of cattle we've cut for the other brands?"

Kim looked up, half awake. "No, why should I? We're through with them."

There must be at least two or three thousand head of KT, Broken Arrow, and Running M cattle in that herd, McQueen thought. That was a big herd, a very big herd.

———

IT WAS ALMOST noon the next day when he rode down to the roundup crew. McQueen had been thinking and checking. Sartain was sitting on a small gray horse, and Jackson was nearby. They had just knocked off for a brief rest.

Perkins and Lopez were sitting on the ground while Gallatin and Jensen were just riding up. Ward dropped from his horse and walked up to Lopez.

"Lopez, what horse did you ride yesterday?" Lopez hesitated. "Bay pony, señor."

"A bay?" Baldy looked around. "You must be forgetful. You rode that blaze-faced black with the broken hind hoof." The Mexican looked at him, then got to his feet, and he suddenly looked sick.

"That's right, Lopez." McQueen's thumbs were tucked in his belt, and around him the other riders were silent. "Now tell me what you were doing moving cattle at midnight."

"I, señor?" Lopez's eyes shifted right and left. "I was moving no cattle. I was in my bunk, asleep."

"A lie!" Ward's tone was brutal and he moved a step nearer. "You took that black horse out again, and you an' somebody else cut some cattle from the unbranded herd and moved them over into those mixed brands!"

"Sleeperin', by golly!" Baldy slapped his leg. "Sleeperin'! Why didn't I figure that? An' nobody ever checks that herd of mixed brands. After we're finished here, they'll just be left to drift back on the range from that long valley where you're holdin' 'em."

"And then these rannies could move in an' brand the unbranded stock for themselves. Nice business." Bud Fox dropped a hand to his six-shooter. "Do we down him, boss?"

"Not if he talks." Ward walked up to the Mexican, whose

face was a sickly yellow now. "Lopez, who's bossin' this show? Tell me an' you can go free."

"Let me have a hand at him!" Gallatin shoved forward, his face grim and his eyes narrow. "I'll fix him for you!"

"Keep out of this!" Ward snapped. "I'll talk to you, later! I've a good notion you're the other one in this mess!"

Gallatin sprang back, his face suddenly wolfish. "Oh, you think so, do you? Well, by—" His hand swept down for his gun.

"Stop!" Ward yelled. "Drop it or I'll kill you!"

Gallatin was crouching and his gun kept lifting. "Drop, nothin'!"

Ward palmed his six-gun in a flashing movement and flame stabbed from the black puzzle. His own gun coming up too slow, Gallatin caught the lead slugs in the stomach. He gulped, then staggered slowly back, his eyes glazing, the gun slipping from nerveless fingers.

———

HOOVES CLATTERED AND a shout went up. McQueen whirled in time to see Lopez streaking away on the horse the Mexican had just freshly saddled. Ward's gun came up, but the rustler was in a direct line with two men on the far side of the herd, and he dared not fire.

"Gone!" He swore. "He got plumb away."

Baldy Jackson reached for his bridle reins. "Boss, we'd better get at that mixed herd. Now they'll probably move in an' try to rustle the works. We'd better start cuttin' her."

"We're not in on any deal with Gally or the Mex," Jensen said. "You can ask Dick Gerber. I rode for him four years."

Ward glanced around at them. "Either of you know their friends? Who did they see in Sotol?"

Jensen hesitated. "Well, I reckon that Black who still rides for Gerber was the only one. They were pretty thick when they both rode for this spread. And then Villani. He worked for Gerber for a while, then left him after some trouble over a bridle, and he went to hangin' out with Ernie Yost."

"That fits." Sartain nodded. "They all run together. The

same brand wears well on them. Let's go coyote huntin', boss."

Ward McQueen hesitated. That was one thing, but the cattle came first. He must at all costs protect Ruth's cattle. "No, we'd better start workin' that mixed herd an' cuttin' our unbranded stock out of it."

"Boss, that Mex didn't head for Sotol," Bud suggested. "He took out for the mountains an' I've a good idea he's more set on gettin' safe away than tellin' Yost what happened here. Why don't we lay low an' check that herd today?"

"All right." Jensen was facing Ward, and he motioned to the body of Gallatin. "Plant him over by those trees, will you? Before anybody sees him. And I don't want it mentioned all day, you hear? Not in front of anybody!"

Sartain crooked a leg around his saddle horn. "Boss, I reckon Buff Colker will be out here soon."

"I said *anybody*." Ward turned to Bud. "I like your idea. We'll start cutting the mixed herd again tomorrow. Today we'll keep on with the branding, and tonight," he glanced at Baldy, then at Kim, "tonight we'll stand guard by that unbranded herd. If anybody starts to move those cattle we'll be ready for them."

The day drew on, hot and dusty. There was no breeze, and Ward nervously glanced at the sky from time to time. It felt like a storm was building up.

A cloud of dust hung over the corral where the branding was done, and the hands kept working up new bunches of cattle from the herd of the unbranded. Sartain was handling a rope, and Baldy was working with a branding iron. Buff Colker had arrived and sat his paint horse near the corral.

"KT, one calf!" Baldy yelled, slapping the iron on the animal, which bawled plaintively. "Tumblin' K! One calf!"

Colker checked the KT in his tally book and wiped the dust and perspiration from his brow. Ward McQueen was studiously avoiding the KT rep. He put his rope on a whiteface steer and spilled the beast close to the fire. Baldy slapped the iron and yelled, "Tumblin' K! One steer!"

Colker slapped his book shut and turned his horse. "Guess

I'll ride along, McQueen," he said, "I've got business in town!"

Ward glanced around, his lips tight. "Go ahead," he said. "We don't need you here."

Buff laughed sardonically. "Maybe there's somebody else that needs me."

McQueen's face flamed. "I don't know what you mean by that, Buff," he said evenly, "but you'd better be ridin'."

"That lady boss of yours seems to like what I say. Pretty little thing, I'll say that for her."

McQueen turned his roan. "If you're goin'," he warned, "you better hightail it while the goin's good."

Colker laughed, his eyes hard and the sneer evident. "Ward," he said, "you're a fool! After I've had my way with her, I'll come back here an' teach you a couple of things!"

He wheeled his horse and started at a gallop toward the Sotol trail. Ward McQueen's face went hard and white, and he wheeled his horse and went after Buff like a streak.

"Lord help that Colker now!" Baldy said. "The boss is sure boilin'. I wondered how much he'd take from that four-flusher!"

"Look!" Kim yelled excitedly. "This is goin' to be good!"

Too late, Buff Colker turned to see what was happening. Ward's roan had covered the ground in a short dash that brought him alongside Colker's galloping horse. Quickly, Ward reached down and grabbed the paint horse's tail and whipped it to one side, shoving the horse hard with his knee.

It was a process used often on the range to throw a steer, and when the animal, whether horse or cow, was traveling at all rapidly, it would invariably be spilled on the head and shoulder. It was known as "tailing," but was rarely used on a horse unless the animal was of little or no value.

Colker and the animal went flying. He sprang to his feet and clawed for his gun, then stopped. Ward was on the ground facing him, and had him covered. Colker had never even seen Ward draw.

A dozen cowhands had crowded around. "Bud," Ward said, "take his gun. I'm goin' to teach this cowboy a lesson!"

"What do you mean?" Colker snarled. His face was white,

but his eyes blazed. "You aimin' to shoot me down like a dog?"

"No, *amigo*," Ward said harshly, "I'm goin' to beat your thick skull in with my fists."

Abruptly, Buff grinned. "You're goin' to fight me with your hands? I'll kill you!"

Fox slid the gun from Buff Colker's holster, and Ward stepped over to Kim Sartain and hung his own gun belts around his saddle horn. Then he turned.

Across the wide ring of horsemen, he faced Buff Colker. Buff was the bigger man, young, wide-shouldered, and tough. He was smiling and confident. Buff paused long enough to strip off his shirt. Ward did likewise. Then the two men moved together.

Colker came fast and lashed out with a left that caught Ward coming in, but failed to stop him. McQueen crowded Colker and threw a short left, palm up, into Buff's midsection as they came together, Ward turning his body with the punch. It jolted Buff, but he jerked away and smashed both hands to Ward's face. Ward tried to duck a left, and caught another right. Then he closed in and threw Colker hard with a rolling hip-lock. Buff came up fast and dived at Ward's knees and they both went down, and then they were up and fighting, toe to toe, slugging. The two men came together, throwing their punches with everything they had in them.

Eyes blazing with fury, Buff sprang close, swinging with both hands. The dust rose from around their feet in a thick cloud, so at times the fighting could scarcely be seen. Neither man would give an inch and they fought bitterly, brutally, at close quarters. This was old stuff to Ward, for he had battled in many a cow camp brawl, and he kept moving in, his head spinning and dizzy with rocking blows, his hands always set to punch.

Blood trickled from a cut lip, and he had the taste of it in his mouth. Overhead the sky was like a sheet of iron, molten with heat. Ward set himself and slammed a right to the body. Again Buff was jolted, and he stepped back, and McQueen moved in, advancing his left foot then his right. He worked in, then threw his right again. Buff's hands came down and

Ward lunged, swinging high and hard with both fists, and Colker went down in the dust and rolled over.

"Put the boots to him!" Baldy said. "He'd give them to you!"

"Let him get up!" Ward panted. "I want more of him!"

Colker staggered to his feet and stood there weaving, the hatred in his eyes a living thing. He lunged, suddenly. But Ward met him with a stiff left hand that stopped him flat-footed and left him wide open for a clubbing right. It caught Colker flush on the ear, and Buff went down to his knees, the ear beginning to puff almost as he hit the ground.

Ward moved in, staggering with exhaustion. He jerked Colker to his feet and, holding him with his left, struck him twice in the wind and then three blows with his right in the face. Then he shoved the man from him, and Buff staggered and tumbled into the dust.

McQueen walked back to his horse and leaned against it for an instant, then picked up his shirt and began to wipe his face and body with it.

"Better get started on those cows," he commented. "We've a lot to do."

Baldy stared at him grimly. "You better go up to the cook shack and get that face fixed up," he suggested. "You look like chopped beef. But not," he added with satisfaction, "near so bad as he does!"

Colker was still stretched on his face, and Bud Fox glanced at him. "Shall we pick him up?" he asked.

"Let him lay!" Baldy told him. "He needs the rest!"

WHEN HE HAD bathed his face and repaired the cuts as best he could, Ward McQueen studied the situation. He was wrong to have let Buff Colker goad him into a fight. Colker was not his problem. He knew that Gallatin and Lopez had been sleepering cattle, and there seemed to be a connection between them and the Yost crowd, and possibly with Black.

He must find something more concrete in the way of evidence. Without returning to the corral, he dropped to a seat on a wooden bench in the shade near the back door of the cook shack. From where he sat he could see the dust rising from the branding corral, and the hills beyond.

The cook stuck his head out of the door and grinned at him. "Coffee, *señor*?"

"You bet, Pedro! An' thanks."

Sleepering cattle by day was a risky job, but it had been done. Baldy and Bud had the right idea, to check the herd by night and watch for the rustlers. Gerber himself might even be in it, but McQueen could not bring himself to admit that, nor could he quite believe that Ernie Yost, crooked as he was, would be the ringleader in any such scheme. Yost might run off forty or fifty head and sell them over the border, but dangerous as he might be at times, he was not a man who planned big.

Sartain had suggested that Colker did not always go to town when he left the roundup. If not to Sotol, where did he go? To a hideout in the hills? Or was he, himself, drifting unbranded stock away from the main herd?

Ward McQueen mounted the roan and headed back for the branding corral. Baldy rode up to him as he approached.

"The boys workin' back in the hills say the stock is mostly down out of the brush," he commented. "Also, Bud seen Old Man Gerber back there in the woods."

"Gerber? Out here?" Ward scowled. "What was he doing? Did Bud talk to him?"

"No, he didn't. Bud found a few more Slash Seven cows for us and was starting them back. They showed no liking for open country, so he had his work cut out for him."

"How long ago?"

"Right after the fight. He must be still back there, because we heard a shot 'way back in the canyon, maybe a half hour ago."

"A shot? What would he be shootin' at?"

Baldy Jackson shrugged. "Want me to ride back an' see? Maybe the old feller is skinnin' you, Ward."

"No, he's honest enough. I think I'll ride back there, though. You come along."

"Kim was tellin' about your run-in with Yost, an' then with Black. You reckon they are in on this steal?"

Ward shrugged. "Could be. Lopez and Gallatin weren't in it alone."

The grass was parched and brown in the valley, and they were leaving the scattered growth of oak, Spanish dagger, and mesquite for higher ground and the cedar. The air felt thick and heavy. Across the shoulder of the mountain they pushed down into the thick brush, and here they ran into Jensen with four head of Slash Seven's, two YT's, and a 21.

"You see Gerber here?" Ward demanded.

"No, I sure haven't. Heard a shot a while back, then two more. I had these critters, though, an' couldn't chase over to investigate. Somebody shootin' at a wolf, maybe, or a panther."

"Start those cattle over the ridge and then come with us. We may need an outside witness."

———

WARD MCQUEEN'S GRAY eyes swept the tangle before him. It would be like hunting for a needle in a haystack to search for anything down there. Still, if Gerber was out here, he was here for a reason.

The sun was blazing hot, and in the chaparral the heat was oppressive. It felt even more like a storm than before. If it rained, it would at least make travel better, and Ward's plan was to start the herd within forty-eight hours if possible. It wouldn't give the men much rest, but he wanted to be driving north to where the grass was better.

Along the trail north they could take their time. He wanted the cattle to feed all the way to Kansas, anyway.

Sweat trickled down his face, cutting a furrow through the dust. It was hot. He wiped his palms dry on his pant legs and let the roan find its way through the brush that now was higher than his head.

"More to the left, I reckon," Jensen said. "You can't always swear to the direction."

"I smell smoke," Baldy said. "Hold up! I smell smoke close to hand."

"Who would want a fire on a day like this?" Jensen asked, of nobody in particular. "This place is like an oven."

"Wait a minute!" Ward lifted a hand. "There's something over here." He turned his horse and pushed through the oak brush, then drew up sharply, and the roan snorted and backed up. "Dead man," he said.

He trailed the bridle reins and dropped to the ground. He needed to go only a step nearer to recognize Dick Gerber. The white-haired old man was lying on his back, one arm thrown across his eyes to shield them from the sun.

Jensen dropped from his horse and bent over the old man. He placed a hand on his heart.

"Dead, all right. That's too bad, he was a pretty good old boy, at that."

"What was he doin' with a fire?" Baldy demanded. "Hey, there's a runnin' iron!"

Ward scowled. "Gerber? With a runnin' iron? What would he be brandin'?" He stared at the man, and then at the fire. "Hunt up his horse, Baldy, while Jensen an' I have a look around."

"He always carried a runnin' iron, Mr. McQueen," Jensen said. "The old man claimed it saved a sight of time to brand stock where he found it. Never went out but what he carried it."

Ward looked around thoughtfully. Obviously, Gerber had used the iron. He bent over it and touched it. It was lying in the shade and it was still warm.

Gerber had been shot twice through the chest, never able to get his gun out.

"He had a critter down, Mr. McQueen," Jensen said. "Here's the tracks. He throwed it, an' from the look hog-tied it."

"Yeah." Ward squatted on his heels. "Here's a piggin' string. But what would he want to brand back in here on a day like this?"

"It wasn't dishonest," Jensen said stubbornly. "I knew the old man well, as I guess you did. He was on the level."

"Sure! But what was he doin' here? An' who shot him?"

Jensen scratched his jaw. "You know what they'll say. They'll say you done it. They'll say after that trouble in town that you had more trouble and that you killed him in an argument over cattle."

McQueen stared at the old man's body. So far as he could see, nothing had been touched. He got up, studying the angle of the shots, but apparently the old man had not died at once, but had moved around some, and it was hard to figure. Yet, when he looked again, there did seem to be one possibility.

On the brow of a hill, not over fifty yards away, was a cluster of boulders. It was worth looking at.

"Baldy, go back to the ranch and get a buckboard," he said. "Come as far as you can, an' we'll pack the body out to it."

"You ought to be havin' a look around, Mr. McQueen," Jensen said seriously. "This here was murder, an' you better find who done it. Folks sure liked this old man."

Who had the opportunity? Jensen, of course. Bud Fox, too. Both of them had been working the brush, and there were probably two or three other hands who had been in the vicinity. But it wouldn't make sense for any of them to kill him. It had to be someone else, and somehow it was sure to tie in with the sleepering of Slash Seven cattle.

Ward turned and fought his way through the brush to the nest of boulders on the hill. From atop a boulder, he studied the earth behind them. From here he could see Jensen standing over Gerber's body, and the unknown murderer could have done the same. Behind the rocks were boot tracks, a number of them. He could find no cartridge anywhere around.

Jensen was waiting for him. "Find anything?"

"Tracks. That's all. Probably whoever shot him did it from there, but that doesn't tell us anything."

Jensen scratched his unshaven jaw. "It does tell you a little, Mr. McQueen. It tells you the chances are that whoever killed him was following him. Nobody gets in this here brush by accident, an' nobody's goin' to convince me that two men are in the brush by accident an' one seen the other down here, then killed him."

"It could be that way, though." Ward pushed his hat back, then removed it and mopped the sweat band. "The thing is, the killer had a reason, an' that's where we've got to think this out. The killer must have seen Gerber down here with that critter thrown, an' he didn't want him to do what he was doin'."

"Well, anybody could say he was rustlin'," Jensen suggested. "I'll never believe it of the old man, but it sure does look funny, him down here with a runnin' iron an' a critter throwed in this heat."

"Or maybe there was something else. Maybe he was inspectin' a brand somebody didn't want him to look at too close. Could that be it?"

Jensen agreed dubiously. "Could be. But what brand?"

Baldy Jackson came up leading a horse. "Got the buckboard. There's a passel of folks at the ranch. Sheriff, too."

"The sheriff? Already?" Ward shrugged. "The law always gets there fast when you don't want him. All right, we'll have a talk."

Ward McQueen rode back to the ranch followed by Baldy with the buckboard, and Gerber's horse and the horse that packed him out of the brush trailing behind. Jensen brought up the rear, his face doubtful.

Buff Colker was there, and not far from him was Ruth Kermitt. Ward glanced quickly at her, but her eyes were averted and he could not catch her glance.

Other men walked up from the corrals and he saw Ernie Yost, Villani, and Black. Taylor was nowhere in evidence. Apparently, he, like Lopez, had decided he had enough.

Kim Sartain loafed nearby, leaning against an old Conestoga wagon. He nodded toward the tall man with the drooping mustache.

"Sheriff Jeff Davis, this is Ward McQueen."

"Howdy." Ward swung around. "What's the trouble, Sheriff?"

"I hear there's been some shootin' around here. Who killed Dick Gerber?"

"That's something I'd like to know," McQueen told him. "We heard the shots, or some of the boys did, and later went to look around. We found Gerber, already dead."

Davis stocked his pipe. "You had trouble with him in town?"

"Nothing serious. We were friends, only somebody told

him I said he lied about the number of cattle we had here and he went off half-cocked. I bought four thousand head, but when we finished our gather the tally showed only a few over three thousand."

"Then what happened?" Davis eyed him thoughtfully. Ward met his eyes and shrugged.

"We had our words in town, then sat down together and straightened things out. I didn't see Dick again until we found him in the brush, dead."

"He had a brandin' iron alongside of him, an' a fire goin'. He'd branded something." Baldy made his offering and then shut up.

Davis glanced at him, one bleak, all-seeing glance. "The killer could have planted that. You could have planted it, McQueen."

"I could have, but I didn't. Dick Gerber never misbranded a cow in his entire life, and I'd bet on it. He drove a hard bargain often enough, but he was honest as they come."

"You ask us to believe," Colker interrupted, "that you parted from Gerber last night on a friendly basis when you had a thousand head missing from the tally? That sounds pretty broad-minded to me."

For a moment Ward looked around at him. "What's his part in this, Sheriff? As you can tell by the expression I pounded into his face, I don't like him!"

"I'm a witness." Colker smiled grimly. "I'll have my say, too."

"Want me to start him travelin', boss?" Sartain asked. "I'd like that."

"I'm in charge here." Davis looked around at Kim. "I'll start who movin' when I want."

Kim Sartain straightened away from the wheel. "Ward McQueen is my boss, and I'll take his orders."

"Are you takin' that, Davis?" Yost thrust forward. "There have been two killin's committed on this place today. Gallatin was shot down by McQueen, and then Gerber was bumped off. That Sartain is a killer; McQueen as much as admitted it the other day."

"Was Gallatin killed?" Davis inquired gently. Ward found

himself liking the man. Obviously, Sheriff Jeff Davis was no fool, and he was a man who knew his own mind.

"Yes, there was a gunfight. I accused Lopez of handling cattle at night. Gallatin interfered, and when I called him on it, he went for a gun. I tried to stop him, but couldn't, so I drew."

"I seen it, Jeff," Jensen said flatly. "Gally asked for it. He was rustlin' cows."

"What about that thousand head?" Davis asked. "Found hide or hair of them?"

"I reckon we did," Ward said, and his eyes swung to Buff Colker. "I think we've found 'em all!"

By the light that leaped suddenly in Colker's eyes, McQueen knew he had guessed right. Buff Colker was the brains of the rustling on the Slash Seven.

"They were sleeperin' 'em, Sheriff. Driving unbranded stock around the pens at night an' mixing them in with the mixed brands we were going to release. Lopez was in on it, an' so was Gallatin. I think that Gerber smelled a rat, an' when the killer trailed him an' saw what he was doin', he killed him."

"Sheriff." Ruth Kermitt spoke gently. "Have you had trouble with rustlers around here before?"

"Sure. Matter of fact, that was the reason Gerber was sellin' his stock. Too much rustlin'."

"And Gerber's brand is a Slash Seven," Ruth continued. "Can you think of a brand that a Slash Seven could be made into, Sheriff?"

"Ma'am, we've been over that here for months," Davis said. "There ain't a brand in this part of the country like that. Not one it could be done with, not anywhere easy."

"There's one brand," she insisted gently. "I refer to the brand that Buff Colker has registered."

Ward happened to have his eyes on Colker, and he saw the man start as if struck with a whip. His head jerked around, and hatred blazed in his eyes, hatred and fear. But then the fear was gone.

"Colker ain't got no brand!" Davis said, frowning. "Nor no cattle I know of."

"He has, though, Sheriff." Ruth glanced at Ward, then away. "I checked with Austin. He has a Box Triangle registered there. Any child could make a Slash Seven into a Box Triangle.

"Mr. Colker spent the whole evening telling me how he didn't have to be a cowhand, that he had a ranch of his own, well stocked with cattle, and that he intended to branch out. When Ward told me of the cattle we were missing, I became curious, and I checked with Austin as to Buff Colker's brand."

"Are you accusin' me of being a rustler?" Colker turned on her, his dark eyes ugly. Then he looked back at the sheriff. "You can see for yourself, Sheriff. This is a cheap plot. They are conniving to hang this on me. McQueen is a known gunman, so is Sartain, and they both work for Miss Kermitt."

Davis chewed his mustache. "Do you have a brand?"

Colker's eyes shifted. "Yes," he said finally.

"Is it a Box Triangle?"

"Well, yes, but that doesn't mean that I'm a rustler."

Davis dropped to his haunches and with a stick drew a Slash Seven in the sand, and then opposite it, a Box Triangle. He glanced up at Colker. "You've got to admit it's awful easily done." He straightened to his feet. "Now, folks, I ain't much on a man havin' an alibi. Them as needs 'em can get 'em, an' them as don't need 'em never has 'em."

"If McQueen has found the Tumblin' K cows, like he says, I don't see no reason for any shootin' on his part. Far's I know, the two of them are friends. There has been some rustlin' here, I can see that. I reckon afore we can do much else we'll have to send a deputy to your ranch an' have a few head of your cows killed so we can check the brands. If we can find any Slash Sevens made over, I reckon we'll have Gerber's rustler, an' maybe a powerful suspect for his murder. Until then we'll hold you."

"That don't figure, Jeff," Yost protested. "Just because this girl figured it that way is no sign that Gerber did."

"He knew." Ruth spoke positively. "I was very careless last night. I was drawing Slash Sevens into Box Triangles at the table, and forgot and left my paper there. When I returned for it, the cook told me that Dick Gerber had picked it up, swore, and went out."

Buff Colker was sweating now, and his face was pale. "That doesn't prove a thing!" he declared. "I demand to be allowed to leave. All you have is a lot of suspicion. I can find fifty brands in Texas that could be made from Slash Sevens."

Ernie Yost had fallen back close to Colker, and Villani had moved toward his horse. A slight movement by Black drew Ward's attention, and he saw that the big gunman was sidling toward his horse and his rifle. And then he saw something else.

Bud Fox had his rope on a steer and he was half leading, half dragging him toward the house. Behind him, Perkins was using his rope as a whip to urge the stubborn steer along.

Ward McQueen shifted his position so he could keep Yost and Colker completely covered if necessary. Out of the corner of his eye he noticed that Kim Sartain and Baldy Jackson were both alert to the shifting of forces. Only the sheriff and Jensen seemed unaware of what was happening.

"Ruth, you'd better get inside," Ward said quietly. "There's going to be trouble." He spoke softly, but he noticed the sheriff's sudden movement and knew he had heard.

Ward shifted his eyes from Buff toward the steer, and for a moment he stared at the weird brand without comprehension, and then it hit him.

"Davis!" he said sharply. "There's your proof of murder!"

Burned with a running iron on the steer's hide was the date, and under it:

SHOT BY BUF CLKR RUSTLER, DYIN

/7 TO BX TRI

HOT AS HELL

D. GRBR.

"There it is! Burned with a runnin' iron as the old man lay dyin' in the brush! Then he cut loose the steer—had him thrown and ready to check his brand when Buff came up on him!"

Buff Colker stepped back quickly and clawed for his gun,

but Ward was faster. Even as Colker's gun started to lift, Ward's first bullet ripped the thumb from his hand and knocked him off balance.

Colker stared at the stub where his thumb had been, now gushing with blood, and with a cry like an animal, rushed for his horse. Ward had swung his gun toward Yost even as a bullet knocked him into the side of the house. He fired, holding his gun low. Sartain had opened up on Black, and the wiry young gunfighter was walking in on him, firing with every step. Villani was out of it. Baldy had fired his rifle right across the saddle bows, and Villani toppled over, clawed at the side of the water trough, and got himself half erect, getting his gun out even as he cursed. Baldy fired again, and the gun slid from Villani's fingers.

Yost screamed as Ward's bullet hit him, and then suddenly, his eyes wild, he ran straight for McQueen, his gun blazing. Ward stepped back and tripped on the stoop. Catching himself on one hand, he looked up into the wild, fear-crazed eyes of Yost as the man threw down on him with a six-shooter at point-blank range! McQueen shot fast, three times, as swiftly as he could thumb the gun.

Ernie Yost went up on his toes, his face twisting in a frightful grimace; then he pitched over on his face, his gun blasting the hard-packed earth within inches of Ward's hand.

McQueen kicked the dying man off his legs and got to his feet, feeding shells into his gun, but the battle was over. In a few seconds four men had died.

Sheriff Davis had fired but one shot, killing Buff Colker as he scrambled to get away.

Ward McQueen holstered his gun and grabbed for support at the well coping. He knew he had been shot; his side felt strangely numb and his mind seemed sluggish, but his eyes were alive and knowing.

Jensen was down, but struggling to get up, with a red stain on his pant leg. Sheriff Davis, in the most exposed position of all, was unharmed.

Ruth rushed to Ward's side. "Darling! You're hurt!"

He put his hand on her shoulder and tried to grin. "Not much," he said. "How's Kim?"

"Never touched me!" Sartain said. "They plowed a furrow over Baldy's ear. Cut off a piece of the last fringe of hair he's got left!"

Neither Fox nor Perkins had managed to get off a shot. Both men came crowding up now, and they helped Ward inside. On examination they found he had only a flesh wound in the side, and while there had been some loss of blood, he was not badly hurt.

Ward looked at Ruth. "I reckon when I get on my feet, we'd better haul out of here. This place looks like trouble."

She laughed, then blushed. "I'm in a hurry to get back, too, Ward. Or shall we wait?"

"No," he smiled, "I've heard that Cheyenne is a good town for weddings!"

WEST OF THE TULAROSAS

T HE DEAD MAN had gone out fighting. Scarcely more than a boy, and a dandy in dress, he had been man enough when the showdown came.

Propped against the fireplace stones, legs stretched before him, loose fingers still touching the butt of his .45 Colt, he had smoked it out to a bloody, battle-stained finish. Evidence of it lay all about him. Whoever killed him had spent time, effort, and blood to do it.

As they closed in for the payoff at least one man had died on the threshold.

The fight that ended here had begun elsewhere. From the looks of it this cabin had been long deserted, and the dead man's spurs were bloodstained. At least one of his wounds showed evidence of being much older than the others. A crude attempt had been made to stop the bleeding.

Baldy Jackson, one of the Tumbling K riders who found the body, dropped to his knees and picked up the dead man's Colt.

"Empty!" he said. "He fought 'em until his guns were empty, an' then they killed him."

"Is he still warm?" McQueen asked. "I think I can smell powder smoke."

"He ain't been an hour dead, I'd guess. Wonder what the fuss was about?"

"Worries me," McQueen looked around, "considering our situation." He glanced at Bud Fox and Kim Sartain, who appeared in the doorway. "What's out there?"

"At least one of their boys rode away still losing blood. By the look of things this lad didn't go out alone, he took somebody with him." Sartain was rolling a smoke. "No feed in the shed, but that horse out there carries a mighty fine saddle."

"Isn't this the place we're headed for?" Fox asked. "It looks like the place described."

Sartain's head came up. "Somebody comin'!" he said. "Riders, an' quite a passel of them."

Sartain flattened against the end of the fireplace and Fox knelt behind a windowsill. Ward McQueen planted his stalwart frame in the doorway, waiting. "This isn't so good. We're goin' to be found with a dead man, just killed."

There were a half dozen riders in the approaching group, led by a stocky man on a gray horse and a tall, oldish fellow wearing a badge.

They drew up sharply on seeing the horses and McQueen. The short man stared at McQueen, visibly upset by his presence. "Who're you? And what are you doin' here?"

"I'll ask the same question," McQueen spoke casually. "This is Firebox range, isn't it?"

"I know that." The stocky man's tone was testy. "I ought to. I own the Firebox."

"Do you now?" Ward McQueen's reply was gentle, inquiring. "Might be a question about that. Ever hear of Tom McCracken?"

"Of course! He used to own the Firebox."

"That's right, and he sold it to Ruth Kermitt of the Tumbling K. I'm Ward McQueen, her foreman. I've come to take possession."

His reply was totally unexpected, and the stocky man was obviously astonished. His surprise held him momentarily speechless, and then he burst out angrily.

"That's impossible! I'm holdin' notes against young Jimmy McCracken! He was the old man's heir, an' Jimmy signed the place over to me to pay up."

"As of when?" Ward asked.

His thoughts were already leaping ahead, reading sign along the trail they must follow. Obviously something was very wrong, but he was sure that Ruth's deed, a copy of which he carried with him, would be dated earlier than whatever this man had. Moreover, he now had a hunch that the dead man lying behind him was that same Jimmy McCracken.

"That's neither here nor there! Get off my land or be drove off!"

"Take it easy, Webb!" The sheriff spoke for the first time. "This man may have a just claim. If Tom McCracken sold out before he died, your paper isn't worth two hoots."

That this had occurred to Webb was obvious, and that he did not like it was apparent. Had the sheriff not been present, Ward was sure, there would have been a shooting. As yet, they did not know he was not alone, as none of the Tumbling K men had shown themselves.

"Sheriff," McQueen said, "my outfit rode in here about fifteen minutes ago, and we found a dead man in this cabin. Looks like he lost a runnin' fight with several men, and when his ammunition gave out, they killed him."

"Or you shot him," Webb said.

Ward did not move from the door. He was a big man, brown from sun and wind, lean and muscular. He wore two guns.

"I shot nobody." His tone was level, even. "Sheriff, I'm Ward McQueen. My boss bought this place from McCracken for cash money. The deed was delivered to her, and the whole transaction was recorded in the courts. All that remained was for us to take possession, which we have done."

He paused. "The man who is dead inside is unknown to me, but I'm making a guess he's Jimmy McCracken. Whoever killed him wanted him dead mighty bad. There was quite a few of them, and Jimmy did some good shootin'. One thing you might look for is a couple of wounded men, or somebody else who turns up dead."

The sheriff dismounted. "I'll look around, McQueen. My name's Foster, Bill Foster." He waved a hand to the stocky cattleman. "This is Neal Webb, owner of the Runnin' W."

Ward McQueen stepped aside to admit the sheriff, and as he did so Kim Sartain showed up at the corner of the house, having stepped through a window to the outside. Kim Sartain was said to be as good with his guns as McQueen.

Foster squatted beside the body. "Yeah, this is young Jimmy, all right. Looks like he put up quite a scrap."

"He was game," McQueen said. He indicated the older

wound. "He'd been shot somewhere and rode in here, ridin' for his life. Look at the spurs. He tried to get where there was help but didn't make it."

Foster studied the several wounds and the empty cartridge cases. McQueen told him of the hard-ridden mustang, but the sheriff wanted to see for himself. Watching the old man, McQueen felt renewed confidence. The lawman was careful and shrewd, taking nothing for granted, accepting no man's unsupported word. That McQueen and his men were in a bad position was obvious.

Neal Webb was obviously a cattleman of some local importance. The Tumbling K riders were not only strangers but they had been found with the body.

Webb was alert and aware. He had swiftly catalogued the Tumbling K riders as a tough lot, if pushed. McQueen he did not know, but the K foreman wore his guns with the ease of long practice. Few men carried two guns, most of them from the Texas border country. Nobody he knew of used both at once; the second gun was insurance, but it spoke of a man prepared for trouble.

Webb scowled irritably. The setup had been so perfect! The old man dead, the gambling debts, and the bill of sale. All that remained was to . . . and then this outfit appeared with what was apparently a legitimate claim. Who would ever dream the old man would sell out? But how had the sale been arranged? There might still be a way, short of violence.

What would Silas Hutch say? And Ren Oliver? It angered Webb to realize he had failed, after all his promises. Yet who could have foreseen this? It had all appeared so simple, but who could have believed that youngster would put up a fight like he did? He had been a laughing, friendly young man, showing no sense of responsibility, no steadiness of purpose. He had been inclined to sidestep trouble rather than face it, so the whole affair had looked simple enough.

One thing after another had gone wrong. First, the ambush failed. The kid got through it alive and then made a running fight of it. Why he headed for this place Webb could not guess, unless he had known the Tumbling K outfit was to be here.

Two of Webb's best men were dead and three wounded, and he would have to keep them out of sight until they were well again. Quickly, he decided the line cabin on Dry Legget would be the best hideout.

Foster came from the woods, his face serious.

"McQueen, you'd better ride along to town with me. I found sign that six or seven men were in this fight, and several were killed or hurt. This requires investigation."

"You mean I'm under arrest?"

"No such thing. Only you'll be asked questions. We'll check your deed an' prob'ly have to get your boss up here. We're goin' to get to the bottom of this."

"One thing, Foster, before we go. I'd like you to check our guns. Nobody among us has fired a shot for days. I'd like you to know that."

"You could have switched guns," Webb suggested.

McQueen ignored him. "Kim, why don't you fork your bronc an' ride along with us? Baldy, you an' Bud stay here and let nobody come around unless it's the sheriff or one of us. Got it?"

"You bet!" Jackson spat a stream of tobacco juice at an ant. "Nobody'll come around, believe me."

Neal Webb kept his mouth shut but he watched irritably. McQueen was thinking of everything, but as Webb watched the body of young McCracken tied over the saddle he had an idea. Jimmy had been well liked around town, so if the story got around that McQueen was his killer, there might be no need for a trial or even a preliminary hearing. It was too bad Foster was so stiff-necked.

Kim Sartain did not ride with the group. With his Winchester across his saddle bows he kept off to the flank or well back in the rear where the whole group could be watched. Sheriff Foster noted this, and his frosty old eyes glinted with amused appreciation.

"What's he doin' back there?" Webb demanded. "Make him ride up front, Sheriff!"

Foster smiled. "He can ride where he wants. He don't make me nervous, Webb. What's eatin' you?"

The town of Pelona for which they were riding faced the

wide plains from the mouth of Cottonwood Canyon, and faced them without pretensions. The settlement, dwarfed by the bulk of the mountain behind it, was a supply point for cattlemen, a stage stop, and a source of attraction for cowhands to whom Santa Fe and El Paso were faraway dream cities.

In Pelona, with its four saloons, livery stable, and five stores, Si Hutch, who owned Hutch's Emporium, was king.

He was a little old man, grizzled, with a stubble of beard and a continually cranky mood. Beneath that superficial aspect he was utterly vicious, without an iota of mercy for anything human or animal.

Gifted in squeezing the last drop of money or labor from those who owed him, he thirsted for wealth with the same lust that others reserved for whiskey or women. Moreover, although few realized it, he was cruel as an Apache and completely depraved. One of the few who realized the depth of his depravity was his strong right hand, Ren Oliver.

Oliver was an educated man and for the first twenty-five years of his life had lived in the East. Twice, once in New York and again in Philadelphia, he had been guilty of killing. In neither case had it been proved, and in only one case had he been questioned. In both cases he had killed to cover his thieving, but finally he got in too deep and realizing his guilt could be proved, he skipped town.

In St. Louis he shot a man over a card game. Two months later he knifed a man in New Orleans, then drifted west, acquiring gun skills as he traveled. Since boyhood his career had been a combination of cruelty and dishonesty, but not until he met Si Hutch had he made it pay. Behind his cool, somewhat cynical expression few people saw the killer.

He was not liked in Pelona. Neither was he disliked. He had killed two men in gun battles since arriving in town, but both seemed to have been fair, standup matches. He was rarely seen with Si Hutch, for despite the small population they had been able to keep their cooperation a secret. Only Neal Webb, another string to Hutch's bow, understood the connection. One of the factors that aided Hutch in ruling the Pelona area was that his control was exercised without being obvious. Certain of his enemies had died by means unknown to either Ren Oliver or Neal Webb.

The instrument of these deaths was unknown, and for that reason Si Hutch was doubly feared.

When Sheriff Foster rode into town with Webb and McQueen, Si Hutch was among the first to know. His eyes tightened with vindictive fury. That damned Webb! Couldn't he do anything right? His own connection with the crimes well covered, he could afford to sit back and await developments.

Ward McQueen had been doing some serious thinking on the ride into town. The negotiations between Ruth Kermitt and old Tom McCracken had been completed almost four months ago. McCracken had stayed on at the Firebox even after the title was transferred and was to have managed it for another six months. His sudden death ended all that.

Webb had said he owned the ranch by virtue of young Jimmy signing it over to pay a gambling debt. This was unlikely, for Jimmy had surely known of the sale. Neal Webb had made an effort to obtain control of the ranch, and Jimmy McCracken had been killed to prevent his doing anything about it.

Sheriff Foster seemed like an honest man, but how independent was he? In such towns there were always factions who controlled, and elected officials were often only tools to be used.

Faced with trickery and double-dealing as well as such violence, what could he do? When Ruth arrived from the Tumbling K in Nevada there would be no doubt that she owned the Firebox and that Jimmy had known of it. That would place the killing of young Jimmy McCracken at Neal Webb's door.

Red Oliver was on the walk in front of the Bat Cave Saloon when they tied up before the sheriff's office. He had never seen either McQueen or Sartain before but knew them instantly for what they were, gunfighters, and probably good.

McQueen saw the tall man in the gray suit standing on the boardwalk. As he watched, Oliver turned in at the Emporium. Ward finished tying his roan and went into the sheriff's office.

Nothing new developed from the talk in the office of the sheriff, nor in the hearing that followed. Young Jimmy McCracken had been slain by persons unknown after a considerable chase. The evidence seemed to establish that several men had been involved in the chase, some of whom had been killed or wounded by McCracken.

Ward McQueen gave his own evidence and listened as the others told what they knew or what tracks seemed to indicate. As he listened he heard whispering behind him, and he was well aware that talk was going around. After all, he and the Tumbling K riders were strangers. What talk he could overhear was suspicion of his whole outfit.

Neal Webb had a bunch of tough men around him and he was belligerent. When telling what he knew he did all he could to throw suspicion on the Tumbling K. However, from what he could gather, all of Webb's riders were present and accounted for.

After the inquest McQueen found himself standing beside the sheriff. "What kind of a country is this, Sheriff? Do you have much trouble?"

"Less than you'd expect. Webb's outfit is the biggest, but his boys don't come in often. When they want to have a blowout they ride down to Alma. They do some drinkin' now an' again but they don't r'ar up lookin' for trouble."

"Many small outfits?"

"Dozen or so. The Firebox will be the largest if you run cows on all of it." Foster studied him. "Do you know the range limits of the Firebox?"

"We figure to run stock from the Apache to Rip-Roaring Mesa and Crosby Creek, south to Dillon Mountain and up to a line due east from there to the Apache."

"That's a big piece of country but it is all Firebox range. There are a few nesters squatted in Bear Canyon, and they look like a tough outfit, but they've given me no trouble."

"Miss Kermitt holds deeds on twelve pieces of land," Ward explained. "Those twelve pieces control most of the water on that range, and most of the easy passes. We want no trouble, but we'll run cattle on range we're entitled to."

"That's fair enough. Watch your step around Bear Canyon. Those boys are a mean lot."

Kim Sartain was somewhere around town but McQueen was not worried. The gunslinging segundo of the Tumbling K was perfectly capable of taking care of himself, and in the meanwhile Ward had business of his own to take care of. He glanced up and down the street, studying the stores. Two of them appeared better stocked than the others. One was Hutch's Emporium, a large store apparently stocked to the doors with everything a rancher could want. The other stores were smaller but were freshly painted and looked neat.

McQueen walked along to the Emporium. A small man with a graying beard looked up at him as he came to the counter. It was an old-fashioned counter, curved inward on the front to accommodate women shoppers who wore hoop-skirts.

"Howdy there! Stranger in town?"

"Tumbling K. We've taken over the Firebox, and we'll need supplies."

Hutch nodded agreeably. "Glad to help! The Firebox, hey? Had a ruckus out there, I hear."

"Nothin' much." Ward walked along, studying the goods on the shelves and stacked on tables. He was also curious about the man behind the counter. He seemed genial enough, but his eyes were steel bright and glassy. He was quick-moving and obviously energetic.

"Troublin' place, the Firebox. Old McCracken seemed to make it pay but nobody else ever done it. You reckon you'll stay?"

"We'll stay."

McQueen ordered swiftly and surely, but not all they would need. There were other stores in town, and he preferred to test the water before he got in too deep. The Firebox would need to spend a lot of money locally and he wanted to scatter it around. Hutch made no comment until he ordered a quantity of .44-caliber ammunition.

"That's a lot of shootin'. You expectin' a war?"

"War? Nothing like that, but we're used to wars. Jimmy McCracken was killed for some reason by some right vicious folks. If they come back we wouldn't want them to feel unwelcome."

The door opened and Neal Webb walked in. He strode swiftly to the counter and was about to speak when he recognized McQueen. He gulped back his words, whatever they might have been.

"Howdy. Reckon you got off pretty easy."

McQueen took his time about replying. "Webb, the Tumblin' K is in this country to stay. You might as well get used to us and accept the situation. Then we can have peace between us and get on with raising and marketing cattle. We want no trouble, but we're ready if it comes.

"We did business with McCracken and I couldn't have found a finer man. His son seemed cut from the same pattern.

"They didn't belong to my outfit, so I'm droppin' this right here. If it had been one of my men I'd backtrail the killers until I found where they came from. Then I'd hunt their boss and I'd stay with him until he was hanged, which is what he deserves."

Behind McQueen's back Hutch gestured, and the hot remarks Webb might have made were stifled. Puzzled, McQueen noticed the change and the sudden shift of Webb's eyes. Finishing his order he stepped into the street.

As he left a gray-haired, impatient-seeming man brushed by him. "Neal," he burst out, "where's that no-account Bemis? He was due over to my place with that horse he borried. I need that paint the worst way!"

"Forget it," Webb said. "I'll see he gets back to you."

"But I want to see Bemis! He owes me money!"

Ward McQueen let the door close behind him and glanced across the street. A girl with red-gold hair was sweeping the boardwalk there. She made a pretty picture and he crossed the street.

As he stepped onto the walk, she glanced up. Her expression changed as she saw him. Her glance was the swiftly measuring one of a pretty girl who sees a stranger, attractive and possibly unmarried. She smiled.

"You must be one of that new outfit the town's talking about. The Tumbling K, isn't it?"

"It is." He shoved his hat back on his head. Kim should see this girl, he thought. She's lovely. "I'm the foreman."

She glanced across the street toward Hutch's store. "Started buying from Hutch?"

"I'm new here so I thought I'd scatter my business until I find out where I get the best service." He smiled. "I'll want to order a few things."

A big man was coming up the walk, a very big man, and Ward McQueen sensed trouble in the man's purposeful stride. His worn boots were run down at the heels and his faded shirt was open halfway down his chest for lack of buttons. His ponderous fists swung at the ends of powerfully muscled arms, and his eyes darkened savagely as he saw Ward McQueen.

"Watch yourself!" the girl warned. "That's Flagg Warneke!"

The big man towered above McQueen. When he came to a stop in front of Ward his chin was on a level with Ward's eyebrows and he seemed as wide as a barn door.

"Are you McQueen? Well, I'm Flagg Warneke, from Bear Canyon! I hear you aim to run us nesters off your range! Is that right?"

"I haven't made up my mind yet," Ward replied. "When I do I'll come to see you."

"Oh! You haven't made up your mind yet? Well, see that you don't! And stay away from Bear Canyon! That place belongs to us, an' if you come huntin' trouble, you'll get it!"

Coolly, Ward McQueen turned his back on the giant. "Why not show me what stock you have?" he suggested to the girl. "I—"

A huge hand clamped on his shoulder and spun him around. "When I talk to you, *face me!*" Warneke roared.

As the big hand spun him around Ward McQueen threw a roundhouse right to the chin that knocked the big man floundering against the post of the overhang. Instantly, Ward moved in, driving a wicked right to the body and then swinging both hands to the head.

The man went to his knees and McQueen stepped back. Then, as if realizing for the first time that he had been struck, Warneke came off the walk with a lunge. He swung his right but Ward went inside, punching with both hands. The big man soaked up punishment like a sponge takes water, and he came back, punching with remarkable speed for such a big man.

A blow caught McQueen on the jaw and he crashed against the side of the store, his head ringing. Warneke followed up on the punch, but he was too eager for the kill and missed.

A crowd had gathered and the air was filled with shouted encouragement to one or the other. Ward's shirt was torn and when he stepped back to let Warneke get up again his breath was coming in great gasps. The sheer power and strength of the big man was amazing. He had never hit a man so hard and had him still coming.

McQueen, no stranger to rough-and-tumble fighting, moved in, circling a little. Warneke, cautious now, was aware he was in a fight. Before, his battles had always ended quickly; this was different. McQueen stabbed a left to the mouth, feinted, and did it again. He feinted again, but this time he whipped a looping uppercut to the body that made Warneke's mouth fall open. The big man swung a ponderous blow that fell short and McQueen circled him warily. The speed was gone from the Bear Canyon man now, and McQueen only sought a quick way to end it.

McQueen, oblivious to the crowd, moved in warily. Warneke, hurt though he was, was as dangerous as a cornered grizzly. McQueen's greatest advantage had been that Warneke had been used to quick victories and had not expected anything like what had happened. Also, McQueen had landed the first blow and followed it up before the bigger man could get set. He stalked him now, and then feinted suddenly and threw a high hard one to the chin. Warneke was coming in when the blow landed. For an instant he stiffened, and then fell forward to the walk and lay still.

McQueen stepped back to the wall and let his eyes sweep

the faces of the crowd. For the first time he saw Sartain standing in front of the store, his thumbs hooked in his belt, watching the people gathered about.

Nearest the porch was a tall man in a gray suit, a man he had observed before when he first rode into town.

"That was quite a scrap," said the man in gray. "My congratulations. If there is ever anything I can do, just come to me. My name is Ren Oliver."

"Thanks."

Ward McQueen picked up his fallen hat and then tentatively he worked his fingers. Nothing was broken but his hands were stiff and sore from the pounding. He gave Sartain a half smile. "Looks like we've picked a tough job. That was a Bear Canyon nester!"

"Yeah." Kim gave him a wry look. "Wonder who put him up to it?"

"You think it was planned?"

"Think about it. You've made no decision on Bear Canyon. You ain't even seen the place or its people, but he had the idea you were going to run them off. And how did he know where you were and who you were? I think somebody pointed you out."

"That's only if somebody has it in for him, or for us."

Sartain's smile was cynical. "You don't think they have? You should have seen how green Webb turned when you said you had title to the Firebox. If the sheriff hadn't been there he'd have tried to kill you.

"And why was the sheriff there? That's another thing we'd better find out."

McQueen nodded. "You're right, Kim. While you're around, keep your eyes and ears open for a man named Bemis. You won't see him, I think, but find out what you can about him."

"Bemis? What do you know about him?"

"Darned little." McQueen touched his cheek with gentle fingers where a large red, raw spot had resulted from Warneke's fist. "Only he ain't around, and he should be."

Sartain walked off down the street and the crowd drifted slowly away, reluctant to leave the scene. McQueen hitched his guns into place and straightened his clothes. He glanced around and saw a sign, Clarity's Store.

The girl had come back into her doorway, and he glanced at her. "Are you Clarity?"

"I am. The first name is Sharon. Did they call you McQueen?"

"They did. And the first name is Ward."

He stepped into the store, anxious to get away from the curious eyes. The store was more sparsely stocked than Hutch's much larger store, but the stock gave evidence of careful selection and a discriminating taste. There were many things a western store did not normally stock.

"I have a washbasin," she suggested. "I think you'd better take a look at yourself in a mirror."

"I will," he said, grinning a little, "but I'd rather not." He glanced around again. "Do you stock shirts by any chance? Man-size shirts?"

She looked at him critically. "I do, and I believe I have one that would fit you."

She indicated the door to the washbasin and then went among the stacks of goods on the shelves behind the counter.

A glance in the mirror and he saw what she meant. His face was battered and bloody, his hair mussed. He could do little about the battered but the blood he could wash away, and he did so. The back door opened on a small area surrounded by a high fence. It was shaded by several old elms and a cottonwood or two, and in the less shaded part there were flowers. He washed his face, holding compresses on his swollen cheekbones and lip. Then he combed his hair.

Sharon Clarity came with a shirt. It was a dark blue shirt with two pockets. He stripped off the rags of his other shirt and donned the new one and dusted off his hat.

She gave him a quick look and a smile when he emerged, saying, "It's an improvement, anyway." She folded some other shirts and returned them to the shelves.

He paid for the shirt she had provided, and she said, "You know what you've done, don't you? You've whipped the toughest man in Bear Canyon. Whipped him in a standup fight. Nobody has ever done that, and nobody has even come close. Nobody has even tried for a long time."

She paused, frowning a little. "It puzzles me a little. Warneke isn't usually quarrelsome. That's the first time I ever saw him start a fight."

"Somebody may have given him an idea. I hadn't had time to even think about Bear Canyon. I haven't even ridden over the ranch, and yet he had the idea we were about to run them off."

She looked at him appraisingly, having grown up with four brawling brothers she knew something about men. This one had fought coolly, skillfully. "You've started something you know. That Bear Canyon outfit is tough. Even Neal Webb's boys fight shy of them."

"Webb has a tough outfit?"

"You've seen some of them. There are two or three known killers in the bunch. Why he keeps them, I couldn't say."

"Like Bemis, for example?"

"You know Harve Bemis? He's one of them, but not the worst by a long shot. The worst ones are Overlin and Bine."

These were names he knew. Bine he had never seen, but he knew a good deal about him, as did any cattleman along the border country of Texas. An occasional outlaw and suspected rustler, he had run with the Youngers in Missouri before riding south to Texas.

Overlin was a Montana gunhand known around Bannock and Alder Gulch, but he had ridden the cattle trails from Texas several times and was a skilled cowhand, as well. McQueen had seen him in Abilene and at Doan's Crossing. On that occasion he himself had killed an outlaw who was trying to cut the herd with which McQueen was riding. The fact that such men rode with Webb made the situation serious.

He purchased several items and then hired a man with a wagon to freight the stuff to the Firebox. Kim Sartain was loitering in front of the saloon when McQueen came down to get his horse.

"Bemis ain't around," he confided, "an' it's got folks wonderin' because he usually plays poker at the Bat Cave Saloon.

Nobody's seen him around for several days." He paused. "I didn't ask. I just listened."

FOR THREE DAYS the Firebox was unmolested, and in those three days much was accomplished. The shake roof needed fixing, and some fences had to be repaired. Baldy had that job and when he finished he stood back and looked it over with satisfaction. "Bud, that there's an elephant-proof fence."

"Elephant proof? You mean an elephant couldn't get past that fence? You're off your trail!"

"Of course it's elephant proof. You don't see any elephants in there, do you?"

Bud Fox just looked at him and rode away.

All hands were in the saddle from ten to twelve hours a day. The cattle were more numerous than expected, especially the younger stuff. Several times McQueen cut trails made by groups of riders, most of them several days old. Late on the afternoon of the third day he rode down the steep slope to the bottom of a small canyon near the eastern end of the Dillons and found blood on the grass.

The stain was old and dark but unmistakably blood. He walked his horse around, looking for sign. He found a leaf with blood on it, then another. The blood had come from someone riding a horse, a horse that toed in slightly. Following the trail he came to where several other horsemen had joined the wounded man. One of the other horses was obviously a led horse.

Men had been wounded in the fight with McCracken. Could these be the same? If so, where were they going? He rode on over the Dillons and off what was accepted as Firebox range. He had crossed a saddle to get into this narrow canyon, but further along it seemed to open into a wider one. He pushed on, his Winchester in his hands.

The buckskin he rode was a mountain horse accustomed to rough travel. Moreover, it was fast and had stamina, the sort of horse a man needed when riding into trouble. The country into which he now ventured was unknown to him, wild and rough. The canyon down which he rode opened into a wider valley that tightened up into another deep, narrow canyon.

Before him was a small stream. The riders had turned down canyon.

It was dusk and shadows gathered in the canyons, only a faint red glow from the setting sun crested the rim of the canyon. Towering black walls lifted about him, and on the rocky edge across the way a dead, lightning-blasted pine pointed a warning finger from the cliff. The narrow valley was deep, and the only sound other than from the stream was a faint rustling. Then wind sighed in the junipers and the buckskin stopped, head up, ears pricked.

"Ssh!" he whispered, putting a warning hand on the buckskin's neck. "Take it easy, boy. Take it easy now."

The horse stepped forward, seeming almost to walk on tiptoe. This was the Box, one of the deepest canyons in the area. McCracken had spoken of it during their discussions that led to his sale of the ranch.

Suddenly he glimpsed a faint light on the rock wall. Speaking softly to the buckskin he slid from the saddle, leaving his rifle in the scabbard.

Careful to allow no jingle of spurs he felt his way along the sandy bottom. Rounding a shoulder of rock he saw a small campfire and the moving shadow of a man in a wide hat. Crouching near a bush he saw that shadow replaced by another, a man with a bald head.

In the silence of the canyon, where sounds were magnified, he heard a voice. "Feelin' better, Bemis? We'll make it to Dry Leggett tomorrow."

The reply was huskier, the tone complaining. "What's the boss keepin' us so far away for? Why didn't he have us to the Runnin' W? This hole I got in me is no joke."

"You got to stay under cover. We're not even suspected, an' we won't be if we play it smart."

His eyes picked out three men lying near the fire, one with a bandaged head. One of those who was on his feet was preparing a meal. From the distance he could just make out their faces, the shape of their shoulders, and of the two on their feet, the way they moved. Soon he might be fighting these men, and he wanted to know them on sight. The man in the wide hat turned suddenly toward him.

Hansen Bine!

Never before had he seen the man but the grapevine of the trails carried accurate descriptions of such men and of places as well. Gunfighters were much discussed, more than prize-fighters or baseball players, even more than racehorses or buckers.

Bine was known for his lean, wiry body, the white scar on his chin, and his unnaturally long, thin fingers.

"What's the matter, Bine?" Bemis asked.

"Somethin' around. I can feel it."

"Cat, maybe. Lots of big ones in these canyons. I saw one fightin' a bear, one time. A black bear. No lion in his right mind would tackle a grizzly."

Bine looked again into the night and then crossed to the fire and seated himself. "Who d'you reckon those riders were who went to the cabin after we left? I saw them headed right for it."

"The boss, maybe. He was supposed to show up with the sheriff."

There was silence except for the crackling of the fire, only barely discernible at the distance. The flames played shadow games on the rock wall. Then Bemis spoke, "I don't like it, Hans. I don't like it at all. I been shot before, but this one's bad. I need some care. I need a doctor."

"Take it easy, Bemis. You'll get there, all in good time."

"I don't like it. Sure, he doesn't want nobody to know, but I don't want to die, either."

Talk died down as the men sat up to eat, and Ward drew care-fully back and walked across the sand to his horse. He swung into the saddle and turned the animal, but as the buckskin lined out to go back along the canyon its hoof clicked on stone!

He had believed himself far enough away not to be heard, but from behind him he heard a startled exclamation, and Ward put the horse into a lope in the darkness. From behind him there was a challenge and then a rifle shot, but he was not worried. The shot would have been fired on chance, as

Ward knew he could not be seen and there was no straight shot possible in the canyon.

He rode swiftly, so swiftly that he realized he had missed his turn and was following a route up a canyon strange to him. The bulk of the Dillons arose on his right instead of ahead or on his left as they should be. By the stars he could see that the canyon up which he now rode was running east and west and he was headed west. Behind him he heard sounds of pursuit but doubted they would follow far.

The riding was dangerous, as the canyon was a litter of boulders and the trunks of dead trees. A branch canyon opened and he rode into it, his face into a light wind. He heard no further sounds of pursuit and was pleased, wanting no gun battle in these narrow, rock-filled canyons where a ricochet could so easily kill or wound a man. He saw the vague gleam of water and rode his horse into a small mountain stream. Following the stream for what he guessed was close to a mile, he found his way out of the stream to a rocky shelf. A long time later he came upon a trail and the shape of some mountains he recognized.

As he rode he considered what he had heard. Harve Bemis, as he suspected, had been one of those who attacked Jimmy McCracken. More than likely Bine had been there as well. That, even without what else he knew of Neal Webb, placed the attack squarely on Webb's shoulders.

With Jimmy McCracken slain and a forged bill of sale, Webb would have been sure nothing could block his claim to the Firebox range.

So what would he do now? Relinquish his attempt to seize the Firebox and let the killing go for nothing? All McQueen's experience told him otherwise. Webb would seek some other way to advance his claim, and he would seek every opportunity to blacken the reputation of the Tumbling K riders.

The men he had seen in the canyon were headed for Dry Leggett. Where was that? What was it? That he must find out, also he must have a talk with Sheriff Bill Foster.

Ruth Kermitt would not like this. She did not like trouble, and yet those who worked for her always seemed to be fighting to protect her interests. Of late she had refused to admit there might be occasions when fighting could not be avoided. She had yet to learn that in order to have peace both sides must want it equally. One side cannot make peace; they can only surrender.

He had been in love with Ruth since their first meeting, and they had talked of marriage. Several times they had been on the verge of it but something always intervened. Was it altogether accident? Or was one or both of them hesitating?

He shook such thoughts from his head. This was no time for personal considerations. He was a ranch foreman with a job to do, a job that might prove both difficult and dangerous. He must put the Firebox on a paying basis.

Their Nevada ranch was still the home ranch, but Ruth had bought land in other states, in Arizona and New Mexico as well as Utah, and she had traded profitably in cattle. One of the reasons for his hesitation, if he was hesitating, was because Ruth Kermitt was so wealthy. He himself had done much to create that wealth and to keep what she had gained. From the time when he had saved her herd in Nevada he had worked untiringly. He knew cattle, horses, and men. He also knew range conditions. The Tumbling K range fattened hundreds of white-faced cattle. The Firebox, further south and subject to different weather conditions, could provide a cushion against disaster on the northern range she had bought, on his advice, for a bargain price. Old Tom and young Jimmy had planned to return to a property they owned in Wyoming. As Tom had known Ruth's father, he offered her a first chance.

On Ward's advice she had purchased land around water holes, ensuring her of water so they would control much more land than they owned.

It was almost daybreak when McQueen rolled into his bunk in the Firebox bunkhouse. Sartain opened an eye and glanced at him curiously. Then he went back to sleep. Kim asked no questions and offered no comments but missed little.

BALDY JACKSON WAS putting breakfast together when McQueen awakened. He sat up on his bunk and called out to

Baldy in the next room. "Better get busy and muck this place out," Ward suggested. "Ruth—Miss Kermitt—may be down before long."

"Ain't I got enough to do? Cookin' for you hungry coyotes, buildin' fence, an' mixin' 'dobe? This place is good enough for a bunch of thistle-chinned cowhands."

"You heard me," McQueen said cheerfully. "And while you're at it, pick out a cabin site for the boss. One with a view. She will want a place of her own."

"Better set up an' eat. You missed your supper."

"Where's the boys? Aren't they eating?"

"They et an' cleared out hours ago." Baldy glanced at him. "What happened last night? Run into somethin'?"

"Yes, I did." He splashed water on his face and hands. "I came upon a camp of five men, three of them wounded. They were headed for a place called Dry Leggett."

"Canyon west of the Plaza."

"Plaza?"

"Kind of settlement, mostly Mexicans. Good people. A few 'dobes, a couple of stores, and a saloon or two."

"How well do you know this country, Baldy?"

Jackson gave him a wry look. "Pretty well. I punched cows for the S U south of here, and rode into the Plaza more times than I can recall. Been over around Socorro. Back in the old days I used to hole up back in the hills from time to time."

Baldy was a good cowhand and a good cook, but in his younger years he had ridden the outlaw trail until time brought wisdom. Too many of his old pals had wound up at the end of a rope.

"Maybe you can tell me where I was last night. I think I was over around what they used to call the Box." He described the country and Baldy listened, sipping coffee. "Uh-huh," he said finally, "that canyon you hit after crossing the Dillons must have been Devil. You probably found them holed up in the Box or right below it. Leavin', you must have missed Devil Canyon and wound up on the south fork of the 'Frisco. Then you come up the trail along the Centerfire and home."

Racing hoofs interrupted. McQueen put down his cup as Bud Fox came through the door.

"Ward, that herd we gathered in Turkey Park is gone! Sartain trailed 'em toward Apache Mountain!"

"Wait'll I get my horse." Baldy jerked off his apron.

"You stay here!" McQueen told him. "Get down that Sharps an' be ready. Somebody may have done this just to get us away from the cabin. Anyway, I've a good idea who is responsible."

Riding swiftly, Fox led him to the tracks. Kim Sartain had followed after the herd. The trail skirted a deep canyon, following an intermittent stream into the bed of the Apache, and then crossed the creek into the rough country beyond.

Suddenly McQueen drew up, listening. Ahead of them they heard cattle lowing. Kim came down from the rocks.

"Right up ahead. Four of the wildest, roughest-lookin' hands I've seen in years."

"Let's go," McQueen said. Touching spurs to his horse as he plunged through the brush and hit the flat land at a dead run with the other two riders spreading wide behind him. The movements of the cattle killed the sound of their charge until they were almost up to the herd. Then one of the rustlers turned and slapped a hand for his six-shooter. McQueen's gun leaped to his hand and he chopped it down, firing as it came level. The rush of his horse was too fast for accurate shooting and his bullet clipped the outlaw's horse across the back of the neck. It dropped in its tracks, spilling its rider. Ward charged into him, knocking him sprawling, almost under the hoofs of the buckskin.

Swinging wide McQueen saw that Sartain had downed his man, but the other two were converging on Bud Fox. Both swung away when they saw Kim and McQueen closing in. One of them swung a gun on Kim and Kim's gun roared. The man toppled from the saddle and the last man quickly lifted his hands.

He was a thin, hard-featured man with narrow, cruel eyes. His hair was uncut, his jaws unshaved. His clothing was ragged. There was nothing wrong with his gun, it was new and well kept.

Now his face, despite its hardness, wore a look of shock. His eyes went from McQueen to Sartain to Fox. "You boys shoot mighty straight but you'll wish you never seen the day!"

Fox took his rope from the saddle tree. "He's a rustler, Ward, caught in the act, an' there's plenty of good trees."

"Now, look!" The man protested, suddenly frightened.

"What gave you the idea you could run off our stock?" Ward asked.

"Nothin'. The stock was in good shape." He looked suddenly at McQueen, who still wore the marks of battle. "You're the gent who whipped Flagg! He'll kill you for that, if not for this. You won't live a week."

"Bud, tie this man to his saddle an' tie him tight. We'll take him into town for the law to handle. Then we'll visit Bear Canyon."

"You'll do *what*?" their prisoner sneered. "Why, you fool! Flagg will kill you! The whole bunch will!"

"No," Ward assured him, "they will not. If they'd left my stock alone they could have stayed. Now they will get out or be burned out. That's the message I'm taking to them."

"Wait a minute." The man's eyes were restless. Suddenly his arrogance was gone and he was almost pleading. "Lay off Bear Canyon! This was none o' their doin', anyway."

"You're talking," Ward said, and waited.

"Neal Webb put us up to it. Promised us fifteen bucks a head for every bit of your stock we throwed into the Sand Flats beyond Apache."

"Will you say that to a judge?"

His face paled. "If you'll protect me. That Webb outfit, they kill too easy to suit me."

———

WHEN THEY RODE down the street of Pelona to the sheriff's office the town sprawled lazy in the sunshine. By the time they reached the sheriff's office nearly fifty men had crowded around. Foster met them at the door, his shrewd old eyes going from McQueen to the rustler.

"Well, Chalk Warneke," he spat, "looks like you run into

the wrong crowd." His eyes shifted to McQueen. "What's he done?"

"Rustled a herd of Firebox stock. He related to Flagg?"

The sheriff nodded. "Brother. Was it him alone?"

"There were four of them. The other three were in no shape to bring back. They won't be talkin'. This one will."

A man at the edge of the crowd turned swiftly and hurried away. McQueen's eyes followed him. He went up the walk to the Emporium. A moment later Ren Oliver emerged and started toward them.

"Who were the others, Chalk? Were they from Bear Canyon?"

"Only me." Chalk's eyes were haunted. "Let's get inside!"

"Hang him!" somebody yelled. "Hang the rustler!"

The voice was loud. Another took it up, then still another. McQueen turned to see who was shouting. Somebody else shouted, "Why waste time? *Shoot him!*"

The shot came simultaneously with the words, and Ward McQueen saw the prisoner fall, a hole between his eyes.

"Who did that?" Ward's contempt and anger were obvious. "Anybody who would shoot an unarmed man with his hands tied is too low-down to live."

The crowd stirred but nobody even looked around. Those who might know were too frightened to speak. On the edge of the crowd Ren Oliver stood with several others who had drawn together. "I didn't see anybody fire, McQueen, but wasn't the man a rustler? Hasn't the state been saved a trial?"

"He was also a witness who was ready to testify that Neal Webb put him up to the rustlin' and was payin' for the cattle!"

Startled, people in the crowd began to back away, and from the fringes of the crowd they began to disappear into stores or up and down the street. There seemed to be no Webb riders present, but Kim Sartain, sitting his horse back from the crowd, a hand on his gun butt, was watching. He had come up too late to see the shooting.

"Webb won't like that, McQueen," Ren Oliver said. "I speak only from friendship."

"Webb knows where to find me. And tell him this time it won't be a kid he's killing!"

Sheriff Foster chewed on the stub of his cigar. His blue eyes had been watchful. "That's some charge you've made, McQueen. Can you back it up?"

Ward indicated the dead man. "There's my witness. He told me Webb put him up to it, and that Bear Canyon wasn't involved. As for the rest of it—"

He repeated the story of the tracks he had followed, of the men holed up in the Box.

"You think they went on to Dry Leggett?" Foster asked.

"That was what I heard them say, but they might have changed their minds. Bemis was among the wounded and he was worried. He had a bad wound and wanted care." Then he added, "Bine did most of the talking."

Ward McQueen tied his horse in front of Sharon Clarity's store, where there was shade. With Sartain at his side he crossed to the Bat Cave.

The saloon was a long, rather narrow room with a potbellied stove at either end and a bar that extended two-thirds the room's length. There were a roulette table and several card tables.

A hard-eyed, baldheaded bartender leaned thick forearms on the bar, and three men loafed there, each with a drink. At the tables several men played cards. They glanced up as the Tumbling K men entered, then resumed their game.

McQueen ordered two beers and glanced at Ren Oliver, who sat in one of the card games. Had Oliver been only a bystander? Or had he fired the shot that killed Chalk?

Oliver glanced up and smiled. "Care to join our game?"

McQueen shook his head. He would have enjoyed playing cards with Oliver, for there are few better ways to study a man than to play cards with him. Yet he was in no mood for cards, and he hadn't the time. He had started something with his comments about Webb. Now he had to prove his case.

He finished his beer and then, followed by Sartain, he returned to the street. Ren Oliver watched them go, then cashed in and left the game. When he entered the Emporium, Hutch glared at him.

"Get rid of him!" Hutch said. "Get rid of him now!"

Oliver nodded. "Got any ideas?"

Hutch's eyes were mean. "You'd botch the job. Leave it to me!"

"You?" Oliver was incredulous.

Hutch looked at him over his steel-rimmed glasses. Ren Oliver, who had known many hard men, remembered only one such pair of eyes. They were the eyes of a big swamp rattler he had killed as a boy. He remembered how those eyes had stared into his. He felt a chill.

"To me," Hutch repeated.

It was dark when Ward McQueen, trailed by Kim and Bud Fox, reached the scattered, makeshift cabins in Bear Canyon. It was a small settlement, and he had heard much about it in the short time he had been around. The few women were hard-eyed slatterns as tough as their men. Rumor had it they lived by rustling and horse thieving or worse.

"Bud," McQueen said, "stay with the horses. When we leave we may have to leave fast. Be ready, and when you hear me yell, come a-runnin'!"

Followed by Kim he walked toward the long bunkhouse that housed most of the men. Peering through a window he saw but two men, one playing solitaire, the other mending a belt. The room was lighted by lanterns. Nearby was another house, and peering in they saw a short bar and a half dozen men sitting around. One of them was Flagg Warneke.

Ward McQueen stepped to the door and opened it. He stepped in, Kim following, moving quickly left against the log wall.

Flagg saw them first. He was tipped back in his chair and he let the legs down carefully, poised for trouble.

"What d' you want?" he demanded. "What're you doin' here?"

All eyes were on them. Two men, four guns, against six men and eight guns. There were others around town.

"This mornin' Chalk and some other riders ran off some of our cows. We had trouble and three men got killed. I told Chalk if he told me who was involved I'd not ride down here.

He didn't much want me to come to Bear Canyon, and to tell you the truth, I hadn't been plannin' on coming down here.

"Chalk started to talk, and somebody killed him."

"*Killed* him? Killed Chalk? Who did it?"

"You make your own guess. Who was afraid of what he might say? Who stood to lose if he did talk?"

They absorbed this in silence and then a fat-faced man at the end of the table spoke. "Those fellers with Chalk? You say you killed them?"

"They chose to fight."

"How many did you lose?"

"We lost nobody. There were three of us, four of them. They just didn't make out so good."

"What're you here for?" Flagg demanded.

"Two things. To see if you have any idea about who killed Chalk and to give you some advice. *Stay away from Firebox cattle!*"

Silence hung heavy in the room. Flagg's face was still swollen from the beating he had taken and the cuts had only begun to heal. His eyes were hard as he stared at McQueen.

"We'll figure out our own answers to the first question. As to the second, we've no use for Firebox cows. As for you and that feller with you—*get out!*"

McQueen made no move. "Remember, friend, Bear Canyon is on Firebox range. What you may not know is that Firebox *owns* that land, every inch of it. You stay if the Firebox lets you, and right now the Firebox is *me!* Behave yourselves and you'll not be bothered, but next time there will be no warning. We'll come with guns and fire!"

He reached for the latch with his left hand, and as the door opened, Flagg said, "I put my mark on you, anyway!"

McQueen laughed. "And you're wearing some of mine. Regardless of how things work out, Flagg, it was a good fight and you're a tough man to whip!"

He opened the door and Kim Sartain stepped out and quickly away. He followed.

Yet they had taken no more than three steps when the door burst open and the fat-faced man lunged out, holding a shotgun in both hands. He threw the shotgun to his shoulder. As one man, Ward and Kim drew and fired. The fat-faced man's shotgun sagged in his hands and he backed up slowly and sat down.

Men rushed from the bunkhouse and Kim shot a man with a buffalo gun. Ward shot through the open door at the hanging lantern. It fell, spewing oil and flame. In an instant the room was afire.

Men and women rushed from the other buildings and the two backed to their horses, where Bud awaited them on the rim of the firelight.

Several men grabbed a heavy wagon by the tongue and wheeled it away from the fire. Others got behind to shove. Of Flagg, McQueen saw nothing.

As the three rode away, they glanced back at the mounting flames. The saloon was on fire, as well as the bunkhouse.

"Think this will move them out?" Kim asked.

"I've no idea. I'm no hand for this sort of thing. Not burning folks out. They'd no right there, and that's deeded land, as I told him. They may have believed it to be government land. If they'd acted half decent I'd have paid them no mind."

"There's no good in that crowd," Kim said.

"Maybe not, but Flagg fought a good fight. He had me worried there, for a spell."

"He didn't get into this fight."

"No, and I think he'd have acted all right. I think he has judgment, which I can't say for that fat-faced gent. He just went hog-wild."

Baldy Jackson was pacing the yard and muttering when they rode in. "Durn it all! You fellers ride away with your shootin' irons on. Then we hear nothin' of you! Where've you been?"

"What do you mean 'we'?" Kim said. "Since when have you become more than one?"

"He was including me, I think." Sharon Clarity got up from the chair where she had been sitting, "But I've only been here a few minutes. I came to warn you."

"To warn us?"

"To warn you, Mr. McQueen. Sheriff Foster is coming for you. He will arrest you for killing Neal Webb."

"For *what*?" Ward swung down from his horse and trailed the reins. "What happened to Webb?"

"He was found dead on the trail not fifteen minutes after you left town. He had been shot in the back."

Neal Webb killed! Ward McQueen sat down in one of the porch chairs. By whom, and for what?

Ward McQueen knew what western men thought of a back shooter. That was a hanging offense before any jury one could get, but more often a lynch mob would handle such cases before the law got around to it.

Kim Sartain had been with him, but he would be considered a prejudiced witness.

"Pour me some coffee, Baldy," he suggested. He glanced over at Sharon Clarity. "And thanks." He hesitated. "I hope your riding to warn me won't make enemies for you."

"Nobody knew," she replied cheerfully. "Anyway, I think you and the Tumbling K are good for this country. Things were getting kind of one-sided around here."

"Neal Webb killed?" Ward mused. "I wonder what that means? I'd sort of thought he was behind all the trouble, but this makes me wonder."

"It does, doesn't it?" Sharon said. "Almost as if he was killed purely to implicate you."

He glanced at her. "That's a shrewd observation. Any idea who would want to do a thing like that? After all, my trouble was with Webb."

She did not reply. She got to her feet. "My father used to box," she said. "Back in the old country he was considered quite good. They had a rule in boxing. I've heard him quote it. It was 'protect yourself at all times.'"

"I am going back to town, but I think you should be very, very careful. And you'd better go. Foster will have about thirty riders in that posse. You'd better start moving."

"I've done nothing. I shall wait for them to come."

She went to her horse. "When you get thirty men together," Sharon said, "you get all kinds. You have to consider their motives, Mr. McQueen."

"Kim, ride along with Miss Clarity, will you? See that she gets safely home."

"Yes, *sir!*" Kim had been tired. Suddenly he was no longer so. "But what about that posse?"

"There'll be no trouble. Take good care of Miss Clarity. She is a very bright young woman."

IN PELONA, OLIVER went to the Bat Cave and seated himself at the card table. The saloon was empty save for himself and the bartender, a man with whom he was not particularly friendly, but the cards were there and he gathered them up and began to shuffle. He always thought better with cards in his hands. He carefully laid out a game of solitaire, but his mind was not on the cards.

He was both puzzled and worried. For some years now he had considered himself both an astute and a wise young man. He made his living with his adept fingers and his skill at outguessing men with cards. He knew all the methods of cheating and was a skilled card mechanic, but he rarely used such methods. He had a great memory for cards and the odds against filling any hand. He won consistently without resorting to questionable methods. He rarely won big. The showoff sort of thing that attracted attention he did not want. He played every day, and when he lost it was only small amounts. The sums he won were slightly larger. Sometimes he merely broke even, but over the months he was a clear and distinct winner. At a time when a cowhand was pulling down thirty to forty dollars a month, and a clerk in a store might work for as little as half that, Ren Oliver could pull down two hundred to two hundred and fifty dollars without attracting undue attention. When a professional gambler starts winning big pots he becomes suspect.

Even Hutch did not realize how well he was doing, and Hutch was providing him with a small income for rendering various services not to be discussed. Over the past year Ren Oliver had built up a nice road stake, something to take with him when he left, for he was well aware that few things last, and many difficulties could be avoided by forming no lasting attachments and keeping a fast horse.

Now Ren Oliver was disturbed. Neal Webb had been

killed. By whom was a question, but an even larger question was why.

It disturbed him that he did not know. The obvious answer was that he had been killed by Ward McQueen, but Oliver did not buy that, not for a minute. McQueen might kill Webb in a gun battle but he would not shoot him in the back.

Moreover, there had been no confrontation between them. The other answer was that Neal had outlived his usefulness and was killed to implicate McQueen.

But who had actually killed him?

It disturbed Oliver that he did not know. Obviously, Hutch was behind it. Had he done the killing? One by one he considered the various men available and could place none of them in the right position. This worried him for another reason. He had considered himself close to Hutch, yet he now realized that, like Webb when he ceased to be useful, he might be killed. He was merely a pawn in another man's game.

For a man of Oliver's disposition and inclinations it was not a pleasant thought. He did not mind others believing he was a pawn, but he wished to be in control so he could use those who believed they were using him. Now he had the uncomfortable sensation that too much was happening of which he was not aware and that any moment he might be sacrificed.

He had no illusions about himself. He was without scruples. It was his attitude that human life was cheap, and like most men engaged in crime he regarded people as sheep to be sheared. He was cold and callous and had always been so.

Outwardly he was friendly and ingratiating. He went out of his way to do favors for people even while holding them in contempt. You never knew when such people might appear on a jury. For the same reason he had allied himself with Hutch.

It was unsettling to realize there was someone more cunning than he himself. He knew Hutch was hunching over his community like a huge spider of insatiable appetite. Within that community he was considered to be something of a skinflint but nothing more. Men came and went from his store because, after all, it was the town's leading emporium, as its name implied. That all those people might not be buying was not considered. Oliver believed Hutch hired his killing done, but whom did he hire?

Bine, of course, but who else? When Oliver looked over his shoulder he wanted to know who he was looking for. The fact that there was an unsuspected actor in the play worried him.

He had the uncomfortable feeling that Neal Webb had been killed not only to implicate McQueen but to serve as a warning to him and perhaps to others. A warning that nobody was indispensable.

Oliver shuffled the cards again, ran up a couple of hands with swiftness and skill, then dealt them, taking several off the bottom with smoothness and ease, yet his mind was roving and alert.

Would Hutch manage it? He had never yet, so far as Oliver knew, encountered such a man as McQueen. Not that Oliver had any great opinion of McQueen. He was typically a cowman, honest, tough, and hardworking. That he was good with a gun was obvious, and that segundo of his, Kim Sartain, was probably almost as good.

Did McQueen have brains? How would he fare against Hutch, particularly when, as Oliver believed, McQueen did not know who his enemy was?

Hutch had planted the Webb killing squarely on McQueen. The timing had been good and there would be witnesses, Oliver was sure. Trust the old man for that.

He watched Sheriff Foster leave town with his posse and knew that several of the men in that posse were owned by Hutch. If the slightest excuse was offered they were to shoot to kill. He knew their instructions as if he had heard them himself.

The door opened and a squat, powerful man entered, his hair shaggy and untrimmed. His square, granitelike face was clean shaved. He had gimlet eyes that flickered with a steely glint. He wore two guns, one in a holster, the other thrust into his waistband. This was Overlin, the Montana gunman.

"Where's Foster goin'?"

"After McQueen, for the Webb killing."

"Webb? Is he dead?"

Oliver nodded. "Out on the trail." Overlin could have done it. So could Hansen Bine, but so far as anyone knew Bine was with the wounded men at Dry Leggett. "There's a witness to swear he did it."

"He might have," Overlin commented, "only I don't believe it. I've heard of McQueen. Made quite a reputation along the cattle trails and in the mining camps. He's no bargam."

"He's only one man. Maybe he'll be your dish one day."

"Or yours," Overlin agreed. "Only I'd like him, myself."

Ren Oliver remembered McQueen and said, "You can have him." He could not understand such men as Overlin. The man was good with a gun, but why would he go out of his way to match skills with a man he believed might be just as good? Overlin had to be the best. He had to know he was best, had to have others know he was the best.

Oliver believed he was faster with a gun than either Bine or Overlin but he was a sure-thing man. He had pride in his skill but preferred to take no chances. He would enjoy killing Ward McQueen if he could do so at no risk to himself.

A horse loped into the street, the rider waving at someone out of sight. It was Sharon Clarity. Now where had *she* been?

"See you around," he said to Overlin, and went into the night.

He dug a cigar from his pocket and lighted it. Sharon Clarity's horse had been hard ridden.

———

WARD MCQUEEN WAS working beside Baldy Jackson, building a pole corral, when the sheriff and the posse rode into the ranch yard. McQueen continued to place a pole in position and lash it there with rawhide. Then he glanced around at the posse.

"Howdy, Foster. Looks like you're here on business."

"I've come for you, McQueen. There's witnesses says you shot Neal Webb, shot him in the back."

McQueen kept his hands in sight, moving carefully so as

not to give any false impressions. His eyes caught the slight lift to the muzzle of a Winchester and he eyed the man behind it, staring at him until the man's eyes shifted and he swallowed.

"All you had to do was send for me, Sheriff. I'd have come right in. No need for all this crowd." He paused. "And you know, Sheriff, I'd never shoot any man in the back. What would be the point? Webb was never supposed to be good with a gun, and if I wanted him killed that bad all I'd have to do would be to pick a fight with him in town. Webb's temper had a short fuse, and killin' him would have been no trick."

"That may be so, but you've got to come in with me and answer charges. There will have to be a trial."

"We'll see. Maybe I can prove I was elsewhere."

"By one of your own men?" The man who spoke had a sallow face and buck teeth. "We'd not be likely to believe *them*!"

"By others, then? Kim Sartain was with me, however, and if you believe he's a liar why don't you tell him so?"

"We want no trouble, McQueen. Saddle a horse and come along." Foster's eyes went to the cabin. Was there somebody inside the window?

"I'll come on one condition. That I keep my guns. If I can't keep 'em you'll have to take me and you'll have some empty saddles on your way back to town."

Foster was angry. "Don't give me any trouble, McQueen! I said, saddle your horse!"

"Sheriff, I've no quarrel with you. You're just doing your duty and I want to cooperate, but you've some men riding with you who would like to make a target of my back. Let me keep my guns and I'll go quiet. In case you'd like to know, there are two men behind you with Winchesters. They will be riding along behind us."

Sheriff Foster studied McQueen. Inwardly, he was pleased. This McQueen was a hard case but a good man. Shoot a man in the back? It was preposterous! Especially Neal Webb.

"All right," he said, "saddle up."

"My horse is ready, Foster. A little bird told me you were coming, and my horse has been ready."

It was a black he was riding this day, a good mountain horse with bottom and speed. As he mounted and settled into the saddle he glanced at the man who had lifted his rifle.

"Just so everybody will understand. Two of my boys are going to follow us into town. Either one of them could empty a Winchester into the palm of your hand at three hundred yards."

He sat solidly and well in the saddle, his black Frisco jeans tight over his thighs, his broad chest and shoulders filling the dark gray shirt. His gun belts were studded with silver, the walnut grips worn from use. "All right, Sheriff, let's go to town!"

He rode alongside of Foster, but his thoughts were riding ahead, trying to foresee what would happen in town, and asking himself the question again: Why kill Neal Webb? Who wanted him dead?

He had believed Webb the ringleader, the cause of his troubles. Most ranchers wanted more range, most of them wanted water, so the attempt to seize the Firebox came as no surprise. In fact, he would have been surprised had it not been claimed. Good grass was precious, and whenever anybody moved or died there was always someone ready to move in. The difference here was that McCracken had been a shrewd man and he had purchased the land around the various water holes, as well as the trails into and out of the range he used. The claim on Firebox range by McCracken was well established.

Webb, he was beginning to suspect, had been a mere pawn in the game, and had been disposed of when his usefulness ceased to be. But Webb's dying had implicated Ward McQueen and apparently somebody had decided to have him killed, either in capturing him or in the ride to town. A posse member could shoot him, claiming McQueen had made a move to escape.

Behind this there had to be a shrewd and careful brain. If there were witnesses to something that had not happened, his supposed murder of Neal Webb, then somebody had provided them.

Who? Why?

The Firebox was valuable range. The only other large ranch was Webb's Running W, and who was Webb's heir? Or did he himself own that ranch?

The Bear Canyon crowd? It wasn't their sort of thing. They might dry-gulch him, steal his horses or cattle, or even burn him out, but the Webb killing was more involved. Anyway, Webb had left the Bear Canyon crowd alone.

Would Sharon Clarity know? She was a handsome, self-reliant girl, yet something about her disturbed him. Why had she ridden out to warn him the sheriff was coming? Had she believed he would run?

Who now owned the Running W? This he must discover. If that unknown owner also owned the Firebox he would control all the range around Pelona and the town as well. It made a neat, compact package and a base from which one might move in any direction.

Ruth Kermitt owned the Firebox now, and Ruth had no heirs. Ward McQueen was suddenly glad his boss was not among those present.

Pelona's main street was crowded with rigs and saddle horses when they rode in. Word had spread swiftly, and the people of the range country—the few scattered small ranchers, farmers, and gardeners—had come in, eager for any kind of a show. All had known Neal Webb, at least by sight. Many had not liked him, but he was one of their own. This Ward McQueen was a stranger and, some said, a killer. The general attitude was that he was a bad man.

A few, as always, had misgivings. Their doubts increased when they saw him ride into town sitting his horse beside the sheriff. He was not in irons. He still wore his guns. Evidently Foster trusted him. Western people, accustomed to sizing up a man by his looks, decided he didn't look like somebody who needed to dry-gulch anybody. It was more likely Webb would try to dry-gulch *him*!

Some of those who came to see drifted up between the buildings into the street. Among these was Bud Fox, with his narrow-brimmed gray hat and his long, lean body, looking like an overgrown schoolboy. The pistol on his belt was man-sized, however, and so was the Winchester he carried.

Kim Sartain, young, handsome, and full of deviltry, they recognized at once. They had seen his sort before. There was something about him that always drew a smile, not of amusement but of liking. They knew the guns on his belt were not there for show, but the West had many a young man like him, good cowhands, great riders, always filled with humor. They knew his type. The guns added another dimension, but they understood those, too.

The pattern was quickly made plain. The preliminary hearing was already set and the court was waiting. McQueen glanced at the sheriff. "Looks like a railroading, Foster. Are you in this?"

"No, but I've nothing against the law movin' fast. It usually does around here."

"When who is to get the brunt of it? *Who's* the boss around town, Foster? Especially when they move so fast I have no time to find witnesses."

"You know as much as I do!" Foster was testy. "Move ahead!"

"If I'd been around as long as you have, I'd know plenty!"

The judge was a sour-faced old man whom McQueen had seen about town. Legal procedures on the frontier were inclined to be haphazard, although often they moved not only swiftly but efficiently as well. The old Spanish courts had often functioned very well indeed, but the Anglos were inclined to follow their own procedures. McQueen was surprised to find that the prosecuting attorney, or the man acting as such, was Ren Oliver, said to have practiced law back in Missouri.

Sartain sat down beside McQueen. "They've got you cornered, Ward. Want me to take us out of here?"

"It's a kangaroo court, but let's see what happens. I don't want to appeal to Judge Colt unless we have to."

The first witness was a cowhand Ward had seen riding with Webb's men. He swore he had dropped behind Webb to shoot a wild turkey. He lost the turkey in the brush and was riding to catch up when he heard a shot and saw McQueen duck into the brush. He declared McQueen had fired from behind Webb.

McQueen asked, "You sure it was me?"

"I was sworn in, wasn't I?"

"What time was it?"

"About five o'clock of the evenin'."

"Webb comes from over east of town when he comes to Pelona, doesn't he? From the Runnin' W? And you say you saw me between you an' Webb?"

"I sure did!" The cowboy was emphatic, but he glanced at Oliver, uncertainly.

"Then," McQueen was smiling, "you were lookin' right into the settin' sun when you saw somebody take a shot at Webb? And you were able to recognize me?" As the crowd in the courtroom stirred, McQueen turned to the judge. "Your Honor, I doubt if this man could recognize his own sister under those circumstances. I think he should be given a chance to do it this evenin'. It's nice an' clear like it was the other night and the sun will be settin' before long. I think his evidence should be accepted if he can distinguish four out of five men he knows under the conditions he's talkin' about."

The judge hesitated and Oliver objected.

"Seems fair enough!" A voice spoke from the crowd, and there was a murmured assent.

The judge rapped for silence. "Motion denied! Proceed!"

Behind him McQueen was aware of changing sentiment. Western courtrooms, with some exceptions, were notoriously lax in their procedure, and there were those who had an interest in keeping them so. Crowds, however, were partisan and resentful of authority. The frontier bred freedom, but with it a strong sense of fair play and an impatience with formalities. Most western men wanted to get the matter settled and get back to their work. Most of the men and women present had ridden over that road at that time of the evening, and they saw immediately the point of his argument.

There was a stir behind them, and turning they saw Flagg Werneke shoving his way through the crowd and then down the aisle.

"Judge, I'm a witness! I want to be sworn in!"

The judge's eyes flickered to Oliver, who nodded quickly.

Warneke still bore the marks of McQueen's fists, and his evidence could only be damning.

Warneke was sworn in and took the stand. Kim muttered irritably but Ward waited, watching the big man.

"You have evidence to offer?" the judge asked.

"You bet I have!" Warneke stated violently. "I don't know who killed Neal Webb but I know Ward McQueen didn't do it!"

Ren Oliver's face tightened with anger. He glanced swiftly toward a far corner of the room, a glance that held appeal and something more. McQueen caught the glance and sat a little straighter. The room behind him was seething, and the judge was rapping for order.

"What do you mean by that statement?" Oliver demanded. He advanced threateningly toward Warneke. "Be careful what you say, and remember, *you are under oath*!"

"I remember. McQueen whipped me that evenin', like you all know. He whipped me good but he whipped me fair. Nobody else ever done it or could do it. I was mad as a steer with a busted horn. I figured, all right, he whipped me with his hands but I'd be durned if he could do it with a six-shooter, so I follered him, watchin' my chance. I was goin' to face him, right there in the trail, an' kill him.

" 'Bout the head of Squirrel Springs Canyon I was closin' in on him when a turkey flew up. That there McQueen, he slaps leather and downs that turkey with one shot! You heah me? One shot on the wing, an' he drawed so fast I never seen his hand move!"

Flagg Warneke wiped the sweat from his brow with the back of his hand. "My ma, she never raised any foolish children! Anybody who could draw that fast and shoot that straight was too good for anybody around here, and I wanted no part of him!

"Important thing is, McQueen was never out of my sight from the time he left town headin' west an' away from where Webb was killed until he reached Squirrel Springs Canyon, and that's a rough fifteen miles, the way he rode! It was right at dusk when he shot that turkey, so he never even seen Webb, let alone killed him."

Ren Oliver swore under his breath. The crowd was shifting, many were getting up to leave. He glanced again toward the corner of the room and waited while the judge pounded for order.

Oliver attacked Warneke's testimony but could not shake the man. Finally, angered, he demanded, "Did McQueen pay you to tell this story?"

Warneke's face turned ugly. "*Pay* me? Nobody lives who could pay me for my oath! I've rustled a few head of stock, and so has every man of you in this courtroom if the truth be known! I'd shoot a man if he crossed me, but by the Eternal my oath ain't for sale to no man!

"I got no use for McQueen! He burned us out over in Bear Canyon, he shot friends of mine, but he shot 'em face to face when they were shootin' at him! The man I'd like to find is the one who killed Chalk! Shot him off his horse to keep him from tellin' that Webb put them up to rustlin' Firebox stock!"

Ward McQueen got to his feet. "Judge, I'd like this case to be dismissed. You've no case against me."

The judge looked at Ren Oliver, who shrugged and turned away.

"Dismissed!"

The judge arose from his bench and stepped down off the platform. Ward McQueen turned swiftly and looked toward the corner of the room where Oliver's eyes had been constantly turning. The chair was empty!

People were crowding toward the door. McQueen's eyes searched their faces. Only one turned to look back. It was Silas Hutch.

McQueen pushed his way through the crowd to Flagg Warneke. The big man saw him coming and faced him, eyes hard.

"Warneke," McQueen said, "I'd be proud to shake the hand of an honest man!"

The giant's brow puckered and he hesitated, his eyes searching McQueen's features for some hint of a smirk or a smile. There was none. Slowly the big man put his hand out and they shook.

"What are your plans? I could use a hand on the Firebox."

"I'm a rustler, McQueen. You've heard me admit it. You'd still hire me?"

"You had every reason to lie a few minutes ago, and I think a man who values his word that much would ride for the brand if he took a job. You just tell me you'll play it straight and rustle no more cattle while you're workin' for me and you've got a job."

"You've hired a man, McQueen. And you have my word."

As the big man walked away Sartain asked, "You think he'll stand hitched?"

"He will. Warneke has one thing on which he prides himself. One thing out of his whole shabby, busted-up life that means anything, and that's his word. He'll stick, and we can trust him."

———

TOUGH AS WARD McQueen felt himself to be, when he rode back to the ranch, he was sagging in the saddle. For days he had little sleep and had been eating only occasionally. Now, suddenly, it was hitting him. He was tired, and he was half asleep in the saddle when they rode into the yard at the Tumbling K's Firebox.

Lights in the cabin were ablaze and a buckboard stood near the barn. Stepping down from the saddle he handed the reins to Kim. No words were necessary.

He stepped up on the low porch and opened the door.

Ruth Kermitt stood with her back to the fireplace, where a small fire blazed. Even at this time of the year, at that altitude a fire was needed.

She was tall, with a beautifully slim but rounded body that clothes could only accentuate. Her eyes were large and dark, her hair almost black. She was completely lovely.

"Ward!" She came to him quickly. "You're back!"

"And you're here!" He was pleased but worried also. "You drove all the way from the ranch?"

"McGowan drove. Shorty rode along, too. He said it was to protect me, but I think he had an idea you were in trouble. Naturally, if that were the case Shorty would have to be here."

"Ruth," he told her, "I'm glad to have you here. Glad for me, but I don't think you should have come. There is trouble, and I'm not sure what we've gotten into."

He explained, adding, "You know as well as I do that where there's good grass there will always be somebody who wants it, and what some of them haven't grasped is that we are not moving in on range. We *own* the water holes and the sources of water."

He put his hands on her shoulders. "All that can wait." He drew her to him. His lips stopped hers and he felt her body strain toward him and her lips melt softly against his. He held her there, his lips finding their way to her cheek, her ears, and her throat. After a few minutes she drew back, breathless.

"Ward! Wait!"

He stepped back and she looked up at him. "Ward? Tell me. Has there been trouble? Baldy said you were in court, that you might have to go on trial."

"That part is settled, but there's more to come, I'm afraid."

"Who is it, Ward? What's been happening?"

"That's just the trouble." He was worried. "Ruth, I don't know who it is, and there may be a joker in the deck that I'm not even aware of."

She went to the stove for the coffeepot. "Sit down and tell me about it."

"The ranch is a good one. Excellent grass, good water supply, and if we don't try to graze too heavy we should have good grass for years. McCracken handled it well and he developed some springs, put in a few spreader dams to keep the runoff on the land, but he wanted to sell and I am beginning to understand why."

"What about the trouble? Has it been shooting trouble?"

"It has, but it started before we got here." He told her about the killing of McCracken, then his own brush with rustlers, and the fight with Flagg Warneke and the killing of Warneke's brother before he could talk. And then the killing of Neal Webb.

"Then he wasn't the one?"

"Ruth, I believe Webb had played out his usefulness to

whoever is behind this, who deliberately had Webb killed, with the hope of implicating me. He'd have done it, too, but for Warneke."

"He must be a strange man."

"He's a big man. You'll see him. He's also a violent man, but at heart he's a decent fellow. Some men get off on the wrong foot simply because there doesn't seem any other way to go.

"Without him, I think that Bear Canyon outfit will drift out and move away. I doubt if they will try to rebuild what was destroyed."

"Ward, we've been over this before. I hate all this violence! The fighting, the killing! It's awful! My own brother was killed. But you know all that. It was you who pulled us out of that."

"I don't like it, either, but it is growing less, Ruth, less with each year. The old days are almost gone. What we have here is somebody who is utterly ruthless, someone who has no respect for human life at all. You're inclined to find good in everybody, but in some people there just isn't any.

"Whoever is behind this, and I've a hunch who it is, is someone who is prepared to kill and kill until he has all he wants. He's undoubtedly been successful in the past, which makes it worse.

"No honest man would have such men as Hansen Bine and Overlin around. They did not ride for Webb—we know that now. They ride for whomever it was Webb was fronting for.

"I've got to ride down to Dry Leggett and roust out those wounded men, but you must be careful, Ruth—this man will stop at nothing."

"But I'm a woman!"

"I don't believe that would matter with this man. He's not like a western man."

"Be careful, Ward! I just couldn't stand it if anything happened to you."

As they talked, they had wandered out under the trees, and when they returned to the house only Baldy was awake.

"Wonder folks wouldn't eat their supper 'stead of standin'

around in the dark! A body would think you two wasn't more'n sixteen!"

"Shut up, you old squaw man," Ward said cheerfully, "an' set up the grub! I'm hungry enough to eat even your food."

"Why, Ward!" Ruth protested. "How can you talk like that? You know there isn't a better cook west of the Brazos!"

Baldy perked up. "See? See there? The boss knows a good cook when she sees one! Why you an' these cowhands around here never knowed what good grub was until I came along! You et sowbelly an' half-baked beans so long you wouldn't recognize real vittles when you see 'em!"

A yell interrupted Ward's reply. "Oh, Ward? Ward McQueen!"

Baldy Jackson turned impatiently and opened the door. "What the—!"

A bullet struck him as a gun bellowed in the night, and Baldy spun half around, dropping the coffeepot. Three more shots, fast as a man could lever a rifle, punctured the stillness. The light went out as Ward extinguished it with a quick puff and dropped to the floor, pulling Ruth down with him.

As suddenly as it had begun it ended. In the stillness that followed they heard a hoarse gasping from Baldy. Outside, all was dark and silent except for the pounding of hoofs receding in the distance.

As he turned to relight the lamp, there was another shot, this from down the trail where the rider had gone. Glancing out, Ward saw a flare of fire against the woods.

"Take care of Baldy!" he said, and went out fast.

He grabbed a horse from the corral, slipped on a halter, and went down the trail riding bareback. As he drew near the fire he heard pounding hoofs behind him and slowed up, lifting a hand.

Suddenly he saw a huge man standing in the center of the trail, both hands uplifted so there would be no mistakes.

"McQueen! It's me! I got him!" the man shouted. It was Flagg Warneke.

McQueen swung down, as did Kim Sartain, who had ridden up behind him. A huge pile of grass, dry as tinder, lay in the center of the road, going up in flames. Nearby lay a rider. He was breathing, but there was blood on his shirtfront and blood on the ground.

Warneke said, "I was ridin' to begin work tomorrow and I heard this hombre yell, heard the shot, so I throwed off my bronc, grabbed an armful of this hay McCracken had cut, and throwed it into the road. As this gent came ridin' I dropped a match into the hay. He tried to shoot me, but this here ol' Spencer is quick. He took a .56 right in the chest."

It was the sallow-faced rider Ward had seen before, one of those who had ridden in the posse. "Want to talk?" he asked.

"Go to the devil! Wouldn't if I could!"

"What's that mean? Why couldn't you talk?"

The man raised himself to one elbow, coughing. "Paid me from a holler tree," he said. "I seen nobody. Webb, he told me where I'd get paid an' how I'd—how I'd get word."

The man coughed again and blood trickled over his unshaved chin.

"Maybe it was a woman," he spoke clearly, suddenly. Then his supporting arm seemed to go slack and he fell back, his head striking the ground with a thump. The man was dead.

"A woman?" Ward muttered. "Impossible!"

Warneke shook his head. "Maybe—I ain't so sure. Could be anybody."

When the sun was high over the meadows, Ward McQueen was riding beside Ruth Kermitt near a cienaga, following a creek toward Spur Lake. They had left the ranch after daybreak and had skirted some of the finest grazing land in that part of the country. Some areas that to the uninitiated might have seemed too dry she knew would support and fatten cattle. Much seemingly dry brush was good fodder.

"By the way," Ruth inquired, "have you ever heard of a young man, a very handsome young man named Strahan?

"When I was in Holbrook there was a Pinkerton man there who was inquiring about this man. He is badly wanted, quite a large reward offered. He held up a Santa Fe train, killing a messenger and a passenger. That was about four months ago. Before that he had been seen around this part of the country, as well as in Santa Fe. Apparently he wrecked another train, killing and injuring passengers. Each time he got away he seemed headed for this part of the country."

"Never heard of him," Ward admitted, "but we're newcomers."

"The Pinkerton man said he was a dead shot with either rifle or pistol, and dangerous. They trailed him to Alma once, and lost him again on the Gila, southeast of here."

They rode on, Ward pointing out landmarks that bordered the ranch. "The Firebox has the best range around," he explained. "The Spur Lake country, all the valley of Centerfire, and over east past the Dry Lakes to Apache Creek.

"There's timber, with plenty of shade for the hot months, and most of our range has natural boundaries that prevent stock from straying."

"What about this trouble you're having, Ward? Will it be over soon or hanging over our heads for months?"

"It won't hang on. We're going to have a showdown. I'm taking some of the boys, and we're going to round up some of the troublemakers. I'm just sorry that Baldy is laid up. He knows this country better than any of us."

"You'll have trouble leaving him behind, Ward. That was only a flesh wound, even though he lost blood. It was more shock than anything else."

They turned their horses homeward. Ward looked at the wide, beautiful country beyond Centerfire as they topped the ridge. "All this is yours, Ruth. You're no wife for a cowhand now."

"Now don't start that! We've been over it before! Who made it all possible for me? If you had not come along when you did I'd have nothing! Just nothing at all! And if my brother had not been killed he could not have handled this! Not as you have! He was a fine boy, and no girl ever had a better brother, but he wasn't the cattleman you are.

"And it isn't only that, Ward. You've worked long and you've built my ranch into something worthwhile. At least twice you've protected me when I was about to do something foolish. By rights half of it should belong to you, anyway!"

"Maybe what I should do is leave and start a brand of my own. Then I could come back with something behind me."

"How long would that take, Ward?" She put her hand over his on the pommel. "Please, darling, don't even think about it! The thought of you leaving makes me turn cold all over! I have depended on you, Ward, and you've never failed me."

They rode on in silence. A wild turkey flew up and then vanished in the brush. Ahead of them two deer, feeding early, jumped off into the tall grass and disappeared along the stream.

"Don't you understand? I'm trying to see this your way. You've told me what has to be done and I'm leaving it up to you. I'm not going to interfere. I'm a woman, Ward, and I can't bear to think of you being hurt. Or any of the other boys, for that matter. I'm even more afraid of how all this killing will affect you. I couldn't stand it if you became hard and callous!"

"I know what you mean but there's no need to worry about that now. Once, long ago, maybe. Every time I ride into trouble I hate it, but a man must live and there are those who will ride roughshod over everybody, given a chance. Unfortunately force is the only way some people understand."

When they dismounted at the cabin, she said, "You're riding out tomorrow?"

"Yes."

"Then good luck!" She turned quickly and went into the house.

Ward stared after her, feeling suddenly alone and lost. Yet he knew there was no need for it. This was his woman, and they both understood that. She had come with a considerable investment, but with too little practical knowledge of range or cattle. With his hands, his savvy, and his gun he had built most of what she now possessed.

Under his guidance she had bought cattle in Texas, fattened them on the trail north, sold enough in Kansas to pay back her investment, and driven the remainder further west. Now she controlled extensive range in several states. Alone she never could have done it.

Kim came down from the bunkhouse. "Tomorrow, Ward?"

"Bring plenty of ammunition, both rifle and pistol. I'll want you, Bud Fox, Shorty Jones, and—"

"Baldy? Boss, if you don't take him it'll kill him. Or you'll have to hog-tie him to his bunk, and I'm damned if I'd help you! That ol' catamount's a-rarin' to go, an' he's already scared you're plannin' to leave him behind."

"Think he can stand the ride?"

Kim snorted. "Why, that ol' devil will be sittin' a-saddle when you an' me are pushin' up daisies! He's tougher 'n rawhide an' whalebone."

DAYLIGHT CAME AGAIN as the sun chinned itself on the Continental Divide, peering over the heights of the Tularosas and across the Frisco River. In the bottom of the Box, still deep in shadow, rode a small cavalcade of horsemen. In the lead, his battered old hat tugged down to cover his bald spot from the sun, rode Baldy Jackson.

Behind him, with no talking, rode McQueen, Sartain, Fox, and Jones. They rode with awareness, knowing trouble might explode at any moment. Each man knew what he faced on this day, and once begun there'd be no stopping. It was war now, a war without flags or drums, a grim war to the death.

For some reason Ward found his thoughts returning time and again to Ruth's account of the Pinkerton who was trailing the handsome killer named Strahan. It was a name he could not remember having heard.

He questioned Baldy. "Strahan? Never heard of a youngster by that name, but there was some folks lived hereabouts some years back named that. A bloody mean outfit, too! Four brothers of them! One was a shorty, a slim, little man but mean as pizen. The others were big men. The oldest one got hisself shot by one o' them Lincoln County gunfighters. Jesse Evans it was, or some friend of his.

"Two of the others, or maybe it was only one of them, got themselves hung by a posse somewhere in Colorado. If this here Strahan is one o' them, watch yourselves because he'd be a bad one."

Their route kept the ridge of the Friscos on their left, and when they stopped at Baldy's uplifted hand they were on the edge of a pine-covered basin in the hills.

Ward turned in his saddle and said, "This here's Heifer Basin. It's two miles straight ahead to Dry Leggett. I figure we should take a rest, check our guns, and get set for trouble. If Hansen Bine is down there, this will be war!"

Dismounting, they led their horses into the trees. Baldy located a spring he knew and they sat down beside it. McQueen checked his guns and then slid them back into their holsters. He rarely had to think of reloading, for it was something he did automatically whenever he used a gun.

"Mighty nice up here," Kim commented. "I always did like high country."

"That's what I like about cowboyin'," Shorty Jones commented. "It's the country you do it in."

"You ever rode in west Texas when the dust was blowin'?" Bud wanted to know.

"I have, an' I liked it. I've rid nearly every kind of country you can call to mind."

"Ssh!" Ward McQueen came to his feet in one easy movement. "On your toes! Here they come!"

Into the other end of the basin rode a small group of riders. There were six men, and the last one McQueen recognized as Hansen Bine himself.

Kim Sartain moved off to the right. Baldy rolled over behind a tree trunk and slid his Spencer forward. Jones and Fox scattered in the trees to the left of the spring.

McQueen stepped out into the open. "Bine! We're takin' you in! Drop your gun belts!"

Hansen Bine spurred his horse to the front and dropped from the saddle when no more than fifty paces away. "McQueen, is it? If you're takin' me you got to do it the hard way!"

He went for his gun.

McQueen had expected it, and the flat, hard bark of his pistol was a full beat before Bine's. The bullet struck Bine as his gun was coming up, and he twisted sharply with the impact. Ward walked closer, his gun poised. Around him and behind him he heard the roar of guns, and as Bine fought to bring his gun level McQueen shot again.

Bine fell, dug his fingers into the turf, heaved himself trying to rise, and then fell and lay quiet.

Ward looked around to find only empty saddles and one man standing, his left hand high, his right in a sling.

"Your name?"

"Bemis." The man's face was pale with shock, but he was not afraid. "I did no shooting. Never was no good with my left hand."

"All right, Bemis. You've been trailing with a pack of coyotes, but if you talk you can beat a rope. Who pays you?"

"Bine paid me. Where he got it, I don't know." His eyes sought McQueen's. "You won't believe me but I been wantin' out of this ever since the McCracken shootin'. That was a game kid."

"You helped kill him," McQueen replied coldly. "Who else was in it? Who ran that show?"

"Somebody I'd not seen around before. Young, slight build, but a ring-tailed terror with a gun. He came in with Overlin. Sort of blondish. I never did see him close up. None of us did, 'cept Overlin." Bemis paused again. "Said his name was Strahan."

That name again! The Pinkerton man had been right. Such a man was in this country, hiding out or whatever. Could it be he who was behind this? That did not seem logical. Strahan by all accounts was a holdup man, gunfighter, whatever, not a cattleman or a cautious planner.

"You goin' to hang me?" Bemis demanded. "If you are, get on with it. I don't like waitin' around."

McQueen turned his eyes on Bemis, and the young cowhand stared back, boldly. He was a tough young man, but old in the hard ways of western life.

"You'll hang, all right. If not now, eventually. That's the road you've taken. But as far as I'm concerned that's up to the law. Get on your horse."

The others were mounted, and Bine was lying across a saddle. Kim looked apologetic. "He's the only one, boss. The rest of them lit out like who flung the chunk. I think we winged a couple here or there, but they left like their tails was a-fire."

Kim Sartain looked at Bemis. "Dead or gone, all but this one. Maybe on the way in—you know, boss, it's easier to pack a dead man than a live one."

Bemis looked from Sartain to McQueen and back. "Now, see here!" he said nervously. "I said I didn't know who did the payin', but I ain't blind. Bine an' Overlin, they used to see somebody, or meet somebody, in the Emporium. There or the Bat Cave. They used to go to both places."

"So do half the men in the county," McQueen said. "I've been in both places, myself." He paused. "How about Strahan?"

"Never seen him before—or since."

"Put him on a horse and tie him," McQueen said. "We'll give him to Foster."

WARD LED THE way toward Pelona. There trouble awaited, he knew, and secretly he hoped Foster would be out of town. He wanted no trouble with the old lawman. Foster was a good man in his own way, trying to steer a difficult course in a county where too many men were ready to shoot. Foster was a typical western sheriff, more successful in rounding up rustlers, horse thieves, and casual outlaws than in dealing with an enemy cunning as a prairie wolf and heartless as a lynx.

They rode swiftly down the S U Canyon to the Tularosa, and then across Polk Mesa to Squirrel Springs Canyon. It was hard riding, and the day was drawing to a close when they reached the plains and cut across toward Pelona. They had ridden far and fast, and both men and horses were done in when they walked their horses up the dusty street to the jail.

Foster came to the door to greet them, glancing from McQueen to Bemis.

"What's the matter with him?"

"He rode with the crowd that killed Jimmy McCracken. Jimmy gave him the bad arm. I've brought him in for trial."

"Who led 'em?" Foster demanded of Bemis.

Bemis hesitated, obviously worried. He glanced around to

see who might overhear. "Strahan," he said then. "Bine was in it, too."

Foster's features seemed to age as they watched. For the first time he looked his years.

"Bring him in," Foster said. "Then I'll go after Bine."

"No need to." McQueen jerked his head. "His body's right back there. Look," he added, "we've started a clean up. We'll finish it."

"You're forgettin' something, McQueen! I'm the law. It's my job."

"Hold your horses, Sheriff. You are the law, but Bine is dead. The boys who were with him are on the run, except for Bemis, and we're turnin' him over to you. Anybody else who will come willin' we'll bring to you."

"You ain't the law," Foster replied.

"Then make us the law. Deputize us. You can't do it alone, so let us help."

"Makes me look like a quitter."

"Nothing of the kind. Every lawman I know uses deputies, time to time, and I'm askin' for the job."

"All right," Foster replied reluctantly. "You brought Bemis in when you could have hung him. I guess you aim to do right."

Outside the sheriff's office, Baldy waited for McQueen. "You name it," he said, as McQueen emerged. "What's next?"

"Fox, you, an' Shorty get down to the Emporium. If Hutch comes out, one of you follow him. Let anybody go in who wants to, but watch *him*!"

He turned to Jackson. "Baldy, you get across the street. Just loaf around, but watch that other store."

"Watch that female? What d'you take me for? You tryin' to sidetrack me out of this scrap?"

"Get goin' an' do what you're told. Kim, you come with me. We're goin' to the Bat Cave."

Foster stared after them and then walked back into his office. Bemis stood inside the bars of his cell door. "I'm gettin' old, Bemis," Foster said. "Lettin' another man do my job."

He sat down in his swivel chair. He was scared—he admitted it to himself. Scared not of guns or violence but of what he might find. Slowly the fog had been clearing, and the things he had been avoiding could no longer be avoided. It was better to let McQueen handle it, much better.

"Leave it to McQueen." Bemis clutched the bars. "Believe me, Sheriff, I never thought I'd be glad to be in jail, but I am. Before this day is over men will die.

"Foster, you should have seen McQueen when he killed Bine! I never would have believed anybody could beat Bine so bad! Bine slapped leather and died, just like that!"

"But there's Overlin," Foster said.

"Yeah, that will be somethin' to see. McQueen an' Overlin." Suddenly Bemis exclaimed, "Foster! I forgot to tell them about Ren Oliver!"

"Oliver? Don't tell me he's involved?"

"Involved? He might be the ringleader! The boss man! And he packs a sneak gun! A stingy gun! Whilst you're expecting him to move for the gun you can see, he kills you with the other one."

Foster was on his feet. "Thanks, Bemis. We'll remember that when you're up for trial."

As Foster went out of the door, Bemis said, "Maybe, but maybe it's too late!"

———

THE BAT CAVE was alive and sinning. It was packed at this hour, and all the tables were busy. Behind one of them, seated where he could face the door, was Ren Oliver. His hair was neatly waved back from his brow, his handsome face composed as he dealt the tricky pasteboards with easy, casual skill. Only his eyes seemed alive, missing nothing. In the stable back of the house where he lived was a saddled horse. It was just a little bit of insurance.

At the bar, drinking heavily, was Overlin. Like a huge grizzly he hulked against the bar. The more he drank, the colder and deadlier he became. Someday that might change, and he was aware of it. He thought he would know when that time came, but for the present he was a man to be left strictly alone when drinking. He had been known to go berserk. Left alone, he usually drank the evening away, speaking to no one, bothering no one until finally he went home to sleep it off.

Around him men might push and shove for places at the bar, but they avoided Overlin.

The smoke-laden atmosphere was thick, redolent of cheap perfume, alcohol, and sweaty, unwashed bodies. The night was chill, so the two stoves glowed red. Two bartenders, working swiftly, tried to keep up with the demands of the customers.

Tonight was different, and the bartenders had been the first to sense it. Overlin only occasionally came in, and they were always uncomfortable until he left. It was like serving an old grizzly with a sore tooth. But Overlin was only part of the trouble. The air was tense. They could feel trouble.

The burning of Bear Canyon, the slaying of Chalk Warneke, and the gun battle in Heifer Basin were being talked about, but only in low tones. From time to time, in spite of themselves, their eyes went to Overlin. They were not speculating if he would meet McQueen, but when.

Overlin called for another drink, and the big gunfighter ripped the bottle from the bartender's hand and put it down beside him. The bartender retreated hastily, while somebody started a tear-jerking ballad at the old piano.

The door opened and Ward McQueen stepped in, followed by Kim Sartain.

Kim, lithe as a young panther, moved swiftly to one side, his eyes sweeping the room, picking up Ren Oliver at once, and then Overlin.

Ward McQueen did not stop walking until he was at the bar six feet from Overlin. As the big gunman reached again for the bottle, McQueen knocked it from under his hand.

At the crash of the breaking bottle the room became soundless. Not even the entry of Sheriff Foster was noted, except by Sartain.

"Overlin, I'm acting as deputy sheriff. I want you out of town by noon tomorrow. Ride, keep riding, and don't come back."

"So you're McQueen? And you got Bine? Well, that must have surprised Hans. He always thought he was good. Even thought he was better'n me, but he wasn't. He never saw the day."

McQueen waited. He had not expected the man to leave. This would be a killing for one or the other, but he had to give the man a chance to make it official. Proving that he had had a hand in the murder of Jimmy McCracken would have been difficult at best.

Overlin was different from Bine. It would take a lot of lead to sink that big body.

"Where's Strahan?" McQueen demanded.

Ren Oliver started and then glanced hastily toward the door. His eyes met those of Kim Sartain, and he knew that to attempt to leave would mean a shootout, and he was not ready for that.

"Strahan, is it? Even if you get by me you'll never get past him. No need to tell you where he is. He'll find you when you least expect it."

Deliberately, Overlin turned his eyes away from McQueen, reaching for his glass with his left hand. "Whiskey! Gimme some whiskey!"

"Where is he, Overlin? Where's Strahan?"

The men were ready, McQueen knew. Inside of him, Overlin was poised for the kill. McQueen wanted to startle him, to throw him off balance, to wreck his poise. He took a half step closer. "Tell me, you drunken lobo! *Tell me!*"

As he spoke he struck swiftly with his left hand and slapped Overlin across his mouth!

It was a powerful slap and it shocked Overlin. Not since he was a child had anybody dared to strike him, and it shook him as nothing else could have. He uttered a cry of choking rage and went for his gun.

Men dove for cover, falling over splintering chairs, fighting to get out of range or out the door.

McQueen had already stepped back quickly, drawn his gun, and then stepped off to the left as he fired, forcing Overlin to turn toward him. McQueen's first bullet struck an instant before Overlin could fire, and the impact knocked

Overlin against the bar, his shot going off into the floor as McQueen fired again.

Overlin faced around, his shirt bloody, one eye gone, and his gun blazed again. McQueen felt himself stagger, shaken as if by a blow, yet without any realization of where the blow had come from.

He fired again, and not aware of how many shots he had fired, he drew his left-hand gun and pulled a border shift, tossing the guns from hand to hand to have a fully loaded gun in his right.

Across the room behind him, another brief drama played itself out. Ren Oliver had been watching and thought he saw his chance. Under cover of the action, all attention centered on McQueen and Overlin, he would kill McQueen. His sleeve gun dropped into his hand and cut down on McQueen, but the instant the flash of blue steel appeared in his hand two guns centered on him and fired: Sartain was at the front door and Sheriff Foster on his left rear. Struck by a triangle of lead, Oliver lunged to his feet, one hand going to his stomach. In amazement, he stared at his bloody hand and his shattered body. Then he screamed.

In that scream was all the coward's fear of the death he had brought to so many others. In shocked amazement he stared from Foster to Sartain, both holding guns ready for another shot if need be. Then his legs wilted and he fell, one hand clutching at the falling deck of cards, his blood staining them. He fell, and the table tipped, cascading chips and cards over him and into the sawdust around him.

At the bar, Overlin stood, indomitable spirit still blazing from his remaining eye. "You—! You—!"

As he started to fall, his big hand caught at the bar's rounded edge and he stared at McQueen, trying to speak. Then the fingers gave way and he fell, striking the brass rail and rolling away.

Ward McQueen turned as if from a bad dream, seeing Kim at the door and Sheriff Foster, gun in hand, inside the rear door.

Running feet pounded the boardwalk, and the door slammed open. Guns lifted, expectantly.

It was Baldy Jackson, his face white, torn with emotion. "Ward! Heaven help me! I've killed a *woman*! I've killed Sharon Clarity!"

The scattered spectators were suddenly a mob. *"What?"* They started for him.

"Hold it!" McQueen's gun came up. "Hear him out!"

Ward McQueen was thumbing shells into his gun. "All right, Baldy. Show us."

"Before my Maker, Ward, I figured her for somebody sneakin' to get a shot at me! I seen the gun, plain as day, an' I fired!"

Muttering and angry, the crowd followed. Baldy led the way to an alley behind the store, where they stopped. There lay a still figure in a riding habit. For an instant Ward looked down at that still, strangely attractive face. Then he bent swiftly, and as several cried out in protest he seized Sharon Clarity's red gold hair and jerked!

It came free in his hand, and the head flopped back on the earth, the close-cropped head of a man!

Ward stooped, gripped the neckline, and ripped it away. With the padding removed, all could see the chest of a man, lean, muscular and hairy.

"Not Sharon Clarity," he said, "but Strahan."

Kim Sartain wheeled and walked swiftly away, McQueen following. As they reached the Emporium, Bud Fox appeared.

"Nobody left here but that girl. She was in there a long time. The old man started out but we warned him back. He's inside."

Ward McQueen led the way, with Sheriff Foster behind him, then Sartain, Jackson, Fox, and Jones.

Silas Hutch sat at his battered rolltop desk. His lean jaws seemed leaner than ever. He peered at them from eyes that were mean and cruel. "Well? What's this mean? Bargin' in like this?"

"You're under arrest, Hutch, for ordering the killing of Jimmy McCracken and Neal Webb."

Hutch chuckled. "Me? Under arrest? You got a lot to learn,

boy. The law here answers to me. I say who is to be arrested and who is prosecuted.

"You got no proof of anything! You got no evidence! You're talkin' up the wind, sonny!"

Baldy Jackson pushed forward. "Ward, this here's the one I told you about! This is the first time I've had a good look at him! He's Shorty Strahan, the mean one! He's an uncle, maybe, of that one out there who made such a fine-lookin' woman!"

"Hutch, you had your killings done for you. All but one. You killed Chalk Warneke."

He turned to Foster. "Figure it out for yourself, Sheriff. Remember the position Chalk was in, remember the crowd, and Warneke on a horse. There's only one place that shot could come from—*that* window! And only one man who could have fired it, *him*!"

Silas Hutch shrank back in his chair. When Foster reached for him, he cringed. "Don't let them hang me!" he pleaded.

"You take it from here, Foster," McQueen said. "We can measure the angle of that bullet and you've got Bemis. He can testify as to the connection between Neal Webb and Hutch as well as that with Chalk. He knows all about it."

Ward McQueen turned toward the door. He was tired, very tired, and all he wanted was rest. Besides, his hip bone was bothering him. He had been aware of it for some time, but only now was it really hurting. He looked down, remembering something hitting him during the battle with Overlin.

His gun belt was somewhat torn and two cartridges dented. A bullet had evidently struck and glanced off, ruining two perfectly good cartridges and giving him a bad bruise on the hip bone.

"Kim," he said, "let's get back to the ranch."

BAD PLACE TO DIE

AFTER THE RIFLE shots there was no further sound, and Kim Sartain waited, listening. Beside him Bud Fox held his Winchester ready, eyes roving. "Up ahead," Kim said finally, "let's go."

They rode on then, walking their horses and ready for trouble, two tough, hard-bitten young riders, top hands both of them, and top hands at trouble, too.

Their view of the trail was cut off by a jutting elbow of rock, but when they rounded it they saw the standing, riderless horse and the uncomfortably sprawled figure in the trail. Around and about them the desert air was still and warm, the sky a brassy blue, the skyline lost in a haze of distance along the mountain ridges beyond the wide valley.

When they reached the body, Kim swung down although already he knew it was useless. A man does not remain alive with half his skull blown off and bullets in his body. The young man who lay there unhappily at trail's end was not more than twenty, but he looked rugged and capable. His gun was in his holster, which was tied in place.

"He wasn't expecting trouble," Bud Fox said needlessly, "an' he never knew what hit him."

"Dry-gulched." Kim was narrow of hip and wide of shoulder. There were places east and south of here where they said he was as fast as Wes Hardin or Billy the Kid. He let his dark, cold eyes rove the flat country around them. "Beats me where they could have been hidin'."

He knelt over the man and searched his pockets. In a wallet there was a letter and a name card. It said he was JOHNNY FARROW, IN CASE OF ACCIDENT NOTIFY HAZEL MORSE, SAND SPRINGS STAGE STATION. Kim showed this to Bud and they exchanged an expressionless look.

"We'll load him up," Kim said, "an' then I'll look around."

When the dead man was draped across his own saddle, Kim mounted and, leaving Bud with the body, rode a slow circle around the area. It was lazy warm in the sunshine and Bud sat quietly, his lean, rawboned body relaxed in the saddle.

Kim stopped finally, then disappeared completely as if swallowed by the desert. "Deep wash," Bud Fox said aloud. He got out the makings and rolled a smoke. He looked again at the body. Johnny Farrow had been shot at least six times. "They wanted him dead. Mighty bad, they wanted it."

Kim emerged from the desert and rode slowly back. When he drew up he mopped the sweat from his face. "They laid for him there. Had him dead to rights. About twenty-five yards from their target and they used rifles. When they left, they rode off down the wash."

"How many?" Bud started his horse walking, the led horse following. Kim Sartain's horse moved automatically to join them.

"Three." Kim scanned the desert. "Nearest place for a drink is Sand Springs. They might have gone there."

They rode on, silence building between them. Overhead a lone buzzard circled, faint against the sky. Sweat trickled down Kim's face and he mopped it away. He was twenty-two and had been packing a six-gun for seven years. He had started working roundups when he was twelve.

Neither spoke for several miles, their thoughts busy with this new aspect of their business, for this dead young man was the man they had come far to see. The old days of the Pony Express were gone, but lately it had been revived in this area for the speeding up of mail and messages. Young Johnny Farrow had been one of the dozen or so riders.

Both Sartain and Fox were riders for the Tumbling K, owned by Ruth Kermitt and ramrodded by Ward McQueen. One week ago they had been borrowed from the ranch by an old friend and were drifting into this country to investigate three mysterious robberies of gold shipments. Those shipments had been highly secret, but somehow that secret had become known to the outlaws. The messages informing the receiving parties of the date of the shipment had been sent in pouches carried by Johnny Farrow. Five shipments had been sent, two had arrived safely. Those two had not been mentioned in messages carried by Farrow.

The mystery lay in the fact that the pouches were sealed and locked tightly with only one other key available, and that at the receiving end. Johnny Farrow's ride was twenty-five miles, which took him an even four hours. This route had been paced beforehand by several riders, and day in and day out, four hours was fast time for it. There were three changes of horses, and no one of them took the allowed two minutes. So how could anyone have had access to those messages? Yet the two messages carried by other riders had gone through safely. And the secret gold shipments had gone through because of that fact.

"Too deep for me," Fox said suddenly. "Maybe we should stick to chasin' rustlers or cows. I can't read the brand on this one."

"We'll trail along," Kim said, "an' we got one lead. One o' the hombres in this trick is nervous-like, with his fingers. He breaks twigs." Sartain displayed several inch-long fragments of dead greasewood. Then he put them in an envelope and wrote across it, FOUND WHERE KILLERS WAITED FOR JOHNNY FARROW, and then put it in his vest pocket.

———

AHEAD OF THEM were some low hills, beyond them rose the bleak and mostly bare slopes of the mountains. Higher on those mountains there was timber, and there were trailing tentacles of forest coming down creases in the hills, following streams of runoff water. The trail searched out an opening in the low hills, and they rode through and saw Sand Springs before them.

The sprawling stage station with its corrals and barn was on their right as they entered. On the left was a saloon and next to it a store. Behind the store there was a long building that looked like a bunkhouse. The station itself was a low-fronted frame building with an awning over a stretch of boardwalk, and at the hitch-rail stood a half-dozen horses. As Sartain swung down he looked at these horses. None of them had been hard ridden.

A big man lumbered out of the door, letting it slam behind him. He was followed by two more roughly dressed men and by two women, both surprisingly pretty. Across the street on the porch of the saloon a tall old man did not move, although Sartain was aware of his watching eyes.

"Hey?" The big man looked astonished. "What's happened?"

"Found him up the road, maybe six or seven miles. He'd been dry-gulched. It's Johnny Farrow."

One of the girls gave a gasp, and Kim's eyes sought her out. She was a gray-eyed girl with dark hair, much more attractive than the rather hard-looking and flamboyant blond with her. The girl stepped back against the wall, flattening her palms there, and seemed to be waiting for something. The blond's eyes fluttered to the big man who stepped down toward them.

"My name's Ollie Morse," he said. "Who are you fellows?"

"I'm Sartain." Kim was abrupt. "This is Bud Fox. We're on the drift."

No one spoke, just standing there and looking, and none of the men made the slightest move toward the body. Kim's eyes hardened as he looked them over, and then he said, "In case you're interested, the mail pouches seem all right. There was a card in his pocket said to notify Hazel Morse." Kim's eyes went to the white-faced girl who stood by the wall, biting her lip.

To his surprise it was not she but the blond who stepped forward. "I'm Hazel Morse," she said, and then turning sharply her eyes went to the two younger men. "Verne," she spoke sharply, "you an' Matty get him off that horse. Take him to the barn until you get a grave dug."

Kim Sartain felt a little flicker of feeling run through him and he glanced at Bud, who shrugged. Both men gathered up their bridle reins. "Better notify the sheriff an' the express company," Kim commented idly. "They'll probably want to know." The faint edge of sarcasm in his voice aroused the big man.

"You wouldn't be gettin' smart now, would you?" His voice was low and ugly. His gun butt was worn from much handling, and he looked as tough as he was untidy.

"Smart?" Kim Sartain shrugged. "That ain't my way, to be smart. I was just thinkin'," he added dryly, "that this young fellow sure picked a bad place to die. Nobody seems very wrought-up about it, not even the girl he wanted notified in case of death. What were you to him?" he addressed the last question to Hazel Morse suddenly.

Her face flushed angrily. "He was a friend!" she flared. "He came courtin' a few times, that was all!"

Sartain turned away and led his horse across the street to the saloon, followed by Bud Fox. Behind him there was a low murmur of voices. The older man sitting on the porch looked at them with veiled eyes. He was grizzled and dirty in a faded cotton shirt with sleeves rolled up, exposing the red flannels he wore. His body was lean and the gun he had tucked in his waistband looked used.

He got up as they went through the door into the saloon, and followed them in, moving around behind the bar. "Rye?" he questioned.

Kim nodded and watched him set out the bottle and glasses. When Kim poured a drink for Bud and himself, he replaced the bottle on the bar, and the old man stood there, looking at them. Kim tossed a silver dollar on the bar and the man made change from his pants pocket. "Any place around here a man can get a meal?" Kim asked.

"Yeah." The older man waited while Kim could have counted to fifty. "Over the road there, at the station. They serve grub. My old lady's a good cook."

"Your name Morse, too?"

"Uh huh." He scratched his stomach. "I'm Het Morse. Ollie, he runs the stage station. He's my boy. Hazel, that there blond gal you talked to, she's my gal. Verne Stecher, the

496 / Louis L'Amour

young feller with the red shirt, he's my neffy, my own brother's boy. Matty Brown, he just loafs here when he ain't workin'."

Kim felt a queer little start of apprehension. He had heard of Matty Brown. The sullen youngster had killed six or seven men, one of them at Pioche only a few months back. He was known as a bad one to tangle with.

"Too bad about that express rider," Bud commented.

"Maybe," Kim suggested to Bud, "we might get us jobs ridin' the mail. With this gent dead, they might need a good man or two."

"Could be," Bud agreed. "It's worth askin' about. Who," he looked up at Het, "would we talk to? Your son?"

"No. Ollie, he's only the station man. You'd have to ride on over the Rubies to the Fort, or maybe down to Carson." He looked at them, his interest finally aroused. "You from around here?"

"From over the mountains," Kim said. "We been ridin' for the Tumblin' K." They had agreed not to fake a story. Their own was good enough, for neither of them had ever been connected with the law; both had always been cowhands.

"Tumblin' K?" Het nodded. "Heard of it. Hear tell that McQueen feller is hell on wheels with his guns. An' that other'n, too, that youngster they call Sarten."

"Sartain," Kim said. "Emphasis on the 'tain' part."

"You know him?" Het studied Kim. "Or maybe you are him?"

"That's right." Kim did not pause to let Morse think that over, but added, "This is the slack season. No need for so many hands, an' Bud here, him an' me wanted to see some country."

"That's likely." Het indicated the darkening building across the road. "Closin' up now, until after grub. They'll fix you a bite over there. I'll let you a room upstairs, the two of you for a dollar."

———

SUPPER WAS A slow, silent meal. The food was good and there was lots of it, but it was heavy and the biscuits were soggy. It was far different from the cooking back on the K, as both punchers remembered regretfully. Nobody talked, for eating here seemed to be a serious business.

The dark-haired girl came and went in silence, and once Kim caught her looking at him with wide, frightened eyes. He smiled a little, and a brief, trembling smile flickered on the girl's face, then was gone. Once a big woman with a face that might have been carved from red granite appeared in the door holding a large spoon. She stared at him and then went back into the kitchen. If this was Het's wife there was little of motherly love around Sand Springs.

Het chuckled suddenly, then he looked up. "You fellers got yourself a high-toned guest tonight," he said, grinning triumphantly and with some malice, too. "That dark-haired one is Kim Sartain, that gunfightin' segundo from the Tumblin' K!"

All eyes lifted, but those of Matty Brown seemed suddenly to glow with deep fire. He stared at Kim, nodding. "Heerd about yuh," he said.

"Folks talk a mighty lot," Sartain said casually. "They stretch stories pretty far."

"That's what I reckoned," Matty slapped butter on a slab of bread, his tone contemptuous.

Kim Sartain felt a little burst of anger within him and he hardened suddenly. Out of the corner of his eye he saw Bud Fox give Matty a cold, careful look. Bud was no gunslinger, but he was a fighting man and he knew trouble when he saw it. As far as that went, they sat right in the middle of plenty of trouble. Kim had guessed that right away, but he knew it with a queer excitement when he saw Ollie reach over and break a straw from the broom and start picking his teeth with it.

Outside on the porch, Fox drew closer to Sartain. "Better sleep with your gun on," he said dryly. "I don't like this setup."

"Me either. Wonder what that dark-haired girl is doin' in this den of wolves? She don't fit in, not one bit."

"We'll see," Kim said. "I think we'll stick around for a

while. When the stage goes on, we'll send a letter to Carson about jobs, but that'll be just an excuse to stay on here."

SARTAIN KICKED HIS feet from under the blankets in the chill of dawn. He rubbed his eyes and growled under his breath, then pulled on his wool socks and padded across the room to throw cold water on his face. When he had straightened, he looked at Bud. The lean and freckled cowhand was sleeping with his mouth open, snoring gently.

Kim grinned suddenly and looked at the basin of cold water, then remembered they would sleep here tonight and thought the better of his impulse. Crossing to the bed he sat down hard and searched under it for a boot. He pulled it on, stamping his foot into place. Bud Fox opened one wary eye. "I know, you lousy souwegian, you want me to wake up. Well, I ain't a gonna do it!" Closing his eyes he snored hard.

Sartain grinned and pulled on the other boot, then crossed to the water pitcher. Lifting it, he sloshed the water about noisily, then looked at the bed. Bud Fox had both eyes wide with alarm. "You do it," he threatened, "an' so help me, I'll kill you!"

Kim chuckled. "Get up! We got work to do!"

"Why get up? What we got to do that's so pressin'?" As he talked, Fox sat up. "When I think of eating breakfast with that outfit I get cold chills. I never did see such a low-down passel o' folks in all my days." He stretched. " 'Ceptin' for that dark-haired Jeanie."

Kim said nothing, but he was in complete agreement. As he belted on his guns he looked out the window, studying the white track of the trail. Nowhere had he seen such a misbegotten bunch of buildings or people.

"You watch that Matty Brown," Fox warned, heading for the basin. "He's pizen mean. Sticks out all over him."

"They're all of a kind, this bunch," Kim agreed. "I reckon we won't have to travel much further to find what we want. Proving it may be a full-sized job. That old man downstairs fair gives me the chills. To my notion he's the worst of the lot."

When they left the room Kim Sartain paused and glanced down the bare and empty hall. Five more doors opened off the hall, but now all were closed. There was a door at the end, too, but that must lead to the stairs he had seen from below.

Turning, they walked down the hall, their boots sounding loud in the passage. The stairs took them to the barroom, where all was dark and still. The dusty bottles behind the bar, the few scattered tables with their cards and dirty glasses that stood desolate and still, all were lost in the half gloom of early day.

Outside a low wind was blowing and they hustled across to the warmth of the boardinghouse. Here a light was burning but there was no one in sight, although the table was set and they could hear sounds from the kitchen, a rattle of dishes, and then someone shaking down a stove.

Kim hung his hat on a peg and glanced into the cracked mirror on the wall. His narrow, dark face looked cold this morning. As cold as he felt. He hitched his guns to an easier place, resting his palms on the polished butts of the big .44 Russians for an instant. There were places where the checking on the walnut butt had worn almost smooth from handling.

There were hurried footsteps and then the dark-haired girl came through the door with a coffeepot. She smiled quickly, glancing from Kim to Bud and back again. "I knew it must be you. Nobody else gets around so early."

"*You* seem to," Kim said, smiling. "Are you the cook?"

"Sometimes. I usually get breakfast. Are . . . are you leaving today?"

"No." Kim watched her movements. She was a slim, lovely girl with a trim figure and a soft, charming face. "We're staying around."

For an instant she was still, listening. Then low-voiced, she said, "I wouldn't. I would ride on, quickly. Today."

Both of the cowhands watched her now. "Why?" Kim asked. "Tell us."

"I can't. But . . . but it . . . it's dangerous here. They don't like strangers stopping here. Especially now."

"What are you doing here? You don't seem to fit in."

She hesitated again, listening. "I have to stay. My father died owing them money. I have to work it out, and then I can go. If I tried to leave now, they would bring me back. Besides, it wouldn't be honest."

Kim Sartain looked surprised. "You think we should leave? I think *you* should leave. At once—by the next stage."

"I cannot. I . . . ," she hesitated, listening again.

Kim looked up at her. "What about Johnny Farrow? Was he in love with Hazel and she with him?"

"He may have been, but Hazel? She loves no one but herself, unless it is Matty. I doubt even that. She would do anything for money."

She went out to the kitchen and they heard the sound of frying eggs. Kim glanced around, reached for the coffeepot, and then filled his cup. As he did so, he heard footsteps crossing the road, and then the door opened and Matty Brown came in, followed by Verne Stecher. They dropped onto the bench across the table.

Matty looked at Kim. "Up early, ain't you? Figure on pullin' out?"

"We're going to stick around. We're writin' to Carson, maybe we can get jobs ridin' with the mail or express. Sounds like it might be interesting."

"You seen Farrow. That look interesting?"

Before Kim could reply, Ollie Morse came in with his father. They looked sharply at Kim and Bud and then sat down at the table. Finishing their meal, Kim scribbled the letter that was to be their cover, then the two cowhands arose and went outside, drifting toward the stable.

"Johnny Farrow," Kim said suddenly, "started his ride ten miles west of here. He swapped horses here, and then again ten miles east, and as the next stretch was all up, and down-hill, rough mountain country, he finished his ride in just five miles on the third horse.

"All this route was mapped out and timed. They know those messages had to be read while in his possession, yet they couldn't have been. Nobody had time to open those pouches, open a message, and then seal both of them again in the time allowed. It just couldn't be done. Unless . . ."

"Unless what?"

"Unless Johnny found a way to cut his time. All the way out here I've been studying this thing. He had to find some way to cut his time. Now he swapped horses here, an' we know that everybody here is in the one family, so to speak. We know that Johnny was sweet on Hazel. No man likes to just wave at a girl; he likes to set over coffee with her, talk a mite.

"Suppose he found a way or somebody showed him a way he could cut his time? Suppose while he sat talkin' to Hazel, these other hombres found a way to open the mail pouch?"

Bud nodded and lit his cigarette. "Yeah," he agreed, "it could have been done that way. Whatever was done, Johnny must have got wise. Then they killed him."

———

THEY SADDLED UP and, mounting their horses, started down the trail to the west. Glancing back, Kim saw Ollie Morse standing on the porch shading his eyes after them. All morning there had been an idea in the back of Kim's mind and now it came to the fore. He swung left into an arroyo and led the way swiftly in a circling movement that would bring them back to the trail east of Sand Springs.

"Where you headed for now?" Bud demanded. "You're headed right into the worst mess of mountains around here."

"Yeah," Kim slowed his pace, "but you know something? I've been drawing maps in my mind. It looks to me like that trail from Sand Springs to the next station at Burnt Rock swings somewhat wide to get around those mountains you speak of. Suppose there was a way through? Would that save time or wouldn't it?"

"Sure, if it would save distance. If there was an easy way through, why, a man might cut several miles off, and miles mean minutes."

"In other words, if a man knew a shortcut through those mountains, and he wanted to stay an' talk to his girl awhile, he could do it. I've seen girls I'd take a chance like that to talk to. That Jeanie, for instance. Now she's reg'lar."

They rode on in silence for several minutes. Before them the wall of the mountains lifted abruptly. It was not exactly a wall in many places, but a slope far too steep for a horse to climb and one that would have been a struggle for a mountain goat. While there were notches in the wall, none of them gave promise of an opening. As far as they could see to the north the mountains were unchanged, a series of peaks, and the wall, staggered somewhat, still.

Twice they investigated openings, but each time they ended in steep slides down which water had cascaded in wet periods. At noon they stopped, built a dry brush fire, and made coffee. But Fox ate in silence until Kim filled his cup for the third time. "Don't look good, Kim. We ain't found a thing."

"There's got to be a hole!" Kim persisted irritably. "There's no other way he could have made it."

He was wishing right now that Ward McQueen was here. The foreman of the Tumbling K had a head for problems. As for himself, well, he was some shakes in a scrap but he'd never been much for figuring angles.

Tired and dusty from travel, they returned to Sand Springs. The street between the buildings was deserted as they approached, not even a sight of Het, who apparently almost lived on the saloon stoop. They stabled their horses and rubbed them down and then started for the boardinghouse. Suddenly Kim stopped. "Bud, watch yourself! I don't like the look of this!"

Bud Fox moved right of the wide barn door, every sense alert. "What's the matter, Kim?" he whispered. "See something?"

"That's the trouble," Kim said. "I don't see anything or hear anything. It's too quiet!"

Carefully, he backed into the shadows and eased over in the darkness along the wall. It was late evening, not yet dusk, but dark when away from the wide barn door. Looking out, Kim's eye caught what was the merest suggestion of movement from a window over the saloon. Although the evening was cool, that window was open. A rifleman there could cover the barn door unseen.

Turning swiftly, Kim ran on soundless feet to the rear of the barn. Opening the door to the corral, he slid outside and scrambled over the fence, then ducked into the desert and circled until he could get across the road. All this took him no more than two minutes, but once across the road, he eased around to the back of the saloon and opened the rear door after mounting the stairs. He crept down the hall, but just as he reached for the doorknob a board creaked under his feet. He grabbed the knob and thrust the door open, hearing a faint sound from within the room as he did so.

Kim stepped into the room, gun in hand, then stopped. It was empty. On the right there was another door and he stepped swiftly to it and turned the knob. The door was locked.

There was a bed here as in his own room; there was also a chair and table, a bowl and pitcher. He stepped to the window and glanced out. There was no sound or movement anywhere. He was turning away when he heard something crunch slightly under his boot. He dropped to one knee and felt around on the floor, then picked up several twigs, broken about an inch long in each case.

Closing the door behind him, he walked along the hall and then went down the stairs. There was nobody in sight. The saloon was empty. Stepping out into the street, Sartain holstered his gun and crossed the street to the stable. "All right, Bud," he said.

As they walked to the boardinghouse he explained swiftly, then he saw a light go on inside the boardinghouse and he pushed open the door. Jeanie was just replacing the lamp chimney after lighting the lamp.

"Oh?" Was that relief in her eyes? "It's you. Did you have a nice ride?"

"So-so." He waved a hand. "Where is everybody?"

"All gone but Hazel and she's asleep. They left right after you did, only they rode the other way. They said they would be back about sundown."

Bud looked inquiringly at Kim, who shrugged his shoulders. If she was the only one around, had it been she who was in the room over the saloon? But how could she have crossed the street unseen?

———

SEVERAL RIDERS CAME up and dismounted in front of the stable and then Ollie and Matty Brown came through the door. They looked sharply at the two cowhands, but neither spoke. After a few minutes the others came in, but the meal seemed to drag on endlessly and the tension was obvious.

Yet as the meal drew to a close, Kim Sartain suddenly found himself growing more and more calm and cool. He felt a new sense of certainty and of growing confidence.

In his own mind he was positive that the killers of Johnny Farrow were here, in this room. He was also convinced that somewhere about was the stolen gold. He had both of these jobs to do: to find how the information on the shipments had been given to the outlaws, and also what had become of the gold. For the authorities were sure that thus far none of it had been sold or used.

With the new sense of certainty came something else, a knowledge that he must push these men. They were guilty and so were doubtless disturbed by the presence of the two cowhands, even though they might not suspect their purpose in being here. Kim was sure that an attempt was to have been made to kill them both that afternoon. The broken twigs were evidence enough that Farrow's killer had stood beside that window, though it could have been at some other time than today. And Ollie Morse used pieces of broom straw for toothpicks, and probably used twigs too.

"Been thinkin'," he remarked suddenly, throwing his words into the pool of silence, "about that poor youngster who was killed. I figure somebody wanted him dead mighty bad, else they would never have filled him with so much lead. Next, I get to wonderin' why he was killed."

Het Morse said nothing, sitting back in his chair and lighting his pipe. Matty continued to eat, but both Verne and Ollie were watching him. "Now I," Kim went on, "figure it must have been jealousy. Which one of you here was jealous of him seein' Hazel?"

Matty looked up sharply. "You throwin' that at me? I'm the only one livin' here who ain't related to her!"

"I figured a girl pretty as Hazel would have men comin' some distance to see her, although I did allow it might be you, Matty."

"Of course, more than one man shot Farrow," Fox contributed.

"I don't need he'p in my killin's," Matty said flatly.

Kim Sartain shrugged. "Just figurin'. Well, I reckon I'll turn in." He got to his feet. "I expect Farrow must have spent a lot of time here," he dropped the comment easily, "seein' he was sweet on Hazel."

"How could he?" Hazel demanded, getting to her feet. "He was an express rider. He only had two minutes to change in, and it rarely took him that long."

"Yeah? Well, I reckoned maybe he found a way." All eyes were on Kim now. "If I was sweet on a girl, *I'd* find a way."

"Such as what?" Ollie demanded.

"Oh, maybe a shortcut through those mountains. Yeah, that would be it. Something that would give me extra time."

Matty leaned back in his chair, and suddenly he was smiling, but it was not a nice smile. Verne was staring at Sartain, his eyes murderous. Het was poker-faced, but Ollie was suddenly sweating.

"Well," Kim said, "good night all. You comin', Bud?"

Outside, Bud mopped his face. "You *crazy*? Stickin' it to 'em that way?"

A shadow moved near the window curtain and Kim heard the door open softly. "The way I figure it," he said loudly, "whoever killed that rider knew something about that gold that was stolen. I figure it must be cached around here somewhere, in the hills, maybe. It was stolen near here and whoever stole it probably didn't take it far. We better have us a look."

They crossed the street to the saloon and entered. A moment later Het came in behind them. "You fellers want a drink?" he asked genially. "Might's well have one. Makes a feller warm to go to bed on."

"Don't mind if we do," Kim replied, "an' you have one with us."

"Sure." Het got out the bottle and glasses. He seemed to be searching for words. "Reckon," he said finally, "you know I heerd what you said about huntin' that there gold. I wouldn't, if'n I was you. Fact is, you two ain't makin' no friends around here: We uns mind our own affairs an' figure others should do likewise."

Kim grinned and lifted his glass. "Gold is anybody's business, amigo. It's yours if you find it, ours if we find it. Here's to the gold and whoever finds it, and here's to the hot place for the others!"

They tossed off their drinks and the old man filled the glasses again. "All right," he said, almost sadly. "Don't say you weren't warned. I reckon it's on your head now, but as long as you're lookin', I'll tell you. There is a shortcut."

"Yeah?" Kim Sartain's face was straight and his lips stiff.

"Uh huh. It's an old Paiute trail. Easy goin' all the way, but known to few around here. I reckon it was me put Farrow up to it. He was sweet on Hazel, so it was me told him. I aimed to he'p the boy. You take the split in the mountains just over that way." He gestured vaguely out the door.

"Thanks." Kim Sartain lifted his glass to the old man. "See you tomorrow?"

Het Morse's Adam's apple bobbed and his eyes looked queer. "I reckon you will."

Upstairs in their room Sartain closed the door and propped a chair under the knob. Bud Fox threw his hat on a peg. "Now I wonder why he told us that?"

In the dim light from the lamp Kim's strongly boned face was thrown into sharp relief. "You know mighty well why he told us. So we'd go there. What better place to kill snoopers than on an unknown trail where nobody but buzzards would find them?"

Bud absorbed that, his freckled face strangely pale. He pulled off a boot and rubbed his socked foot. Then he looked up. "What we goin' to do, Kim?"

"Us?" Kim chuckled softly, warmly, and with real humor. "Why, Bud, you wouldn't disappoint 'em, would you? We're goin', of course!"

———

THE MORNING SUN lay warm upon the quiet hills, and the cicadas that hummed in the greasewood seemed drowsily content. Between the knees of Kim Sartain the Appaloosa stepped out gaily, head bobbing, knees lifting, stepping as if to unheard music. And Kim Sartain sat erect in the saddle, a dark blue shirt tucked into gray wool trousers which were tucked into black, hand-tooled boots with large Mexican spurs. Kim Sartain rode coolly, and with a smile on his lips.

The mountains seemed split asunder before him, and where the sunlight fell upon the gigantic crack, the shadows lay before him, and he rode down into darkness with a hand on his thigh and a loose and ready gun inches from his hand. There was no sound, there was no movement. A mile, and the crack widened, then opened into a wide green valley across which the track of the ancient Paiute trail left a gray-white streak among the tumbled boulders and broken ledges. There was a sound of running water, and a freshness in the air, and at the fording of the stream, Kim Sartain swung down, allowing his horse to drink.

There were trees at the base of a big-as-a-house boulder, and from the shelter of these boulders stepped Matty Brown.

He stepped into the bright sunlight and stood there, and Kim Sartain saw him. And Matty Brown took another step forward and said, speaking clearly, "I reckon that gun rep o' yours is all talk, Sartain! *Let's see!*"

His right hand slapped down fast and the gun came up smoothly and his first shot blasted harmlessly off into the vast blue sky, and then Matty turned halfway around and fell, rolling over slowly with blood staining his shirtfront and the emptiness in his eyes staring up at the emptiness in the sky, and Kim Sartain's .44 Russian lifted a little tendril of smoke toward the sky. And then Kim saw Het Morse step from the brush, with Ollie off to his right, and Verne Stecher spoke from behind him.

"Matty," Stecher said, "he allus did figure hisself faster than he was. He wanted to have his try, so we let him. Now you, snooper, we plant you here."

"Hey, where's your partner?" Ollie suddenly demanded. The big man was perspiring profusely. Only Het was quiet, negligent, almost lazy; that old man was poison wicked.

Bud's voice floated above them. "I'm right up here, Ollie. S'pose you drop your guns!"

Ollie's head jerked and fear showed on his face, stark fear. Where the voice came from he did not know, but it might have been a dozen places. Kim Sartain could feel the panic in him but his own eyes did not waver from Het's.

"Guess we better drop 'em, Pop." Ollie's voice shook. "They got us."

The old man's voice was frosty with contempt. "We're three to two. They got nothin'. Let Verne get that other'n. We'll take Sartain."

"No!" Ollie's fear was strident in his voice. The death of Matty Brown, the body lying there, had put fear all through him. "No! Don't—!"

Kim saw it coming an instant before Het squeezed off his shot, and he fired, smashing two quick ones at Het. He saw the old man jerk sharply, heard the whine of the bullet past his own head, and then he fired again, throwing himself to the right to one knee, the other leg stretched far out. Then he swung his gun to Ollie. Other guns were smashing around him, and a shot kicked dirt into his mouth and eyes. Momentarily blinded, he rolled over, lost hold on his gun and clawed at his eyes. Something tugged at his shirt and he grabbed for his left-hand gun and came up shooting. Old Het was half behind a rock and had his gun resting on it.

Kim lunged to his feet and ran directly at the old man, hearing the hard bark of a pistol and the shrill whine of a rifle bullet, and then he skidded to a halt and dropped his gun on Het. Het tried to lift his own six-shooter from the rock as Kim fired. Dust lifted from the old man's shirt and the bullet smashed him to the ground and he lost hold on his gun.

And then the shooting was past, and Kim glanced swiftly around. Bud was near the boulder where he had waited for the ambush, and Ollie was down, and Stecher was stretched at full length, hands empty.

Kim looked down at Het. The oldster's eyes were open and he was grinning. "Tough!" he whispered. "I told Matty you was tough! He wouldn't listen to . . . to an . . . to an old man . . .

"Ollie," he whispered, "no guts. If I'd o' spawned the likes o' you . . . !" His voice trailed away and he panted hoarsely.

"Het," Kim squatted beside him, "the Law sent us down here. The United States Government. That gold was rightly theirs, Het. You're goin' out, and you don't want to rob the Government, do you, Het?"

"Gover'ment?" He fumbled at the word with loose lips. He flopped his hand, trying to point at the boulder where they had waited. "Cave . . . under that boulder . . ."

His words trailed weakly away and he panted hoarsely for a few minutes, and then Kim Sartain saw a buzzard mirrored in the old man's eyes, and looking up, he saw the buzzard high overhead, and looking down, he saw that Het Morse was dead.

Bud Fox walked up slowly, his freckles showing against the gray of his face. "Never liked this killin' business," he said. "I ain't got the stomach for it." He looked up at Kim. "Reckon you pegged it right when you had me come on ahead."

"An' you picked the right spot to wait," Kim agreed dryly.

"It was the only one, actually." Bud Fox looked around. "Reckon we can load that gold on their horses. You goin' to stop by for that Jeanie girl?"

"Why, sure!" Kim whistled and watched the Appaloosa come toward him. "We'll take her to Carson. I reckon any debt she owed has been liquidated right here." Then he said soberly, "I was sure the first day we rode in. Behind the bottles on the back bar I saw an awl an' a leather-worker's needle. They opened the stitching on those pouches while Farrow was sparkin' Hazel. They got the information that-away, then put the letters back and stitched 'em up again."

Behind them they left three mounds of earth and a cross

marking the grave of Het Morse. "He was a tough old man," Bud Fox said gloomily.

Kim Sartain looked at the trail ahead where the sunlight lay. A cicada lifted its thin whine from the brush along the trail. Kim removed his hat and mopped his brow. "He sure was," he said.

GRUB LINE RIDER

THERE WAS GOOD grass in these high meadows,
Kim Sartain reflected, and it was a wonder they were
not in use. Down below in the flatland the cattle looked
scrawny and half-starved. He had come up a narrow, little-
used trail from the level country and was heading across the
divide when he ran into the series of green, tree-bordered
meadows scattered among the ridges.

Wind rippled the grass in long waves across the meadow,
and the sun lay upon it like a caress. Across the meadow and
among the trees he heard a vague sound of falling water, and
turned the zebra dun toward it. As he did so, three horsemen
rode out of the trees, drawing up sharply when they saw him.

He rode on, walking the dun, and the three wheeled their
mounts and came toward him at a canter. A tall man rode a
gray horse in the van. The other two were obviously cowhands, and all wore guns. The tall man had a lean, hard face
with a knife scar across the cheek. "You there!" he roared,
reining in. "What you doin' ridin' here?"

Kim Sartain drew up, his lithe, trail-hardened body easy in
the saddle. "Why, I'm ridin' through," he said quietly, "and
in no particular hurry. You got this country fenced against
travel?"

"Well, it ain't no trail!" The big man's eyes were gray and
hostile. "You just turn around and ride back the way you
come! The trail goes around through Ryerson."

"That's twenty miles out of my way," Kim objected, "and
this here's a nice ride. I reckon I'll keep on the way I'm
goin'."

The man's eyes hardened. "Did Monaghan put you up to
this?" he demanded. "Well, if he did, it's time he was taught

a lesson! We'll send you back to him fixed up proper! *Take him, boys!*"

The men started, then froze. The six-shooter in Kim's hand wasn't a hallucination. "Come on," Kim invited mildly. "Take me!"

The men swallowed, and stood still. The tall man's face grew red with fury. "So? A gunslinger, is it? Two can play at that game! I'll have Clay Tanner out here before the day is over!"

Kim Sartain felt his pulse jump. Clay Tanner? Why, the man was an outlaw, a vicious killer, wanted in a dozen places! "Listen, Big Eye," he said harshly, "I don't know you and I never heard of Monaghan, but if he dislikes you, that's one credit for him. Anybody who would hire or have anything to do with the likes of Clay Tanner is a coyote!"

The man's face purpled and his eyes turned mean. "I'll tell Clay that!" he blustered. "He'll be mighty glad to hear it! That will be all he needs to come after you!"

Sartain calmly returned his gun to its holster, keeping his eyes on the men before him without hiding his contempt. "If you hombres feel lucky," he said, "try and drag iron. I'd as soon blast you out of your saddles as not.

"As for you"—Kim's eyes turned on the tall man—"you'd best learn now as later how to treat strangers. This country ain't fenced, and from the look of it, ain't used. You've no right to keep anybody out of here, and when I want to ride through, I'll ride through! Get me?"

One of the hands broke in, his voice edged. "Stranger, after talkin' that way to Jim Targ, you'd better light a shuck out of this country! He *runs* it!"

Kim shoved his hat back on his head and looked from the cowhand to his boss. He was a quiet-mannered young drifter who liked few things better than a fight. Never deliberately picking trouble, he nevertheless had a reckless liking for it and never sidestepped any that came his way.

"He don't run me," he commented cheerfully, "and personally, I think he's a mighty small pebble in a mighty big box! He rattles a lot, but for a man who runs this country, he fits mighty loose!"

Taking out his tobacco, he calmly began to roll a smoke, his half smile daring the men to draw. "Just what," he asked, "gave you the idea you did run this country? And just who is this Monaghan?"

Targ's eyes narrowed. "You know durned well who he is!" he declared angrily. "He's nothin' but a two-by-twice would-be cattleman who's hornin' in on my range!"

"Such as this?" Kim waved a hand around him. "I'd say there ain't been a critter on this in months! What are you tryin' to do? Claim all the grass in the country?"

"It's my grass," Targ declared belligerently. "Mine! Just because I ain't built a trail into it yet is no reason why . . ."

"So that's it!" Sartain studied them thoughtfully. "All right, Targ, you an' your boys turn around and head right out of here. I think I'll homestead this piece!"

"You'll *what*?" Targ bellowed. Then he cursed bitterly.

"Careful, Beetle Puss!" Kim warned, grinning. "Don't make me pull your ears!"

With another foul name, Targ's hand flashed for his gun, but no more had his fist grabbed the butt than he was looking into the muzzle of Kim's six-shooter.

"I'm not *anxious* to kill you, Targ, so don't force it on me," he said quietly. The cattleman's face was gray, realizing his narrow escape. Slowly, yet reluctantly, his hand left his gun.

"This ain't over!" Targ declared harshly. "You ride out of here, or we'll ride you out!"

As the three drifted away, Kim watched them go, then shrugged. "What the devil, Pard," he said to the dun, "we weren't really goin' no place particular. Let's have a look around and then go see this Monaghan."

While the sun was hiding its face behind the western pines, Kim Sartain cantered the dun down into the cuplike valley that held the ranch buildings of the Y7. They were solidly built buildings, and everything looked sharp and clean. It was no rawhide outfit, this one of Tom Monaghan's. And there was nothing rawhide about the slim, attractive girl with red hair who came out of the ranch house and shaded her eyes at him.

He drew rein and shoved his hat back. "Ma'am," he said,

"I rode in here huntin' Tom Monaghan, but I reckon I was huntin' the wrong person. You'd likely be the boss of any spread you're on. I always notice," he added, "that redheaded women are apt to be bossy!"

"And I notice," she said sharply, "that drifting, no-good cowhands are apt to be smart! Too smart! Before you ask any questions, we don't need any hands! Not even top hands, if you call yourself that!

"If you're ridin' the grub line, just sit around until you hear grub call, then light in. We'd feed anybody, stray dogs or no-account saddle bums not barred!"

Kim grinned at her. "All right, Rusty. I'll stick around for chuck. Meanwhile, we'd better round up Tom Monaghan, because I want to make him a little deal on some cattle."

"You? Buy cattle?" Her voice was scornful. "You're just a big-talking drifter!" Her eyes flashed at him, but he noticed there was lively curiosity in her blue eyes.

"Goin' to need some cows," he said, curling a leg around the saddle horn. "Aim to homestead up there in the high meadows."

The girl had started to turn away, now she stopped and her eyes went wide. "You aim to *what*?"

Neither had noticed the man with iron-gray hair who had stopped at the corner of the house. His eyes were riveted on Sartain. "Yes," he said. "Repeat that again, will you? You plan to homestead up in the mountains?"

"Uh-huh, I sure do." Kim Sartain looked over at Tom Monaghan and liked what he saw. "I've got just sixty dollars in money, a good horse, a rope, and a will. I aim to get three hundred head of cows from you and a couple of horses, two pack mules, and some grub."

Rusty opened her mouth to explode, but Tom held up his hand. "And just how, young man, do you propose to pay for all that with sixty dollars?"

Kim smiled. "Why, Mr. Monaghan, I figure I can fatten my stock right fast on that upland grass, sell off enough to pay interest and a down payment on the principal. Next year I could do better. Of course," he added, "six hundred head of stock would let me make out faster, and that grass up there would handle them, plumb easy. Better, too," he added, "if I had somebody to cook for me, and mend my socks. How's about it, Rusty?"

"Why, you insufferable, egotistical upstart!"

"From what you say, I'd guess you've been up there in the meadows," Monaghan said thoughtfully, "but did you see anyone there?"

"Uh-huh. Three hombres was wastin' around. One of them had a scar on his face. I think they called him Jim Targ."

SARTAIN WAS ENJOYING himself now. He had seen the girl's eyes widen at the mention of the men, and especially of Jim Targ. He kept his dark face inscrutable.

"They didn't say anything to you?" Monaghan was unbelieving. "Nothing at all?"

"Oh, yeah! This here. Targ, he seemed right put out at my ridin' through the country. Ordered me to go around by Ryerson. Right about then I started lookin' that grass over, and sort of made up my mind to stay. He seemed to think you'd sent me up there."

"Did you tell him you planned to homestead?"

"Oh, sure! He didn't seem to cotton to the idea very much. Mentioned some hombre named Clay Tanner who would run me off."

"Tanner is a dangerous killer," Monaghan told him grimly.

"Oh, he is? Well, now! This Targ's sort of cuttin' a wide swath, ain't he?"

The boardinghouse triangle opened up suddenly with a deafening clangor, and Kim Sartain, suddenly aware that he had not eaten since breakfast, and little of that, slid off his horse. Without waiting for further comment, he led the dun toward the corral and began stripping the saddle.

"Dad," Rusty moved toward her father, "is he crazy or are we? Do you suppose he really saw Targ?"

Tom Monaghan stared at Sartain thoughtfully, noting the two low-slung guns, the careless, easy swing of Kim's stride. "Rusty, I don't think he's crazy, I think maybe Targ is. I'm going to let him have the cows!"

"Father!" She was aghast. "You wouldn't! Not three hundred!"

"Six hundred," he corrected. "Six hundred can be made to pay. And I think it will be worth it to see what happens. I've an idea more happened up there today than we have heard. I think that somebody tried to walk on this man's toes, and he probably happens to have corns on every one of them!"

When their meal was finished, Monaghan looked over at Kim, who had had little to say during the supper. "How soon would you want that six hundred head?" He paused. "Next week?"

The four cowhands looked up, startled, but Kim failed to turn a hair. "Tomorrow at daylight," Kim said coolly. "I want the nearest cattle you have to the home ranch and the help of your boys. I'm goin' to push cattle on that grass before noon!"

Tom Monaghan's eyes twinkled. "You're sudden, young fellow, plumb sudden. You know Targ's riders will be up there, don't you? He won't take this."

"Targ's riders," Sartain said quietly, "will get there about noon or after. I aim to be there first. Incidentally," he said, "I'll want some tools to throw together a cabin—a good strong one. I plan to build just west of the water," he added.

He turned suddenly toward Rusty, who had also been very quiet. As if she knew he intended speaking to her, she looked up. Her boy's shirt was open at the neck, and he could see the swell of her bosom under the rough material.

"Thought about that cookin' job yet?" he asked. "I sure am fed up on my own cookin'. Why, I'd even marry a cook to get her up there!"

A round-faced cowhand choked suddenly on a big mouthful of food and had to leave the table. The others were grinning at their plates. Rusty Monaghan's face went pale, then crimson. "Are you," she said coolly, "offering me a job, or proposing?"

"Let's make it a job first," Kim said gravely. "If you pass the exams, then we can get down to more serious matters."

Rusty's face was white to the lips. "If you think I'd cook

for or marry such a pigheaded windbag as you are, you're wrong! What makes you think I'd marry any broken-down, drifting saddle tramp that comes in here? Who do you think you are, anyway?"

Kim got up. "The name, ma'am, is Kim Sartain. As to who I am, I'm the hombre you're goin' to cook for. I'll be leavin' early tomorrow, but I'll drop back the next day, so you fix me an apple pie. I like lots of fruit, real thick pie, and plenty of juice."

Coolly, he strolled outside and walked toward the corral, whistling. Tom Monaghan looked at his daughter, smiling, and the hands finished their supper quickly and hurried outside.

———

It WAS DAYBREAK, with the air still crisp, when Rusty opened her eyes suddenly to hear the lowing of cattle, and the shrill Texas yells of the hands. Hurriedly, she dressed and stopped on the porch to see the drive lining out for the mountains. Far ahead, her eyes could just pick out a lone horseman, headed toward Gunsight Pass and the mountain meadows.

Her father came in an hour later, his face serious. He glanced at her quickly. "That boy's got nerve!" he said. "Furthermore, he's a hand!"

"But Dad," she protested, "they'll kill him! He's just a boy, and that Tanner is vicious! I've heard about him!"

Monaghan nodded. "I know, but I heard this Sartain was *segundo* for Ward McQueen of the Tumbling K when they had that run-in with rustlers a few months back. According to the stories, Sartain is hell on wheels with a gun!"

She was worried despite herself. "Dad, what do you think?"

He smiled. "Why, honey, if that man is all I think he is, Targ had better light a shuck for Texas, and as for you, you'd better start bakin' that apple pie!"

"Father!" Rusty protested. But her eyes widened a little, and she stepped farther onto the porch, staring after the distant rider.

KIM SARTAIN WAS a rider without illusions. Born and bred in the West, he knew to what extent such a man as Jim Targ could and would go. He knew that with tough, gun-handy riders, he would ordinarily be able to hold all the range he wanted, and that high meadow range was good enough to fight for.

Sartain knew he was asking for trouble, yet there was something in him that resented being pushed around. Targ's high-handed manner had got his back up, and his decision had not been a passing fancy. He knew just what he was doing, but no matter what the future held, he was determined to move in on this range and to hold it and fight for it if need be.

There was no time to waste. Targ might take him lightly, and think his declaration had been merely the loud talk of a disgruntled cowhand, but on the other side, the rancher might take him seriously and come riding for trouble. The cattle could come in their own good time, but he intended to be on the ground, and quickly.

The dun was feeling good and Kim let him stretch out in a fast canter. It was no time at all until he was riding up to the pool by the waterfall. He gave a sigh of relief, for he was the first man on the ground.

He jumped down, took a hasty drink, and let the dun drink. Meanwhile he picked the bench for his cabin and put down the ax he had brought with him. Monaghan had told him there was a saddle trail that came up the opposite side of the mountain and skirted among the cliffs to end near this pool. Leaving the horse, Kim walked toward it.

Yet before he had gone more than three steps, he heard a quick step behind him. He started to turn, but a slashing blow with a six-gun barrel clipped him on the skull. He staggered and started to fall, glimpsed the hazy outlines of his attacker, and struck out. The blow landed solidly, and then something clipped him again and he fell over into the grass. The earth crumbled beneath him, and he tumbled, over and over, hitting a thick clump of greasewood growing out of the cliff, then hanging up in some manzanita.

The sound of crashing in the brush below him was the first thing he remembered. He was aware that he must have had his eyes open and been half-conscious for some time. His head throbbed abominably, and when he tried to move his leg, it seemed stiff and clumsy. He lay still, recalling what had happened.

He remembered the blows he had taken, and then falling. Below him he heard more thrashing in the brush. Then a voice called, "Must have crawled off, Tanner. He's not down here!"

Somebody swore, and aware of his predicament Kim held himself rigid, waiting for them to go away. Obviously, he was suspended in the clump of manzanita somewhere on the side of the cliff. Above him, he heard the lowing of cattle. The herd had arrived, then. What of the boys with it?

It was a long time before the searchers finally went away and he could move. When he could, he got a firm grip on the root of the manzanita and then turned himself easily. His leg was bloody, but seemed unbroken. It was tangled in the brush, however, and his pants were torn. Carefully, he felt for his guns. One of them remained in its holster. The other was gone.

Working with infinite care and as quietly as possible, he lowered himself down the steep face of the rocky bluff, using brush and projections until finally he was standing upright on the ground below. A few minutes' search beneath where he had hung in the brush disclosed his other pistol, hanging in the top of a mountain mahogany.

Checking his guns, he limped slowly down into the brush. Here weakness suddenly overcame him, and he slumped to a sitting position. He had hurt his leg badly, and his head was swimming.

He squinted his eyes, squeezing them shut and opening them, trying to clear his brain. The hammering in his skull continued, and he sat very still, his head bulging with pain, his eyes watching a tiny lizard darting among the stones. How long he sat there he did not know, but when he got started moving again, he noticed that the sun was well past the zenith.

Obviously, he had been unconscious for some time in the brush, and had lost more time now. Limping, but moving carefully, he wormed his way along the gully into which he had fallen and slowly managed to mount the steep, tree-covered face of the bluff beyond where he had fallen.

Then, lowering himself to the ground he rested for a few minutes, then dragged himself on. He needed water, and badly. Most of all, he had to know what had happened. Apparently, Targ was still in command of the situation. The herd had come through, but Monaghan's riders must have been driven off. Undoubtedly, Targ had the most men. Bitterly, he thought of his boasts to Rusty and what they had amounted to. He had walked into a trap like any child.

It took him almost an hour of moving and resting to get near the falls. Watching his chance, he slid down to the water and got a drink, and then, crouching in the brush, he examined his leg. As he had suspected, no bones were broken, but the flesh was badly lacerated from falling into the branches, and he must have lost a good deal of blood. Carefully, he bathed the wound in the cold water from the pool, then bound it up as well as he could by tearing his shirt and using his handkerchief.

When he had finished, he crawled into the brush and lay there like a wounded animal, his eyes closed, his body heavy with the pulsing of pain in his leg and the dull ache in his skull.

Somehow, he slept, and when he awakened, he smelled smoke. Lifting his head, he stared around into the darkness. Night had fallen, and there was a heavy bank of clouds overhead, but beyond the pool was the brightness of a fire. Squinting his eyes, he could see several moving figures, and no one sitting down. The pool at this point was no more than twenty feet across, and he could hear their voices clearly and distinctly.

"Might as well clean 'em up now, Targ," somebody was saying in a heavy voice. "He pushed these cattle in here, an' it looks like he was trying to make an issue of it. Let's go down there tonight."

"Not tonight, Tanner." Targ's voice was slower, lighter. "I

want to be sure. When we hit them, we've got to wipe them out, leave nobody to make any complaint or push the case. It will be simple enough for us to tell our story and make it stick if they don't have anybody on their side."

"Who rightly owns this range?" Tanner asked.

Targ shrugged. "Anybody who can hold it. Monaghan wanted it, and I told everybody to lay off. Told them how much I wanted it and what would happen if they tried to move in. They said I'd no right to hold range I wasn't usin', an' I told them to start something, an' I'd show 'em my rights with a gun. I'll get the cattle later. If any of these piddlin' little ranchers want trouble, I'll give it to 'em."

"Might as well keep these cows and get the rest of what that Irishman's got," Tanner said. "We've got the guns. If they are wiped out, we can always say they started it, and who's to say we're wrong?"

"Sure. My idea exactly," Targ agreed. "I want that Monaghan's ranch, anyway." He laughed. "And that ain't all he's got that I want."

"Why not tonight? He's only got four hands, and one of them is bad hurt or dead. At least one more is wounded a mite."

"Uh-uh. I want that Sartain first. He's around somewhere, you can bet on that! He's hurt and hurt bad, but we didn't find him at the foot of that cliff, so he must have got away somehow! I want to pin his ears back, good!"

Kim eased himself deeper into the brush and tried to think his way out. His rifle was on his horse, and what had become of the dun he did not know. Obviously, the Monaghan riders had returned to the Y7, but it was he who had led Tom Monaghan into this fight, and it was up to him to get him out. But how?

The zebra dun, he knew, was no easy horse for a stranger to lay hands on. The chances were that the horse was somewhere out on the meadow, and his rifle with him. Across near the fire there were at least six men, and no doubt another one or two would be watching the trail down to the Y7.

It began to look as if he had taken a bigger bite than he could handle. Maybe Rusty was right after all, and he was just a loud-talking drifting saddle bum who could get into trouble but not out of it. The thought stirred him to action. He eased back away from the edge of the pool, taking his time and moving soundlessly. Whatever was done must be done soon.

The situation was simple enough. Obviously, Monaghan and some of the small flatland ranchers needed this upper range, but Targ, while not using it himself, was keeping them off. Now he obviously intended to do more. Kim Sartain had started something that seemed about to destroy the people he called his friends. And the girl too.

He swallowed that one. Maybe he wasn't the type for double harness, but if he was, Rusty Monaghan was the girl. And why shouldn't he be? Ward McQueen had been the same sort of hombre as himself, and Ward was marrying his boss—as pretty a girl as ever owned a ranch.

While he had decided to homestead this place simply because of Targ's high-handed manner, he could see that it was an excellent piece of range. From talk at the Y7 he knew there were more of these mountain meadows, and some of the other ranchers from below could move their stock up. His sudden decision, while based on pure deviltry, was actually a splendid idea.

His cattle were on the range, even if they still wore Monaghan's brand. That was tantamount to possession if he could make it stick, and Kim Sartain was not a man given to backing down when his bluff was called. The camp across the pool was growing quiet, for one after another of the men was turning in. A heavy-bodied, bearded man sat near the fire, half dozing. He was the one man on guard.

Quietly, Kim began to inch around the pool, and by the time an hour had passed and the riders were snoring loudly, he had completed the circuit to a point where he was almost within arm's length of the nearest sleeper. En route he had acquired something else—a long forked stick.

With infinite care, he reached out and lifted the belt and holster of the nearest rider, then, using the stick, retrieved those of the man beyond. Working his way around the camp, he succeeded in getting all the guns but those of the watcher, and those of Clay Tanner. These last he deliberately left behind. Twice, he had to lift guns from under the edges of blankets, but only once did a man stir and look around, but as all was quiet and he could see the guard by the fire, the man returned to his sleep.

Now Kim got to his feet. His bad leg was stiff, and he had to shift it with care, but he moved to a point opposite the guard. Now came the risky part, and the necessity for taking chances. His Colt level at the guard, he tossed a pebble against the man's chest. The fellow stirred, but did not look up. The next one caught him on the neck, and the guard looked up to see Kim Sartain, a finger across his lips for silence, the six-shooter to lend authority.

The guard gulped loudly, then his lips slackened and his eyes bulged. The heavy cheeks looked sick and flabby. With a motion of the gun, Kim indicated the man was to rise. Clumsily, the fellow got to his feet and at Sartain's gesture, approached. Then Sartain turned the man around, and was about to tie his hands when the fellow's wits seemed to return. With more courage than wisdom, he suddenly bellowed, *"Targ! Tanner! It's him!"*

Kim Sartain's pistol barrel clipped him a ringing blow on the skull, and the big guard went down in a heap. Looking across his body, Kim Sartain drew his other gun. "You boys sit right still," he said, smiling. "I don't aim to kill anybody unless I have to. Now all of you but Tanner get up and move to the left."

He watched them with cat's eyes, alert for any wrong move. When they were lined up opposite him, all either barefooted or in sock feet, he motioned to Tanner. "You get up, Clay. Now belt on your guns, but careful! Real careful!"

The gunman got shakily to his feet, his eyes murderous. He had been awakened from a sound sleep to look into Sartain's guns and see the hard blaze of the eyes beyond them. Nor did it pass unnoticed that all the guns had been taken but his, and his eyes narrowed, liking that implication not a bit.

"Targ," Kim said coldly, "you and your boys listen to me! I was ridin' through this country a perfect stranger until you tried to get mean! I don't like to have nobody ridin' me, see?

So I went to see Monaghan, whom I'd never heard about until you mentioned him. I made a deal for cows, and I'm in these meadows to stay. You bit off more than you could chew.

"Moreover, you brought this yellow-streaked, coyote-killin' Tanner in here to do your gunslinging for you. The rest of you boys are mostly cowhands. You know the right and wrong of this as well as I do! Well, right here and now we're goin' to settle my claim on this land! I left Tanner his guns after takin' all yours because I figured he really wanted me. Now he'll get his chance; afterwards if any of the rest of you want, you can buy in, one at a time! When the shootin's over here tonight, the fight's over."

His eyes riveted on Targ. "You hear that, Jim Targ? Tanner gets his chance, then you do, if you want it. But you make no trouble for Tom Monaghan, and no trouble for me. You're just a little man in a big country, you can keep your spread and run it small, or you can pull your freight!"

As he finished speaking, he turned back to Tanner. "Now, you killer for pay, you've got your guns. I'm going to holster mine." His eyes swung to the waiting cowhands. "You," he indicated an oldish man with cold blue eyes and drooping gray mustaches, "give the word!"

With a flick of his hands, the guns dropped into their holsters. Jim Targ's eyes narrowed, but his cowhands were all attention. Kim Sartain knew his Western men. Even outlaws like a man with nerve and would see him get a break.

"Now!" the gray-mustached man yelled. "Go for 'em!"

Tanner spread his hands wide. "No! No!" He screamed the words. "Don't shoot!"

He was unused to meeting men face to face with an even break. The very fact that Sartain had left his guns for him, a taunt and a dare as well as an indication of Sartain's confidence, had wrecked what nerve the killer had.

Now he stepped back, his face gray. With death imminent, all the courage went out of him. "I ain't got no grudge agin you!" he protested. "It was that Targ! He set me on to you!"

The man who had given the signal exploded with anger. "Well, of all the yellow two-bit, four-flushin' windbags!" His words failed him. "And you're supposed to be tough!" he said contemptuously.

Targ stared at Tanner, then shifted his eyes to Sartain. "That was a good play!" he said. "But I made no promises! Just because that coyote has yellow down his spine is no reason I forfeit this range!"

"I said," Sartain commented calmly, "the fighting ends here." Stooping, he picked up one of the gun belts and tossed it to Targ's feet. "There's your chance, if you want a quick slide into the grave!"

Targ's face worked with fury. He had plenty of courage, but he was remembering that lightning draw of the day before, and knew he could never match it, not even approach it. "I'm no gunfighter!" he said furiously. "But I won't quit! This here range belongs to me!"

"My cattle are on it," Kim said coolly. "I hold it. You set foot on it even once, and I'll hunt you down wherever you are and shoot you like a dog!"

Jim Targ was a study in anger and futility. His big hands opened and closed, and he muttered an oath. Whatever he was about to say was cut off short, for the gray-mustached hand yelled suddenly, "Look *out*!"

Kim wheeled, crouched and drawing as he turned. Tanner, his enemy's attention distracted, had taken the chance he was afraid to take with Sartain's eyes upon him. His gun was out and lifting, but Kim's draw was a blur of motion, then a stab of red flame. Tanner's shot plowed dust at his feet. Then the killer wilted at the knees, turned halfway around, and fell into the dust beside the fire.

Sartain's gun swung back, but Targ had not moved, nor had the others. For an instant, the tableau held, and then Kim Sartain holstered his gun.

"Targ," he said, "you've made your play, and I've called you. Looks to me like you've drawn to a pair of deuces."

For just a minute the cattleman hesitated. He had his faults, but foolishness was not one of them. He knew when he was whipped. "I guess I have," he said ruefully. "Anyway, that trail would have been pure misery, a buildin'. Saves us a sight of work."

He turned away, and the hands bunched around him. All but the man with the gray mustache. His eyes twinkled.

"Looks like you'll be needin' some help, Sartain. Are you hirin'?"

"Sure!" Sartain grinned suddenly. "First thing, catch my horse—and then take charge until I get back here!"

———

THE BOARDINGHOUSE TRIANGLE at the Y7 was clanging loudly when the dun cantered into the yard.

Kim dismounted stiffly and limped up the steps.

Tom Monaghan came to his feet, his eyes widened. The hands stared. Kim noted with relief that all were there. One man had a bandage around his head, another had his arm in a sling, his left arm, so he could still eat.

"Sort of wound things up," Sartain explained. "There won't be any trouble with Targ in the high meadows. Figured to drop down and have some breakfast."

Kim avoided Rusty's eyes and ate in silence. He was on his second cup of coffee when he felt her beside him. Then, clearing a space on the table, she put down a pie, its top golden brown and bulging with the promise of fruit underneath.

He looked up quickly. "I knew you'd be back," she said simply.

About Louis L'Amour

"I think of myself in the oral tradition—as a troubadour, a village taleteller, the man in the shadows of the campfire. That's the way I'd like to be remembered—as a storyteller. A good storyteller."

I T IS DOUBTFUL that any author could be as at home in the world re-created in his novels as Louis Dearborn L'Amour. Not only could he physically fill the boots of the rugged characters he wrote about, but he literally "walked the land my characters walk." His personal experiences as well as his lifelong devotion to historical research combined to give Mr. L'Amour the unique knowledge and understanding of people, events, and the challenge of the American frontier that became the hallmarks of his popularity.

Of French-Irish descent, Mr. L'Amour could trace his own family in North America back to the early 1600s and follow their steady progression westward, "always on the frontier." As a boy growing up in Jamestown, North Dakota, he absorbed all he could about his family's frontier heritage, including the story of his great-grandfather who was scalped by Sioux warriors.

Spurred by an eager curiosity and desire to broaden his horizons, Mr. L'Amour left home at the age of fifteen and enjoyed a wide variety of jobs, including seaman, lumberjack, elephant handler, skinner of dead cattle, miner, and an officer in the transportation corps during World War II. During his "yondering" days he also circled the world on a freighter, sailed a dhow on the Red Sea, was shipwrecked in the West Indies, and stranded in the Mojave Desert. He won fifty-one of fifty-nine fights as a professional boxer and worked as a journalist and lecturer. He was a voracious reader and collector of rare books. His personal library contained 17,000 volumes.

Mr. L'Amour "wanted to write almost from the time I could talk." After developing a widespread following for his many frontier and adventure stories written for fiction magazines, Mr. L'Amour published his first full-length novel, *Hondo,* in the United States in 1953. Every one of his more than 120 books is in print; there are more than 300 million copies of his books in print worldwide, making him one of the bestselling authors in modern literary history. His books have been translated into twenty languages, and more than forty-five of his novels and stories have been made into feature films and television movies.

His hardcover bestsellers include *The Lonesome Gods, The Walking Drum* (his twelfth-century historical novel), *Jubal Sackett, Last of the Breed,* and *The Haunted Mesa.* His memoir, *Education of a Wandering Man,* was a leading bestseller in 1989. Audio dramatizations and adaptations of many L'Amour stories are available from Random House Audio publishing.

The recipient of many great honors and awards, in 1983 Mr. L'Amour became the first novelist ever to be awarded the Congressional Gold Medal by the United States Congress in honor of his life's work. In 1984 he was also awarded the Medal of Freedom by President Reagan.

Louis L'Amour died on June 10, 1988. His wife, Kathy, and their two children, Beau and Angelique, carry the L'Amour publishing tradition forward with new books written by the author during his lifetime to be published by Bantam.

FORGET THE LAW OF THE JUNGLE...

The Worst
Drought In
Memory . . .

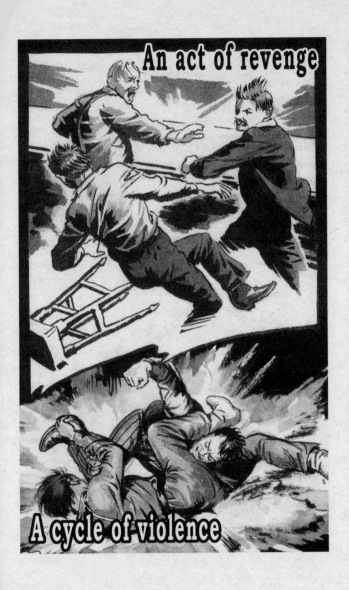

In Louis L'Amour's classic tale of loyalty and betrayal . . .

BASED ON THE STORY BY
LOUIS L'AMOUR
LAW OF THE DESERT BORN
A GRAPHIC NOVEL
Adapted by CHARLES SANTINO
Script by BEAU L'AMOUR
and KATHERINE NOLAN
Produced by BEAU L'AMOUR
Illustrated by
THOMAS YEATES